MW01077335

BISON
BOOKS

HOW SI CAME OUT.

HOW SI STARTED IN.

Corporal Si Klegg and His "Pard"

WILBUR F. HINMAN

Introduction to the Bison Books edition by
Allan R. Millett

Illustrations by
George Y. Coffin

UNIVERSITY OF NEBRASKA PRESS

LINCOLN AND LONDON

Library of Congress Cataloging-in-Publication Data
Hinman, Wilbur F. (Wilbur Fisk), d. 1905.
Corporal Si Klegg and his "pard" / Wilbur F. Hinman;
introduction to the Bison Books edition by
Allan R. Millett; illustrations by George Y. Coffin.
p. cm.
Includes bibliographical references.
ISBN 978-0-8032-2473-5 (pbk. : alk. paper)
1. United States—History—Civil War, 1861–1865—Fiction.
I. Millett, Allan Reed. II. Coffin, George Yost, 1850–1896.
III. Title.
PS1929.H78C67   2009
813'.4—dc22
2009012156

This edition of *Corporal Si Klegg and His "Pard"* is dedicated to the memory of Private Stanley J. Kahrl, 3rd Marine Volunteers, professor of English, the Ohio State University, and Captain Brian Pohanka, 5th New York Volunteers ("Fire Louaves"), champions of the reconstruction of Civil War soldier life.

INTRODUCTION

ALLAN R. MILLETT

I saw my first Civil War battle in April 1961 and finally fought in one in March 1989. No, it was not a *Twilight Zone* moment—only the world of Civil War reenacting. A Marine infantry lieutenant stationed at Camp Lejeune and a modest Civil War buff, I drove to Virginia to see the reenactment that memorialized the one hundredth anniversary of the First Battle of Bull Run or Manassas, depending on your sectional politics. I took notes and wrote a newspaper feature on that experience, so I remember what I saw—a comic muddle that resembled a toga party in blue and gray. Perhaps that is how the real battle looked. I doubt it, for the participants of 1861 at least fought with deadly as well as ignorant enthusiasm. The 1961 soldiers certainly did not look or act as if they really wanted to recreate the battle. Some looked like Army Guardsmen on a bad drill weekend. I was amused and put off by Civil War reenacting.

Twenty-eight years later, having reached mandatory retirement as a colonel, U.S. Marine Corps Reserve, I went into the Civil War reenacting closet as a lieutenant, 54th Massachusetts Volunteer Infantry Regiment, as a nonspeaking, often-dying extra in the movie *Glory*. My war was a week of assaulting Battery Wagner, which had slid south from Morris Island, South Carolina, to Jeykll Island, Georgia. Totally ignorant of Civil War drill, which also meant tactics, I fell under the patient tutelage of Greg Urwin, Tim Kinreid, and Jack Thompson, all of whom had joined the late Brian Pohanka's "Band of Blue Brothers," a group dedicated to doing the Civil War *right* in look and language. My look that week hardly passed muster. I kept buying the wrong hat and rank insignia, appearing as a doctor and assistant adjutant general. I wore an enlisted four-button jacket, and my shoes were World War II "boondocker" knockoffs, not Jefferson brogans. My pistol was a nonfiring Navy Colt, but at least I carried an original Model 1860 light cavalry saber, lent to me by my brother Stephen, an antique collector. The saber was in excellent condition since it had belonged to a Confederate surgeon who hadn't carried it much. Cary Elwes liked it when we played sword mumblety peg between takes. I tripped often over the scabbard.

I went to Jekyll Island as a stand-in for my friend the late professor Stanley Kahrl, who had organized and equipped the Columbus-The Ohio State University company for *Glory*. Stan, who later died "on the field" at Franklin, Tennessee, in December 1989, would not abandon his classes to lead the company, so he recruited me since I had an academic leave. He must have known I had posttraumatic stress disorder from no longer going to drill weekends or active duty periods in Washington and Quantico. Stan had participated in a reenactment at Gettysburg the year before, so he was hooked on fake war and real camp camaraderie. Always persuasive, after *Glory* he talked me into becoming a private in something called "Vincent's Brigade." We joined the brigade for a reenactment of the battles of the Wilderness and Spotsylvania in Louisa County, Virginia, in May 1989. The 3rd Maine, Stan's host, proved to be a shadow unit of three or four taciturn people, so I gravitated to Company E, 15th New Jersey, a unit of lively competence and considerable knowledge of Civil War history. I had grown up in northern New Jersey, so I understood the loud marshland-mafia patois spoken in the company. My only regret since that day is that I have not had more weekends to sacrifice in the service of the Union. By also joining the 49th Ohio, however, I fought at Perryville, Shiloh, and Chickamauga with my own pard now-professor William B. Feis, Buena Vista University, Storm Lake, Iowa, who had a real incentive to keep me alive so I could sign his dissertation. We made cameo performances with the 15th New Jersey for Cedar Creek, Antietam, Gettysburg, and (again) Spotsylvania. We never got promoted, but we never fell out. We often ran into Greg Urwin, who kept getting promoted until he made colonel, and we campaigned with Stan Kahrl's son Ben because we needed someone to order around and to fill blank cartridges. We *always* cleaned our own rifles.

Throughout that halcyon war era of the 1990s, Bill and I conducted "participatory research" interviews on Union army soldier life. What did *real reenactors* read to shape their impressions of Union infantrymen? (We hold cavalry and artillery in contempt because they are *dangerous* to be near, and who loves horses?) Well, being military history professors, we already knew the answers, right? The books must be Bell Wiley's *Billy Yank* and John Billings's *Hardtack and Coffee*, which was actually written by a veteran. (But Billings was an artilleryman!) No, said our veteran comrades, the book to read was Wilbur Fisk Hinman's *Corporal Si Klegg and His "Pard."* Who? What? I had never heard of the book, and I thought I had a fair grasp of the volumes of personal memoirs written by Civil War veterans. *The Red Badge of Courage* had been one of my favorite books since childhood, even if Stephen Crane hadn't been shot at until 1898. I had read most of Ambrose Bierce's noir short stories, but saying Bierce is a representative soldier-author is like saying that Norman Mailer was a typical World War II GI. *Corporal Si Klegg and His "Pard"*? So I tracked down a copy of this iconic book, read it, and joined the ranks of the Wilbur Fisk Hinman fan club.

Except for the Civil War reenactor army, which numbers in the tens of thousands, *Corporal Si Klegg* does not receive

much attention from the academic authorities on the so-
cial life of Civil War armies. Si and his pard Shorty (who is
tall and thin) don't seem to be interested in subjects that
attract contemporary historians. They do not ponder the
relationship of virtue to survival since there is none. They
quickly learn that personal character has little to do with
life and death. Death is capricious, pitiless. It is important
to fall in and become a "2" in the countoff since that en-
sures a rear rank position when the company comes on
line. Such cleverness is no match for a cannonball, but it
does mean the "1" catches the first bullet—maybe. Perhaps
that fits Drew Gilpin Faust's argument that Civil War deaths
traumatized the whole nation, but Si and Shorty don't
seem obsessed with fear or death because they know such
anxiety is useless and consumes energy that can be better
used for scrounging food and avoiding sentry or kitchen
duty. They do not reflect on the morality of killing, either,
because in the noise and smoke of infantry combat, one
can seldom tell whether one's bullet has hit anything at all.
No doubt a sensitive minority of soldiers experienced the
angst of killing. No doubt another minority of sociopaths,
temporary or permanent, gloried in being death-dealers.
Si and Shorty are in the majority. "It's them or us" with no
guilt and no apologies.

Si and Shorty are also disinterested in religious beliefs
and practices. They are not atheists or agnostics, just soldiers who hope that Oliver Cromwell's prayer applies to
them, too. They do not worry about splits in the Protestant
churches or whether the war will advance or hinder the in-
terests of any institutional church. They do not believe God
chose sides, even though Confederate flags sported crosses
of varied design and rebel politicians favored the language
of evangelistic crusaders.

The irrepressible duo of the fictional 200th Indiana
Volunteers would not understand the term "gender relations," and their world of war excluded women except as

bystanders. Women lived on the edge of Civil War armies as Sanitary Commission nurses, sutler's clerks, and whores. No doubt the Union army had its share of Romeos and sexual predators of varied tastes. The incidence of venereal disease in Civil War armies suggests that celibacy was not a requirement. Sex of any kind—and real liquor—was mostly available to officers and the garrisons of Washington and Nashville. In the field the usual prurient experience peaked with pornographic postcards or stereopticon peep shows. Si and Shorty regard women, mostly Southern, as a curiosity unrelated to their most cherished desires, which center on food, sleep, liquor, and staying dry and warm. If they worry about anything below their waist, it is coping with diarrhea, a most powerful agent in reducing one's libido. The cure for almost any infliction was more liquor, sometimes laced with opium, which made it laudanum. The nickname for unpopular medical officers was "loose bowels." Si and Shorty are silent on the issue of soldier sex, in line with Victorian convention. On the other hand, they worry a great deal about their bowels; thirty-eight thousand Union soldiers died of diarrhea or dysentery.

They are only mildly more open about what the war is about and why they volunteered for the Union army. Si thinks he will look marvelous in a uniform despite a flabbiness he never sheds. He loves the look of corporal's chevrons. He cannot think of any reason he should *not* march off to war, especially since he can escape his parents' close supervision and a long list of chores. He does miss his mother's cooking. When he partners up with Shorty, he finds his pard even less focused on cause and comrades, but he is deeply concerned about his next meal and a warm campfire. They are mildly moved by the need to preserve the Union. They are indifferent to the issue of slavery because the fate of the black man has no relevance for them.

If Si and Shorty are such poor examples of noble Union soldier culture, why should Wilber Fisk Hinman bother to write a book about their adventures? More importantly, why is the book memorable? The answer is simple: *Corporal Si Klegg and His "Pard"* became the book of choice for Union army veterans because they believed it was the most accurate portrayal of their wartime experiences, physical and spiritual.

Assessments of Civil War literature ignore *Corporal Si Klegg* because literary critics favor "high" literature, which through most of the twentieth century meant fiction, essays, and poetry written in an Anglo-American, Christian, humanistic tradition. It is no wonder that Hinman does not rank with Melville, Holmes, Whitman, Bierce, Alcott, and Dickinson. The best he can do is to be identified as a possible source for Crane's *The Red Badge of Courage*. Crane never admitted any debt to Hinman, only that he had been influenced by the war writing of Leo Tolstoy. *Corporal Si Klegg* even suffers as a historical document. In the 1960s the Civil War Centennial Commission asked Allan Nevins, James I. Robertson Jr., and Bell I. Wiley to compile an annotated, critical bibliography of Civil War books, generously defined. Along with Bruce Catton, Nevins and Wiley were the reigning popular historians of the war in the 1960s, filling the gap created by the fading of Douglas Southall Freeman. Shelby Foote, Tom Connelly, and Jim McPherson were just marching onto the literary battlefield, and Bud Robertson, a new professor at Virginia Tech, had just joined the ranks of the Generation of the Bicentennial as it emerged from the academic woods into the bookstores.

As part of the project, Robertson compiled a section of writing on "Military Aspect—Soldier Life," and forty years later it is still a useful source. Robertson included fiction if the book or collection of short stories was written by a veteran or contemporary observer. Ambrose Bierce makes the listing, and so does Wilbur Fisk Hinman, but not as the author of *Corporal Si Klegg and His "Pard."* Instead, Robertson notes Hinman's *Camp and Field: Sketches of Army Life Written by Those Who Followed the Flag, '61–65* (1892) as "a hodge podge of anecdotes and alleged personal experiences." In other words, at best exaggerated soldiers' tales and at worst fantasized hearsay. *Corporal Si Klegg* receives no entry. Nevertheless, Robertson then calls Hinman's *The Story of the Sherman Brigade* "one of the top ten narratives by a Federal soldier; a necessity [for] any study of the Western theater." Yet, all three of Hinman's books are the same book or at least the same story—the Civil War experience of two Ohio Volunteer Infantry regiments—told three different ways by the same person and using the same sources. The difference is that *The Sherman Brigade* provides attribution, direct quotes, statistics, and references to official reports by the brigade and regimental commanders, as if that avoids fiction.

Rather than simply accepting the testimony of enthusiastic Civil War reenactors, who in turn echoed the praise of Union army veterans for the book, I reviewed the letters and postwar memories of veterans of four Indiana Volunteer Infantry regiments: the 14th, 31st, 85th, and 97th Indiana. Members of my mother's family, who settled in southern Indiana in 1819, served in each of these regiments. In all, seven served, and four survived the war. Of the four veterans, two had normal postwar lives, but one died of "consumption" in 1873, and the other, psychologically stricken by the war, lived as a ward of the extended Letsinger family with a small pension, a mental and physical ruin until dying in 1933 at the age of eighty-nine. Another family member became an officer. The experience of Alfred F. Phillips, my great-grandfather, Company C, 97th Indiana, is documented by the letters of his regimental commander, Aden G. Cavens, and his company commander, Capt. Joseph W. Young. Captain Young's letters ended when an errant Union shell blew him apart in the rifle pits below Kennesaw Mountain on June 27, 1864. A former orderly sergeant and lieutenant, Phillips commanded the company for the rest of the war. My great-grandfather's experience paralleled Hinman's service. Wilbur Hinman's 200th Indiana may be fictitious, but its soldiers could have been in the four Indiana regiments I know well.

WILBUR FISK HINMAN'S CIVIL WAR

Born in 1840 and raised in Berea, Ohio, Wilbur Fisk Hinman entered the Union army in November 1861 when it became clear that the Southern rebellion would not be quickly suppressed. He was a typical recruit except that he was better educated than most of his comrades. From 1848–52 he attended Baldwin University (now Baldwin-Wallace College) in his home town. He did not graduate. He returned to college in 1854, but Baldwin-Wallace's records do not show him as a graduate. The curriculum was literary and philosophical. It is likely that Hinman wanted a journalism career or some sort of local government job. At the age of twenty-one he joined the 65th Ohio Volunteer Infantry Regiment, a three-year regiment organized under Lincoln's call for troops, the Volunteer Act of July 1861, which called for five hundred thousand men to fight for the Union for three years or less, if they won the war sooner. They didn't.

The 65th Ohio was drawn from Ohio's northeastern counties. Hinman's Company E came from Cuyahoga County, the Cleveland area. His portrait photograph of the time shows him as a serious, sober private, clean-shaven, with dark, curly hair framing a strong face with nose and chin to match. His eyes are steady and almost piercing, but that may reflect the photographic technology of the 1860s. His long, thin-lipped mouth does not appear to be made for smiling. Wilbur Hinman looks soldierly and he knows it.

The 65th Ohio Volunteers had been recruited as part of the "Sherman Brigade," a force of legionary organization that also included the 64th Ohio, the 6th Battery of Ohio

Light Artillery, and a cavalry squadron. Its sponsor, Senator John Sherman, Republican of Lancaster and older brother of Gen. William Tecumseh Sherman, was supposed to command the 64th Ohio, but he wisely passed his colonelcy to James Forsyth, an Ohioan who graduated from West Point in 1856 and then served as an infantry lieutenant in the Washington Territory. Forsyth returned to Ohio to muster in the 64th Ohio and train it at its assembly point, Camp Buckingham, Mansfield, Ohio. Confusion over the status of regular officers' rank in the Volunteer Army convinced Forsyth, promoted to captain, U.S. Army, to look elsewhere for service. He spent the rest of the war in important staff positions and finished the war as Philip Sheridan's chief-of-staff and a brigadier general of Volunteers.

Senator Sherman followed the same method in finding a colonel for the 65th Ohio. He recruited Charles G. Harker, a New Jersey orphan who had been adopted by a congressman. A West Point graduate (1858), Harker also served in the Northwest before he followed Forsyth to Ohio to be the mustering officer and instructor of the 65th Ohio. He became its colonel on November 11, 1861, first surrendering his commission as a captain in the U.S. Army. He was twenty-six years old and noted for his temper, energy, physical courage, high military standards, tactical knowledge, and relentless demands on his troops. The soldiers of the 65th Ohio did not like their commander, but in time he won their respect. In less than a year he became the brigade commander. Lt. Col. Horatio Whibeck, a twenty-five-year-old militia officer and former store clerk, became the acting regimental commander.

The 65th Ohio moved from Ohio to Kentucky in December 1861, still part of the Sherman Brigade. The regiment became part of the 3rd Brigade, First Division (Brig. Gen. Thomas J. Wood, USV and USMA, 1845) in the Army of the Ohio (Brig. Gen. Don Carlos Buell, USV and USMA, 1841). Wood was a Kentuckian, Buell a native of Ohio who grew up in Indiana. Both had seen combat in the Mexican War and had been brevetted for their exemplary service. Neither would end the war as a conspicuous success as a field commander, but in 1862 their immediate challenge was to train, discipline, and equip an army of civilians that could hold Kentucky in the Union. The 3rd Brigade included not only the 64th and 65th Ohio but also the 51st Indiana, 73rd Indiana, and 13th Michigan infantry regiments. The 6th Ohio Battery served as the brigade artillery, although it and two Indiana batteries normally deployed under Wood's direct control. The 3rd Brigade's organization remained constant until 1863.

The process of training and deploying culled the ill and the faint-of-heart from the ranks of the 65th Ohio, but it also created a stable, experienced cadre of company officers and noncommissioned officers (sergeants and corporals). Company E's commander, Capt. Thomas Powell, served in that position for almost two years. His younger brother, Edward G. Powell, served as a corporal and sergeant until he became a lieutenant in September 1864. Joseph H. Willsey became the orderly (first) sergeant, then regimental sergeant major until commissioned in January 1863. Wilbur F. Hinman began his field service as a corporal, then sergeant, and became the Company E orderly sergeant in November 1861. By war's end Hinman had become a captain and commander of Company F.

In its first year of service, the 65th Ohio trained, marched, and rode trains and steamboats throughout the upper South without much fighting. The brigade moved into Tennessee and occupied Nashville and marched in March and April to reach the battlefield of Shiloh (April 6–7, 1862), arriving too late for much combat. In May 1862 it reached Corinth, Mississippi, in Maj. Gen. Henry W. Halleck's combined western army, then advanced east toward Chattanooga, but raids on Buell's supply lines by John Hunt Morgan's Confederate cavalry forced the Army of the Ohio to fall back into Kentucky in July–August 1862. By September Buell's army had returned to the Louisville area to defend the city from an invading Confederate army led by Gen. Braxton Bragg. On October 8 the two forces fought each other to a tactical draw at Perryville, Kentucky, but Bragg abandoned his march on Louisville and returned to Tennessee. The campaign cost Don Carlos Buell his command since Halleck and Secretary of War Edwin M. Stanton decided that two lackluster battle performances were enough.

On October 30, 1862, Maj. Gen. William S. Rosecrans (usv and usma, 1842), an engineer officer who had left the army in 1854 to manage a kerosene refinery in Cincinnati, took command of the army in Kentucky. A native Ohioan, Rosecrans had returned to the army as colonel of the 23rd Ohio but demonstrated his political influence by rejoining the officer corps of the U.S. Army as a brigadier general. His service in the eastern theater and Mississippi valley showed enough ability to impress Stanton. The patronage of a friend, Maj. Gen. George B. McClellan, did not hurt either. Rosecrans showed considerable administrative ability in his new command, and he renamed his force the Army of the Cumberland (which meant it would march south) and divided it into four corps. Wood's division became part of the IV Corps (Maj. Gen. Thomas L. Crittenden, usv). A Mexican War veteran whose greatest accomplishment had been being born a Kentucky Crittenden and son of a U.S. senator, Crittenden won Lincoln's favor by taking command of Kentucky's unionist forces and holding Louisville and Frankfort in 1861. As a division commander in the Army of the Ohio, Crittenden showed no special competence, but Rosecrans respected his political ties and personal loyalty.

Wilbur F. Hinman seldom touched on issues of high command and strategy when he began sending letters from Kentucky to his parents and friends back in Berea. He reported the details of camp life, training, and news of Company E soldiers. He described the regiment's travels to Tennessee and Mississippi and its lack of action, not without a little regret. He recorded the novel details of train and steamboat travel. He protested a Halleck order to have soldiers' letters censored since any operational information would be useless by the time a letter reached Ohio. He theorized that Halleck did not like criticism of his generalship and the army's supply system. In September Hinman entered a hospital in Louisville for respiratory problems and dysentery, but he quickly concluded he would survive only if he returned to Company E. He did not report how many of his comrades were already out of action from accidents and health problems. Even without major battle casualties, the 65th Ohio ended November 1862 at half strength, or about five hundred officers and men. If noncombat deaths were tolerable, the sick noneffectives were an administrative burden and tactical limitation.

The 65th Ohio fulfilled its destiny at Stones River, or the Battle of Murfreesboro, Tennessee, December 31, 1862–January 2, 1863. Having secured Nashville without much resistance, Rosecrans—under insistent orders from Washington—started his army south along the axis of the Nashville-Murfreesboro Pike and the gateway to Chattanooga, the advance Buell had not made in the summer of 1862. Rosecrans expected that Braxton Bragg's Army of Tennessee would not let him move far without a battle, but he did not know that Jefferson Davis had answered Bragg's pleas for reinforcements, provided Bragg march north to stop Rosecrans. The two armies finally found each other three or four miles north of Murfreesboro and deployed on a line east to west. Bragg's army massed just north of Stones River, Rosecrans's in the woods and farm lots between the Franklin Road and Nashville Turnpike. Each convinced that his enemy would soon attack, both generals planned preemptive mass assaults on December 31.

Bragg concentrated against Rosecrans's left (eastern)

flank; Rosecrans massed his "Right Wing"—four divisions—to attack Bragg's left (western) flank. Crittenden's "Left Wing" of three divisions would hold Rosecrans's left, deployed on either side of the Nashville-Murfreesboro Pike. Anticipating an attack, Bragg shifted the weight of his attack to his left (western) flank, which would preempt Rosecrans's advance, but Rosecrans in turn had shifted the seven divisions of his "Left" and "Center" wings to an attack straight toward Murfreesboro. The result was a battle that began on an east-west axis and developed as a north-south struggle for control of the Franklin and Murfreesboro roads.

Rosecrans rushed troops from the "Center Wing" and "Left Wing" to halt the Confederate attacks from the west, and they held the Murfreesboro Pike. However, as the Confederate brigades advanced (eleven of them headed for the pike at noon), they opened the way for additional attacks from the south, and Rosecrans's piecemeal commitment of Crittenden's corps created gaps and salients in his defenses. In the rush, Harker's five regiments marched to the aid of two other brigades, who, facing south, were about to be flanked by three Confederate brigades. Harker, however, took a position on a hill (the Widow Burris House Ridge) that proved too far from the threatened brigades to stop the Confederate envelopment. Harker's position, though, allowed him to deploy four regiments in a *u*-shaped firing line, with the 65th Ohio holding the southeast slope against the attack of five regiments of Tennessee infantry. Under Rosecrans's direction, Harker surrendered the ridge and marched his confused regiments back to the Murfreesboro Pike and a new straight Union line. The Confederate division they faced stalled in greater disarray from exhaustion around 3 p.m. The battle continued elsewhere, but the 65th Ohio had passed its crisis.

Orderly Sergeant Wilbur F. Hinman emerged from his first battle stunned by the noise, the confusion, and the carnage. In two letters to his family and friends on January 3 and 11, he tried to describe the battle, but he found his "language . . . utterly incapable" of conveying the experience of watching his regiment shelled and blasted with musketry. He called the battle a "trial hardship," the shelling the source of "fearful anxiety." After a desperate thirty minutes of battle the 65th Ohio, which went into line with four hundred officers and men, mustered ninety-seven effectives. It had lost fifty-two dead and mortally wounded, around one hundred wounded, and the rest stragglers or detailed to evacuate the wounded. Company E entered the battle with twenty-three effectives and suffered eleven wounded, two or three of whom, Hinman reported, would probably die.

The Battle of Stones River, the most deadly fight in the 65th Ohio's war service, brought a new fatalism and determination to Hinman's letters. In February he asserted that "we must quell the rebellion at all hazards" but admitted the next month that the war "hardens and brutalizes us." In April 1863, as another campaign beckoned, he reported that only he remained of the ten company orderly sergeants who had reached Kentucky in 1862. Four orderly sergeants had become lieutenants. Three of them, sick or wounded, had resigned their commissions in 1862. The fourth had died at Stones River. Of the remaining five, one had been reduced to the ranks and had deserted, two had been discharged for disability, and two had died "in camp" or at home of illness. Even though the company was now guarding railroads and wagon trains, Hinman faced a sure future: "My turn must certainly come next."

As the first lieutenant in Company E, 65th Ohio, Hinman marched out of Nashville on June 16, 1863, again headed for Chattanooga. The Army of the Cumberland sought another chance to destroy Braxton Bragg's Army of Tennessee and thus open the trans-Appalachian Confederacy to occupation and political purification. If the war had become a struggle to abolish slavery, Hinman's letters do not reflect much interest in the issue except as a means to destroy the economic base of the Confederacy. Instead he felt pleased to be an officer, the last of the original orderly sergeants to become a lieutenant. He had been the victim in 1862 of a tie vote in Company E for the position, resolved by drawing straws. He had lost, but the winner soon resigned his commission and returned to Ohio, an honorable and much-taken road out of the war. Still part of Harker's 3rd Brigade, Wood's First Division, Crittenden's XXI Corps, the 65th Ohio marched hard and far, but it fought only Confederate rear guards as Rosecrans's army outmaneuvered Bragg's in the Tullahoma campaign and reached the Tennessee River near Chattanooga.

By mid-September 1863 Harker's brigade had marched past Chattanooga and found itself with the rest of Rosecrans's army along a wood-choked stream with a strange Creek name: Chickamauga, translated as "River of Death." In the battle that began on September 18, 1863, Wood's division occupied a position in the center of Rosecrans's army at Lee and Gordon's Mill and fought hard to stop the probing Confederate attacks on its front. Most of the serious fighting on September 19 occurred to the north, where Bragg tried to flank and drive back George H. Thomas's XIV Corps, astride the main road to Chattanooga. Confederate brigade attacks forced countermanuevers by Union brigades. Harker's brigade fought its way north to halt a Confederate attack on Thomas's right flank. During the afternoon's fighting, the 65th Ohio lost Lieutenant Colonel Whitbeck, shot from his horse with a serious body wound. Maj. Samuel C. Brown took command.

The thick woods and broken terrain made larger deployments difficult to control. Slowly the Confederate corps of Lt. Gen. D. H. Hill forced the XIV Corps back west beyond Chickamauga Creek by force of numbers. Desperate for a quick victory, Bragg ordered a night attack by Brig. Gen. Patrick Cleburne's division, but even this veteran force could not break the Union line. Still desperate, Bragg decided to extend his attacks to the south and turn Rosecrans's right (southern) flank, if he could find it. He had the uncommitted force for this maneuver—Lt. Gen. James Longstreet's corps from Lee's Army of Northern Virginia. For once, Jefferson Davis had overruled Lee and ordered Longstreet's corps, less Pickett's division, to entrain in Virginia and hurry to Bragg's assistance. Still smarting from its defeat at Gettysburg, Longstreet's corps relished the chance to crush a Yankee western army. While waiting for Longstreet's corps to arrive in full, Bragg ordered the remaining division of Leonidas Polk's corps to attack the Union center along the north-south Lafayette Road on the morning of September 20. Again the Confederate attacks came against Thomas's XIV Corps, fully committed and hard-pressed but fighting with skill and cohesion. Bragg thought he saw a chance to break across the Lafayette Road behind Thomas and ordered one of Longstreet's divisions to join the attack on the XIV Corps. This deployment forced Longstreet to change his plan of attack and reorient his advance (three divisions of ten thousand men) to the north against Crittenden's XXI Corps, not against McCook's XX Corps to the south.

Rosecrans knew his army might have a dangerous gap between the XIV and XXI corps, a gap that the Confederates discovered in the early attacks of September 20 and opened in repeated attacks by late morning. Since Rosecrans's headquarters was less than a mile from the battle, a captain from his staff checked the situation and confirmed the gap. With Rosecrans's approval and Crittenden's knowledge, Thomas redeployed two brigades of Brig. Gen. John M. Brannan's division of the XIV Corps to reinforce his menaced flank, which allowed two of his divisions, the bloodied commands of Maj. Gen. James S. Negley and Maj. Gen. Joseph J. Reynolds, to shift to the north and to tighten their lines. At this point Rosecrans and his chief-of-staff, James A. Garfield, lost track of their army's deployment, in part because Thomas had to respond promptly and successfully to the new threat on his southern flank at the intersection of the Lafayette and Brotherton roads. Unaware that Brannan had entered the battle and given the XIV Corps a new southern flank, Rosecrans ordered Crittenden to extend his left flank division (Wood) to restore contact with the XIV Corps, presumably with some part of Reynolds's division. Reynolds's division, however, had shifted north to allow Brannan to join the battle line. Neither Crittenden nor Wood challenged the order or Rosecrans's assumptions about the position of the XIV Corps. Thomas knew of the order but not of Rosecrans's confusion on where the XIV Corps's right flank now rested. Rosecrans's single order snatched defeat from the possibility of victory.

Receiving Rosecrans's order to "close up on Reynolds," Crittenden and McCook reassured Wood, whose division would execute the order, that Rosecrans must know something they did not about the enemy. The army commander might not have known that Brannan's division now occupied Reynolds's former position, but two of his corps commanders and the affected division commander all knew that to execute the order Wood's division would have to leave the front by brigades in column and march around Brannan's division to find Reynolds's division. Perhaps they thought Rosecrans intended for Van Cleve's division, the third and reserve division of the XX Corps, to replace Wood's. In any event, at around 11 a.m. Wood's division basically faced left and marched off to the north with Harker's brigade in the middle of the column. Col. George P. Buell's four-regiment 1st Brigade formed the rearguard. Before it could move, Buell's brigade found itself under fire from a fully formed Confederate division that had just marched through the gap created by Wood's division's departure.

Already in motion, Longstreet's grand assault found the

gap created by the departure of Wood's division, and the Confederate attack fell upon the open flanks of the XXI and XIV corps. Longstreet's advance broke Rosecrans's army in half. The southern half of Rosecrans's army (most of the XX and XXI corps) never managed a coherent rally and left the field in various stages of disarray, taking Rosecrans with it. Wood's division, though losing its rear brigade, managed to reach the XIV Corps, which Thomas redeployed to meet attacks from the east and south. In the withdrawal Harker's brigade actually counterattacked a Confederate division then fell back, facing the enemy and firing until it reached Thomas's "last stand" position on Snodgrass Hill.

Harker's brigade fought a desperate rearguard action against two brigades of Longstreet's corps that allowed the XIV Corps to occupy Snodgrass Hill and Horseshoe Ridge. Led by the 125th Ohio Volunteers, commanded by the redoubtable Emerson Opdycke, the brigade held long enough for Union artillery to blunt the Confederate advance. The battle cost the 65th Ohio dearly. Major Smith went down with a mortal wound. Although not the senior surviving officer, Capt. Thomas Powell took command of a regiment already one-third smaller than it had been when it began the battle. Hinman became the acting commander of Company E but lost his strongest leader, First Sergeant John Cooper, dead on the field. For the remainder of a very long day the 65th Ohio, often short of ammunition, held the northeastern slope of Snodgrass Hill with the rest of Harker's shrunken brigade. Reinforcements from the Reserve Corps of the Army of the Cumberland brought welcome ammunition and stiffened Thomas's defenses. The battle withered away with darkness. Under Rosecrans's orders, Thomas withdrew that night to join the rest of the army near Chattanooga. The 65th Ohio left the field less fifteen dead, sixty-eight wounded, and eighteen missing, presumed captured. Eight of the wounded later died. The regiment now mustered 9 officers and 169 men, or one-sixth its mustering-in strength.

Wilbur Hinman's letters about the battle of Chickamauga have all the emotion of someone who watched the battle from the moon. The regiment and Company E fought bravely under severe pressure. All the officers and men did their duty and fell in crippling numbers, especially the officers and sergeants so critical to unit cohesion. The shortage of water and ammunition made the defense of Snodgrass Hill a touch-and-go matter. The army had survived and would hold Chattanooga. The regiment's current duty was to protect the railroad. In sum, Lieutenant Hinman had entered the world of psychological numbing, fatalism, suppressed grief, and constant exhaustion that could be countered only by relief from combat and the daily demands of military routine. He did not report that he had been slightly wounded. His state-of-mind reflected the condition of the Army of the Cumberland, its commander relieved and its troops penned by Bragg's army in the trenches around Chattanooga.

Fresh from its campaign in Mississippi, U. S. Grant's western army, reinforced with two corps from the Army of the Potomac, massed around Chattanooga and drove off Bragg's army in November 1863. The battered Army of the Cumberland, now commanded by George H. Thomas, played a limited role in its own rescue. In the winter reorganization, the 65th Ohio, strengthened by some late recruits and returning wounded, remained in Harker's brigade, now part of the 2nd Division (Maj. Gen. John C. Newton), IV Corps (Maj. Gen. Gordon Granger). To keep Harker's command at reasonable strength, roughly 1,600 officers and men, the 65th Ohio became one of nine miniature regiments assigned to the brigade. Wilbur Hinman knew that "winter quarters" would end in the spring of 1864 when the combined western armies (Cumberland, Ohio, and Tennessee), commanded by Maj. Gen. William T. Sherman, would strike south for Atlanta and the destruction of Bragg's army.

For Hinman the new campaign brought his promotion to captain. The promotion reflected several changes in the 65th Ohio. Probably worn and sick of the responsibility of leading men to their deaths, Capt. Thomas Powell resigned his commission—but stayed with the regiment as its chaplain in the same rank. His brother Edward remained in Company E as its orderly sergeant. Hinman, however, left Company E to command Company F, which had no officers. The new Company E commander was Capt. Joseph F. Sonnanstine, the former lieutenant of Company K, who was promoted a month after Hinman. The two companies were much alike—a handful of veterans and a group of new soldiers. Company E joined twenty "replacements," of whom eight volunteered for a bounty, three came as paid substitutes for affluent draftees, and nine joined as draftees. Company F numbered fifteen veterans and twenty substitutes and draftees. Captain Hinman did not command a company of strangers, but he no longer wrote about his men as friends and neighbors. He wrote of them instead as simple soldiers who had no other duty than to obey his orders and fight.

Hinman reported to his friends that the 65th Ohio marched long miles and dug earthworks as it moved on Atlanta against the reorganized Army of Tennessee (Lt. Gen. Joseph E. Johnston). Engaged at Resaca and Dallas, Georgia, Company F lost eight more dead. Its next trial came at Kennesaw Mountain, June 27, 1864, when Sherman ordered a frontal assault on a heavily fortified Confederate trench system. To reach the first rebel rifle pits, Harker's brigade in a column of regiments would have to cross four hundred yards of open field, only to enter a maze of rocks and felled trees. Harker protested the attack, to no avail. In a sense, he continued his protest by leading the hopeless charge on horseback from the front, an act of suicidal courage—or rage. The charge went forward and actually reached the Confederate rifle pits at the base of the hill. The regiment then tried to climb Cheatham Hill, the heart of the defense. Harker fell mortally wounded in a blast of shrapnel, and the advance stopped. The brigade continued to endure plunging rifle and artillery fire for forty-five minutes before it cracked and fled back to its own trenches. Hinman, Sergeant Major George S. Pope, and three lieutenants saved the 65th Ohio's colors and rallied twenty-five to thirty men from the regiment. When the regiment reassembled, it counted its losses again: ten dead and wounded. It seemed like more.

The 65th Ohio fought on at Marietta, Peach Tree Creek, the first battle of Atlanta (July 22, 1864), and the siege of the city, abandoned by the Confederates on September 1–2. Eight more members of the regiment died in the summer fighting, but not from Company F. The regiment, however, was close to collapse, dramatized by the resignation of Lieutenant Colonel Whibeck, who had returned from the hospital to take command for the 1864 campaign, only to be wounded a third time at Kennesaw Mountain. Only a handful of stalwarts, such as the Powell brothers, Maj. Orlow Smith, Capt. Joe Willsey, Sonnanstine, and Hinman, chose to stay with the flag when the regiment mustered out some of the surviving 1861 enlistees in October 1864. Enough men reenlisted, however, for the 65th Ohio to retain its regimental identity and qualify for thirty days leave. It also became the 65th Ohio Infantry, Veteran Volunteers. Some twenty thousand Ohio volunteers of 1861 chose to stay with their colors in the autumn of 1864. The total strength of the 65th Ohio on November 1, 1864, was 130 officers and men.

Had the 65th Ohio known it would not join Sherman's "march to the sea" in the fall of 1864, the remaining veterans might have chosen to go home. The Army of the Cumberland occupied Atlanta after Sherman's two other armies departed to tear out the spiritual and economic heart of Georgia. Later, Thomas's army faced its old foe, the Army of Tennessee, now commanded by the crippled, drug-soaked John Bell Hood. The regiment fought at Spring Hill and Franklin in the Tennessee campaign of 1864–65 and lost six more dead and forty-four wounded. In the battle of Franklin, as part of Brig. Gen. David Wagner's division, the regiment occupied a ridge in front of the final Union lines and became swamped in Hood's grand assault of November 30. Fleeing to the trenches in front of the Carter house and gin mill, the 65th Ohio lost more than forty soldiers wounded or captured, about half the regiment. Those who escaped rallied to Opdycke's 125th Ohio and joined the "Tigers" for the furious assault that cleared the Union position, breached near the Carter house. After the battle of Nashville, which destroyed Hood's army, the 65th Ohio remained on occupation duties in Tennessee. It did participate in the Army of the Cumberland's greatest victory but saw little combat.

Hinman continued to write his "Dear Friends" and "Laura" on sporadic and limited occasions as he waited for the war to end. He wrote in April 1865 that his company was shocked and saddened by Lincoln's assassination but that he saw Lincoln as just another casualty. He did not reflect upon the death of Lincoln's peace policy. Instead he repeatedly worried about avoiding his own and his company's death in accidents. Ironically, he almost died in a train wreck while on leave in July 1865. After the Confederate surrender, the 65th Ohio joined the occupation forces in exotic New Orleans, then it traveled to Texas to join the army massed there for intervention in Mexico. During these travels Hinman became a major of Volunteers (October 1865). He served six days (November 24–30, 1865) as a lieutenant colonel before the regiment mustered out at Camp Chase, Columbus. Wilbur Fisk Hinman's war had ended, and he returned to Berea. He was twenty-five years old.

Looking back on the war, Hinman certainly remembered the losses of Company E, by his calculation twenty-one officers and men killed in battle or mortally wounded. The official record says the company had eight combat deaths and eleven deaths from other causes. By either accounting, one-fifth of the 126 men who served in Company E died in the service. Its losses were about average for the regiment, whose deaths by company ranged between fifteen (Company F) and thirty (Company G). Arduous service, however, left only eleven "originals" in Company E to muster out in 1865. Three veterans died in transportation accidents on the way back to Ohio. Instead, Hinman stressed the distances the regiment had traveled: 3,315 miles on foot, 3,115 miles by rail, and 3,585 by steamship. It had not only been a long war but a war of great distances for men who might never have left their native Ohio.

THE BIRTH OF SI KLEGG AND HIS PARD

Even if Wilbur Hinman had wanted to put the war behind him, his skill as a writer and his position as a veteran leader in the 65th Ohio Volunteers made him the memorialist of his old regiment. No one used the term "posttraumatic stress disorder" in 1865, but the condition seems to have been common among Civil War veterans. The first sign that Hinman had found some sense of normalcy came in 1870 when he married Sarah M. Everett, age twenty-eight. He was thirty. They became parents of two sons and a daughter before the end of the decade. The Hinmans settled in Cleveland, where Wilbur worked as a newspaper reporter and editor. He was well known enough to be elected clerk of the Common Pleas Court, Cuyahoga County, in 1875. He was reelected in 1878. He served concurrently on a committee formed by the Cleveland Board of Education to establish a library system for the city's public schools. Hinman's local political career apparently ended in 1881, and he left the city sometime in 1885 for Washington DC, which suggests some sort of appointment linked to Grover Cleveland's election as president.

There were two projects in Washington that would have interested Hinman: the organization of the Bureau of Pensions and Records and the compilation of the *Records of the War of the Rebellion*. By 1890, however, the Hinmans had moved back to northeastern Ohio and settled in the small city of Alliance, Stark County, not far from his own and his wife's families. At the time of the 1900 census, the Hinman family, reduced to three with the departure of the two Hinman sons, still resided in Alliance. Five years later Wilbur Fisk Hinman died on March 21. He must have had some political connections since he is buried in Arlington National Cemetery. The cemetery records call him "major, U.S. Army," a status he did *not* have in life. The widow Hinman, according to the census records, lived in Washington until her death on March 10, 1921. The Hinmans' common gravesite is marked with a large stone, and the inscription identifies Hinman as major, 65th Ohio Volunteer Infantry.

Either during or just after Hinman's time in Washington, N. G. Hamilton and Company of Cleveland published the first edition of *Corporal Si Klegg and His "Pard"* in 1887, followed by reprintings in 1889, 1890, and 1898. As Hinman promised, he told the story of how Union soldiers "lived and talked, and what they did and suffered, while fighting for the Flag." By one estimate the book sold more than thirty-five thousand copies, predominately to veterans. Si and Shorty belong to the fictitious Company Q, 200th Indiana Volunteers, but they really tell the story of Company E, 65th Ohio. Hinman's choice of Company Q was droll since many Union infantry regiments referred to those soldiers who were sick, lame, lazy, under punishment, absent without leave, detached, or generally invisible as "Company Q." Si and Shorty had begun their march to immortality.

Not all the veterans of the 65th Ohio wanted to be represented by Si and Shorty and their adventures. As Hinman later recounted his journey away from biographical-historical fiction to documented history, his comrades did not challenge the realism of *Corporal Si Klegg*. They simply wanted their families and descendants to read real names and learn about real battles and the challenges of dealing with the rebels, the terrain, the weather, and their own army. Like a good journalist and storyteller, Hinman had started to collect anecdotes and personal memories from his comrades in the 1880s. In 1892 the Hamilton Company published *Camp and Field: Sketches of Army Life Written by Those Who Followed the Flag, '61–65*, an anthology of stories told by veterans of the 64th and 65th Ohio. Hinman himself wrote seven of the anecdotes, but he edited the entire collection. Many of the stories had already found their way into *Corporal Si Klegg*.

Hinman found his audience still unsatisfied, and now the veterans of the Sherman Brigade were holding regular annual reunions and urging the Thucydides of Alliance to write a *real* unit history. Wilbur Hinman did his duty and applied his skills as an author, editor, and researcher until he finished *The Story of the Sherman Brigade*, published in 1897. The book fulfilled Hinman's promise to tell the true story of the brigade's war in "The Camp, the March, the Bivouac, the Battle, and how 'the Boys' lived and died, during four years of active service." The book covers the histories of the 64th and 65th Ohio Volunteer Infantry regiments and the 6th Battery, Ohio Light Artillery, attached to Harker's brigade until the 1864 campaign. The book also covers the service of an Ohio cavalry squadron that did not serve with the brigade as planned. Whatever the veterans thought of the book—and Hinman did find a commercial publisher—*The Story of the Sherman Brigade* remains one of the more notable regimental histories for understanding the Union army in "the west." At its heart, however, *The Sherman Brigade* is just a cleaned-up, repackaged version of *Corporal Si Klegg and His "Pard,"* complete with period photographs and company rosters. As fine a book of its type as *The Sherman Brigade* is, it is only one of several comparable regimental histories.

Corporal Si Klegg and His "Pard" is one of a kind.

NOTES ON SOURCES

I have used the Wilbur Fisk Hinman correspondence, 1861–65, in the archives of the Western Reserve Historical Society, Cleveland, Ohio, to reconstruct Hinman's military service. I received additional assistance from the library and archives of Baldwin-Wallace College, Berea, Ohio, and the library and archives of the Ohio Historical Society, Columbus, Ohio. I am indebted to the staff of these three repositories for their assistance.

In addition to Hinman's own books, I consulted Roster Commission, General Assembly, State of Ohio, *Official Roster of Soldiers of the State of Ohio in the War of the Rebellion, 1861–1865*, 12 vols. (Akron: Werner Printing and Manufacturing, 1887). Volume 5, pages 479–515, includes the regimental records of the 65th Ohio Volunteers. The initial deployment roster of the regiment is the monthly return, December 1861, 65th Ohio Volunteer Infantry Regiment, Records of the Adjutant General, Ohio Archives, Ohio Historical Society.

I consulted the online records of *The Encyclopedia of Cleveland History*; Arlington National Cemetery; the Civil War Pension Records (NARA); the U.S. Census; Ancestry.com; and the *War of the Rebellion Records* as posted by eHistory, a source managed by the Department of History, The Ohio State University, and sponsored by military history's great friend and my former student Mr. Scott Laidig. I also consulted the online Cornell University "Making of America" Project and a website for the *Official Records of the War of the Rebellion*. I depended upon the maps and order-of-battle information in *Blue and Gray* magazine, Columbus, Ohio, managed with care by the Dave Roth family. I thank Michael Edwards, Eisenhower Center, University of New Orleans, for his assistance. My pard Bill Feis reviewed the manuscript to my benefit.

For the possible linkage between *Corporal Si Klegg and His "Pard"* and *The Red Badge of Courage*, see H. T. Webster, "Wilbur F. Hinman's *Corporal Si Klegg* and Stephen Crane's *Red Badge of Courage*," *American Literature* 11 (November 1989): 285–93. For the literary context, see Daniel Aaron, *The Unwritten War: American Writers and the Civil War* (Madison: University of Wisconsin Press, 1987).

FURTHER READING

The descriptivist classics of Union army soldier life begin with John D. Billings, *Hardtack and Coffee: The Unwritten Story of Army Life* (1887; repr., Lincoln: University of Nebraska Press, 1993), held in high esteem by later historians since Billings was an articulate, observant veteran of the 10th Massachusetts Battery of Light Artillery, Army of the Potomac. Billings enlivened his book with sketches by Charles W. Read, also a Massachusetts gunner. The book was reprinted seven times and inspired Bell Irvin Wiley's *The Life of Billy Yank: The Common Soldiers of the Union* (Baton Rouge: Louisiana State University Press, 1952), a composite portrait of soldier life woven from the veterans' letters, diaries, and memoirs as well as regimental histories.

Both Civil War armies included literate and literary soldiers of all ranks who understood that they were part of America's greatest historical event since the Revolution, and they wrote about it during and after their service. The voluminous primary source material, complemented by pension records, allows historians to write "literary reconstructions" of soldier life that include impressions of the *mentalité* of those soldiers on the issues of political commitment, combat motivation, and psychological stress. At the time of this writing, the most influential of these studies are James M. McPherson, *For Cause and Comrade: Why Men Fought in the Civil War* (New York: Oxford University Press, 1997); Gerald F. Linderman, *Embattled Courage: The Experience of Combat in the American Civil War* (New York: The Free Press, 1987); James I. Robertson Jr., *Soldiers Blue and Gray* (Columbia: University of South Carolina Press, 1988); Reid Mitchell, *Civil War Soldiers* (New York: Simon & Schuster, 1988); and Gregory A. Coco, *The Civil War Infantryman* (Gettysburg PA: Thomas Publications, 1996). See also Gerald J. Prokopowicz, *All for the Regiment: The Army of the Ohio, 1861–62* (Chapel Hill: University of North Carolina Press, 2001). The most ambitious efforts to reconstruct the realities of combat from veterans' testimony are Earl J. Hess, *The Union Soldier in Battle: Enduring the Ordeal of Combat* (Lawrence: University Press of Kansas, 1997) and Hess, *The Rifle Musket in Civil War Combat: Reality and Myth* (Lawrence: University Press of Kansas, 2008), the latter book a useful corrective to the exaggerated accounts of the effects of Civil War ordnance on combat. Notable for its use of statistical analysis, although limited to Indiana regiments, is Eric T. Dean Jr., *Shook Over Hill: Post-Traumatic Stress, Vietnam, and the Civil War* (Cambridge MA: Harvard University Press, 1997).

The impact of military service on faith and values is probed in Steven E. Woodworth, *While God Is Marching On: The Religious World of Civil War Soldiers* (Lawrence: University Press of Kansas, 2001) and Randall M. Miller, Harry S. Stout, and Charles Reagan Wilson, eds., *Religion and the American Civil War* (New York: Oxford University Press, 1998). The issues of gender relations are the focus of Catherine Clinton and Nina Silber, eds., *Battle Scars: Gender and Sexuality in the American Civil War* (New York: Oxford University Press, 2006) and Thomas P. Lowry MD, *The Story the Soldiers Wouldn't Tell: Sex in the Civil War* (Mechanicsburg PA: Stackpole Books, 1994). For a recent, prize-winning "literary construct" about the cultural impact of Civil War deaths, see Drew Gilpin Faust, *This Republic of Suffering: Death and the American Civil War* (New York: Knopf, 2008), a monument to necromancy that draws too little distinction between common soldiers, officers, and civilians in its selective quotations that favor Oliver Wendell Holmes, Ambrose Bierce, Walt Whitman, Herman Melville, and Emily Dickinson.

THE AUTHOR TO HIS READERS.

MANY books have been written—and many more will be—upon subjects connected with the war for the Union. There is no end of histories—of campaigns and battles and regiments—and lives of prominent generals; but these do not portray the every-day life of the soldier. To do this, and this only, has been the aim of the author in "Corporal Si Klegg and his 'Pard.'"

This volume is not a history; nor is it a "story," in the usual acceptation of the word. "Si Klegg" and "Shorty," his "pard," are imaginary characters—though their prototypes were in every regiment—and Company Q, 200th Indiana, to which they belonged, is, of course, fictitious. Their haps and mishaps while undergoing the process of transformation that made them *soldiers*, and their diverse and constantly changing experiences on the march, the battle-field and the picket-line, in camp and bivouac, in hospital and prison, were those that entered directly into the daily life or observation of all the soldiers.

Carefully avoiding everything in the nature of burlesque or extravagance, the writer has aimed to present a truthful picture of "soldiering." He feels justified in the belief that such of his comrades as may read these pages will, at least, give him the credit of fidelity to the actual life of a million volunteers.

This book has not been written from hearsay. It was the writer's fortune to serve four years at the front, in a regiment which, with eleven hundred men on its rolls, from first to last, was reduced by the casualties of battle and the ravages of disease to one hundred and thirty, officers and men, present for duty at the time it was mustered out. It had traveled fifteen thousand miles—more than six thousand on foot. During the first year of his service the writer carried a musket and knapsack. These facts are mentioned only to show that he had abundant experience, without which it would be folly to attempt such a book as this.

The vivid memories of those four eventful years have supplied all the material. No other source has been drawn upon for information or suggestion. The author has made no attempt at literary embroidery, but has rather chosen the "free and easy" form of language that marked the intercourse of the soldiers, and therefore seemed most appropriate to the theme. He has tried to flavor the narrative with the spice of army life—for there was some "fun," though a great deal more of the reverse character—endeavoring to present the picture in all its varied hues.

Thinking it possible that some may read this volume who have no experimental knowledge of life in the army, the author has devoted pages, here and there, to information of an explanatory nature, which he hopes will assist them in appreciating, perhaps as never before, how the soldiers lived—and died.

The patriotism, the sacrifice and the suffering were not confined to the army. The home scenes herein presented were common to every city and village and hamlet, from Maine to California.

It is believed that the illustrations will prove an attractive feature. They were all drawn expressly for this work, and cover every phase of the subject. They will bring to the eyes of the veterans many scenes that were familiar in days long past. The author wishes to express his obligation to Mr. George Y. Coffin, whose ready pencil and fertile mind have so faithfully carried out his designs. He appreciates the more highly this assistance, because he could never, himself, "draw" anything except rations.

With fraternal greetings to all his late comrades-in-arms the author sends out this volume, indulging the hope that they may find pleasure and interest in living over again the stirring scenes of a quarter of a century ago, in the experiences of "Si Klegg" and "Shorty."

WILBUR F. HINMAN.

Washington, D. C., September, 1887.

CONTENTS.

CHAPTER I.

CHAPTER XXXIX.

CHAPTER XL.

CHAPTER XLI.

CHAPTER XLII.

CHAPTER XLIII.

CHAPTER XLIV.

CHAPTER XLV.

CHAPTER XLVI.

CHAPTER XLVII.

CHAPTER XLVIII.

LIST OF ILLUSTRATIONS.

Corporal Si Klegg.

CHAPTER I.

IN WHICH SI KLEGG, CARRIED AWAY BY HIS TUMULTUOUS EMOTIONS, ENLISTS IN COMPANY Q, OF THE TWO HUNDREDTH INDIANA.

LATE in the summer of 1862, a smart-looking young man made his appearance in a little village in the hoop-pole region of Indiana. On his shoulders were the straps of a second lieutenant. His brand-new uniform, faultless in cut and make, fitted him "like the paper on the wall." His step was brisk, and he cultivated a military air with untiring assiduity. His padded coat bulged out over his patriotic bosom like the mainsail of a ship scudding before a spanking breeze; and this was made the more conspicuous by his extreme erectness of carriage as he strutted among the quiet village folk. He was proud of his new clothes, with their shining brass buttons, and proud of himself. His face wore a fierce and sanguinary look, as if he chafed under the restraint which kept him beneath peaceful northern skies. His eyes seemed longing to gaze upon the lurid flames of war. Everybody imagined that he was consuming with a desire to rush to the front, that he might plunge into scenes of carnage.

He was a recruiting officer.

As he will soon disappear from the narrative, it may be remarked here that he did not want to wade in blood half as badly as people thought he did, nor, quite possibly, as he thought himself. He had no occasion to invest in rubber boots to wear on the battlefield. He did not get

so much as a sniff of powder in a state of violent combustion. Before the regiment was organized his health
suddenly gave way and he resigned.

But at this time he appeared the very embodiment of
martial ardor—an ideal soldier. The simple-hearted gray-
beards of the village put on their spectacles to look at
him; the lasses blushed at their own admiring glances as he
passed in his ma-
jestic splendor;
the young men, in
jeans and home-
spun, gazed with
envy upon his
symmetry of
shape and gor-
geous apparel,
and wished they
might be like him;
the small boys
looked upon him
with unutterable
awe, and trailed
after him through
the streets as
though he were
the drum-major
of a brass band.

Such was the
advent of the re-

THE RECRUITING OFFICER.

cruiting officer into this quiet hamlet. A few of its ready
sons had gone to the war in '61, moved by the mighty
feeling that so profoundly stirred the north after the fall
of Sumter; but this was the first effort there to raise a
company, under the great call for volunteers in 1862,
which seemed to say to every one, "Thou art the man!"

The officer procured a room over the village postoffice,

and hung out of the window a big flag that brushed the heads of the passers-by. Buildings and fences far and near were decorated with flaming posters, which set forth in startling type the unequaled advantages guaranteed to those who should enlist in Company Q of the 200th Indiana regiment. After reading the placard the confiding youth would imagine that the patriots of that company would always have carriages to ride in and feather beds to sleep on; they would be clad in purple and fine linen and fare sumptuously every day, with cream in their coffee and "soft bread" all the year round. None of them would get hurt, as many of the less fortunate soldiers did; they would while away the time in guarding prisoners or on provost or headquarters duty. In short, Company Q would have for three years little else than a protracted picnic.

This was the alluring idea conveyed by the posters and the advertisement conspicuously displayed in the village paper. The worthy editor, who believed that the pen was mightier than the sword, wrote a notice highly commending the smart young officer, and calling attention to the rare privileges that would be enjoyed by all who joined his company. Of course, he knew all about it because the smart young officer told him. The oracular words of the editor were not without effect in stimulating the spirit of enlistment in the village and the region round about. The grand impulse of '61 had spent its force in this community as elsewhere, and a little urging was often found to be necessary. The recruiting officer who could hold out the most seductive inducements was likely to reap the most abundant harvest. At least such was the theory that governed recruitment after the first spontaneous rush to arms.

Having thus adroitly scattered the seed, the officer hired a fifer and drummer to stand on the sidewalk at the foot of the stairs and play "Yankee Doodle" and other inspiring tunes, and then sat down in his office to gather in the crop. As soon as a recruit was enlisted he was arrayed in baggy blue clothes and sent forth as a missionary to bring in others. Under all these favorable conditions the roll of Company Q lengthened rapidly.

One day while this was going on Si Klegg drove into the village with a lot of butter, eggs and other farm truck, which his mother had commissioned him to exchange for sundry groceries needed to replenish the larder of the Klegg household. He was a red-cheeked, chubby-faced boy who had some distance yet to go before getting out of his teens. He had worked hard ever since he was large enough to make himself useful. The demand for his services upon the farm, increasing as he grew older, had confined within narrow limits his opportunities for education. These had not gone beyond a few winters at the "district school." He had seen nothing of the great world that lay beyond the bounds of his immediate neighborhood.

Si had a frenzied attack of war fever in '61, when the drums beat in response to the President's first call. His parents were not willing that he should go on account of his youth. He was a good lad—his father's pride and his mother's joy. He pleaded that the war would only last a few weeks and that his whole future life would be embittered by the thought that he had no hand in it. But the parental heart was for the time inexorable, and Si obediently yielded, secretly indulging the hope, however, that the rebels would not be whipped until he should be old enough to go.

As the weeks sped away none were more eager than he to hear the news. When he read of a little skirmish that had resulted favorably to the Union troops he swung his hat and shouted with the rest; but there was a sinking of his heart, because he thought the war was about over and he was going to "get left." Then when he heard of another brush—people called them all battles then—in which half a dozen Union pickets had been captured, he lamented the success of the foes of his country, but his spirits rose as he thought that possibly, after all he might yet be a soldier and with the soldiers stand; a knapsack on his back and a musket in his hand.

Then when the President called for three hundred thousand men for three years, Si's heart gave a great leap. Three years in the army would just suit him; and surely his parents would not refuse now that the demand was so urgent. Here re-opened the debate with great enthusiasm; but father and mother were still inflexible, and again he submitted. He did this the more willingly because of his growing belief that the affair would not blow over in a few days and he would patiently bide his time to get in.

SI KLEGG.

Si's patriotic emotions, animated by the fiery ardor of youth, bubbled with constantly increasing fury in his swelling breast, and at the time the brass buttons of the

recruiting officer twinkled in the village he was almost at
the point of bursting. In his fervid zeal he

> "Scorned the lowing cattle;
> He burned to wear a uniform,
> Hear drums and see a battle."

Such was Si's mental condition when he drove into
town that day. It became still more inflamed when
he read one of the recruiting officer's big posters; and
his passionate eagerness almost overcame him when
two or three of his friends sauntered up in full uniform.
He felt that he could not endure the pressure much
longer.

"Hello, Si," said one of the military fledgelings, "what
d'ye stan' there gawpin' at that han'bill fer? Why don't
ye come down to the 'cruitin' office an' 'list, 'long with the
rest o' the boys?"

Si had never in his life wanted half so badly to do anything as he did to walk straight to where the flag was
flying and the fife and drum playing, sign his name to the
roll of Company Q, and get inside of a blouse and sky-blue
trousers. He had more than half a mind to carry out his
ardent impulse at once and take the chances on his action
being ratified by the home authorities.

"I want ter jine yer comp'ny mighty bad but—"

Si had not the heart to finish the sentence. His thoughts
might have been easily read in his eyes as he gazed long-
ingly at the bright brass buttons on the clothes of his
friends and the nodding plumes that decorated their
enormous hats.

"'Fore I'd be tied to my mammy's apurn string!" was
the derisive reply. "Why don't ye be a man! All the
boys is goin', an' ye don't want ter stay behind fer the
gals to p'int their fingers at and say ye was 'fraid ter
go. Come 'long, an' never mind yer dad an' the old
woman!"

"Look a-here, Bill," and Si began to show symptoms of a furious eruption, "you 'n' me has allus bin good friends; but if you say 'nother word agin me er my father 'n' mother ye won't have ter wait t'll ye git down among the seceshers—if ye ever *do* git thar—to have the biggest kind of a fight. One er t'other on us 'll git the all-firedest lickin' ye ever hee rn tell of. P'r'aps ye'll find out that ef I ain't a very big pertater I'm kind o' hard to peel. I ain't no coward. I'm goin' ter try 'n' git inter this comp'ny. I don't b'lieve in braggin', but ef I do go with ye, ye'll never git court-martialed fer hangin' back er runnin' the wrong way ef ye jest keep right up 'longside o' Si Klegg!"

It may be fairly said that the circumstances justified the warmth and earnestness of Si's manner. Involuntarily his fat fists clenched, and he assumed an attitude of hostility that alarmed his comrade. The latter prudently retired out of range.

"Ye don't need ter git spunky 'bout it, Si," he said from a safe distance. "Ye know I didn't mean nothin'. Ye'd make a bully soljer, an' the boys 'd like fust rate to have ye 'long. Comp'ny Q 's goin' ter have a soft thing, 'cause the officer says he's got it all fixed. She's a-fillin' up purty fast, an' we're goin' ter leave in a few days, so ye'll have ter hustle 'round!"

"I don't know ner care nothin' 'bout the easy time ye say ye're goin' ter have. Ef I knowed Comp'ny Q wouldn't never do nothin' but stay back in the rear I'd jine some other rijiment. Ef I'm goin' ter be a soljer I want ter *be* one 'n' do suthin' more'n strut 'round in a uniform. But I reckon as how Comp'ny Q 'll have ter take its chances 'long with the rest."

Si wanted to go down to the headquarters but he scarcely dared trust himself to do so. He feared that the temptation to "jine" would be stronger than his power of resistance. Just at that critical moment the fife and drum struck up a lively air and that settled it. His friends were already on the way to the recruiting office.

"Hold up," shouted Si, "I'm goin' that way," and he started after them at a brisk pace.

"I thought ye'd come to it," said one of them, as they stopped for him to join them.

"I sha'n't 'list to-day," replied Si, "I jest thought I'd look in thar 'n' see what's goin' on."

The truth is that, notwithstanding this positive declaration, he "felt it in his bones" that he would go home that afternoon wearing blue clothes. He was badly broken up when he thought of the consternation that he was sure his appearance at the old farm in the garb of a soldier would produce. He did not want to enlist without parental consent, as he had promised, and he kept trying to make himself believe that he was not going to. His conscience told him that he ought to turn around and go to his wagon and drive straight home, but the magnet that was drawing him along in spite of himself was irresistible He couldn't help it; he *had* to go. His feet caught the step of the drum-taps and he marched to what he felt would be his fate, borne along by a tide of emotions as resistless as the flood of a raging river.

The discordant sound of the squeaky fife and rattling drum was the sweetest music that had ever greeted the ears of Si Klegg. He mingled in the crowd of old and young that stood around the musicians talking about the war — the one subject that was first upon every tongue. They all knew Si, and again and again he was asked if he was going to enlist. He could not say no and he dared not say yes, although he felt away down in his heart that there were nineteen chances out of twenty that within the next thirty minutes there would be another "K" added to the roll of Company Q, and he would be trying on his regimentals.

The only thing that prevented Si from rushing at once into the presence of the recruiting officer was the ever haunting thought of father and mother. He tried to argue himself into the belief that his duty to his country was first, and that in responding to her call in the time of her extremity he was doing no violence to the fifth commandment. Aided by the persuasive influences that surrounded him, he so far succeeded in quieting his

STIMULATING VILLAGE PATRIOTISM.

conscience that when one of his companions, who was in a similar state of mind, said to him, "I'll 'list if you will," Si replied, "Come on," and started at once up the stairs. The flood had carried him completely over the dam.

A moment later Si stood, with his hat under his arm, in the presence of the recruiting officer. Dazzled by the splendor of his appearance, Si shrank back abashed for a moment. The officer was busily engaged in superintending the efforts of two or three recruits to fit themselves out of an assortment of army clothing that lay scattered about the room. Si had a chance to recover and brace himself for the trying ordeal.

"Ah, my man," said the lieutenant, extending his hand to Si, "you've come to join my company, haven't you? You do not need to answer, for I know it by your looks. You'll make a splendid soldier, too—just the sort of brave fellows we want. Walk right up to the table and sign your name. We're going to have the finest company that ever left the state."

"Say, mister, I jest wants ter ax ye ef a feller kin git out agin ef he *has* ter arter he's jined."

At the last moment a sense of his filial obligations prompted Si to provide, if possible, for keeping open a line of retreat. Fearful lest his motive might be misconstrued, however, he hastily added:

"'Tain't 'cause I wants ter back out, fer I don't; but ye see I'm 'feard pap 'll kick. He made me promise I wouldn't 'list 'less he was willin', 'n' I know he aint."

"Oh, that 'll be all right," said the officer. "We'll fetch the old man around easy enough. You put your name right down and get your uniform on. When he sees how fine you look he'll pat you on the head and tell you to go right along like a man and fight for your bleeding country."

"Gimme the pen 'n' I'll chance it."

Si sat down to the table and with much effort succeeded in producing his autograph on the roll of Company Q. His heart thumped violently as he looked at his name and began to realize that he was going to be a soldier. It is true that the chickens he was counting were not yet fully hatched, for he could not rid himself of the vague fear that there would be trouble at the farm-house. But he persuaded himself that it would end as he so fervently desired; and when he arose he felt that he was taller by a foot than when he entered the room.

"Now, Mr. Klegg," said the lieutenant, "just step into that room and let the doctor examine you."

"What's that fer?" asked Si.

"To see if you are sound and able to discharge the duties of a soldier."

"The doctor 'll only be wastin' his time 'zaminin' me," replied Si. "I'm sound 's a hicker'-nut."

"No doubt of it; but the army regulations require it, and we have to obey them, you know."

Si had a foggy idea that obedience was one of the cardinal virtues of a good soldier, and without further objection he passed into the apartment, where the village doctor, duly invested with the proper authority, was inspecting the physical condition and "prior soundness" of those who were about to enter the military service.

"Now, young man, strip yourself," said the doctor, in a business-like way, when Si's turn came.

It seemed to Si that there was a good deal of foolishness about such a performance. The doctor evidently shared this opinion as he looked upon the robust form and well-turned limbs of the farmer-boy. A single glance told his experienced eye that Si would fill the bill. He passed his hands over the limbs of the recruit, looked at his feet, drummed on his chest and ribs, and then pressed his ear against his breast.

"Your heart beats a little hard and rapidly," said the doctor, "but I guess it's only because you're a bit excited. I think you'll do, my lad, and I'm greatly mistaken if you do not make a good, brave soldier. Just one thing more, let me see your teeth."

Si thought it was very much as if he was a colt and somebody wanted to buy him. But he was pleased with the doctor's verdict, and only said with a laugh:

"I don't see what teeth 's got ter do 'th bein' a soljer."

"You will be wiser after a time, my young friend," said the doctor with a smile. "You will find good teeth very useful in biting cartridges and chewing hardtack."

"What's hardtack?" said Si, his face not less than his words betokening his curiosity.

"Oh, that's what the soldiers call the bread they get in the army. But you hadn't better ask any more questions; you'll know all about it in a little while."

"Nice boy!" the doctor said to the lieutenant. "A little too much flesh just now, but a few weeks of active campaigning will bring him down to good marching weight. I'd like to be colonel of a regiment of such fellows."

AN AVERAGE ARMY "FIT."

"You can put these on if you like, Mr. Klegg," said the officer, handing him a pair of pants and a blouse. "I guess they are about your size."

No five-year-old boy was ever prouder when he laid aside his pinafore and donned his first pair of breeches than was Si when he arrayed himself in the habiliments of a soldier. It mattered little that the trousers were several inches too long, and the blouse so small that it embraced him like a corset. As his eyes feasted upon the blue garments and the burnished brass buttons, his fears all gave way before the confident belief that his appearance would sweep aside all the objections of his father and mother and sister Maria and pretty Annabel, the neighbor's daughter.

CHAPTER II.

WHEN Si Klegg left the recruiting office and tripped gayly down the stairs with his farm clothes in a bundle under his arm, he was greeted with loud cheers by the crowd on the sidewalk. He was a favorite in the village, where he had been known from a child. The people thronged about him and took him by the hand, all uniting in the cordially expressed hope that he would "come out all right." No one had any fear that he would make other than an honorable record.

By this time the day was well spent, and Si began to think about getting home. A cloud of seriousness crept over his face as he wondered what his "folks" would say and do. His first impulse was to go into somebody's barn and change his clothes, to relieve the surprise of its suddenness. He thought it might be better to go home in his accustomed garments and then, by clever diplomacy, let the cat out of the bag little by little. The effect would be less startling than if she jumped out all at once. Then came the thought that this would be cowardly, and he at once resolved to go right ahead and face the music like a man. He believed he was not afraid to meet rebels with guns in their hands, and surely he must not quail before his father and mother and sister Maria.

"I'll lay the gad on the old mare, too!" he said to himself, half aloud. "I'm in fer it, 'n' the sooner the thing's over with the better. I ain't goin' ter go sneakin' 'n' beatin' 'round the bush, nuther!'"

Si was soon on his way. His activity in the use of the "gad" produced a degree of speed that the mare, who was in the sear and yellow leaf of her existence, only attained on extraordinary occasions. She laid back her ears and forged ahead, as if conscious that something of unusual importance was in the wind.

It was only a couple of miles from the village to the Klegg farm, and the ride took but twenty minutes. As Si neared the house he drew rein that he might, if possible, calm his agitation. His heart beat fast at the thought of meeting his mother—and then of bidding her good-bye to march away to the war. He had not realized before how hard this would be.

Looking away he saw his father slowly coming from his toil in a distant field. The story of the Prodigal Son came up before him. While he could not admit the justice of comparing himself to the wayward wanderer, yet at that moment he would have given the world, had he possessed it, to be assured that his father would receive him as the father in the parable received the son who "was lost and is found." Si had not intended to be undutiful, or to do anything wrong.

Turning his eyes and looking through the soft, shadowy twilight that was already falling, he saw his sister coming slowly up the lane with the cows. Again his heart throbbed wildly. He had not thought what it would be to leave her whose loving companionship had been a part of his daily existence. How *her* heart would ache when he should be far away amidst scenes of hardship, suffering and death.

Such a moment had never come to Si as that when he alighted from the wagon, took his parcels in his arms, and walked toward the house. With a mighty effort to control his feelings he opened the door and entered. He passed directly to the kitchen, where he knew he would find his mother engaged in the preparation of the evening meal.

"Mother," he said—and he knew that his voice was tremulous, hard as he tried to keep it steady—"I've brought you the things you wanted from the store."

She was busy at her work, with her face from him. For a moment she did not look at him, only remarking, with a shade of anxiety in her gentle tones:

"You've been gone a long time, Josiah. I've looked for you these two hours. What's goin' on in the village? Any news from the war?"

"Mother!"

None but a mother can know what was in that word as it fell from the lips of Si. Her maternal instinct told her, quick as the lightning's flash, that she must make the sacrifice that thousands of mothers had made before her. The knife dropped from her trembling hand. For an instant she stood, with face still averted, as if to gather strength for the trial which she had long felt she must face sooner or later. Day and night she had prayed that the cup might pass from her. It had come, and in that moment she resolved, with the spirit of the mothers of Sparta, to meet it with a patriot's devotion.

Then she turned and cast a look of unutterable tenderness upon her boy, already a soldier. He sprang toward her and she folded him in her arms. Tears trickled from the eyes of both. Their hearts were too full for words. As her soft kisses fell like a benediction on brow and cheek, Si felt that his mother was tenfold dearer than ever before.

"My son," she said, "I feel that it is right. You cannot know how hard it is for me to say that. But it is duty that calls, and I'm proud of ye for bein' so brave and manly. I knew ye'd be goin' one o' these days, an' I'd kinder got my mind made up to it; but it aint an easy thing for a mother to send her only boy off to war."

"But—father—" said Si, inquiringly.

"Father won't be hard on ye, Si," she replied. "We've talked it over many an hour when ye've been asleep, an'

SI AND HIS MOTHER.

he feels a good deal like I do. I guess he'd a *leetle* rather you'd spoke to him 'bout it 'fore ye' listed, but if I don't mistake he'll give ye his blessin' an' tell ye to go an' do yer duty like a hero, just as I know ye will."

The outer door opened and a familiar step was heard in the adjoining room.

"Stay here a moment, Si," said his mother, as she hastily withdrew her arms from him and brushed away her tears. "Let me say a word to father first."

Si still dreaded to meet his father, although this feeling had yielded in some measure before the loving words of his mother. His heart filled with gratitude to her for the delicate tact which prompted her to shield him from a possible harsh word.

"Thank ye, mother!" he faltered.

"Father," she said, as she went in to meet her husband. She was trying to control herself, but her trembling lip and misty eyes betrayed the emotions she could not conceal.

"Why, mother," he interrupted, "what's the matter? Anything gone wrong to-day? Hasn't Si got back from town?"

"Yes, Si's here—but—he's got a new suit o' clothes on—and they're *blue!* Now, father, I told him you wouldn't be hard on him, an' I know ye won't. He's *my* boy as much as *yours*, an' if I can bear it you can."

For a moment he did not speak; a shade passed over his face, but it gradually melted away before the pleading gaze of the wife and mother. Then he said:

"You know we've been expectin' it, mother, for a good while. Si haint said much 'bout it lately, but it was plain to see that he was just achin' to go all the time. If we had half a dozen other boys it wouldn't be any easier to let him go; but we could get along better without him than we can bein' as he's the only one. If he'd waited till I'd ha' give my consent I reck'n he wouldn't ha' gone at all, for I don't b'lieve I could ha' made up my mind to say he might jine the army. But it looks 's though they'd need all the men they can git 'fore they bring them seceshers to their senses, an' I persume we'd ought ter be willin' to let Si go an' help 'em. Lookin' at it on all sides I guess it was best for him to 'list in the way he did, 'cause as I was sayin', I couldn't ha' screwed myself up to the point o' tellin' him he might."

A glad smile, though it was not without a tinge of sadness, lighted up the countenance of Si's mother. With the sacrificing heroism that so grandly characterized the women of that time, she had fully accepted the truth that she must give up her boy. She knew that his heart, like her own, was full almost to bursting, and she rejoiced to

know that he would not have to bear the added burden of
a father's displeasure.

"Josiah, come here!"

Si had stood trembling where his mother left him, during
the interview between his parents. He could not hear the
words, but the tones of his father's voice were not those
of an angry man, and he felt that if he had done wrong he
would be forgiven. When his father called him his hand
was already upon the latch. Quickly opening the door he
advanced to meet the outstretched arms of his father.
Tears that were not unmanly dimmed the eyes and wetted
the brown cheeks of the old farmer as he folded his boy to
his breast.

"I aint goin' to say a word agin it, Si," he said, after a
long embrace. "Other folks has to let their boys go, an' I
musn't think I'm better 'n anybody else. But it makes me
feel like a baby to think of ye goin' down 'mong the soljers
an' likely's not we shan't never——"

"Don't, father," said his wife, gently, "we musn't talk
of that now. If I didn't believe God 'd let Si come back to
us, I couldn't let him go; that 'd be askin' too much."

"Well, well, dear, I couldn't help thinkin' what a dangerous place it is down there, an' how many other people's
boys wont never see home agin. There's jest one thing I
want to say to ye, Si. Ye know somethin' 'bout how dear
ye are to me—I don't need to tell ye that—but I'd a hunderd times rather ye'd get killed when ye was standin'
up to your duty like a brave soljer, an' be buried with
nothin' but a blanket 'round ye, than to hear anybody
say that my boy was a coward. But I aint afeard that
we'll ever be 'shamed of ye, Si. Mother, hadn't we better
have supper?"

"Why, bless me, if I didn't forgit all 'bout supper!" exclaimed the good woman, as she started for the kitchen,
"but Si comin' in so sudden with them soljer clothes on,

jest upsot me an' driv all thoughts o' cookin' clean out o' my head."

When she reached the culinary department she found things in a disastrous plight. The potatoes in the oven were baked to a crisp, the pork in the spider had fried to cinders, and the teakettle was boiling over with great fury, emitting a volume of steam that filled the room. Mrs. Klegg had to begin all over again.

It was a matter of small concern to Si whether he had any supper at all or not. A great load had been lifted from his heart. At last his ambition was to be realized. In a few days he would march away to the field of glory, and he would go with his mother's prayers and his father's blessing. It was the happiest moment he had ever known. His fervent imagination saw only the lights of an untried life. None of its deep shadows darkened the picture that his fancy painted.

"Father," he said, "I'll go out 'n' tell Marier the news 'n' then I'll help ye do the chores."

"Sister Marier," a rosy lass, two years older than Si, was coming from the barnyard with a pail of milk in either hand. As she bent beneath the load her eyes were upon the ground, and she did not observe the approach of Si through the gathering dusk until he said, in a cheerful tone:

"Let me carry 'em fer ye, Marier."

"That you, Si?" she said, as she raised her eyes.

In an instant the pails dropped from her grasp and the milky flood inundated the ground at their feet. Raising her hands in surprise, she exclaimed:

"For the land's sake, Si, what are ye doin' with them clothes on? Borrered 'em from one o' the boys, didn't ye, to see how ye'd look in 'em?"

"These clothes is mine. I'm a soljer now!"

"What, you?" Then as the truth burst upon her she added, in a tone that touched his heart, "Oh, Si!"

Circling her arms about his neck, her feelings found vent in a flood of tears.

Si felt that he was having a rather sloppy time of it, and he was really glad that the family was no larger, and that he had now got around. Yet his experience during the half hour since he reached home had been to him in the nature of a revelation. There had been nothing in the every-day farm life of the family to test the strength of the cord that bound them together. Si supposed, as a matter of course, that his father and mother and sister loved him, as it was their duty to do. He had always been conscious of a reciprocity of feeling toward them. Now he knew, as never before, how strong are the ties of affection, and how heavily falls the blow that severs them.

CALAMITOUS EFFECT OF THE NEWS UPON "SISTER MARIER."

"There, don't cry any more, sister," he said, kissing her tenderly. "You know I couldn't help doin' it. But I made ye spill all the milk 'n' I'll go down 'n' pump some fer supper. S'pose I'll have to git 'long without milk in the army, 'n' I'd better fill up while I've got a chance."

There were some of the cows whose lacteal fountains had not been drawn upon, so that the catastrophe that had befallen Maria promised to result no more seriously than to make the next "churning" a trifle short.

"Well, old Brindle, don't ye wish you was me?" exclaimed Si, in the exuberance of his spirits. "H'ist, there, why don't ye! Now, so, Bossy, so!" and he was soon milking away with all his might, singing to himself:

"We are coming, Father Abraham, three hundred thousand more."

"That's so," he soliloquized, " 'n' I'm one o' them bully three hunderd thousan'. Yes, Father Abraham, Si Klegg's comin'. Jest have the army wait t'll he gits thar 'n' then ye can drive ahead."

When Si entered the house with brimming pail he found supper waiting. Mother and sister greeted him with fond looks and gentle words. They had placed upon the table every delicacy that the house afforded. Jars and cans, such as hitherto had only been brought forth on state occasions, were opened and their contents dished out with a prodigality that under any other circumstances would have been amazing.

A thrifty housewife is moved by an impulse of no ordinary magnitude when she scatters her precious jellies and preserves and pickles and things in such reckless profusion. If Si had stopped to think of this he would have needed no stronger evidence of the place he held in the estimation of at least the female members of the family.

"Si always did like these little knick-knacks so," his mother said to Maria, "an' goodness knows he won't have any of 'em down there. Whatsomever 's in this house is his 's long 's he's here. I'd jest enj'y seein' him eat up the last bit of 'em. If any comp'ny comes they can go without."

Meanwhile, "Father" had come in from his "chores," and the four sat down to the evening meal. Thrice each day for many a year they—father, mother, sister, brother—had gathered around that table, but never before had there been such an all-pervading spirit of gentleness and affection. The very air seemed fragrant with the incense from those loving hearts. The little spark had kindled into a fierce flame the latent fires of love in the breasts of that household.

The sudden rush of feeling had subsided, giving way to a calm determination to make the best of the situation. Gradually the members of the little group regained a measure of their wonted cheerfulness. Si's elastic spirits rebounded the instant the pressure upon them was relaxed.

"You haven't told us yet how you came to 'list," said his mother, as she heaped again with preserves a dish that he had already emptied.

This started Si's tongue, and he rattled off the story of the day's adventures.

"I'll tell ye how 'twas," he said. "I druv straightwise to the store and done all the arrands ye wanted me to. Then I thought I'd look 'round a bit 'fore I started hum. I heerd right away thar was a 'cruitin' ossifer 'n town. I tell ye he's a daisy, too; must be a big gin'ral er suthin' like that. I seen lots o' the boys that had 'listed walkin' 'round with their uniforms on. Some on 'em told me I'd better jine if I didn't want ter be grafted, as they was goin' ter begin graftin' purty soon. There was a fife 'n' drum a-playin' at the 'cruitin' office, 'n' when I heerd 'em I jest *had* to go down. There was a crowd there, and everybody was a-cheerin' 'n' shoutin' 'n' the flag was a-flyin'. I kep' sayin' to myself I wouldn't jine till I'd been hum 'n' axed ye agin; but while I was stan'in' thar Tommy Smith says to me, says he, 'Si, I'll dar' ye to 'list; ef you will I will.' I says, 'Tom, who's afeard?'—jest that way. ''Tain't me,' says I, ''n' if you ain't nuther walk up to the scratch.' He didn't back out, ner I didn't, 'n' in 'bout ten minutes we both b'longed to Comp'ny Q. She's goin' ter be the boss comp'ny, too. That's the way it happened, 'n' I don't see how a boy like me could ha' done any different. Jest one spoonful more o' that currant jell', mother, please."

"The fact is, Si," said the head of the family, "I s'pose I could get ye out by goin' to law, 'cause ye're a long ways under age an' I didn't give my consent fer ye to 'list."

"But ye won't do that, will ye, father?" said Si quickly, with a look of alarm.

"No, Si. Ye've done it an' I aint goin' to find no fault. I don't quite see how I'm goin' to git 'long without ye on the farm."

"I'll send home to ye all the money I 'arn," said Si, "'n' ye can hire a man to take my place."

"Uncle Sam 'll make ye work purty cheap, Si. Thirteen dollars a month aint very much, 'n' I reckon what ye'll have left arter usin' what ye need won't 'mount to a great deal. The men 'round here 's all goin' to the war. Farm hands is gittin' skurce an' wages is high an' goin' higher."

"But ye never got such big prices afore fer yer wheat 'n' corn 'n' pork," observed Si, to whom it seemed that, in a financial point of view, the case was not without its compensating features.

"Mother an' me can help ye, father," said Maria, who had sat quiet and thoughtful, taking little part in the conversation. "There isn't anybody feels wuss 'bout Si's goin' 'n I do, but all the same I'm proud of him! An' if we work a leetle harder an' fill his place we'll all feel that we're doin' somethin' for the country. A woman can't shoulder a gun an' march an' fight, but there's a good many ways she can help."

So it was all settled that Si should go to the war. He arose from the table happy in heart and in stomach. He bustled around for a time, bringing in a bountiful supply of water and wood and kindlings, and doing everything he could think of for his mother and sister. Then he put on his hat and started for the door.

"Where ye goin', Si?" asked his mother.

"I'll be back after a bit," he replied, evasively. The light of the tallow candle was too faint to reveal the blush that mantled his tingling cheeks.

"Don't be too inquisitive, mother," said Maria, as Si made a hasty exit.

Si bent his steps toward the home where Annabel lived, a quarter of a mile away. He walked very fast at first, so anxious was he to see the neighbor's pretty daughter and tell her all about it. He wondered if she would feel badly about his going away. He couldn't help hoping she would—just a little.

Si and Annabel had been playmates from childhood. They had grown up together, and Si had come, little by little, to feel a sense of proprietorship in her—almost impalpable, and yet to him an existing reality. No other boy in the neighborhood had so well-established a right as he to take Annabel sleigh-riding in winter and to the circus in summer. Up to the time of his enlistment not a word had ever passed between them that could make their relations any more definite than would naturally result from a childish fancy. Among their companions she was recognized as Si's "girl" and he as her legitimate "beau."

As Si paced along that night he was conscious that he had that day made a long stride toward manhood. He felt that he was a boy no longer, and with this came a feeling toward Annabel that he had never experienced before. He had heard of people being "in love," but up to this time had only a vague idea of what that meant. After thinking it over he made up his mind that he was in that condition, whatever it was. On no other hypothesis could he satisfy himself regarding the sensations that thrilled him more and more as he drew nearer, step by step, to her father's door. In fact, by the time he reached the gate it was about an even race between his country and Annabel for the first place in his affections.

Si did not at once rush into the house. The agitation of his heart was such as to utterly destroy his courage. He walked some distance past and then turned around and walked as far the other way, striving to quiet the turmoil in his breast; but the more he tried the more he couldn't do it. The symptoms were those of a malignant case.

For half an hour he patrolled the beat in front of the house, as if it were the headquarters of a general and he the guard. At every turn, ashamed of his timidity, he resolved that he would march straight to the door, but as often, by the time he reached the gate, his courage had all oozed out at the ends of his fingers and toes. Then he would keep on, gathering strength again as the distance increased, and at length face about and repeat the performance. Once the watch-dog came out and barked at him until he felt that he would like to kill the animal had he not known Annabel's fondness for him. The farmer opened the door and looked out to see what it was that had provoked such a breach of the peace. Si dropped into a fence corner and lay trembling until quiet was restored.

He had more than half a mind to give it up and go home, but as soon as he could bring his perturbed thoughts to bear upon this proposition he spurned it as unworthy of him. What would he ever amount to as a soldier if he was afraid to face so harmless a thing as the neighbor's daughter? This view of the case was like an elixir to him. His courage came back to stay. He opened the gate, walked boldly up to the door, and rapped with no uncertain sound.

"Come in!"

Si's heart beat like a trip-hammer as he raised the latch and entered.

"Hello, Si, how d'ye do?" was the farmer's greeting.

"Good evenin'!" said Si in response, with some shyness of manner. His coy salutation was addressed in a general way to the family group, although, judging from his eyes, it was aimed more particularly at Annabel. She smiled and Si thought she blushed—probably she did. There was a tinge of sadness on her face that for the moment he could not understand. She did not express the surprise he had supposed she would at seeing him in the uniform of a soldier.

"I was in town this arternoon," said the farmer, "an I heerd ye'd jined the company they're raisin'."

Annabel bent down her head and looked very hard at her sewing. So she had already heard of it, thought Si. He wondered if the relation of cause and effect existed between her knowledge and the sad, quiet manner so unusual to her.

"Them clothes is becomin' to ye, Si," continued Annabel's father, in his bluff, hearty way, "an' ye'll make a fine lookin' soljer. We'll all be sorry to have ye go——"

Si cast a quick glance at Annabel to see if he could read in her face the extent to which she would share in the general grief. She did not look up, and he thought he saw something that glistened in her eye, but he may have been mistaken.

"——an' we hope there won't nothin' happen to ye down there. Ye must be spry an' dodge the bullets of them pesky rebels."

Annabel got up and went to a cupboard in the corner of the room to look for something. She seemed to have a good deal of difficulty in finding it. Once Si saw her put her kerchief to her eyes. It was no doubt merely accidental and had no connection with the subject of conversation. After a while she went back to her seat, but she appeared not to have found what she was looking for.

Si's stay was brief. He had in his mind some things he

thought he wanted to say in Annabel's ear, but no opportunity was offered, owing to the perverse blindness of the
"old folks"—so often a source of exasperation to young
hearts palpitating with the tender passion. It may be
seriously doubted, however, whether Si could have mustered courage enough to say anything confidential to the
rosy-cheeked girl if he had had a chance to do so. Be this

AT THE NEIGHBOR'S.

as it may, he was not in his usual loquacious mood for
general conversation. So the kind-hearted old farmer did
most of the talking, Si only responding now and then in
monosyllables. But what his busy eyes had seen, aided by
an active imagination, had given him a measurably satisfactory answer to the question his throbbing heart had
silently asked.

When Si arose and bade the family good night, Annabel stepped quickly to the door and followed him outside for a single moment.

"Si," she said softly, "I know it's right fer ye to go, but —ye don't know—how bad—it makes me feel!"

Putting her arm around his neck she kissed his hot cheek. Before he could recover his senses she had fled into the house like a frightened fawn. Si pinched himself two or three times to see whether it was he or somebody else. Then he walked rapidly home, the happiest boy in all Indiana.

––––––

CHAPTER III.

In Which Si is Provided with a Bountiful Outfit, Makes Satisfactory Progress with Annabel, and Starts for the War.

SI KLEGG was very impatient to get away to the front. It was only a week after his enlistment that Company Q left for the regimental rendezvous to become a part of the 200th Indiana, but a month had never seemed so long to him. Every day he went to town to see how the work of recruiting was getting on. He assisted, to the utmost of his ability and influence, in filling the ranks by persuasive efforts among his comrades.

Si had now little taste for the plodding work of the farm. Possibly he felt that such plebeian toil was not in keeping with the dignity that properly belonged to a soldier. Now and then the thought would come that he ought to lend a willing hand to help his father while he could; but he was so thoroughly imbued with the war spirit, and so restive at the delay, that he could give no serious consideration to anything else. There was little to do to put him in marching order. He had no incumbrances, and could just as well have marched away the morning after his name was added to the company roll. Indeed, nothing could have pleased him better.

His feelings were saddened sometimes when he allowed himself to picture the parting from parents and sister, and thoughts of Annabel made his heart twinge with even greater violence. With the philosophy of a stoic, however, he persuaded himself that the sundering of these ties was but a part of the sacrifice that every soldier must make, and to which he had already become reconciled. On the whole he would be glad rather than otherwise when the farewells were over. He did not desire frequent repetition of the tearful scene that was caused by his return from the village on that eventful day.

Among Si's relatives, irrespective of age or sex, great zeal was manifested in fitting him out for his first campaign. They had heard much about the sufferings of the soldiers for lack of home comforts, and it was unanimously voted that Si should want for nothing that could minister to his external or internal welfare. If he suffered it should not be their fault. His female friends were particularly active in the good work. In preparing his outfit they displayed that marvelous discrimination that characterized the patriotic women of America in this respect during the early part of the war, before they had learned better. Feminine ingenuity exhausted itself in conjuring up all sorts of things, describable and indescribable, that could make life a burden to a recruit in active service. When they could not think of anything more to make, they ransacked the stores for something to buy and load him down.

Si's mother and sister devoted to this labor of love all

their time and energies not employed in ministering to his appetite. Not an hour passed but they thought of something else that he would need for his health and comfort, and there was no rest till it was provided. By the time the contributions of friends and neighbors had been sent in there was a large wheelbarrow-load, without taking into account the stock he would receive from the government.

"There, Si," said his good mother, with evident satisfac-

tion, as she showed him the result of the labor of loving hearts and hands, "we've got this clothes-basket purty nigh full. I reckon them things 'll fix ye out tollable well. If ye're keerful an' don't lose any of 'em ye can keep yerself kind o' comfortable like."

"That'll be jest gorjus," replied Si. "Marchin' 'n' campin'

A MODEL OUTFIT.

won't be nothin' but fun 's long 's a feller 's got everythin' he wants. I 'low the boys wouldn't have sich hard times if they all had mothers 'n' sisters like I've got."

"I've heerd, Si, that they only give the soljers one blanket apiece. I s'pose ye'll have to sleep on the ground a good deal o' the time, an' ye'll want plenty o' kivers; so I've got ye an extry blanket an' this heavy quilt—ye must take good care o' that 'cause it's one o' my best ones, an', if ye can, I'd like ye to fetch it back in good shape when the war 's over. I guess they'll keep ye warm. I'd feel awful to be all the time 'fraid ye was ketchin' cold. I'll give ye one o' my best pillers if ye want, to lay yer head on. I've made ye a pair o' nice undershirts. Ye'll want 'em after a while an' ye'd better take 'em 'long now, 'cause I don't s'pose I'll git a chance to send 'em to ye. Here's three pair o' good woolen socks. I don't reckon them they has in the army is any great shakes. Yer Aunt Samanthy knit 'em fer ye. Marier's made ye a purty needle case full o' needles an' buttons an' thread an' a pa'r o' scissors. Them things 'll come mighty handy. Ye won't have no mother to mend up yer clothes an' sew on yer buttons an' darn yer stockin's. Here's a harnsom' portfolio yer sister bought fer ye. It's got lots o' paper an' envelopes an' pens an' pencils an' ink an' postage stamps. I know ye ain't a great hand to be writin' letters, but ye mus'n't forgit that we'll want ter hear from ye reel often. Yer father bought ye a pa'r o' boots. They won't weigh more'n five or six pounds, an' ye can carry 'em 'long to wear when yer guv'ment shoes gives out. They say that the army shoes drops all to pieces in a few days. I 'xpect the contractors gits rich out of 'em.

"We want ye to keep yerself lookin' nice an' slick, an' yer Cousin Betsey got ye a toilet-case, with a comb an' brush an' lookin'-glass an' a bottle o' ha'r ile. Here's half a dozen cakes o' sweet-smellin' soap to keep yer han's an' face clean, an' a couple o' towels. I don't s'pose Uncle Sam 'll give ye any. An' I've put in a clothes-brush; ye'll have plenty o' use for that. Ye mustn't forgit to black up yer shoes every mornin'. I've got ye a good new brush an' a couple o' boxes o' blackin'. Here's a big pin-cushion full o' pins from Aunt Polly. A pin 's a purty small thing, but sometimes when ye want one ye want it mighty bad. These ought to last ye a year or two, if ye have ter stay that long, which goodness knows I hope ye won't. I've fixed up a box o' medicine for ye. I know ye don't very often git sick, but then ye might git took sudden, an' them army doctors won't know what ye want to bring ye 'round half 's well 's yer mammy does. Here's a bottle o' Number Six, an' 'nother o' rewbarb, an' a box o' headache pills, an' a bunch o' pennyr'yal. Ye know pennyr'yal tea 's powerful good when one gits under the weather.

"The parson didn't forgit ye, nuther. He sent over a Bible fer ye to read an' a hymn-book fer ye to sing out of when ye feels like singin'. Ye'd better take 'long the Bible ye got last Christmas, too, 'cause suthin might happen to one on 'em, and I'd feel sorry to think ye hadn't none. Like enough a good many o' the soljers won't have Bibles an' they'll all want to be borryin' yours. I don't think ye'll care ter tote a very big library, but I jest wanted ter give ye my 'Pilgrim's Progress.' 'Tain't very heavy, an' ye'll be a sort of a pilgrim yerself. P'r'aps ye'll have purty nigh 's hard a time 's the man John Bunyan writ 'bout. Here's somethin' I know ye'll like, Si. We've all had our fortygraphs took, an' Marier got ye this album in town yisterday. The picturs is all in there and there's room fer a few more.

"Yer Cousin Jim bought ye a couple o' boxes o' paper collars, and Marier made some neckties that'll go well with 'em. Here's a roll o' bandages an' a bundle o' lint. I hope and pray, Si, ye won't have any use fer 'em yerself, but I reck'n they're desperate car'less with all their different kinds o' shootin' things, an' it'll be a good idee to have 'em if ye do git hurt. Then I couldn't think o' yer goin' 'thout takin' 'long a few cans o' peaches, an' jell', an' some o' that cramberry jam ye're so fond of. An' I've put ye up four or five pounds o' nice butter. I guess ye can carry it. I s'pose I'll think o' lots more things afore ye go, but we've got 'nough here fer a fair start."

Si expressed in the warmest terms his gratitude for his mother's thoughtfulness in providing so bountifully for him. Neither of them had the faintest conception of the actual capacity of a soldier's knapsack; nor did they imagine that he would soon see the time when every pound he carried would seem to weigh a ton.

Si's Sunday school teacher gave him a barbarous bowie-knife with a blade a foot long. It was provided with a leather sheath and a belt, so that he could wear it around his body. The presentation was made at a Sunday school picnic, which took place just before Company Q got march-ing orders. The teacher delivered an impressive speech as he handed Si the hideous weapon. The women and children shuddered as they looked upon the horrible thing, and were deeply affected at the thought of Si roaming around through the south like a murderous brigand, plunging the reeking steel into the bowels of everybody he met.

A DELUSION OF THE WAR.

The young soldier was greatly pleased with so practical and useful a gift. He assured his teacher that he would never bring dishonor upon the shining blade, and that he would make as much havoc with it as possible among the foes of his country.

Some of those good people seemed really to believe that whole battalions of rebels would be gathered to their fathers, and the south would be filled with widows and orphans, through the devastating agency of that knife, wielded by the avenging arm of Si Klegg; in short, that he would soon end the war when he had a fair chance to use it. He would throw himself upon the enemy and cut and hew and slash, covering the field with ghastly heaps of the slain. All that the rest of the 200th Indiana would have to do would be to follow him with picks and shovels, and bury the dead. Such were the notions of war, that prevailed during the first year or two of the great struggle.*

And what of the neighbor's daughter? How did Annabel pass the week between Si's enlistment and departure? The most marked effect upon her of his entering the service was a rapid crystallization of her feelings toward him. Si had not said anything to her about it, nor did there seem to be any pressing need that he should do so. When he called at her father's house the evening of the day he enlisted, she became vividly conscious that she was more to him than any other of the neighborhood girls, and equally so that she had a reciprocal feeling toward him. No premeditation on either side had contributed to bring about this happy state of affairs between them. Like Topsy, it had "just growed," and neither of them realized it until it developed so rapidly under the ripening influence of Si's blue uniform.

Annabel cried herself to sleep that night, and then dreamed all sorts of awful things about Si away down in the army. In the morning her reddened eyes and sad face betrayed her. Her mother was not long in understanding the case. She had noted the symptoms, from time to time, and it was not difficult to arrive at the cause of her daughter's

---

* The writer deems it not inappropriate to say that on the eve of his departure for camp he and several comrades were each presented with one of these tremendous implements of destruction. The presentation was made by a college professor, in a church, before a tearful and shuddering audience. The general feeling appeared to be, as we buckled on those knives, that they would cause a speedy collapse of the Southern Confederacy. Candor compels the statement that no blood ever stained them save that of vagrant pigs and chickens; and that their chief function in putting down the rebellion was to slice bacon for the frying pan or the ramrod.

dejection. She thought well of Si and made no effort to disturb the amatory relations that were evidently fast becoming established. True, both were yet too young to be "engaged," but there seemed to be no occasion for parental interference.

In the Klegg family it was much the same. Si's mother and sister had not been blind to his boyish partiality for Annabel. Their keen eyes and instincts read through the flimsy mantle of concealment with which Si tried to hide his feelings. If they had questioned him on the subject he would probably have lied about it, as young people usually do when they have reached the mellow stage of love's enchantment. The matter was quietly talked over, at odd moments, and it was decided that the best thing to do was to do nothing and let matters take their own course.

The situation was, however, somewhat embarrassing to both Si and Annabel, in their intercourse with each other, and with their respective families. Their natural coyness at first placed the seal of silence upon their tongues. Whatever the future might have in store for them, their relations were as yet too immature to become a theme for conversation. But the rules which custom has laid down for affairs of the tender passion would not apply to such extraordinary cases as the one in question. Si was going to the war, and this soon swept away the barrier.

"Si," said his sister Maria one day, "I've asked Annie over to supper to-night."

"Annie who?" exclaimed Si, assuming dense ignorance, but at the same time growing very red in the face.

"Annie who! Wall I declare to goodness if I ever heerd the like! Anybody 'd think ye knowed a thousand Annies an' ye couldn't tell which of 'em I'm talking about. Annie who! Oh, Si!" And Maria gave him a suggestive nudge, as if to quicken his perceptions and assist him to identify the particular Annie who had been invited to supper.

"Why, yes—that is—of course," said Si, while the hot

blood mantled his cheeks, "how sh'd I know what gals ye've asked. 'Tain't nothin' to me, nohow!"

"Now, Jo-si-er Klegg, ye ought ter be 'shamed o' yerself, an' I b'lieve ye are, too; I'm sure I'd be if I was you. But reely, Si, layin' all jokes aside, Annie 's a nice girl an' we're all glad ye think so much of her. Ye needn't try to keep it to yerself any longer, 'cause ye can't do it. We know all 'bout it just the same 's if ye'd told us. We had an idee it 'd please ye to ask her over and let us all git sort o' 'quainted like 'fore ye go off to the war. We've got ye cornered an' ye may as well give in. Don't ye think it 'll be the best way?"

Si rather thought, on the whole, that it would. After a little more parleying he decided upon an unconditional surrender. Then he told his sister how kind it was of her, and how glad he was for what she had done.

"But ye didn't tell me," he said, "whether she accepted yer invite."

"She was a bit shy at first, an' she asked me if I thought you'd like to have her. I told her I knowed ye would, an' then she looked kind o' smiley an' said right away she'd come. I s'pose Si," Maria added with a sly twinkle in her eye, "you'll see to gittin' her home all right."

Si did not answer in words, but the look upon his face sufficiently indicated the alacrity with which he would discharge this pleasing duty.

Annabel came, pretty as a peach blossom. She blushed a good deal and so did Si, but father and mother and sister Maria gave no heed to the bright carnation hues that kept coming and going on those two pairs of cheeks. They just rattled away and tried to make Annabel feel that Si was not the only friend she had in the family. Si frequently cast furtive glances across the table at the fair guest, though he did not take any part in the conversation worth mentioning. He scarcely spoke to Annabel during the whole time of her stay. He made some earnest speeches with his eyes, but reserved his vocal forces for the walk home with her.

Si was glad when she remarked that she guessed it was time for her to go. His services as escort were promptly offered. She told him coyly that he didn't *have* to go; it wasn't very dark and she knew the way. She didn't mean it at all. She would have cried her eyes out if Si had taken her at her word and hung up his hat again. But she did not think he would do that, and he didn't.

It is not a matter of public concern what passed between them during that walk—whether they talked about the weather, the crops and the stars, or whether they maintained the same eloquent silence that marked their manner toward each other at the supper table. It may fairly be presumed, however, that they found something to say

A SATISFACTORY STATE OF AFFAIRS.

of an interesting nature, for Si's absence from home was protracted to a degree that was out of all proportion to the distance between the two houses.

"Have they moved, Si?" asked Maria with a smile, as her brother at length entered.

"N—no, I reck'n not," he replied rather dubiously, turning his face to hide his confusion. The fact is, he could not have told whether the house of Annabel's father stood where it used to or had been moved over into the next township.

"Seems 's though ye'd been five mile," said Maria. "Better set down 'n' rest; ye must be tired!"

Si said he wasn't tired a bit, and he didn't know that he had been gone very long. He was happy in the well-grounded belief that no stay-at-home rival could "cut him out" in the good graces of the farmer's fair daughter while he was "gone to the war."

Annabel's nimble fingers were not idle during these days. She worked a pair of slippers for Si, which she thought would be comfortable for him to put on at night after a hard day's march. She stitched his name into the corners of half a dozen nice handkerchiefs, and worked a fancy bookmark, so that he would not lose the place in his Bible. Then she went to the photographer's and sat for her picture. This she had enclosed in a pretty locket, with a wisp of her hair, and a red ribbon fastened to it so that he could wear it around his neck, if he wanted to, and she hoped he did. All these things helped to make Si happy. A soldier couldn't help having a gay time of it with such an elaborate outfit.

One day Si returned from town greatly elated. The roll of company Q had reached high-water mark. A hundred sturdy young men had filled its ranks, and they were ordered to be ready to take the train on the following day for the rendezvous. There were sad hearts that night in the farmer's humble home. Only a few hours, now, and father, mother and sister must say farewell to their boy—

"It may be for years and it may be forever."

Little sleep came to their eyes, and tears moistened the pillows. Si's head was filled with romantic visions of the new life upon which he was about to enter, but even these gave place now and then to thoughts of the separation. As he lay there he wondered if Annabel was asleep. He would have felt comforted in a measure had he known that through the too swiftly passing hours, she often. wiped from her soft cheeks the tears that flowed for sake of him.

Before break of day the family were astir and, with sad faces, busily engaged in the final preparations. Si's baggage had been for days hourly augmented by sundry articles of clothing, and gimcracks of various kinds. When they were all packed into a big box there seemed to be everything that he could need or desire—and a good deal more. He never had so much in his life before. His mother put in a lot of pies, cookies, etc., that she had baked for him, and Annabel brought over a large fruit-cake, which Si knew would taste good because she had made it with her own hands.

"Bully for you, Annie," he exclaimed as she handed him the fragrant loaf. His words startled her, for she had never heard him speak in that way before. Si hastened to explain that it was time for him to begin to talk like a soldier and he felt that he ought to practice a little, so that he could be getting his hand in.

Then farmer Klegg hitched the team to the big wagon, the box of quartermaster and commissary stores was loaded, and all got in. Si hoped Annabel would ride with them, but her diffidence overruled his suggestion to this effect. She would be there. Everybody for miles around was going to see the boys off, and she would ride with her own family.

As the hour of departure approached, a great crowd gathered at the railway station. There were fathers, mothers, sisters, sweethearts and friends, to say the parting word and give the farewell embrace to their loved ones. None in that throng whose heart was not moved as it had never been before.

The company formed at the headquarters and with fife and drum and waving banner, marched down the street, filling the air with shouts. At the station the soldiers were permitted to break ranks and a few minutes were given for hasty adieus. Can words depict the scene—the streaming eyes, the clinging clasp of loving arms, the tender words of affection and of admonition?

"All aboard!"

OFF TO THE WAR.

Rudely the sacred ties are sundered. War is only hard and cruel, and its demands are inexorable.

Si's face is wet with the tears of mother and sister, and his cheek is warm with their kisses. Tearing himself from their enfolding arms he takes for an instant the hand of Annabel and looks into her brimming eyes. No word passes their quivering lips. Then he dashes away. He is going to be a soldier now.

The great pile of baggage—enough for a brigade two years later—has been put on board, and at the signal the train moves off, amidst cheers and shouts and farewell waving of handkerchiefs.

Faster flow the tears of those who watch the receding train that is bearing sons and brothers and husbands away to scenes of suffering and death. Many of those brave boys will not come back. Who of them will go down in the fierce storm of battle? who will join the endless procession that day by day moves from the hospitals to the populous cities of the dead?

Ah, how like mountains they were piled—the pangs of mothers and sisters and wives at parting with those they loved; and, through the long bitter years that followed, the dropping tears and the hearts crushed with grief for the unreturning ones, in a million homes forever clouded by the dark shadows of war!

CHAPTER IV.

CONTAINS SOME OBSERVATIONS ON A SOLDIER'S EQUIPMENTS, AND SEES THE TWO HUNDREDTH INDIANA OFF FOR THE FRONT.

SI KLEGG soon forgot the sad parting as the train swiftly bore him away. Visions of his new life took entire possession of his mind and heart, crowding out all other thoughts. The brightly-colored picture that his fancy painted was but the frontispiece to the volume whose dark pages were yet sealed to him.

This feeling was universal among the members of Company Q. Moved by the excitement of the occasion they indulged in the wildest hilarity. They jested and laughed and shouted and sang, manifesting a convulsive enthusiasm that promised great things for the future if they could only keep up the head of steam that was now lifting the safety-valve. With valorous words those lion-hearted patriots recounted to one another the prodigious deeds of heroism that they would perform as soon as they met the enemy—and they all hoped that they wouldn't have long to wait.

At all the stopping places crowds cheered the volunteers, the boys responding with tremendous power of lungs. As they went whirling along, the wave of a kerchief from a farm-house by a rustic lass or matron—particularly the former—was always the signal for a tempestuous response. The impression seemed to prevail among the people along the route that the country was safe now that Company Q was on its way to the field, and it was high time for the rebels to quit and go home; they doubtless would as soon as they learned that the company had started. So far as might have been judged from surface indications, those on board the train were even more strongly impressed with this belief.

An hour's ride brought Company Q to the place of rendezvous, where the 200th Indiana regiment was being rapidly organized. Most of the companies were already on the ground, and the full complement arrived during the day. There was a great and pressing emergency across the border, and the utmost activity prevailed in rushing the new levies to the front. The President's call for "three hundred thousand more" had been promptly and cheerfully met, and the railroads were choked with trains bearing fresh regiments to the point of danger to reinforce the veteran army that was vainly striving to check the northward sweep of the enemy's confident legions. Every city and hamlet was wrought up to the highest pitch of excitement and patriotic fervor.

Immediately upon alighting from the train the members

of Company Q learned that orders had been received for the regiment to perfect its organization at once and hold itself ready to move at a moment's notice. It was understood that the 200th would leave that evening.

Si was glad of it. He was burning with a desire to fight the rebels. To his mind everything indicated that the commander of the Union army was only awaiting the arrival of Company Q to fall upon the enemy and smite him hip and thigh. Si was confident that before another day had passed he would be charging around on the field of battle, climbing over heaps of slaughtered rebels, and surrounding the name of Klegg with a halo of immortal renown.

Language cannot describe the excitement that prevailed that day among the thousand impetuous recruits who were being crystallized into a regiment—for there was not a man of them that did not feel just as Si did. Nobody thought of anything but hastening the work of preparation. Officers in gorgeous uniforms, on horseback and on foot, were hustling around with that consciousness of importance that comes to most men when they first find themselves clothed with authority over those otherwise their equals, and able to say, in the language of the Centurion of old: "For I am a man having soldiers under me; and I say to this man, Go, and he goeth; and to another, Come, and he cometh; and to my servant, Do this, and he doeth it"—if he don't he goes to the guard-house or is tied up by the thumbs. The inestimable privilege of commanding one's fellow-men, and possessing the power to compel prompt and unquestioning obedience, is a luxury to be found nowhere but in the army.

Everybody was at high pressure, and displayed an energy befitting the crisis. The wildest rumors concerning the movements of the rebel army and the desperate state of affairs at the front, went from lip to lip and found plenty of believers. The more absurd and preposterous they were

the more ready credence was given to them. In this way
fresh fuel was constantly added to the fires that raged
with quenchless fury in the breasts of those men—they
were far from being soldiers yet. The climax was reached
when somebody started the rumor that the rebels had set
fire to the Ohio river and burned it; that they were marching over dry-shod, in swarms as countless as the locusts
of Egypt or the grasshoppers of Kansas, and were sweeping up through Indiana at the rate of twenty miles an hour.
In calmer moments the incongruities of this intelligence
might have been detected, but in the seething excitement
they were not thought of, and the startling news was received as gospel truth. Every one who repeated it added
thousands to the invading host and miles to the hourly
rate at which it was approaching. Then the men began
to inquire impatiently about their guns, but were informed
that these would not be furnished until they reached the
army. There was a good deal of grumbling at this, for the
first thing that a recruit always wanted was to get hold
of something to shoot with. The prospect that in their
defenceless condition they would be immediately attacked
by the enemy had a highly inflammatory effect.

Company Q went through the form of "electing" its
officers, though it was already understood who they
would be, and their commissions had been duly issued by
the Governor. It was a harmless fiction, to make the
members of the company think they had something to say
in the matter. Then the boys listened very attentively
while the newly "elected" Captain read out the appoint-
ments of non-commissioned officers—five sergeants and
eight corporals. No major-general was ever prouder of his
well-earned stars than were some of those corporals of the
chevrons that within half an hour decorated the sleeves
of their blouses. They had but a vague notion of the
official functions of corporals, but they stood a round higher
on the military ladder than the privates, and this knowl-

edge brought with it a consciousness of superiority, and a feeling that they were indispensable to the prosecution of the war.

Si Klegg stood with ears agog while the list was being read. He did not expect to hear his name called out and so he suffered no disappointment. In this respect he was more fortunate than many others, who thought that the captain showed very poor judgment in making his selections. Si had no more thought of being a corporal than he had of being a brigadier, and he was perfectly content to let his name remain among the K's, down in the body of the company roll. The captain did not hit the bull's-eye every time in appointing the non-commissioned officers --no captain ever did in organizing a new company. External appearances were often deceitful, and it was not easy to say from a man's looks how good a soldier he would make. Like tallow, he had to be tried—and in the fire, too. A year or so of real solid service, with a battle or a skirmish now and then, aided greatly in a proper solution of the question.

The quartermaster was up to his ears in business, issuing such clothing and other articles as the men needed to complete their equipment. When the new orderly of Company Q called up the boys to get their overcoats there was a great scramble. The orderly handed them out just as they came, without reference to size, leaving the men to fit themselves as best they could by "trading" with one another. It really made little difference, for there was not much "fit" to them anyway; but when a fat man found himself in possession of a coat that would not come together, while his lean comrade had one that reached half way around the second time; when a tall man drew a very short coat and a short man a very long one, there was need for a harmonious adjustment. This was measurably accomplished by a system of exchange, but of necessity there were some odd ones who had to take such as they could get.

Si's circumference of body, in consequence of the plenitude of his mother's commissariat, was somewhat in excess of its due proportion to his height. It was very likely that after a while a smaller garment would hold him, but the present needs of his well-rounded form required one of large capacity. When he found one that he could button over his stomach the "tails" reached to his

ankles. His sister Maria would have laughed herself into hysterics if she could have seen him in that big blue coat. Si said confidentially to one of his comrades that he didn't want to begin grumbling right off, but he should think they might have measured him and made him a coat that would fit instead of giving him such a thing as that. He learned in time that Uncle Sam did not run his tailor shop on that principle. And then the great unwieldy cape that flapped about his arms—he could not imagine what that was for. His first impulse was to cut it off, but he finally thought he

THE ARMY OVERCOAT.

would wait and see, as they were all made that way, and there must be some mysterious purpose in it. He did, however, shorten the tails a foot or so by amputation with his knife.

There was less difficulty with the blankets, as they were all alike and there was no choice. Si thought they were much the same as the horse blankets in his father's barn. He wondered if they would get curry-combs with them. When he first spread his blanket upon the ground to see how it looked his eye caught the "U. S." in the center.

"I s'pose that means they b'long to *us*," he said, "'n' they've marked 'em so nobody won't steal 'em!"

He thought this was an excellent idea, and showed the care and thoughtfulness of the government in providing for the soldiers. He contemplated with satisfaction the fact that, so far as the blanket was concerned, he would have an advantage over the tall men, as he could more easily keep his feet warm.

Then the knapsacks were distributed. Si had never seen one before. He had only heard there was such a thing that a soldier carried his surplus clothing in. He had an idea it was built something like a trunk, such as other people used when they traveled. He opened it out and examined with curious eye its great "pocket" on one side and its flaps and straps on the other. He stuffed his blanket into the pocket, buckled in his overcoat, and then tried to put it on to see how it would feel. The first time he stuck his arms through what he conceived to be the places intended for them, the knapsack landed squarely in front of him. This, he was sure, could not be right, and he tried it again. He got mixed up in a chaos of straps and buckles and the riotous knapsack dangled under one of his arms. Extricating himself, he laid it upon the ground and prepared for another trial.

"I'll git the durned thing on 'f it takes t'll Christmas!" he exclaimed.

After another examination of the perverse contrivance, he thought he had found the correct theory of putting it on. Swinging it up to his shoulders, and leaning far forward that it might the more easily be kept in its position until he could make the necessary connection, he thrust one arm through the closed strap, holding it up from the rear with his other hand, almost unjointing his shoulder. Then he tried to fasten the hook and had nearly succeeded when the knapsack gave a great lurch, as the cargo of a ship shifts in a storm, and rolled to leeward. It carried him off his balance, and knapsack and Si went down upon the ground all in a heap.

Si was not in the habit of losing his temper, but as he again got upon his feet there were symptoms of fermentation. He began to utter language as expressive as his Sunday school instruction would permit, when one of his comrades approached, laughing heartily at the result of his tussle with the knapsack.

SI FINDS HIS MATCH.

"Lemme help ye git the hang of it, pard!" he said.

The speaker was lank and lean, and his well-tanned face gave evidence of much exposure to wind and sun. He was a kind of "black sheep" in the company. Whence he came no one knew. He entered the recruiting office one day and enlisted in Company Q in a business-like way, as if he knew just what he was doing. The boys dubbed him "Shorty" because he was so tall—or rather he looked so on account of his thinness. Si had no acquaintance with him, and they had not even spoken together before.

"Thank'ee; don't keer 'f ye do!" replied Si. "I didn't s'pose the thing 'd floor me that way. Sh'd think they mout git up some better contraption 'n that!"

"I reck'n they couldn't do no better considerin'," said

Shorty. It's easy 'nough when ye larn how. Ye see I was out a while when the war fust started 'n the three months' sarvice, 'n' I picked up a little suthin 'bout soldierin'. I hap'n'd ter strike the town that day I jined Comp'ny Q, 'n' I jest tuk a notion ter give her 'nother turn. Now this 's the way ter sling a knapsack."

Shorty first put it on himself, showing Si how to take hold of it, swing it up into position and fasten the end of the strap under his arm.

SHORTY.

"I don't see nothin' the matter with that," exclaimed Si. "I kin do that 'n' not half try!"

Shorty took it off in soldierly style and laid it upon the ground. Si then renewed the encounter, determined that he would not let it get away with him this time. With a little help from Shorty he succeeded, and marched around with the great lump on his back, and a smile of satisfaction at the achievement of his first victory.

"It's goin' ter be jest fun ter carry this thing," he said. "I've heern tell 't some o' the soljers makes a right smart o' fuss 'bout luggin' the'r knapsacks, but 't seems 's if I'd jest enj'y it."

"I hope ye will," was Shorty's only answer. He did not want to dampen the ardor of the ambitious young recruit.

"P'r'aps ye kin tell a feller what this is," Si said to Shorty, as the orderly handed him a piece of rubber cloth, six feet long by four feet wide, with a slit eighteen inches in length running crosswise in the center. Si thought there was no end to the curious things he was getting for his outfit.

"That's a poncho," replied Shorty.

"What makes 'em call it that, 'n' what's it fer?"

"I reck'n they calls it a poncho 'cause that's its name," said Shorty. "Ye don't want ter stick up yer nose at it, nuther, fer it'll come 'bout 's handy to ye 's anything ye'll git. It's mighty good ter spread on the ground under yer blanket when ye goes ter bed. Ye know wet won't soak through Injy-rubber, 'n' it'll help pervent ye ketchin' the rumaticks. 'Sides that, when ye have ter lie down 'n the mud it keeps yer blanket clean. Then when ye're marchin' in the rain it beats 'n umbreller all holler. Ye jest take it this way."

Shorty proceeded to illustrate his lecture on the value of the article by thrusting his head through the slit. The poncho fell loosely around him from his shoulders, extending as far down as the knees, before and behind, and covering him as a mantle—not wholly unlike that fantastic achievement of the modern dressmaker, the "Mother Hubbard." With the "gum" side outward it gave promise of excellent protection from rain.

Then Si put it on and promenaded around as proud as a peacock. He could hardly find words strong enough to express his admiration for a government that had provided so bountifully for him.

"I don't keer 'f it rains pitchforks," he said, "'s long 's I've got this thing."

Every hour Si felt more and more glad that he had enlisted; he was going to have such a nice time of it.

Shorty did not exaggerate the value of this item in the soldier's wardrobe. Its official name was the "poncho," but this word had no meaning to the boys, few of whom were supplied with dictionaries, and they always called it the "gum blanket." The specific purposes for which it was made were those described by Shorty, but it had many other uses. It was convenient to wrap around a quarter of pork or mutton which it was desired to smuggle into camp. It was provided with a flap and buttons to close the aperture in the center, and was handy to carry upon the shoulder half a bushel or so of apples or sweet potatoes. About half the ponchos, after they had been in service a few months, had "checker-boards" penciled or painted on them, and the other half had the necessary squares and figures for "chuck-a-luck," "sweat," "Honest John," and other fascinating games that tended to impoverish those who were addicted to them.

Another detail returned from a visit to the quartermaster, and the orderly began to hand around to each man a white canvas bag that would hold about a peck, with a strap attached to opposite sides.

"What's this?" asked Si of his new acquaintance, who was standing near as one of the bags was given to him.

"That's yer haversack!"

"But what's it *fer?*"

"Ter carry yer grub in!" replied Shorty. "If ye've got 's good a appetite 's I think ye hev f'm yer looks, ye can't git 'long 'thout that, nohow. Ye may see the time 't ye'll wish ye had more ter put in it; but jest let me tell ye ter hang onter yer haversack through thick 'n' thin. It'll be the best friend ye'll find in the army."

Si readily coincided with his comrade's views concerning its value, and inwardly resolved that whatever might betide he would stick to his haversack, and defend it with his life. He thought it was very nice, it looked so white and clean.

There were haversacks—and haversacks. Theoretically they were all water-proof, but practically they were quite the reverse, particularly after they had become a little worn.

A penetrating rain storm was very likely to make a sorry mess of their contents. Some of them were black and some were white—that is to say, they were white when new. By the time one of these had been in use for a few weeks as a receptacle for chunks of fat bacon and fresh meat, damp sugar tied up in a rag—perhaps a piece of an old shirt—potatoes and other vegetables that might be picked up along the route, it took on the color of a printing-office towel. It would have been alike offensive to the eyes and nose of a fastidious person. Very likely he would have gone hungry a good while before he could bring himself to eat anything out of it. But the educated taste of the veteran soldier disdained all such squeamishness. When his regiment halted he would drop by the roadside, draw his grimy and well-greased haversack around in front of him, and from its dark and odorous recesses bring forth what tasted better to him than the daintiest morsel to the palate of an epicure. It was all in getting used to such things.

If at this time one of the war-worn haversacks that went through "to the Sea" had been laid before Si Klegg at dinner time, he would have placed his fingers to his nose and turned away in dire disgust, saying: "Is thy servant a *dog* that he should do this thing?" It would be all right after a while, but he would have to come to it gradually. "Rome was not built in a day;" no more did a soldier learn in that limited time to eat a campaign meal out of one of those fearful haversacks and be thankful. Sometimes a stray recruit joined a veteran company. His hands were white, his face clean, and his appetite had been pampered by home diet. For a time he was altogether too "nice" and particular, and the old soldiers treated with withering scorn such symptoms of effeminacy.

Now and then, in a spasm of reform, a man would try to wash his haversack, but the laundry facilities of the army were sadly defective, and only indifferent results were attained. The original whiteness of that haversack was gone forever. If it showed an improved appearance, it was but brief and delusive. It was soon blacker than before, and the last state of that haversack was worse than the first.

The only superiority of the haversack made of black material lay in the fact that the effects of use were not so plain to the eye. The grease and dirt were there just the same, but they did not show, and less violence was done to one of the senses. As far as the nose was concerned, there was no difference. Indeed, the combination of smells from the black haversack was apt to be the more pungent and overwhelming, because its uncleanness was less apparent to the eye, and, therefore, liable to be neglected. It should be understood that these conditions did not exist to such a degree when the soldiers were lying in camp, with opportunities to keep themselves and their belongings in a state of cleanliness, and to supply themselves with new articles of equipment when needed. It was when, for weeks at a time, they were on the march and the picket-line, and lying in the trenches, day and night—when considerations of personal comfort were sunk in the one all-pervading purpose to fight the enemy and end the war.

A new officer generally provided himself with a shiny, patent-leather haversack that would hold a day's rations, and had a convenient pocket in which he might carry a flask—for medicinal purposes—while his reserve supplies were transported in a wagon or upon the strong shoulders of a burly "contraband." A thorough soaking was enough to use up one of these dainty affairs, and during the long campaigns the officer was glad enough to throw one of the regulation haversacks over his shoulder and take "pot-luck" with the boys.

The next addition to Si's outfit was a canteen. This was a simple article, made of tin and covered with cloth, shaped like the earth, except that it was a good deal more "flattened at the poles," and with a cloth strap running around at the equator by which it was suspended over one shoulder and carried against the opposite hip. It would hold about three pints. Of course, Si had to put it on and wear it a while. Every new thing he received was a source of wonder and delight to him, gratifying his curiosity and making him feel more like a soldier. Ever since he signed the roll of Company Q he had been impatient for the day when he should be arrayed in all the panoply of war.

The canteen was the natural complement of the haversack. These two articles of equipage were as inseparable and as necessary to each other as the two boots of a pair. When a soldier lost either of them by the casualties of war, he gave no sleep to his eyes nor slumber to his eyelids until the vacuum in his accouterments was filled. If a soldier *had* to have anything, he generally got it by fair means or foul.

The uses of the canteen were manifold. Its chief duty as a factor in the war was the transportation of water, although it was found equally adapted to carrying some other things. It came handy to the forager for milk, cider or molasses. In very rare instances it was also used for liquids of a more vigorous and searching character than any of these—for now and then a man found his way into the army who was not a member in good standing of a temperance society.

A peculiarity of the canteen was that its usefulness did not end when it was no longer fit to serve in its legitimate sphere. When a lot of them became battered and leaky, and the company commander wanted to drop them from his monthly return of government property for which he was responsible, he would have them duly condemned by a board of officers appointed to hold a solemn inquest upon them. These regulation forms having been complied with, the old canteens were eagerly sought after by the soldiers, who were now at liberty to make such use of them as their ingenuity might suggest.

The necessities and deprivations of active campaigning developed among the veterans a wonderful fertility of resource. Under such circumstances men become intensely practical. Everything that could in any way contribute to human welfare and comfort was brought into play, and the makeshifts resorted to were often startling and ludicrous.

The old canteen was thrown into the fire and the heat soon melted the solder by which the halves were joined, and the soldier found himself in possession of two tin basins eight or ten inches across and in the center about two inches deep. One of these he carried day after day in his haversack. It was not often that the latter was so full of provisions that there was not plenty of room for it. Its weight was nothing, and he found it useful in ways that the man who made it never thought of.

The government forgot to supply the soldiers with wash-basins, and the half-canteen made a convenient substitute. It was a trifle small, it is true, but by being frequently replenished it answered the purpose admirably. After the man had finished his ablutions he would rinse it out with a dash of water—or if he was too hungry to do this it was a matter of small moment—split the end of a stick for a handle, and he had a frying-pan—a prime article. Tons and tons of the flesh of swine were fried in the half-canteen, not to mention the pieces of chicken and the succulent vegetables that were in this way prepared for eating. If he drew coffee in a "raw" state, the half-canteen was an excellent roaster. Now and then it came handy for cooking "flapjacks," when he chanced to get hold of something of which to make them. In the fall, when the corn in the fields was hardening, he took a half-canteen, stabbed it full of holes with his bayonet, from the inside, and the convex surface made an excellent grater, and a dish of "samp"

relieved the everlasting monotony of regulation diet. Even
ripe corn was thus grated into a sort of meal from which
mush and indescribable cakes were fearfully and wonderfully made.

Indeed, for months at a time, a half-canteen and an old

USEFUL CAREER OF THE CANTEEN.

fruit-can, in which to boil coffee, comprised his entire
culinary "kit." They were simple but they were enough,
and in their possession he was happy. The nice coffee-pot
and frying-pan that he once owned had long since succumbed to the vicissitudes of army life.

Sometimes the veteran found himself suddenly placed in a position where he wanted something between himself and the muskets of the enemy, and he wanted it right off. There was no time to send back to the rear for picks and shovels. With a bayonet to loosen the dirt he scratched out a hole with his half-canteen, and, with the aid of a log or two or three rails or a few stones, against which he threw the earth, he had a safe protection from bullets. In this way a line of experienced skirmishers would burrow into the ground and almost disappear from sight with a quickness that was amazing.

Illustrations of the clever uses of the old canteen might be almost indefinitely multiplied. Si Klegg had but the faintest idea of the many ways in which that simple article of his outfit would prove to him "a friend in need" during his devious wanderings as he followed the flag of the 200th Indiana.

Toward evening came by telegraph the expected order to take the cars at once for the front. The emergency was becoming hourly more pressing. There seemed a strong probability that the regiment would be called into immediate service of the most active kind. If so, it would take the field at a disadvantage, not having had an hour's drill or a syllable of military instruction. Most of the regiments had been drilled in camp a few weeks before leaving their respective States. The members of the 200th Indiana would, however, be spared much of the mental anxiety and suffering that was endured through the slowly-dragging days by hundreds of thousands while they were held in camp like impatient hounds in leash, lest the war would be over before they could get there.

So the order to move was received with uproarious cheering. The fledgelings were panting to "see the elephant," and there was good prospect that they would soon gaze upon him in all his glory and magnitude. There was much hubbub during the brief time allowed the men to get themselves in readiness. The officers seemed to consider it necessary to make a good deal of fuss, and they stormed around in a convulsive way, shouting their orders to the men. The sergeants and corporals had a misty idea that they ought to do something by virtue of their positions and the honors that had been heaped upon them, and their voices helped to swell the din. A day's ration of "soft bread" and cooked meats was issued to supply the wants of the men during the trip by rail. Most of them had no need for this, however, as they had brought from home that morning pie and cake and other food, as much as they could eat in a week.

Si thought he had better take all the provisions he could get, and stowed his portion carefully in his haversack. Then he filled his new canteen and thought he would take a "pull" at it just to see how it worked. It was a very small thing—learning how to drink out of a canteen—but there were many whose first effort to do this was not wholly satisfactory. It was so with Si. Without a thought that there was anything to learn about so simple a matter, he gayly swung up the canteen, threw back his head, rolled his eyes, puckered his lips, and placed the "nozzle" at the opening. He did not get his lips fixed just right, and from the sides of his mouth streams of cold water went streaking down his neck and thence traversing his warm body and bringing up in his shoes. He gave a little shiver as the canteen came down quicker than it went up. After experimenting with some caution for a minute or two, he caught the "knack" of suction and of staying the downward rush of water, and the problem was solved. Then he took a long drink, and never in his life had water tasted half so good to him as when it came gurgling and fizzing from the neck of that canteen.

Si hastily packed in his knapsack the few articles of clothing he had drawn, rolled up his blanket and strapped it in its place, and he was ready to advance upon the enemy.

"Company Q—Fall in!" shouted the captain, impressively, as the drum at headquarters gave the signal. "Orderly, form the company!"

Now the orderly sergeant knew just as much about calculating the time and duration of the next eclipse of the moon as he did about "forming the company."

"Git into a string, you fellers!" he exclaimed, and the men huddled together in a state of almost hopeless anarchy. They swayed and bulged and surged forward and backward in the vain attempt to form a line. The orderly bustled up and down the front with great zeal, judiciously distributing pushes and punches to the more perverse ones, all the time exercising his tongue in a manner that was highly encouraging for future usefulness. The captain was about as ignorant as the orderly, but it was the latter's duty to form the company, and this fact let the captain out, affording a convenient cloak to hide his lack of knowledge. He kindly went to the orderly's assistance, backed by the two lieutenants, and the combined efforts of the four finally brought the men to anchor in two tolerably straight "rows."

"Dress up, there, you Klegg!" yelled the captain with terrifying vehemence.

Si tremblingly began to examine his clothes. A hasty inspection showed him that they were in proper order.

"Please, sir," he said with some hesitation, "I don't see how I can be any more 'dressed up' 'n I am, 'thout I gits some nicer clothes!"

"Silence!" roared the captain. "Don't you know that 'dress up' means to get into a straight line?"

"Nobody never told me," replied Si.

"Not another word, sir. I've told you now and that's enough. Ye've got to learn that there ain't to be any back talk, either."

Si was naturally impulsive and quick to resent any attempt to impose upon him. He wanted to say something in reply, but on second thought concluded he had better keep quiet. He did think, however, that the captain need not have made so much ado about it.

Si had met at the very threshold—as did many others—one of the most difficult lessons to be learned before he could be a perfect soldier. It was not an easy matter for volunteers of such a class as largely composed the Union army to submit, without question or reply, to the moods and whims of those who were in no way their superiors, save in a military sense, and to yield implicit obedience to their commands—to sink the individual in the soldier. Some never succeeded in this.

The adjutant and sergeant-major had as much trouble in forming the regiment as the orderly did in getting company Q into line, but it was accomplished after much tribulation.

Before starting it was necessary—according to "Regulations"—that the men should be formally mustered into the service of the United States. Under the circumstances it was determined to muster the whole regiment in a "lump," instead of in detail by companies. As soon as the line was formed the pompous mustering officer appeared, in tow of the colonel.

"What they goin' ter do now?" Si Klegg asked of Shorty.

"I reck'n we're goin' ter git mustered," was the reply.

"It'll be kind o' nice," said Si, "ter have mustard t' eat on biled ham—fer I s'pose the guvment 'll give us ham once 'n a while—but I hain't got nothin' ter carry it in."

"'Taint that," replied Shorty, laughing; "it's only jest a leetle red-tape pufformance 't clenches the nail 't the 'listin' ossifer druv into ye, 'n' fixes ye so ye can't git out 'less ye git shot out. That's what they calls gittin' mustered. But come ter think on't, yer idee wa'n't fur out o' the way. Ye gits mustered now 'n' ye're likely ter git peppered when ye strike the rebils, 'n mebbe ye'll get salted down for keeps. There ain't much danger 't ye won't be purty well seasoned 'fore ye git through 'th this thing."

The ceremony lasted but a few minutes and then all was ready for the start. The colonel and the field and staff officers, on gaily caparisoned horses, pranced around, the band struck up a lively march, and, amidst the cheers of the spectators and the responsive shouts of the soldiers, the column moved off.

The knapsacks were not very heavy, as they contained nothing but clothing. Si had not opened the box he brought from home, and had some concern respecting its fate. He was reassured by the information that, as there had been no opportunity for the men to put their things in order, all the baggage would accompany the regiment to its first stopping place, where its equipment would be fully provided.

The train had been reported to be in readiness at the railway station, but of course it wasn't; nobody ever heard of such a thing. The regiment had to wait and stand around for two hours before it received the welcome order, "All aboard!" It was after dark when the eager men packed themselves into the cars for an all-night ride. The two engines whistled and coughed, the people hurrahed and waved hats and handkerchiefs, the soldiers thrust their heads out of the windows and yelled —and the 200th Indiana was off to the war.

CHAPTER V.

In Which the Bright Colors that Fancy Painted Begin to Fade—
The Soldier and his "Pard"—How Si was Led From the Straight
and Narrow Way of Soldierly Rectitude.

THERE was little sleep on the train that night. The
boys fought imaginary battles and yelled and sang
and laughed at one another's jests. It was a long time
before the members of the 200th Indiana found another
occasion for such hilarity—not till those that were left of
them went home at the close of the war.

"There won't be so much laughing in a few days," said
the colonel, "let 'em enjoy themselves while they can!"

A few were sober and thoughtful, realizing that every
moment was bringing them nearer to scenes of danger and
death. Some wanted to sleep as best they could in the
crowded seats, but this was impossible in the universal
tumult of mirth and jollity that prevailed. At frequent
intervals the soldiers stirred up the musicians to play martial airs, and the roar of the fast speeding train was drowned
by rattling drums and screaming fifes and the shouts evoked
by the inspiring strains. One would hardly have thought
those men were going to war to kill and be killed; but
that was the way all the regiments went out.

Si had for his seat-mate his new friend Shorty, who had
volunteered to help him out of his quandary with the knapsack. He was taken with his kindly ways, notwithstanding his rough exterior, and was quite disposed to improve

the acquaintance. Si was an active and noisy participant in the night's merriment, and in the morning he felt considerably fagged. He told Shorty that he thought on the whole they had had a pretty hard time of it.

About breakfast time the regiment reached its immediate destination. As the men alighted from the train they found themselves surrounded by reminders of war. They had reached the grand army of which each of them was to become an atom. Thenceforward they were to be identified with its history—its triumphs and its defeats. There were soldiers everywhere, engaged in the various duties incident to preparation for a great campaign. The streets of the city were full of wagons loaded with ammunition, food, clothing, forage and army supplies of all kinds. On every hand were heard the yell of the mule-driver and the crack of his whip. There were officers of every grade dashing about, cavalrymen with clanking sabers galloping hither and thither, artillery rumbling over the pavements, and bodies of infantry moving from point to point. All was bustle and confusion, such as the eyes of these new soldiers had never looked upon before.

Si Klegg was keenly interested in all that he saw and heard. To him there was a fascination in this pomp and display—the uniforms, the glittering bayonets, the men marching with measured tread, and the bespangled officers—that bound him as with a spell. At last had come the realization of his romantic dreams. He could scarcely wait until he should have a gun to put on his shoulder.

"Hello, sonny, does yer mother know ye're out?"

It was very cruel to say this to Si, as he stood with his hands in his pockets and with open mouth and eyes gazing in astonishment at the scenes around him. The man who said it was a rusty-looking soldier who, with a few of his comrades, chanced to pass that way.

"Yes, mother said I might come!" said Si, innocently.

Then the veterans laughed loudly and stopped to "have some fun." Si could not for his life see anything for them to laugh at.

"Say, bub, give us a hunk o' gingerbread!"

"Look at the big ridgment o' tenderfoots! Won't they be a-humpin' one o' these days?"

"Jest see them paper collars!"

"Had any hardtack yet?"

Si did not comprehend the army lingo. It was as if

they had spoken to him in an unknown tongue. But he found that they were making game of him and then his wrath began to rise. In fact, he went so far as to express a willingness to fight the entire squad. His eyes flashed as he said to them:

"I've come down here to do some fightin', 'n' I'd jest like to git my hand in!"

SI'S FIRST ENCOUNTER WITH THE VETERANS.   This warlike demonstration was greeted with jeers and shouts of laughter.

"Better save what sand ye've got, young feller," said one of them, "ye'll have need fer it 'fore long."

A hand was laid upon Si's arm, and Shorty drew him aside.

"I don't blame ye fer gittin' mad, Si," he said, "but it don't allus pay. When the odds is too big ye can't do nothin' but grin 'n' b'ar it. Them fellers don't mean no harm. They has ter have the'r fun when they gits a chance; they look 's if they hadn't been havin' much on it lately. Ef ye was hungry, they'd divide their last cracker with ye; 'n' ef ye was lyin' sick er wounded they'd give ye all the blankets they had, ef ye needed 'em. Soldiers is queer bein's 'n' ye have ter git so ye kin understand 'em."

Shorty's homely philosophy had its designed effect and Si soon recovered his equanimity. When his tormentors found him laughing at their good-natured badinage, they left him and turned their fire upon others.

These men had been in active service for a year. Their clothing and their faces and hands gave abundant evidence that they had been somewhere. Si eyed them curiously and he wondered if he would ever be like them.

"Attention, Company Q!"

The regiment formed and marched out two or three miles to the place assigned it for a camp. It was not far to march, and the men had little to carry, but for some reason they were all very glad when they got there. They had a slight foretaste of how hard it was to travel "in harness." After reaching the outskirts of the city they saw nothing but camps. As far as the eye could reach in every direction, the white villages of regiments and brigades dotted every field, wood and hillside. Si wondered where so many soldiers came from.

The aspect of the 200th Indiana "gave it away" completely. The men were without arms, their clothes were new and their faces clean. The full ranks had not been scorched and shriveled by the hot blast of war. There could be no mistaking the fact that it was a new regiment just from home.

The veterans would always rather go without a dinner than to miss a chance to "nag" a fresh arrival of green soldiers. It was the height of enjoyment to stand by the roadside as they trudged by and assail them in front flank and rear with pungent remarks and questions clothed in all the luxuriant beauty of the army vernacular. It was great sport for the veterans, but not quite so funny for their victims.

All the way out the long-suffering members of the 200th Indiana had to run the gauntlet of the tanned and bearded soldiers of the crop of '61. The band at the head of the column kept playing defiantly, but it did not take the men long to learn that it was the part of wisdom to receive in silence the "slings and arrows" that were constantly hurled upon them. Perhaps it was this experience, quite as much as the fatigue of the march, that induced the feeling of satisfaction with which they saw first the colonel and then the band file off the road, indicating that the halting place had been reached. A cheer started at the head of the column and the whole regiment joined in a wild shout of joy.

The most desirable spots for camping were already occupied, and the 200th was obliged to content itself with a cornfield. Unfortunately the rain began to fall just as it broke ranks. It was not a hard rain, but one of those exasperating drizzles so destructive to the Christian virtues. When it *had* to rain—and the frequency of the storms seemed wholly unnecessary—the soldier would rather have it pour down while it was about it and then quit, than to endure one of those protracted seasons when the water oozed slowly from the low-hanging clouds, and dribbled down, filling the air with a heavy mist that made everything cold and wet and clammy. Possibly the human race may have been in some degree regenerated since the war, but at that time there were few men living —and they all stayed at home—who could pass through a day or two of such experience and not lose control of tongue and temper.

The members of the 200th Indiana were indeed in a sorry plight. They were without shelter, as their tents had not yet arrived. They could only stand around, with their heads sticking through their ponchos, churning the soft earth into mud with their restless feet. This dismal and unlooked for visitation had a most depressing effect upon their spirits. Their mental condition was in marked contrast to the revelry of the previous night. Most of them looked as if they would like to take the next train for Indiana, if the matter of return tickets had not been entirely overlooked.

There was a great deal of justifiable grumbling because tents were not awaiting the regiment upon its arrival, as its coming was known. Such a thing, however, never occurred during the war. It was unheard of and unthought of, except by the soldiers who happened to be caught as was the 200th Indiana. A great many things might have been but were not, on account of the kinks in the red-tape in which every department of the army was tangled.

So a thousand men, wet and disconsolate, had to wait while the colonel and quartermaster galloped back to town after tents. They went straight to headquarters and made application for them, but were promptly informed that business was not done in that way. A requisition must be made in due form, according to regulations, and must be approved by the various intermediate commanders —brigade, division, corps and army. In vain the Colonel stormed, and declared it was an outrage to keep his men, who were not used to such things, standing out in the rain while that performance was being gone through with. He wanted the tents and would furnish the papers afterward. But the laws of war had no elasticity, and the colonel and quartermaster were obliged to go back and start in at the bottom. It took them two hours to get around. The regiment had no wagons yet, and the head quartermaster did consent to send a couple of teams out to the camp with the tents.

Meanwhile, the men of the 200th had been sloshing

about in a deplorable state of mind and body. It was a
rude awakening from their dreams to the stern reality of
"soldiering."

"Are we goin' ter have very much o' this kind o' thing?"
asked Si, as he stood with the water slowly trickling from
the rim of his hat and the corners of his poncho, while
drops just ready to fall hung from his nose and chin.

"Wall, I can't 'zactly tell," replied Shorty. "There's
all kinds o' weather, 'n' a good deal *on* it down 'n this

A BAPTISM.

kentry. I can't think
o' nothin' we kin do
'bout it, 'n' I reck'n
we'll have to let 'er
rain 's long 'n' 's of'n
's she wants ter."

"I s'pose that's so;
but seems ter me 't ef
I was a-runnin' this
war I'd have things
a leetle diff'runt when
the rijiments comes in.
I don't see no use 'n
keepin' us fellers stan'-
in' 'round here all day
half way to our knees
'n mud 'n' gittin' wuss
every minit."

"Si," said Shorty,
"ye'll larn arter a while. Course, this 'ere 's a damp shame,
but it's jest the way they allus does things 'n the army.
But ther' ain't no good gittin' cranky, 'cause ye can't help
yerself. Ef ye'd hired out to work fer a man to home 'n'
he didn't treat ye squar', ye could jest up 'n' quit, but
ther' ain't no gittin' out o' this. They've got ye dead to
rights!"

"Who said anything 'bout wantin' ter quit?" exclaimed

Si, piqued a little at Shorty's implied insinuation that he was deficient in staying qualities. "Mebbe I'm younger 'n some o' the soljers, but I ain't no baby. I kin stan' jest 's much 's the next un."

Shorty hastened to assure him that he had no intention of casting slurs upon him. "I b'lieve ye've got grit," he said. "I don't know whether I've got 'nough myself ter last me through, but I like ter see it 'n somebody else."

This smoothed Si's ruffled feelings, and put him at once into as good a humor as was possible under such doleful conditions. He summoned to his aid all the "pluck" he could command, determined to show his comrade that he could and would face like a brave soldier whatever might come. The slight pricking that Shorty gave him was just what he needed. He had nailed his colors to the mast, so to speak, and they were going to stay there. Under the spur of his resolute will he became cheerful, and even tried a few jokes at the expense of his comrades. There was but a feeble response, however, for the dripping men of the 200th Indiana were not in a mood for jesting. What little was said was of a different character.

They had had no breakfast that was worthy of the name. There was no danger of immediate starvation, as they had eaten liberally during the night, and since then the contents of their haversacks had sufficed to appease the mild gnawings of hunger. They were beginning to feel the need of something warming, and were most agreeably surprised when they were waited upon by a delegation from the regiments of a veteran brigade encamped near by, inviting them over to have some coffee.

"We've been thar, boys," they said, "an' we know jest how ye feel. 'Tain't a bit funny. We can't give ye no fancy lay-out, but we've made a lot o' hot coffee fer ye, an' that'll feel good to yer insides. Ye're welcome to the best we kin give ye."

"Si," said Shorty, "how's that fer a *in*vite? What'd I

tell ye 'bout them soljers? These 's some o' the same fellers as was hootin' 'n' yellin' at us 's we come up the road. I told ye they didn't mean nothin'. They'd jest turn theirselves inside out ter do anything fer them that's sufferin' 'n' needin' help. They don't draw no more coffee 'n they want, 'n' they'll have ter go 'thout it one meal on 'count o' what they're a-doin' fer us. The vet'rans is a hard lookin' lot, but ye kin tie to 'em, Si."

The hospitable invitation was accepted with alacrity, and with a profusion of thanks that came from the innermost recesses of those drooping hearts. The companies were formed and marched to the neighboring camp, two or three to each of the regiments, and were cordially welcomed by the very soldiers who had jeered them without mercy two hours before. Shorty had not over-stated the case. Beneath those ragged blouses were big hearts full to the brim with the "milk of human kindness."

The guests were scattered through the camp and invited into the tents in little squads, where they laid off their wet ponchos.

"We hain't got no cheers," said one of the hosts, as Si and Shorty and two or three others entered one of the tents. "Thar's a cracker box a couple of ye kin sit on, an' the rest of ye 'll have ter git down tailor-fashion on these 'ere blankets."

The dispositions were quickly made and tin cups full of steaming coffee were brought in. The odor was sweeter than incense to the nostrils of those Hoosiers.

"Here's plenty o' sugar," said one of the veterans. "This 'mess' is a little short o' spoons; there 's only one an' ye'll have to pass it 'long—that's the way *we* does. The cows hain't come up yet, an' we hain't got no milk fer ye. Want some hardtack?"

"What's it like?" asked Si.

"Oh, that's the stuff we gits fer bread," replied the veteran. "I s'pose ye hain't struck any on it yet. Hardtack tastes mighty good sometimes, but it's when a feller's reel hungry an' hain't got nothin' else to eat. If ye've got any soft bread in yer haversacks, I reck'n that'll taste better to ye jest now."

The boys had plenty of bread, and the excellent coffee was most refreshing.

"Purty tough beginnin' fer ye, boys," said one of their

HOSPITALITY.

entertainers, "but ye've got to git broke in, same's all on us had to. We don't mind it now, 'cause we've got used to it. Ye're stan'in' it bully, bein' its the fust time, an' if ye stick to it ye'll make soljers arter a while."

Si did not quite like the intimation that he was not a soldier already. He was certain, at least, that he would be one as soon as he had a gun on his shoulder and a car-

tridge-box buckled around his waist. He did not yet realize
the difference there was between a recruit and a soldier,
and the long and severe process that was necessary to complete the transformation. His first impulse was to argue
the question, but a wink from Shorty, who seemed to divine his thoughts, told him that he had better hold his
peace.

The members of the 200th Indiana were profoundly grateful to the veterans for their kindness, and expressed the
hope that they might sometime have the opportunity to
pay the debt. They had a vastly better opinion of the
old soldiers than they formed two hours before when
receiving the volleys of taunts and gibes.

Soon after their return to their own camping-ground
the wagons with the tents arrived, under convoy of the
colonel and quartermaster. The camp was hastily laid
out and all hands fell to with a will. Not a quarter of
the men had ever seen a tent before that day, and very few
knew anything about "pitching" one. But they all
thought that was easy enough. They hadn't anything
to drive stakes with, but they borrowed axes and hatchets
from their neighbors and were soon pounding away with
great energy. They were not long in finding out that a
good many things are easy—after you have learned how
to do them. Even the pitching of a tent required at
least a limited amount of knowledge and experience. They
were directed to place them in straight rows, by companies,
but they got them up askew and "every which way."
The "flaps" at the front perversely refused to come together,
leaving great yawning gaps, making it impossible to "shut
the door." The boys gladly accepted a few suggestions
from some of the veterans who came over and stood around,
first exhausting their stock of jokes on the new men, and
then taking hold in the kindest possible way and showing
them how to do it.

With the tents up the camp assumed a rather more cheerful aspect. It would be more nearly correct to say that it was a little less miserable, for the two conditions were only comparative degrees of woe. The prospect for the night was dismal enough.

"Now, men," said the captain, encouragingly, "get divided off, one 'mess' for each tent, and make yourselves as comfortable as you can." And then the captain went to the surgeon and told him he didn't feel very well, got an excuse to go into town, and stayed all night at a hotel.

"'Pears ter me, Shorty, we're in 'bout 's bad a 'mess' now 's we kin git!" said Si, as he looked despairingly down at his legs, which were elaborately frescoed with that red clay mud so peculiar to the South and as adhesive as patent glue.

The order of the captain to "make themselves comfortable" had but little meaning to the men of Company Q. It seemed a very preposterous thing to talk of manufacturing "comfort," when so destitute of the necessary elements. As yet the word conveyed to them no other idea than a well spread table, a rocking-chair before a blazing hearth, and a good bed to sleep in.

There was absolutely nothing in sight, not under guard, that could give them relief in their extremity. Boards, rails, limbs of trees—anything on which to spread their blankets would have been hailed as a favorable dispensation of providence, but the last vestige of available material had long since disappeared among the thousands of soldiers in the densely populated camps. A crow might have scanned that field in vain for material with which to build a nest.

There were barns and outbuildings and fences in the vicinity, but bristling bayonets warned off all who sought to lay violent hands upon them. They were as tempting to those gloomy-hearted Hoosiers as was the forbidden fruit to the ancestral pair in the Garden of Eden—and they were a great deal more securely protected. The destructive propensity, which seemed to be an instinct in the breast of the soldier, showed itself at the very outset in the 200th Indiana, and foreshadowed great activity in this direction whenever the restraint should be removed. As the murky twilight began to deepen they would have torn down half the city, if they had been turned loose, and used the debris to keep themselves out of the mud. But the time for this had not yet come.

The truth is that the soldiers fully adopted the confiscation theory long before the statesmen and the generals did, though not permitted by the latter to carry out their eminently practical ideas of how to conduct a campaign. But the boys planted their flags there, and after a while the lawgivers and the men with stars twinkling on their shoulders "dressed up" to the line in fine style. After trying it for about two years the beautiful theory of carrying on a war without hurting anybody—in pocket—was abandoned.

The field occupied by the 200th was surrounded by a rail fence. More properly speaking, it had been so surrounded before the war. Whatever value for other purposes there might be in the few scattering rails that stretched around the camp, as a fence they were no longer of any account. Nor did it seem at all likely that any fence would be needed there while the war lasted. When the flame of the guns at Sumter lighted up the heavens with its lurid glare, about the first thing the government did was to place a guard over that sacred fence, and it had been kept up ever since. Judging from the faithfulness with which the sentinels paced their beats around that field, successively relieving one another through all the weeks and months, the protection of those rails—that no soldier might lay them down to sleep on, or make fires of them to cook his coffee and bean-soup—seemed to be the chief purpose for which the army was sent down there. The condition of the fence at this time gave abundant evidence of the fact that the vigilance of the guards had not been wholly successful in preventing depredations. Numerous forays on dark nights, the moment of attack being when a guard was at a remote point on his beat, had resulted in a slow but sure process of dissolution. But still the men in blue trudged to and fro, by day and by night, over the well-worn path, with the same orders that were dinned into the astonished ears of the first men who were stationed to guard it: "If any man attempts to take a rail from that fence, shoot him on the spot!" By the time the 200th Indiana moved away, there were no rails left to speak of; but in the absence of any testimony on the subject it is safe to say that from sheer force of habit the guard was kept up along the line where that fence *was* until Lee surrendered at Appomattox.

"Purty hard place ter sleep, ain't it, Shorty?" said Si, as he stood within the tent, surveying the muddy ground and calculating the chances on getting a night's rest.

"Purty *soft*, ye mean, don't ye?" replied Shorty.

Si laughed, more at the thought of a jest from such an unexpected source than from the brilliancy of the joke itself.

"Ther' ain't no diff'rence," he said, "we're both drivin' 't the same idee. What 'd mother 'n' sister Marier say 'f they c'd see whar we've got ter lay down, 'nless we stan' up to 't all night, 'n' I d'no but that's the best way out o' the scrape. Even Dad's hogs 's better off ner we be, fer they *kin* git out o' the mud 'f they wants ter, 'n' that's mor'n we c'n do!"

In making up the "messes" these two had naturally entered the same tent, and drawn by a mutual attraction they had "paired."

With rare exceptions every soldier had his "pard." New troops on taking the field and adjusting themselves to the peculiar situations of army life, mated as naturally as birds in springtime. The longer they remained in the service the

more did they appreciate the convenience of this arrangement.   During the arduous campaigns two constituted a
family, eating and sleeping together.   They "pooled"
their rations and made an equitable division of labor.   On
the march, if a patch of sweet potatoes, a field of "roasting
ears," or an orchard in fruit was reached, one would carry
the gun of his comrade while the latter would lay in a supply of forage for their evening meal, and then hasten forward to his place in the column.

On going into camp one would look for straw while the
other went on a hunt for a chicken or a piece of fresh pork.
Then while one filled the canteens at the spring or stream,
the other gathered wood and made a fire.   All became
prime cooks, and this part of the work was shared.   If it
was to be a "regulation" meal, one superintended the
coffee, pounding up the roasted grains in a tin cup or can
with the butt of his bayonet while the water was coming
to a boil, and the other fried or toasted the bacon.   If
either was detailed for guard or fatigue duty, he knew that
the wants of his inner man would be provided for, and his
portion of any choice morsel would be scrupulously saved
for him.   If one was ill or worse "played out" than the
other after a toilsome march, his companion cared for him
with all the tenderness of a brother.   If one was imposed
upon by quarrelsome comrades he could always safely depend upon his "pard" to stand by him to the last extremity.   At night they lay together upon one blanket with
the other as a cover.   It is not probable that Solomon
ever snuggled up to his "pard" under a "pup" tent; but he
seems to have had the correct idea when he wrote (Ecclesi-
astes IV: 11): "Again, if two lie together, then they have
heat: but how can one be warm alone?"   There were
many times when they hugged each other like two pieces
of sticking-plaster, in the vain effort to generate heat
enough for even a measurable degree of comfort.   When
two congenial spirits were thus brought together nothing

but death or a separation at the call of duty could sever the ties that bound them.

It will not be thought strange that many, after "living together" for a few days or weeks, found themselves mismated. In fact it was about as much of a lottery as getting married is popularly believed to be; and divorces were as frequent as in the hymeneal experience of mankind.

A fruitful source of domestic eruptions was the development and gradual growth of a disposition on the part of one member of the firm to "play off" on his more energetic comrade, and shirk his part of the labor so indispensable to their welfare. The soldier was constitutionally lazy, so far as the performance of irksome toil was concerned. This was considered proper and right when applied to general fatigue duty, but when a man was too lazy to help get his own dinner or go foraging for sweet potatoes, he placed himself outside the pale of Christian forbearance. Then his "pard" went back on him, and sometimes a riot occurred that aroused the whole camp. The upshot of it all was that the "drone" was left to shift for himself, while the industrious bee, finding it easier to provide for one than for two, buzzed around until he could pick up a more congenial mate.

Incompatibility of temper broke up many of these hastily formed partnerships. Sometimes the appetites were not evenly balanced, and in times of scarcity one ate more than his share of the common stock of rations. Then there *was* trouble, and plenty of it. These and other causes often disturbed for a time the harmony of intimate association, and it generally took about a year to get the "pards" properly adjusted.

The ravages of disease and the deadly missiles of battle made sad havoc with these ties of brotherhood. Few bereavements are more keenly felt than were those among the comrades of months and years.

Here and there, in every company flock, was a black sheep

who seemed to be a misfit everywhere. Nobody paired
with him, and—perhaps as much from his own choice as
from the fact that he seemed to have no "affinity"—he
lived like a crusty old bachelor in civil life. He made
his own fire, boiled his coffee in a kettle holding just enough
for one, and ate his meal alone. Then he rolled himself
up in his blanket like a mummy and lay down, having, at
least, the satisfaction of knowing that no bed-fellow would
kick the cover off in the night and expose him to the
copious and chilling dews.

In the company to which the writer belonged there was
a little fellow of Teutonic birth, who had a snore that was
like the sound of a fish-horn. When he was asleep it was
never silent. He would begin to tune up his bazoo as soon
as he closed his eyes, and by the time he was fairly asleep
it would be at full blast. Enough imprecations to sink a
ship were nightly heaped upon that unfortunate youth.
Sometimes the boys made it so warm for him that he
would get up in high dudgeon, seize his blanket, and go off
back of the camp and crawl into a wagon. Then when
he got to snoring again it would set all the mules to braying. Once when the company was sent, at night, to occupy a position near the enemy, and silence was a necessity,
this man was actually left behind as a prudential measure.
It was feared he would go to sleep and his snoring would
convey intelligence to the enemy. But he snored his way
through the war to the very end. In all the hard fighting
only one bullet ever touched him—and that did not in the
slightest degree impair his snoring machinery. Of course
he never had a "pard." A chap tried it the first night in
camp, but half an hour after they lay down he got
up in a rage and left the Dutchman's "bed and board"
forever.

"Si," said Shorty, as if an idea had struck him with
unusual force, "come 'long 'th me!"

"What fer?" asked Si.

"Never you mind," was the reply; "jest foller me 'n' don't say nothin' ter nobody!"

Si did as he was bidden, for he was already learning to pin his faith to his companion. When they had passed outside the rows of tents, Shorty unfolded his scheme.

"Ther' ain't no use lyin' 'n the mud," he said, "'n' them rails out thar rottin'."

"Why, Shorty," exclaimed Si, astonished at so flagrant a violation of orders, "ye know what they told us; 'n' them fellers's out thar 'th their bay'nets! I don't want ter have none o' them things punched into me jest yet; I want ter see suthin' more o' this war!"

"Bay'nets be blowed!" said Shorty. "I ain't goin' ter git *you* inter no scrape, so don't ye be 'feard. You stand whar I tell ye 'n' I'll fotch ye some o' them rails, sure's yer born."

Si promised to obey, with a dubious hope that it would all come out right. He took his position at a safe distance from the fence, though not without some smitings of conscience. He felt very much as he did once when, beguiled at night into a neighbor's melon-patch, he trembled with fear lest the old man should turn loose the dogs.

The darkness favored Shorty's foray. Creeping carefully up he saw the sentinel face about at the end of his beat and start in the opposite direction. Two or three minutes later Shorty darted up to the fence, seized a couple of rails, bore them back and delivered them to Si.

"Now wait t'll I get 'nother load," he said.

"Won't these do?" asked Si. "I don't like ter have ye try it agin. I'm 'feard they'll cotch ye!"

"We can't sleep on one rail apiece. I'll be back 'n a minit!"

In an instant he had disappeared. Si stood breathlessly awaiting his return. Shorty slipped a figure in his calculation this time, and as he was lifting the rails to his shoulder he was confronted by the guard.

Now the truth is the guard did not care how many rails were taken. He did not want to see what might be going on, for it was not unlikely that the next night, if it was dark and he was not on duty, he would be doing the same thing himself. But when he came suddenly upon Shorty in the very act he could not let him pass unnoticed. Shorty, with a grip on the rails, bounded off into the darkness.

"Halt, there! Halt, or I'll blow ye into the middle o' next week!"

Si heard the awful words, followed by the ominous click of the gun lock. He sank upon the ground all in a heap, quaking with fear.

"O-o-oh, Sh-sh-shorty!" he exclaimed in a hoarse whisper, as his comrade came dashing up.

"Git up, Si, *quick!* Grab yer rails 'n' run. Don't lie thar 'n' let 'im stab ye er plug a hole through yer liver!"

STEALING A BED.

In frantic desperation Si seized the rails. Shorty led the way some distance off at a right angle from the line leading to the camp.

"Thar, now, git down 's low 's ye kin!" said Shorty. "It'll be only a chance 'f the pesky guard finds us here, 'n' ef he does, all we kin do is ter take the consekences. I don't b'lieve he'll shute anybody."

The sentinel tramped around a few minutes in the darkness and then, glad that the raiders had escaped, turned to his beat.

"Thar it's all right," said Shorty, " ye mustn't git scar't at a little thing like that. Now let's go in."

Si was too frightened yet to talk. He once more shouldered his rails and followed his comrade to the camp. Just outside the outermost row of tents they threw them down and Si stayed with them while Shorty hunted up an axe. He chopped them in two and they carried the pieces in triumph to their tent.

Si and Shorty laid down the rails, spread their blankets upon them, placed their knapsacks for pillows, and stretched themselves out. It was a hard bed. Si's bones were well cushioned with flesh, but the sharp corners of the rails made great furrows in his body.

"Shorty," said Si, after they had lain quiet for a few minutes, "what 'll the ossifers do to us 'f they finds these 'ere rails 'n our tent?"

"Don't let that worry ye," replied Shorty, "we'll jest keep 'em kivered wi' the blankets, t'll we gits a chance ter burn 'em up!"

Just before dark several wagon loads of green oak logs had been dumped at various points through the camp. After long effort, that exhausted the patience of several successive "reliefs," a few feeble fires were started. Around these, wet and shivering and blinded by the smoke, the disconsolate men of the 200th Indiana crowded and elbowed one another. Patriotism was at zero.

CHAPTER VI.

"WALL, Si, how d'ye feel?" said Shorty to his comrade, as they got up at an early hour next morning.

"Fust rate," was the cheery answer. "But I'll tell ye what 'tis, pard, I don't hanker much arter that kind o' bed-slats 'n' no matrus ter put on 'em. I never did like ter git up 'n the mornin' to hum, but you kin depend on me fer a early riser 's long 's I sleep on sich a bed 's that." And Si rubbed his legs and moved about briskly to limber up his stiffened joints.

When company Q fell in for roll-call, the men looked as if they had just been to a funeral in the capacity of chief mourners. Most of them had scarcely slept at all, but had spent the long hours of the night that they thought would never end, in hovering around the smoking fires. The sun rose bright, and the genial warmth of his rays gradually dispelled the gloom that had settled over the camp.

It was a busy day. Wagons arrived loaded with rations, which were promptly issued to the various companies. There was an abundance of the articles that went to make up the nourishing regulation *menu*, except that soft bread was furnished in lieu of "hardtack." There seemed to be a humane desire to let the boys down to bed-rock by easy stages.

Si felt a lively personal interest in the commissary department, to which he must look for his daily bread. He volunteered to help unload the wagons, and as he saw the seemingly bountiful supplies of bread, bacon, sugar, coffee, beans, etc., a quiet joy filled his heart.

"Shorty," he said, "this don't look much like starvin' the soljers. I'll do jest anything Uncle Sam wants me ter 's long 's he gives me 'nough ter eat."

Then other wagons came with a supply of camp-equip-age—axes, shovels, camp-kettles and other articles neces-sary to a company outfit. The word "necessary" is here used because all these things were so considered at that time. The camp-kettle, as indicated by its name, was a good and useful article of furniture when the troops were lying in camp, but did not figure largely in the long, active campaigns of the later years of the war. It was chiefly used for making coffee and bean soup, and for laundry purposes—for the soldiers had to boil their clothes the same as their mothers and sisters did the family wash, though for a different reason, which will appear in due time.

The camp-kettle was an odd looking affair, of heavy sheet-iron, very tall, and of the same diameter from top to bottom. All were of the same height, but there were three or four sizes of them, so that they could be conveniently "nested" for transportation. They rapidly fell victims to the casualties of active service. Like everything else the sol-diers used or wore, they were "made by contract." Some of them soon became leaky from causes known only to the men who made them. The idea seemed to be paramount in the minds of those self-sacrificing patriots who helped to save the country by supplying the army with camp-kettles and other things, that if they made them so that they would not last long, there would be a speedy demand for more, and this would make business brisk. Other camp-kettles had their usefulness impaired by various accidents to which they were liable. Wagons ran over them, and the boys,

in their mirthful moods, kicked them about the camp. On
the whole, the camp-kettles had a hard time of it. During
the last year of the war thousands of the soldiers did not
so much as see one for months together. A little ingenuity
and activity in foraging supplied substitutes that answered every purpose.

Then came the event of the day. Half a dozen wagons
drew up to the camp and the detail of men began to unload
long heavy boxes that looked as if they were made to
enclose coffins—an appearance not wholly inappropriate.
They contained bright, new Springfield muskets for the
200th Indiana. This arrival was greeted with an outburst
of cheers, for the men were painfully conscious that as yet
they were soldiers only in name. Without arms they did
not amount to "a row of pins."

More big boxes were tumbled out of the wagons. These
contained the cartridge-boxes, waist and shoulder belts,
cap-boxes, and other "traps" that went to make up the
long list of accouterments. One of the wagons was loaded
with small boxes of about the capacity of a half-bushel
measure. Si sprang forward to toss them out, but when
he took hold of one he found it was as much as he could
do to lift it. It fairly made his bones creak as he lowered
it to the ground. It was full of ammunition—cartridges
ready for use.

Things now began to look like business, and the men
moved about with the utmost eagerness. Rumors flew
through the camp that the rebel army was close at hand
and a conflict was hourly expected. The members of the
200th Indiana felt that if the impending battle could only
be staved off until they should get their guns and fill up their
"pill-boxes" it would be all right. There could no longer
be any doubt as to the result, and the band might at once
begin to play.

When Company Q's turn came it was marched up to
headquarters, and in a few minutes each man was the

happy possessor of a brightly burnished musket and bayonet, and all the accessories needful to complete his warlike array, including forty rounds of ammunition. To the
regiment forty thousand cartridges were issued—enough to
destroy the entire opposing army, provided they all went
to the right spot. Little wonder that these valiant new
soldiers believed that the end was now near at hand.

The colonel superintended the distribution of the arms,
and noted with pride the eagerness with which his men
grasped their muskets and accouterments. He had no doubt
that they would manifest equal promptitude in using them
when occasion required, and there passed before him visions
of the glory that would cause the name of the 200th
Indiana to shine with conspicuous luster.

The captain of Company Q had to sign a receipt for the
arms and equipments issued to his men, as he did for the
tents and everything appertaining to the company's outfit. The officers who went out in '62 were wiser in their
generation than those who took the field the year before. They had the benefit of the latter's experience. It
was on this wise: It was decreed in the "Revised Army
Regulations"—a big blue-covered book, impressively let-
tered, that was both law and gospel to all who entered
the army in any capacity—that the commanding officer of
a company should, under all circumstances, be held strictly
responsible for every penny's worth of government property in the possession of his men. Monthly returns of
clothing and "camp and garrison equipage," as it was
called in a lump, and quarterly returns of ordnance and
ordnance stores had to be made to the Grand Moguls at
Washington. In these returns everything in the way of
baggage, down to a hatchet or a tent-pin, had to be accounted for, as well as every article in the line of ordnance,
from a musket to a belt-plate. Even the tompions—tiny
wooden plugs to stick into the muzzles of the guns and
keep out the dust and rain, worth about two-for-a-cent—

had to be momentously entered in the long columns of items and figures. If one of the little things disappeared it had to be accounted for, with an imposing array of certificates and affidavits, as though the salvation of the country hung by a thread on the fate of that lost tompion. If he could not account for it in a way that was perfectly satisfactory to the high and mighty authorities at the National capital, he had to pay for it in cash. In collecting debts of this kind Uncle Sam "had the bulge" on the officer, by an overwhelming majority. He just sent the account to the paymaster, and that pompous officer promptly lopped off the amount from his pay.

To the unsophisticated volunteer it *did* seem as though, in thus holding him pecuniarily accountable for these paltry things, through all the vicissitudes of war, our great and glorious government was straining at very small gnats, while it was at the same time gulping down so many double-humped camels without a qualm. But it was "Regulations," and that settled it. The pains and penalties laid down in that terrible book were as inflexible as the law of the Medes and Persians, "which altereth not."

The officers of '61 devoted themselves with commendable assiduity to "Hardee's Tactics," but they sadly neglected the "Regulations." At least they did not give such heed to its teachings as the welfare of their pockets required. The making of returns at stated periods was all well enough, they thought, for "Regulars," permanently stationed in forts and barracks, but they did not for a moment imagine that such punctilious duties would be exacted of those who had left the plow, the bar, the counter, the office, for the sole purpose of putting down the rebellion. Whatever of government property disappeared was destroyed or lost in the service, any way, and the idea of their being compelled to pay for it was too preposterous to be entertained for a moment. So they pursued the even tenor of their way, trudging over the stony pikes and leading their men into battle, and didn't make any returns at all.

But there came a day of rude awakening from their dreams of fancied security. In many cases the pay of the officers of an entire regiment was stopped, with the strictest orders that the spigot in Uncle Sam's "bar'l" should not be withdrawn and the flow of money resumed until full returns from the beginning were made, as it was "nominated in the bond." Shylock was not more exacting in the demand for *his* "pound of flesh." The effect of an order of this kind from Washington was like that of an unexpected shell from a masked battery. It threw the officers who had commanded companies, into a convulsive state which continued for days and weeks, while they were trying to get themselves out of the snarl. By this time most of the companies had been reduced to half their original strength. Forty or fifty guns and their accouterments, and camp and garrison equipage in proportion, were gone, and not a scrap of writing to show for them. Many things had been worn out, and most of the guns had irregularly found their way into the hands of ordnance officers from the hospitals where the men were left; but these facts did not help them out of their dilemma, in the absence of receipts and other documentary evidence. It would have absorbed many an officer's pay for a year to square his accounts.

This was where the swearing came in. The making of searching and comprehensive affidavits is the kind of swearing intended to be understood, although the widest possible latitude may be given to the word in this connection without doing violence to the truth. In a case of this kind the orderly-sergeant was the captain's sheet anchor. His memory was taxed to the utmost, and, when its resources were exhausted, his imagination was drawn upon for accidents and casualties that would account for the missing property. Some of the affidavits almost blistered the paper upon which they were written.

When one officer had been continuously in command of a company and the same orderly had stuck by him, time, patience and stationery only were necessary. But in the great majority of cases, through the casualties of disease and battle, two or three officers had successively commanded, with perhaps as many different first sergeants at

the wheel, and there was long floundering in the mire. In many instances it took months to get the accounts sufficiently straightened so that the paymaster pulled out the plug and again started the stream of greenbacks to irri- gate the well-parched pocket- books of the exasperated officers. Thousands will recognize this as a truthful picture of their experi- ence in learning Uncle Sam's rule that "business is business."

When Si got back to his tent he could not rest until he had tried on the latest addition to his equipment. With Shorty's assist- ance he managed to get the vari- ous parts together and buckled on his cartridge-box. Then he shouldered his musket and

IN PANOPLY OF WAR.

marched up and down the company street with a feeling of pride and satisfaction that he had never felt before. He wished his mother and Annabel could see him now.

The bayonet was an object of peculiar interest to him. It was a savage-looking thing. He ran his fingers up and down its three fluted sides, touched its sharp point, and wondered if he could ever have the heart to stab anybody with it. He finally concluded that he could and would if he ever got a chance; and then he "fixed" it on the muzzle of his gun and charged around the camp, lunging at imaginary foes in a manner highly suggestive of sanguinary results. Then he remembered that the rebels had bayonets, too, and he tried to imagine how it would feel to have one of them penetrate *his* anatomy. The bare thought of it made the cold shivers chase each other over his body.

A few random observations on the uses of the bayonet during the war, theoretical and practical, may not be out of place here, even though they should, for the moment, carry our young defender of his country some distance ahead in his military career. Si Klegg fully shared the popular delusion in regard to the devastation wrought by the bayonet. He had an abiding faith in its efficacy as an aggressive weapon. His young blood had been curdled by reading harrowing descriptions of bayonet charges. He had seen

WHAT SI EXPECTED TO DO WITH HIS BAYONET.

pictures of long lines of gorgeously dressed soldiers advancing upon the enemy with their bayonets sticking out in front, and he imagined that when they reached the other fellows they just used their bayonets like pitchforks, tossing about their unhappy foes as he had pitched pumpkins from a wagon. He thought this was the way fighting was done. There is no doubt that some bayonet wounds were given and received on both sides during the four years of war. It would have been strange indeed if, with all those two or three million keen shafts, somebody did not get hurt. But the number of men who were "prodded" was small. There were many surgeons of large experience in field hospitals who never dressed a bayonet wound.

None will deny the "moral force" of a well-directed bayonet charge. Providence gives to few men pluck enough—sufficient as to both quantity and quality—to enable them to stand long in open field before the onward sweep of a compact, serried line, bristling with points of shining steel. An important factor is the unearthly yell that always accompanies the charge, or rather is a necessary part of it. A bayonet charge without a yell would be as incomplete as a dance without music. The yell itself was usually terrifying enough to bleach the hair of an ordinary man. The combined effect was to greatly stimulate the natural impulse to break to the rear. So it was that only in very rare cases was the bayonet long enough to reach for purposes of blood-letting.

Some companies with ambitious officers spent a great deal of time and perspiration in learning the picturesque "bayonet-drill." This drill was a Frenchy affair—with its "parry" in "prime," "se-conde," "tierce" and "high quarte;" its "guard," "lunge," and "blow with the butt;" its "advance," "retreat," and "leap to the rear, kneel and over the head, parry"—that kept the men jumping around like so many animated frogs. It was a sort of gilt-edged drill and, like a ring in a Fiji Islander's nose, much more ornamental than useful. Companies that had become proficient in this manual, used to give impressive exhibitions on Sundays and idle days, before admiring crowds of soldiers whose military education was defective in this respect. Perhaps they fight on these scientific principles in France, but in "our war" nobody ever heard any of these commands given in battle. An officer who attempted to put the drill into actual practice would have been sent to the rear and clothed in a strait-jacket. The fancy drill was as useless as a blanket to a Hottentot.

But the bayonet was not by any means a superfluous appendage. After Si Klegg got fairly started into the field his experience ripened rapidly. "Necessity is the mother of invention," and his daily needs constantly suggested new uses for the bayonet that were unknown to military tactics.

The first blood that stained Si's bayonet was not that of a fellow-man. Company Q was on picket. Rations had been short for a week and his haversack was in a condition of emptiness that caused grave forebodings. Strict orders against foraging had been issued. Si couldn't quite get it straight in his head why the general should be so mighty particular about a few pigs and chickens and sweet potatoes; for he was really getting hungry, and when a man is in this condition he is not in a fit mood to grapple with fine-spun theories of governmental policy.

So when a fat pig came wabbling and grunting toward his post, it was to Si like a vision of manna to the children of Israel in the wilderness. A wild, uncontrollable desire to taste a fresh spare-rib took possession of him. Naturally his first idea was to send a bullet through the animal, but the discharge of his piece would "give him away" at once. Then he thought of the bayonet, and the problem was solved. After a few strategic movements he got the pig into a corner and a vigorous thrust of the steel did the work silently and effectually. The *pig* made a good deal of noise, but a well directed blow with the butt of the gun silenced him forever.

Si wrote to his mother that his bright new bayonet was stained with Southern blood, and the old lady shuddered at the awful thought. "But," added Si "it wasn't a man I kild only jest a pig."

"I'm so glad!" she exclaimed.

By the time Si had been in the service a year there was

less zeal in the enforcement of orders of this kind, and he had become a very skillful and successful forager. He had still been unable to reach with his bayonet the body of a single one of his misguided fellow-citizens, but he had stabbed a great many pigs and sheep. In fact Si found his bayonet a most useful auxiliary. He could not well have got along without it. He often came into camp with a

THE ACTUAL USES HE FOUND FOR IT.

ham or a fresh "flitch" of bacon impaled on it. That was a convenient way to carry such things.

Uncle Sam generally furnished Si with plenty of coffee—roasted and unground—but did not supply him with a coffee-mill. He thought at first that the Government had forgotten something. He saw that several of the old veterans of '61 had coffee-mills, but he found on inquiry that they had been obtained by confiscation. He determined to supply himself at the first opportunity, but in the meantime he was obliged to use his bayonet as a substitute, just as all the rest of the soldiers did. This innocent use of the "cold steel" was universal. On going into bivouac, or halting for dinner during the day's march, about every other man squatted on the ground or knelt beside a log, and with the butt of his bayonet pounded up the kernels of coffee in a tin cup, spreading one hand over the top to prevent the escape of the pieces. True, the pulverizing was not as thoroughly done as if the berries had been run through a mill, but it was sufficient.

Once in a while Si's mess "drew" a candle, but the Regulations did not provide for any candlestick. The bayonet was an excellent substitute. It could not have been more "handy" if made for that particular purpose. The hollow shank was always ready to receive the candle, while the point could be thrust into the ground or a log or cracker-box in an instant, and nothing more was necessary. This was one of the general spheres of usefulness found by the bayonet during the war. Barrels of candle-grease flowed down its furrowed sides for every drop of human blood that dimmed its luster. The soldiers had little to read, and it might be imagined that they had not much use for candles or candlesticks; but it must be remembered that there were millions of games of euchre and "old sledge" that had to be played, and it was necessary to have light enough so that a player could not with impunity slip aces and "bowers" up the sleeve of his blouse, or "turn jack" from the bottom of the "deck." To protect its brave defenders from these fraudulent practices was no doubt the object of the Government in issuing candles, as that was about all they were used for. Si found his bayonet a good thing to dig sweet potatoes with, and it answered well for a tent-pin in a sudden emergency. In many other ways it contributed to his well-being—but it was a long time before he hurt any rebels with it.

CHAPTER VII.

"IF 'twasn't fer one thing, Shorty," remarked Si, "I'd like ter drive one o' them ar' mule teams. I allus was a good hand at drivin' team, 'n' it 'd be big fun ter jest sit on a mule's back 'n' ride all the time. I never druv no mules, though I s'pose they're purty much same 's hosses. But ther' ain't no glory 'n bein' a mule-driver; *he* ain't no soljer. I reck'n somebody has to do it, but carryin' a gun 's what *I* 'listed fer!"

These patriotic observations were suggested by the arrival of the quota of wagons and mules for the 200th Indiana. The allowance of transportation had been greatly reduced since the previous year. In 1861 each company had its wagon, with three or four in addition to each regiment for headquarters and general purposes. The wagon train of a division composed of a dozen regiments stretched out for miles. A year later only half as many were allowed, and the camp and garrison equipage and personal baggage of officers and men were proportionately reduced.

The mules for the regiment might at this time have been properly classified as "raw material." They were taken at random from the great government corral, led over to the camp, and delivered to the quartermaster. Then the men who had been enlisted or detailed as "wagoners" began the work of organizing their teams.

94

Most of the mules that were braying and exercising their heels in the camp of the 200th Indiana were as raw as the men. Few of them had yet been broken to harness, and they resented in the most vigorous manner the least approach to familiarity. Coaxing, beating and swearing were alike fruitless. The adventures of the teamsters in trying to educate those depraved and obdurate mules into a state of docility, afforded a rich entertainment to a large and appreciative audience.

After protracted effort they succeeded in getting the refractory animals geared up, and the wagons were dispatched to the city after the baggage the men had brought from Indiana. The trip was only made through much tribulation, but they finally got back with all the boxes and barrels and "gripsacks" that contained the home contributions to the outfit of the regiment. The colonel thought it would do no harm to humor the boys and let them have these things while they lay in camp.

Si was delighted to get his box. Shorty did not have anything except what he had drawn from the government, but Si had enough for both. They fixed up their part of the tent in a style that was regal magnificence compared with their condition the night before. They built a "bunk" a foot high out of the rails they had purloined from the interdicted fence, and their abundant supply of blankets and quilts made a luxurious couch.

"Now this 's reel nice 'n' humlike," said Si to his comrade, as he surveyed the result of their labors. "'*Twas* kind o' discouragin' last night, but now we've had a chance ter git things fixed, I don't see nothin' ter growl 'bout. Ye know we'll take all these things 'long 'th us when we go anywhere, 'n' I'm goin' ter sheer 'em 'th you, Shorty. We'll have a bully time!"

Shorty thanked him for his kind offer but made no further reply. He had a pretty correct idea of what would be the early fate of all the nice things Si's friends had given him.

During the afternoon, Company Q was ordered to fall in, and the orderly marched it up to the quartermaster's tent. Si wondered what they were going to get this time.

"Now, men, git into them coats," said the orderly.

"Them coats" were the regulation "dress coats," the only thing necessary to complete their wardrobes.

The dress coat was another of the delusions of the war. It was a close, tight-fitting garment, with an impressive row of brass buttons extending up to the chin, and a stiff standing collar that rasped the ears, save when an unusually long neck lifted those appendages to a safe height. The sleeves were small and left little freedom of motion to the arms. This coat, as its name indicates, was to be worn on state occasions. In the early part of the war it was considered as indispensable at dress-parade, inspection or review as a claw-hammer coat at a swell dinner. Of course, when worn, every button must be in its button-hole. A company looked as stiff as a row of statues. When the mercury was up in the nineties it was a terrible sweat-box. Not a breath of air could reach the sweltering body.

THE "SWEAT-BOX."

When the hot work of the war came the dress coat had to go, except among the troops which were permanently stationed at posts in the rear. On a "shelter-tent" campaign inspections and reviews were unheard of, and the soldiers were wise enough to follow the injunction given the apostles, to "provide neither two coats"—the overcoat being excepted. For all ordinary wear the blouse was the garment that filled the bill. On the first hard march the dress-coats disappeared rapidly. They were recklessly flung away to lighten knapsacks and ease aching shoulders, or were traded off to the negroes for chickens and other eatables.

But Si thought it was a splendid thing. He succeeded in getting one with about the right length of sleeve, but owing to his tendency to corpulence, it was a very tight squeeze to get it buttoned. When he had accomplished it he felt as if he had a sheet-iron coat riveted around him. His eye followed down the row of shining buttons with its graceful swell and the blue-corded seams, and he thought it was the nicest coat he had ever seen. He only lacked the shoulder-straps to look like an officer.

Shorty smiled at Si's enthusiasm. He drew one of the coats only because he had to; he did not want it, and mentally resolved that he would get rid of it at the first opportunity.

The camp of the 200th Indiana swarmed with venders of medicines, razors, coffee-pots, tin and sheet-iron ware, underclothing, combs and an endless variety of useless things which they labored to convince the new soldiers were indispensable to them. Most of the men were well supplied with money, which they spent lavishly. Of course they wanted to take the field in good shape, prepared to make themselves as useful as possible, and they fell an easy prey to the peddlers, who did a thriving business.

Si was determined to be thoroughly equipped and proved a good customer. He bought a frying-pan and a patent coffee-pot warranted to make as delectable a beverage as he ever drank at home. These he was sure he would need. For some time he had observed, with emotions of pleasure, that his face was beginning to show symptoms of a hairy growth, marking the threshold of manhood. He had said nothing about it at home because, like all other boys, he was ashamed of it. But he was sure he would need a razor before he got back, and so he bought a complete shaving apparatus. He would carry it along until he should find occasion to use it.

At length a man made his appearance with a wonderful life-saving contrivance. It was a breastplate of steel, shaped to fit the contour of the body, to be worn under the clothing when in battle, as a protection against bullets. It was suggestive of the armor worn by knights in the olden time. The vender expatiated with great eloquence and pathos upon the merits of this concern. He said it was a duty that every man owed to himself, to his family and to his country to buy one. It was better than a life insurance policy. "You can jest walk right through a brigade o' rebels and they can't phaze ye!"

"Will—will she stop cannon balls?" asked Si, who had listened with keen interest to the graphic portrayal of its virtues, and had put one under his blouse to see how it would fit.

"It might, but I can't say for sartin, as I've never tried it. I rayther think, my young friend, that if a cannon ball hits ye fair an' square you're a goner. But it's the bullets as does most o' the mischief, an' it'll turn *them* like a duck's back sheds water. Jest think, young man, how much more contented yer mother'd be if she knowed ye had one o' these life-savers."

The delusive idea was not a little captivating, and Si really believed it was a good thing. He would have bought one but for a veteran soldier who was standing by.

"They ain't no good," he said. "A lot of our boys got fooled on 'em. Most on 'em was throwed away 'fore we ever got near a fight. When we did strike a battle a few wore 'em in, but some on 'em got killed jest the same. The bullets went right through them things. The other fellers made so much fun o' them that wore 'em, for bein' cowards, that they flung 'em away and that's the last we ever seen on 'em. Ye'll be wastin' yer money if ye buy it."

The idea that fear was the principle underlying the use of the breastplate settled the question with Si. He had not thought of that. He declined to purchase, telling the man that he guessed he was not afraid to go in and take his chances along with the rest. He didn't believe the rebels had them, and it wouldn't be hardly fair, anyway. Some of them were bought by members of the 200th, but the only use ever made of them was as a substitute for frying-pans.

Among the numerous devices to catch the money of the soldiers, a few were really valuable. One of these, which will be kindly remembered by many, was an ingenious combination of knife, fork and spoon, which, when not in use, could be folded up into small compass and car· ried in the haversack or pocket. The novel contrivance pleased Si and he bought one, although his mother had fitted him out with cutlery. It turned out to be the best of all his investments, doing him good service long after the pretty knife and fork his mother gave him had gone the way of all things in the army.

"Fall in, Company Q, lively, in undress uniform!"

Toward evening this command of the orderly startled the company. Si rushed into his tent, threw off his blouse, and was making further hasty efforts to disrobe, when Shorty entered.

"What on arth ar' ye doin', Si?" he said. "'Taint no time ter be goin' ter bed! Anybody'd think ye was crazy."

"Mebbe I didn't understand the ord'ly jest right," replied Si; "but I thought he said we was to come out'n undress uniform, 'n' I didn't know what that meant 'less it was ter take our clothes off. It did seem kind o' queer, but orders is orders, 'n' I didn't stop ter ax no questions."

"You git into yer clothes agin!" said Shorty, as he threw himself upon the bunk almost bursting with laughter.

"Oh, Si, but that's a good joke on ye!" and Shorty rolled over and over in a paroxysm of merriment.

"I don't see nothin' ter laugh at," said Si. "I was only tryin' the best I knew how ter do what the ord'ly said."

"Ye wants ter scratch gravel, 'cause the comp'ny 's formin'. I hain't got time now; but I'll 'splain it to ye arter a while." And Shorty went off into another spasm.

"I sh'd think it was *you* that's crazy," said Si, as he put on his blouse. He was a little piqued that his comrade should be so mirthful at his expense, particularly when he was so thoroughly conscious of the rectitude of his motives.

Si and Shorty hurried to their places in the company, just as the orderly was getting ready to yell at them for being behind. The captain told the men that there was to be a dress-parade of the regiment that evening, and he was very desirous that Company Q

A LITERAL INTERPRETATION.

should make a creditable showing. He hoped each man would feel a pride in his personal appearance and have his hair combed, his clothes brushed, and his shoes nicely blackened. He wanted to show the rusty old veterans how soldiers ought to keep themselves.

As Si walked back to the tent with Shorty, he thought of the episode a few minutes before but said nothing. He realized that he had misinterpreted the orderly's command, and seemed disposed to drop the subject. But Shorty felt that he ought to enlighten him and he said, while Si be·gan to brush his shoes:

"When ye puts on the Sunday-go-to-meetin' coat with the long row o' brass buttons, 't ye drawed f'm the quartermaster a little bit ago, they calls that yer 'dress uniform.' 'Undress uniform''s when ye wear jest yer everyday duds. Now d'ye understand what I was laughin' at? I'm sorry Si, but I couldn't help it 'f I was to ha' been shot fer it!"

"That's all right, pard," said Si, "I'd ha' laughed myself 'f I'd knowed what you did. A feller what ain't used ter these things can't larn 'em all in a minit. Ef the ord'ly wanted us ter wear our blouses why didn't he say so. How sh'd I know that 'undress' didn't mean the same 'n the army reggelations 's it does to hum. That day I 'listed the doctor made me shuck myself, 'n' I s'posed this was goin' ter be some such a pufformance as that. I reck'n I'll be larnin' suthin' new almost every day fer quite a spell."

"Shouldn't wonder 'f ye would," said Shorty.

At the hour appointed the call was sounded for dress-parade. It was the first attempt the 200th Indiana had made at anything in the line of tactics. There had not yet been an hour's drill, but the officers thought they could manage to get their men out to the line in some way. The colonel wanted to put his command on exhibition, that the old soldiers might see what a large, fine regiment he had. He thought the veterans must be getting a good deal discouraged by this time, and the sight of such a reinforcement would cheer them up.

The regimental flags, fresh and new, with their bright stripes and gleaming stars, were stationed on the color line, and "markers" with fluttering guidons were posted on either flank to direct the formation. The drum-major, arrayed like Solomon in all his glory, with a towering shako on his head, and fantastically twirling and bobbing his gilded and tasseled baton, marched the band to its place at the right of the line.

Many of the veteran regiments had outgrown such frivolities as dress-parades, and only indulged in them at long intervals. Just now their external appearance was so shabby for lack of clothes, that a dress-parade would

have been a painful spectacle. So the ragged veterans turned out by hundreds to give the new regiment a good send-off, bent on getting out of the display all the fun they could. The lordly drum-major drew their fire in a way that made him feel as if he would like to have the ground open under his feet and let him drop in out of sight.

"Hello, Gineral, when's the army goin'to move?"

"Howly Saint Pathrick, but did yez iver see the loikes av the way he handles that shillaly! Give us a chune, will yez?"

"Stand back, boys, an' give 'im room. Here

THE DRUM-MAJOR.

comes the boss of all creation!"

The drum-major could hardly be blamed for wishing he hadn't come. Up in Indiana, when, on public occasions, he appeared in magnificent pomp, he had always received an ovation from the admiring populace who gazed upon him with the profoundest awe, wondering how one man could hold so much dignity. He thought these scoffing veterans must belong to some different branch of the human family.

Throughout the camp of the 200th all was confusion as the companies were formed for the momentous event. The men were imprisoned in their new dress-coats, and, with their shining muskets and clean, new accouterments, presented an appearance at once both attractive and war-like. They looked more like soldiers than at any previous time in their as yet brief military career.

Si Klegg was promptly in his place. His make-up was faultless. His face was clean, his shoes were nicely pol-ished, and around his neck was a new paper collar. He seemed to be well satisfied with himself, as he had a right to be. It is true he had slipped his cartridge-box on his belt upside down, and had his bayonet-scabbard on the wrong side; but these little irregularities were quickly cor-rected when his attention was called to them by one of the file-closers.

The captain talked to the men in a fatherly way, ex-pressing the hope that they would carry themselves like soldiers, and reminding them that the eyes of the veterans would be upon them. His faith was a little shaky as to the appearance they would make when in motion. He thought that if he could only get them out to the color-line, they would be all right.

"Attention, company! Right—Face!" The captain had been studying up a little and had learned a few simple commands.

The men faced to all points of the compass, but the officers and sergeants at length got them headed the right way. They did not know anything about "doubling up" yet. In fact the captain was not very clear about it himself, and he thought it wise to move the company "in two ranks."

"Forward—March!"

The fife squeaked and the drum rattled and away went

Company Q. Most of the men had a theory that they must step with the beat of the drum, but there was a lack of uniformity in carrying it into practice. Part of them who happened to start that way properly brought down the left foot at the accented beat; some had the right foot —which was the wrong one—to the drum; while others, who seemed to have no music in their soles, just tramped along as though they were going to mill, without any reference to the measure.

"Left!—Left!—Left!" exclaimed the captain sharply, stamping his left foot on the ground to give force to the word. "Get the step there, men!"

"Getting the step," was an easier thing for the tongue to say than for unlearned feet to do. In the effort to "change step" Si had a hard time of it. He hopped along and stumbled, and kicked the shins of the man behind him and the calves of the one in front, finally settling down again into the same step with which he started.

"Hayfoot—Strawfoot! Hayfoot—Strawfoot" shouted the iniquitous veterans as Company Q's wriggling labyrinth of legs came in sight.

"Hey, young feller, take off that 'ere paper collar an' tie it 'round your left leg so 's ye can learn to march!"

Si knew intuitively that he was the person at whom the harrowing gibe was aimed. His young spirit rebelled and his tongue got the better of him before he could curb its impatience.

"You fellers thinks ye're smart, but if I——"

Whatever may have been the dreadful thought of retribution in Si's mind, its utterance was suddenly cut off, for the captain came down on him like a thunderbolt.

"Don't you know, sir, that you must not talk in ranks? I'll teach you in a way that you'll remember. Orderly, have Klegg put through an hour's knapsack drill as soon as the parade is dismissed—no, I guess half an hour will do for the first time. See that the job is well done."

"Yes, sir," replied the orderly, although he had no idea what a "knapsack drill" was. The anger and stern words of the captain had a crushing effect upon poor Si. He grew white and red by turns with shame and mortification, wondering, meanwhile, what the dire punishment was that he had been sentenced to undergo.

"Shorty," he said in a tremulous whisper, after the company had got into line, "what's knapsack drill?"

"Don't ax me," replied his comrade, "ye'll find out if Cap. don't weaken!" It was only by great effort that Shorty suppressed a laugh.

So Si stood there, pale and trembling, while the band played "Hail Columbia" down the line and came skipping back to the lively strains of "The Girl I Left Behind Me." This tune drove the iron deep into Si's suffering soul. Suppose Annabel could see him while he was going through that knapsack drill—whatever it was! He would ask the boys not to write home anything about it.

Then the adjutant marched from the right flank down to the colors and out to within a few paces of the colonel who was standing with folded arms like a brass-mounted statue. Then he faced about and gave the order:

"Battalion! Present—Arms!"

The adjutant had "skipped" opening the ranks according to the tactics, because few of the officers and fewer still of the men understood the movement. For a similar reason the men had stood with their muskets at a "shoulder"—in the tactics of more modern days known as a "carry"—because in this position they could not well help holding them in a uniform way. The colonel was so apprehensive of chaos if the "order arms" and "parade rest" were attempted that he had directed their omission from the program.

But the "present arms" could not be left out of a dress-parade. The colonel's heart sank as the adjutant gave the command. The result fully justified his fears. The captains had been ordered to instruct their men how to do it before marching out to the color-line, but in the hurry and excitement most of them had forgotten it. It took about five minutes to get all the guns into the prescribed position.

Then the adjutant faced about, saluted the colonel, and told him the parade was formed; and the colonel looked as though he were glad of it, after it had taken so long to do it.

The orderly sergeants, who had been carefully "coached" by the sergeant-major, massed in the center of the line, charged upon the adjutant, and informed him that the men of their respective companies were "all present or accounted for." They returned to their posts and the officers executed a similar movement, marching up to within speaking distance of the colonel, where they halted and made a profound salute. The colonel congratulated them upon the fine appearance of their men. He told them that drilling would begin at once, and he hoped no effort would be spared to bring the 200th Indiana up to the highest state of efficiency for active service. The parade was dismissed, and the orderly sergeants piloted their companies back to their respective grounds as best they could.

Si Klegg had taken very little interest in the solemn proceedings. His thoughts were centered on the knapsack drill. He hoped the captain and the orderly would forget all about it—but they didn't.

CHAPTER VIII.

"NOW, Klegg," said the orderly, as soon as Company Q had broken ranks, "git yerself ready. Ye know what the captain said."

"I dunno—what ye want—me ter do!" said Si, who could hardly have felt worse if he had been ordered to be shot.

The orderly didn't know, either, but he went and asked the captain, who in a few words explained to him the mysteries of a knapsack drill.

"And detail a guard, orderly," he said, "to see that the young rascal keeps moving."

Returning, the orderly found Si sitting on the edge of his bunk, with his face buried in his hands—a picture of despair. The orderly considerately remarked that he was sorry for him, "but I can't help it, ye know."

Si said it was all right, he guessed he would live through it.

"'Tain't nothin' Si," said Shorty, "lots on 'em has ter do it. Mebbe ye'll be a bit tired 'fore ye git done, but 'twon't hurt ye any."

Si arose with the air of a malefactor about to start for the scaffold, and in a subdued voice remarked that he was ready.

"Empty out yer knapsack!" said the orderly.

Si took out all his things and piled them on his bunk. Shorty said he would take care of them till he came back.

"Now pick 'er up and come on!"

The orderly led the way and Si meekly followed, nerving himself for the trial. It was the first case of discipline in the company, and all the boys turned out to see the sport. A little way from the camp was a pile of old bricks. Thither the orderly bent his steps, and as he stopped beside the heap an idea of what a knapsack drill was flashed across Si's mind.

"Fill up yer knapsack with them bricks!" said the orderly.

If the orderly had been the person responsible for this indignity, Si would probably have knocked him down. As it was he began slowly to lay in the bricks, registering a vow that he would keep a sharp lookout for a chance to square accounts with the captain.

It would take a large volume to hold all the oaths of vengeance that were made under similar circumstances during the war. A page would contain all of them that were ever carried out.

When Si had stowed away four or five of the bricks he looked up appealingly at the orderly, as if to inquire whether they were not sufficient to appease the demands of justice and the wrath of the captain.

"That ain't more'n half full. He said to fill 'er as full as she'd hold."

"I didn't 'list ter be a hod-carrier," said Si. "Ef I wanted a job o' that kind I c'd git it 'thout comin' this fur huntin' arter it!"

"Now buckle 'er up," said the orderly, after Si had laid in a few more. "I reck'n ye can't sling 'er alone. Here, a couple o' you men, give him a lift!"

The knapsack with its hateful load was lifted upon Si's shoulders and the straps duly secured. Then the orderly escorted him back to the company street .

"March up and down here for thirty minutes," said the orderly, taking out his watch, "an' ye'll have to keep goin', too, 'cause the guard 'll stick ye with his bay'net if ye don't. I'll let ye know when the time 's up."

Si began his tramp, and the orderly detailed a guard who, with fixed bayonet, was instructed not to permit the culprit to stop for a single moment. The captain had impressed upon the orderly the necessity of carrying out his orders to the letter, as it would have a salutary effect upon the company.

Si had already become a favorite among his comrades, and there was a universal feeling of sympathy for him in the hour of his calamity. A few rude jests were ventured, but they were promptly rebuked. It was not long till his shoulders began to ache, but he uttered not a word of complaint. He was determined to show his grit, and

SI'S FIRST PENANCE.

patiently trudged to and fro, leaning forward more and more as the burden grew heavier, until his penance was done. Once the captain came out, viewed the scene with satisfaction for a minute or two, and then returned to his tent. Si would have given a month's pay for the privilege of making *him* shoulder that knapsack full of bricks.

He would volunteer to serve as the guard, and he would do his duty "right up to the handle."

Shorty had stayed in the tent while his "pard" was paying the penalty of his "conduct prejudicial to good order and military discipline," not desiring to witness his humiliation. "Hello, Si," he exclaimed, as the latter entered and threw himself upon the bunk to rest.

"Ef I don't fix the cap'n for this, one o' these days!" said Si.

"Oh, no, ye won't do no sich a thing," replied Shorty. "The boys always says that, but they mostly fergits it the next day. Sich things has ter be did in the army — leastwise the ossifers thinks they does. But my notion is that Cap. piled it onto you purty heavy fur the little mistake ye made. He mout ha' knowed ye didn't mean no harm."

"I s'pose *'twan't* jest 'cordin' to Hoyle fer me ter sing out the way I did, but them fellers was mighty aggravatin', 'n' I couldn't help it. It hollered itself."

"Ye don't want ter fergit" said Shorty, "'t them's the same boys 't gin us that coffee yisterdy."

"That coffee," replied Si, "like suthin' I used to read 'bout 'n the Bible, 'covers a multitude o' sins,' but seems ter me they mout be a leetle more civil like."

Si lay for a few minutes and thought of the ludicrous features of the case.

"It *was* funny, wasn't it, Shorty," he said, bursting into a laugh, "anyhow, I'd ha' thought it was ef some other feller 'd had ter do it. The idee o' marchin' out there with a knapsack full o' bricks on my back!"

"That's a fack," answered Shorty, "but 'tain't a patchin' ter what they does ter them that's reel ugly; and there's some o' the soljers that's chuck full o' the old Nick. Ye'll have ter eddicate yer tongue a leetle, Si, er it'll git ye inter wuss trouble 'n this. You're used ter allus sayin' jest what ye think, but ye can't do it in the army—that is ye can ef ye *want* ter, but it don't pay."

After supper Si got permission to visit the camp of one of the old regiments not far away, to see some of his friends who had enlisted the year before. The veterans were having a frolic. Si elbowed his way into a crowd in the center of which a dozen men were standing around an outstretched blanket, with their hands firmly grasping its edges. He stood for a moment, with his hands in his trousers' pockets, wondering what it all meant. Then he ventured to ask one of the spectators what they were doing.

"O, jest havin' a little sport!" was the answer.

"I'd like ter know," said Si, "whar's the fun in them fellers stan'in' like so many stoughton-bottles hangin' on ter that blanket, 'n' the crowd jest lookin' at em'! Mebbe its fun but I can't see it."

"Keep yer eye on that blanket 'bout five seconds an' p'r'aps ye'll see suthin' wuth lookin' at!"

The veteran drew back a step and winked to one or two of his comrades. Seizing Si by the legs they pitched him over, a helpless heap, upon the blanket. There was a quick outward pull in all directions upon the edges of the blanket which straightened it suddenly and he went up four or five feet in the air. The tension was relaxed for an instant as he came down. Then with a fiendish delight the men braced their feet, swaying their bodies outward, and their victim bounded up, with sprawling limbs, higher than before. Powerless to help himself in the slightest degree, he was wholly at the mercy of the barbarians.

"O-o-o-oh!—Ou-ou-ouch! Sa-a-ay! Hold on! Don't k-k-kill a feller!"

Si was not suffering any serious personal damage, but never before had he been so badly frightened.

He yelled and begged and pleaded, while the tossers and the bystanders screamed in their enjoyment of the scene.

They bounced him in the air a dozen times and then released him. Flushed, trembling and breathless, he hardly knew for a while whether he was standing on his feet or on his head. None found a more genuine pleasure in the spectacle than a few raw soldiers who, having just been "tossed" themselves, shouted over the discomfiture of other victims.

VETERANS ON A FROLIC.

Si was pretty thoroughly shaken up, but finding that he was not hurt soon recovered his composure.

"Do ye understand it now?" asked the veteran.

Si replied that he believed he did. The information he sought had come to him with a suddenness and completeness that fully satisfied his curiosity.

"An' d'ye see now whar the fun comes in?"

"Ya-a-a-s!" said Si, with a feeble attempt to smile. "'Peared like 'twas big fun —fer you fellers!"

"Ye know when ye jines a serciety," said the veteran, "ye has ter be 'nishiated. This is how we 'nishiates the boys that jines the army."

"Say, pard," remarked Si, scratching his head reflectively, as a remembrance of the knapsack drill flitted across his mind, "I'd like ter have a lot o' ye come over to the 200th Injianny 'n' 'nishiate the cap'n 'n' ord'ly of Comp'ny Q. I dunno anybody 't needs it wuss 'n they does. I'll let ye have my blanket ter go through the cerrymony."

"We has ter go kind o' light on the officers, but if we had the orderly here we'd fix 'im."

"Thar he comes now, true's I'm alive," said Si, as a little squad of men approached the scene of hilarity.

Sure enough, there was the executive officer of Company Q sauntering over to make a friendly call.

"Got a grudge agin the orderly?" asked the veteran.

"I'll tell ye how 'twas. I s'pose ye know what a knapsack drill is?"

"Reck'n I ought ter. Been through it times 'nough."

"That's what I thought," said Si. "Wall, this arternoon, 'twan't nothin' ter speak of 't I done, but the cap'n got mad 'n' said I'd have to be put through a knapsack drill. The ord'ly he bossed the job 'n' made me fill my knapsack clear full o' bricks. Now ye know why I'd like ter see 'em 'nishiated. I'd a leetle ruther it'd be the cap'n, but the ord'ly 'll do. I'll jest give ye five dollars, cash down, ef ye'll bounce him."

"Hand over yer spondulix. I'll give it back to ye ef we don't give him the liveliest tossin' he ever had."

Si was as good as his word, and at once placed a five dollar bill in the veteran's ready hand.

"'Tain't counterfeit, I reck'n?"

"No, *sir!*" said Si, with some asperity.

"All right, that's a bargain. Now ye'll see some reel fun d'reckly."

The orderly entered the crowd and pushed to the front to see what was going on. He was just as ignorant as Si had been of the dark ways of the old soldiers. The latter were no respecters of persons who did not wear shoulder-straps, and the bright chevrons of a "green" first sergeant afforded the wearer no protection.

Watching their opportunity they tipped over the orderly into the blanket, and in an instant he was kicking and clawing as he bounded and rebounded into the air.

Si lay down and rolled over and screamed with delight. No financial investment he ever made had paid him such enormous and immediate dividends as did that five dollar bill. When he got back to camp he told Shorty about it. Both agreed that as between Si and the orderly the account was balanced.

The story of the five dollars was too good to keep. The veteran immediately told it to his comrades, and the orderly got wind of it. No sooner had the latter returned to his company than he learned that one of the camp-guards had been taken suddenly ill and it was necessary to detail a man to fill the vacancy.

"Klegg you'll have to go on guard right off, so git your traps on quick!" he said as he stuck his head into the tent where Si and Shorty were still laughing over the affair of the blanket.

"How d'ye figger it bein' my turn, ord'ly?" asked Si in surprise. "When ye made the detail fer guard to-day ye only jest got through the B's. K didn't come next after B 'n my spellin' book. They must have a diff'runt kind o' alfybet 'n the army."

"You do as I tell ye, an' be smart about it, too, or I'll report ye to the cap'n, an' he'll give ye 'nother dose. Ye'll have to put in more bricks next time than ye did to-day."

"Oh, that's all right, ord'ly," said Si, springing to his

feet and displaying the utmost alacrity in getting himself into harness, "I was only jokin'. I'd jest 's lief go on guard 's not. Got ter begin sometime. I'll be ready 'n a minute."

"Si," said Shorty, after the orderly had gone, "d'ye spose he heerd anything 'bout yer givin' that chap five dollars to bounce 'im?"

Si gave a long, low whistle. "I wouldn't ha' thought that feller 'd go back on me that way."

"Looks 's if he did" said Shorty, "I shouldn't wonder 'f that's the reason why the ord'ly jumped from B to K. I guess he's a leetle ahead arter all."

Si really had little objection to going on guard. The weather was pleasant, and he was constantly hungering and thirsting after new experiences. In fact this was the first time he had been called upon to do duty in any military capacity, and it was with sensations of pride and satisfaction that he shouldered his musket and marched to the headquarters of the guard, to take the place of a man who had been doubled up by the colic. At last he was going to do something to help save the country. He could hardly wait till his "trick" began. His turn would not come till midnight, but he dared not go to sleep for fear they would forget to wake him.

"Second relief, fall in!" shouted the sergeant of the guard.

Si was prompt to respond, and a moment later the squad was on its way around the line, each guard, as he was relieved, falling in at the rear of the squad.

When the guards were detailed early in the day—for twenty-four hours, each man being on beat two hours out of six—they had been instructed as to their duties, and an extract from the articles of war was impressively read to them, in which was set forth the fact that death was the awful penalty for sleeping on post. Si had heard nothing of this, so that he unfortunately went on duty with only a foggy notion that walking to and fro on his beat was all there was of it. He got an idea of the ceremony of relieving a guard from seeing it a few times, and when he was given the countersign and duly posted, with his bayonet fixed and his gun at a right-shoulder-shift, he felt that he had really entered upon the work of putting down the rebellion. He did so with a determination that so far as Si Klegg was concerned the war should be vigorously prosecuted.

Just before the sergeant left him to meet the "Who comes there?" of the sentinel on the next beat, he cautioned him to be alert and vigilant, as the "grand rounds" would soon visit him. Si had not the faintest idea what the "grand rounds" was. He first thought he would ask the sergeant, but he did not like to expose his ignorance and concluded to wait and learn. Whatever it was, he felt fully competent to give it a warm reception.

The "grand rounds" was usually composed of an officer, a sergeant, and two privates. Its function was to take a trip around the entire line, to see that the guards were attentive to their duties. It generally started soon after midnight. Of course at the regular time all the sentinels were watchful, zealous and full of business. Sometimes the officer took an insane notion to make his appearance at unexpected hours, and then he was very likely to catch some of the boys napping.

Si had not been patrolling his beat more than half an hour when his ear caught the sound of footsteps. By the dim starlight he saw a body of men approaching. He correctly surmised that they must be the "grand rounds."

"Hello, there!" he shouted.

He was too much flustered to recall the form of the challenge, but he knew he had to say something. The squad paid no attention to this irregular observation, but kept marching toward him.

"Hold on," said Si, "or I'll blow a hole through some

on ye!" bringing down his gun with his thumb on the hammer.

The officer thought it about time to halt, and did so.

"Who are ye, anyway, 'n' what d'ye want?"

Then the officer gave Si a lecture, and after instructing him in the forms for such cases made and provided in the army regulations, he marched the squad back some distance and once more advanced upon Si, to give him a little practice. He got through it to the satisfaction of the officer and the grand rounds went on its way

For an hour Si walked his beat. The time seemed very long to him; he was sure that the third relief had forgotten to come around. He began to feel tired and at length sat down beside a stump. Then his eyelids grew heavy and before he knew it they had closed. He did not mean to go to sleep, but he was not used to working at such unseasonable hours,

SI FORGETS HIMSELF.

and it is not strange that drowsiness overcame him.

When the relief came around the sergeant found Si sleeping soundly. The first thing he did was to disengage the musket from the relaxed grasp of the slumberer. Then giving him a vigorous shake the sergeant exclaimed:

"Wake up, the rebels are coming!'

Si leaped to his feet in an instant and began to scratch

around for his gun, while the rising hair almost lifted the hat from his head.

"Wh–wh–where's my g–g–gun? Wh–what's the matter?" he said in trembling tones, as his knees threatened to give way under him.

"Young man," said the sergeant in tones that pierced his very marrow, "*I've* got yer musket. I took it from

A RUDE AWAKENING.

ye while ye was sound asleep. That's what's the matter, and it'll be a serious matter for ye, too! Don't you know, sir, that the penalty for sleeping on post is death?"

"Wh–a–a–a–t!" said Si, and his limbs began to shake as he stared at the sergeant in blank amazement. "Ye m–m–must be j–j–jokin', ain't ye?"

"No, sir, I am not, what I told ye is true as gospel. Didn't ye hear it read from the articles o' war when ye went on guard to-day? It is my duty to report ye to the colonel for sleeping on post, and I suppose ye'll have to be shot. It's tough, but ye shouldn't have gone to sleep."

Poor Si was overwhelmed as thoughts of the awful consequences of his unwitting lapse from duty rushed over him. He sank to the ground in an agony of wretchedness. As soon as he could recover his speech he told the sergeant in appealing tones that he was detailed that night to take the place of a man who was sick, and protested that he had heard nothing of what was read to the guards, and did not even know that there were such things as "Articles of War." His gun and cartridge-box and knapsack were the only "articles" he knew anything about.

This gave a different aspect to the affair, mitigating, in some degree at least, the enormity of his offense. The sergeant's voice softened as he handed Si his gun and told him that he would report the explanation to the officer of the guard, and if what he had said was true, he hoped and believed that the punishment would not be inflicted.

Si fell in behind the relief and marched around to the headquarters of the guard, in a state of mind bordering on distraction. The officer, satisfying himself of the truth of his statements, told him that the matter should go no further; but in earnest words he impressed upon him the turpitude of such a violation of military law.

"I'm ever so much 'bleeged to ye," said Si, "I didn't mean ter do nothin' wrong. I shan't forgit what I've larned to-night ef I stay 'n the sarvice a thousan' years. Ef anybody ever ketches me asleep agin when I ought ter be awake, he may shoot me 's full o' holes 's a pepper-box."

CHAPTER IX.

IT was with genuine satisfaction that Si Klegg heard the order of the captain one evening at roll-call, for Company Q to begin the work of drilling the following day. It must be confessed that Si's conceptions of the "school of the soldier" and the various company and battalion evolutions were at this time exceedingly vague. He knew that a "drill" was something to make holes with, and as he understood that he had been sent down South to make holes through people, he supposed drilling had something to do with it. He handled his musket very much as he would a hoe. A "platoon" might be something to eat, for all he knew. He had a notion that a "wheel" was something that went around; and the only "file" he knew anything about was a screeching thing that his father used once a year to sharpen up the buck-saw.

But Si's ignorance was no indication that he would not make a good soldier. His mind was in a plastic state, ready to receive impressions of duty. He was more than willing to learn—his heart was burning with a desire to know all about the mysterious things of which he had heard so much, that he might speedily attain to the fullest measure of usefulness in his humble sphere of martial life.

"I s'pose I kin do jest's good fightin' 'thout havin' all the tic-tacs 'n my head," he said to Shorty. "I've bin used ter handlin' a gun ever sence I was knee high to a grasshopper, 'n' I b'lieve I kin load 'n' shoot 's fast 's the next un. I don't reck'n drillin' makes a feller have any more sand, nuther, but its reggelations, 'n' the ord'ly'll allus find me on hand. I hope they won't fool away too much time drillin' us t'll the rest on em gits the rebils licked, 'n' we don't have no chance fer some o' the fun."

Then Shorty gave his buoyant comrade some idea of the value of drill and discipline to a soldier. Si assured him that he would be a diligent pupil, and expressed the utmost confidence that he would make rapid and satisfactory progress.

The situation was critical, and all signs pointed to active operations in the very near future. It might be a week, it might not be an hour; but a general order had been promulgated for the army to hold itself in perfect readiness for an arduous campaign against the enemy, who was known to be at hand in large force. The colonel of the 200th Indiana, who had seen a year's service in one of the earlier regiments, was solicitous for the highest possible efficiency of his raw command, and directed that every moment should be improved. The time was too short for thorough, detailed instruction and practice in all the intricacies of the science of war; this must be postponed to a more convenient season. His men were liable to be called into action, and he determined that they should be first given a few of the simple and necessary lessons in the school of the soldier, the company and the battalion.

The work was to begin with the lark. Reveille was ordered at daybreak, and there was to be an hour of "squad drill"—for instruction in the manual of arms— while the company cooks were getting breakfast. This would give the men a good appetite, and assist in reconciling their stomachs to army diet; for the hungrier a man is the less particular he is about his food. So the colonel thought the arrangement an admirable one, as it would serve a double purpose. Some of the boys thought it was rather crowding matters, but the great emergency at hand was pretty well understood, and the general verdict was one of approval.

The men turned in early. Two or three days and nights of excitement, with little sleep or rest, had severely taxed their as yet undeveloped powers of endurance, and they were glad enough to stretch their limbs upon a blanket on the unyielding ground.

They sprang up at the first tap of the drum, buckled on their accouterments, seized their muskets, and took their places in line. The company was told off in squads of six or eight men each. Most of the line officers of the 200th were wholly inexperienced. In order that the seed sown among those patriotic Hoosiers might be of the best, and yield an immediate harvest, a number of sergeants from the old regiments had been detailed to teach the men how to handle their arms. These non-commissioned officers considered themselves veterans, and knew—or thought they did—all about war that was worth knowing. The one who took Si's squad was a grizzled sergeant, who had been "lugging knapsack, box and gun" for a year. He fully realized his important and responsible functions as instructor of these innocent youths, having at the same time a supreme contempt for their ignorance.

"Attention, squad!" and they all looked at him in a way that indicated a thirst for knowledge.

"Load in nine times—Load!"

Si couldn't quite understand what the "in" meant, but he had always been handy with a shotgun, to the terror of the squirrels and coons in the neighborhood of his father's farm, and he thought he would show the sergeant how spry he was. So he rammed in a cartridge, put on a cap, held up his musket and blazed away, and then went to loading again as if his life depended upon his activity. For an instant the sergeant was speechless with amazement. At length his tongue was loosed and he roared out:

"What in the name of General Jackson are ye doing, ye measly idiot! Who ordered ye to load and fire yer piece?"

"I—I—th—thought you did!" said Si, trembling as if he had the Wabash ague. "You said fer us to load nine times. I thought nine loads would fill 'er chuck full and bust 'er, and I didn't see any way but to shute 'em off as fast as I got' em in."

"No, sir! I gave the command according to Hardee,* 'Load—in—nine—times!' and ef yer hadn't bin in sich a hurry you'd 'a' found out what that means. Yer'll git along a good deal faster ef yer'll go slower. Ye ought ter be made ter carry a rail, and a big one, for two hours."

"LOAD IN NINE TIMES—LOAD!"

Si protested that he was sorry and didn't mean to and wouldn't do so again, and the drill went on. The master went through all the nine "times" of "Handle—Cartridge!" "Draw—Rammer!" etc., each with its two or three "motions." It seemed like nonsense to Si.

* The authorized text-book for infantry at the time the war broke out, and for two or three years thereafter, was "Hardee's Tactics." The author, W. J. Hardee, was an officer of the United States Army before the Rebellion, but espoused the Confederate cause and was a distinguished corps commander under Bragg, Johnston and Hood. Toward the close of the war two revised "Tactics"—by General Silas Casey and General Emory Upton, respectively—were published, and were used by some of the late regiments. The "old soldiers" knew only "Hardee."

"Boss," said he, "I kin git'er loaded in jest half the time ef yer'll let me do it my own way!"

"Silence!" thundered the sergeant. "If you speak another word I'll have ye gagged 'n' tied up by the thumbs!"

Si had always been used to speaking out when he had anything to say, and had not yet got his "unruly member" under complete subjection. He saw, however, that the drill sergeant was a sort of military buzz-saw that it was

"OUCH!"

not safe to fool with, and he held his peace. But he kept thinking that if he got into a fight he would ram in the cartridges and fire them out as fast as he could, without bothering his head with the "one time and three motions."

"Order—Arms!" commanded the sergeant, after he had explained how it was done. Si brought his gun down along with the rest like a pile-driver. The pencil of the artist conveys a better idea of the immediate effect than can be expressed in words.

"Ou-ou-ouch!" remarked the victim of Si's inexperience.

"Didn't do it a-purpose, pard," said Si compassionately; "'pon my word I didn't. I'll be more keerful arter this."

His suffering comrade, in very pointed language, urged upon Si the propriety of exercising a little more care. He determined that he would manage to get some other fellow to stand next to Si after that.

"Shoulder—Arms!" ordered the sergeant, and the guns came straggling up into position. Then, after a few words of instruction, "Right shoulder shift—Arms."

"Don't you know your right shoulder?" said the sergeant, with a good deal of vinegar in his tone, to Si, who had his gun on the "larboard" side, as a sailor would say.

"Beg yer parding," said Si; "I allus was left-handed. I'll learn if yer only gimme a show!"

"Silence!" again roared the sergeant. "One more word, sir, and I *will* tie ye up, fer a fact!"

The sergeant got his squad down to an "order arms" again, and then,

"RIGHT SHOULDER SHIFT—ARMS!"

after showing them how, he gave the command, "Fix—Bayonet!"

There was the usual clicking and clattering, during which Si dexterously managed to stick his bayonet into the eye of his comrade, whose toes were still aching from the blow of the butt of his musket. Si assured him he was sorry, and that it was all a mistake, but his comrade thought the limit of patience had been passed. He confidentially informed Si that as soon as drill was over he was going to "pound the stuffin'" out of him, and there wouldn't be any mistake about it, either.

When the hour was up the captain of the company came around to see how the boys were getting along. The upshot of it was that Si and a few other unfortunates were

organized into an "awkward squad," and sentenced to an extra hour of drill.

"We'll see, Mr. Klegg," said the captain, " if you can't learn to handle your arms without mashing the toes and stabbing the eyes out of the rest of the company."

The first thing on the program after breakfast was company drill. The captain thought the smattering he

"FIX—BAYONET!"

had of Hardee was enough to justify him in undertaking the job. As Company Q marched out to the drill-ground and began operations the veteran soldiers from the adjacent camps gathered to enjoy the sport, forming a ragged border around the field. As occasion was offered they stimulated the "freshmen" by exasperating comments and suggestions. The captain acquitted himself as well as could have been expected, but it was very much like the blind leading the blind, and now and then they "both fell into the ditch." Si Klegg had been so awkward in the first drill that he was ordered to take his place at the tail of the company.

The captain first exercised the company in the simple facings, without "doubling." He deemed it essential that they should be able to get their toes turned the right way.

Si was one of those who required line upon line and precept upon precept. There were some who "took to it" naturally, and easily learned the multifarious movements. Others, just as brave and patriotic and faithful, tried diligently for three or four years, and then failed to master them. The true military instinct is much like the gifts of the poet and the artist, "born, not made."

"LEFT—FACE!"

"Left—Face!" shouted the captain.

Si was zealous in the pursuit of knowledge, and when he really learned anything he tried hard that it should not get away from him, and generally succeeded. As yet, however, he was as likely to face one way as the other. He knew that the sonorous words of the captain required him to do something. When he had done it he found himself looking squarely into the eyes of the man who had stood next to him. Observing his mistake he quickly turned himself around, stepping heavily on the toes of his comrade. He was just in time to escape a reproof from the captain, who ran his eye down the line to see how well the order had been executed. Si was in good shape when the official glance reached him, and the captain nodded approvingly.

"RIGHT—FACE!"

"Front!"

This was not difficult, as everybody knew it meant to face toward the captain.

"Right—Face!"

Si promptly faced to the left. Being at the end of the line, with no one now in front of him, he did not detect his error. He did not know that he was standing back to back with the next man. Company Q was as large then as the whole regiment "present for duty" was two years later, and the captain, who had gone to the head of the long line to direct a movement by the flank, did not notice that Si was out of position.

"Right shoulder shift—Arms!"

The lesson of the early morning had not proved altogether unfruitful, and the men, in the course of two or three minutes, got their muskets into position satisfactorily. When Si first came into possession of his gun he wanted to carry it in his left hand, but he soon found that this would not do at all. By carrying it with the other, as the rest did, he was enabled to identify his right shoulder with fair success.

"Forward—March!"

The company started off; but the captain was not a little surprised, on looking back, to see Si trudging away in the opposite direction. The captain asked him with great vehemence where he was going. This caused him to look around, and he scampered back to overtake the column, while the old soldiers who stood or lay about watching the proceedings, yelled with delight.

The captain marched the company around awhile so that the men might "get the hang" of keeping step to the tap of the drum and the "Hep!" "Hep!" of the orderly. At intervals he ventured "By file left" or right, to change the course of the column. Si was glad he did so, for if they kept right on in one direction they would soon be among the veterans. This was easy, as the captain only needed to steer the orderly, and the men had nothing to do but follow.

Then he thought he would try the "double-quick." He knew that when Company Q got near where any fighting was going on, the anxiety of the men to get in would urge them to a rapid gait. Perhaps at a later period they would be satisfied with "common time" when moving into the vortex of battle, but now nothing short of a double-quick would meet the demands of their quenchless ardor.

After a few words of rather uncertain instruction, the necessary command was given and away went the men at a gallop. There was no thought of "keeping the step," and the company formation dissolved into a wildly rushing mass, having no more semblance of order than a stampeded flock of sheep. Si Klegg was not built for speed, and he brought up the rear, puffing and blowing with great energy. Repeated shouts from the captain at length brought the company to a halt. The officers and sergeants had all they could do for the next ten minutes in getting the men straightened out and once more in their places. From a tactical point of view, the experiment was not a success, but it clearly demonstrated the ability of the company to make time when necessary.

"About—Face!"

This was the next command given, after the captain had told the men how to do it. This change of position was executed by properly adjusting the feet and then quickly swinging the body to the right half way around, leaving the soldier faced in the opposite direction. It was very easy—after it had been learned.

The first attempt to obey the command convulsed Company Q like an earthquake. Some wriggled around one way and some the other. Here and there one gave himself too much whirling motion and went spinning around too far before he could stop, or lost his balance and went down among the squirming legs of his comrades. Men bumped against one another and muskets and heads came in collision. When the company tried the "Right about," —the same movement as the above, except that it is executed while marching at common or double-quick time, without losing the step—the consequences were even more disastrous.

"Right—Wheel!"

It was here that the real trouble came in. No infantry movement is more difficult than the wheel. None is more graceful when executed with precision, nor more ungraceful when badly done. A perfect wheel, preserving the alignment, can only be accomplished after long practice.

It is scarcely necessary to say that the first trial was a sad failure. The line bulged out in the centre, and the outer flank, unable to keep up, fell behind, the company assuming nearly the shape of a big letter C. Then the boys on the outer end took the double-quick, cutting across the arc of the proper circle, which soon resulted in a hopeless wreck of the whole company. The captain halted the chaotic jungle of struggling men, and with the help of the orderly finally succeeded in getting them untangled and into line again. The men had often seen practiced soldiers going through this movement, and it seemed easy enough; they did not see why they could not do it just as well as the other fellows.

"COMPANY—RIGHT WHEEL!"

The second time the company tried it those in the center of the line went to the other extreme and did not step out fast enough, and the moving flank forged ahead, taking the short cut and coming in on the home-stretch with a wild rush that threw the ranks into a confusion worse confounded than before.

By this time the men were getting badly winded, and the captain was hoarse from yelling at them. All hands were glad to hear the recall sounded, that gave them an hour of rest. The day was warm and much of their clothing was soaked with perspiration.

Si hurried to his tent when the company was dismissed, threw off his traps, and stretched himself on his bunk.

"It's all fer yer country, Si," said Shorty.

"That's all right," replied Si, "but ef there's any fun 'n drillin' I can't see much on it yet. I'd a heap ruther fight!"

Shorty smiled.

That evening Company Q was ordered on picket. As soon as the men were in line ready to start, the colonel addressed them solemnly on the importance of the duty assigned them. He was ardently desirous that they should acquit themselves with credit in case an emergency should arise. The men were profoundly impressed, and marched to the line of outposts feeling that the whole burden of the war rested upon their shoulders.

The company relieved part of an old regiment which had been on duty for twenty-four hours. These veterans had watched upon the outposts of the army many a day and night, in field and brake and wood, through heat and cold and storm. They saw at a glance that the men who were to take their places for the night were innocent lambs who had never seen a picket-line before. In low, hoarse whispers they told blood-curdling stories of the awful danger that surrounded them. The trembling Hoosiers stood with staring eyes and mouths agape, cold sweat starting from their bodies, as they listened with breathless eagerness to the astounding recital.

"Why, young feller," said one of them, talking into the ready ear of Si Klegg, as if he were pouring water into a funnel, "there's more 'n fifty brigades o' rebels right over thar in them woods. They've been shootin' bushels o' bullets at us all day. Jest look a-here an' see how my clothes is riddled."

His garments were ragged and torn by long usage. It was getting dark and Si could not see distinctly, but he took it for granted that all the rents and holes were made by the bullets. True, Si had not heard any firing that day, nor had there been any commotion in camp such as would inevitably have resulted. But he did not think of this; the veteran knew he wouldn't. Si did not see any dead or wounded lying around, but he supposed they had all been sent back to the rear.

"N-n-narrer 'scape fer ye, w-w-wa'n't it?" said Si, vainly striving to quiet the chattering of his teeth.

"Bet yer life 'twas," replied the malignant old soldier. "You take my advice an' jest lay low. Ye don't want ter talk ner make no noise, fer they'll hear ye. I had ter sneeze once to-day, 'cause I couldn't help it, an' the bullets come spatterin' 'round me like hail-stuns on a tin roof. All them trees is full o' sharp-shooters; there's two or three of 'em sittin' on every limb. They've got rifles that'll carry furder 'n you ever hearn tell of. Them fellers kin shute, I tell ye; they kin hit a fly a mile off four times out o' five."

Si was now fully prepared for his duty. There was no danger that he would go to sleep. He moved about with the greatest caution lest his foot should snap a twig and those fifty brigades of rebels should concentrate their fire upon him. He did not talk unless it was necessary, and when he had to say something he spoke only in a whisper. The veterans formed their companies and tramped off toward camp in a very unconcerned way. Si wondered that they were not all shot down in their tracks.

"What was that chap givin' ye, 'twas talkin' to ye like a Dutch uncle?" Shorty asked Si after they had gone.

"Sh-sh-sh!"—and Si held up his hand imploringly—"Don't talk so loud, Shorty, er we'll all be dead men"—and he repeated to his comrade the important information that the veteran had imparted to him.

"Dead fiddlesticks!" said Shorty, "Cap. says ther ain't a rebel within five miles o' here."

"Beats all how them old soljers kin lie, don't it Shorty?"

CHAPTER X.

R-r-r-r-r-r-rap-r-r-r-r-rap-r-rap-r-r-r-r-rap-rap-r-r-r-rap-rap-rap!

It was the long roll, sounding for the first time through the camp of the 200th Indiana. It is not necessary to remind an old soldier what the "long roll" was. For the information of those whose ears have never been startled by its wild alarm, it may be said, to use the phrase of the day, it "meant business." It betokened a sudden emergency that required immediate action. Whenever a soldier heard it, at any hour of the day or night, it was his duty, without waiting for orders, to spring for his "traps," harness himself up, sieze his musket and get into line—and to do it with all possible haste. After he heard the long roll once he never forgot it.

"Taps" had sounded, the camp-fires burned low, and the thousand patriotic Hoosiers had "turned in." Si and Shorty had just lost themselves in "the first sweet sleep of night," when the sharp rattle of the drum at regimental headquarters broke upon the stillness. Both were awake in an instant.

"Wonder what that's fer!" said Si.

"That's the long roll," replied Shorty, who had already kicked off the blankets and was putting on his blouse.

"Ye're actin' like ye'd lost yer wits, Shorty. What's up, anyway?"

134

"I d'know what's the matter," said Si's comrade, "but ye don't want ter wait ter ax no questions. Git yerself hitched up, 'n' ye'd better hustle, too. Whenever ye hear that kind o' racket ye don't want to fool away no time monkeyin' 'round."

Without knowing why, except that Shorty had told him to, Si began to scratch around for his things. Then came the shout of the orderly: "Turn out, men, promptly! Fall in, fall in! Be lively!"

THE LONG-ROLL.

Officers came tearing out of their tents, buckling on their swords as they ran. Orderly sergeants rushed through the company streets stirring up the men. The whole regiment was thrown into a panicky condition. If a volley of musketry had burst upon the camp, it could scarcely have produced greater commotion and alarm.

"Is ther g-g-goin' ter be a f-fight, Shorty?" said Si, as they, among the first to be ready, took their places, with their muskets at a "shoulder." Si's hands trembled, and his knees seemed to be a little shaky. It was probably nothing but the chill of the cool night air. "Hadn't we better—load our—g-guns?" he continued.

"Naw," replied Shorty, "wait t'll ye git orders. I don't see nothin' 't looks like a fight, nuther. Hold on a bit 'n' we'll see what it's all 'bout."

Si was reassured by the coolness of Shorty, and by the fact that there was no sound within ear-shot that indicated immediate trouble.

In their excitement many of the men came out half dressed, dragging their muskets by the "slings," their waist-belts and cartridge-boxes trailing behind, completing their hasty toilets after getting into line. Some had their blouses on inside out, and others had their belts buckled upside-down. A good many of them were affected by the night air in the same manner that Si was.

"Orderly, call the roll!" said the captain.

"Reck'n they wouldn't stop ter call the roll 'f thar was anything ser'us on hand," said Shorty to Si in an undertone.

Si thought this a sensible view of the case. By the time his name was reached the chill had entirely passed away, and when the orderly called out "Klegg!" he responded "Here!" in a loud, clear voice.

As a matter of fact there was no occasion for creating such a riot in the camp of the 200th Indiana. The colonel had received marching orders, and he thought he would try the long roll on the boys just to see how it would strike them. It was a way the officers had of gently "breaking in" the new troops.

After Company Q had been duly formed, with "all present or accounted for," the captain announced that the regiment would march at daylight. Each man was to have three days' rations in his haversack, and sixty rounds of ammunition. Tents would be left behind, and only one baggage-wagon to the regiment would be allowed. Reveille would sound at three o'clock.

The necessary instructions having been given, the companies were dismissed. Few of the soldiers returned to their beds. In the excitement of the hour there was no thought of sleep. They piled wood on the smouldering fires and gathered in groups around them to talk it over. Everybody asked everybody else where they were going and what they would do when they got there; but as all were in the same state of dense ignorance no light was thrown on the subject. The company officers were besieged with inquiries, but they were equally in the dark, or if they did know they wouldn't tell. The boys imagined that the colonel knew all about it, but none of them dared to ask him.

Si and Shorty sat on a log before a comfortable fire discussing the situation. Si wanted to have a big fight more than he wanted anything else in the world, or at least he believed he did. He thought he would not be of any possible account as a soldier until he had been through a battle, and the bigger it was the better it would suit him. Hourly, since leaving home, he had given free utterance to his desires in this direction.

"P'r'aps ye'll git 'fore long what ye've bin wantin' so bad," observed Shorty. "Things looks kind o' squally ahead. But say, Si, what made ye shake so when that pesky drum routed us out a little while ago? Ye'll have ter git over that sort o' thing."

"Oh, that wan't nothin," replied Si, trying to conceal his chagrin at having shown, even at such a time, any symptom of weakness unbecoming a brave soldier. "It come on us so sudden like, 'n' all the ossifers a-yellin' at us, a feller couldn't help it."

"Quinine 's what they take fer the shakes up in Injianny."

"I don't need no quinine, Shorty. Jest lemme git my second wind. I ain't goin' ter blow, but I don't mean ter let anybody in this 'ere rijiment go any furder 'n Si Klegg does."

"I was only jokin', Si. I b'lieve ye; 'f I didn't I wouldn't have ye fer my pard. But what ye goin' ter do with all the nice things ye fotched from home? Yer knapsack won't begin ter hold 'em, 'n' ef it would yer couldn't tote 'em. Ye know ye can't have nothin' but what ye lug on yer back."

"I was jest thinkin' 'bout that," said Si; and the fire-light showed upon his face a look of anxiety. He bowed his head upon his hand and sat for a moment in deep thought, as if earnestly wrestling with the problem that confronted him.

"I s'pose I'll have ter leave some on 'em behind," he said, sadly. "I didn't know 's it was goin' ter be this way. I thought they had plenty o' baggidge waggins fer the sol-jers. I hate ter fling away them things that mother 'n' Marier 'n' An— that is, I mean the rest o' the folks give me. I b'lieve I c'n carry the most on 'em. I'm goin' ter try it, anyway. I shan't let go on 'em till I *haf* ter."

"I didn't have nobody ter cry over my goin' away er to load me down," replied Shorty, "'n' I'm glad on it. What I got f'm the quartermaster 's all I want ter lug. I've got an idee that you'll git shet o' purty much everything else 'fore ye've tramped a thousan' mile. But 'f I was you I'd stick to 'em 's long 's I wanted ter. You're a nice boy, Si, 'n' has lots o' relations 't thinks a heap on ye. I'm a black sheep, as hain't got no friends, 'n' 'cordin' ter my notion that's the best thing fer a soljer. Ther' ain't nobody in a stew 'bout me all the time. Ef I gits killed I won't be missed, 'n' 'twon't break nobody's heart. I don't have to bother with writin' no letters, nuther!"

"I don't 'zactly agree with ye, Shorty," replied Si. "Ef I thought I didn't have no friends I wouldn't keer ter live. Ef I've got ter git killed 'n this war, I'll be a leetle more reconciled to it fer knowin' that ther's somebody 't 'll feel bad 'n' wish the bullets 'd missed me. But I 'low we'd better be a gittin' down ter business. I don't s'pose they'll wait fer us in the mornin' ef we ain't ready. I was jest goin' to ax yer, Shorty, how we're goin' ter carry 'long sixty rounds o' ammernish'n; catridge-boxes don't hold but forty."

"In our britches pockets, I reck'n."

Si scarcely knew how he would manage it, he had so many other things that would test the capacity of all his pockets. Shorty suggested that perhaps he could put the extra twenty rounds in his knapsack, but Si didn't think he would have any room in that to spare. The conclusion arrived at was that the cartridges had the right of way and something else would have to yield. What it would be Si could not yet determine. It was dawning upon him that a sacrifice would have to be made.

The whole camp was soon astir with the work of preparation for the march. Rations were issued, and each man filled his haversack with hardtack, bacon, coffee and sugar. Cartridge-boxes were inspected and replenished and the extra twenty rounds per man distributed in pursuance of the order.

Si's first business was to lay in his commissary supplies. Then he betook himself to the serious job of packing his knapsack. When he realized the great disparity between the heap of things he had brought with him and the space to put them in, he found himself in a most perplexing quandary. After figuring on it for a while without finding a way out of the woods, he determined to fall back on Shorty, whose practical ideas would, he thought, prove valuable to him in his dilemma. Si was overstocked with sentiment; Shorty had none. By striking an average a solution of the puzzle might be reached.

"The trouble is," said Shorty, "ye can't put two bushel o' stuff inter a peck measure. Ye'd ought ter got a knap-sack made to order, 'bout four times 's big 's the reggelation size, and *then* ye'd had ter have a mule ter carry it fer ye. I never done much marchin', but I've had jest 'nough so 's I know how heavy a knapsack gits, even if ther' ain't much in it. I know ye wont take my word fer it, ye'd better find it out fer yerself—an' it won't take ye long, nuther."

But Si was active, strong and well, and had unbounded faith in his physical abilities. He inwardly resolved that he would demonstrate to Shorty what he could do, without wishing to spurn the well-meant suggestions of his comrade. Shorty had stowed away, in about five minutes, his simple change of army clothing, and that was all. His knapsack being ready, he was at liberty to bestow upon his ardent young friend such assistance as the latter might be willing to accept.

"Less see," said Si, as he began in detail upon his outfit, "I'm goin' ter take this fortygraph album, 'cause it's got all the folks's pictur's; an' this 'ere portfolio, 'n' the slippers, 'n' this rig fer mendin' up my clothes, 'n' the pincushion, 'n' the soap 'n' towels—I don't see how I can git 'long without them. I don't want ter live like a heathen."

"Ef I was you, Si," observed Shorty, "I'd put in yer reg'lar army duds fust. Ye've *got* to have them, an' ye can see how much room ye've got left. Then ye can tackle yer knicknacks 'n' fill er up 's much 's she'll hold."

A moment's reflection convinced Si that there was a strong element of common sense in this suggestion, and he began the packing process in that way, with great zeal.

"Thar," he said, crowding down the dainty garments to compress them into the smallest possible space, "they're all in 'n' ther's lots o' room left. Reck'n I'd better chuck in the undershirts 'n' socks 't mother 'n' Ant Samanthy made fer me. They'll be mighty comf'table one o' these days. This pa'r o' boots I kin hang on the outside."

Then Si began on the miscellaneous collection. The slippers and handkerchiefs that Annabel had given him, went in first. He would stick to them while he was able to lift an ounce. Other articles rapidly followed, as one by one they were taken up and duly considered. He thought how handy they would be, and of the loving hands that had wrought them for him, and the verdict in each case was that it could not be spared, and in it went. It was not long, however, till the knapsack began to show signs of fullness, and not half his things were in yet.

"Better buckle 'er up," said Shorty, "'n' see how she looks."

Si closed the flaps and fastened the buckles, though not without labor. He kneaded it down like dough with his fists, and got upon it with his knees, in the effort to make himself believe that it would hold a good deal more.

"If these straps was only injy-rubber," he said in a tone of disappointment, "but they're leather, 'n' they won't stretch a bit!"

THE TUG OF WAR.

At length he got it buckled and Shorty suggested that he put it on just to see how it felt, and he might be able to judge how much more he could stand.

"Fiddlesticks," said Si, "'tain't heavy; I c'n lift it with one hand. I c'd carry the hull caboodle well 'nough 'f the thing 'd only hold 'em."

"Ye don't want ter fergit 't yer overcoat 'n' yer blankets

'n' quilts, 'f ye take 'em all, has got ter go on top yit. They'll make 'er a right smart heavier."

Even this did not weaken Si's faith in himself. What if his knapsack did weigh forty or fifty pounds; that would be a mere feather's weight on the shoulders of a strong boy like him. Then Si unfastened the straps, determined to put in other articles—they had *got* to go.

"Hadn't ye better give 'way one o' yer Bibles, 'f ye can find anybody 't 'll take it?" asked Shorty. "'Pears ter me 'f ye gits all the good out o' one on 'em ye'll be a heap better 'n' the av'ridge."

"I'd like ter give it to you, Shorty!"

"I reck'n 'f you 'n' me 's goin' ter be pardners, we c'n git 'long purty well with one Bible 'tween us. I don't s'pose I'll read it much, anyway, 'n' when I do want it you c'n lend me yourn."

But Si could not bring himself to part with either of them. One was a Christmas present from his mother and the other the parson had given him.

"Never mind," he said, "I c'n carry one of 'em in my pocket 'n' I wont feel it there." He did argue with himself whether it would not be best to try and rub along without Bunyan and the hymn-book. He believed he could remember all the hymns he would want to sing.

"I'd let 'em slide 'f I was you," said Shorty. "They're fust class fer a Sunday school libery but they don't b'long in a knapsack. If I had to tote 'em I'm afeard the s'warin' I'd do 'd spile all the good I'd git out of 'em. I ain't goin' ter say nothin' agin yer Bible, but right thar's whar I draw the line on books. Ef ye was a mule-driver, er 'f ye had a hoss to ride, ye mout manage 'em, but don't ye try ter carry 'em along. Ye'd better give 'em to some cavalryman. I don't know of anybody 't needs that kind o' readin' more'n they do."

Si seemed to be favorably impressed with this suggestion, and said he would bear it in mind. He thought it quite

possible that he might find somebody whose spiritual condition was worse than his own, and if he could benefit
him by these volumes it would ease his conscience for discarding them from his outfit. He said he would take them
along at first, and if he found them too burdensome he
would watch for an opportunity to dispose of them in
that way. So he jammed them into the knapsack and got
on them with all his weight to crowd them down.

"Here's this blackin' kit," he remarked. "Mother told
me ter keep myself lookin' slick, 'n' of course I want ter do
it. The brush won't pack very well 'n' I'll tie it on the
outside with a string. I c'n put the box o' blackin'
'n my pocket. This clothes-brush I c'n hang on somewhere."

The "housewife" that his sister had made for him both-
ered him sorely. He was profoundly impressed with its
value for keeping his garments in repair, to say nothing of
the feeling he had toward it for Maria's sake.

"I'll leave it to you, Shorty," he said, "'f it wouldn't be
durned mean to sling that away."

"Looks so," replied Shorty, "but 'fore ye git home,
'nless the war ends sooner 'n I think 'twill, ye'll have ter
do a good many things 't goes agin the grain. Ye might
's well begin now 'n' be gittin' used to it. As I told ye
'afore, I'm glad I hain't got a lot o' sich traps to bother my
head about."

"I wish Marier hadn't made it big 'nough fer a hull
fam'ly," said Si, as he squeezed it in under the straps of
the knapsack. "I ain't goin' back on her yet, though!"

Then he came to the toilet-case—a pretty box fitted with
hair-brush, tooth-brush, combs, glass and hair-oil. With
the utmost deference to the affection that prompted Cousin
Betsey to make this contribution to Si's museum, no old
veteran, whose shoulders ached under the load he tried to
carry when he started out, will for a moment take issue
with the proposition that such a thing ought not to have

a place in a soldier's knapsack. Its utility was not proportionate to its weight or the space it required.

"Cousin Betsey gimme that," said Si, sorrowfully, "but I don't see how I'm goin' ter git it in, nohow. It'd be nice ter have."

"If ye'd put some wheels to it ye mout hitch a string to it 'n' draw it 'long behind ye," said Shorty, with a laugh.

Si felt that his feelings were being trifled with, but when he really came to think of it he could not help agreeing with Shorty that it "wouldn't pay."

"Ther' ain't nothin' ye need in thar," said Shorty, as he inspected the contents of the box, "'cept that ar' fine comb. *That'll* come mighty handy to ye arter a while, 'n' I'd 'vise ye ter hang to it. It'll be the usefullest thing, fer its weight 'n' bigness, in yer hull outfit. That glass ain't no 'count. Ye've got a purty face ter look at now, but bime-by ye'll look so tough 't ye won't want ter see yerself. Ye'd think 'twas somebody else 'sides Si Klegg. Wait t'll ye've been goin' it stiddy fer a year 'n' ye'll feel like smashin' yer lookin'-glass. Talk 'bout brushes! Ye've got a clothes-brush 'n' a blackin'-brush 'n' a ha'r-brush 'n' a tooth-brush, 'n' I don't know how many more. The boys 'll think ye're the travelin' agent fer a brush fac't'ry. We'll have a 'brush' with the Rebs one o' these fine days, and then ye won't be thinkin' 'bout no other kind. What's all them fancy wipes good fer?"—as Si handled over the pretty handkerchiefs, with his initial worked in the corners, that Annabel had given him. "They ain't no 'count. As fer ha'r-ile"— and Shorty lifted his nose and turned away his face in extreme disgust. "Ef ye've got any notion o' bein' a dandy, Si, ye want ter git 'pinted on some gin'ral's staff. Ther' aint no other place fer the like o' them."

Si listened thoughtfully to Shorty's long speech. He began to think that, so far as the toilet-case was concerned, his pard was not far from right.

"I b'lieve," he said, after thinking it over, "I won't try ter carry that box. I c'n scatter the things 'round 'n my pockets."

"If ye don't look out," said Shorty, "yer pockets 'll fool ye 's bad 's yer knapsack did. Catridges is made o' lead, 'n' ye've got ter lug two big bunches of 'em, 'sides them in yer box."

But Si's faith in his pockets was unshaken. He said he guessed they'd hold all he wanted to put in them.

"What'd I better do with this rewbarb 'n' pennyr'yal, 'n' them bottles o' stuff 't mother put up fer me 'f I sh'd git sick? Prob'ly I orter have 'em, but I don't see no place. I wouldn't mind carryin' 'em but ther' ain't room."

"Ye've got a good mother, Si. I 'low she's one o' the best wimmen 'n the world."

"You bet she is, Shorty!"

"That's all right, 'n' I'm glad of it, but she don't know no more 'bout soljerin' 'n you do. Ther' ain't no sense 'n tryin' to carry a drug store on yer back all through the war. The doctors 've got dead loads o' medicine, 'n' 'f ye git under the weather, they'll cram it into ye t'll ye can't rest. 'Twon't cost ye nothin', nuther."

Si did not enjoy taking medicine. He had never had any sickness to speak of, and he thought there was little likelihood that he would need the remedies which his mother had so kindly put up for him. The "drug store," as Shorty termed it, was the first thing he had found that he thought he could do without. If it had been possible he would have taken it along, but he was brought face to face with the stern necessity of cutting off something, and he concluded this was the best place to begin. He thought he would take the chances with the doctors. So he flung the bottles one by one against a log, and threw the "yarbs" into the fire. He did not do it without some compunctions of conscience, and he hoped his mother would never know the rude fate that befell his medicine chest.

"That's the sensiblest thing ye've done to-night, Si," said his comrade. "Now what ar' ye goin' ter do with them cans o' peaches 'n' bottles o' pickles 'n' that butter? Ye'll find *them* heavy 'nough 'f ye try ter carry 'em."

Si "hefted" them and was forced to admit that they would add too much to his burden, even were it possible to stow them away.

"Ye'd better eat 'em up 'fore ye start, 'f ye kin," said Shorty, "Ye won't be likely ter git no more soft bread fer a while, 'n' butter ain't no good on hardtack."

Large as was Si's capacity for anything good to eat, it was out of the question for him to dispose in that way of all the toothsome dainties with which his mother had supplied him. Up to this time he had shared them freely with Shorty, but still further assistance was necessary. So ne invited six or eight of his friends to join them, and by the light of the fire they emptied the cans and bottles of their contents.

"I guess I'm fixed, Shorty," said Si. "We'll only have a couple o' hours ter sleep; lets go ter bed!"

CHAPTER XI.

"HELLO, Si, wake up, wake up!"

"Oh, quit! Lemme 'lone! I'm sleepy!"

"Don't ye hear 'em beatin' the drums 'n' tootin' the bugles?" said Shorty. "It's the revel-*lee*,* 'n' ye have ter turn out, right quick. Ye know we've got ter march to-day."

By this time, aroused by sundry shakes and nudges, Si was fairly awake, and sprang up in an instant, happy in the thought that he was to move upon the enemy. In his dreams, during his brief sleep, he had fought a whole war through.

"Fall in fer roll-call, Company Q!" yelled the orderly.

"Seems ter me," said Si, as he hurriedly threw on his blouse, "we hain't done much since we've been in camp but fall in fer roll-call. I can't see no use doin' it six or eight times a day. Wonder 'f they stop right in the middle of a big fight 'n' call the roll when it comes time—do they

---

* Wise men who made the dictionaries say that "reveille" should be pronounced "re-*vel*-ye" or "re-*val*-ya," but it was never heard so in the army. The word was always spoken "rev-el-lee." This pronunciation would be fatally disastrous to the cadence of Scott's smoothly flowing lines, in the "Lady of the Lake":

> "Huntsman, rest! thy chase is done,
>   While our slumbrous spells assail **ye;**
> Dream not with the rising sun
>   Bugles here shall sound reveillé."

147

Shorty? An' does the rebels quit shootin' t'll they gits through?"

"Wall now, Si, ye've got ter l'arn not to fret. Ye don't want ter know nothin' ner ax no questions. Ye mus'n't think 'bout nothin' 'cept ter jest do what the ossifers tells ye to. Ef ye does that ye'll make a soljer; 'f ye don't ye won't 'mount ter shucks."

One of the first things an orderly sergeant had to learn was to call the roll of his company from memory, so that he could go through the ninety or a hundred names in the darkest night without a skip. A man who could not master the long list in a week was not considered fit to be an orderly. The first sergeant of Company Q had not yet learned his roll, and was compelled to call it from his book, by the feeble light of a candle.

"The 'general' will sound in an hour," said the captain, "and you must be through with your breakfast and ready to strike tents. Then you will pack the wagons and roll up your blankets, and at five o'clock, when you hear the 'assembly,' every man must promptly fall in."

"Shorty," said Si, after the company was dismissed, "what does the Gin'ral say when he yells out fer us to strike tents? The cap'n said we'd hear the Gin'ral 'sound' in an hour."

"Ye're 'way off, Si. The Gin'ral don't say nothin'. It's the drums 'n' bugles as does the soundin'. That's only the name they gives ter that call. Ye'll find it if ye'll read the army reggelations."

"Oh, I didn't know," said Si, "but I thought the Gin'ral 'd have to yell purty loud to make 'em all hear."

The whole army was to move. Ten minutes later the darkness that had brooded over the great camp was dispelled by the gleaming light of countless fires. It was a wild, weird scene. Fifty thousand men were bustling about, busy in the final preparations for the march. To break camp and strip an army of its incumbrances for an active campaign was a prodigious task, only accomplished by the combined labors of all its multitude of men When completely mobilized and upon the road, it would drop for rest by the way-side, in field or forest, as circumstances permitted, always ready, by day or night, to spring at sound of drum or bugle, to march or fight.

Making coffee and frying bacon were the only culinary processes required to make ready the frugal breakfast, and the morning meal was soon over. The boys ate the last of their soft bread, and not for many a day did they see any more.

Then, amidst a very Babel of shouts and distracting commands, the tents were taken down, and the company baggage, that was to be left behind, was loaded into the wagons.

When Si had finished his part in the general work, he addressed himself once more to his personal belongings. The job of getting his knapsack ready for the march, so auspiciously begun some hours before, was not finished. Each part of the receptacle was crammed to its utmost capacity. When he brought them together his whole weight was not sufficient to make the straps and buckles connect. He was obliged to call Shorty to his assistance. By dint of much tugging and squeezing, their united efforts were at length successful in making the ends meet.

"There," said Si, viewing the great round heap with undisguised satisfaction, "I reck'n she'll do. I c'n carry that jest 's easy 's rollin' off a log. All these other contraptions I'm goin' ter hitch on the outside."

Having provided himself with strings, he tied on his frying-pan, coffee-pot, hatchet, assortment of brushes and the boots. Then he rolled up the two blankets, the quilt and his overcoat, making a bundle nearly as large as the knapsack itself. This he strapped upon the top, and the work was complete. Si was ready to take the road.

Promptly at five o'clock the "assembly" sounded through

the camp, and cries of "Fall in, men!" were heard on every hand. The new soldiers of the 200th Indiana were determined to toe the mark in the most approved manner, and they began to hustle around with the greatest activity. At the first note of the bugle Si bounded from the ground, where he had been resting from his labors. He buckled on his cartridge-box; then gayly tossed the strap of his canteen over one shoulder, and that of his bulging haversack over the other. Then he took hold of his knapsack and tried to "sling" it. He had done this half a dozen times before, just for practice, but it did not then weigh a quarter as much as now. Seizing it with his strong arm he gave it a long, upward swing, and it came down upon his shoulders like an avalanche. He staggered under the shock, while the coffee-pot, frying-pan and other articles upon the outside dangled about and jingled a merry tune. Si leaned forward until his back was nearly horizontal, so that the unwieldy hump would stay in its place until he could fasten it. He wriggled and twisted in his abortive efforts to reach the strap and make the connection.

"Guess ye want a leetle lift," exclaimed Shorty with a laugh, as he came to his assistance and fastened the hook. "Ye ll want more help 'fore night 'f I ain't badly mistook."

"Oh, this ain't nothin'," said Si, cheerily, as he slowly straightened up, the knapsack almost pulling him over backward. "It's jest 's light 's a feather. I c'n carry that a hull day 'n' not half try."

Then taking his musket, Si moved with a wabbling gait to his place in Company Q. There were many other very large knapsacks, but his unquestionably would have been awarded the first prize at a county fair.

"Mr. Klegg, fall back into the rear rank!" shouted the orderly, who was fussing around in the usual way, trying to meet the responsibilities that rested so heavily upon him.

The company had only been formed a few times, but Si

had always taken his place in the front rank. He naturally belonged there; he wanted to be where he could see all that was going on, and could be one of the first to "go in," without having anybody in his way. It sorely wounded his pride to be ordered into the rear rank.

"What's that fer, ord'ly?" he said, unable to conceal his chagrin.

"'Cause I tell ye to; that's all the reason you want."

The orderly had been one of the "big" boys of the town—a size larger than Si—and was already manifesting a fondness for exercising the authority which was vested in him by virtue of his position. Si felt that he was just as good as the orderly, and was on the point of raising an issue with him on the spot.

READY FOR THE MARCH.

"Don't ye say nothin', Si," said Shorty, in a low voice. "Ye want ter recolleck what I told ye 'n' jest obey orders, er ye'll git yerself into a sling 'fore ye know it! I 'low 't he put ye 'n the rear rank on 'count o' the big knapsack 'n' tin-shop on yer back. If ye was in front ther' couldn't nobody stan' behind ye 'thout gittin' way out o' line. When yer load shrinks mebbe ye c'n git back 'f ye want ter."

Si took the place assigned him without any further attempt to have a rumpus with the orderly. But his "spunk" was up, and he was determined to stick to that knapsack, whether the Union was saved or not. His grotesque appearance called forth many jests from his comrades, but these only contributed to the further development of his "nerve."

"They think I've bit off more'n I c'n chaw," he said to himself, "but I'll show 'em! Si Klegg knows what he's 'bout."

When the company was ready, the captain came out to take it off the orderly's hands. He had no personal baggage except his dainty patent-leather haversack, and something over the other shoulder that looked like a flask.

"Don't *he* have to carry no knapsack?" Si asked of Shorty. The distinctions and inequalities of rank had not yet found their way into his understanding.

"Course not!" replied Shorty. "Don't ye know 't the ossifers has everything done fer 'em? If ye don't ye'll find it out purty quick. Ye know the orders 't was read las' night said ther' wouldn't be but one baggidge-wagin fer the hull rijiment. That's fer the ossifers."

"The ossifers has a soft thing, don't they?" said Si, whose shoulders were even now beginning to twinge a little.

"Company, Right—Face! Forward—March!" and Company Q started for its place on the color line. The well-stuffed knapsacks bobbed up and down like humps on the backs of so many camels. The colonel and the other field and staff officers, booted and spurred, came out on their prancing horses. The adjutant rode wildly up and down the line, directing the formation of the battalion.

"Right—Dress!"

In the effort to get into a straight line, the ranks surged to and fro, like the surface of a body of water when there is a "sea on."

"Front!"

A fairly satisfactory result having been obtained, the adjutant saluted the colonel and told him the regiment was formed. The colonel sent an orderly to brigade headquarters with word that the 200th Indiana was ready, and the work of putting down the rebellion could now begin in earnest.

When forty or fifty regiments were ordered to march at the same hour on the same road, some of them had to wait. It was three hours before the 200th Indiana pulled out—and long, tedious hours they were. The men who composed it had not yet been educated in the school of patience. During the first hour they were kept standing in line, that there might not be a moment's delay when the order should come to join the long procession that was moving upon the pike.

Ten minutes had not passed when Si's back and shoulders began to ache. Furtively slipping his gun around behind him, he placed the butt upon the ground and braced the muzzle under his knapsack. This gave slight temporary relief, but whenever a galloping horseman was seen, the colonel commanded "Attention!" and there was no more resting until official vigilance was relaxed.

At length it dawned upon the colonel's mind that the men could just as well be taking it easy, as far as circumstances would permit. So he told them they might break ranks and rest at will. Knapsacks were not to be unslung, however, and every man must be ready to spring into his place at the word of command. Then those already tired Hoosiers experienced for the first time in their lives what a blessed relief it was to a soldier burdened with all the paraphernalia of war, to lie on his back with all his traps on, slide down a few inches to loosen the straps, and rest, with his head pillowed on his knapsack. There were few things in the army that yielded as much solid comfort to the square inch as this. It has no existence in the memory of a cavalryman.

The men of the 200th Indiana watched with jealous eyes the column of troops, that seemed to have no end, passing in the road. They were sure there would be a fight that day, and what possible chance would they have to get any of it, with so many ahead of them? They were all anxious to have front seats at the first entertainment they were to witness, however much this desire might be modified in the future.

Si Klegg was greatly disturbed by the apprehension that it would be all over before he got there. He did not know then how long they had to chase over the country some- times when they were looking for somebody who wanted to fight, nor what a disappointment awaited his expecta- tion of pleasure in a battle.

"Looks like they warn't goin' ter give us no show 't all," he said, as he tried to roll over so that he could talk to Shorty.

"Now don't git in a sweat," replied his comrade. "I know ye've got lots o' sand in yer gizzard, but ye're goin' ter git filled chuck full 'fore ye gits through with this thing. Ye won't be half so hungry arter a while!"

Nothing could dampen Si's ardor, and as regiments and brigades swept by, he felt that his chance to win military renown was growing slimmer and slimmer. There cer- tainly would not be any batteries left for him to help cap- ture.

"Attention, Two Hundredth Indiana!"

The long looked-for order had come at last. Si got up at once—or rather he tried to do so, for it was very much as if a millstone were hanged about his neck. His knap- sack weighed twice as much as when he put it on in the early morning. He only succeeded in reaching an erect posture by rolling over and getting up by degrees, with the aid of his hands and knees. He was a little "groggy," but he knew he would be all right after he got fairly started.

The colonel's sword swished through the air as he drew it from its scabbard and gave the order "Forward—March," and the raging patriots turned their faces in the direction of the foe—or where he was supposed to be. The 200th had been assigned to a brigade of four or five regiments of veterans, who for twelve or fifteen months had been doing some hard fighting and a great deal of hard marching. They had learned much of war. Their romantic fictions had long since disappeared and they had got down to the reality of army life.

The 200th was to lead the brigade that day, and as it marched past the old regiments the boys made the acquaintance of those who were to be their companions in camp and field. The few knapsacks that still remained among the veterans looked scarcely larger than postage-stamps stuck on their backs, compared with the huge masses that were borne on the shoulders of the Indianians. Listen to those ragged and depraved old soldiers as the men of the 200th Indiana, with their fresh faces, clean new clothes and burnished arms, go tramping by:

"Here's yer mules, boys! Look at the loads they're packin'!"

"Fresh fish!"

"Ther' hain't no dew fell on 'em yet."

"I say, how'd ye leave Mary Ann 'n' all the folks to hum?"

"Look at the fellers with fortifications on their backs."

"Here's a hull rijiment o' knapsacks with legs to em!"

"Ye'll be a sheddin' them things 'fore night."

"Hello, thar, Bub, how d' ye sell tin-ware?"

This heartless question was aimed at Si Klegg, whose

ponderous and picturesque outfit was a conspicuous target for the raillery of the brown and bearded veterans. Si's feelings were outraged. He wondered why men who were so lost to all decency were not court-martialed and shot. He straightened himself up and cast upon his tormentors a look of unutterable scorn. Sharp words of retort flew from his tongue, but they were lost in the chorus of wild yells of derision that greeted him.

"Better dry up, Si," said Shorty "them chaps is too many fer ye. Wait t'll ye git a little more practice 'fore ye try to talk to sich duffers 's they be."

Si checked his combative impulses, and marched on in silence.

Once upon the road the column stretched away at a brisk gait. The colonel of the 200th was determined that his regiment should not fall behind, while the men wanted to show the fleet-footed veterans that they could get over the ground as fast as anybody. They indulged the hope that they would soon have an opportunity to show the old soldiers—who had not yet succeeded in whipping the rebel army—how to fight as well as how to march.

Meanwhile the sun was rapidly climbing the eastern sky, and his rays were beginning to beat down fiercely upon the now perspiring patriots. Si had not gone a mile till his tongue was hanging out and he found himself panting for breath. Already his shoulders were aching as they had never ached before in all his life. And the day's march had but just begun!

"How 're ye makin' it, Si?" inquired Shorty, with tender solicitude. He had noticed that his pard seemed to have lost his usual vivacity. He had not spoken a word for a quarter of an hour; and when Si's tongue was so long quiet there must be something out of gear.

"Oh! I'm g–gettin' 'long b–bully!" replied Si; but the slow and labored utterance did not quite tally with his words.

Si did not evince a disposition to continue the conversation. He appeared to have other uses for all his energies. He noticed many of his companions leaning forward to ease their burdens, now and then hitching up their knapsacks to give a moment's ease. It was evident that a feeling of fatigue was already pervading the regiment. All this only strengthened Si's pluck. Whatever anybody else might do he was bound to peg it through to the end,

A SERIOUS MISCALCULATION.

and carry every pound he had taken upon himself. He would get used to it directly and then it would be easy enough.

So he trudged bravely on, with teeth firmly set, and the grip of a vise upon the butt of his musket. The perspiration streamed from his nose and chin, and flowed in tickling streams down his body and legs. He was warming up to his work.

"Sh–Shorty,' he gasped, as he reached the end of the second mile, "d–don't they give a feller any restin' spells? Dad used ter put us through when we was pitchin' hay 'n' hoein' corn, but he'd let us b–blow once 'n a while."

"Ye ain't playin' out a-ready, are ye, Si?"

"No-sir-ee, I ain't," he replied, bracing himself up by a

great effort. "I c'n go it all day 'f I *haf* ter, but it 'd be a heap easier 'f I c'd jest stop a minute er two 'n' lay in a fresh supply o' wind."

"I'll tell ye one thing, Si, ye've got too much meat on yer bones fer a fust-class roadster. Ye know hosses can't travel when they 're fat, 'n' I reck'n it's the same way with soljers. When ye gits rejuced twenty er thirty pounds— an' 'twon't take hard marchin' 'n' hard-*tack* long ter do it —ye'll git over the ground a mighty sight better. By that time ye won't be luggin' so many traps, nuther. 'F I was you I'd begin purty quick ter git shet o' some on 'em!"

But Shorty's advice was still premature. The most careless observer could have seen that Si was slowly but surely approaching the point when the exigencies of the service would overcome his sentimental devotion to his "traps and calamities," as Shorty flippantly called them, in spite of mother and sister and Annabel.

At length the drum gave the signal for a halt. With a sigh of inexpressible relief the weary, panting men sank to the ground by the roadside, to find such rest as they might in the few allotted moments.

Si Klegg was more nearly exhausted than he was willing to admit, even to himself. As he dropped into a fence-corner, trembling in every nerve and fiber of limb and body, there came into his mind the fleeting wish that his load were not so heavy.

The single hour's experience on the road had served to remove the scales from the eyes of a goodly number of the members of Company Q. They began to foresee the inevitable, and at the first halt they made a small beginning in the labor of getting themselves down to light marching order—a process of sacrifice which a year later had accomplished its perfect work, when each man took nothing in the way of baggage save what he could roll up in a blanket and toss over his shoulder. It was but a small beginning. They "yanked" open their knapsacks and flung away a book or an album, or an extra garment, choosing such articles as could best be spared. The sacrifice was not made without a twinge of regret, for all had their cherished keepsakes—affection's gods, that they well-nigh worshiped for the sake of the loving hands that fashioned them.

Shorty was lean in flesh and in baggage, and in good shape for traveling. Although he had shared in the general fatigue and was glad enough to rest with the others, the march thus far was to him but a pleasant exercise as compared with what it had been to those who staggered beneath their burdens. While the reducing process was going on he looked at Si to see whether *he* was yet learning the wisdom that in time came to every soldier. Some did not learn it as soon as others.

"Goin' ter try it 'nother heat, ar ye Si?" he said, observing that the latter gave no sign of casting off any of the weight that encumbered him.

"Course I am," he replied, cheerfully, "I feel 's fine 's a fiddle now 't I've rested a bit 'n' had a chance ter git up steam. 'Tain't goin' ter be so hard when a feller gits broke in!"

"It's the breakin' in 't hurts," said Shorty. "I s'pose ye've heern tell o' the hoss 't was fed on sawdust. Jest as he was gittin' used to it he up 'n' died. I sh'd be sorry ter have it work that way with you, Si."

At the call the soldiers fell in and resumed the march. Si was quick to obey, feeling greatly refreshed by his five minutes of rest. He started off very courageously, whistling "Columbia, the Gem of the Ocean," and keeping time to the music. But he did not whistle a great while. He did not feel like it, much as he tried to make himself think he did. Hotter and hotter beat down the sun's rays as it mounted to the zenith. In streams more copious flowed the perspiration that oozed from every pore. The air was thick with dust from the countless feet of men and horses that had gone before. It gathered upon Si's face; it permeated his clothes and was ground into the skin under the straps and belts that bound him. At every step his knapsack grew heavier. His heated, sweating back smarted under the pressure. Lower down his cartridge-box, with its leaden load, bobbed up and down with every footfall, chafing and grinding until that particular spot felt as if in contact with a red-hot iron. His canteen and haversack rubbed the skin off his hips; the bunches of cartridges in his pockets scraped his legs; and his musket lay like a section of railroad iron upon his shoulder.

Then a new trouble came to Si, as though he had not enough already. He was young and tender—a sort of "spring chicken," so to speak. There was a sharp, smarting sensation at different points on his feet; it did not take long to blister such soft feet as he had. They felt as if somebody had poured scalding water on them, and was rubbing on salt and pepper and horse-radish, varying the treatment by thrusting in a dozen needles. What a keen, maddening pain it was! How it thrilled every nerve, as the rough shoes tore off the tender skin; and the great load of knapsack and cartridge-box and gun pressing the needles farther in at every step!

There are not many things in this world of sorrow more utterly and wildly exasperating than tramping with blistered feet on a hot day, carrying a big knapsack. A blister is not always as large as a barn-door, but for stirring up all the latent depravity of a boy's heart, it has few successful rivals.

Si began to limp, and, in spite of his efforts to prevent it, an expression of pain now and then escaped his lips. Still he kept up in his place, strong in his determination not to straggle. His efforts may have been somewhat stimulated by a blood-curdling rumor, which started at one end of the regiment and quickly ran its entire length, that a body of rebel cavalry was following leisurely along at the tail of the column, massacring all the stragglers. But the tax that he had imposed upon his physical forces was too great. The spirit indeed was willing but the flesh was weak.

"Shorty," he said to his comrade, "I wonder how fur we've got ter hoof it to-day; did ye hear?"

"Some o' the ossifers was sayin' this mornin' we'd have ter make twenty mile 'fore we'd camp, 'n' we *mout* have ter keep right on all night."

"Seems ter me," said Si, groaning inwardly at the prospect, "we've traveled much 's twenty mile a-ready, hain't we?"

"Skurcely," replied Shorty. "I'm sorry fer ye, pard, but we hain't come more 'n five er six mile yit."

Shorty saw that Si was rapidly approaching the point where he would break down. His sympathies were aroused in his comrade's behalf.

"Si," he said, "lemme carry yer gun a piece; that'll ease ye up a leetle bit!"

"'Bleeged to ye, Shorty" he replied, "but I guess I c'n pull through. Ye've got all ye want ter tote."

But when Shorty reached up and relieved him of his musket he yielded without objection. At the next halt Si told Shorty that he had made up his mind to take his advice and lighten his load.

"I knew ye'd have ter come to it," said Shorty, "'cause ye ain't no mule 'n' ye can't stand it. There's lots o' them things ye don't need, 'n' ye'll git 'long a heap better 'thout 'em when ye're marchin'. I know ye hate ter fling 'em away, 'n' I think all the more of ye 'cause ye've got sich feelin's, but if yer mother 'n' yer sister 'n' all the rest on 'em had knowed how it 'd be they wouldn't ha' guv 'em to ye to load ye down. It's got ter be did, Si."

Shorty's logic was unanswerable. Si's blistered feet and aching limbs and smarting shoulders told him, even more plainly than his comrade's words, that the sacrifice was inevitable. He first tossed his hatchet over the fence. Then his clothes-brush and shoe-brush went; true they did not weigh much, but every ounce would help. His frying-pan and coffee-pot he decided to be necessities. Opening his knapsack he held a melancholy inquest upon its contents. The hymn-book he speedily disposed of without carrying out his intention of bestowing it upon a wicked cavalryman. The "Pilgrim's Progress" quickly followed.

THE SHRINKAGE BEGINS.

It was as much as he could do to look after his own progress as a pilgrim. He threw away the cakes of fancy soap and his sister's pin-cushion, after sticking half a dozen pins in his blouse. He discarded the photograph album, first taking out the pictures and putting them in his pocket. Some of the nice articles of clothing he flung upon the ground. As the weather was then, he did not feel that he would ever want them. He looked at his big roll of blankets and decided that an advantageous reduction could there be made. His first plan was to abandon his blankets and keep the pretty quilt he had brought from home.

"Don't do that," said Shorty. "Ye'll be sorry 'f ye do. Ther' ain't nothin' so good 's an army blanket. I know ye don't like to heave away that quilt, but you jest let 'er slide."

Si was coming to have a good deal of confidence in Shorty's judgment, and it was settled that the broad expanse of beautiful patchwork, on which his mother had spent so many hours of toil, would have to go.

People who lived along the line of march followed the moving army for miles, gathering up the things that the new soldiers threw away. Men, women and children loaded themselves with quilts, clothing and articles of every description. A happy thought entered Si's head. Drawing out the big knife that his Sunday school teacher gave him, he began to slash the quilt into strips.

"What ye up ter now?" asked Shorty in surprise.

"I tell ye what 'tis, Shorty," was the reply, "ef I can't have any good o' this kiver ther' ain't no secesh goin' ter sleep under it," and he continued the work of destruction.

By the same process the home blanket was disposed of. Shorty told him to keep only his overcoat and the blanket furnished him by the quartermaster, and he concluded that Shorty knew better than he did.

Si had learned his first practical lesson in making himself a soldier. It had come to him through much pain and tribulation. Two or three million other men were taught by the same educator—Experience. Precepts and theories went for naught. The shrinkage of the knapsack was the first symptom of the transformation that changed the raw recruit into an effective soldier, ready at any moment for a fight or a foot-race.

CHAPTER XII.

AT the call to resume the march Si jumped nimbly to his feet, notwithstanding the general stiffness of his joints and the large and varied assortment of aches and pains that darted and dodged through every part of him. With renewed confidence he slung his knapsack, which had been very materially lightened. But it was a big knapsack yet, and destined to be flattened a good deal more in the near future. It was not clear to Si how any further reduction was possible; and indeed, as he started off again he experienced such relief that not a lingering doubt remained in his mind that he could now go as far and as fast as any man in the army.

The blisters on his feet, which at once became lively, were his greatest cause of grief. The old ones remained as vigorous as ever, and new ones were constantly forming on sole and toe and ankle.

"Ouch!"

This was the laconic observation that Si involuntarily made every now and then, in a voice of agony. Whenever he said this his companions in misery knew that another blister had "busted," as they expressed it. How his nerves tingled with the sharp pain!

But on and on tramps the remorseless column. The army cannot pause for aching limbs to rest and blistered feet to heal.

The knapsack bears down again upon Si's chafed and smarting shoulders. It seems heavier than before, and with each mile grows heavier still. How glad he would be if he could pitch it into a fence corner and leave it there. He wonders if he could possibly get along without it. But no, this cannot be seriously thought of—at least not yet. So he braces himself up and plods along his weary way. Thoughts of home—he can't help it—that he left scarcely more than a week ago flit through his mind. Mother, father, sister—and Annabel, he knows they are all thinking and talking about him and wondering how he fares. How glad he is that they cannot see him now. How their hearts would bleed for him if they knew.

But Si was not going to be one of the many poor boys who actually died in the army from "homesickness." Dashing the sleeve of his blouse across his eyes to brush away —perhaps it was only perspiration, he banished the haunting thoughts.

"Now, Si," he said to himself as he trudged on, "ye ain't goin' ter make a fool o' yerself. It 'd be jest heaven 'f ye c'd lie down with yer head on yer mother's knee, 'n' have her soft hand strokin' yer hair, but ye can't have that now 'n' ther' ain't no use worryin' yerself 'bout it. Ye're goin' ter be a soljer, 'n' a good 'un' too, but ye want ter fergit fer a while 't ye've got any mother 'n' sister. Thar's Shorty, he's glad 'cause he hain't got nobody, 'n' I d'know but he's purty nigh right. Anyhow ye've got jest all ye c'n think 'bout 'n' 'tend to now. It's a mighty sight harder 'n ye thought, but ye're goin' ter stick to it, Si, 'n' be a man 't yer folks won't be 'shamed of."

How slowly the hours dragged, and how long were the last few miles! Hundreds of the new soldiers dropped by the roadside, utterly unable to keep their places in the column that swept on and left them. Many who in the morning were in the flush of strength and vigor, lay panting and exhausted upon the ground. At every stream and

spring the men crowded one another for the blessed privilege of bathing their smarting feet, and filling their canteens.   Strict orders, with the most severe pains and penalties, had been given against straggling; but obedience
was not within the bounds of human possibility.   The

THE RUSH FOR WATER.

rear-guard, with fixed bayonets, sought to force onward
those who had fallen by the way.   Some, at sight of the
cruel steel, got upon their feet and hobbled painfully on,
but to many it seemed that even death, in the face of their
sufferings, had no terrors.   The ambulances were full to
overflowing of worn and wretched men.   The few wagons

that accompanied the troops were heaped with knapsacks and muskets, of which the soldiers had been permitted by the surgeons to relieve themselves. The clothing of the men was white with dust, and saturated with the moisture from their sweating bodies.

Si was determined to keep with the colors, and he did; but he was profoundly thankful when the 200th Indiana, with scarcely half its men in ranks, filed into a field to bivouac for the night. If all the haying and harvesting and corn-hoeing and wood-chopping that he had ever done in a whole year, could have been compressed into the hours of a single day, he could not have been more completely "used up" than he was when the regiment stacked arms and received the welcome order to "break ranks." When he unslung his knapsack and let it fall to the ground, it was like getting out from under a mountain. And what a relief it was to lay off cartridge-box, haversack and canteen! Who that has not experienced it can know the restful feeling that came to limb and body, as he unfastened the strap and flung down the last of his accouterments! What an unspeakable luxury to take off his shoes and throw himself upon the ground. No bed of softest down was ever half so welcome. Si began to wish that he had enlisted in a cavalry regiment, so that he could ride.

Shorty, for the good and sufficient reasons already given, stood the march better than most of his companions. He was, however, by no means free from aches and blisters, though his feet had more skin left on them than Si's had. It was simply the difference between carrying a big knapsack and one that wasn't so big.

After they had rested a little time, Shorty suggested that they go to the stream near by and bathe their feet. "It'll be the best kind o' medicine fer 'em," he said.

"That's a good idee!" said Si, "but I'm afeard I can't git down thar. I jest feel 's though I couldn't budge an inch. I'm 's sore all over 's if I'd been run through a thrashin' machine. I don't b'lieve I could 'a' gone 'nother mile ter save my life."

"I'm purty much that way myself," replied Shorty, "'n' I know you feel a good deal wuss ner I do; but I tell ye ther' ain't nothin' like water ter bring us 'round. Try 'n' limber up."

After painful effort Si managed to get himself up "on end." Taking their shoes in their hands and treading gingerly, they slowly made their way to the creek. The banks were lined with soldiers enjoying the reviving influence of the water. Si and Shorty slipped off their trousers, and oh, how delicious the cooling water felt to their chafed limbs and smarting feet! They had but fairly begun to enjoy it when the ominous voice of the orderly fell upon Si's unwilling ears.

AFTER A DAY'S TRAMP.

The orderly sergeant in the army was generally regarded by the other non-commissioned officers and the privates as a necessary evil, but none the less a palpable and unmitigated nuisance.*

Next below the grade of a commissioned officer, he out-

* This is not, to the writer, an abstract theory. For a year his arms were decorated with the chevrons of a first sergeant, composed of three V stripes and a diamond, and he speaks from personal knowledge gained by abundant experience.

ranked all the rest of the enlisted men, so that his authority—unless in its exercise he transcended his legitimate
functions—could not be called in question. By his superiors
he was held directly responsible at all times for the condition of his company and the whereabouts of its members.
All must be "present or accounted for." It was his business to see that all orders were duly enforced and obeyed,
to draw and issue to his company supplies of rations,
clothing and ammunition, to see that the men kept their
persons and their clothing clean, and their arms and tents
—when they had any—in good condition, and to make all
details for fatigue, guard and other duty; besides numberless minor things that no one can understand or appreciate
except those who have served in that thankless and exasperating position.

It was impossible to do all this without more or less
friction—generally more. There were many very brave
and in every way excellent soldiers who were not the embodiment of all the Christian virtues. Indeed, it may be
safely said that the "old Adam" theory of the theologians
found more ample illustration in the army than in any
other sphere of active life. The circumstances were not
favorable to the development of gentleness, meekness, patience, long-suffering and the other beautiful adornments
of human character. Exception may perhaps be taken by
some of the veterans to the last of the attributes mentioned, for it cannot be denied that there was plenty
of "long suffering," if the words be given a literal interpretation.

Upon the head of the orderly was poured a great deal
more than his share of profanity. Scarcely a day
passed that he was not deluged with it. If anything went
wrong with the company he caught "Hail Columbia" from
the officers. When enforcing discipline and making details of men for duty, particularly after fatiguing marches
or on rainy days, he rarely failed to provoke the wrath

of those whose "turn" it happened to be. The curses and
maledictions were not always loud, for prudential reasons,
but they were deep and fervent. The longer the men remained in service the more fluent they became in the use
of pungent words, making it warmer and warmer for
the orderly. Swearing at *him* was the sovereign balm
for the soldier's woes. When the hardtack was wormy,
or the bacon maggoty, or the bean-soup too weak, or
rations scanty; when the weather was too hot or too
cold, or it rained, or the company had to go on picket after
a hard day's tramp, or any fatigue duty had to be done;
when the buttons flew off their clothes and seams ripped
the first time they were worn, or the shapeless "gunboats"
scraped the skin from their feet; when the company had
to turn out for drill, with the mercury in the nineties, and
swelter and charge around capturing imaginary batteries
—for all these and much more the persecuted orderly was
to blame. He was ground to powder between the upper
and nether millstones—the officers and the men. His life
was a continual martyrdom.

Then he was expected to be, himself, in every way, an
example to the men worthy of their imitation—a pattern
of soldierly perfection, in his bearing, his person, and "all
appurtenances thereunto belonging," as the lawyers say.
The only redeeming feature in the orderly's wretched existence was that he did not have to detail *himself* to go
on guard or chop wood or load the colonel's wagon.
From these the "Regulations" exempted him.

"Hey, there, Mr. Klegg!" shouted the orderly of Company Q.

The orderlies addressed the men as "Mister" at first, but
they soon got over that.

"Hello!" replied Si, "what d' ye want o' me?"

"Report immejitly fer fatigue duty.   Go to headquarters an' help put up the colonel's tent.   Hurry on with

yer duds an' be lively, 'cause the colonel's waitin', an' he'll stan' ye on yer head if ye don't come to time!"

Si's first thought was to make another issue on the question of his "turn." He was sure that all whose names preceded his on the roll had not been detailed for fatigue duty. He wondered if he was to suffer still further punishment for his part in the conspiracy to have the orderly tossed in a blanket. Remembering his former experience he said nothing, but he "chalked it down" in his memory for future use.

"That's purty tough, ain't it Shorty?" said Si, as he sadly drew his feet out of the water and began to put on his trousers. "'Tween you 'n' me, I think it 's mighty mean, too. The colonel rid a hoss all day while we was a-trampin', 'n' 't seems ter me 's if he mout put up his own tent. He's got a nigger ter help him, too. Ef I was colonel o' this 'ere rijiment I bet ye I wouldn't make none o' the soljers that hain't got no skin left on their feet, put up *my* tent. I wish 't I was colonel 'n' he was Si Klegg fer jest one day so he c'd know how 't feels."

"Growlin' don't do no good," replied his comrade. "The ossifers 'n' the orderlies has all the trump keerds 'n' they takes the trick every time. Better let me go 'n yer place, Si. I ain't used up 's bad 's you. I'll be glad ter do it fer ye."

"It's reel kind of ye, Shorty, but I'll do it ef I c'n make the riffle. I ain't goin' ter shirk nothin' 's long 's I c'n stan' up. Ef I can't I *can't*, 'n' that's the end on 't. But I sh'd think the colonel mout git 'long 'thout any tent. The rest on us has ter, 'n' I don't see how he's any better 'n we are, jest 'cause he's got shoulder-straps 'n' we hain't!"

The subtle questions of distinction between carrying a sword or a musket, between commanding and being commanded, were too much for Si's philosophy. Nor was there time to pursue the discussion. Two minutes had sufficed for putting on his clothes and shoes, though the latter caused him much pain and still further ruffled his temper.

At headquarters Si found half a dozen men who had been detailed from other companies for the work in question. All were in a similar condition as to their feet and limbs; and judging from the emphatic observations that fell from their lips, there was no dissent from the views Si had expressed to Shorty. They had not yet learned the "knack" of pitching a tent, and not till after repeated trials, under the pressure of pointed rebukes from the colonel for their awkwardness, did they get it up to suit him.

Fortunately, Shorty's information that the march might have to be continued through the night, proved to be incorrect. The tired soldiers were directed to make themselves as comfortable as possible, but to be ready to move at an early hour in the morning. When Si got back to his company he found that his faithful friend had kindled a fire, upon which the coffee was already boiling and the bacon sizzling in a manner most gratifying to one as hungry as he. During the day there had been no halt for coffee. The gnawings of hunger had only been partially appeased by an occasional nibble at the flinty hardtack. As Si limped down from the colonel's tent he had been wondering how he would manage about the supper, and he was delighted at Shorty's prompt and efficient services. The grateful odor of the steaming coffee did much to revive his drooping spirits.

"Shorty," he said, "I think I was mighty lucky to git such a good pardner 's you be. I never knowed ye t'll ye jined the company, 'n' when I fust seen ye I 'lowed ye wa'n't much 'count nohow. I thought ye'd be the last man I'd ever want ter tie to. But now I wouldn't swap ye off fer any man 'n the hull rijiment."

"Ye can't most always tell 'bout folks f'm what ye see on the outside," replied Shorty. "I couldn't tell ye how 'twas 'f I sh'd try, but somehow I kind o' took to ye, Si. f'm the start, 'n' 's long 's ye keep on the way ye've begun, I'll stick by ye. I never had much bringin' up, 'n' I've knocked 'round fer myself ever sence I was a little shaver, but I've got *some* feelin's, 'n' it does me good ter have somebody to think 'bout 'n' do suthin' fer when I kin. But the coffee 's done 'n' this ere pig-meat 's fried 'nough; let's eat."

The ties that bound near comrades and associates in the army were more than those of friendship. In constant companionship, bearing one another's burdens and sharing the toil and danger and suffering and the hard-earned glory of a soldier's life, their hearts were drawn together by a feeling that can find a parallel only in the tenderest relations of life. These cords were fast tightening around Si and Shorty. Si's innocence, frank good-nature and cheery chatter had completely captured his comrade, and thawed out the heart that lay beneath his forbidding exterior. Shorty's repeated kindnesses had won Si's ardent affections, and his hard sense and helpful, practical ways were just what was needed by one who had had so little experience with the world as his young companion.

"Shorty," said Si, as they spread down their blankets, "that 'cruitin' ossifer kind o' fooled the boys when he blowed so much 'bout Comp'ny Q havin' sich a soft thing, didn't he?"

"He did so—them as b'lieved it."

"I didn't take no stock in 't," Si continued, "fer I wasn't lookin' fer no soft snap, anyway. I jined the army with the idee o' seein' the elephant."

"Purty good-sized animile, ain't he, Si?" said Shorty with a laugh.

"Wall—yes—'n' gittin' bigger all the time; but I'm goin' ter have a good squar' look at him. I'd jest like ter seen that feller 't 'listed us humpin' 'long 'th this **rijiment.** What ever become on 'im, Shorty?"

"Oh, he didn't never 'low to do any soljerin'. His pa-trit'ism—I b'lieve that's what they calls it—swelled up so big that it busted. When he got his comp'ny raised he sold us to the man 't 's our capt'n. Ef I'm any jedge Cap. 's wuth a dozen like t'other chap!"

CHAPTER XIII.

WHICH ILLUSTRATES THE DEPRAVITY OF THE VETERAN SOLDIERS.

FAR into the night the weary stragglers, by ones and twos, dragged themselves into camp, inquiring the whereabouts of the 200th Indiana. Suffering in body, discouraged and sick at heart, they flung themselves upon the ground with no thought of anything but rest. Their needs were supplied by kind-hearted comrades who had been more fortunate in enduring the fatigue of the day. The doctors found plenty of work in administering reviving cordials, and applying soothing emollients to blistered feet and stiffened limbs. Gradually the fires of the great bivouac burned low as the soldiers lay down to sleep. The hum and bustle grew quiet, and the mantle of night spread over the sleeping army.

This was the time for the wicked veterans to make their predatory forays upon the new troops. A year of hard campaigning had made sad havoc with the clothing of the old soldiers. Many of them had no blankets or over-coats. Such of these necessary articles as still remained were much the worse for the service they had seen. They had not stood it as well as the men. They were worn and tattered, blackened by the smoke and burned by the sparks of many a camp-fire. The elaborate outfit of the raw sol-diers afforded an opportunity that could not be permitted

to pass unimproved. The march of twenty miles, that **h**ad so nearly used up the 200th Indiana, had been nothing to the veterans, with their light burdens and nimble, hardened feet. With laugh and jest and song they had made their coffee, toasted their bacon and munched their hard-tack, and then smoked and spun yarns as they squatted around the fires, in the happy-go-lucky style that characterized the seasoned soldiers. Some of them were so kind of heart as to go over to the bivouac of the aching, smarting, groaning and grumbling Indianians and proffer their advice and personal services in preparing supper and making such arrangements for comfort as the circumstances would permit. Their ministrations were most gratefully received by the sufferers, who had not the faintest conception of the real errand of these good Samaritans. This was to reconnoiter and determine the most promising place to strike—after a deep sleep should have fallen upon those unsuspecting Hoosiers—to replenish their wasted stock of overcoats and blankets. The men of the 200th Indiana warmly thanked the veterans for their timely assistance. The latter, while cherishing their diabolical schemes of plunder, assured their neighbors that they were heartily welcome. They had been there themselves, and knew just how it felt to be "played out."

Two hours later, when the fires had burned to smoldering embers, dark forms glided noiselessly about among the prostrate soldiers of the 200th. Here an overcoat was adroitly prigged from under the head of a sleeper, and there a blanket was gently drawn from the forms it covered. The men generally slept by twos, spreading one blanket upon the ground and the other over them. Fortunate was he who had no "pard," and wrapped himself in his solitary blanket, lying upon part of it and covering himself with the rest. For obvious reasons he was safe from the operations of the raiders. Sometimes the prowler would leave in place of the article taken one that had been battered by storms and burned full of holes, quieting his conscience—if he had any—with the recognized commercial axiom that "an even exchange is no robbery," or the more flexible one that "all is fair in war." True, it required a stretch of imagination to consider the exchange an even one, but the veteran was not accustomed to split hairs in such trifling matters. If he had none to leave in exchange he simply walked off with his plunder, leaving to be settled hereafter whatever moral questions might be involved. To take care of number one was a cardinal principle in the mind of the old soldier. If it now and then ran foul of the decalogue, the latter had to give way. A few of the Hoosiers had struggled through with extra blankets or quilts brought from home. In such cases one of them was taken without compunction. It was not considered fair for one soldier to have two while another had none; and besides, it was a blessing to him to relieve him of part of his burden.

FLEECING THE LAMBS.

Si and Shorty did not escape the doom that befell so many of their comrades. They slept so soundly that they knew nothing of the midnight raid that left them without a blanket save that upon which they lay. The dew fell heavily upon their garments that were still damp from the perspiration of the day. The night air chilled them to the very marrow. Si at length awoke, with teeth chattering, and shivering in every limb.

"Hello, there, Shorty," he exclaimed, poking him with his elbow, "ye've pulled all the blanket off 'n' I'm purty nigh friz. Ef ye don't quit doin' that I'll ketch my death cold. Ugh!" and Si shook till his bones fairly rattled.

"I hain't got no kiver, nuther," replied Shorty, as he roused up with a shiver. "Whar is the pesky thing, anyway?"

"She's gone!" said Si, sadly, after they had fruitlessly explored the adjacent territory. "D'ye s'pose somebody stole it?"

"Shouldn't wonder!" Shorty scratched his head reflectively and continued: "I'll bet ye I know whar 't went to, Si. You remember seein' one o' them Ohio chaps sneakin' 'round when we was gittin' into shape last night, 'n' tellin' us how ter do it?"

"Yes," said Si, who was beginning to comprehend the mysterious disappearance, "'n' he had the cheek ter ax me 'f we had plenty o' blankets so 's we'd sleep warm. I told him we did, 'n' he said he was glad of it."

"I 'low that feller 's got our blanket," said Shorty.

"Wall, ef that ain't dog-goned ornery!" exclaimed Si. "I'm goin' ter lick him termorrer. I don't keer 'f he 's twicet 's big 's I am!"

With this idea of retributive justice uppermost in his mind, Si dragged himself to the remains of the fire and tried to get a little warmth into his chilled body. Shorty threw on some wood, and in a few minutes a bright blaze diffused a glow of good cheer. Drowsiness soon overcame them, and spreading their only remaining blanket near the fire, they again lay down and in a moment were fast asleep.

Long before daylight the pitiless drum and bugle sounded the reveille into the unwilling ears of Company Q. Si had not slept half as long as he wanted to, but the orderly was yelling for the tardy ones to fall in for roll-call, and there was no alternative. He was very stiff and sore. It seemed as if all his joints had grown together during the night and his bones, from head to foot, were united in a solid mass.

"Great Scott, Shorty," he said, as he rolled over and made an effort to get upon his feet, "I reck'n ye'll have ter git a rail 'n' pry me up. I'm jest 's sore 's a bile all over, 'n' 's stiff 's a poker. It seems like I hadn't got no j'ints."

"I don't feel very frisky myself," replied Shorty, "but I s'pose we'll have ter turn out. Lemme give ye a lift."

Si gave him his hand, and by their combined efforts he succeeded in reaching an erect posture. When he tried to step he tottered and would have fallen but for the supporting arm of his comrade. His feet were insubordinate and would not do as he wanted them to. Every attempt to move extorted an involuntary groan.

"Stick to it, Si," said Shorty, "ye'll git limbered up arter a while."

Si was courageous and determined. He knew that other men, thousands of them, had gone through such an experience. It was true that a good many had died in bravely trying to "get used to it," and many more had thronged the hospitals along the track of the army; but Si never for a moment entertained the thought that he could not do what anybody else had done. He kept up a cheerful spirit, notwithstanding his bodily woes. To do this was always worth more than barrels of medicine to a soldier.

A little exercise loosened his joints, and after roll-call he began to stir about in the work of preparing for the day's march, with more briskness than he had thought possible when he was so rudely awakened from his slumbers.

The disappearance of so many overcoats and blankets created a great stir among the members of the 200th Indiana. There was much speculation as to what had become of them. There were few who had not lost one or the other, and some had been despoiled of both. Daylight revealed the members of the old regiments of the brigade suddenly possessed of new articles of this kind, and by putting this and that together, a simple process of reasoning soon brought to the minds of the forlorn Hoosiers a plausible solution of the mystery. Vows of vengeance were heard on every hand.

After breakfast Si began to consider the advisability of still further lightening his knapsack. He was partially consoled for the loss of his blanket by the thought that he would not have to carry it. The nocturnal foragers had kindly spared his overcoat. He thought he could manage to rub along with that until the fortunes of war—or the quartermaster—should provide him with another blanket. His knapsack, reduced though it was, seemed very heavy when he lifted it. He had but little sentiment left after the experience of the previous day. He was more and more convinced of Shorty's good sense in the matter of baggage.

"Pard," he said, as if once more seeking counsel of his friend, "I don't b'lieve I want these 'ere traps 's much 's I thought I did. I've 'bout made up my mind ter sling away some more on 'em."

"Ko-rect," replied Shorty, "now ye're talkin' kind o' sensible like. I tell ye a soljer don't want ter 'lug a single ounce more 'n he has ter. I'd clean 'em *all* out ef 'twas me."

Si went through his stock with a remorseless determination to spare not. Everything went except such articles as were absolutely necessary to his well-being, and two or three precious mementoes of home which he felt that he could not part with. When he came to the pretty slippers that Annabel gave him, Shorty sniffed contemptuously.

"What on airth d'ye want o' them things?" he said. "Ye hain't no more use fer 'em nor a mule has fer kid gloves."

But logic had no bearing upon such a subject, and Si,

without making any reply, tucked them back into his knapsack, saying to himself that they weren't very heavy, anyway.

"Shorty," he said, "what 'd I better do 'th these 'ere boots; they feel 's heavy 's ef they was poured full o' lead. Them 's extry nice boots 'n' its wicked ter throw 'em away. They must ha' cost father nigh ten dollars."

"Ef the ole man 'd ever toted a knapsack he wouldn't ha' guv 'em to ye. He meant well, but he throwed away his money 'n' you can't do nuthin' but throw away the butes. 'Sides, ye can't march in 'em. They ain't no good 'longside o' shoes. Ye wouldn't have no feet left arter ye 'd marched in 'em fer a week. I'll tell ye, Si, try 'n' sell 'em ter some ossifer 't rides a hoss. Don't be pertickler 'bout the price; take jest what ye c'n git fer 'em."

This was a good suggestion and Si acted upon it at once. After a brief negotiation with the quartermaster, whom the boots happened to fit, a bargain was made, and Si returned to his comrade with three dollars in money.

"Thar, pard," he said, gleefully, "I'm goin' ter spend that buyin' chickens 'n' you 'n' me 'll go snacks on 'em. They won't 'low us ter steal 'em, but I reck'n they won't hender a feller f'm gittin' 'em by payin' fer 'em."

By the time Si got through, his knapsack looked as if an elephant had stepped on it. Those of the entire regiment presented a similar appearance, varying only in the extent to which they had been flattened. A few of the men were still inclined to overestimate their carrying abilities, and needed one or two more days of tramping to convince them of their error. The ground was strewn with gim-cracks of every conceivable kind. An army wagon might have been heaped with the debris.

Some of the soldiers from other regiments strolled through the camp of the 200th to see how their new com-rades were getting on. As they scornfully kicked about the castaway articles, they indulged in many a cruel jest at the expense of the Indianians. The latter kindly offered them books and "housewives" and albums, but the old veterans spurned the gifts.

"We don't want 'em no more'n you do!" said a tall, lank Illinois soldier, who looked as if he had slept in a smoke-house. "We all had 'em when we started in but we wasn't long sheddin' 'em. When I seen you fellers humpin' up yer backs yisterdy I knowed what ye'd all be a doin' this mornin'. Soldierin' 's easy 'nough arter ye git the hang of it."

Si tried to give away one of his Bibles, but he did not succeed in finding anybody who was hungering and thirsting after righteousness sufficiently to be willing to put upon his back the pound or so that it weighed. It seemed to him that there were plenty of the veterans who showed the need of it. He thought particularly of the degenerate individual who stole his blanket, and felt that he would like to give it to *him*—although he wanted the pleasure of "licking" him first—if he could ever find the guilty man. He would not throw the Bible away, and finally turned it over to the chaplain, who promised to find a place where it would do good to somebody. The chaplain gathered up a score of others upon the ground, which the men had thrown away. When it came to the point of choosing between blisters and Bibles, it did not take long to reach a conclusion. The chaplain's reverential ideas were shocked, and he ventured to distribute in a general way words of mild reproof. Their effect was somewhat modified, however, by the fact that he had a horse to ride.

"I jest wonder how many Bibles he'd carry," Shorty said to Si, "'f he had ter hoof it 'long 'th the rest on us, 'n' tote a knapsack 'n' gun 'n' catridge-box 'n' all the rest of the traps 't we has ter; then he'd know a good deal better how to preachify ter the soljers."

There was yet some little time before the fall-in would be sounded, and Si thought he would go over to the Ohio regiment and see if he could find his blanket. He did not think Shorty would approve of the expedition, and therefore said nothing to him about it. He limped around among the veterans, hoping that his eye might catch the face of the man who visited him the evening before. He believed that person was the culprit, and was confident that he could recognize him.

The old soldiers were lazily loitering around the fires, for the chill of the night had not yet been dissipated. From the moment that Si crossed the line he was the target of a constant fire of good-natured badinage. No person could possibly have been mistaken in supposing that Si was one of the new crop. His fresh, ruddy face had not yet been darkened by sun and storm and smoke, nor had the bright color faded from his garments. You could have picked him out for a recruit among a thousand.

Si was not long in finding the object of his search. Sitting upon a new blanket, which he had twisted up ready to throw over his shoulder at tap of drum, was the man who had called upon Si and Shorty. Si was sure he was not mistaken as to the soldier's identity, and he had not a shadow of doubt that that blanket rightfully belonged to himself. His first impulse was to move immediately upon his works and mete out to the Ohio man condign punishment, in accordance with his declaration to Shorty. On second thought he didn't know but he might be mistaken after all; perhaps somebody else had taken his blanket, and besides this man seemed to be in good health and thoroughly able to defend himself.

"Good mornin'," said Si, rather timidly.

"How ar' ye, pard," replied the Ohio man.

"Nice mornin'."

"Yup!"

"I thought I'd come 'n' see—that is, I was goin' ter ax ye —I mean I wanted ter tell ye how much 'bleeged I am ter ye for comin' over 'n' helpin' us last night. It was mighty good of ye ter do it."

"Oh, that ain't nothin'," said the veteran. "I knowed ye'd be purty well played out, fer I've been jest that way myself, 'n' I thought I mout give ye a hint er two 't 'd come in sort o' handy. Ye pulled through bully, yisterdy, but I don't reck'n ye feel very spry this mornin', do ye? Feet a leetle sore? Bones ache? Feel's if ye didn't care whether school kep' er not?"

This gave Si an opening to introduce the subject uppermost in his thoughts.

"Wall, I'm fa'r to middlin', considerin' the way they put us through all day."

"That wa'n't no march 't all! One o' these days ye *will* cotch it fer a fact. It was yer big load 't come nigh bustin' ye up. I seen you fellers all physickin' yer knapsacks this mornin', 'n' I 'low ye'll get 'long easier to-day."

"I wouldn't ha' been so stiff," said Si, "'f I hadn't cotched cold last night. Somebody borrered my blanket 'thout axin' me, 'n' 'long to'rd mornin' I waked up shakin,' 's if I'd got the ager."

"That *was* a scurvy trick," said the old soldier, with feigned indignation. "Ef I was you I'd punch his head fer him, 'n' punch it hard, too, 'f I could find the feller 't done it. Ef ye git yer eye on him, 'n' he's too big fer ye, jest cal' on me 'n' I'll help ye. We'll polish him off beautiful."

"That's what I come over here fer," said Si, who found his courage rising. "I was kind o' thinkin'—mebbe I'm wrong—but—that 'ere blanket you're a-sittin' on looks jest like mine!"

At this palpable assault upon his integrity the soldier sprang to his feet and assumed a warlike attitude that for the moment demoralized Si and caused him to fall back. In a moment, however, the veteran's hostile appearance vanished, and the scowl upon his face gave way to a "smile that was childlike and bland."

"I don't blame ye, pard," he said, "fer tryin' to find yer blanket. I'd feel the same way 'f I was in yer place. But this 'ere one ain't yourn! I drawed it f'm the quartermaster last night. I'd jest's lief let ye look at it," and he unrolled it and spread it before Si, feeling secure in the fact that all blankets were alike.

Si surveyed it critically and then said: "Ye don't object to turnin' it over, do ye?"

A PRIMA FACIE CASE.

"Course not!" was the ready reply, and over it went.

Si's quick eye detected in one corner a rude "K" that he had been thoughtful enough to put in the first day he had his blanket. His "housewife" furnished the necessary materials.

"There," he exclaimed triumphantly, as he took it up and pointed to the letter, "I guess that blanket b'longs to a feller 'bout my size. D'ye see that K? My name's Klegg, 'n' that means me. I done that myself."

Appearances were rather against the veteran, but he had been in tight places before, and he was not in the least disconcerted by the evidence that Si had made out his case.

"Why, man alive," he said, "my name begins with a K, too. When I drew this blanket last night I thought some durned fool 'd come 'long 'n' say 'twas hisn, 'n' so I jest made my 'nitial thar 'n the corner. I'll leave it to the boys 'f I didn't."

The interview between Si and the veteran had attracted to the spot a number of the latter's comrades, most of whom had supplied themselves with new blankets in the same manner as did the one who said his name began with K. When appealed to in behalf of the monstrous statement, of course they all stood by their comrade.

"That's so, Johnson," said one of them thoughtlessly, "I seen ye doin' it with my own eyes. Ye was sittin' right on that ar' log."

Si thought it was queer to spell "Johnson" with a K. He wanted to say so, but in the presence of such monumental assurance and so great numerical odds he concluded that it would be the part of discretion not to press his claim. There was nothing more to be said, and he turned away. The soldiers laughed heartily at his discomfiture.

"Ef I was you, Johnson," he heard one of them say, "the next time I went fer a blanket I'd try 'n' cabbage one 't wa'n't marked, er 't had a J on it."

And then they all went to inspecting those which they had acquired, to see if they were liable to be caught in the same trap as Johnson, spelled with a K.

Si walked slowly back to Company Q, meditating on the depth to which human depravity could reach, and wondering if he would ever be like those terrible veterans.

"Hello, Si, whar ye been?" said Shorty, as his comrade came up. "What makes ye so solemn? Ye look 's though ye'd come f'm a fun'ral."

"Shorty, I've found my blanket 'n' the chap 't stole it."

"Did ye lick 'im?"

"N–no, I can't say 's I did. I never wanted ter thrash anybody so bad in my life, but—ther' was too many on 'em, Shorty. I knew I couldn't lick a hull rijiment, 'n' so I didn't try. Jest wait t'll I ketch 'im alone some time 'n' I'll—"

"But why didn't ye bring along yer blanket?"

"Oh, I kind o' thought I wouldn't, fer the same reason 's why I didn't give him the lickin'. He said 'twas hisn 'n' stuck to it, 'n' half the rijiment backed 'im up."

"Ye know ye had a mark in the corner o' yer blanket, Si; did ye find that?"

"You bet I did, but that feller had more cheek 'n a hull team o' mules. He said *his* name begun that way 'n' he put that mark thar hisself. An' then I heern one o' the boys call him Johnson!"

Shorty laughed as his comrade told of the treatment he had received among the Philistines.

"Tell ye what 'tis, Si," he said. "Ye never seen sich funny fellers 's these 'ere vet'rans is. They're up ter all kinds o' shenanigan. Ye've got ter larn how ter git 'long with 'em. The best thing fer ye is ter do jest 's they do 'n' then they'll respect ye 'n' ye won't have no bother with 'em. They're a bad crowd, 'n' they allus makes it warm fer the greenies. Ye wants ter watch out fer a chance ter git even with 'em."

"I'd take my blanket 'f I could, but ye know, Shorty, I couldn't steal nobody else's."

"I ain't so squeamish 's you be," said Shorty. "I'll git ye a blanket jest 's good 's the one ye had, 'fore termorrer night. I ain't goin' ter rob nobody in the 200th Indiana, nuther."

The colonel of the 200th stormed around and talked with great vehemence about the robbing of his men; but there were very few of the losers who could prove their property and nothing came of it. The colonel declared that he would keep a guard around the regiment with loaded muskets and fixed bayonets, with orders to shoot or stab any man who should attempt to cross the line.

The second day's march was much like the first. With his greatly reduced load Si got along better. But for the blisters upon his feet, which caused acute pain at every step, he would have made the journey with comparative ease. The division to which the 200th belonged was ahead that day, and the men were kept in a constant fever of excitement by the reports of rebels ahead, that filtered through each successive regiment of the long column. Now and then a shot was heard in the distance that caused the new soldiers to prick up their ears in anticipation of the slaughter they thought was about to begin. They did not find any fighting to do, however, and at dark, weary and footsore, they filed off the road and went into bivouac.

"Shorty," said Si, as they threw themselves upon the ground to breathe a few minutes before setting about the work of getting supper, "I'm *awful* glad termorrer 's Sunday!"

"What fer?" asked Shorty.

"So 's we kin have a chance ter rest. I never *was* so glad ter have Sunday come!"

Shorty laughed softly to himself but said nothing.

———

CHAPTER XIV.

In Which, Overcome by his Aches and Blisters, Si Falls out
and Finds How Hard it is to "Ketch up."

AN hour before daylight the reveille aroused Si from his deep slumber. When he lay down the evening before he had nothing but his overcoat to serve as a cover; now he was pleased to find himself lying under a blanket which, if it had no "K" stitched in the corner, was as good as the one he had lost.

"Whar 'd this come from?" he asked his comrade.

"Don't ax too many questions," replied Shorty, "ye

had ter have one 'n' I jest got up 'n the night 'n' 'drawed' it fer ye.''

"But, Shorty—"

"Now, pard, never you mind the buts. Ther' ain't nothin' ter be said 'bout it. Ye've got a good blanket 'n' ye wants ter freeze to it. Ye'll have ter larn ter look out fer yerself, same 's all the rest on 'em does."

Si was so stiff and sore that it was as much as he could do to get into his place for roll-call. He felt comforted when he remembered that it was Sunday, and he would not have to march. How he would enjoy a day of rest!

"Ye'll have ter stir 'round lively this mornin'," said the orderly, after he had got through the Z's in calling the roll. "We're goin' to pull out early, 'cause we've got to make a long march. I want ye to be ready to fall in when ye hear the drum. Ye've all got to keep in ranks, too; ther' ain't goin' to be any stragglin' 'lowed!"

"Did the ord'ly say we'd got ter march *to-day*, Shorty?" asked Si, who thought his ears must have deceived him He did not believe so monstrous a thing could be true.

"That's jest the bigness of it," replied Shorty.

"I didn't s'pose they marched Sundays," said Si, "I sh'd think it 'd be wicked 'n' our chaplain 'd make a fuss 'bout it."

"Ye won't be long findin' out 't when men goes to war they've got ter leave Sunday to home. The chaplain won't git no chance ter preach to-day 'less he preaches on hoss back. I reck'n his sarmon 'll keep."

"Wall," said Si, with an air of resignation. "I don't see no way but ter go 'th the rijiment, but it's purty hard ter put a feller through right along, Sundays 'n' all. It 'd make mother feel bad, but I ain't ter blame."

Soon after breakfast the column was on the road, moving at a rapid pace. The veterans didn't mind it. They stretched their legs and went swinging along, cheerful and happy, as if they were having a holiday. The men of the

200th Indiana started bravely, and for the first hour or two kept in fair, compact shape.

At the outset Si groaned as he loaded himself up, and the straps and belts began to rub the tender spots on his body. But there was no limit to his pluck, and he tramped away with a determination to keep up with the old soldiers at all hazards.

"Them fellers that's bin in the sarvice longer 'n we have thinks they're smart," he said to Shorty as they plodded on, both already a little blown. "We'll show 'em that we kin scratch gravel jest 's well 's they kin."

"Seems to me we're gittin' over the ground purty lively to-day," replied Shorty, who was in a grumbling mood. "Wonder if the Gin'ral thinks we're hosses! I'm a little short o' wind, and these pesky gunboats is scrapin' the bark off'n my feet; but I'll keep up or bust a-tryin'."

Si soon began to limp badly, and the smarting of his feet became almost intolerable. But he clenched his teeth, humped his back to ease his shoulders from the weight of his knapsack, screwed up his courage, and trudged on over the stony pike. He thought the breathing spells were very short and a long way apart.

Before noon the 200th began to show signs of going to pieces. The column stretched out longer and longer, like a piece of India rubber. The ranks looked thin and ragged. Lame and foot-sore, with woe-begone faces, their bodies aching in every part, and overcome with a weariness that no language can describe, the men dropped out one by one and threw themselves into the fence-corners to rest. The officers stormed and drew their swords in vain. Nature—that is, the nature of a new soldier—could endure no more. The ambulances were filled to their utmost, but these would not hold a twentieth part of the crippled and suffering men.

"How're ye gittin' on, Shorty?" said Si, as he and his comrade still struggled along.

"Fa'r to middlin'," replied Shorty. "I'm goin' ter **pull** through!"

"I thought *I* could," said Si, "but I'm 'bout played out! I am, fer a fact! I guess ef I rest a bit I'll be able to ketch up arter a while."

Si didn't know, till he found out by experience, how hard it was to "ketch up" when a soldier once got behind on the march.

He crept up to the orderly and told him that he would have to stop and puff awhile and give his blisters a rest. He'd pull up with Company Q in an hour or so.

"Better not, Si," said the orderly; "ye know it's agin orders, and the rear-guard 'll punch ye with their bay'nets if they catch ye stragglin'."

But Si concluded that if he must die for his country it would be sweeter to do so by having a bayonet inserted in his vitals, and have it all over with at once, than to walk himself to death.

So he gradually fell back till he reached the tail of the company. Watching his opportunity he left the ranks, crept into a clump of bushes, and lay down. Soon the rear-guard of the 200th came along, with fixed bayonets, driving before them, like a flock of frightened sheep, a motley crowd of limping, groaning men, gathered up by the roadside.

Si lay very still, hoping to escape discovery; but the keen eye of the officer detected the blue heap among the bushes.

"Bring that man out!" he said, sternly, to one of the guards.

Poor Si scarcely dared to breathe. He hoped the man would think he was dead, and therefore no longer of any account. But the soldier began to prod him with his bayonet, ordering him to get up and move on.

"Look a-here, pard," said Si, "don't stab me with that **thing**! I jest *can't* git along any furder till I blow a little.

You please lemme be, 'n' I'll do as much fer you. P'r'aps sometime you'll git played out and I'll be on the rear-guard. The cap'n 'll tell me ter fotch ye 'long, an' I'll jest let up on ye, so I will!"

This view of the case struck the guard with some force. He was in much the same condition himself, and had that "fellow-feeling" that made him "wondrous kind." He turned away, leaving Si to

"DON'T STAB ME."

enjoy his rest. Si threw aside his traps, took off his shoes and stockings, and bathed his feet with water from his canteen. He ate a couple of hardtack, and in the course of half an hour began to feel more like Si Klegg. He put on his accouterments, shouldered his gun, and started to "ketch up."

HYDROPATHIC TREATMENT.

All this time the stream of troops — regiments, brigades and divisions — had flowed on. Of course, soldiers who were with their colors had the right of way, and the stragglers were obliged to stumble along as best they could, over the logs and through the bushes at the sides of the road, or skirt along the edges of the fields and woods adjoining. It was this fact, added to their exhausted and crippled condition, that made it almost impossible for them to overtake their regiments until after they had halted for the night. Even then it was often midnight before the last of the wayfarers, weary and worn, reached the end of the day's journey.

Si started forward briskly, but soon found it was no easy matter to gain the mile or more that the 200th Indiana was now ahead of him. It was about all he could do to keep up with the fast moving column and avoid falling still farther to the rear. Presently the bugles sounded a halt for one of the hourly rests.

"Now," said Si to himself, "I'll have a good chance ter git along tor'd the front. The soljers 'll all lie down in the fence corners an' leave the road clear. I'll jest git up and dust!"

The sound of the bugles had scarcely died away when the pike was deserted; and on either side, as far as the eye could reach, the prostrate men that covered the ground mingled in a long fringe of blue.

Si got up into the road and started along the lane between these lines of recumbent soldiers. His gait was a little shaky, but he trudged pluckily along, limping some, though on the whole making very good headway.

Pretty soon he struck a veteran regiment from Illinois, the members of which were sitting and lying around in all the picturesque and indescribable attitudes which the old soldiers found gave them the greatest comfort during a "rest." Then the fun commenced—that is, it was great sport for the Sucker boys, though Si did not readily appreciate the humorous features of the scene.

"What rijiment is this?" asked Si, timidly.

"Same old rijiment!" was the answer from half a dozen at once. A single glance told the swarthy veterans that the fresh-looking youth who asked this conundrum belonged to one of the new regiments, and they immediately opened their batteries upon him:

"Left—Left—Left!"

"Hayfoot—Strawfoot! Hayfoot—Strawfoot!" keeping time with Si's somewhat irregular steps.

"Grab a root!"

"Hello, there, *you!* Change step an' ye'll march easier!"

"Here comes one o' the persimmon-knockers!"

"Look at that 'ere poor feller; the only man left alive of his rijiment! Great Cæsar, how they must ha' suffered! *Say*, what rijiment did ye b'long to?"

"Paymaster's comin', boys; here's a chap with a pay-roll 'round his neck!" Si had put on that morning the last of the paper collars he had brought from home.

"Ye'd better shed that knapsack, or it'll be the death of ye!"

"I say, there, how's all the folks to home?"

"How d' ye like it 's fur 's ye've got, anyway?"

"Git some commissary and pour into them gunboats!"

"Second relief's come boys; we kin all go home now."

"How 'd ye leave yer sweetheart?"

"Hep—Hep—Hep!"

Si had never been under so hot a fire before. He stood it as long as he could, and then stopped.

"Halt!" shouted a chorus of voices. "Shoulder—Arms! Order—Arms!"

By this time Si's wrath was at the boiling point. Casting around him a look of defiance, he exclaimed:

"Ye cowardly blaggards; I kin jest lick any two on ye, an' I'll dare ye to come on. Ef the 200th Injianny was here we'd clean out the hull pack of ye quicker'n ye kin say scat!"

This is where Si made a mistake. He ought to have kept right on and said nothing. But he had to find out all these things by experience, as the rest of the boys did.

All the members of the regiment now took a hand in the

game. They got right up and yelled, discharging at Si a volley of expletives and pointed remarks that drove him to desperation. Instinctively he brought up his gun.

"Load in nine times—Load!" shouted the tramps.

If Si's gun had been loaded he would have shot somebody, regardless of consequences. Thinking of his bayonet, he jerked it quickly from its scabbard.

"Fix—Bay'net!" yelled the ragged veterans.

SI DEFIES A REGIMENT OF VETERANS.

And he did, though it was more from the promptings of his own hostile feelings than in obedience to the orders.

"Charge—Bay'net!"

Si had completely lost control of himself in his overpowering rage. With blood in his eye, he came to a "charge," glancing fiercely from one side of the road to the other, uncertain where to begin the assault.

Instantly there was a loud clicking all along the line. The Illinois soldiers, almost to a man, fixed their bayonets. Half of them sprang to their feet, and aimed their shining points at the poor little Hoosier patriot, filling the air with shouts of derision.

It was plain, even to Si in his inflamed state of mind, that the odds against him were too heavy.

"Unfix—Bay'net!" they yelled.

Si concluded he had better get out of a bad scrape the best way he could. So he took off his bayonet and put it back in its place. He shouted defiant words at his tormentors, but they could not be heard in the din.

"Shoulder—Arms! Right—Face! Right shoulder shift —Arms! Forward—March!" These commands came in quick succession from the ranks amidst roars of laughter.

Si obeyed the orders and started off.

"Left—Left—Left! Hayfoot—Strawfoot!"

Forgetting his blisters, Si took the double-quick, while the mob swung their caps and howled with delight.

Si didn't "ketch up" with the 200th Indiana until it had been some time in bivouac. Shorty had a quart of hot coffee waiting for him.

"Shorty," said Si, as they sat by the fire, "I'm goin' ter drop dead in my tracks 'fore I'll fall out agin."

"Why, what's the matter?"

"Oh, nothin'; only you jest try it," said Si.

Had it not been for the occasional "fun" the soldiers had in the army to brighten their otherwise dark and cheerless lives, they would all have died. They made the most of every opportunity, and Si was a true type of those who had to suffer for the good of others until they learned wisdom in the school of experience.

CHAPTER XV.

THE one thing that troubled Si Klegg more than everything else during the first few weeks of his service in the army was his appetite. It was a very robust, healthy one that Si had, for he had never known what it was to be hungry without abundant means at hand to satisfy his cravings. His mother's cupboard was never in the condition of Old Mother Hubbard's, described in the nursery rhyme. His flourishing state at the time he enlisted showed that he had been well fed, and that nature had made good use of the ample daily supplies that were provided. His digestive organs were kept in perfect condition by constant exercise.

During the short time that the 200th Indiana lay in camp before starting on its first campaign there had been no lack. The toothsome dainties that had been so lavishly provided by the home-folk supplemented the plentiful rations of soft bread, meat, coffee, beans, etc., furnished by the commissary department, and Si enjoyed a continual feast. When he was put on campaign diet he had a hard struggle to bring his rebellious stomach into a state of subjection. He began to realize what it was to suffer for his country.

When the regiment got orders to pull out, Company Q drew several boxes of hardtack that the boys had heard so much about. As the orderly pried open the boxes preparatory to distributing the "staff of life," they gathered around, eager to gratify their curiosity.

"Them looks 's ef they was reel nice—jest like sody crackers. I don't b'lieve the grub 's goin' ter be so bad arter all."

Si said this with a smile of serene satisfaction, as he stood looking at the long rows of crackers standing edgewise.

"Better taste one an' see how ye like it!" said a ragged Indiana veteran who had come over to see the boys of the 200th and hear the latest news from "God's country."

It happened that this lot was one of extra quality as to hardness. The baker's watch had stopped, or he had gone to sleep, and they had been left in the oven or dry-kiln too long. Si took one of them and carried it to his mouth. He first tried to bite it in the same way that he would a quarter section of custard pie, but his incisors made no more

A TEST OF JAW-POWER.

impression upon it than if it had been cast-iron.

"Ye'll have ter b'ar down hard," said the veteran, with a grim smile.

"Je-ru-sa-*lem*!" exclaimed Si, after he had made two or three attempts, equally barren of results.

Then he tried his "back teeth." His molars were in prime order, and his jaw power was sufficient to crack a hickory nut every time. Si crowded one corner of the hardtack as far as he could between his grinders, where he could get a good purchase on it, shut his eyes, and turned on a full head of steam. His teeth and jaws fairly creaked under the strain, but it gave no sign of yielding.

"Ef that ain't old pizen!" he said. "It beats anything I ever seen up in the Wabash country."

But his blood was up, and laying the cracker upon a log, he brought the butt of his gun down upon it with the force of a sledge-hammer.

"I thought I'd fix ye," he said, as he picked up the fragments and tried his teeth upon the smaller ones. After chewing upon them for two or three minutes he felt qualified to give a just verdict.

"Wall — I'll — be — durned! I didn't spose I'd got ter live on sich low-down fodder 's that. The guvyment must think I'm a grist-mill. I'd jest 's soon be a billy-goat 'n' eat circus-posters 'n' tomater-cans 'n' old hoopskirts."

THE LAST RESORT.

"Ye'll get used to 't arter a while, same 's we did," said the veteran. "Ye'll see the time when ye'll be mighty glad to get as hard a tack as that!"

Si's heart sank almost into his shoes at the prospect, for the taste of his mother's pie and Annabel's fruit cake were yet fresh in his mouth. But he was fully bent on being a loyal and obedient soldier, determined to make the best of everything, without any more "kicking" than was the inalienable right of every man who wore a uniform.

Si went to bed hungry the first night of the march, an affliction he had never before suffered. Impelled by the gnawings of his appetite he made repeated assaults upon the hardtack, but the result was wholly insufficient to satisfy the longings of his stomach. Before going to bed he began to exercise his ingenuity on various schemes to reduce the hardtack to a condition in which it would be more gratifying to his taste and better suited to the means

with which nature had provided him for digesting his rations. Naturally Si thought that soaking in water would have a beneficial effect. So he laid five or six of them in the bottom of his frying-pan, anchored them down with a stone, and covered them with water.

He felt a little blue as he lay curled up under his blanket. He thought some about his mother and sister Maria and pretty Annabel, but he thought a good deal more about the beef

THE EFFECT OF "GETTING USED TO IT."

and potatoes, the pies and the puddings, that were so plentifully spread upon the table at home. While he was thinking it over, before he went to sleep, there came to his mind uses to which it seemed to him the hardtack might be put, which would be much more consistent with its nature than to palm it off on the soldiers as alleged food. He believed he could now understand why, when he enlisted, the doctor examined his teeth so carefully, as if he was going to buy him for a mule. He had been told that it was necessary to have good teeth in order to bite "catridges" successfully, but now he knew it was with reference to his ability to eat hardtack.

Si didn't want to be killed if he could help it. While he was lying there he thought what a good thing it would be to line one of his shirts with army crackers, and put that on whenever there was going to be a fight. He didn't believe the bullets would go through them. He wanted to do all he could toward paralyzing the rebels, and with such a protection he could be very brave, while his comrades were being mowed down around him. The idea of having such a shirt struck Si as being a brilliant one. The peddler's patent breastplate would be nothing to it.

Then he thought hardtack would be excellent for half-soling his shoes. He didn't think they would ever wear out. If he ran short of ammunition he could ram pieces of hardtack into his gun, and he had no doubt they would do terrible execution in the ranks of the enemy.

All these things, and many more, Si thought of, until finally he was lost in sleep. Then he dreamed that somebody was trying to cram stones down his throat.

In the morning Si went to look after the crackers he had put to soak the night before. He thought he had never felt so hungry in his life. He fished them out and carefully inspected them, to note the result of the submerging and to figure out the chances on his much-needed breakfast.

It would be unnecessary to describe to any old soldier the condition in which Si found those crackers. For the information of any who never soaked a hardtack it may be said that they were transformed, to all appearances, into sole-leather. They were flexible, but as tough as the hide that was

> "Found in the vat when the tanner died."

Si tried to bite off a piece to see what it was like, but he couldn't get his teeth through it. In sheer desperation he laid it on a log, drew his Sunday school bowie-knife, and chopped off a corner. He put it in his mouth, but found it as tasteless as cold codfish.

He thought he would try the frying pan. He cut the hardtack into bits, put in some water and two or three slices of bacon, sifted over the mixture a little salt and pepper, and then gave it a thorough frying. His spirits rose during the gradual development of this scheme, as it seemed to offer a good prospect for his morning meal. When it came to the eating, he found it good, comparatively speaking, though it was very much like a dish compounded of the sweepings from around a shoemaker's bench. A good appetite was indispensable to a real enjoyment of it, but Si had the appetite, and he ate it with a thankful heart.

"I thought I'd get the bulge on them things some way er ruther," said Si, as he drank the last of his coffee and arose from his meal, feeling like a giant refreshed with new wine.

For the next two or three months Si largely devoted his surplus energies to further experimenting with the hardtack. He applied every conceivable process of cookery he could think of, that was possible with the outfit at his command in the way of utensils and materials. Nearly all of his patient and persevering efforts resulted only in vexation of spirit. He continued to eat hardtack from day to day, in various forms, but it was only because he had to do it—it was that or nothing.

Si's chronic aversion to the hardtack was not fully overcome until he went through another "experience." It fell upon a day that the line of communication was broken by the enemy and the cracker supply was cut off. The commissary happened to have a lot of flour on hand, and this was issued to the men for a week.

"That 'll be tip-top," Si said to Shorty.

"How ye goin' ter cook it?" asked Shorty.

Si had not thought as far as that. At the moment he only remembered the delicious bread and biscuit that his mother and sister Maria used to make. It did not occur to him, until suggested by Shorty's practical question, that in his case both the skill and the means by which so desirable a result could be attained were wholly wanting.

"I guess we kin manage it some way," he said, hopefully.

To get that flour into eatable shape, with the extremely meager facilities at his command, proved a severe strain upon Si's culinary resources. The fearful flapjacks that he made, and the lumps of dough, mixed with cold water and dried on flat stones before the fire, as hard as cannon-balls, wrought sad havoc with his internal arrangements. During that week he was a frequent visitor at the doctor's tent, where he was liberally dosed with blue-mass.

"Ther' ain't nothin' so good as hardtack," said Shorty.

By this time Si thought so too. He had had enough of flour, and hailed with delight the reappearance of the exasperating but wholesome hardtack. The only grumbling he afterward did on this score was when, owing to the exigencies of the service, he could not get as much of it as he wanted. About six months taught him, what all the soldiers learned by experience, that the best way to eat the hardtack was to take it "straight"—just as it came out of the box. When the crackers were extra hard they were softened—a curious fact—by toasting, and in no other way could this be satisfactorily accomplished. The soaking and frying and stewing were but a delusion and a snare.

Early in the war there was a benevolent but Utopian scheme to supply the soldiers with "soft bread" while engaged in active campaigning. Inventive genius produced a great bake-oven on wheels, that could be hauled around and fired up whenever the troops halted. In the goodness of its heart the United States government ordered several hundred of these perambulating ovens, equipped them in gay style with mules and drivers and scientific bakers, and distributed them around, one to each regiment. At first the boys thought they were a great thing, and they were—for the contractor who furnished them. They started out in fine trim and for a few days, when the roads were good, they kept up with the army and turned out loaves by the hundred. The troops were in high feather at the prospect. True, the bread was often sour and sodden, but the new soldiers ate it thankfully, under the mistaken idea that it was better than hardtack. The bread went rapidly from bad to worse. Sometimes the unwieldy machine would stick in the mud and perhaps not reach camp till midnight; or the baker would so far forget his duty to his suffering country as to get drunk, and then there would be no bread, good or bad. With their full rations of flour the soldiers, at such times, had no hardtack to fall back upon, and to avert a disastrous famine they were forced to make such shift as they could by cooking, each for himself, in the most rude and primitive manner. So the pleasing illusion of the traveling bakery was gradually dispelled, and there was a sad awakening from the dream of soft bread. One by one the ponderous vehicles got out of repair, or were capsized and wrecked, or were abandoned as a useless incumbrance. They had wholly disappeared before the 200th Indiana took the field.

Si did not have such serious trouble with that other staple of army diet, which was in fact the inseparable companion and complement of the hardtack. It took its most popular name from that part of the body of the female swine which is usually nearest the ground. Much of Si's muscle and brawn was due to the fact that meat had always been plenty at home. When he enlisted he was not entirely free from anxiety on the question of meat, for to him it was not even second in importance to bread. If bread was the "staff of life," meat was life itself. It didn't make much difference what kind it was, only so it was meat. He didn't suppose Uncle Sam would keep him supplied with quail on toast and porterhouse steaks all the time, but he did hope he would give him as much as he wanted of something in that line.

"Ye won't git much 'sides pork, 'nless ye're a good forager," said Shorty to him one day, when they were giving the subject thoughtful consideration.

Si thought he might, with practice and a little encouragement, be fairly successful in foraging, but he said he

wouldn't grumble if he could only get plenty of pork. Fortunately for him he had not been imbued with the teachings of the Hebraic dispensation, which declared "unclean" the beast that furnished so much food for the American soldiers.

Before starting on the march, the bacon received by Company Q was of prime quality, and Si thought it would always be so.

THE FLESH OF SWINE.

"I don't see nothin' the matter with sich grub as that!" he said. "Looks to me 's though we was goin' ter live like fightin' cocks."

"Ye're jest a little bit brash," said his veteran friend. "Better eat all ye kin lay yer hands on now, while ye've got a chance. One o' these days ye'll git 'n a tight place 'n' ye won't see 'nough hog's meat in a week ter grease a griddle. I've bin thar, myself! Jest look at me and see what short rations 'll bring ye to."

But Si thought he wouldn't try to cross a bridge till he

got to it, nor lie awake nights worrying over troubles that were yet in the future. He had a philosophical streak in his mental make up, which was a good thing for a soldier. "Sufficient unto the day is the evil thereof," was an excellent rule for him to follow.

So Si assimilated all the pork that fell to his share, with an extra bit now and then from a comrade whose appetite was less vigorous, and thrived under it. No scientific processes of cookery were necessary to prepare it for immediate use. A simple broiling or frying or toasting was all that was required.

Sometimes fresh beef was issued. It is true that the animals slain for the soldiers were not always fat and tender, nor did each of them have four hind-quarters. This last fact was the direct cause of a good deal of inflammation in the 200th Indiana, as in every other regiment. The boys who got sections of the forward part of

A SIMPLE PROCESS.

the "critter," usually about three-quarters bone, always growled, and fired peppery remarks at those who got the juicy steaks from the rear portion of the animal. Then, when *their* turn came for a piece of hind-quarter, the other fellows would grumble. Four-fifths of them generally had to content themselves with a skinny rib or a soup-shank. Si shared the common lot, and did his full quota of grumbling because his "turn" for a slice of steak didn't come every time beef was issued.

The flesh of the swine was comparatively free from this

cause of irritation. It was all alike, and was simply "Hobson's choice." Si remembered, however, the fragrant and delicious fried ham that so often garnished his mother's breakfast table, and sometimes wondered if the hogs slaughtered for the army were all "belly" and no ham, for he never drew any. One day he asked Shorty about it.

"Thunder!" was the answer. "Hams don't grow fer anybody but ossifers!"

"Oh," said Si, "I didn't think o' that. Pity we can't all be ossifers!"

Now and then a few pigs' shoulders were handed around among the boys, but the large proportion of bone they contained was aggravating, and was the cause of much profanity.

There were times when, owing to circumstances which it could not control, the army in the field was put on short rations. Often in these straits bacon was issued that had outlived its usefulness, except, perhaps, for the manufacture of soap. Improperly cured, it was strong and rancid, and sometimes so

"ALL RIGHT, BOSS, DAT'S A GO."

near a condition of putrefaction that the stench from it offended the nostrils of the whole camp. At other times it was full of "skippers," that tunneled their way through and through it and grew fat with riotous living. Si in time reached the point where he could eat almost anything, but he drew the line at putrid and maggoty meat. Whenever he got any of this he would trade it off to the darkies for chickens.

By a gradual process of development his palate became so educated that he could eat his fat pork perfectly raw. During a brief halt when on the march he would squat in a fence corner, go down into his haversack for supplies, cut a slice of bacon, lay it on a hardtack, and munch them with a keen relish.

Not less indispensable to the soldier than either of the articles already mentioned was coffee. If he had a reasonable supply of these three the veteran was satisfied, even though for weeks at a time he got nothing else. It would be difficult to decide which he prized most; but it is safe to say that if forced to strike one of them from the bill of fare, not one in a hundred would have marked out coffee. If hardtack or bacon ran short, it could be eked out with odds and ends picked up by foraging, but there was nothing to take the place of coffee. It was an elixir to the weary body and drooping spirit after a fatiguing march; it warmed the soldier into new life when soaked by drenching rains or chilled by winter's cold. There was usually sugar enough to sweeten the draught, but if this ran out it made little difference. The men soon learned to drink it without any "trimmings." The refreshing and invigorating effect that made it more than drink was the same, though the taste was not pampered by sugar and milk. The latter was only seen at rare intervals, and by a fortunate few. Cows were never plenty in the South, and the ravages of war for two or three years made them exceedingly scarce. Now and then a forager filled his canteen with milk, and a dash of it in the coffee-cups of his comrades gave to the beverage a doubly delicious flavor. Occasionally a can of "condensed milk" was recklessly bought of the sutler, at the price of a week's wages.

As a general thing, coffee was issued to the army roasted, but unground. This was the most convenient form for transportation in sacks or barrrels. More than that, it insured to the soldier the genuine article. Had ground coffee been furnished, the virtue of the contractors would hardly have been proof against the temptation to put money in their pockets by liberal adulteration. Whatever strength it had would soon have wasted by evaporation. So it was sent down in the berry, by the hundred thousand pounds, and the bayonet and tin-cup served for crushing purposes.

Foraging never yielded coffee, because during the war the people of the "Confederacy" had none to speak of. They were always eager to get it in the way of "dicker." When the Union soldiers drew full rations they often had more coffee than they needed, and with the surplus they could buy whatever anybody had to sell. Chiccory, peas and even beans were used for the Confederate army, as very poor and stale substitutes. During brief periods of "grace, mercy and peace" between the hostile pickets, commercial relations were often established. The men in gray gladly exchanged tobacco, of which they had plenty, for coffee. The former was often scarce among the chewers and smokers in the Union army, and such a barter was equally satisfactory to both.

Another beverage that used to cheer but not inebriate, was bean-soup. The army bean will be remembered to the end of life's longest span as one of the features of the war period. It was not that the beans which found their way to the front were radically different from contemporaneous beans, or from those of the present day—it was the cooking and its results that caused the bean to be so deeply imbedded in the soldier's memory. It will readily be admitted that beans skillfully baked and flavored on the Boston plan are seductive, wholesome and nutritious. It may be charitably believed that whoever gave the flatulent bean a place in the army ration was deluded with the New England idea. Owing to the lack of facilities for cooking, however, particularly during active campaigns, it proved a vexatious disappointment. Soldiers lying long in camp were partially successful in their prolonged struggle with the bean. In some cases ovens were built that yielded satisfactory returns. But soup was the almost universal form in which the bean was prepared. And *such* soup as most of it was! If a camp-kettle could be had it was usually made in a wholesale way to supply a mess or an entire company. The men took their turns at such kinds of cooking, and there were as many radically different varieties of bean-soup as there were men to make it. No two of them ever tasted alike, and it was hard to tell which was the worst. It was not more than half cooked, or else it was burnt; it was as thick as pudding, or the ratio of water to beans was so large as to make it pitifully feeble; it was either salty enough to pickle pork in, or the cook that day had forgotten to season it at all; one cook poured in vinegar to suit his own erratic taste and spoiled it for everybody else; one didn't put in any pork, while another boiled so much grease into the soup that it could be taken into few stomachs with safety. So it was that a kettle of bean-soup rarely failed to set everybody to grumbling. As the men filed past and dipped their cups into the kettle, they turned up their noses and sniffed contemptuously and indulged the most pointed remarks reflecting upon the skill of the cook who had made such a mess. During the weeks and months of marching and fighting the bean fell into disuse. It was "every man for himself," and if beans were issued at all—which was not often—each man was forced to put his little handful into his coffee-kettle and make his own soup. One disadvantage of this necessity was that if the soup did not suit him he was deprived of the pleasure of grumbling at somebody else. If, at such times, rations were short the soldier contrived some way to utilize his beans; if he had plenty of other food he threw them away.

Rice was issued at stated periods when the proper connections were kept up and things ran smoothly. It was a healthy article of diet, but the cooking caused almost as much tribulation as in the case of the bean. An inexperienced hand, ignorant of its habit of "swelling," would fill his kettle with rice and hang it over the fire. Pretty soon it would begin to flow over the top and down the sides of the kettle like the eruption of a volcano, while the amateur cook looked on in amazement.

The pungent and tear-starting onion was a favorite esculent. Few of them found their way to the front, however, till the last year or two of the war, when thousands of barrels were sent to the soldiers by the sanitary commission. The doctors said they were good to prevent scurvy. They were not a part of the ration furnished by the government. Onions were seized with avidity and eaten, generally raw, with a keen zest.

In the fall of 1863 the soldiers in the field began to receive queer looking slabs about a foot square and an inch thick. The many colors and shapes of their component parts gave them much the appearance of the modern "crazy quilt." At first they were a stubborn conundrum to the boys, who, after a critical inspection with eye and nose, concluded they must be some new style of forage for the mules. They were "desiccated vegetables," for the human stomach. They contained a little of almost everything in the vegetable world—potatoes, corn, cabbage, beets, carrots, parsnips, onions, peppers, etc., to the end of the list, together with what seemed to be cornstalks, potato-tops and pea-vines. The ingredients were cut into slices and mixed with the utmost impartiality. They were pressed by steam or hydraulic power into cakes of the size described, and thoroughly dried. In this form they would "keep" for an indefinite time. Every drop of juice was squeezed or evaporated out of them, so that there was little left except the fiber. The veterans made no end of sport of the motley mixture. . Its scientific name was immediately changed to "desecrated" or "consecrated" vegetables, and it was rarely called by any other. But they liked the soup it made. This was both palatable and nourishing, and was a most welcome change from the stereotyped fare. It "swelled" in the kettle even more than rice. A cubic inch of the "stuff" would make a quart of soup.

It may interest the reader to give the "ration"—the established daily allowance of food for one person—as provided by the army regulations at that time. It was composed as follows: twelve ounces of pork or bacon or twenty ounces of salt or fresh beef; twenty-two ounces of soft bread or flour, or one pound of hard bread—[hardtack]—or twenty ounces of corn meal; and to every one hundred men fifteen pounds of beans or peas, ten pounds of rice or hominy, eight pounds of roasted coffee, or twenty-four ounces of tea, fifteen pounds of sugar, four quarts of vinegar, twenty ounces of candles, four pounds of soap, four pounds of salt, four ounces of pepper, thirty pounds of potatoes and one quart of molasses. This was the ration as it existed when the war broke out. During the first year, however, evidently to meet the wants of such lusty fellows as Si Klegg, Congress passed an act increasing the allowance of several of the items—notably potatoes, of which each man was to have one pound three times a week, "when practicable." This sounded well, but the condition spoiled it. Rarely indeed was it "practicable" to issue a pound of potatoes once in six months. The only potatoes the soldiers in the field had were those they got by foraging. Tea, as an optional alternative for coffee, did not figure largely in the war. A few nice young men fresh from home called for it, but the veteran spoke of it only with scorn. Tea was too "thin" a beverage on which to put down the rebellion. Most of the less important items in the "ration" were only seen at long intervals during the last or "fighting" year. It was hardtack, bacon and coffee, with sugar and salt for condiments, that furnished the nerve and muscle to carry on the war.

Like all raw soldiers, Si Klegg learned with exceeding great joy, that there was such a person in the army as the sutler. It was usually many weeks—months in some cases—before the new troops could become reconciled to the regulation diet, and this gave the sutler his opportunity. He reaped a rich harvest and made a fortune, provided he had a fair chance at a new regiment for six months. But his business enterprise had its drawbacks. When the army was on the jump he often had a hard time of it. He usually had a couple of large wagons, in which he transported his goods and the big tent that he pitched as often as circumstances would permit. Of course he had to furnish his own teams, and half a dozen men, black and white, to manage them and do his work. He always had to look out for himself and take his own chances. A sutler's wagon was a "bonanza" to a band of rebel "looters," and he often suffered in this way from the capture of his entire outfit. This was, however, but a temporary reverse, for he would mark up the prices on his next load of goods and thus retrieve his loss.

If his wagons stuck in the mud, or his mule-power was insufficient to pull them up a steep hill, the boys might lend a hand to help him out; but if they did they wanted a good share of what he had as compensation for their services. If he demurred they would settle the matter by helping themselves. He was regarded as an Ishmaelite, and every man's hand was against him. If a wagon capsized, the scattered boxes and cans and bottles of eatables and drinkables were deemed legitimate plunder, and a nightly foray upon the "shebang" was considered justifiable larceny. When the soldiers ran out of money the sutler issued "checks," to be redeemed the next pay-day. When a battle intervened, or the hardships of campaigning sent scores to the hospitals, the sutler failed to realize.

Then up would go the prices again, to make good the deficit. The sutler did not like the smell of powder, and when a fight was imminent he prudently stayed behind. When all was quiet again he would crack his whip, push to the front, and open up his seductive stock. The sutler of a full, new regiment sometimes took desperate chances in following it closely, for the money rolled in at a rate most gratifying to that worshiper of mammon. When the paymaster was around he never failed to be there.

CHAPTER XVI.

Si Gets a Letter from Annabel and Answers It under Difficulties.

"ORDERLIES for your mail!" shouted the sergeant-major of the 200th Indiana one afternoon. The regiment had just turned into a tobacco patch to bivouac for the night. It had been marching for a week, and this was the first mail that had caught up with it. During all this time the boys had not heard a word from their mothers, sisters, wives and sweethearts. It was only a fortnight since they left home, but it seemed to them as if they had been gone a year. If Si Klegg had been Robinson Crusoe he could not have felt more lonesome and forsaken.

The eagerness of the soldiers to receive letters could have been equaled only by the anxious watching of those at home for tidings from their loved ones. There was no literature in the army worth mentioning. The men were not long in learning that they could not carry books on their backs. There was nothing in the way of reading matter for those in active service save an occasional volume picked up here or there, or a chance newspaper, generally a week or two old. These circulated among the soldiers until they were literally read to pieces. Correspondence and "keeping diaries" were the means resorted to by thousands to while away hours and days that would otherwise have hung heavily. There was never a lack of "something to write about," although circumstances were often unfavorable. Frequently, for weeks at a time, only the briefest letters were possible. In moments snatched during intervals of respite from duty—in a fence-corner, while resting from the march, or during the "off" hours of guard and picket; under the blazing sun, or in drizzling rain; by the light of a bit of candle stuck in the shank of a bayonet, or the flame of the camp-fire, a vast multitude of messages of affection and friendship were written.

Writing materials were often scarce—sometimes they could not be procured at all. He was fortunate who had pen and ink; generally a pencil was used, going around from one to another until worn out. In times of scarcity odd bits of paper, of every kind and color, were pressed into the service. The envelopes of letters received were "turned" and sent back to Northern homes inclosing missives from the front. The sutlers kept supplies of stationery, which they sold at a profit of about a thousand per cent., but they did not often "show up" during active campaigns. The soldiers could not get far enough to the rear to find them. Postage-stamps were a necessity, for Uncle Sam did not relax his thrifty rule requiring prepayment. At times it was almost impossible to obtain them, and they commanded a high premium. To keep the boys supplied with stationery—or to *try*, at least—was considered to be one of the duties of the chaplains. Few of them had a chance to preach a great deal, so they did not have to spend much time in theological study. Many devoted themselves very faithfully to the temporal comforts of the men; some drew their pay with great promptness, three-fourths of the time far in the rear. The constant demand for stationery was partially met by supplies sent to the soldiers by their friends, but these were freely shared with comrades and soon disappeared.

Great irregularity in the transmission of the mails was unavoidable. When lying quietly in camp, on or near a line of railroad, a daily mail was the rule, with occasional exceptions when a body of the enemy's cavalry swooped down and captured a train, tore up the track, or burned a bridge. In the confusion following a great battle, a week or ten days sometimes elapsed before letters reached the soldiers, or any could be sent by them to relieve the suspense of their friends at home. On the long campaigns, when the army was constantly shifting about, miles from its line of communication, mails rarely averaged oftener than once a week; frequently no letters were received or sent for two or three weeks at a time. Enormous quantities then accumulated, and when opportunity offered were sent to the front by the wagon load and distributed to the various corps, divisions and brigades. Each of these had its postmaster, whose duty it was to attend to the distribution and collection of mail matter. During the last year or two of the war the postal service of the army reached a high state of efficiency, affording to the soldiers every facility that circumstances would permit for communicating with their friends. Efforts to this end were well applied, for nothing contributed more to promote cheerfulness and content among the soldiers.

When the intervals were long, much anxiety and impatience were manifested. Perhaps toward the close of a fatiguing day's march the long-looked-for brigade postmaster was seen on a sprightly mule, galloping beside the toiling column.

"Mail when you git to camp, boys!"

Then what a wild yell went up! How the weary men straightened their backs and stretched away for the halting place! No general was ever received with more tumultuous huzzas than was the brigade postmaster.

Sometimes the mail was taken to the front and distributed to the men as they stood in the trenches. The shouts that greeted the orderlies with their armfuls of letters were enough to make the rebels quake in their shoes. Then if word was passed along the line that the mail would "go out" in a couple of hours, everybody engaged

"MAIL WHEN YOU GIT TO CAMP, BOYS!"

in the quest for writing materials. Hastily they indited their messages, in all conceivable postures—standing, sitting, kneeling or lying flat upon the ground—perhaps now and then dropping the pencil and taking up the musket to fire at a "Johnny" who was getting too free with his bullets. Occasionally a mail was captured by the enemy. Tidings of such a calamity generally prompted the boys to put an extra charge or two of powder into their guns by way of revenge.

Thousands of soldiers had "unknown" correspondents of the tender sex, scattered all over the North, the result of advertising in the newspapers. It may be admitted that under ordinary conditions such a custom ought not to be encouraged, as trenching on dangerous ground; still it is true that in the great majority of cases the correspond-

EPISTOLARY WORK IN THE TRENCHES.

ence of this kind during the war was innocent and harmless. The soldiers in long periods of inaction needed entertainment and occupation, and hundreds of thousands of patriotic and sympathetic young women were ready to aid them through the medium of pen, ink and postage stamps. A single insertion of "Wanted, correspondence" in a largely circulating paper, often brought a shower of two or three dozen dainty missives. To answer them all would keep their recipient busy for a week. No doubt some of these epistolary acquaintanceships matured into the closest and dearest relations when the war was over; though it is not probable that more than one in a hundred gave to such correspondence a thought beyond a passing pleasure, spiced with a flavor of romance. If some of the soldiers secured good wives in this irregular way it was well, for is it not a recognized axiom that "none but the brave deserve the fair?"

Nearly every soldier started out with a firm determination to keep a diary, and began the daily record with commendable zeal. Possibly one in fifty held out faithful to the end. It was easy enough to do it while lying in camp, but on a hard campaign the diary would get so far behind that it was too great a job to bring up the arrears, and the enterprise was very likely to be abandoned in disgust. Another discouraging feature was the fact that the accidents of marching and fighting often caused the loss of diaries. The persistent and methodical diary-keeper wrote concisely in a small book that he carried in his pocket. When it was full he sent it home by mail or by the hand of a comrade, and started a fresh one. Many were lost in transmission, and that man was fortunate who had both the perseverance to "keep up" his diary, and the good luck to lose none of his volumes. If the soldiers had foreseen the uses for such records that have been developed since the war, half a million diaries that died early would have survived.

"Now tumble up here, Company Q, an' git yer letters!" yelled the orderly, as he came down from headquarters.

In the excitement of distributing the mail everything else was forgotten. The boys were all busy getting their suppers, but at the thought of letters from home even the demands of hunger were not considered.

Si left his coffee-pot to tip over into the fire, and his bacon to sizzle in the frying-pan, as he elbowed his way into the crowd that huddled around the orderly.

"If there ain't more 'n one letter for me," he said to him-self, "I hope it'll be from Annabel; but, of course, I'd like to hear from ma and sister Marier, too!"

The orderly, with a big package in his hand, was calling out the names, and as the boys received their letters they scattered through the camp, squatting about on rails or on the ground, devouring with the greatest eagerness the welcome messages from home. The camp looked as if there had been a snow storm.

Si waited anxiously to hear his name called, as the pile of letters rapidly grew smaller, and began to think he was going to get left.

"Josiah Klegg!" at length shouted the orderly, as he held out two letters. Si snatched them from his hand, went off by himself and sat down on a log.

He looked at his letters and saw that one of them was ad-dressed in a pretty hand.

SI'S FIRST LETTER.

He had never received a letter from Annabel before, but he "felt it in his bones" that this one was from her. He glanced around to be certain nobody was looking at him, and gently broke the seal, while a ruddy glow over-spread his beardless cheeks. But he was secure from observation, as everybody else was similarly intent.

"Deer Si," the letter began. He didn't have to turn over to the bottom of the last page to know what name he would find there. He read those words over and over a dozen times, and they set his nerves tingling clear **down** to his toe-nails. Si forgot his aches and blisters as he read on through those delicious lines.

She wrote how anxious she was to hear from him, and how cruel it was of him not to write to her real often; how she lay awake nights thinking about him down among those awful rebels; how she supposed that by this time he must be full of bullet holes; and didn't he get hungry sometimes, and wasn't it about time for him to get a furlough? how it was just too mean for anything that those men down South had to get up a war; how proud she was of Si, because he had 'listed, and how she watched the newspapers every day to see something about him; how she wondered how many rebels he had killed, and if he had captured any batteries yet—she said she didn't quite know what batteries were, but she read a good deal about capturing 'em, and she supposed it was something all the soldiers did; how she hoped he wouldn't forget her, and she'd like to see how he looked now that he was a real soldier, and her father had sold the old "mooley" cow, and Sally Perkins was engaged to Jim Johnson, who had stayed at home, but as for herself *she* wouldn't have anybody but a soldier about the size of Si, and 'Squire Jones's son had been trying to shine up to her and cut Si out, but she sent him off with a flea in his ear—"Yours till deth, Annabel."

There was a postscript, as a matter of course; no truly patriotic young woman during the whole war ever wrote a letter to her soldier-lover without one. This contained an irregular diagram intended as an unsatisfactory sub- stitute for a kiss. She wrote that if he did not know what that meant she would explain it to him when he got home. Si was not versed in the subtleties of amatory correspond- ence, and the diagram was a serious conundrum to him. Once he thought he would ask Shorty about it, and then he concluded on the whole, he had better not.

The fact that there was a word misspelt now and then did not detract in the least from the letter, so pleasing to Si. In fact, he was a little lame in orthography himself, so that he had neither the ability nor the disposition to scan Annabel's pages with a critic's eye. He was happy, and as he began to cast about for his supper he even viewed with complacence his bacon burned to a crisp and his capsized coffee-pot helplessly melting away in the fire.

"Well, Si, what does she say?" said one of his comrades.

"What does *who* say?" replied Si, getting red in the face, and bristling up and trying to assume an air of indifference.

"Just look here now, Si, ye can't play that on me. How about that rosy-cheeked gal up in Injianny?"

It was Si's tender spot. He hadn't got used to that sort of thing yet, and he felt that the emotions that made his heart throb like a saw-mill were too sacred to be trifled with. Acting upon a sudden impulse he

ANOTHER CASE OF DISCIPLINE.

smote his comrade fairly between the eyes, felling him to the ground.

The orderly, who happened to be near, took Si by the ear and marched him up to the captain's quarters.

"Have him carry a rail in front of my tent for an hour!" thundered the captain. "Don't let it be a splinter, either; pick out a good heavy one."

The order was carried out immediately. It was **very**

mortifying to Si, and he would have been almost heart-broken had he not been comforted by the thought that it was all for Annabel.

As soon as the hour was up and he had eaten supper, he set about answering his letter. When he cleaned out the surplusage from his knapsack, he had hung on to the pretty portfolio that his sister gave him. This was stocked with postage stamps and writing materials, including an assortment of the envelopes of the period, bearing in gaudy colors national emblems, stirring legends, and harrowing scenes of slaughter, all intended to quicken the patriotic emotions and make the breast of the soldier a very volcano of martial ardor.

When Si got out his nice portfolio he found it to be an utter wreck. It had been jammed into a shapeless mass, and, besides this, it had been soaked with rain; paper and envelopes were a pulpy ruin, and the postage stamps were stuck around here and there in the chaos. It was plain that this memento of home had fallen an early victim to the hardships of campaign life.

"It's no use; 'tain't no good!" said Si, sorrowfully, as he tossed the debris into the fire, after vainly endeavoring to save from the wreck enough to write his letter.

Then he went to the sutler—or "skinner," as he was better known—and paid ten cents for a sheet of paper and an envelope, on which were the cheerful words, "It is sweet to die for one's country!" and ten cents more for a 3-cent postage stamp. He borrowed a lead pencil, hunted up a piece of cracker-box, sat down and began his work by the flickering light of the fire.

Deer Annie.

There he stopped, and while he was scratching his head and thinking what he would say next, the orderly came around detailing guards for the night, and directed Klegg to get his traps and report at once for duty.

"It hain't my turn," said Si. "There's Bill Brown, and

Jake Schneider, and Pat Dooley, and a dozen more—I've been on since they have!"

But the orderly did not even deign to reply. Si's shoulder still ached from the rail he had carried, so he quietly folded up his paper and took his place with the detail.

The next morning the army moved early, and Si had no chance to resume his letter. As soon as the regiment halted, after an eighteen mile march, he tackled it again. This time nothing better offered in the way of a writing-desk than a tin plate, which he placed face downward upon his knee. Thus pro-vided, Si plunged briskly into the job before him, with the following result:

I now take my pen in hand to let you no that I am well, except the dog-goned blisters on my feet, and I hope these few lines may find you enjoyin the same blessins.

Si thought this was neat and a good start for his letter. Just as he had caught an idea for the next sentence a few scattering shots were heard on the

"SIT STILL, PLEASE."

picket-line, and in an instant the camp was in commotion. Cries of "Fall in!" "Be lively, men!" were heard in every direction.

Si sprang as if he had received a galvanic shock, cramming the letter into his pocket. Of course there wasn't any fight. It was only one of the scares that formed so large a part of the early campaigns. But it spoiled Si's letter-writing for the time.

It was nearly a week before he got his letter done. He wrote part of it using for a desk the back of a comrade who was sitting asleep by the fire. He worked at it whenever he could catch a few minutes between the marches and the numerous details for duty. He said to Annie:

Bein a soljer aint quite what they crack it up to be when they're gittin a fellow to enlist. It's mity rough, and you'd better believe it. You ought to be glad you're a gurl and don't haf to go. I wish't I was a gurl, sometimes. I haven't kild enny rebbles yet. I haint even seen one except a fiew raskils that was tuk in by the critter soljers, they calls em cavilry Me and all the rest of the boys wants to hav a fite, but it looks like the Ginral was afeard, and we don't git no chance. I axed the Ordly couldn't he get me a furlow. The Ordly jest laft and says to me, Si, says he, yer don't know as much as a mule. I made one of the boys see stars tother night because he was a-talkin 'bout you. The Captn made me walk up and down for a hour with a big rail on my sholeder. You tell Square Joneses boy that he haint got sand enuff to jine the army, and if he dont keep away from you Ile bust his eer when I git home, if I ever do. Whattle you do if I shouldn't never see you agin? But you no this 'glorus Govyment must be pertected, and the bully Stars and Strips must flote, and your Si is goin to help do it.

My pen is poor my ink is pale
My luv for you shall never fale.
Yours affeckshnitly,

Si Klegg.

CHAPTER XVII.

In Which Si's Cherished Desire to Drive a Mule Team is Fully Satisfied.

"I'VE got to have a man to drive the colonel's team for a few days," said the orderly of Company Q one morning at roll-call. "The teamster's sick, and he's got to go to the hospital to-day."

He didn't tell the boys what ailed the teamster, thinking, perhaps, that if he did no one would want to take his place. The fact was that the heels of the "off-wheeler" caught the teamster in the pit of the stomach and doubled him up so badly that he wouldn't be fit for duty for a week. It was worse than the colic.

"'Tisn't everybody," continued the orderly, "that's gifted with fust-class talent fer drivin' team. I'd like to find the best man to steer them animals, an' if there's a real scientific mule-whacker in this comp'ny let him speak up, and I'll detail him right off. It'll be a soft thing fer somebody; them mules are daisies!"

Somehow they didn't all speak at once. The regiment had only had its teams two or three weeks, but the boys were not dull of hearing, and ominous sounds had come to them from the rear of the camp at all hours of the night—the maddening "Yee-haw-w-w!" of the long eared brutes, and the frantic ejaculations of the teamsters, spiced with oaths that would have sent a shudder through "our army in Flanders."

So they did not apply for the vacant saddle with the alacrity that might have been expected, when so good a chance was offered for a soldier to ride and get his traps on a wagon. Whenever an infantryman threw away such an opportunity it is safe to assume that there was some good reason for it.

The motive power of an army wagon usually consisted of six mules. Two large animals, called the "wheelers," one of which the charioteer bestrode, were "hooked" to the wagon. Next were two of medium size, designated in the drivers' parlance as the "swing team." Ahead were two small mules known as the "leaders." These were sometimes called "rabbits," by reason of their diminutive size and great length of ears. The menagerie was "steered" by a single line, fastened to the bit of the "nigh leader." The driver managed the rein with one hand and his whip with the other. Practice made him equally adept in the use of both. The whip was a barbarous affair, with a long, stinging lash, that, when there came a hard pull, would fairly singe the quivering flanks of the mules, or crack like a pistol-shot

as the driver snapped it above their heads. A man was
not thought fit to drive a team unless he could, four times
out of five, pick a fly from the ear of a swing mule with
the tip of his lash.

But the tongue of the muleteer was, after all, his chief
reliance as a stimulating force. The whip and rein had
their uses, but when pulling up steep and stony hills,
through miry sloughs and over "corduroy" roads, the
driver brought into play all
his reserve power of lungs,
and the effect was magical.
Without those unearthly
yells and howls, those awful oaths and imprecations,
the supply-trains never
could have reached the

AN ARMY TEAM.

front ; the army
would have starv-
ed to death and
the war have been
a failure.

The idea of riding for a few days and letting his blisters
get well was too much for Si Klegg. Besides, he thought
if there was any one thing he could do better than another
it was driving team. He had been doing it on his father's
farm all his life. He did not think there would be a fight
that day, and so was willing to serve as a substitute for
the charioteer.

"I'm yer man!" he said.

"All right!" said the orderly. "Company, Right—Face! Break ranks—March!"

"There ain't no trouble about it!" Si said to Shorty as they walked back to the tent. "I reckon it's easy 'nough ter manage mules ef ye go at 'em right. It'll be jest fun for me to drive team. And say, Shorty, I'll carry all yer traps on my waggin. That'll be a heap better 'n totin' 'em!"

"Thank'ee, pard," said Shorty, "I'll b'ar it 'n mind ef I gits played out. I reck'n ye'll git 'long 'thout no trouble. It'll give ye a chance ter find out the diff'runce 'tween mules 'n' hosses."

Si gathered up his outfit and started to enter upon his new sphere of usefulness.

"Shall I take my gun 'n' bay'net 'long?" he asked the orderly.

"Guess you'd better; they might come handy!" replied the orderly, as he thought of the regular teamster's disastrous encounter with the "off-wheeler."

After Shorty had eaten his breakfast he thought he would go back of the camp and see how Si was getting on. With thoughtful care Si had fed his mules before appeasing his own appetite, and Shorty found him just waiting for his coffee to cool a bit.

"Why, them 'ere mules is jest 's gentle 'n' peace'ble-like 's so many kittens. Look at 'em, Shorty!" and Si pointed with a proud and gratified air to where the six "daisies" were standing, three on each side of the wagon-pole, with their noses in the feed-box, quietly munching their matutinal rations, and whisking their paint-brush tails about in evident enjoyment.

Indeed, to look at those mules, one who was ignorant of the peculiar characteristics of the species would not have thought that beneath those meek exteriors there were hearts filled with the raging fires of total depravity.

Shorty thought how it would be, but he didn't say any-thing. He was sure that Si would find out all about it.

The brigade to which the 200th Indiana belonged was to march in the rear of the procession that day. This was lucky for Si, as it gave him an hour or two more than he would otherwise have had to get hitched up. But he thought he would begin early, so as to be on hand with his team in good time.

"Want any help?" asked Shorty.

"No," said Si; "I kin hitch 'em up slick 's a whistle. I can't see why they makes sich a fuss 'bout handlin' mules!"

Shorty lighted his cob pipe and sat down on a stump to watch Si. "Kind o' think there'll be a circus!" he said to himself.

Si got up from his coffee and hardtack, and addressed himself to the business of the hour. It proved to be just as much as he could attend to. When he poured half a bushel of corn into the feed-box it was all very nice, and the ani-mals rubbed their heads against him to give expression to their grateful emotions. But when it came to putting on the harness, that was quite a different thing. The mere touch of a strap was enough to arouse into activity all the evil passions of mule nature.

"Now, Pete 'n' Jeff 'n' Susan, we must git ready to pull out!" said Si to his charge, in a familiar, soothing tone, preliminary to getting down to business. It was his evi-dent desire to maintain the friendly relations that he thought he had already established. At the first rattle of the harness Pete and Jeff and the rest, as if with but a single thought, laid back their ears and began to bray, their heels at the same time showing symptons of impatience.

"Whoa, there—whoa!" exclaimed Si, in a conciliatory way, as he advanced with a bridle in his hand toward one of the big wheelers, whose ears were flapping about like the fans of a windmill.

Si imprudently crept up from the rear. A flank movement would have been better. As soon as he got fairly within range the mule winked viciously, lowered his head, and let fly both heels. Si was a spry boy, and a quick dodge saved him from the fate of his predecessor. One of the heels whizzed past his ear with the speed of a cannon ball, caught his hat, and sent it spinning through the air.

Shorty, who was whittling up a piece of Kentucky twist to recharge his pipe, laughed till he rolled off the stump all in a heap. A few of the other boys had strayed out to see the fun, and were lounging around the outskirts of the corral.

"Go for 'em, Si!" they shouted.

Si was plucky, and again advanced, with more caution. This time he was successful, after a spirited engagement, in getting the bridle on. He thought he would ride the animal down to the creek for water,

A CLOSE SHAVE.

and this would give him a chance to get acquainted with him, as it were. He patted his neck, called him pet names, and gently stroked his stubbly mane. Si didn't know then what an utter waste of material it was to give taffy to an army mule.

With a quick spring he vaulted upon the mule's back. He started off in good style, waving his hand exultingly to the boys, with the air of a general who has just won a great battle.

All at once the animal stopped as suddenly as if he had run against a stone wall. He planted his fore feet, throwing his ears back and his head down. There was a simultaneous rear elevation, with the heels at an upward angle of about forty-five degrees. Si went sprawling among the bushes. This performance was greeted with great enthusiasm by the fast-increasing crowd of spectators.

Si's temper began to show signs of fermentation. He had hung on to the bridle-rein, and after addressing a few impressive words to the obstreperous mule, he again leaped upon his back. The mule then took a docile turn, his motive having apparently been merely to show Si what he could do when he took the notion.

"A MAN OVERBOARD."

It would be tedious to follow Si through all the details of "hitching up" that team. He did finally succeed after much strategic effort. The mules brayed and kicked a good deal, and Si's wrath was fully aroused before he got through. He became convinced that soft words were of no account in such a contest, and he enforced discipline by the judicious use of a big club, together with such appropriate language as he could think of. He hadn't learned to swear with that wonderful and appalling proficiency that was so soon acquired by the army teamster.

At last Si climbed into the saddle, as proud as a king. Seizing the long line he shouted, "Git up thar, Pete! G'lang Susan!" and the caravan started.

But those unregenerate brutes didn't go far. Si was

gayly cracking his whip, trying to hit a big blue-bottle fly that was perched on the ear of one of the "swing" mules.

As if by a preconcerted plan, the establishment came to a sudden halt and the mules began to rear and kick and plunge around in a state of riotous insurrection. It didn't take more than a minute for them to get mixed in a hopeless tangle. They were in all conceivable shapes—heads and tails together, crosswise and "every which way," tied up with the straps of the harness. The air in all directions was full of heels. There was a wild chorus of discordant braying.

In the course of the scrimmage Si found himself on the ground. Gathering himself up, he gazed in utter amazement at the twisted, writhing mass. At this moment a message came from the colonel to "hurry up that team," and poor Si didn't know what to do. He wished he could only talk like the old mule drivers. He thought it would make him feel better. There was no one to help him out of his dilemma, as the members of the company were all getting ready for the march.

A veteran teamster happened along that way, took in the situation at a glance, and volunteered his assistance.

"Here, young feller," said he, "Lemme show ye how to take the stiffenin' out o' them ere dod-gasted mules!"

Seizing the whip at the small end of the stock he began laying on right and left with the butt, taking care to keep out of range of the heels. During these exercises he was shouting at the top of his voice words that hissed through the air. Si thought he could smell the brimstone and see the smoke issuing from the old teamster's mouth and nostrils. This is a section of what that experienced mule-driver said, as nearly as types can express it:

"—— ——!! —— —— ——!!!***†††!!!!—— ???——— — *†‡!!!!"

Si thanked the veteran for these timely suggestions in the

way of language, and said he would remember them. **He** had no doubt they would help him out next time.

They finally got the team untied, and Si drove over to headquarters. The regiment had been gone some time, a detail having been left to load the wagon. After getting out upon the road the mules plodded along without objection, and Si got on famously. But having lost his place in the column in consequence of the delay, he was obliged to fall in rear of the division train, and it was noon before he got well started.

TOTAL DEPRAVITY.

Along toward evening Si struck a section of old corduroy road through a piece of swamp. The passage of the artillery and wagons had left it in a wretched condition. The logs were lying at all points of the compass, or drifting about in the mire, while here and there were seas of water and pits of abysmal depth.

To make the story short, Si's mules stumbled and floundered and kicked, while he laid on with the whip and used some of the words he had learned from the old teamster before starting.

At length the wagon became hopelessly stalled. The wheels sank to the hubs, and Si yelled and cracked his whip in vain. Perhaps if he had had the old teamster there to talk for him he could have pulled through, but as it was he gave it up, dismounted, hunted a dry spot, and sat down to think.

Just before dark a large detail from the regiment which had been sent back on an exploring expedition for the colonel's team, reached the spot. After hours of prying and pushing and tugging and yelling they at length got the wagon over the slough, reaching camp about midnight.

The colonel was a good deal excited because his wagon was so late in getting up. It contained his mess-chest and he had been compelled to wait for his supper, fain

IN THE SLOUGH.

to stay his hunger by begging a hardtack or two from the boys. He made it very uncomfortable for the amateur teamster.

Early next morning Si went back to the company. "Orderly," said he, "I b'lieve I'd like ter resign my place as mule-driver. It's a nice, soft thing, but I'd jest 's lief let s'm other feller have it, an' I'll take my gun an' go ter hoofin' it agin!"

CHAPTER XVIII.

"SEEMS to me it's 'bout time ter be gittin' into a fight!" said Si Klegg to Shorty one night as they sat around the fire after supper, with their shoes and stockings off, comparing the size and number of their respective blisters. Neither of them had left on their feet much of the skin with which they started out. "I always s'posed," he continued, "that bein' a soljer meant fightin' somebody; and here we are roamin' over the country like a lot o' tramps. I can't see no good in it, nohow!"

"Don't be in a hurry, Si," replied Shorty; "I reck'n we'll ketch it soon 'nough. F'm what I've heern the old soldiers tell, a battle ain't such a funny thing as a feller thinks what don't know nothin' 'bout it. The boys is always hungry at fust for shootin' and bein' shot at, but I've an idee that it sort o' takes away their appetite when they gits one squar' meal of it. They don't hanker arter it no more. It's likely we'll git filled full one o' these days! I'm willin' ter wait!"

"Wall," said Si, "I sh'd think we might have a little squirmish, anyhow. I'd like ter have a chance ter try my gun, 'n' hear what kind of a noise bullets makes. Of course I'd ruther they'd hit some other feller 'sides me, but I'm ready ter take the chances. I don't b'lieve I'd be afeard!"

Si was ambitious, and full of the martial ardor that blazed in the breast of every young volunteer. He was really glad when the orderly came around presently and told them that the 200th Indiana would have the advance next day, and Company Q would be on the skirmish line. He told the boys to see that their cartridge-boxes were all full and their guns in good order, as they would be very likely to run foul of the rebels.

Before Si went to bed he cleaned up his gun and made sure that it would "go off" when he wanted it to. Then he and Shorty crawled under the blankets, and as they lay "spoon fashion," thinking about what might happen the next day, Si said he hoped they would both have "lots of sand."

All night Si was dreaming about awful scenes of slaughter. Before morning he had destroyed a large part of the Confederate army.

It was yet dark when the reveille sounded through the camp. Si and Shorty kicked off the blankets at first blast of bugle, and were quickly in their places for roll-call. Then, almost in a moment, fires were gleaming, and the soldiers gathered around them to prepare their hasty breakfast.

Before the sun was up the bugles rang out again upon the morning air. In quick succession came the "general," the "assembly," and "to the color." The 200th marched out upon the pike, but soon filed off into a cornfield to take its assigned place in the line, for the advance division was to move in order of battle, brigade front, that day.

Moving in line of battle was a very different thing from marching in column on a well-defined road. The former mode of advancing was customary when in the immediate presence of the enemy, to be in readiness for action at any moment. In case of sudden attack, a body of men marching by the flank would almost inevitably be thrown into confusion before it could be formed in order of battle. Sometimes the leading corps of an army, disposed in two or three parallel lines, with a front of a mile or more, marched all day with this formation, directly "across country," through field and wood and bramble patch, leveling every fence in its course, fording streams and swamps, stopping for nothing, except, perhaps, a fortified position of the enemy. A march of this kind was extremely fatiguing, and night found the men with clothing torn and hands and faces bleeding from the effects of bush and brier. During the early hours of the day, when moving through thick underbrush or fields of standing grain wet with the heavy dews of night, the garments of the soldiers became as completely saturated as if they were marching in a rain-storm.

In obedience to orders Company Q moved briskly out and deployed as skirmishers, covering the regimental front. The movement was not a scientific "deployment," for that point in the tactics had not yet been reached; but a few directions enabled the men to spread themselves out in good shape. As the line advanced through field and thicket Si Klegg's heart was not the only one that thumped against the blouse that covered it.

It was not long till a squad of cavalrymen came galloping back, yelling that the rebels were just ahead. The line was halted for a few minutes, while the generals swept the surrounding country with their field-glasses, and took in the situation.

' The skirmishers, for fear of accidents, took advantage of such cover as presented itself. Si and Shorty found themselves to leeward of a large stump.

"D'ye reckon a bullet 'd go through this 'ere stump?" said Si.

Before Shorty could answer, something happened that absorbed their entire attention.

Boom–m–m–m!

"D–d–d'ye hear that?" said Si through his chattering teeth.

"Yes, and there's suthin comin' over this way," replied Shorty.

A shell came screaming and swishing through the air. The young Hoosiers curled around the roots of that stump and flattened themselves out like a pair of griddle-cakes. If it was Si and Shorty that the rebel gunners were after they timed the shell to a second, for it burst with a loud bang just over them. The fragments flew all around, some striking the stump and others tearing up the dirt on every side.

To say that for the moment those two soldiers were demoralized would be drawing it very mildly. They showed unmistakable symptoms of a panic. It seemed as though they would be hopelessly stampeded. Their tongues were paralyzed, and they could only look silently into each other's white faces.

NEARLY A PANIC.

Si was the first to recover himself, although it could hardly be expected that he could get over his scare all at once.

"D–d–did it hit ye, Sh–Shorty?" he said.

"N–no, I guess not; b–b–but ain't it aw–awful, Si? You looked so b–b–bad I th–thought ye was k–k–killed!"

"Who's afeard?" said Si. "I was only skeered of you, Shorty. Brace up, pard! It's all right so 's we ain't hurt. But say, Shorty, does all the bullets do that way?"

"That was a shell a-bustin', Si, 'n' that big noise jest 'fore it was a cannon. I've heerd 't shells was powerful fer skeerin', 'n' I 'low ther' ain't no mistake 'bout it."

"I've read 'bout shells 'n' things," said Si, "but I never heerd one afore. Ef they're all like that un I don't guess

I'm goin' ter like 'em very much. We hain't got no use fer 'em, 'n' I wish they'd keep 'em to theirselves. 'Tain't a fa'r way ter fight, nuther; a feller hain't got no show 'th a muskit agin a cannon 't heaves them things a mile."

Several more shells were sent over, but they exploded to the right and left and in the rear.

"Givin' the rest o' the boys a chance ter smell 'em," said Shorty.

"'Pears to me they'd orter be divided 'round. I ain't no pig, 'n' I'm willin' ter wait t'll it's my turn."

After a brief consultation the generals determined to push on. "Skirmishers—Forward!" was heard along the line.

SI'S FIRST SHOT.

"Come on, Shorty," said Si, and they plunged bravely ahead.

Emerging suddenly from a thick wood, they came upon the rebel skirmishers in full view, posted on the opposite side of a field.

Crack! Crack!—Zip! Zip!

"Guess there's a bee-tree somewhere around here, from the way the bees is buzzin'," said Si.

"'Tain't no bees," replied Shorty, "them's bullets, Si. Nice music, ain't it? Don't ye see the durned galoots over yonder a-shootin' at us?"

Si was not a coward, and he was determined to show that he was not. The shell, a little while before, had taken the starch out of him for a few minutes, but that was nothing to his discredit. Many a seasoned veteran found himself exceedingly limber under such circumstances.

"Let's give the raskils a dose," said he; "the best we've got 'n the shop!"

Suiting the action to the word Si crept up to a fence, thrust his gun between the rails, took good aim and fired. A bullet from the other side of the field made the splinters fly from a rail a foot or two from his head, but he was getting excited now, and he didn't mind it any more than if it had been a paper wad from a pea-shooter.

It makes a great difference with a soldier under fire whether he can take a hand in the game himself, or whether he must lie idle and let the enemy "play it alone."

"Did ye hear him squeal?" said Si, as he dropped upon the ground and began to reload with all his might. "I hit that feller, sure pop! Give 'em pertickler fits, Shorty. We'll show 'em 't the 200th Injianny 's in front to-day!"

"Forward, men!" shouted the officers. "Go right for 'em!"

The skirmishers sprang over the fence and swept across the field at a "double-quick" in the face of a sputtering fire that did little damage. None of them reached the other side any sooner than Si did. The rebels seemed to have found out that the 200th was coming, for they were already on the run, and some of them had started early. Pell-mell through the brush they went, and the blue-blouses after them.

"Halt, there, or I'll blow a hole clean through ye!" yelled Si, as he closed up on a ragged specimen of the Southern Confederacy whose wind had given out. Si thought it would be a tall feather in his hat if he could take a prisoner and march him back.

The "Johnny" gave one glance at his pursuer, hesitated, and was lost. He surrendered at discretion.

"Come 'long with me; ye're my meat!" said Si, his eyes glistening with pleasure and pride. He conducted his prisoner back and delivered him to the colonel.

"Well done, my brave fellow!" said the colonel. "This is a glorious day for the 200th Indiana, and you've taken its first prisoner. What's your name, my boy?"

"Josiah Klegg, sir!" said Si, blushing to the very roots of his hair.

"What company do you belong to?"

"Company Q, sir!" and Si saluted the officer as nicely as he knew how.

"I'll see your captain to-night, Mr. Klegg, and you shall be rewarded for your good conduct. You are the kind of stuff we want for non-commissioned officers, and we must have you promoted. You may now return to your company."

It was the proudest moment of Si's life up to date. He stammered out his thanks to the colonel, and then, throwing his gun up to a right–shoulder–shift, he started off on a canter to rejoin the skirmishers.

The fight was over. It was only the rebel rear-guard making a stand to check the advance of the Union troops, led by the impetuous 200th Indiana. The main body of the Confederate army was getting out of the way as fast as possible.

A GOOD BEGINNING.

That night Si Klegg was the subject of a short conversation between his captain and the colonel. They agreed that Si had behaved very handsomely, and deserved to be promoted.

"Are there any vacancies in your non-commissioned officers?" asked the colonel.

"No," was the reply, "but there ought to be. One of

my corporals skulked back to the rear this morning and crawled into a wagon. I think we had better reduce him to the ranks and appoint Mr. Klegg."

"Do so at once, " said the colonel.

Next morning, when the 200th was drawn up in line, an order was read by the adjutant reducing the skulker and promoting Si to the full rank of corporal, with a few words commending the gallantry of the latter. These orders announcing rewards and punishments were sup- posed to have a salutary effect by inspiring the men to deeds of glory, and as a warning to those who were a little short of "sand."

Si bore his unexpected honors with becoming modesty. The boys of Company Q cheered him on the march that day, shouting and yelling for "Corporal Klegg" with great effusiveness. In the evening, after supper, in spite of his protests, they placed him on a cracker-box mounted on two rails, and four sturdy men carried him around in triumphal state on their shoulders, led by fife and drum, and followed by the members of the company in grotesque procession. It may have been accidental,—possibly it was part of the plan for the celebration—but one of the rails slipped and the new corporal tumbled to the ground in a promiscuous heap, amidst the shouts of his comrades. He was informed that he would be required to "set 'em up" at the first opportunity.

Promotions in the army were celebrated by demonstra- tions of this kind, with every conceivable variation of style, and few who had stripes put on their arms were per- mitted to escape. The solemn awe with which the soldiers at first regarded their commissioned officers gradually melted away, and they, too, had to come in for their share of attention when they stepped up a round in the ladder. When a soldier was commissioned from the ranks he was an especial object of boisterous congratulation; nor was he permitted to wear his shoulder-straps in peace until they had been properly "moistened."

Si hunted up some strips of cloth and needle and thread, went off back of the tent, rammed his bayonet into the ground, stuck a candle in the socket, and, with Shorty's assistance, sewed chevrons on his sleeves.

CORPORAL SI KLEGG.

"Thar," said Shorty, as his comrade put on his decorated blouse, "them stripes 's mighty becomin' to ye, 'n' ye *armed* em, too, fa'r 'n' squar'. I ain't 'shamed ter have ye fer my pard."

Then Si thought of somebody whose heart he hoped would flutter with pleasure to know of his promotion, and before going to bed he wrote a short letter:

DEER ANNIE: I once more take my pen in hand to tell you theres grate news. I'm an ossifer. We had an awful fite yisterdy. I don't know how menny rebbles I kild, but I guess thare was enuff to start a good sized graveyard. I tuk a prizner, too, and the Kurnal says to me bully fer you Mister Klegg, or sumthin to that effeck. This mornin they made me a Corporil, and red it out before the hull rijiment. I guess youd been prowd if you cood a seen me. To-night the boys is hollerin hurraw fer Corporil Klegg all over camp. I aint as big as the Ginrals and sum of the other ossifers, but thars no tellin how hi I'll get in three years.

Rownd is the ring that haint no end,
So is my luv to you my frend.

Yours, same as before,

CORPORIL SI KLEGG.

CHAPTER XIX.*

ONE day just before Si left home with Company Q he was sitting on the sugar barrel in the corner grocery, gnawing a "blind robin," and telling how he thought the war wouldn't last long after the 200th Indiana got down there and took a hand in the game. One of the town boys, who had been a year in the service, had got a bullet through his arm in a skirmish, and was at home on furlough, entered the store and accosted him:

"Hello, Si; goin' for a soljer, ain't ye?"

"You bet!"

"Wall, you'd better b'lieve it's great fun; it's jest a picnic all the time! But say, Si, let's see yer finger-nails!"

"I'd like ter know what finger-nails 's got to do with soljerin'!" said Si. "The 'cruitin' ossifer 'n' the man 't

---

* Before entering upon this chapter the writer is moved to a few words of explanation—he will not say apology. Under ordinary circumstances the "grayback" would be a theme with few attractions for a refined and sensitive reader. Possibly these pages may be scanned by some for whose information it is well to say that the "grayback" was a very large factor in the discomfort of the soldier. In the usual conditions of life the abiding presence of this pestiferous insect might well be considered an evidence of uncleanly habits. In the army it was not so—that is to say, there were times when everybody, from generals down, "had 'em" more or less, and no power on earth could prevent it. To "skip" the subject in these pages would be deemed by the old soldier an unpardonable fault; and the writer believes that any person who will put himself in the place of the soldier may read this chapter without offending his sense of literary propriety.

243

keeps the doctor shop made me shuck myself, 'n' then they 'xamined my teeth, 'n' thumped me in the ribs, 'n' rubbed down my legs, 'n' looked at my hoofs, but they didn't say nothin' 'bout my finger-nails."

"You jest do 's I tell ye; let 'em grow 'n' keep 'em right sharp. Ye'll find plenty o' use fer 'em arter a while, 'n' 'twon't be long, nuther. I know what I'm talkin' 'bout."

Si wondered a good deal what the veteran meant about the finger-nails. He did not even know that there existed in animated nature a certain active and industrious insect which, before he had been in the army a great while, would cause his heart to overflow with gratitude that nature had provided him with nails on his fingers.

If the 200th Indiana had been quartered for a while in long-used barracks, or had pitched its tents in an old camp, Si would very soon have learned the delightful luxury of finger-nails. But the regiment had moved out quickly with the army and always camped on new ground. Under these circumstances the insect to which allusion has been made did not begin its work of devastation with that suddenness that usually marked its attack upon soldiers entering the field.

One afternoon, when a few days out, a regiment of Wisconsin veterans bivouacked next to the 200th. Their strange antics, as they threw off their accouterments, attracted Si's attention.

"Look a' thar," he said to Shorty. "What 'n the name of all the prophets 's them fellers up to?"

"Seems like they was scratchin' theirselves!"

"I s'pose that's on account o' the dust 'n' sweat," said Si.

"It's a mighty sight wuss 'n that!" replied Shorty, who knew more about these things than Si did. "I reckon we'll all be doin' like they are 'fore long."

Si whistled softly as he watched the Wisconsin boys. They were hitching and twisting their shoulders about, evidently enjoying the friction of the clothing upon their skins. There was a general employment of fingers, and often one would be seen getting some other fellow to scratch his back around where he couldn't reach himself. If everybody was too busy to do this for him, he would back up to a tree and rub up and down against the bark.

Life has few pleasures that can equal the sensations of delightful enjoyment produced, in those days when gray-backs were plenty, by rubbing against a tree that nicely fitted the hollow of the back, after throwing off one's "traps" at the end of a day's travel.

Directly the Wisconsin chaps began to scatter into the woods. Si watched them as they got behind the trees and threw off their blouses and shirts. He thought at first that perhaps they were going in swimming, but there was no stream of water at hand large enough to justify this theory in explanation of their partial nudity. As each man sat down, spread his shirt over his knees, and appeared to be intently engaged with eyes and fingers, Si's curiosity was very much excited.

"Looks 's if they wuz all mendin' up their shirts an' sewin' on buttons," said Si. "Guess it's part o' their regular drill, ain't it, Shorty?"

Shorty laughed at Si's ignorant simplicity. He knew what those veterans were doing, and he knew that Si would have to come to it, but he did not want to shock his tender sensibilities by telling him of it.

"Them fellers ain't sewin' on no buttons, Si," he replied, "they're skirmishin'."

"Skirmishin'!" exclaimed Si, opening his eyes very wide. "I hain't seen no signs o' rebils 'round here, 'n' there ain't any shootin' goin' on, 'nless I've lost my hearin'. It's the funniest skirmishin' I ever heern tell of!"

"Now, don't ax me nuthin' more 'bout it, Si," said Shorty. "All I'm goin' to tell ye is that the longer ye live the more ye'll find things out. Let's flax 'round 'n' git supper!"

A little while after, as Si was squatting on the ground holding the frying-pan over the fire, he saw a strange insect vaguely wandering about on the sleeve of his blouse. It seemed to be looking for something, and Si became interested as he watched it traveling up and down his arm. He had never seen one like it before, and had a desire to know what it was. He would have asked Shorty, but his comrade had gone to the spring for water. Casting his eye around he saw the first lieutenant, who chanced to be

sauntering through the camp. The lieutenant had been the principal of a seminary, and at home was looked upon by the simple villagers as a man who knew about all that was worth knowing. Si thought he might be able to tell him something of the harmless-looking little stranger. So he put down his frying-pan and stepped

A LESSON IN NATURAL HISTORY.

up to the officer, holding out his arm and keeping his eye on the insect so that it should not get away.

"Good evenin', Lieutenant!" said Si, touching his hat.

"Good evening, Corporal Klegg," said the officer, returning the salute.

"Look a-here, pard," said Si, familiarly, forgetting in the interest he felt in the subject of inquiry the chasm of rank that yawned between them, "you've bin ter collidge, 'n' got filled up with book-l'arnin'; p'raps ye kin tell me what kind o' bug this is. I'm just a little bit curus ter know." And Si pointed to the insect, that was leisurely creeping toward a hole in the elbow of his outer garment.

" Well, Josiah," said the lieutenant, after a brief inspection, "I presume I don't know quite as much as some people think I do; but I guess I can tell you something about that insect. I never had any of them myself, but I've read of them."

"Never had 'em himself!" thought Si. "What 'n the world does he mean?" And Si's big eyes opened with wonder and fear at the thought that whatever it was he had "got 'em."

"I suppose," continued the captain, "you would like to know the scientific name?"

"I reck'n that'll do 's well 's any."

"Well, sir, that is a *Pediculus*. That's a Latin word, but it's his name."

"Purty big name fer sich a leetle bug, ain't it, Perfessor?" observed Si. "Name's big enough for an el'fant er a 'potamus."

"It may seem so, Corporal; but when you get intimately acquainted with him I think you will find that his name isn't any too large for him. There is a good deal more of him than you think."

The young soldier's eyes opened still wider.

"I was going on to tell you," continued the lieutenant, "that there are several kinds of *pediculi*—we don't say *pediculuses*. There is the *pediculus capitis*—Latin again, but it means the kind that lives on the head. I presume when you were a little shaver your mother now and then harrowed your head with a fine-tooth comb?"

"Ya-as" said Si; "she almost took the hide off sometimes, 'n' made me yell like an Injun."

"Now, Mr. Klegg, I don't wish to cause you unnecessary alarm, but I will say that the head insect isn't a circumstance to this one on your arm. As you would express it, perhaps, he can't hold a candle to him. This fellow is the *pediculus corporis !*"

"I s'pose that means they eats up corporals!" said Si, with a terrified glance at the two stripes on his arm.

"I do not think the *pediculus corporis* confines himself exclusively to corporals, as his name might indicate," said the lieutenant, laughing at Si's literal translation and personal application of the word. "He no doubt likes a juicy and succulent corporal, but I don't believe he is any respecter of persons. That's my opinion, from what I've heard about him. It is likely that I will be able to speak more definitely, from experience, after a while. *Corporis* means that he is the kind that pastures on the human body. But there's one thing more about this fellow. They sometimes call him *pediculus vestimenti;* that is because he lives around in the clothing.

"But we don't wear no *vests*," said Si, taking a practical view of this new word; "nothin' but blouses, 'n' pants, 'n' shirts."

"You are too literal, Mr. Klegg. That word means any kind of clothes. But I guess I've told you as much about him as you care to know at present. If you want any more information, after two or three weeks, come and see me again. I think by that time you will not find it necessary to ask any more questions."

Si went back to his cooking, with the *pediculus* still on his arm. He wanted to show it to Shorty. The lieutenant's explanation, with its large words, was a little too much for him. He did not yet clearly comprehend the matter, and as he walked thoughtfully to where Shorty was boiling the coffee he was trying to get through his head what it all meant.

"Hello, Si," said Shorty; "whar ye bin? What d'ye mean, goin' off 'n' leavin' yer meat half done?"

"Sh-h!" replied Si. "Ye needn't git yer back up about it. Been talkin' to the leftenant, Shorty; look at that 'ere bug!" And Si pointed to the subject of the officer's lecture on natural history that was still creeping on his arm. Shorty slapped his thigh and burst into a loud laugh.

"Was *that* what ye went to see him 'bout?" he asked as soon as he could speak.

"Why—ya-as," replied Si, surprised at Shorty's unseemly levity. "I saw that thing crawlin' 'round, 'n' I was a-wonderin' what it was, fer I never seen one afore. I knowed the leftenant was a scholard 'n' a perfesser, 'n' all that, 'n' I 'lowed he c'd tell me 'bout it. So I went 'n' axed him."

"What 'd he tell ye?"

"He told me lots o' big, heathenish words, 'n' said this bug was a *ridiculus*, er suthin' like that."

"'Diculus be blowed!" said Shorty. "The ole man was a-stuffin' of ye. I'll tell ye what that is, Si," he added solemnly, "that's a grayback!"

"A grayback!" said Si. "I've hearn 'em call the Johnnies, graybacks, but I didn't know 's there was any other kind."

"I reck'n twon't be long, now, t'll yer catches on ter the meanin' of what a grayback is. Ye'll know all 'bout it purty sudden. This ain't the fust one *I* ever seen."

Si was impressed, as he often had been before, by Shorty's superior wisdom and experience.

"See here, Si," Shorty continued, as his eye suddenly lighted up with a brilliant thought, "I guess I kin make ye understand what a grayback is. What d'ye call that coat ye've got on?"

"Why, that's a fool question; it's a blouse, o' course!"

"Jesso!" said Shorty. "Now, knock off the fust letter o' that word, 'n' see what ye got left!"

Si looked at Shorty as if he thought his conundrums were an indication of approaching idiocy. Then he said, half to himself:

"Let's see! Blouse—blouse—take off the fust letter, that's

'b'—'n' she spells l-o-u-s-e, louse. Great Jemimy, Shorty, is that a louse?"

"That's jest the size of it, Si. Ye'll have millions on 'em 'fore the war's over 'f they don't hurry up the cakes."

Si looked as if he would like to dig a hole and get into it and have Shorty cover him up.

"Why didn't the leftenant tell me 'twas that? He said suthin' about *ridiculus corporalis*, and I thought he was makin' fun o' *me*. He said these bugs liked to eat nice, fat corporals."

"I reck'n that's so," replied Shorty; "but they likes other people jest as well—even a skinny feller like me. They lunches off'n privits, 'n' corp'rils, 'n' kurnals, 'n' gin'rals, all the same. They ain't satisfied with three square meals a day, nuther; they jest eats right along all the time 'tween reg'lar meals. They allus gits hungry in the night, too, and chaws a feller up while he's asleep. They don't give ye no show at all. I rayther think the graybacks likes the ossifers best if they could have their ch'ice, 'cause they's fatter 'n the privits; they gits better grub."

Si fairly turned pale as he contemplated the picture so graphically presented by Shorty. The latter's explanation was far more effectual in letting the light in upon Si's mind than the scientific disquisition of the "perfesser." He had now a pretty clear idea of what a "grayback" was. Whatever he lacked to make his knowledge complete was soon supplied in the regular way. But Si was deeply grieved and shocked at what Shorty had told him.

"Shorty," he said, with a sadness in his tone that would almost have moved a mule to tears, "who'd a-thought I'd ever git as low down 's this, to have them pesky graybacks, 's ye call 'em, crawlin' over me. How mother 'd feel if she knew about 'em. She wouldn't sleep a wink fer a month?"

"Ye'll have ter come to it, Si. All the soljers does, from the major-gin'rals down to the tail-end o' the mule-whack-ers. Ye mind them 'Sconsin chaps we was lookin' at a little bit ago?"

"Yes," said Si.

"Wall, graybacks was what ailed 'em. The fellers with their shirts on their knees was killin' on 'em off. That's what they calls 'skirmishin'.' There's other kinds o' skirmishin' besides fightin' rebels! We'd better git rid o' that one on yer arm, ef he hain't got inside a-ready; then ther'll be one less on 'em; but ef ye don't watch out ther'll be a thousan' comin' ter the fun'ral!"

Si found him after a short search, and proposed to get a chip, carry him to the fire and throw him in.

"Naw!" said Shorty in disgust, "that's no way. Lemme show ye how!"

Shorty placed one thumb-nail on each side of the insect. There was a quick pressure, a snap like the crack of a percussion cap, and all was over.

Si shuddered, and wondered if he could

PRACTICAL INSTRUCTION.

ever engage in such a work of slaughter.

"D'ye s'pose," he said to Shorty, "that there's any more of 'em on me?" And he began to hitch his shoulders about, and to feel a desire to put his fingers to active use.

"Shouldn't wonder," replied Shorty. "Mebbe I've got 'em, too. Let's go out 'n' do a little skirmishin' ourselves."

"We'd better go off a good ways," said Si, "so the boys won't see us."

"You're too nice and pertickler for a soljer, Si. They'll all be doin' it, even the cap'n himself, by termorrer er nex' day"

They went out back of the camp, where Si insisted on getting behind the largest tree he could find. Then they sat down and engaged in that exciting chase of the *pediculus* up and down the seams of their garments, so familiar to all who wore either the blue or the gray. Thousands of nice young men, who are now preachers and doctors and lawyers and statesmen, felt just as badly about it at first as Si did. But they all became very expert in the use of the thumb-nail.

"Shorty," said Si, as they slowly walked back to eat

their supper, which had been neglected in the excitement of the hour, "afore Company Q started ter jine the rijiment a feller 't was home on furlough told me ter let my finger-nails grow long 'n' sharp. He said I'd need 'em. I didn't know what he meant then, but I reck'n I do now."

"SKIRMISHING."

Among the memories of the war few are more vivid than those of the numerous little pests that, of one kind or another, day and night, year in and year out, foraged upon the body of the soldier. In every new locality there seemed to be a fresh assortment of ravenous insects, to cause bodily discomfort and drive away sleep. Bullets and screaming shell were not desirable companions, but as a rule they only came now and then; while the bugs and worms and insects, in every form that flies or creeps, were with the soldier always. Many of them, though annoying, were harmless, while others seemed to have been created for the especial purpose of spoiling men's tempers and getting them into the habit of using bad language.

Every man who marched and scratched will place the *pediculus* at the head of the list, and keep him there. He was everywhere—the soldier's close and intimate companion, in camp and hospital and prison, on the march and the battlefield. The faithful portrait here given represents a robust specimen of this sportive insect. It is of heroic size, having been enlarged twenty times by the aid of a microscope. No doubt the scientific name would be mystifying to most of the veterans of the war, but no practiced eye can fail to recognize in the work of the artist an old acquaintance that was ever present. It would appear not unlikely that the naturalists christened the insect by this sounding name — *pediculus vestimenti* — so that it could be used in any company of polite people with perfect safety, as not one person in a hundred would know what it meant. If doubt

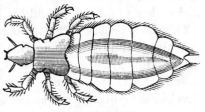

THE PEDICULUS.

[This portrait is many times larger than he really was, but not half as big as he sometimes seemed to be.]

exists in the mind of any respecting the identity of the *pediculus*, it will be removed by the following, from the *American Entomologist*—a magazine in which the wise men tell all they know, or can guess at, about bugs and insects. It says:

This is the species which, during the late war, infested so grievously both Union and rebel soldiers, from whom it received the characteristic name of "grayback."

This is the name that strikes the veteran. It has the old, familiar sound, and there can be no mistake about it. The learned writer goes on to discuss the theme in this way:

The reason that it was so prevalent in the late war was that the soldiers, from the necessities of the service, were unable to wash their clothing as often as they would have done at home, and nineteen times out of twenty had nothing but cold water to wash it in. Now, almost every species of insect will revive after an immersion of several hours in cold water, whereas water of such a temperature that you cannot bear your finger in it for one second will immediately destroy any insect, whatever, that is immersed in it.

One of the great problems of the war was how to get rid of the *pediculus*. It was decidedly a practical question, and personally interested the soldiers far more than those of state sovereignty, confiscation and the negro, which agitated the minds of the statesmen. Probably the intellects of most of the soldiers were exercised far more in planning successful campaigns against the *pediculus* than in thinking about those which were directed against Lee and Jackson and Bragg and Joe Johnston.

This arch enemy of the soldier preyed incessantly upon "Yankee" and rebel alike. But for this fact it might have been imagined that the *pediculus* was a diabolical invention of the enemy, more to be dreaded than Gatling guns, Greek fire or breech-loading rifles. As it was, he feasted and fattened with equal enjoyment upon those who wore the blue and the gray, officer and private. *

Sometimes for weeks the soldiers tramped through heat and dust, night and day, with but very rare opportunities for washing either their clothes or their persons. Water, soap, and leisure time were equally scarce. It was then

---

* During a long midsummer march, the writer saw a robust brigadier-general, who was afterward President of the United States, engaged in hunting the *pediculus*, with his nether garment spread out upon his knees in the popular style. It was just after the army had bivouacked for the night at the end of a hard day's march. The soldiers had no tents, nor anything else to speak of—except graybacks. These were exceedingly numerous and active. The general had wandered out back of his headquarters, and, squatting behind a large tree, applied his energies to the work of "skirmishing," while the setting sun cast a mellow glow over the touching scene. Not far away, behind other big trees, were two of his staff officers similarly engaged—cracking jokes and graybacks.

that the *pediculus* had a prolonged season of sumptuous living. There was little chance for the effective boiling process. When a few afflicted men were so fortunate as to secure the use of a kettle, they wandered about *in puris naturalibus* above the latitude of the waistband, while they crowded the fire and suffered the boiling water to do its purifying work. It was useless to try to drown the insects. In boiling lay the only hope of extermination, and even this gratifying effect was but temporary, for it did not take long to "catch 'em" again. Scalding water also brought to an un-

timely end all the eggs or "nits," thus pre-venting the birth of a new generation to join the marauding forces. Therein lay the advan-tage of hot water over that universal weapon, the thumb-nail, which slew its millions. This was none the less effec-tive as far as it went, but it was a good deal slower, requiring time and patience. The thumb-nail could not

ONE OF LIFE'S PLEASURES.

reach out into the future, as it were, like the foaming camp-kettle, and prematurely cut off myriads yet unborn.

In the southern prisons, where thousands of Union sol-diers were huddled together, with no change of clothing and only the most limited cleansing facilities, the swarms of lice that preyed constantly upon the wretched, starving men, added immeasurably to their sufferings.

It was a source of continual wonder to the soldiers where the countless multitudes of graybacks came from.

A German naturalist has brought his mathematics to bear upon the subject, and finds that two female *pediculi* will in eight weeks become the mothers and grandmothers of a posterity numbering not less than *ten thousand!* Some people might not believe this, but no old soldier will have the slightest doubt of the entire correctness of the statement. Indeed, if the professor had said ten million he could have found a cloud of witnesses ready to sustain him with affidavits.

The second place on the list of pests may be awarded to the mosquito—more familiarly known as the "skeeter." This insect was often quite as numerous as the *pediculus*. In low, damp regions, during warm weather, swarms of these bloodthirsty insects drove the soldiers to the borders of distraction. They came in literal clouds, filling the air, the hum of a million wings swelling in maddening chorus. The naturalists say a mosquito's wings vibrate three thousand times a minute. The soldier who has heard them buzzing in his ears will certify that this is not an overestimate. How many times he found sleep possible only by curling up under his blanket and covering every inch of feet, hands and head, at the imminent risk of being smothered! Sometimes the mosquitoes would not be baffled even in this way, and they would prod their bills through the blanket and pierce their victim. Then he would rush wildly out and heap on the fire something that would make a great smudge. Sitting down in the thickest of the smoke, he would weep and cough and sneeze and strangle and swear—even this deplorable condition being preferable to the torments of the "skeeters." This picture is not overdrawn. Such scenes were common in many localities, from the Chickahominy to the Rio Grande.

The mosquito reached his highest state of physical and carniverous development on the arid plains of Texas. Those who spent the summer and fall months in that forsaken region are fully prepared to defend the affirmative of this proposition. During September and October, in the evening, the visitations were simply appalling. A few of the soldiers had foreseen the impending evil and provided themselves with netting, but to the great mass of them the remembrance of those nights is like a hideous dream. They frequently sat up a good part of the night, their "pup" tents tightly buttoned, and a smudge of weeds and grass within. In addition to this every man had his pipe filled with "navy plug" or "niggerhead," and the viler the tobacco the more effective was the smoke upon the mosquitoes.

The writer one afternoon rode a horse over the prairie, a distance of about ten miles. Before starting he took the precaution to cover his hands with gauntlets, tying them closely around the wrists, and to wind cloths around his head until he looked like a mummy. By the time his destination was reached he and portions of his horse were completely covered with masses of mosquitoes, clinging to one another and hanging in festoons from every point. He avers, with full knowledge of the fate of Ananias for telling a lie, that he could have scraped off four quarts of them from his person and the beast he rode.

The woodtick was worthy of note for his patient industry and the quiet manner in which he fulfilled his mission. He did not make any fuss, like the mosquito, to give warning of his designs and enable his victim to take preventive measures. He had a most persistent way of getting in under one's clothes. When a southern tick made up his mind to have a taste of Yankee, access to the body was not difficult through the holes in the garments left by the tailor, or those resulting from the wear and tear of the service. Then he would look around to find some tender spot, and settle down to his work. The victim was not often aware of his presence until he had burrowed nearly or quite under the skin. He could easily get there in the course of a night, for the tick neither slumbered nor slept. On getting up in the morning the soldier would feel, perhaps on the arm or the fleshy part of the leg, an itching sensation. Applying his hand to the spot, he would detect a small lump that he instinctively felt did not belong there. In fact, after a little experience he would know right away that he "had a woodtick."

The insect's industrious habits made it desirable to muster him out of the Confederate service as soon as possible. There was no telling where he would not plow his way if left free to carry on his little campaign. So the sufferer would

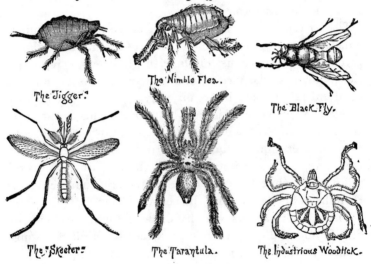

The "Jigger."

The Nimble Flea.

The Black Fly.

The "Skeeter."

The Tarantula.

The Industrious Woodtick.

A FEW OLD ACQUAINTANCES.

at once prepare for an inspection by taking off his shirt or trousers, according to the location of the lump. If it happened to be around where he could not reach it, he would get a comrade to diagnose the case and apply the remedy. If the tick had only his head under the skin, it was not a difficult matter. A grasp with thumb and finger and a quick jerk would separate the blood-distended body from the head, leaving the latter to be removed by a little heroic treatment with a jack-knife. The woodtick never let go, and could not be drawn out any more easily than a fish-hook after it has entered past the barb. He could only be disposed of by pulling him in two and getting rid of him in sections. Occasionally one burrowed so far that the knife of the surgeon was found necessary. The woodtick is not venomous. It is not likely that he ever killed anybody, but he was an unmitigated nuisance.

That exasperating insect commonly known as the "jigger," could make as much trouble for his size as any of the pests that disturbed the peace of mind and body of the soldier. The only redeeming feature about the jigger was that he was confined to certain localities, and did not insist on sticking by and traveling right along with the soldiers, like the vengeful *pediculus*. Whenever they camped where he was, he would do all in his power to make it lively and interesting, but when they rolled up their blankets and moved away, he stayed behind. The jigger dwelt chiefly among the leaves on the ground and in the bark of old logs. If the camp was kept thoroughly policed, there was comparatively little trouble from this source.

The correct orthography of the name, according to the books, is "chigoe." The big dictionaries, however, allow "jigger," and this sounds more natural than the other. The jigger is a very small insect, often not more than half as large as the head of a pin. When the soldiers remem· ber how much he could do, small as he was, toward making life a burden, their hearts are filled with gratitude that the jigger wasn't any bigger. The fact is there were two or three wholly different insects, about equally pestiferous, which were grouped under the convenient name of "jiggers." One of them was of a bright red color, and so small that a person had to look twice to see him. But there was no trouble in feeling him after he had made his way under the skin, causing a keen smarting sensation that—when a man had half a dozen of them at once— would almost drive him frantic. The soldiers often got up in the night and lighted a candle or torch to hunt jiggers.

This category would be incomplete without the nimble flea—the kangaroo of the insect world. The peculiarity of the flea is his jumping propensity, and the consequent difficulty of catching him. In this respect the flea is wiser and smarter than his fellows. Most of the bugs and insects that pester the human family become so absorbed in their biting and blood-sucking that they are wholly oblivious of personal safety. While they are gorging themselves they think of nothing else, till there comes a well-directed slap, and they are no more. But it isn't so with the flea— "put your finger on him and he isn't there." He is a believer in the Hudibrastic theory, that

> He who bites and runs away
> May live to bite another day.

He keeps the danger flag flying when upon his forays, and if his quick eye detects a hostile demonstration he gives one of those jumps that have made his name a proverb.

There are said to be ten distinct varieties of fleas, infesting different animals. The one known as the "human flea," is very fastidious in his tastes. He does not like the flavor of dog or mule, and preys only upon the human race. It is not often that he gets so good a chance as the army afforded him. At some times and places the fleas were exceedingly annoying, infesting clothing, blankets and old straw, biting and hopping around in a way that was most trying to the temper. It was their agility in getting away that made a soldier mad in spite of himself. Even after the lapse of more than twenty years, it is impossible for him to think of the army flea with any degree of calmness.

The "black fly" is scarcely an eighth of an inch in length, but he is gifted with wonderful abilities in the way of annoying man or beast. The soldiers rarely found them in the open country or on high ground, but in the swamps and canebrakes they were terrible. Their peculiar method of torture was to get into the ears and nose—and the mouth, if it was not kept tightly closed—and bore and bite and buzz until the victim was well nigh crazed. Horses and mules were sometimes so beset by countless thousands of these tiny insects, that they became almost unmanageable in their desperate efforts to escape from their tormentors. When circumstances compelled a body of troops to bivouac among the black flies, there was no sleep worth mentioning for anybody.

The repulsive and deadly tarantula is too large to be called an insect and may be classed among reptiles. It is an exaggerated spider, frequently reaching the size of a man's hand. Its bite is venomous and often fatal. Comparatively few of the northern soldiers formed its acquaintance, as it is only found in the extreme southern portion of the United States, and rarely outside of Texas. It lives in the ground and comes out of its hole to wander about in quest of prey. When the camps were thoroughly policed out to the guard-line, the tarantula did not often find his way across the beat. It was common to meet tarantulas when walking over the prairie, but they could always be killed without difficulty. It is well known that copious draughts of whisky are considered an antidote for the bite of a venomous reptile. For a few days after reaching Texas the soldiers worked the tarantula for all it was worth. One of them would prick his foot or hand with a knife, just enough to bring the blood, and then he would start on a wild run for the doctor's tent, shouting that he had been bitten by a "tarantler." The doctor would pour whisky down his throat until he had filled him up, and the man would go away happy. This worked very nicely until the trick was discovered.

CHAPTER XX.

THE chevrons on Si Klegg's arms had raised him several degrees in the estimation of not only himself, but the other members of the company. His conduct in the skirmish had shown that he had in him the material for a good soldier, and even the orderly began to treat him with that respect due to his new rank as one of the "noncommish."

Like every other man who put on the army blue and marched away, "with gay and gallant tread," Si could not tell whether he was going to amount to anything as a soldier until he had gone through the test of being under fire. There were many men who walked very erectly, talked bravely, drilled well, and made a fine appearance on dress parade, before they reached "the front," who wilted at the "zip" of bullets like tender corn blades nipped by an untimely frost. A good many continued in that wilted condition. Some of them wore straps on their shoulders.

It must be confessed that Si was somewhat unduly elated over his achievements as a skirmisher and his success in starting up the steep hill of military rank and fame. It is true it wasn't much of a fight they had that day, but he thought it was pretty fair for a beginning, and enough to prove to both himself and his comrades that he wouldn't be one of the "coffee coolers" when there was business on hand.

262

"Corporal Klegg, you will go on duty to-night with the camp-guard!" said the orderly one evening as the 200th Indiana went into bivouac, a few days after Si had been promoted.

Si responded with ready promptness. He had walked a beat once or twice as a common tramp, and had not found it particularly pleasant, especially in stormy weather; but now he was a peg higher, and he thought as corporal he would have a better time. He had already observed that the rude winds of army life were tempered, if not to the shorn lambs, at least to the officers, in a degree proportionate to their rank. The latter had the first pick of everything, and the men took what was left. The officers always got the softest rails to sleep on, the hardtack that was least infested by worms, the bacon that had the fewest maggots, and the biggest trees in a fight.

"Forward—March!" shouted the officer in command, when the detachment was ready. Si stepped off very proudly, thinking how glad his good old mother and sister Maria and pretty Annabel would be if they could see him at that moment. He was determined to discharge his official duties with rigorous fidelity and make the boys stand around and toe the mark in the most approved manner.

When the guards reached the place selected for headquarters, the officer briefly lectured them in regard to their duties, impressing upon them the necessity of being alert. There was only a thin picket-line between them and the enemy. The safety of the army depended upon the faithfulness of those appointed to watch while others slept. He gave them the countersign, "Bunker Hill," and ordered them under no circumstances to allow any person to pass without giving it, not even the commanding general himself.

Then the "beats" were laid off and numbered, and the guards posted, and as the fast-gathering shadows deepened among the trees the sentinels paced to and fro around the tired army.

For an hour or two after the guards were stationed all was quiet along the line. The noise of the great camp was hushed for the night, and no sound broke the stillness of the gloomy forest. The moon arose and peeped timidly through the branches.

"Corporal of the guard—Beat number six!"

Si's quick ear, as he lay curled up at the foot of a tree, caught these words, rapidly repeated by one sentinel after another. It was his first summons. He sprang to his feet gun in hand, his heart beating at the thought of adventure, and started on the run for "beat number six."

"What's up?" he said to the guard, with a perceptible tremor in his voice.

"There's one o' the boys tryin' to run the guards!" was the answer. "He's been out foragin', I reckon. He's got a lot o' plunder he wants to git into camp with. See him, out there in the bush?"

The forager, for such he proved to be, was nimbly dodging from tree to tree, watching for a chance to cross the line, but the alertness of the guards had thus far kept him outside. He had tried to bribe one or two of the boys by offering to "whack up" if they would let him pass, or give him the countersign so that he could get in at some other point in the cordon. But the guards were incorruptible. They were "fresh" and had not yet learned the scheme of accepting an offered chicken, a juicy section of pig, or a few sweet potatoes, and then walking off to the remote limit of the beat, with eyes to the front, while the forager shot across the line in safety. All this came to them in the fullness of time.

The raider tried in vain to negotiate with Si. Raising his gun to a "ready," the corporal ordered the man to come in or he would put a bullet through him. The best thing to do under the circumstances was to obey. The forager, who belonged to Si's company, crept up to Corporal Klegg and in a conciliatory tone opened a parley.

"You jest lemme in 'n' you may have yer pick o' this stuff," said he, holding up a fowl in one hand and a ham in the other. "It'll be all right, and nobody'll never know nothin' 'bout it!"

Si hesitated; it was an assault upon his weak point. The offer was a tempting one, but he remembered his responsibility to his country, and his stomach appealed in vain. Duty came before stewed chicken or roasted spare-rib.

"Can't do it!" said Si. "Ye've got hold o' the wrong man this time. I ain't goin' to have nobody monkeyin' 'round while I'm corporal o' this 'ere guard. Come 'long 'th me, 'n' step out lively, too!"

Si marched the culprit back and delivered him up to the officer, who commended Si for his fidelity. The officer sent the prisoner to regimental headquarters, and the next day the ground back of the colonel's tent was strewn with feathers, chicken bones, ham rinds and potato skins, while the unlucky forager who had provided the field officers' mess with such a royal meal had to carry a rail for two hours.

An hour later Si had another experience. The captain of Company Q felt a kindly interest, and not a little pride, in him, since the skirmish, and thought he would take a turn that night and see whether his newly-made corporal was "up to snuff."

"Beat number three" was Si's second call. As he approached the guard the latter said:

"Corporal, here's the cap'n, and he wants to *in!* He hain't got the countersign; shall I pass him?"

"Good evening, Corporal!" said the captain, as Si came up, at the same time extending his hand.

Si was thrown completely off his guard. Dropping the butt of his gun carelessly to the ground he replied cheerily,

"Good evenin', Cap'n," touching his hat by way of salute,
Then he took the proffered hand, pleased at the captain's
mark of kindly recognition. He didn't understand the
dark plot against his official integrity.

"How are you getting on, Mr. Klegg?"

"Fust rate!" said Si, with the air of one conscious that
he has done his duty well. "I captured a forager a little
bit ago and took him to headquarters!"

"Well done, Corporal. I have no doubt you will honor
the good name of the 200th Indiana in general, and Company Q in particular.
I got caught outside
to-night, and I want
to get back into camp.
Of course you know
me and it's all right!"

"Certainly, sir!"
said Si, as he stood
leaning on his gun,
and allowed the offi-
cer to pass the magic
line. "Good night,
Cap'n!"

"Good night, Cor-
poral!"

"By the way," said
the captain, retracing

CORPORAL KLEGG GETS CAUGHT.

his steps, "I notice that you do not carry your gun just
right. Let me show you how to handle it!"

Si didn't know what a flagrant offense it was for a soldier on guard to let his gun go out of his hands; nor had
he the faintest suspicion that the captain was "playing
it" on him. So he promptly handed his piece to the officer
who immediately brought it down to a "charge," with the
bayonet at Si's breast.

"Suppose, now, I was a rebel in disguise," said the cap-tain, "what kind of a fix would you be in?"

Light began to dawn upon Si, and he started back in terror at the thought of the mistake he had made.

"Of course, I wouldn't let anybody else have it," he stammered; "but I knowed you, Cap'n!"

"That makes no difference to a man on duty, Corporal. You hang on to your gun the rest of the night, and if any-body—I don't care who it is—insists on your giving it to him, let him have two or three inches of your bayonet. Don't let anybody pass without the countersign, either! Come to my quarters when you are relieved to-morrow."

All this illustrates a way the officers had of testing new soldiers and teaching them a thing or two, when, as was frequently the case, they were not yet up to the mark. A trick of extra duty for the hapless novitiate was generally the penance for his simplicity.

The cold chills ran up and down Si's back as he took his gun and slowly returned to the guard-fire. He felt that he had utterly spoiled his good record.

"Lieutenant," he said to the officer, "I wish ye'd please detail a man to kick me for about an hour!"

The lieutenant wanted to know what the matter was, and Si told him all about it, ending with:

"So now I s'pose Cap 'll yank the stripes off'n my blouse!"

The officer quieted his fears by assuring him that there was no cause for alarm. The captain knew that he was trying to do his duty, and what he had done was for Si's own good.

Si sat down by the fire and was thinking it over when there was another call, "Corporal of the guard!" He was soon at the point indicated, and found two officers on horseback, whom he recognized as the colonel and adju-tant of the 200th Indiana. Si's pard, Shorty, was the guard who had halted them.

"Now, Corporal Klegg," said Si to himself, laying his

finger alongside his nose, "you jest watch out this time. Here's big game! Shouldn't wonder if them ossifers 'd been out skylarkin', 'n' they're tryin' to git in. Don't ye let 'em fool ye 's the cap'n did!'"

Si was right in his surmise. The colonel and adjutant had been enjoying a good supper at a house half a mile

away, and had not the faintest idea what the counter-sign was.

Si was determined not to get caught this time. As he approached, the colonel saw that it was the soldier he had commended for his gallantry at the time of the skirmish.

"Ah, Corporal Klegg, I'm glad to see you so prompt in your duty. I was sure we had made no mistake when we promoted you. Of course, you can see who I am. I'm your

"NOT 'LESS YE SAY 'BUNKER HILL!'"

colonel, and this is the adjutant. We are, unfortunately, outside without the countersign; but you can just let us through."

The "taffy" had no effect upon Si. He brought himself into a hostile attitude, with his bayonet in fair range of the officer, as he replied:

"Colonel, my orders is ter pass no livin' man 'less he says 'Bunker Hill.' I'd be glad ter do ye a good turn, but there's no use talkin'. I'm goin' ter 'bey orders, 'n' ye can't git in here."

The colonel chuckled softly as he dismounted and came up to Si.

"It's all right," he said. "Of course I know what the countersign is. I was only trying you."

"Hold on, there," said Si, "don't come too close. If ye've got the countersign, advance 'n' give it. If ye hain't got it, I'll jest call the ossifer o' the guard!"

Leaning over the point of Si's bayonet the colonel gently whispered "Bunker Hill!"

"Correct!" said Si, and bringing his gun to a "shoulder" he respectfully saluted the colonel. The latter started to remount, but turned back as he said:

"Just let me show you how to hold your gun. You don't——"

"Not ef the court knows herself," said Si, again menacing the colonel with his bayonet. "That's been played on me once to-night, and if anybody does it agin my name ain't Si Klegg!"

"That's right, Corporal," said the colonel, as he sprang into the saddle: "but don't tell anybody what the countersign is again! Good night!"

"Good night, Colonel," said Si, touching his hat.

As the officers rode away Si began to think he had put his foot in it after all. He was confirmed in this opinion by seeing Shorty sit down on a log in a paroxysm of laughter.

"Ye give yerself away *bad* that time!" said Shorty, as soon as he could speak. "What did ye tell him the countersign fer?"

"Whew-w-w-w!" observed Si, with a prolonged whistle. "Shorty," said he, "I wish ye'd take a club and see 'f ye can't pound a little sense into me; I don't b'lieve I've got any!" Without another word he shouldered his gun and returned to the guard headquarters, in a very uncomfortable frame of mind. "Now I'm a goner, sure!" he said to himself.

"Corporal of the guard!" was heard again, sometime after midnight. "If they try any more measly tricks on me to-night somebody 'll git hurt!" thought Si as he walked briskly along the line in response to the call.

This time it was a "contraband"—an old negro, who stood shivering with terror as the guard held him at the point of the bayonet. Recalling the unlucky adventures

of the night, Si imagined that it was one of the officers, who had blackened himself like a minstrel, and had come there purposely to "catch" him.

"Ye can't git through 'nless ye've got the countersign," he said decisively; "and I shan't give it to ye, nuther! And ye needn't try ter show me how ter hold my gun! I kin handle it well enough ter shoot and punch the bay'net!"

SI AND THE CONTRABAND.

"Don' know what dat all means, boss," said the frightened negro; "but fer de good Lawd's sake don't shove dat t'ing frew me. Ise only been ober to de nex' place to er possum roast and Ise jist gwine home. I didn't know dese yer ge-yards was heah!"

Si didn't propose to take any chances, and so he marched the old negro to the guard headquarters and delivered him to the officer, who kept him till daylight, and then suffered him to go his way.

Once more, toward morning, Si was called out, in addition to his tramps with the "reliefs" and the "grand rounds." It was, perhaps, an hour before daylight, and Shorty was the guard who called him. He told Si there was something walking around in the woods, and he believed it was a rebel trying to creep up on them. He had challenged two or three times, but got no answer. The moon had gone down, and in the dark wood objects at any distance could not be distinguished.

"There, d'ye hear that?" said Shorty, as there came a sound of crackling sticks and rustling leaves.

"Halt!" exclaimed Si. "Who comes there?"

There was no response, and Si challenged again, with like result.

"Shorty," said Si, "let's fire, both together," and crack went their muskets.

For a moment there was a great floundering, and then all was still.

A DEAD SHOT.

As soon as it was light, and Shorty was relieved, he and Si went out to see the result of their fire. What they found is shown by the artist.

On the whole it was a busy and interesting night for Si. He did not lose his chevrons on account of his mistakes. But he learned something, and the lesson was impressed upon his mind by a few kindly words of caution and advice from the captain.

CHAPTER XXI.

Sı has a Varied Experience in Camp, and Goes upon an Exasperating "Wild Goose Chase."

"YOU can take it easy to-day, boys, for we ain't goin'
to move," said the orderly of Company Q, one
morning. "The orders is for to put the camp in nice shape,
and for the men to wash up. We're goin' to have an extra ration of soap this mornin', and you fellows want to
stir around lively and fix yerselves as if it was Sunday and
ye was goin' to meetin'. The fust thing after breakfast all
hands 'll turn out and police the camp, 'cause the capt'n
says we're goin' to stay here, mebbe, fer two or three
weeks."

The order to "take it easy" was most gratefully received. Ever since they took the field they had been kept
"on the jump," with only now and then a brief halt of a
few hours, or a day at most. This was the first time that
even an attempt had been made to establish a well-ordered
camp.

"What 'n the world did the ord'ly mean by p'leecin' the
camp?" Corporal Klegg asked Shorty, as they stood by
the fire making coffee and warming up some fragments of
chicken that had been left over from supper the night before. "I didn't s'pose," said Si, "that we 'listed to be
p'leecemen!"

As soon as breakfast was over the orderly directed each
man to provide himself with a small bundle of sticks, made

by putting together a dozen bits of brush or "switches" three or four feet long, such as are used by rural pedagogs to enforce discipline. These were the implements used in policing camp, which meant brushing the leaves and loose debris outside the grounds.

"Does corporils have to do that sort o' thing?" asked Si. He thought army regulations and camp usage ought to show some consideration for his rank. "What's the use o' wearin' stripes," he said to himself, "ef it don't give a feller a chance to play off once 'n a while?"

"Corporals ain't no better 'n anybody else," replied the orderly, " an' you can jest git some brush and go to work, 'long with the rest!"

Si was disposed to grumble a little, but he obeyed orders and was soon scratching up the leaves and dust with great zeal. He did not find it a particularly pleasant occupation, but the camp looked so much better when the job was done, that he

" POLICING " CAMP.

thought it was not a bad thing after all.

"Now, Si," said Shorty, "let's go down to the creek and do our washin'. My clothes has got to be biled, and I shouldn't wonder if yourn had, too!"

"Yes, that's a fact!" said Si, sadly.

They took a camp-kettle that had been used, and no doubt would be again, for making bean-soup, and started for the stream back of the camp. They had no change of clothing with them. One by one their surplus garments had been flung away during the march, or had been "traded" to the natives for poultry. They expected to have an opportunity to stock up for the winter when the campaign was over.

"Fall in for battalion drill!"

These cruel words fell upon their ears just as they were starting for the stream. The colonel had suddenly bethought himself that it would be a good idea to put the boys through for an hour. He told the adjutant to turn out the regiment, and the rattle of drums and the yells of the orderly sergeants carried dismay to the hearts of the men. They had had just enough battalion drill, during the halts, to acquire a chronic aversion to it that never forsook them.

"So that's the kind of an 'easy time' we're goin' ter have to-day!" exclaimed Si, as he and Shorty turned back in response to the summons. "Ef there's anything 't I hate the wust, it's battalion drill. I sh'd think the colonel might let up on us a leetle 'n' give the skin a chance to grow ag'in on our feet."

There was a general chorus of grumbling as the men geared themselves up and took their places in line. The colonel galloped them around in the various regimental evolutions, winding up with a wild charge upon a hypothetical line of intrenchments that left everybody, except the officers who were on horseback, panting and breathless. Then the regiment was dismissed for the day, after the cheering announcement that while they remained in camp there would be four drills daily.

Shorty proposed to his comrade that they make their projected trip to the creek, but Si's attention was absorbed in another direction. The camp was fast filling with people, black and white, from the region round about, with corn "pones," alleged pies, boiled eggs and truck of various kinds, which they sought to dispose of for a valuable consideration. They struck a bad crowd, however, in a financial sense. The members of the 200th Indiana were not at this time in a condition of opulence, as they had not been out long enough to receive a visit from the paymaster. The lank men and scrawny women cried their wares vociferously, but with indifferent results. The boys wanted the stuff, but they were "broke" and trade was dull.

Si looked wistfully at the "pies," and suggested to Shorty a joint investment. Their purses were almost empty, but the temptation was great, and he thought they might raise enough to buy one.

"Them looks nice," said Si. They were the first pies he had seen since leaving home, and his judgment was a little warped. Indeed it was only by the greatest stretch of courtesy that they could be called pies at all. But the word touched Si in a tender spot, and he thought only of such as his mother used to make.

Si and Shorty "pooled in" and bought a pie. Impatiently whipping out his pocket knife Si tried to cut it in two. It was hard work, for the "crust"—so called—was as tough as the hide of a mule. By their united efforts they at length succeeded in sawing it asunder. It was a fearful and wonderful specimen of culinary effort. It was made of two slabs of sodden, leathery dough, with a thin layer of stewed dried-apple sandwiched between them. Si tried his teeth on the pie, but it was like trying to chew an old boot-leg.

"I say, old lady," said he, turning to the female of whom he had bought it, "is these pies pegged er sewed?"

"Look a hyar, young feller," said the woman, with considerable vinegar in her tone, "p'raps you-all thinks it's right smart to insult we-uns; it shows how yer wuz broughten up. I don't 'low yer ever seed any nicer dog-goned pies 'n them is. Ye needn't try ter argefy 'long 'th me, fur I kin jest knock the spots off'n any woman thar is 'round here a-cookin'."

Si saw that it would be profitless to discuss the matter,

and concluded to make the best of a bad bargain. But he couldn't eat the pie.

On the whole the hucksters fared rather badly. The boys confiscated most of the stuff that was brought in, promising to pay next time they came that way. There was a good deal of friction, but the trouble always ended in the soldiers getting the plunder.

The climax was reached when a putty-faced citizen drove into camp a bony mule, tied with straps and ropes and strings to a crazy cart, on which was a barrel of cider, which he "allowed" to sell out to the boys at ten cents a drink, or a quarter a canteen full. He had a spigot rigged in one end, and an old tin cup, with which he dealt out the seductive beverage to such as would buy.

A thirsty crowd gathered around him, but sales were slow, on account of the scarcity of money. Si and Shorty mingled with the boys, and then drew aside and engaged in a whispered consultation.

"That'll be jest bully!" said Shorty. "Ef ye kin raise an auger somewhere we'll bamboozle that old chap."

Si returned after a brief absence, with an auger which he had borrowed from the driver of an ammunition wagon.

"Now, Shorty," said Si, "you git the boys ter stand 'round 'n' keep up a racket, and I'll crawl under the cart and bore a hole inter that 'ere bar'l. Then pass in yer canteens and camp kettles 'n' we'll show the old man a trick!"

Shorty quietly broached the scheme to a few of his comrades, who fell in with it at once. Gathering around the cart they cheered and chattered so as to drown any noise Si might make while carrying out his plan, and which would "give it away."

It was not more than a minute till a gurgling sound was heard, and Si began to pass out to the boys the buckets and canteens, which they so freely furnished him, filled with the fast-flowing contents of the barrel. It did not take long to empty it entirely, nor did the citizen discover the state of affairs until the cider no longer ran from the spigot.

He had not sold more than a gallon or two, and was amazed when the liquid ceased to respond. Then he re solved himself into an investigating committee, and after a protracted search he discovered the fraud that had been played on him.

"Wall, I'll be gosh-durned!" he exclaimed, "I've heern tell 'bout Yankee tricks, but dog my cats if this 'ere don't beat 'em all! I'd like to cut the gizzard outen the rascal that bored the hole 'n that bar'l!"

"A LITTLE MORE CIDER, TOO."

"I declar', old pard, that was mean!" said Si, who stood looking on, with his hands in his trousers' pockets, the picture of innocence. "I'm jest goin' ter flax 'round 'n' help ye find that feller. If I was you I'd jest wallop him—when ye cotch him!"

The citizen, in high dudgeon, poured into the ears of the colonel the story of his grievance, protesting with great vehemence his loyalty to the old flag. The colonel told him that if he could identify the culprits they should be brought to justice. Of course he could do nothing, and he finally mounted his cart and drove away with the empty barrel.

"Ef that old covey loves his country 's much 's he says he does," remarked Si, "I guess he kin 'ford ter give her a bar'l o' cider!"

After dinner Si and Shorty took the camp-kettle and again started for the stream.

"Seems ter me," observed Si, "'tain't hardly a fair shake for Uncle Sam ter make us do our washin'. They'd orter confisticate the niggers 'n' set *them* at it; er I don't see why the guvyment can't furnish a washin' masheen for each comp'ny! 'Twouldn't be no more 'n the squar' thing!"

"The wimmen does the washin', ye know, Si, up whar we live," said Shorty, "'n' I don't quite like the notion o' doin' that kind o' work, but I can't jest see how we're goin' ter git out of it. It's got ter be done, that's sure!"

On the bank of the stream they quickly threw off their clothes for a bath. Si cast rueful glances at his garments as he laid them on the ground.

"Hadn't we better pile some rocks on 'em, Shorty?" said he. "I'm afeard 'f we don't they'll crawl off inter the bush."

"Guess we had," replied Shorty. "I b'lieve mine's started a-ready!"

Having made sure that they would not find them "absent without leave" when they wanted them, they plunged into the water. Far up and down the stream were hundreds of men, swimming and splashing about. The soldiers availed themselves of every opportunity to enjoy this luxury.

Having thoroughly performed their ablutions, Si and Shorty turned their attention to the clothes, which were in such sore need of soap and hot water. Putting their trousers into the kettle and filling it with water, they built a roaring fire under it. After half an hour of vigorous boiling they concluded the clothes were "done." Plenty of soap, rubbing and rinsing finished the work, and they presented a quite respectable appearance.

"How 're we goin' ter git 'em dry?" asked Si as he wrung out his "wash."

"Hang 'em on the fence in the sun!" replied Shorty.

"But what'll we wear while they're dryin'?"

"Nothin', I reckon!"

So they spread them on the rails, put their shirts into the kettle, and then dashed again into the water. After splashing awhile they came out and drew on their half-dried trousers. All along the stream were soldiers in every stage of *dishabille*, similarly engaged. Shorty lighted his pipe as he and Si lay down upon the grass, after making a fresh fire under the kettle.

THE ARMY LAUNDRY.

"Say, Shorty," said Si, "'tain't very wicked ter smoke, is it?"

"Guess not!" was the reply.

"That's the way it 'pears ter me, 'n' I've been kinder thinkin' lately that I'd larn how. The soljers all seems ter enjoy their smokin' so much. You know, Shorty, that I was allus a reel good boy—never smoked, nor chawed terbacker, nor cussed, nor done nothin' that was out o' the straight an' narrer way. When I jined the rijiment my good old mother says to me: 'Now, Si,' says she, 'I do hope ye'll 'member what I've always taught ye. I've heern 'em tell that they does drefful things in the army, and I want ye to see if ye can't be as good a boy as ye've been at home.' Of course I told her I would, 'n' I mean ter stick to it; but I don't b'lieve she'd keer 'f 1 sh'd smoke. Is it hard ter learn?"

"Wall, I d'know; ye can't most always tell till ye try. Take a whiff, and see how she goes. I reck'n ef ye go through the war 'n' don't larn nuthin wuss 'n smokin', ye'll do purty well." And Shorty handed him his pipe, which he had just refilled with whittlings of black plug.

"I b'lieve I'll jest try it," said Si. "I s'pose I kin quit easy 'nough, 'f I want ter, when I go home."

He took the pipe and began to puff with great energy. He made a few wry faces at first, but Shorty told him to stick to it, and he bravely pulled away, while the clouds of smoke curled above him. Soon the color left his face, his head was in a whirl, and his stomach began to manifest eruptive symptoms.

"Shorty," he gasped, "I'm awful sick. If smokin' makes a feller feel like this, I don't want any more of it in mine."

"Whar's all yer sand ye brag so much 'bout?" said Shorty, laughing. "Ye're mighty poor timber for a soljer if ye can't stan' a little pipe o' terbacker like that. Ye'll get over it purty soon, and it won't bother ye any next time ye try it."

Si found that he had about as much as he could manage with his dizzy head and the internal rebellion that was so actively going on. He rolled and writhed about in a state of abject misery.

Suddenly there came from the camp a sound that brought Shorty to his feet.

"Hello, Si," he shouted, "don't ye hear the drums rattlin' 'n' the bugles tootin'? Ther's suthin up fer *sure*. Git up, pard, we'll have ter skin out o' here right quick!"

From far and near the alarm came to their ears, and on

every hand were seen half-dressed officers and men running toward their respective regiments.

Shorty seized the kettle in which the shirts were being boiled, turned out the water, and dashed toward camp. Si followed as fast as he was able, though his head seemed to spin like a top. The exercise made him feel better, and by the time he reached the regiment he had nearly recovered. Officers were shouting "Fall in!" and orderlies were tearing around in frantic zeal urging the men to "be lively."

A SCAMPER IN DISHABILLE.

There was no time to ask or answer the questions that were in everybody's mouth in regard to the cause of the sudden alarm.

"What'll we do 'bout our shirts?" asked Si of his comrade. "How 's a feller goin' ter march 'n this kind of a fix?"

"We'll have ter tote 'em 'long t'll we git a chance ter cool 'em off 'n' put 'em on," replied Shorty. "Git into yer blouse 'n' sling on yer traps, quick 's ever ye kin!"

Just before stepping into ranks Si and Shorty fished their steaming and dripping shirts out of the kettle and hung them on their bayonets. They cut a grotesque figure, and were the target of many a jest from those of their comrades who had not been similarly caught. At the first halt they managed to put on their shirts, and resumed the march in a most uncomfortable condition. They had reason to repent their attempt to check the ravages of the *pediculi.*

A small detail from each company was ordered to remain to strike the tents, load the wagons, and serve as a guard for the train. The hastily formed column filed out upon the road and started off at a plunging gait.

"Is this what they calls havin' 'n easy day, thrashin' 'round on battalion drill, 'n' then marchin' off 't a hoss-trot?" said Si, struggling and puffing in his efforts to keep his place in the ranks. "They said we was goin' ter stay awhile 'n that camp 'n' git rested up. Looks like it, don't it?"

"The best way fer ye ter do," replied Shorty, "is jest ter b'lieve nothin' 't anybody tells ye 'n the army. 'Tain't half the time 't the ossifers knows theirselves, 'n' ef they do like as not they'll tell ye t'other way. Soljerin' 's queer kind o' business!"

This was not the last time that the men of the 200th Indiana, after fixing up a nice camp under the delusive belief that they were going to "take it easy" for a few days or weeks, had their work for nothing. Sometimes in mid-summer they put up awnings of boughs over their tents to temper the sun's fierce heat; or in winter they built fire-places and chimneys of brick or stones or sticks and clay, which added greatly to the comfort of their frail tenements. "Marching orders" were usually delayed until just as these improvements were finished, but if, within twenty-four hours after this, the regiment did not "pull out" it was an exception to the rule. An order for the men to put the camp in good shape and make themselves comfortable, came to be considered as the equivalent of an order to move—if it was only over to the next field, where all the work had to be done over again

The rushing column swept on with undiminished speed, halting a few minutes at long intervals for the panting soldiers to get their breath. The shuffling of many feet on the dry limestone road filled the air with a thick cloud of dust that enveloped the men, covering their garments, entering their eyes, mouths and noses, and clinging to their sweating faces. A soldier could not recognize the muddy countenance of his nearest comrade. Knapsacks and cartridge boxes grew heavy, and the straps and belts ground the dust into the smarting flesh.

At sundown there was a halt of half an hour. The men were directed to make coffee and brace themselves for an all-night march. They washed the dirt from their hands and faces, lighted fires, and hurriedly prepared their evening meal. Wild rumors flew from mouth to mouth that they would charge upon a large body of the enemy at daylight, and the rising sun would no doubt look upon a bloody scene of carnage. These were the more readily believed from the fact that such a furious march was considered *prima facie* evidence that something extraordinary was about to happen, and it was more likely to be a fight than anything else.

It was nearly dark when the column was again formed. Backs and shoulders and legs were already aching, and hearts sank at the prospect of the long, weary night's tramp; but nerved by the thought of a battle the men of the 200th stepped firmly and briskly, bent on keeping up with the veterans who were stretching ahead of them, and out of the way of those who were close upon their heels. Again the cloud of dust enveloped them, hanging heavily in the damp night air, through which they groped their way. Covered with a mantle of white they looked like a procession of ghosts as they plodded on.

Nine o'clock—ten—eleven—midnight, and on they march, with now and then a few minutes of rest. The officers speak words of sympathy and encouragement to the toiling men. It is a critical emergency and they *must* keep in their places. How the muscles twinge with pain, and what torture to the tender feet as they tread, hour after hour, the hard pike! No laugh or jest is heard. Save an occasional moan or cry extorted by keen suffering, there is no sound but the clatter of horses' hoofs upon the flinty road and the ceaseless tramp—tramp—of the tottering soldiers.

One—two—three o'clock, and still "forward" is the word. Exhausted and bent and racked with pain, the burdened forms mechanically drag themselves along. Overcome by fatigue and drowsiness men fall asleep and march in their dreams. They stumble one against another and in this rude way are brought back to consciousness. Sometimes they are awakened by rolling into the ditch by the roadside, or coming in collision with protruding fence-rails. *

During the night there was no opportunity for refreshment except such as could be derived from the dry hardtack, eaten on the march or at the halts by the wayside. Morning dawned at length, upon a struggling mass of men, fainting and footsore, exhausted to the verge of human endurance. The column halted and was formed in order of battle. The 200th Indiana appeared to be all there, but it was in the poorest possible condition for action, if there had been any fight to go into—which of course there was not. It was a hard night for Si Klegg, but Shorty had helped him along by carrying his gun now

* It was a common thing, when soldiers went for days and nights without rest, for infantrymen to sleep as they marched and cavalrymen as they rode their horses.

and then, and daylight found him "here," ready to do anything that was asked of him. It was more severely trying than anything he had been through before. He did not say much; there was nothing to be said, and he had not a breath to spare for unnecessary words.

For two hours the soldiers lay on their arms while the general sent out some men on horseback to reconnoiter. He had heard that several hundred rebel troopers were encamped in that vicinity, and the brilliant expedition was for the purpose of surprising and capturing them. Part of the Union forces had been marched around so as to close in on all sides of the camp, and it was scientifically planned that not a man should escape to tell the tale. But the rebels were gone—and had been for two days. They were only a squad of a few dozen guerrillas, anyway. The 200th Indiana and the rest of the regiments were there "holding the sack," but the game had fled.

Then the men were told to stack arms, break ranks, and get their breakfast. Two hours later they started back for the same spot they left in such mad haste the day before. It took them two days to return the thirty miles they had traveled. The wagons, which were met slowly trailing along, were turned about and followed in the rear. When the soldiers reached their camp and pitched their tents on the old ground they were physically "used up," and mentally in a state of supreme disgust over the inglorious result of their impetuous march. Si tried to give Shorty his opinion of such a "wild goose chase," but for once language failed him and he said it wasn't any use to try. But he had a good many similar experiences before the war was over, and when he became more skilled in the use of unparliamentary language he succeeded better in expressing his opinions concerning such strategic maneuvers.

CHAPTER XXII.

FROM twelve to sixteen miles was an easy day's march. To a person wholly unincumbered this would be no more than a pleasant stroll. But when a soldier, with the burden he was obliged to carry even when stripped of all unnecessary weight, had tramped that distance, he was glad enough to "call it a day." On long journeys, when there was no occasion for haste, the troops were not often pushed to greater speed; though at critical times, when the need was urgent, thirty and even forty miles were made within twenty-four hours, but it taxed to the utmost the power of endurance. When not under pressure, it was customary to start early in the day and go into camp by two o'clock. Occasional marches of this kind, with changes of camp, were greatly conducive to health and comfort, and were far preferable to occupying the same ground for months at a time. The soldiers never grumbled at these pilgrimages, unless they were made in bad weather. Nor did they complain of the severest marching when it was necessary; but there was a great deal of wild cavorting over the country that, to the untutored mind of the rank and file, seemed wholly needless. It may have been an essential factor in bringing the final victory, but the soldiers could not understand it that way. It sent many men to the hospitals, and seriously impaired the tempers of those who were able to endure it.

Those regiments were fortunate which were permitted by circumstances to pass gradually through the seasoning process that made men *soldiers,* capable of enduring the exposure and hardships of active campaigning. A harder fate had fallen to the lot of the 200th Indiana. While yet "raw" in the largest sense, it was forced to begin at the "butt end." Its ranks had thinned rapidly. In every town through which the army passed, the buildings were turned into hospitals and filled with sick and crippled men from the new regiments, who had fallen by the way. Not half of these ever rejoined their commands for duty. Many regiments were thus as much reduced in a few weeks as others had been in twice as many months. The 200th had jogged along bravely, but had suffered its share of decimation. Not less than a third of its men had "given out," and were taking quinine and blue-mass, and rubbing arnica on their legs along the tortuous route.

Corporal Si Klegg and Shorty proved to be "stayers." Full of life and ambition, they were always prompt for duty and ready for a fight or a frolic. No one was more quick than Si to offer a suffering comrade the last drop of fresh water in his canteen, or to give him a lift by carrying part of his load for an hour.

One day the regiment started out for a comfortable march. The coast was clear of rebels, and, there being no excuse for crowding on the steam, the boys were allowed to take their own gait, while the horses of the officers and the cavalry had a chance to recover their wind.

It was a warm day, late in October. The nights at this time were keen and frosty, but the sun at mid-day still showed much of his summer vigor. Perspiration flowed freely down the faces of those wandering Hoosiers—faces that were fast assuming the color of half-tanned leather under the influence of sunshine and storm.

Once an hour there was the customary halt, when the boys would stretch themselves by the roadside, hitching their knapsacks up under their heads. When the allotted time had expired the bugler blew the "fall in," the notes of which during the next two years became so familiar to their ears. All were in good spirits. As they marched they pelted one another with jests, and laughter rippled along the column.

The only thing that troubled them was the emaciated condition of their haversacks, with a corresponding state of affairs in their several stomachs. The commissary department was thoroughly demoralized. The supply train had failed to connect, and rations were almost exhausted. There was no prospect that the aching void would be filled, at least in the regular way, for two or three days, until they reached a depot of supplies.

At this stage of the war strict orders against foraging were issued almost daily. These were often read impressively to the men of the 200th Indiana, who, in their simplicity, "took it all in" as military gospel. The effect was somewhat depressing upon the ardor with which, otherwise, they would have pursued the panting pig and the fluttering fowl, and reveled in the orchards and potato-fields. A few irrepressible fellows managed to get a choice meal now and then—just enough to show that the 200th Indiana was not without latent talent, which only needed a little encouragement to become fruitful of results.

These sounding proclamations against foraging were received by the veterans with less solemnity. They had been heard so many times that they had lost their force. By long and successful practice these old soldiers had become skilled in the many ingenious arts by which such regulations were evaded. When rations were short the "will" to supply the deficiency always found a "way," if there was anything to be had; or if the appetite craved a change from the monotonous regulation diet, the means to do so were not wanting. Many a regimental and company officer, who proclaimed these orders to his men, and in words of thundering sound avowed his determination to enforce them, was moved to condone a flagrant offense by a propitiatory offering of a leg of mutton, a spare-rib, a chicken or a "mess" of sweet potatoes. Indeed, some of the generals seemed to feel that they had filled the measure of duty in the issuance of orders, permitting the soldiers to put their own interpretation upon them. The latter were not slow to construe them in the most liberal manner. The new troops proved apt learners. For the first few days, with the orders ringing in their ears, they marched along without daring so much as to pluck an apple. But when they saw the old soldiers throttling fowls, bayoneting fatlings, and filling their haversacks with the fruit of orchard and field, they naturally felt that there ought to be a more equitable adjustment of things. It was not long till they were able to get their full share of whatever the country afforded.

During the early stage of the war the only authorized foraging was done in an official way. There were times when supplies for men and animals were necessary. Expeditions were sent out under the direction of quartermasters, who gave receipts for all property taken from loyal men, and these were honored in cash by the government. As the armies pushed their way farther into the rebellious states the restrictions upon fence-rails, straw stacks, and forage of every kind fell into what a modern chief magistrate of the nation would call "innocuous desuetude." A year before the war closed they had practically disappeared. The enemy was assaulted in purse as well as in person, and if a soldier—or an officer—saw anything that he needed he "went for it." If he could not see what he wanted he hunted until he found it.

On the day in question a few hints were thrown out to the 200th Indiana which resulted in a tacit understanding that, in view of the actual need of the soldiers, if they got a good chance to pick up something the eyes of the officers would be closed. In fact the latter were as hungry as the men, and hoped to come in for a "divide."

Soon after starting in the morning a persimmon tree, well laden with fruit, was seen in a field not far from the road. About fifty men started for it on a run, and in five minutes it was as bare as the barren fig tree.

The persimmon has some very marked peculiarities. It is a toothsome fruit when well ripened by frost, but if eaten before it has reached the point of full maturity, the effect upon one's interior is unique and startling. The pungent juices take hold of the mouth and pucker it up in such a manner as to make even speech for a time impossible. The tongue seems as if it were tied in a knot. If the juice be swallowed similar results follow all along its course. But the novice does not often get far enough for that.

The boys soon found that the 'simmons, although they looked very tempting, were too green to be eaten with any degree of enjoyment. So they filled their pockets with them to pucker up the mouths of their comrades. Shorty had joined in the scramble, telling his comrade he would bring him a good supply.

"Ain't them nice?" he said to Si, holding out three or four of the greenest ones he could find. "Eat 'em; they're jest gorjus! Ye can't help likin' on 'em!"

Si had never before seen a persimmon. Eagerly seizing them he tossed one into his mouth and began to chew it vigorously. The persimmon at once took hold with a mighty grip, wrinkling him up like the skins on scalded milk.

After sputtering furiously a few minutes, while Shorty laughed at him, Si managed to get his tongue untwisted.

"Yes," said he, "them things *is* nice—in a horn! 'Twouldn't take many on 'em to make a meal!"

A little farther along Si's quick eye noticed a row of beehives standing on a bench in the yard of one of the natives. He had a weakness for honey.

"Shorty," said he, "see them hives over thar? How'd ye like ter have some honey fer supper?"

Shorty "allowed" that it would be a good thing. Si stopped and waited a few minutes until his own regiment got past, thinking his plan would be less liable to interruption. Then he leaped over the fence, went up to the hives, and boldly tipped one of them over, hoping he could get out a comb or two, fill his coffee-kettle, and effect his retreat before the bees really found out what he was doing. But the bees instantly rallied their forces and made a vigorous assault upon the invader. Si saw that it would be too hot for him, and without standing upon the order of his going he went at once, in a decidedly panicky condition. The bees made the most of their opportunity, using their "business ends" on him with great activity and zeal. They seemed to fully share the common feeling in the South toward the "Yanks."

THE BUSY BEE.

A disheveled woman, smoking a cob-pipe, had watched Si's raid from the door-way, with a stormy face. As he fell back in utter rout she screamed, "Sarves ye right!" and then sat down on the doorstep and laughed till she cried. She enjoyed it as much as the bees did. The latter took hold of Si in various places, and by the time he caught up with the regiment one eye was closed, and there was a

big lump on his nose, besides several more stings which the
bees had judiciously distributed about his person. It was
very evident that he had been overmatched, and had come
out second best in the encounter. Corporal Klegg presented a picturesque appearance as he reached Company
Q, and the boys screamed with delight.

"Whar's yer honey?" said Shorty. "'Pears like ye
waked up the wrong passenger that time!"

Si laughed with the rest, rubbed salt on his stings, and
plodded on, consoling himself with the thought that his
was not the only case in which the merit of earnest effort
had gone unrewarded.

During the march a large stream was reached, the bridge
over which had been burned. The water was waist deep.
If the regiment had been moving rapidly to meet an emergency the men would not have stopped for a moment.
Unclasping their cartridge-box belts they would have
plunged into the water without removing a single garment,
carrying their muskets and ammunition so as to keep them
dry. But at this time the regiment was not under pressure and a halt was ordered. The colonel directed the men
to strip, and they quickly divested themselves of their
clothes. These and their numerous "traps" were bundled
up and hoisted upon fixed bayonets or carried upon the
head. Then the bugle sounded and the fantastic procession
entered the water. The grotesquely ridiculous appearance
of the men provoked shouts of laughter.

Short men were at a disadvantage, and Corporal Klegg
had as much as he could do to resist the sweep of the current that threatened to carry him off his feet, as he carefully felt his way along the stony bottom. It was difficult
for one to assist another, as each had his hands fully occupied in the carriage of his clothing and accouterments.
When about midway Si's foot slipped on a treacherous
stone and he went down with a great splash, submerging
himself and his burden, while everybody yelled.

Shorty had thoughtfully arranged his load so as to have one hand free, and had kept near Si, that he might be of service in case of accident. He seized his unfortunate comrade just in time to save him from being borne away by the rushing stream, and got him upon his feet again. Si came up half strangled and spouting like a whale. But for Shorty's timely aid he would have been forced to jetson his cargo and swim for his life. Shorty kept his hand until the bank was safely reached. Si had clung to all his things, but they were well soaked. Many others of the regiment

THE 200TH INDIANA TAKES TO THE WATER.

had similar watery experiences, and some of them were less fortunate, losing their guns and equipments. Loss of life while crossing streams in this way was not an uncommon occurrence.

During the brief time allowed the men to "dress up," Si wrung out his dripping garments and drew them on. The warm sun quickly dried them, and he was none the worse for his mishap.

"I reck'n they'd let me jine the Babtist church now," he said to Shorty.

Soon after noon the regiment came to a large patch of

sweet potatoes. Si and Shorty, as well as many of the
rest, thought it would be a good place to lay in a supply
for supper, as they might not have another such chance.
From all parts of the column the soldiers, by dozens, dashed
into the field. In a moment there was a man at every hill,
digging away with his bayonet, and chucking the tempting tubers into his haversack. The artist has pictured the
scene in a manner that will touch a responsive chord in
the memories—not to mention the stomachs—of the veterans of the war.

Two hours before going into camp the regiment passed

A PREMATURE HARVEST.

a small spring, around
which a crowd of sol-
diers were struggling to
fill their canteens. There
had been a long stretch
without fresh water, and
Si thought he would sup-
ply himself.

"Gimme your canteen,
too, Shorty, and I'll fill
it," he said, "ef ye'll jest
carry my gun."

"Here, Si, you're a
bully boy, take mine!"
"Mine, too!" "And

mine!" said one after another of his comrades. Si good-
naturedly complied, and they loaded him down with
a dozen canteens.

"All right," said Si, "I'll be 'long with 'em full d'reckly!"
He had to wait for his turn at the spring, and by the
time he had filled all the canteens he was half an hour behind. Slinging them around his neck he started on, with
just about as big a load as he could carry. He forged
ahead, gradually gaining a little by the tardy movement
of the column that generally preceded going into camp.

The canteen straps chafed his shoulders, his back ached, and perspiration flowed in streams. The smoke of the campfires ahead told that the end of the day's march was near. He kept on and finally came up with Company Q just as the 200th was stacking arms on the bank of a clear stream. He threw down his burden of canteens, well-nigh exhausted.

"Purty good load, wa'n't it, Si?" said Shorty. "But what made ye lug all that water in here? When ye seen they was goin' into camp ahead ye might ha' knowed there was plenty o' water. Why in blazes didn't ye turn the water out o' them 'ere canteens?"

"I never thought o' that," said Si, while the boys joined in a hearty laugh.

At the command "Break ranks" there was a general scamper to engage in the work of getting supper and preparing to spend the night. The members of each mess scattered in all directions, some

A "BULLY BOY'S" BURDEN.

for water, rails and straw, while others scoured the adjacent region for edibles. The utmost activity characterized these operations. It was "every one for himself," and he who stirred around with the greatest zeal was likely to fare best.

Si threw off his traps and dropped on the ground to rest a few minutes, but got up presently to scratch around with the rest. As he took hold of his haversack he was surprised at its lightness. When he laid it down it was bulging out with sweet potatoes, and a glance showed him that these were all gone.

"Durn my buttons!" exclaimed Si, as he forgot his weariness, and his eyes flashed fire. "Ef I *am* a corporil, I kin jest mash the feller 't stole my 'taters, I don't keer if he's ten foot high. Won't somebody show 'im to me? Thar won't be 'nuff of 'im left to hold a fun'ral over!"

Si pranced around in a high state of indignation, and there is little doubt that if he had found the purloiner of his provender there would have been a harder fight, in proportion to the forces engaged, than any that had yet occurred during the war.

The boys winked slyly at one another, and all said it was too bad. It was a startling case of turpitude, and Si determined to have revenge by getting even on some other fellow, without pausing to consider questions which appertain more to theology than to war.

"Come 'long with me, Shorty!" he said to his friend, and they strode away. Just outside the camp they came upon two members of some other new regiment coming into camp, with a fine pig slung over a pole and two or three chickens in their hands. Shorty suggested to Si that this was a good chance for him to even up.

"Halt there!" shouted Si to the foragers. "We're sent out ter pick up jest sich fellers 's you!"

The effect was like a shot from a cannon. The men dropped their plunder and fled in wild confusion.

"Take hold o' that pole, Shorty!" said Si, and laying it upon their shoulders they made a triumphant entry into camp.

There seemed to be no danger of immediate starvation in the ranks of the 200th. Each man had supplied himself abundantly. Fires gleamed brightly in the gathering twilight, and around them crowded the hungry soldiers intent upon making ready the feast.

Up to this time the doctors of the 200th Indiana had

found little to do, aside from issuing salve and arnica to assuage the pain of blisters and lame legs and shoulders. The men had started out in good physical condition, and there had been scarcely time for disease to make serious ravages among them.

Si Klegg was a good specimen of a robust Hoosier lad— for he could scarcely be called a man yet. Since he lay in his cradle and was dosed with paregoric and catnip tea like other babies, he had never seen a sick day. He had done all he could to starve the doctors.

LAYING IN SUPPLIES.

When the regiment took the field it had the usual outfit of men who wrote their names sandwiched between a military title in front and "M. D." behind. It had a big hospital tent, and an apothecary shop on wheels, loaded to the guards with quinine, blue-mass, castor oil, epsom salts —everything in fact that was known to medical science as a cure for the ills to which flesh is heir. As yet the doctors had not done much but hold a continual dress-parade in their shiny uniforms.

The next day the march was continued. On going into camp the 200th, being well in the advance, struck a field of late corn with a good crop of ears just at the right stage for roasting or boiling. Adjoining this was an apple orchard loaded with fruit. The boys quickly laid in an enormous supply, lighted fires, and an hour later were enjoying a royal feast.

"Now this is suthin like!" said Si, as he squatted on the ground along with Shorty and half a dozen messmates. They surrounded a camp-kettle full of steaming ears, and half a bushel or so of apples heaped on a poncho.

"Wish we had some o' mother's butter to grease this

corn with," observed Si, as he flung a cob into the fire and seized a fresh ear.

All agreed that Si's head was level on the butter question, but under all the circumstances they were glad enough to have the corn without butter. The ears went off with amazing rapidity. Every man seemed to be afraid he wouldn't

A RED-LETTER DAY.

get his share. When the kettle was empty the boys turned themselves loose on the apples, utterly reckless of results. When Si got up he burst half the buttons off his clothes. It was not long till he began to wish he had eaten an ear of corn and an apple or two less. He didn't feel very well. He turned in early, thinking he would go to sleep and be all right in the morning.

Along in the night he uttered a yell that came near stampeding the company. An enormous colic was raging in his interior, and he fairly howled with pain. He thought he was going to die immediately.

"Shorty," he said, between the gripes, to his comrade, "I'm afeard I'm goin' up the spout. Arter I'm gone you write to—to—Annie, and tell her I died fer my country, like a man. I'd ruther been shot than die with the colic, but I s'pose 'twon't make much diff'runce arter it's all over!"

"I'll do it," replied Shorty. "We'll plant ye 'n good shape; and, Si, we'll gather up the corn-cobs and build a moniment over ye!"

But Si wasn't cut off in the bloom of youth by that colic. His eruptive condition frightened Shorty however, and, though he was in nearly as bad shape himself, he went up and routed out one of the doctors, who growled a good deal about being disturbed. The debris of the supper scattered about the camp told the doctor what was the matter, and he had no need to make a critical diagnosis of Si's

A CLEAR CASE OF COLIC.

case. He administered a dose of something that eased the pain a little, and Si managed to rub along through the night.

Fortunately for Si, and for more than half the members of the regiment, the army did not start early the following day. At the usual hour in the morning the bugler blew the "sick-call." A regiment of grizzly veterans lay next to the 200th Indiana, and as Si lay groaning in his tent he heard them sing the words that became so familiar to him afterward.

"Fall in fer yer ipecac!" shouted the orderly. Si joined the cadaverous procession and went wabbling up to the "doctor's" shop with a discouraged air.

Git yer qui - nine! Git yer qui - nine!

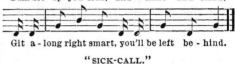

Tum-ble up you sick, and lame and blind;

It was a regular matinee that day. The surgeon and his assistants were all

Git a - long right smart, you'll be left be - hind.

"SICK-CALL."

on hand, as the colicky squads came to a focus in front of the tent. The doctors worked off the patients at a rapid rate, generally prescribing the same medicine for all, no matter what ailed them. This was the way the army doctors always did, but it happened in this case that they were not far wrong, as the ailments, arising from a common cause, were much the same. When Si's turn came he received a liberal ration of medicine from the

SI INTERVIEWS THE DOCTOR.

hospital steward, and the doctor gave him a "pass" to ride that day in an ambulance.

CHAPTER XXIII.

DURING the very few days that the 200th Indiana lay in camp before entering upon the campaign, nothing was thought of except getting the regiment into condition for immediate service. There was no opportunity to learn the customary details of camp life. Then it spent three or four weeks cantering over the country, trying without success to find a battle to get into. Now that the chase after the fleet-footed rebels had been abandoned, attention was given to the prescribed daily routine of duty. The wagons that were left behind when the army moved had rejoined the regiment, and the men once more had tents to sleep in.

The campaign had been a disappointment to Si Klegg. When the troops entered upon it, in such imposing array, he fully expected that the opposing rebel army would be exterminated. One insignificant brush with the enemy was the nearest approach to a battle that he had seen. His impatience knew no bounds when, at the sound of half a dozen shots on the skirmish-line, the whole army halted, performed grand maneuvers, formed line of battle, threw up intrenchments and solemnly waited to be attacked by the enemy, who was all the time trying so hard to get away.

"I'd jest like ter show 'em how ter run a war," he said to Shorty. "I wouldn't have so much tomfoolery goin'

on. We walks our legs off tryin' ter find the Johnnies so 's
we kin thrash 'em, 'n 's soon 's we cotches 'em we don't
do nothin' but stan' 'n' make faces at 'em, 's ef we was a
lot o' boys. Now they've got away fer good 'n' ther' ain't
nobody hurt on ary side. Wish 't they'd make *me* a gin-
'ral. Mebbe I wouldn't whip the rebels but I'd *try* my
level best. Ther' 'd be a fight, anyway."

After a while the "gin'rals" fell into Si's way of thinking. Then came fierce fighting, and at last the end. Si was
glad when he heard that a new commander had been appointed to lead that army. He did not have to wait much
longer to know what it was to go through a great battle.

"Fall in, Company Q, for retreat!" shouted the orderly
one Saturday evening, as the drums rattled at sunset.

"What we goin' to retreat fer, Shorty?" asked Si, with
alarm. "The rebils hain't whipped us, have they? I'm
mighty sartin 't I ain't licked yet. The folks to home 'll
think we're all a pack o' cowards ef we go ter runnin' back
'thout havin' a fight."

"It don't mean that, Si," replied his comrade. "When
ye hear the bugles blowin' 'n' the drums beatin' fer roll-call
at sundown, that 's what they calls 'retreat.'"

"I can't see no sense 'n givin' 't that name," said Si.
"I allus thought retreat meant runnin' the wrong way.
'Pears like words don't have the same meanin' 'n the army
't they does up 'n Injianny."

Si had new cause for wonder two or three hours later
when another call was sounded and the company was
ordered to fall in for "tattoo." In his eagerness for information he asked Shorty if they had all got to be tattooed
like the cannibals he had seen pictures of, and if so what
it was for. Shorty told him that "tattoo" was the name
given by the army regulations to the call for everybody to
go to bed.

"I hope I'll git all these curus things larned arter a
while," said Si.

As a matter of fact the army did get pretty thoroughly "tattooed" during the war. Every regiment had its tat-tooers, with outfits of needles and India-ink, who for a consideration decorated the limbs and bodies of their com-rades with flags, muskets, cannons, sabers, and an infinite variety of patriotic emblems and warlike and grotesque devices. Some of these men were highly artistic and did their work in a manner that would have been creditable to a South Sea Islander. Thousands of the soldiers had name, regiment and residence "pricked" into their arms or legs. In portions of the army this was recommended in general orders, to afford means of identification if killed in battle. It was like writing one's own epitaph, but the custom prevented many bodies from being buried in "un-known" graves.

"Tomorrow's Sunday, ye know!" said the orderly at "retreat."

This was in the nature of news to the boys. But for the announcement very few of them would have known it. The orderly was not distinguished for his piety, and it is not likely that the approach of Sunday would have oc-curred to him if the sergeant-major had not come around with orders from the colonel for a proper observance of the day. The colonel himself would not have thought of it, either, if the chaplain had not reminded him of it. Everybody wondered how even the chaplain could keep track of the days well enough to know when Sunday came. It was the general impression that he either carried an almanac in his pocket, or else a stick in which he cut a notch every day with his jack-knife, and in that way man-aged to know when a new week began.

The 200th Indiana had been kept particularly active on Sundays. Probably this regiment did not manifest any more than the average degree of enthusiasm and fervor in religious matters, but there were many in its ranks who, at home, had always sat under gospel ministrations, and

to tramp on Sundays, the same as other days, was, at
first, a rude shock to their moral sensibilities. These were
yet keen; the edges had not been worn off and blunted
and battered by the hard knocks of army life. True, they
could scarcely tell when Sunday came, but they knew that
they kept marching right along every day.

"There'll be guard-mountin' at 9 o'clock," continued
the orderly, "regimental inspection at 10, preachin' at 11,
an' dress-parade at 5 in the evenin'. All of ye wants to
tumble out right promp'ly at revellee an' git yer breakfast, an' then clean up yer guns an' put all yer traps in
apple-pie order, 'cause the colonel's goin' to look at 'em.
He's got sharp eyes, an' I reck'n he'll be mighty pertickler.
If there's anything that ain't jest right he'll see it quicker'n
lightnin'. Ye know we hain't had any inspections yet, an'
the cap'n wants us to be the boss company. So ye've got
to scratch around lively in the mornin'."

"Shorty," said Si, after they had gone to bed, "seems
like it'll be sort o' nice ter keep Sunday ag'in. At the rate
we've bin goin' on we'll all be heathens by the time we git
home—if we ever do. Our chaplain hain't had no chance
ter preachify yet. The boys w'at knows him, says he's a
staver, 'n' I b'lieve it'll make us all feel better ter have him
talk to us once. 'Twon't do us no harm, nohow. I'd like
ter be home termorrer 'n' go to church with mother, 'n'
sister Marier, 'n' the rest o' the folks. Then I'd jest eat
all the arternoon. I ain't goin' ter git homesick, Shorty;
but a feller can't help feelin' a leetle streaked once 'n a
while. Mebbe it's a good idee fer 'em to keep us on the
jump, fer then we don't git no chance to think 'bout it. I
don't s'pose I'm the only boy 'n the rijiment that 'd be
glad ter git a furlough jest fer termorrer. I sh'd want ter
be back bright 'n' arly terfall in Monday mornin', fer I calkilate ter stick ter the 200th Injianny through thick 'n'
thin. Say, Shorty, how d'ye feel, anyway?"

But Shorty was already fast asleep. Si spooned up to him and was soon at home in his dreams.

The sound of bugle and drum, at daylight, fell upon unwilling ears, for the soldiers felt the same indisposition to get up early Sunday morning that is everywhere one of the characteristics of modern civilization. Their beds were hard, but to their weary limbs no couch ever gave more welcome rest than did the rough ground on which they lay. But the wild yell of the orderly, "Turn out for roll-call!" with the thought of the penalties for non-obedience —which some of them had abundant reason to remember — quickly brought out the laggards.

Si and Shorty were, as usual, among the first to take their places in line. They were pleasantly greeted by the captain, who had come out on the run at the last moment, and wriggled himself into his coat as he strode along the company street. The captain did not very often appear at

THE CAPTAIN AT EARLY ROLL-CALL.

morning roll-call. Only one officer of the company was required to be present, and the captain generally loaded this duty upon the lieutenants, "turn about." If he did show up, he would go back to bed and snooze for an hour while the cook was getting breakfast. If one of the men did that, he would soon be promenading with a rail on his shoulder or standing on a barrel with a stick or a bayonet tied in his mouth.

"I think that's a fust rate notion ter mount the guards," said Si to Shorty, as they sat on a rail by the fire making coffee and frying bacon. "It'll be so much better 'n walkin' back 'n' forrard on the beats. Wonder 'f they'll give us hosses or mules to ride."

"I'd like ter know what put that idee into yer head?" said Shorty.

"Why, didn't the ord'ly say las' night 't there 'd be guard-mountin' at 9 o'clock this mornin'? I s'posed that fer a man ter be mounted meant straddlin' a hoss or s'mother kind of an animil."

"SIR, THE GUARD IS FORMED."

"*Ain't* ye never goin' to larn nuthin'," said Shorty, with a laugh. "Guard-mountin' don't mean fer the men ter git on hosses. It's only the name they gives it in the reggelations. Dunno why they calls it that, 'nless it's 'cause the guards has ter 'mount' anybody that tries ter pass 'thout the countersign. But don't ye fool yerself with thinkin' ye're goin' ter git to ride. We'll keep pluggin' along afoot, on guard er anywhere else, same 's we have all the time."

"I sh'd think they might mount the corporils, anyway," said Si.

Thus rudely was shattered another of his bright illusions.

The whole regiment turned out to witness the ceremony of guard-mounting. It was the first time the exigencies of the campaign had permitted the 200th Indiana to do this in style. The adjutant was the most important personage, and he stood so straight that he narrowly escaped falling over backward. In order that he might not make a mess of it, he had spent half the night rehearsing the various commands in his tent. Thus prepared, he managed to get through his part quite comfortably, though the non-commissioned officers and privates made awkward work of it.

The next thing on the program for the day was the inspection. The boys had been industriously engaged in cleaning up their muskets and accouterments, and putting their scanty wardrobes in presentable condition. In arranging his knapsack for the colonel's eye, each man carefully laid a clean shirt, if he had one, on the top. The garments that were not clean he either stowed away in the tent or put at the bottom of the knapsack. In this he was actuated by the same principle that prompts the thrifty farmer to put the biggest apples and strawberries at the top of his measure.

The clothing of the regiment was already in an advanced stage of demoralization. It was of the "shoddy" sort, that a good hard wind would almost blow to pieces.

Corporal Klegg was anxious that not only his person, but all his goods and chattels, should make as creditable an appearance as possible. He put on the best and cleanest garments he had, and then betook himself to fixing his knapsack so it would pass muster.

"Them duds is a bad lot," he said to Shorty, casting rueful glances at the little heap of soiled and ragged clothes. "Purty hard to make a decent show with them things!"

"Wait a minute," said Shorty, "an' I'll show ye a leetle trick."

Taking his poncho under his arm, Shorty went to the rear of the camp, where the mules were feeding, and presently returned with a bunch of hay.

"What ye goin' to do with that?" asked Si.

"You jest do 's I tell ye, and don't ax no questions. Cram some o' this hay into yer knapsack 'n' fill 'er up, 'n' then put a shirt or suthin, the best ye kin find, on top, 'n' the colonel 'll think she's full o' clothes right from the laundry. I'm goin' ter fix mine that way."

"Shorty, you're a trump!" said Si approvingly. "That 'll be bully!'"

It required but a few minutes to carry out the plan. The hay was stuffed into the knapsacks, and all vagrant spears were carefully tucked in. Then a garment, folded so as to conceal its worst features, was nicely spread over the hay, the flaps were closed and buckled, and the young Hoosiers were ready for inspection.

"S'posen the colonel sh'd take a notion to go pokin' down into them knapsacks," said Si; "don't ye think it 'd be purty cold weather fer us?"

"P'r'aps it mout" answered Shorty; "but we've got ter take the chances. He's got six er seven hunderd knapsacks to 'nspect, 'n' I don't b'lieve he'll stick his nose down into very many on 'em!"

At the appointed time the battalion was formed and the inspection was gone through with in good style. The colonel and the field and staff officers, escorted by the captain of each successive company, moved grandly between the ranks, their swords dangling around and getting mixed up with their legs. The soldiers stood facing inward like so many wooden men, with their open knapsacks lying upon the ground at their feet. The colonel looked sharply right and left, stopping now and then to commend a soldier whose "traps" were in particularly good condition, or to "go for" another whose slouchy appearance betokened untidy habits. If a button was missing, or a shoe untied, his eye was keen to detect it, and a word of reproof was administered to the delinquent.

As the colonel started down the line of Company Q, Si watched him out of the corners of his eyes with no little anxiety. His heart thumped as he saw him occasionally stoop and fumble over the contents of a knapsack, evidently to test the truth of Longfellow's declaration that "things are not what they seem." What if the colonel should go down into the bowels of *his* knapsack! He shuddered at the thought.

Si almost fainted when he saw the colonel stop in front of Shorty and make an examination of his fat-looking knapsack. Military dignity gave way when the removal of the single garment exposed the stuffing of hay. The officers burst into a laugh at the unexpected revelation, while the boys on either side almost exploded in their enjoyment of Shorty's discomfiture.

SHORTY'S COLD DAY.

"Captain," said the colonel, with as much sternness as he could command, "as soon as your company is dismissed, detail a guard to take charge of this man. Give him a stiff turn of fatigue duty. You can find something for him to do; and make him work hard, if it is Sunday. Keep him at it till church-call, and then take him to hear the chaplain. He needs to be preached to. Perhaps, between the fatigue duty and the chaplain, we can straighten him out."

Corporal Klegg heard all this, and he wished the earth might swallow him. "These stripes is gone this time, sure !" he said to himself, as he looked at the chevrons on his arm. "But there's no use givin' yerself away, Si," he continued, in his mental soliloquy. "Brace up, 'n' mebbe the colonel 'll skip ye."

Si had been badly shaken up by the colonel's episode with Shorty, but by a great effort he gathered himself together and was at his best, externally, when the colonel reached him, though his thoughts were in a raging condition. He stood as straight as a ramrod, his face was clean and rosy, and his general make-up was as good as could be expected under the circumstances.

The colonel had always remembered Si as the soldier he had promoted for his gallantry. As he came up he greeted the corporal with a smile and a nod of recognition. He was evidently pleased at his tidy appearance. He cast a glance at the voluptuous knapsack, and Si's heart seemed to sink away down into his shoes.

But the fates were kind to Si that day. The colonel turned to the captain and told him that Corporal Klegg was the model soldier of Company Q. Si was the happiest man in the universe at that precise moment. It was not on account of the compliment the colonel had paid him, but because his knapsack had escaped a critical examination.

The inspection over, Company Q marched back to its quarters and was dismissed. Poor Shorty was soon hard at work chopping wood, with a guard on duty over him. Si was sorry for him, and at the same time felt a glow of pleasure at the thought that it was not his own knapsack instead of Shorty's that the colonel had examined. He could not help feeling, too, that it was a great joke on Shorty to be caught in his own trap.

Shorty took his medicine like a man, unheeding the gibes and jeers of his hard-hearted comrades.

The bugle sounded the call for religious services. Shorty was not in a frame of mind that fitted him for devout worship. In fact, few in the regiment had greater need of the regenerating influence. He had never been inside of a church but two or three times in his life, and he really felt that to be compelled to go and listen to the chaplain's sermon was the hardest part of the double punishment the colonel had inflict-ed upon him.

The companies were all marched to a wooded knoll just outside the camp. Shorty had the companion-ship of a guard with fixed bayo-net, who escorted him to the place chosen for the services. He was taken to a point near the chaplain, that he might get the full benefit of the preacher's words.

CALLING TO REPENTANCE.

Under the spreading trees, whose foliage was brilliant with the hues of autumn, in the mellow sunshine of that October day, the men seated themselves upon the ground to hear the gospel preached. The chaplain, in his best uniform, stood and prayed fervently for Divine guidance and protection and blessing, while the soldiers listened, with heads reverently bowed. Then he gave out the familiar hymn,

"Am I a soldier of the cross,"

and all joined in the old tune "Balerma," their voices swelling in mighty chorus. As they sang,

"Are there no foes for me to face?"

there came to the minds of many a practical application
of the words, in view of the long and fruitless chase after
the rebels, in which they had been engaged.

The chaplain had formerly been an old-fashioned Meth-
odist circuit-rider in Indiana. He was full of fiery zeal,
and his vivid portrayal of the horrors of future punishment ought to have had a salutary effect upon Shorty,
but it is greatly to be feared that he steeled his stubborn
heart against all that the chaplain said.

It was difficult not to feel that there was something
contradictory and anomalous about religious services in
the army. Brutal, hideous war, and all its attendant circumstances, seemed so utterly at variance with the principles of the Bible and the teachings of Him who was meek
and lowly, that few of the soldiers had philosophy enough
to reconcile them.

The men spent the afternoon in reading what few stray
books and fugitive newspapers there were in camp, mend-
ing their clothes, sleeping, and some of them, it is painful
to add, in playing euchre and old sledge. Dress parade
closed the day that had brought welcome rest to the way-
worn soldiers.

"Shorty," said Si, after they had gone to bed that night,
"I sh'd be mighty sorry if I'd ha' got up that knapsack trick
this mornin', 'cause you got left on it so bad."

"There's a good many things," replied Shorty, "that's
all right when ye don't git ketched. It worked tip-top
with you, Si, 'n' I'm glad of it. But I put ye up to it, 'n' I
shouldn't never got over it ef the colonel had caught ye, on
'count o' them stripes on yer arm. He'd ha' snatched
'em mity quick, sure's yer born. You're my pard, 'n' I'm
jest as proud of 'em as you be yerself. I'm only a privit',
'n' they can't rejuce me any lower! 'Sides, I 'low it

sarved me right, 'n' I don't keer so 1 didn't git *you* inter no scrape."

The forms of punishment in the army were many and unique. Some of them were grotesque and ridiculous in the extreme—particularly those for minor offenses, which came within the discretion of regimental and company commanders. Commissioned officers could only be punished by the sentence of a court-martial. They could not be "reduced" in rank. Reprimand and forfeiture of pay were common penalties for the milder forms of their trespasses and sins. In flagrant cases the usual punishment was "cashiering" or "dishonorable discharge," often with forfeiture of all pay and allowances due the officer. For desertion, sleeping on post, and all the graver offenses, non-commissioned officers and privates were also tried by court-martial. Only in extreme cases was the death penalty imposed. The most common punishments were reduction to the ranks—in the cases of non-commissioned officers—loss of pay, confinement in military prison, hard labor with ball and chain at the ankle, shaving the head and "drumming out of camp"—sometimes with a permanent decoration in the shape of a brand on the hip.

For minor infractions of discipline, often committed through ignorance and without wrong intent, there was no limit to the variety of penalties suggested by the whims and caprices of colonels and captains and even orderly sergeants. In many cases they appeared unreasonable, in view of the trifling character of the offenses. The "guard-house" was a retributive institution that existed everywhere. At permanent stations this was usually a building of some kind, which was made to serve the purposes of a jail. In the field it was often a tent—perhaps only a fence-corner. Wherever the headquarters of the camp-guard were fixed, there was the "guard-house." Often just before go'ng into action prisoners were released and sent to their companies. If they behaved well in battle it served as an atonement for their transgressions.

The "buck and gag" was a severe corporeal punishment. The "bucking" was done by securely tying the wrists, seating the culprit on the ground and placing the arms

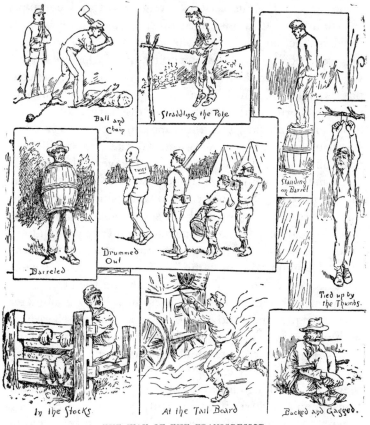

THE WAY OF THE TRANSGRESSOR.

over the knees, which were drawn up close to the body, and then thrusting a stout stick—frequently a musket— through under the knees and over the arms at the elbow. It is impossible to imagine a more utterly helpless condition in which a man can be placed. The "gag" was a piece of wood, or more often a bayonet, pushed as far back as possible between the open jaws and fastened with a cord on either side of the face, tied at the back of the neck. To be kept in this position for two hours was extremely painful. Frequently, instead of being "bucked," the offender was "tied up by the thumbs" to the side of a building or the limb of a tree, the arms being stretched upward by cords fastened around the thumbs, the culprit's heels just reaching the ground. The "gag" was usually applied in addition. This position was also very painful, and the thumbs often became black and swollen. Sometimes a man was tied by the wrists to the tail-board of a wagon during a day's march.

The "knapsack drill" and carrying a rail upon the shoulder, which were very common, have entered into the disciplinary experience of Si Klegg. In the milder class of punishments were: promenading the camp with a headless barrel around the body, suspended by cords from the neck; sitting for a stated period "straddle" of a horizontal pole, five or six feet from the ground; standing for hours, like a statue, on a barrel; confinement in the "stocks," and many others. Extra fatigue duty—for hours or days, gauged by the enormity of the offense—was universally in vogue as a corrective measure.

It would have been strange if the army did not contain many who were turbulent, lawless and insubordinate. Some were an absolute injury to the service, fomenters of disturbance, and corrupting and demoralizing in their influence. These were the ones who were dishonorably discharged and drummed out of camp to the tune of the "Rogue's March." In many cases severe punishments were necessary, but it is true, on the other hand, that they were sometimes barbarously cruel. Authority to prescribe and enforce penalties at will is a dangerous power. It was conferred, by virtue of military rank, upon some whose lack of judgment and of the "quality of mercy" should have disqualified them for official position.

CHAPTER XXIV.

" THE cap'n says we've got a mighty hard road to travel to-day," said the orderly of Company Q one morning. "Our company 's detailed to march with the wagons 'n' help 'em along. I reck'n the mules 'll have more 'n they can manage, 'n' we've got to give 'em a lift when they need it."

There seemed to be no limit to the physical possibilities of the soldiers. Leaving bullet and shell and bayonet out of the account, the successful manner in which men withstood the tests of endurance to which they were subjected was simply marvelous. Excessive and long protracted exertion, exposure and hunger destroyed the lives of many thousands, but other thousands are today illustrations of what a man may pass through and yet live. It is often said that those were "the times that tried men's souls," but a cloud of witnesses will sustain the additional statement that they tried men's bodies as well. Indeed, to those who marched so many weary miles, the familiar quotation would seem more applicable if the last word were spelled "soles."

It was often demonstrated that men could endure more than horses, or even mules. On those long and arduous marches, day and night, through cold and storm, with but scant rations, the soldiers plodded along, patiently and even cheerfully, while the animals lay down by the roadside with their heels in the air, and forever ceased from their labors. So it was that when supplies ran short the horses and mules were first looked after. A cavalryman was always expected to have his horse fed and cared for, whether he got anything himself or not. When there was a job of hauling that was too heavy for the mules, the men were called to their assistance, and this never failed of the desired result.

"That 'll be jest fun, to march with the waggins," said Corporal Klegg to Shorty, as they were getting their breakfast. "We'll pile our knapsacks 'n' things on 'n' make the mules haul 'em, 'n' we'll have a picnic."

"Don't be too sure o' that," replied Shorty. "Better wait t'll night 'n' see how ye feel by that time. I guess ye won't be quite so frisky as ye ar' this mornin'. I've got a notion how it'll be today, 'n' my advice is to fill yerself up with grub, 'cause ye'll need it 'fore ye git through."

It was not necessary to tell Si to do this, because he always did it. He ate all of his own rations, and whenever a man got sick Si would immediately enter into negotiations for his hardtack and bacon.

After the usual amount of scrambling and yelling the wagons were loaded and the men were in line ready for the road. The 200th Indiana stepped off at a lively gait, in the fresh morning air, the band playing "John Brown's Body," "Red, White and Blue," and other tunes calculated to stimulate the flagging zeal of such as were getting faint at heart and weak in the knees.

But few of the new regiments were permitted to have brass bands. The 200th had, however, been made an exception. In view of the glorious career that was anticipated for it, this congregation of patriots started on its travels with a large and well-equipped band of blowers. The veteran regiments had found that bands were a luxurious superfluity. Every company soon developed men who were so gifted in the art of "blowing" that there was little need for brass horns.

It is true that music had charms for the soldier. In the early days of the war, when the head of a regiment entered a straggling town and the band struck up a lively air, the effect was magical. Bent backs involuntarily straightened up, arms were brought to a "right-shoulder-shift," stragglers fell into their places, every soldier caught the step, aches and blisters were for the moment forgotten, and the column went swinging along under the inspiration of the martial strains. Every old infantryman will remember how it gladdened his heart and seemed to lighten his load when he heard the band play. Nor can he forget how, at night, when quiet had settled down upon the bivouac, his very fingers and toes tingled, as the strains of "The Bowld Soger Boy," or "The Girl I Left Behind Me," fell upon his ear; nor how the tears flowed unbidden down his tanned and roughened cheeks, as the tender melody of "Annie Laurie" or "Home, Sweet Home" floated through the evening air and came to him like a blessed benediction.

But the bands did not last long. The horn-blowers, as a class, were not "stayers." They appeared to use up all their wind in blowing, and didn't have any left for marching. Like most of the non-combatants, they got all their traps carried on the wagons, had no guard, picket, fatigue or other duty to perform, and were popularly believed to have a "soft thing," but they always made more fuss than anybody else. They thought they ought to have carriages to ride in, and restaurants on wheels to supply them with food.

Up to this time the band of the 200th had held its own pretty well. An occasional colic or other ailment had created a temporary vacancy, but those who were left blew all the louder, and the vacuum caused by the absence of a horn or two was not noticed in the general racket. But it was not long till the band that was the pride of those roving Hoosiers shared the fate of all the rest. The B-flat bass took an overdose of green corn, went to the hospital, and his horn was heard no more. The E-flat cornet proved to be a "tenderfoot," and after hobbling along on his blisters for a few days, he gave it up and quit. The clarionet player gradually weakened and finally went to the rear, without anything the matter, on the face of the returns, except that his "sand" had run out. The piccoloist knew when he had got enough and deserted. A wagon wheel ran over the trombone and reduced it to a chaotic wreck. The man who rattled the snare drum was taken in "out of the wet" by some rebel troopers while he was eating pie at a house a mile away from camp. Other casualties followed, and there were not enough musicians to play an intelligible tune.

In fact, there wasn't much left of the band but the drum-major. He continued to strut in the full effulgence of his glory. But he looked like a hen wandering about the barn-yard with two or three forlorn little chicks—all of her brood that had escaped the ravages of rats and the "pip." So at last the drum-major and the survivors of the band were sent back and mustered out, and the 200th saw them no more.

But during this autopsy on the late lamented brass band of the 200th Indiana, the regiment is stumbling along the stretch of bad road, and Company Q has entered upon the active duties of the day. Si Klegg is in the enjoyment of the "picnic" he told Shorty they would have.

Soon after leaving camp the column filed off the pike and struck into one of those barbarous country roads or trails that are so common in the South. They do not seem to begin or end anywhere in particular. Often the devious course runs through woods and swamps and over rough hills, the path filled with ruts and obstructed by logs and stumps and stones.

"What sort o' road 's this?" asked Si of a woman who

stood swabbing her mouth with snuff at a squatter's cabin by the wayside.

"Wall, it's fa'r to middlin'," was the reply. "Ye've seen better 'n' I reck'n ye've seen wuss. I 'low ye kin git through, but it'll take a powerful sight o' pullin' in spots."

This diagnosis proved to be correct. The soldiers managed to "git through" because they always did that, but the "powerful sight o' pullin'" was an important and prominent factor in the operation.

Company Q was distributed along the regimental train, eight or ten men to each wagon. When one of the wagons "stuck," the men took hold of the wheels, the teamster cracked his whip with extra force, and threw additional vehemence and fervor into his exhortations to the straining, panting mules. If all this failed to produce the desired effect, there was a general muster of reinforcements. Axes, levers, ropes and other appliances were brought into requisition, and the combined efforts of men and mules, with much prying and lifting and yelling, were generally successful. The yelling was considered especially valuable as an accessory. The greater the tug the louder everybody yelled. The shouts and exclamatory words were chiefly addressed to the mules. Those who were not within convenient earshot of the team went in on general principles and did their "level best" to swell the din.

Corporal Klegg, with a squad of men which, of course, included Shorty, accompanied the headquarters' wagon, containing the colonel's outfit. Si, by reason of his rank, was in charge, and determined to spare no effort to bring the colonel's wagon through in good shape, whatever might be the fate of the others. The team was one of the best in the train; the muleteer was an artist in his profession, singularly gifted in language; and for a time all went well. A lift and a yell now and then sufficed to keep the wagon moving most of the time.

The soldiers always yelled on the slightest provocation.

Day or night, in camp or on the march, they exercised their lungs whenever anything gave them an excuse for doing so. If a favorite general came in sight he received a boisterous greeting; if a frightened "cotton tail" rabbit started up it was enough to set a whole division yelling. One of those mighty choruses would sweep in a tumultuous wave for miles through a great camp or along a marching column, when not one man in ten had any idea what he was yelling at or about. It was violently contagious, and one regiment or brigade yelled just because its neighbor did. No great undertaking that required united physical effort was accomplished without the inevitable yell. The men yelled when the bugle sounded for a rest from the toilsome march, and when the head of column filed off the road betokening the end of the day's tramp; they yelled at the sutler, the commissary, the quartermaster and the paymaster; they yelled with equal ardor at the sight of a pig, a chicken or a woman—for there were times when a woman's face was not seen for weeks.

Si and Shorty chattered as they trudged along, occasionally giving their backs and shoulders a rest by hanging their knapsacks on behind, or underneath, where the teamster could not see them, and sliding their muskets in among the baggage and tent poles that filled the wagon to the very roof of the canvas. Once, when stopping for a brief rest, the teamster dismounted and went to the rear of his vehicle. This was prompted by seeing the men comfortably walking without their customary burdens. Waiving all ceremony, he quickly jerked the knapsacks from their fastenings and flung them on the ground. These were followed a moment later by the guns, which he drew from their places of concealment.

"Ye ought ter be 'shamed o' yerselves, ye lazy lubbers," he said. "There's every pound on that waggin that them 'ere mules kin pull. You fellers gits paid fer carryin' them knapsacks 'n' guns, 'n' ye've got to arn yer money. Ef I cotch ye puttin' 'em on the waggin I'll report ye to the colonel. Ye knows it's agin orders."

"S'posen you puts on my traps 'n' carries 'em awhile, 'n' see how ye like it, while I ride yer mule!" said Si, who was inclined to be a little spunky about it, and for the moment forgot that he was a corporal.

"Ye'd better be a little keerful," said the teamster, "er ye'll git them stripes snatched off 'n yer arms. You *hear* me!"

Si knew that the mule-driver had the best of the argument, and thought it wise not to continue the debate. He told the men to sling their knapsacks and shoulder their guns, and the procession again moved forward. But the boys soon had their knapsacks hanging on the wagon again, being careful to snatch them off whenever the team stopped.

Trouble came at length. They reached a slough where the mules sank to their knees and the wheels went down to the hubs. The driver yelled and cracked his whip, but all to no purpose. The wagon was immovable. After each repeated effort it was only more hopelessly bemired. A council of war was held, and it was decided that the only way was to unload. Half the members of the company were summoned to their assistance.

There was no alternative, and the men plunged into the mud. Five or six climbed upon the wagon, threw off the cover, and passed down tents, baggage, and all the paraphernalia of the colonel's "mess." The men carried them, splashing through mud and water, to solid ground ahead, where they would have to be reloaded.

Si stood with his hands in his pockets, with the evident intention of confining his efforts to "bossing" the job. The wagonmaster, mounted on a mule, came galloping up to see what the trouble was all about. He was bustling and fussy, like all wagonmasters, and made a great deal of unnecessary noise.

"What ye standin' there for, like a bump on a log?" he said to Si. "Why don't ye take hold and do something?"

"Sir, I'm a corporil!" said Si.

"Wall, that don't make no difference. You jest wade in an' help unload that wagon, or you won't be a corporal any longer 'n tomorrow."

The man on the mule appeared to be master of the situation, and Si reluctantly obeyed the order.

"Thought ye'd have to come to it," said Shorty, as Si took one corner of the colonel's mess-chest, and went half way to his knees in the mud.

As soon as it was empty the wagon was pried up and the mules succeeded in getting it upon *terra firma*. Then it was reloaded and started again upon its winding way. The tired and bespattered men

"SIR, I AM A CORPORIL!"

slung knapsacks, shouldered muskets, and plodded on.

In some places the way was very stony and uneven. More than once the wagon was only kept from overturning by the efforts of those on the upper side of the road with ropes fastened to the bows. There was much tugging and lifting, and the men became thoroughly "blown."

At length a steep and rugged hill was reached. A glance was enough to show that the mules, unaided, could not pull up the load, and that a combination of all the physical forces at hand would be necessary.

The whole of Company Q was ordered to the scene of action. The men stacked arms and stripped off their accouterments. A stout rope, big enough to anchor a ship, which had been provided for such an emergency, was fastened in the middle to the pole of the wagon, and run out ahead in two lines a hundred feet long.

"Every man to the ropes!" shouted the wagonmaster.

Corporal Klegg looked despairingly at his chevrons, as if he thought they ought to protect him from such indignities.

"I didn't 'list fer a mule!" he growled to Shorty, as they took their places at the rope.

The men stretched away up the hill, like the volunteer firemen of a generation ago hauling their "masheen" to a fire. Those who were unable to find room at the ropes swarmed around the wagon, some at the tail-board and others at the wheels, ready to lift and push when the word was given. A few, who had not rushed with alacrity to the various posts of duty, were left out, and they rather seemed to be glad of it. These stationed themselves at convenient points to yell at the mules, this department of especial usefulness being still unoccupied.

"Are you ready? Now, all together—Git!" shouted the wagonmaster.

Company Q, as one man, set up a wild, unearthly yell and braced for the tug. Like a fusillade of pistol-shots, the teamster cracked his whip as he touched up alternately the "leaders" and "swings," at the same time plunging his long spurs into the reeking sides of the saddle "wheeler," while from somewhere in his interior there came forth a series of piercing whoops that would have done credit to a Comanche warrior. The captain of the company pranced up and down the hill, cleaving the air with his sword, and screaming to the men to remember their suffering country.

He confidentially informed the first lieutenant that if he should accidentally get in range of a mule's heels during the engagement, he wanted to be wrapped in the old flag and buried where he fell.

It would have been strange if such a union of vocal and muscular forces did not yield immediate results.   The wagon went up that hill almost as quickly as if it had been shot out of a mortar.   When the summit was reached and the laurels of victory, as it were, crowned the perspiring brow of Company Q, there went up one tremendous shout of triumph.

"NOW, ALL TOGETHER!"

"Now for the next one!" said the wagonmaster. "That was well done, an' we'll snake 'em all up in jest no time."

The boys hadn't thought of the other wagons to be pulled up, and their hearts sank within them at the prospect.   But in an hour or so the work was done.   Each wagon was "yanked" up by the tugging and yelling process already described.   The teams had, however, an obvious advantage over the men.   Each of them had to pull up but once, while the men had to apply their energies a dozen times.   Si Klegg noticed this odious discrimination, and it led him to remark to Shorty that on the whole he believed he'd rather be a mule than a soldier.

Once the experiment of doubling teams was tried, and twelve mules were strung out ahead of the wagon. But they proved unmanageable, plunging and kicking and tangling themselves into a knot, to untie which required the combined ingenuity of half a dozen talented teamsters.

By the time the last wagon was at the top the men were thoroughly "tuckered out," as they expressed it. The day was warm, and perspiration streamed from their bodies. But there had already been so much delay that there was no time to be lost. Slinging their loads upon their aching backs they started on.

Soon the road led down the other side of the ridge. The descent was so steep that it was not considered safe to trust to the brakes, and the former operation was reversed. The rope was fastened to the rear of each wagon, and the men applied their muscles to the work of retarding its speed. They went dragging, slipping and skating along on their gambrels as the wagon pulled them to the bottom. It was, if possible, worse than the getting-up process.

A dire calamity befell the colonel's wagon. Near the foot of the hill one forward wheel went into a rut and the other struck a stone, and the effect was instantaneous. The wagon toppled for an instant, balancing on two wheels, and then, before aid could reach it, went over with a mighty crash. The cover and bows were dashed away like straws, and there was a general spill of the load. The colonel's mess-chest, and sundry bags and boxes containing his table supplies, were broken open and their tempting contents exposed to the gloating eyes of the soldiers. There were cans of preserved fruit, and vegetables, and pickles, and lobster, the sight of which drove the boys half crazy. There were also some dark looking bottles, but what was contained therein can only be conjectured. It was not possible to withstand such a temptation. The soldiers furtively snatched up these things and stowed them into their haversacks.

Si hesitated a moment, while a brief argument was going on between his conscience and his stomach. The latter prevailed, and he went in for his share of the spoils of war.

"Guess we'll have that picnic, arter all!" he said to Shorty, stuffing a box of sardines into his breeches pocket.

By the time the captain—who had stayed at the top of the hill to superintend operations—reached the wreck, all the loose edibles had disappeared, and the men were busily engaged in clearing away the debris, preparatory to righting and reloading the vehicle. This was accomplished in due time, and the wagon finally reached the end of the day's journey without further mishap.

"LOOTING" THE COLONEL'S MESS-CHEST.

By this time it was nearly dark. The colonel had long been waiting for his supper, and was in a famishing condition. Rumors of the disaster to the wagon had reached him, but the possibility of a raid on his commissary department did not for a moment enter his imagination.

There was a sudden and alarming rise in the temperature around headquarters when the wagon was unloaded. If the weather bureau had been in operation then and there, it would have displayed the storm flag over the territory occupied by Company Q, warning its members to look out for an immediate tornado, of unusual violence.

"Adjutant!" thundered the colonel, "have **Company Q** formed at once, with haversacks and knapsacks, and march 'em to headquarters, *promptly*. Do not delay an instant!"

Shorty, half expecting something of this nature, had been smart enough to loiter about the colonel's quarters to see what shape things would take. He hurried back to the company and told Si to "get shut" of his plunder as quick as possible.

"There's goin' ter be the biggest row ye ever seen!" he said.

Si and Shorty hastily took out of their haversacks and pockets the fruits of their pillage. Their first impulse was to put them into some other fellow's haversack. They agreed, however, that this would be too mean a thing, and they hurriedly hid them under a log.

They were not a moment too soon, for the order, "Fall in, Company Q," was already being shouted by the orderly. The company was marched to headquarters where the colonel ordered every one to be searched, himself giving personal attention to the operation. The net result was a miscellaneous heap of cans and bottles and boxes taken from the persons of half the men in the company.

"Ah! Corporal Klegg, I'm glad that none of this stuff was found on you!" said the colonel to his "model soldier," in whose faithful and efficient performance of duty he felt such a kindly interest. "I shall not forget you, sir."

Si's face became as red as a boiled beet, but it was growing dusk, and if the colonel noticed it at all he doubtless imagined it to be the blush of pride at being again so conspicuously commended. Si didn't say anything.

Details from Company Q did all the hard, extra duty of the regiment for a week. Thus was the colonel's wrath appeased.

Si's conscience smote him that night, and he wanted to

carry the plunder and put it where the colonel's cook would find it in the morning, but Shorty said there was no danger of their being found out now, and they might as well eat it up. So they went off among the trees and had their "picnic."

A NOCTURNAL PICNIC.

"Si," said Shorty, as he took a mouthful of canned lobster, "it's jest 's I've told ye before; these things ain't so bad as they seem, pervidin' ye don't git ketched. Do ye know whar the colonel got them things?"

"No; I s'pose he bought 'em, didn't he?" said Si, innocently.

"Nary–*time!*" was the reply. "The sutler guv 'em to him fer the priv'lege o' skinnin' us boys!"

CHAPTER XXV.

NIGHT had cast her mantle over the camp of the 200th
Indiana. The details for guard and picket had
been made. Videttes, with sleepless eye and listening ear,
kept watch and ward on the outposts, while faithful sentries trod their beats around the great encampment. All
day the army had marched, and was to take the road
again at an early hour in the morning. Supper had been
eaten, and the tired soldiers were gathered around the
campfires that glimmered far and near through the darkness.

For two or three weeks, since the pursuit of the rebels
was abandoned, the army had been aimlessly drifting
about, marching and camping a few days by turns,
evidently looking for a place to come to anchor until the
next campaign.

"Si," said Shorty to his chum, as they sat on a log beside the dying embers, "how d'ye like soldierin', as fur as
ye've got?"

"It's purty hard business," said Si, reflectively, "an' I
s'pose we hain't seen the worst on it yet, either, from what
I've heern tell. Pity the men that got up this 'ere war
can't be made ter do all the trampin' 'n' fitin'. An' them
fellers up in old Injianny that come 'round makin' sich
red-hot speeches ter git us boys ter 'list, wouldn't it be fun
ter see *them* a-humpin' 'long with gun 'n' knapsack, 'n'

330

chawin' hardtack, 'n' stan'in' guard nights, 'n' pourin' water on their blisters, 'n' pickin' graybacks off their shirts, 'n' p'leecin' camp, 'n' washin' their own clothes?"

"I think we'd enj'y seein' em' do all that," said Shorty, laughing at the picture Si had drawn. "I reck'n most on 'em 'd peter out purty quick, and I'd like ter hear what sort o' speeches they'd make *then*. I tell ye, Si, there's a a big diff'runce 'tween goin' yerself an' tellin' some other feller to go."

"Mebbe they'll git ter graftin' arter a while," observed Si, "'n' if they do, I hope that'll ketch 'em!"

"Wall, we're in fer it, anyway," said Shorty. "Let's make down the bed 'n' turn in!"

It did not take long to complete the arrangements for the night. They spread their "gum" blankets, or ponchos, on the ground, within the tent, and on these their wool blankets, placed their knapsacks at the head for pillows, and that was all. It was warmer than usual that evening, and they stripped down to their nether garments.

"Feels good once 'n a while," said Si, "to peel a feller's clothes off, 'n' sleep in a Christian-like way. But Great Scott! Shorty, ain't this ground lumpy? It's like lyin' on a big wash-board. I scooted all over the country huntin' fer straw to-night. There wasn't but one little stack within a mile o' camp. Them durned Missouri chaps gob-bled every smidgin of it. They didn't leave 'nuff ter make a hummin'-bird's nest. The 200th Injianny 'll git even with 'em some day."

Si and Shorty crept in between the blankets, drew the top one up to their chins, and adjusted their bodily protu-berances as best they could to fit the ridges and hollows beneath them.

"Now, Si," said Shorty, "don't ye git to fitin' rebels in yer sleep and kick the kiver off, 's ye did last night!"

As they lay there their ears caught the music of the bu-gles sounding "lights out," or "taps." Far and near floated through the clear night air the familiar melody that warned every soldier not on duty to go to bed. Next to the 200th Indiana lay a regiment of wild Michigan veterans, who struck up the words, following the strains of the bugles.

During the night there came one of those sudden storms that seemed to be sent by an inscrutable Providence especially to give variety to the soldier's life. A well-developed cyclone struck the camp, and Si and Shorty were soon awakened by the racket.

Say, oh Dutchy, will ye fight mit Si-gel?

Zwei glass o' la-ger, Yaw! Yaw!! Yaw!!!

Will ye fight to help de bul-ly ea-gle?

Schweitzer-kase und pret-zels, Hurraw!—*raw!* RAW!

"GO TO BED."

The wind was blowing and whirling in fierce gusts, wrenching out the tent-pins or snapping the ropes as if they were threads. Everywhere was heard the flapping of canvas, and the yells and shouts of the men as they dashed about in the darkness and confusion. Many of the tents were already prostrate, and their demoralized inmates were crawling out from under the ruin. To crown all, the rain began to fall in torrents. The camp was a vast pandemonium. The blackest darkness prevailed, save when the scene was illumined by flashes of lightning. These were followed by peals of thunder that made the stoutest quake.

Si jumped at the first alarm. "Git up here, you fellers!" he shouted. "We'd better go outside and grab the ropes, er the hull shebang 'll go over!"

There was not a moment to spare. Si dashed out into the storm and darkness, followed by his comrades. Seizing the ropes, some of which were already loosened, they

braced themselves and hung on for dear life, in the drenching rain, their hair and garments streaming in the wind.

Their prompt action saved the tent from the general
wreck. The fury of the storm soon abated, and Si and
his comrades, after driving the pins and securing the ropes,
re-entered the tent, wet and shivering—for the mercury had
gone down with a tumble, or rather it would have done so
had they been supplied with thermometers. But their
scanty costume afforded a weather indicator sufficiently accurate for
all practical pur-
poses.

The ground was
flooded, and their
blankets and gar-
ments were fast
absorbing the
water that flowed
around in such an
aggravating way.
Sleep under such
conditions was
out of the ques-
tion. The boys put
on their clothes
and tried to make
the best of their
sorry plight.

A CYCLONE IN CAMP.

By this time the rain had nearly ceased. Fortunately,
they had laid in a good stock of fuel in the evening, and
after a little patient effort they succeeded in getting a fire
started. Around this they hovered, alternately warming
their calves and shins.

"This is a leetle more 'n I barg'ined fer," said Si. Then,
taking a philosophical view of the case, he added, "But
there's one good thing about it, Shorty, we'll be all fixed

fer mornin', 'n' we won't have ter git up when they sound the revellee. The buglers kin jest bust theirselves a-blowin' fer all I keer!"

In this way the soldiers spent the remainder of the night. Before daybreak the blast of a hundred bugles rang out, but there was little need for the reveille.

In the gray dawn of that murky morning the long column went trailing on its way. The weather gave promise of a sloppy day, and the indications were fully verified. A drizzling rain set in and continued without cessation. The boys put their heads through the holes in their ponchos, from the corners of which the water streamed. With their muskets at a "secure" they splashed along through the mud, hour after hour. In spite of their "gums," the water found its way in at the back of the neck and trickled down their bodies. Their clothes became saturated, and they were altogether about as miserable as it is possible for mortals to be.

It seemed to Si that the maximum of discomfort had been reached. He had experienced one thing after another during the few weeks since he left home, and he thought each in turn was worse than the last, and about as bad as it could be. But he learned a good deal more before he graduated.

All through the long, dreary day the soldiers plodded on. There was little comfort to be derived from the "rests," for the ground was soaked with water.

"Why didn't we think of it, Shorty," said Si, "'n' make it part o' the barg'in when we 'listed that we was ter have umbrellers. These gum things don't 'mount ter shucks, nohow, ter keep the rain off. I sh'd think Uncle Sam might do that much fer us!"

"I reckon our clothes 'll be purty well washed by the time we git out o' this mess," said Shorty.

"Feels that way," said Si; "but how about the bilin'?"

It was nearly night when the 200th, dripping and dis-

couraged, turned into a field of standing corn to pass the
night. The men sank to their shoe-tops in the soft earth.
Si remarked to Shorty that he didn't see why the officers
should turn them loose in such a place as that. But the
longer he lived the more he found out about those things.
That was the way they usually did.

In five minutes after arms were stacked not a cornstalk
remained standing in the field. During the afternoon the
troops had gone over a long stretch of swamp road that
was almost im-
passable for teams.
Fears were enter-
tained that the
wagons of the regi-
ment would not be
up that night, and
they would not
have their tents to
shelter them from
the weather. In an-
ticipation of such
a calamity the
boys gathered in
the cornstalks, be-
lieving that they
would help out in
their extremity.
Then there was

GOING FOR THE "TOP RAIL."

a scramble for the fences. Recognizing the need of good
fuel, an order from the general was filtered through
the various headquarters that the men might take the
top rails, only, from the fence enclosing the field. This
order was literally interpreted and carried out, each
man, successively, taking the "top rail" as he found it.
The very speedy result was that the bottom rails became

the "top," and then there weren't any. Almost in the twinkling of an eye the entire fence disappeared.

The drizzle continued through the evening, and by the sputtering fires the soldiers prepared and ate their frugal suppers.

Si was crouching over the fire making coffee for himself and his "pard." After much blowing of the struggling flame, and strangling in the smoke, he had succeeded in bringing it to a boil, when the fagots on which the kettle stood gave way

and it tipped over, deluging the fire with the coffee and sending up a cloud of steam and ashes that well-nigh smothered him. Si stood speechless, in utter despair. He felt that no greater catastrophe could have befallen

SUPPER UNDER DIFFICULTIES.

him. He realized, as never before, the poverty of language at times of extreme provocation.

"Shorty," he said sadly, "it makes me feel bad sometimes ter hear ye sw'ar, but ther' can't nuthin' else do jestice ter this c'lamity. Ef ye'd say a few o' them words, seems ter me it 'd be kind o' soothin'.''

The idea of swearing for his comrade made Shorty laugh so that he could not have done it if he had wanted to.

"The wust on it is," said Si, "I put in the last particle o' coffee we had, 'n' now we'll have ter go 'thout. The rest o' the boys hain't got none, so we can't borry. This 's 'bout the hardest row o' stumps 't we've struck.''

There was no help for it, and they were obliged to eat what little they had for supper without the solace of coffee.

Word came that, as was feared, the wagons were hopelessly stalled three or four miles back, and the men would have to get along as best they could. The prospect was dreary and cheerless enough. It was little wonder that many of the young Hoosiers felt as if they would rather quit and go home. But with that wonderful facility for adapting themselves to circumstances that marked the volunteer soldiers, they set about the work of making shift for the night. No one who has not "been there" can imagine how good a degree of comfort—comparatively speaking, of course—it was possible to reach, even with such surroundings, by the exercise of a little patience, ingenuity and industry.

Si and Shorty and the others of the "mess" bestirred themselves, and it did not take them long to build, out of rails and cornstalks, a shelter that was really inviting. Shorty, who was fertile in resource, directed the work as chief architect. He was ably seconded by Si, who engaged in the enterprise with great ardor. "I jest tell ye," he said, viewing it with satisfaction, "that ain't no slouch of a shanty!"

They kindled a big fire in front of it, laid some rails within, covered them with stalks, and on these spread their blankets. It was unquestionably the best that could be done under the circumstances, but as a dormitory it had its drawbacks. The rain continued to drizzle down during the dismal night, and trickled upon their faces and soaked through their blankets as they lay in their saturated garments, under their rude and imperfect shelter. Wet, clammy and altogether wretched, they passed

the long hours, and were glad when morning came. As the daylight struggled through the misty air, the sound of bugles and drums fell upon the ears of the soldiers.

"Don't see no use gittin' up so arly this mornin'," said Si, as Shorty threw off the blanket. "I hain't got nuthin' fer breakfast, no-

"NO SLOUCH OF A SHANTY."

how, 'n' if 'twan't fer roll-call I'd jest lie here t'll time ter start. The ord'ly said we wouldn't git no rations to-day. I feel mighty empty, 'n' I don't quite see how I'm goin' ter make the riffle. I s'pose I'll git thar some way er ruther. I heerd the ajitant tellin' the cap'n las' night we'd got ter pull through twenty miles 'fore we got

LUBRICATING OIL NEEDED.

ter the next campin' place. Looks t' me like we was goin' ter have a mighty tough row ter hoe today. Jiminy, but

I'm 's stiff this mornin' 's if I'd laid in the starch all night."

"Wall, I reck'n ye've *got* ter git up," said Shorty, "'n' there ain't no use lyin' here growlin'."

Si's joints creaked as he raised himself, and seemed to be sorely in need of lubricating oil.

"Tell ye what, Shorty," he said, as he tried to double himself enough so that he could tie his shoes, "we'll have ter bore some holes at the j'ints 'n' carry 'long an ile-can so 's we kin limber up once 'n a while. I need greasin' this mornin' 's bad 's ever our old waggin did."

Shorty was more provident than Si. He had saved something over from supper the night before, so that he might at least partially fortify himself for the day's march.

"I've got a leetle left," he said. "'Tain't much, but I'll go cahoots with ye. It 'll be a purty slim meal fer two, but 's long 's I've got a cracker half on it's yourn, ef ye need it!"

"Pard," said Si, "I don't see how I'd git along without ye. I'd do 's much fer you, only—ye know, Shorty—I don't never have nuthin' left."

This state of destitution was universal throughout the regiment. Breakfast was marked by the most extreme frugality. The men turned their haversacks inside out and devoured the last crumb they contained. No miraculous power interposed, as when the five loaves and two fishes were spread before the multitude and they "ate and were filled." Few indeed of the soldiers had a "trust in Providence" sufficiently strong and well defined to take the place of hardtack.

With long, sour faces, and tempers sadly out of joint, the men fell into their places and the column drew out. The clouds hung heavy and dark, like great sponges from which the water oozed unceasingly. Everybody was in a condition of abject misery. Every old soldier will remember many such days—how he went sloshing along through the mire, with soaked and dripping garments, the water squirting up inside his trousers legs at every other step, while the maddening drizzle seemed gradually to extinguish the fires of patriotism that before had burned so fiercely in his breast. It was so that day with the 200th Indiana. Their clothing was saturated, they were benumbed by the cold, the water slowly trickled from their blue fingers and noses, and they felt themselves growing sadly indifferent as to what fate might befall the old flag.

"Durned if I'm ever goin' ter love another country!"

It was Si that said this. It is true that he did not at that time have any patriotic affection to spare for bestowal elsewhere. He needed all he had for immediate use. His remark was a fair index to the feeling that prevailed from front to rear of that bedraggled column. This became more marked when, soon after noon, there came one of those sudden changes so characteristic of the South at certain seasons, and the temperature began to fall rapidly. It kept going down, below the freezing point, and the boys thought it never would stop. The rain changed to sleet and then to snow, while a keen and bitter wind chilled the very marrow in their bones. Their clothes were soon frozen and their sleeves and trousers legs were like joints of stove-pipe.

Mile after mile, with shivering limbs and chattering teeth, hungry and forlorn, the men trudged on through blinding snow, facing the pitiless blast. None but those who have experienced it can realize the utter and absolute wretchedness of such a situation. The hearts of many who may read this will yearn with sympathy and compassion for Si and Shorty, and their comrades of the 200th Indiana.

Minutes stretched into hours, and hours that seemed interminable dragged along in slow procession, as if they, too, were chilled and stiffened. The regimental flag had been rolled around its staff and covered with its sheath of black. The twinkle of its stars and the rustle of its silken folds no longer cheered the drooping spirits of those who had sworn to follow and defend it.

"It'll be askin' a good deal of a feller to love his own country, if this sort o' thing keeps up much longer!" said Corporal Klegg, as a kind of appendix to his former observation.

When Si weakened there was little hope for anybody else. His exuberant spirits did not yield to ordinary discouragements. His remark elicited no reply, for as the men trudged along it seemed that they didn't want to do anything except commune with their own thoughts. But they all felt that Si had hit the bull's-eye.

Night came on and darkness settled down upon that band of despondent patriots. The snow fell thicker and heavier, and already lay inches deep upon the ground. More bitter and relentless blew the biting blast. There were yet miles to be traveled before reaching the place of bivouac.

Two hours more the column pulled itself along, and then turned into a field. The half-dead soldiers set up a straggling yell, rather feeble, it is true, but expressive in some degree of the delight with which they hailed the end of the toilsome day's march. A detail was immediately sent to the town near by for rations. The men had eaten nothing since their scanty breakfast. Pending the arrival of supplies, the soldiers betook themselves to the unpromising task of preparing for the night.

There may be some among those who have formed the acquaintance and followed the fortunes of Si Klegg and Shorty, who have no experimental knowledge of "soldiering." Let such, if they can, imagine themselves members of the 200th Indiana as it broke ranks that night. Cold, hunger and fatigue were doing their work. Clothes were frozen stiff. Icicles hung from the men's garments, the rims of their hats and their beards. The snow was still falling, and covered the ground ankle deep. The wind blew fiercely, nipping ears and noses and fingers with its frosty breath. Could there be a more cheerless and forbidding prospect for a night's lodging?

Fires were the first thing thought of. Through the darkness and blinding storm the men groped their way, seeking the nearest fences. No order against depredations would have been observed that night, though it came from a general with all the stars in the firmament upon his shoulder-straps.

Back with their burdens of fuel came the men, and in

A POLAR EXPERIENCE.

a few moments the kindling flames began to glimmer feebly through the darkness. Soon great heaps of rails were all ablaze. Around them, in ghostly array, hovered the shivering soldiers, eager to catch the warmth that was given out by the now roaring fires. Ah, who does not remember what a blessed privilege it was at such a time to stand before those burning piles! How thankful those half-frozen Hoosiers were for even thus much of comfort!

Si's elastic spirits were among the first to rise under the genial warmth that was gradually diffused, in spite of wind and snow.

"Let's brace up, Shorty," he said, as he stood warming first one side and then the other, while the steam from his thawing clothes enveloped him like a cloud of incense. "It's a good deal wuss 'n we thought 'twould be this mornin', but we're livin' yet, and I reck'n after what we've been through ter day we kin stand anything. We're goin' ter git some rations d'reckly, 'n' we won't have ter go off huntin' fer water, nuther, 'cause we kin jest melt snow to make coffee of. By that time mebbe the waggins 'll be up, 'n' we'll scrape away the snow, 'n' stick up the tent, 'n' build a big fire 'n front of it, 'n' have a bully time!"

Shorty did not fully share Si's enthusiasm over the prospect, but cheerfully stirred around to assist in doing what they could. Si felt that in the experience of that day they had touched bottom. He did not think it possible to reach any lower point in the scale of human misery. But there were yet greater depths which he and Shorty and the rest were very soon to fathom.

"Company Q, get ready to go on picket immediately!"

This cheerful command was shouted by the orderly, on receiving a message from the sergeant-major that it was Company Q's "turn." The sergeant-major did not linger around among the boys of that company. He went back to his quarters in a hurry, as if in mortal fear of his life.

"Git yer traps on, men, an' fall in, lively!" exclaimed the orderly.

"We hain't had nuthin' to eat yet!" said Corporal Klegg, aghast at the prospect of continuing his fast; "can't we hold on t'll the grub comes?"

"We're all jest as hungry as you be, Mr. Klegg," replied the orderly, "but we've got to go all the same, an' there's no use in kickin'. You git in yer place as sudden as ye can."

"Shorty, I don't b'lieve it 'd be very wicked to *kill* the ord'ly, would it?" said Si, who thought it might be considered justifiable homicide.

"Mebbe not," replied his comrade, "but 'twouldn't do no good 'cause they'd 'pint 'nother one right away. 'Sides, ye ought to 'member 't *he* ain't ter blame. The sargent-major 's the man ye're after."

It was hard lines for the boys, but there was no help for it. With much grumbling, and with longing glances at the cheerful fires, they marched away in the darkness. The company was ordered to establish its reserve on the pike, a mile from camp, posting its videttes at proper points on either side.

Through the deepening snow they moved to their station. The biting cold and the piercing blast took a fresh grip upon them. After the grateful warmth of the blazing rail-piles it was even more keenly felt than before. Scarcely a word was spoken as they traversed that dreary mile. A haystack near the pike was chosen for the headquarters, and sentinels were thrown out in front and on either flank within hailing distance.

Those upon the reserve began casting about to see if anything could be done in the way of making themselves in any measure comfortable. Si proposed to build a fire and began operations in that direction, but the scheme was promptly knocked in the head by the captain, who told him he had been in the service long enough to know that fires were never permitted on the picket-line at night, under any circumstances. Si made no reply to the captain, but he told Shorty that he thought such a night as that ought to be an exception to any rule that ever was made.

A shelter from the storm was made by leaning rails against the sides of the stack and covering them with hay. More hay was placed upon the ground within, after the snow had been scraped away, and upon this the men threw themselves, more dead than alive.

It was a long, long night. Minutes seemed hours as they slowly dragged away. Chilled and benumbed through and through by the cold, now and then taking a turn outside to keep their joints in working condition, the men shivered and waited for the dawn.

Si and Shorty covered themselves with hay and hugged each other affectionately, in the vain hope of generating a little warmth, but they were like two blocks of ice packed in an ice-house. Their clothing actually froze together, so that when they were called to go on duty it required no little effort to get themselves separated and find out how much of the heap was Si and how much was Shorty.

"Seems to me there ain't much glory in dyin' here in the snow," said Si. "If we gits killed in a fight, that's all right; it's what we 'listed fer. But them speechifyers 't come round didn't say nothin' 'bout freezin' to death, 'n' I don't see a bit o' fun in it, nuther."

"Keep up yer Ebenezer, Si," said Shorty, through his chattering teeth. "Ye're wuth mor 'n half a dozen corpses yet. It's purty tough, but ye'll be 'live 'n' kickin' termor-rer, jest the same."

Shorty had to go out and take his "trick" as vidette, and Corporal Klegg went with the squad to relieve a portion of the line.

"Good-by, Shorty," said Si, as he left his pard standing in a fence corner; "keep a stiff upper lip."

"Upper lip 's purty near froze stiff now, 'n' I guess there won't be much trouble 'n keepin' it that way while I'm on post."

"Ye'll have ter keep movin' 'round," said the man whom Shorty had relieved, "er the next relief 'll find ye friz solid!"

At the pike Si found a forlorn citizen who was pleading for permission to pass through the lines to his house, a short distance beyond. Si promptly took him in charge and marched him to the haystack. He was shaking with the cold, and begged piteously that the captain would let him go home. The officer told him his orders were imperative to pass no one, and he would have to be held till morning. He placed him in charge of Si for safe keeping. He crawled in upon the hay, and Si felt a fiendish delight in listening to his groans and curses.

Morning came at length. At the first streak of dawn everybody turned out and gathered around a heap of rails and hay that had been made ready.

"Who's got a match?" shouted Si, cheerily. "Mine's all wet 'n' they won't go!"

All the matches in the party were found to be in the same useless condition. It was necessary to send a man to the nearest house, a quarter of a mile away, before a fire could be started. Then in a moment the pile was ablaze, and never was cheerful warmth more welcome.

The members of Company Q gradually thawed themselves out, and then came a realizing sense of the fact that they had eaten nothing for twenty-four hours. They felt that their situation was really growing desperate. Daylight revealed a barn not far away, and thither went a detachment of foragers. A "razor-back" pig was found which, by some miraculous intervention, had thus far escaped the ravages of war. A bayonet was instantly plunged through the animal's vitals, and he was borne off in triumph. Half a bushel of frozen apples completed the results of the foray. On these and fresh pork the soldiers breakfasted. Two hours later they were relieved by another company and returned to camp, where they found awaiting them an abundant supply of hardtack, bacon and coffee.

"Feel's though I c'd git away 'th a pile o' this stuff," said Si, as he and Shorty sat upon a rail with a kettle of steaming coffee, a dozen slices of toasted bacon, and a pile of crackers before them. "I've got a mighty big hole ter fill up, 'n' I ain't goin' ter quit till she's full, nuther!" And he didn't.

CHAPTER XXVI.

"SAY, Shorty, have ye heerd the news?" said Corporal Klegg one morning, as he came back from the spring with a couple of canteens of water for breakfast. Shorty was toasting some strips of swine's flesh on the end of a ramrod, his comrade's function being to make the coffee. Si had come up on a run, with a smile that expanded over every part of his round face, and it was evident that he was the bearer of good tidings.

"What's up now?" asked Shorty, as he blew out the blaze that was too rapidly consuming the bacon.

"Goin' ter git paid off to-day! Bill Jinkins told me down ter the spring 't he heerd the cap'n say so ter the ord'ly. I come 's quick 's ever I could ter tell ye, 'cause I knowed ye'd be glad ter hear it."

Si sat down on a log to recover his wind, and think about what he would do with all the money he was going to get.

"Tell ye what, Shorty," he said, "I'll feel kind o' proud-like ter send some money home, though I don't 'spose they're sufferin' fer it. Dad said when I 'listed he'd have ter hire some feller t' work 'n my place, but I reck'n he's able ter pay him. I'm goin' ter send five dollars apiece ter mother 'n' sister Marier jest fer a present, so they'll know I don't forgit 'em. Then I want ter send another fiver, er

347

a ten-spot"—here Si checked his tongue and finished the sentence in his thoughts, for he didn't dare tell it even to Shorty—"fer Annabel. I'd git suthin purty 'n' send to her 'f I could, but the sutler hain't got nothin' o' that kind, 'n' if he had he'd charge me fifteen times too much. So I'll jest send her an X, 'n' tell her ter git a nice ring er suthin ter remember me by. There's no tellin' but this 'll be the last chance I'll ever have!'"

Shorty laughed as he read Si's thoughts. "Better wait," he said, "'n' see how much ye git. Don't count yer chickens t'll after they's hatched!"

For some time Si and Shorty had been financially insolvent. Their liabilities—all to the sutler—were an unknown quantity, and their assets could have been expressed by a single cipher. They had shown the same reckless disregard of expense that characterized all the new troops, and what money they brought from home had rapidly found its way into the cash-box of the "skinner." Si's empty pocket-book was a source of serious alarm to him until Shorty told him that he could get "checks" of the sutler "on tick," to be paid for the first pay-day. Si thought the sutler was very kind to "trust" the boys. Every day or two he bought "another dollar's worth o' checks, please," and they were duly charged up to him. In this way the pickles and cheese and canned peaches did not seem to cost anything, and he was lavish in his investments, without a thought of the day of reckoning.

But it was a happy time for them when the paymaster came. It did not occur to Si to figure up how much he would get, nor had he any idea what amount he owed the sutler.

"I don't need ter pay him this time fer all them checks," he said, "he kin jest 's well wait t'll next time fer part on it."

"Ye kin bet the skinner don't git left!" replied Shorty. "The paymaster stands in with him 'n' snatches ye bald-headed; he takes right out o' yer pay 's much 's the skinner says, 'n' that settles it. Ye can't help yerself."

Si and Shorty had pooled their resources while they lasted, for their mutual advantage, but the last five-cent scrip had disappeared.

"I've fergot how money looks," said Shorty. "Ef this 'ere hull camp was sellin' fer a dime shinplaster, I couldn't buy a tent-pin. I reck'n we ain't goin' ter git enough to hurt us any. A feller don't git rich very fast on thirteen dollars a month. Then, ye know, the sutler 'll git the fust grab at it, to pay fer all them checks we've been havin' of him. What thar 'll be left won't scare ye!"

Si hadn't thought of this. When he brought his mind to bear upon the cold facts he realized their truth, and it reduced several degrees the temperature of his enthusiasm.

"Guess you're right, Shorty," he said, and then added, philosophically, "but it 'll be jest 's good 's a mint 's long as it lasts. When it's gone we kin go to buyin' checks agin."

Theoretically, the money purveyor came around once in two months, and the muster-rolls for payment were made out covering that period. But the paymaster, although he always wore a gorgeous uniform and put on more style than the general commanding, was not a fighter. When there was danger of hearing bullets whistle he kept well to the rear. The exigencies of active service not infrequently delayed getting "paid off" for four or six months at a time. "Chuck-a-luck," "Honest John," and other curious and exciting games, that the boys engaged in when they were "flush," languished, and for the time almost disappeared. The possession of cash became a matter of tradition. At length, when all was quiet at the front, the paymaster would slip up, unlock his box, and feed the boys with a half year's rations. For a few days everybody rolled in wealth.

The 200th Indiana had not yet been two months in ser-

vice, but at the first regulation pay-day its account was
to be settled up to that time, so that it might start even
on the next bi-monthly period.

Early in the day the regiment went through the ceremony of being mustered for pay. The paymaster—with
shoulder-straps and brass buttons that shone as if
they were right from the foundry, and with that swelling air of importance that is always assumed by a man
who handles and pays out large amounts of money—occupied a tent at regi-
mental headquar-
ters, surrounded by
a cordon of guards
with bristling bay-
onets.

"PAYING OFF."

Each company
in turn was march-
ed up to the tent.
The men were at
their best. They
had brushed their
clothes, washed
their faces and
combed their hair
in honor of such an
important and rare
occasion. The pay-
master was the big-
gest man in camp that day, and the next in size was his fussy
clerk. The sutler, who was the chief beneficiary of the
paymaster's visit, was on hand with his accounts against
the men for the checks they had got since their funds ran
out. If two or three dollars apiece were charged up all
around for checks they never had, few of them were any
the wiser, and it was so much more clear profit for the
sutler.

The clerk called the expectant patriots one by one from the rolls, showed each man where to sign his name, and swore volubly at those who couldn't write as fast as *he* could. When a man succeeded in getting his autograph on the wrong line, the clerk fired a sulphurous volley at him that made him turn pale with fear. Then the clerk figured out the amount due him, after deducting the claim of the sutler, and the paymaster counted it out in crisp, crackling bills and scrip. With a bow and an involuntary "Thank'ee, sir!" he received his money and turned away, an object of supreme envy, for the moment, to those whose names began with W and Y and were therefore at the end of the roll.

"Attention, Company Q!"

The boys had been standing in line half an hour, waiting to be summoned into the solemn and awful presence of the paymaster. They responded briskly as these words of command fell from the lips of the orderly. A moment later the company stood, carefully right-dressed, in front of the pay-tent. The captain and the lieutenants were first attended to. For their six or seven weeks of service they got about two hundred dollars apiece. Si thought the nimble fingers of the paymaster would never get through counting out the ten-dollar bills to them. He was a little deficient in mathematics, but he had a vague notion that it wouldn't take quite as long to count out *his* money as it did the captain's.

The orderly came next on the roll after the officers. Si noticed that there was a very sudden shrinkage in the size of the "pile." The captain and the lieutenants got whole handfuls of bills, that made their pockets bulge out like the bay-windows of a house, when they stowed them away. Two or three spry flips of the paymaster's fingers quickly made up the thin parcel that was handed to the orderly as his stipend—and Si supposed that *he* got a good deal more pay than a corporal.

It did not take long to go through the sergeants and then the clerk struck the corporals. Although Si Klegg's name was at the end of the list—as he was only eighth corporal—his heart throbbed with pleasurable emotions at the thought that his impoverished condition would be relieved several minutes sooner than if he was a poor private, and his name was away down among the K's.

"Corporal Josiah Klegg!" at last called out the clerk.

Si took off his hat, put it under his arm, and walked shyly up, with a scared look on his face, to the table on which the financial business was being transacted. On the other side of it sat the paymaster, overpowering in his dignity, with his big tin box full of money. Next to him was the fidgety clerk, and at one end of the table that man of gall and iron-plated cheek, the sutler.

"Take this pen and sign yer name there," said the clerk, indicating the place with the tip of the holder.

"On this line?" asked Si.

"Yes, right there where I told ye!" replied the clerk, with a flavor of mustard and pepper in his voice.

Si carefully dipped the pen in the ink-bottle and, in doing so, lost the line on the muster-roll. The roll was nearly as large as a barn-door, and it was almost necessary for one to have a chart and compass in order to keep his bearings on its broad expanse and among its multitudinous columns.

"Which line?" asked Si, timidly, for he saw indications of a storm on the face of the impatient clerk.

"Why, *there!* Haven't ye got any eyes in yer head?"

"Oh, this 'ere 's the one ye mean?" said Si, putting his finger down in such a way as to cover two or three adjacent lines.

Then he seized the pen with a grip like the claws of a lobster, screwed up his mouth, and began to build a J. Some of the corporals not being present there were vacant lines, and Si managed, after all, to start in wrong.

"*That* ain't the place!" said the clerk, snappishly. "How many times have I got to tell ye?" And he viciously stabbed his pencil through the paper at the right spot. "If all of Company Q are as slow as you we won't get 'em paid off in a week. Now hustle, you—"

"Gently, gently, there!" interrupted the colonel, who was sitting in the tent exercising a fatherly supervision over the operations. "Have a little patience with Corporal Klegg. Perhaps he ain't as smart as you are with a pen, but he is one of my best soldiers, and I'm not going to have him abused." Then, turning to Si, he added: "Start right, Corporal, and then just go ahead and sign your name."

Si blushed at the colonel's compliment, and was reassured by knowing that he had such good backing. For an instant he felt that he would like to have the paymaster's clerk out back of the tent for a few minutes, and he would polish him off so thoroughly that they would have to carry him to the hospital on a stretcher. He was tempted to give the clerk a piece of his mind, but was afraid that if he did he wouldn't get his money. So he pocketed his wrath, mentally resolving that he would lie low for the clerk that night and try and get a chance to "punch his head."

Once more applying himself to his task, he had, after much labor, finished "Josiah," when he heard the clerk figuring out the amount due him.

HIS AUTOGRAPH.

"Let's see," mused the clerk, "one month and sixteen days. One month is thirteen dollars, and—"

"How much did ye say?" asked Si, as he stopped and looked at the clerk with astonishment.

"I said one month was thirteen dollars," replied the

testy clerk. * "Don't interrupt me again, sir, if you please!"

"But—but don't—c-corporils—git any—more 'n that? That's same 's—privits!"

"Thirteen dollars a month, sir!" and the clerk took up the thread of his calculation. "Sixteen days at forty-three and one-third cents a day is—6 times 3 's 18; 6 times 4 's 24 'n' 1 's 25; 5 'n' 3 's 8; 4 'n' 2 's 6—6.88, ⅓ of 16 's 5⅓, makes six dollars 'n' ninety-three 'n' one-third cents. We'll have to dock the third of a cent, 'cause the government can't afford to give ye the other two-thirds. Add thirteen for one month, whole amount 's nineteen dollars 'n' ninety-three cents. How much does this man owe ye, Mr. Sutler?"

"Eight dollars fifty," was the prompt answer.

"All right; subtract eight fifty, leaves eleven forty-three. That's right, major!"

Si had felt some inclination to continue the argument with the clerk. It seemed to him a glaring inconsistency to pay a man with stripes on his arms no more than a private. But he realized that debate would be useless. So while the clerk was engaged in his mathematics Si finished his autograph. Then, almost before he could think, the paymaster whisked upon the table two five-dollar bills, a one-dollar, four ten-cent scrips and three pennies.

The government started out to pay the soldiers in gold and silver. But the specie ran out in less than a year, and money that "chinked" was not again seen during the war —except by those who bought United States bonds, and clipped off their coupons at stated intervals. Greenbacks, at a discount of from twenty to sixty per cent., were considered good enough for the soldiers. Patriotism was ex-

---

* In the infantry arm of the service corporals received the same pay as privates until May, 1864. Then the pay of privates was increased to sixteen dollars per month, and the valor and efficient services of such men as Corporal Klegg were recognized by fixing the pay of that grade at eighteen dollars per month.

pected to supply the deficiency. Fractional parts of a dollar were issued in the form of scrip — "shinplasters" the soldiers called them.

"Next!" said the clerk, as he began to call up the privates.

Si picked up the money and walked slowly away. He felt as though something had struck him—he hardly knew what. A misty idea floated through his brain that in some way he had "got left." It is true that as compared with his previous indigent condition he felt now as if he owned a bank, but still the thought that he had not been fairly treated by the government he had tried to serve so faithfully, caused a temporary depression of spirits. He went off by himself, sat down behind a tree, and went into executive session.

"'Leven dollars 'n' forty-three cents," he exclaimed, as he counted it over, "fer nigh 'bout two months of a mighty sight harder work 'n I ever done on the old farm. Choppin' wood 'n' hoein' corn 'n' hayin' ain't a patchin' to it. It's purty small pay fer all this drillin' 'n'

"'LEVEN DOLLARS 'N' FORTY-THREE CENTS!"

marchin' 'n' stan'in' picket 'n the rain 'n' lyin' 'round 'n the mud. 'Leven dollars 'n' forty-three cents! An' that pesky old sutler; he looked jest as if he was sorry he couldn't grab the rest on it. I'll never buy 'nother thing of the skinner 's long 's I'm in the sarvice!"

This was a rash thing to say, but it is what the boys always said. And two hours later they would swarm around the sutler's "shebang" like flies around a molasses barrel.

The sutler's figures had fairly staggered Si. He knew he had bought a few checks now and then, but he could not remember half that amount. He had not kept any account, but somehow it seemed to him that the sutler and the paymaster, who had even clipped off that third of a cent, were like the two jaws of a vise, and between them they had squeezed him pretty hard.

It was a deep humiliation to Si to find that he got no more pay than a private. He really felt that the extra mental and physical wear and tear caused by the arduous duties and responsibilities of a corporal, ought to be recompensed by several dollars a month additional. He did not know, until he found out by experience, that the glory of a soldier's first promotion was considered to be an ample equivalent for all official requirements. But before Si had succeeded in adjusting his feelings to this view of the case he was more than half inclined to try and organize among the corporals a strike for higher wages, in the hope of securing justice.

Si was soon joined by Shorty, who, after getting his money, hunted up his comrade. It was a sort of holiday in camp, in view of the extraordinary nature of the occasion.

"How much 'd ye git, Shorty?" asked Si, as his "pard" sat down beside him.

"'Bout the same 's you did."

"'Tain't very hefty, is it?"

"I sh'd ruther say not," replied Shorty; "but it's 's much 's I thought there 'd be after the sutler 'd had *his* grab."

"Wall, it's all right," said Si, whose elastic spirits soon rebounded to their natural level; "we ain't doin' all this eatin' hardtack 'n' trampin' 'round fer fun nor fer money. As fur 's that goes, I wouldn't do it fer all a jigadier-brindle gits. 1 'spose it's what the spouters calls patri'tism. You 'n' me 's goin' ter stick to this thing, anyhow, t'll we gits them rebils licked out o' their boots. But say, Shorty, I'd like ter git a good crack at that 'ere snappin'-turtle of a clerk 't the paymaster has ter do his figgerin'. He'd think he'd bin kicked by a hull mule team. Wouldn't I dance ter see him marchin' with a gun on his shoulder?"

Already the various industries that showed so much activity immediately after pay-day had begun to thrive around the 200th Indiana. The fresh troops, the first time they were paid off, fell an easy prey to the seductive allurements of "chuck-a-luck." This is a game not especially calculated to promote intellectual or moral improvement. A novice thinks he can see through it right away, but there is where he makes a mistake. The more he tries it the less he knows about it. Experience is also likely to be expensive. The other fellow always seems, in the long run, to get the money.

The innocent youths of the 200th laid in a stock of experience that day. Hardened reprobates from some of the veteran regiments gathered in the woods about the camp, spread their "lay-outs" under the trees, with piles of money in front of them, and began to rattle their dice in a tantalizing way. The boys gathered about, like minnows nibbling at a hook baited with the first angle-worm of spring. Within an hour scores of these games were in full blast.

Si and Shorty loitered around to see what was going on. Si became a good deal interested, especially when he saw a member of Company Q win several times in succession. He wondered if luck wouldn't favor him so that he could make up what the paymaster ought to have given him because he was a corporal, but didn't, and the amount that had gone into the voracious maw of the sutler. He had a somewhat indefinite idea that chuck-a-luck was wrong, and it would make his mother feel bad, but, if the truth must be told, Si's conscience had been severely burdened since he left home, and was getting a little tired.

"I've a notion ter give her a turn," he said to Shorty.

"Better not," replied his comrade. "Them fellers 'll hornswoggle ye, 'n' they 'll bust ye sartin 'f ye play long 'nuff."

But Si never wanted to take anybody's word for anything. He would rather find out for himself.

"I'll jest go them four ten-cent shinplasters I've got, 'n' if I lose 'em, I'll quit," said Si. "What number 'll I try first?"

"I ain't goin' ter give ye no advice, 'cept ter quit 'fore ye begin," said Shorty. "Besides, ef I pick a number fer ye it'll be dead sure ter lose. That's the way it allus was with me when I used ter buck agin it."

"Here goes on the 4," said Si, and he laid one of his

CHUCK–A–LUCK.

scrips on that figure. It disappeared at the first throw of the dice.

"Now I'll try the 6," and the second scrip went to keep company with the other.

It took just four throws to get rid of his change. As the "banker" raked in the money Si began to get excited. His losses already reached the limit he had fixed, but he could not think of stopping there.

"I've *got* ter git that back, Shorty," he said, "'cause I

an't spar' it. I'll jest go a quarter, 'n' ef I c'n win a
couple o' times I'll be even 'n' then I'll sw'ar off. Here,
pard," he said to the man with the dice, "gimme change
fer this dollar! Now"—laying down a quarter—"sling yer
ivories. I'll go that on the 3."

This time Si won. "Thar, Shorty," he said, "I knowed
't 'd come my way arter a while. Here goes a half, fer
luck."

The banker got it, and in two or three minutes had
what remained of the dollar. Si began to feel for one of
his five-dollar bills when Shorty took him by the arm.

"Now, Si," he said, "I ain't goin' ter stan' here 'n' let
them fellers skin ye 'live. Ye won't have a cent left 'n a half
hour. You jest mosey 'long 'th me."

Si got up without a word and walked away with his
friend. Shorty gave him a lecture that lasted him till
the war was over, and he never tried "chuck-a-luck"
again.

Notwithstanding Si's resolution that he would break off
all commercial relations with the sutler, his appetite got
the better of him. It was nearly supper time, and he
thought some of those things the sutler had would taste
good. He concluded, upon reflection, that he could not
spend his money better than for something to eat. By a
unanimous vote he and Shorty at once passed an appro-
priation bill, and started for the sutler's.

There was a great crowd around the big tent. Everybody seemed anxious to spend his money as fast as possible. It went about as easily and rapidly as it did in playing chuck-a-luck. The sutler had spread out in tempting
array a stock of new goods, and marked up the prices to
keep pace with the active demand. His clerks were all on
the jump and the money poured in.

Si and Shorty made a few investments that they considered to be judicious. A re-count of their funds after the
purchases, however, warned them that at that rate of out-

lay they would very soon be again shivering in the chilling air of penury.

One of the uses of a chaplain was to take home, after a pay-day, the money that the members of the regiment wanted to send. He usually got back in the course of two or three months. The chaplain of the 200th went on this errand, but the boys did not load him down very heavily. The sutler went, too, and he carried a good deal

THE SUTLER'S HARVEST.

more money than the chaplain did. He was going to "salt down" part of it, and with the rest lay in a supply of goods for the next pay-day.

It became painfully evident to Si that his cherished plan of making liberal remittances to various members of his family must be abandoned.

"I guess mother 'n' Marier 'll have ter wait t'll next time," he said to himself, "but—" and an hour later Si placed in the chaplain's hand a letter. It said:

KY., Nov. 1800 and 62.

DEER ANNIE: We was pade off to-day. I dident git vary much only **a**
little more 'n leven dollers. They give me jest the saim what a privit gits
and Ime a Corporil. I think its almite y mean dont yew. And the sutler
the boys calls him Skinner cause he takes the hide rite off he got purty ni
haff my money. He sed I ode it to him fer checks. Checks is what the
boys gits from the sutler wen they aint got enny money to bye pikles an
sardeens an things. I gess the sutler puts down too dollers on his
book evry time a man byes one dollers worth of checks. Then it dont
take more'n 5 minits to spend the checks. You hav to pay 10 sents fer
a peece of cheese that aint enny biggern a postidge stamp. Thats the kind
of a harepin the sutler is. Shorty sez he gives the kurnel lots of stuff but
we cant all be kurnels fer thar woodent be ennyboddy to lik the rebbles.
Now Annie this is the furst money I ever urned fer myself and I jest
wanted to cend part of it fer yew to git sumthing thattle allways make
ye think of Si. Yew may as well have it cause if ye doant Ime afeered
the sutler will git it. Take this $5.00 and bye a wring to ware on yer
finger. Yew no wich finger to put it on. If ennyboddy asks ye hoo
give ye that wring and what yer warin it fer jist tell em nun of thare
bizness. We has sum awfle hard times but Ime goin to stick by the star
strangled banger as longs thares a rag of her left.

The rose is red the vilets blew
Sugar is sweet and bully fer yew.

Always yourn   SI KLEGG.

That night, after Si and Shorty had gone to bed, the rec-
ollection of how the paymaster's clerk had treated him
rankled in Si's breast. He felt that the great law of compensation required that he should in some way "get even"
with him. As he lay thinking over various schemes for
revenge, a brilliant idea flashed through his mind. He
thought he would ask his comrade about it.

"Shorty, wake up a minnit!"

And Si rose and shook his bedfellow, who was already
snoring.

"Whatcher want?" said Shorty, with his temper somewhat ruffled at being so rudely aroused.

"I've got an idee!" said Si.

"Wall, don't let it git away," said Shorty; "'cause ye
don't have many on 'em to spare."

"Much obleeged t' ye, pard. But say, hev ye got any
o' them little *pediculuses?* Ye know what I mean."

"I reck'n so," said Shorty; "but s'posin' I hev, w'at of it?"

"Lemme tell ye 'bout a scheme I've got in my head. Ye know that smart feller that 's clerk fer the paymaster?"

"Yaas!"

"An' ye know how he sailed into me 'cause I kicked on gittin' only privit's pay, and 'cause I couldn't write fast enough ter suit him? I s'pose he hain't got any sand 'n' was in a hurry ter git back to the rear agin fer fear he'd git hurt."

"Yaas!"

"Wall, Shorty, he don't look 's if he'd ever seen one o' them leetle bugs 't makes things so lively fer us. I'd jest like ter corral a few on 'em 'n' go up ter the tent whar he's sleepin' 'n' see 'f I can't turn 'em loose in his clothes. I'm goin' ter try it, anyhow!"

By this time Shorty was fully awake and entered with considerable enthusiasm into Si's plan.

"That'll be tip-top, Si, ef ye can make it," he said. "I'll see what I kin do fer ye!"

So Si and Shorty stripped off their nether garments, lighted a candle, and began the search. It will be sufficient to say that they did not have to hunt a great while. They secured a dozen or so robust and healthy specimens, that seemed to have good appetites. Si carefully imprisoned them in a piece of paper, hurriedly drew on his clothes and started on his mission.

"Be keerful ye don't git ketched," said Shorty; "ye know there's a guard there 'n' they'll think ye're tryin' to burgle the paymaster's money-box."

Fortunately the night was dark, and this favored Si's infamous plot. He crept cautiously up to the rear of the tent occupied by the paymaster and his clerk. A light was burning dimly within, and a guard was lazily pacing to and fro in front.

Si raised the canvas and peeped under. The disbursers

of greenbacks were lying upon cots, one at each side of the tent, with their clothes at their heads. Si could distinguish the major's uniform at one cot and he knew the other fellow was the clerk—the man he was after.

"I s'pose he's got his shirt *on*," he said to himself, "but it'll do jest 's well to put 'em inside his britches. They'll git thar jest the same."

Si carefully drew down the clerk's trousers and in an instant the work was done. He returned the garment to its place and quietly went back to his quarters.

"Guess I've got the bulge on *him!*" he said, as he entered the tent, where Shorty was waiting to learn the result of his trip.

"Fixed him, did ye, Si?"

"Bet yer bottom dollar I did," and Si told him all about it.

"Sarves him right!" said Shorty. "He thinks he's a heap better 'n the rest on us, but he ain't. He'll have 'bout a thousand of 'em in a couple o' days."

"I kinder wanted ter stick two or three on 'em in the paymaster's duds; he puts on so much style around here," said Si.

"That'll be all right," replied Shorty, "he'll ketch 'em from the clerk quick 'nuff!"

CHAPTER XXVII.

In Which Si goes Foraging, is Caught in a Spider's Web, and has a Close Call.

THE 200th Indiana had been lying in camp for two or three days, and the ambitious heroes who composed that regiment were getting tired of loafing. Nothing chafed the spirit of the new troops like a condition, however brief, of masterly inactivity. They refused to be comforted unless they were on the war-path all the time. Their ideal of a soldier's life was to take a rebel battery every morning before breakfast, storm a line of works to give them an appetite for dinner, and spend the afternoon charging with cold steel the serried columns of the foe, climbing over heaps of slain, and wading around through seas of gore.

"Company Q 's been detailed to help guard a forage train tomorrow," said the orderly one evening. "We've got to light out early, so ye want to be up 'n' dressed, with yer catridge-boxes full 'n' a day's rations in yer haversacks. Be sure yer guns is in good order, fer likely 's not we'll have a skirmish 'fore we git back!"

Members of the other companies watched the preparations with jealous eyes, envious because they were not detailed for the expedition instead of Company Q.

"Say, Shorty," remarked Si, thoughtfully, "hadn't I better write a letter home? Who knows but we'll be 's dead 's mackerels tomorrer night!"

"Fiddlesticks!" said Shorty. "What's the use o' havin'

a fun'ral afore there's any corpse! We've bin through one fight 'n' didn't git hurt, 'n' I've made up my mind there's no use gittin' into a stew over a thing that may hap'n 'n' may not. Time 'nuff to fret 'bout it when it comes. Ef we're goin' to be killed we can't help it, so let's not fret our gizzards!" And Shorty crammed a handful of hardtack into his haversack.

Shorty's view of the matter was not without its effect upon Si. Indeed, it cannot be denied that there was a great deal of common sense in his homely philosophy. Sooner or later every soldier came gradually to adopt Shorty's idea as the governing principle of his military career.

"Shouldn't wonder if you was 'bout right," said Si, as he sliced up some bacon to have it ready for an early breakfast. "You're better'n medicine ter keep a feller f'm gittin' the blues."

In the morning the orderly came around and stirred the boys up an hour before reveille, as they were to start at daylight. The primary object of the expedition was forage for the animals, the supply of which had run short. Besides this each man had a secondary purpose, and that was to gather in something on his own hook that would satisfy his longing for a change of diet. This was always the unwritten part of an order to "go foraging."

Daylight was just streaking over the camp when Company Q, equipped in light marching order, leaving knapsacks behind, moved out to where the two dozen wagons detailed from the brigade transportation were ready for the start. Each regiment in the brigade furnished a company to serve as guards. The impatient mules were braying and flapping their ears, as if they understood that they were to be the chief beneficiaries of the raid.

"Pile in, boys!" said the orderly, and they clambered into the wagons. The guards were permitted to ride until there were symptoms of danger.

Then the muleteers, bestriding the big "wheelers," cracked their long whips, addressed to the mules the usual words of exhortation, and the procession drew out upon the stony pike and took a brisk trot. Considerable foraging had already been done in the vicinity, and it was expected the train would have to go out several miles in order to accomplish its object. The boys were in fine spirits and enjoyed their morning ride, albeit the jolting of the wagons gave them a thorough shaking up.

"I guess they forgot to put any springs in when they

A SOUTHERN "MOSSBACK."

built these waggins!" said Shorty, as he shifted his position so that he might catch the bumps in a new place for a while.

"Jest thinkin' that way myself," replied Si; "but all the same, it beats travelin' on the hoof all holler!"

Three or four miles out from camp the train was halted while the officers in command made inquiries of a cadaverous native who was sunning himself on the fence, and whose principal occupation seemed to be chewing tobacco and distributing the resultant liquid around in a promiscuous way.

"Good morning, stranger," said the officer; "have you any corn on your place?"

"Hain't got a dog-goned ear left!" was the surly answer. "Some o' you-unses men wuz out here yisterdy 'n' tuk every bit I hed."

This may or may not have been true. Inquiries of this nature always developed the fact that it was a man's neighbors who had plenty of corn; he never had any himself.

"Thar's ole man Scroggs," he continued; "he lives a matter o' two mile from hyar. I 'low ye'll git sum if ye go thar. He growed a power o' cawn this yeah; he sold a heap, but I reckon he's got a right smaht left."

During this time a couple of men, sent for that purpose, had been making a hasty examination of the outbuildings on the place. They reported that they could find nothing in the way of forage. If the man had any corn he had carefully concealed it. The train started on to pay a visit to "ole man Scroggs."

"Say, pard," asked Si as his wagon drove past, "is there any rebs 'round here?"

"There wuz a few Confedrit critter-men ridin' 'bout hyar this mawnin';—mebby ye'll run agin 'em afore night."

"How many o' your boys is among 'em?"

"We-uns is all Union."

"Jest as long as we're 'round, I s'pose!" said Si.

A mile further on those who were in the lead, rising to the crest of a hill, saw—or thought they saw—a few vagrant cavalrymen far ahead. The train was halted and dispositions were made to meet any emergency likely to arise. The men were ordered to "tumble out" of the wagons. The main body was formed in advance. A line of skirmishers was deployed in front and flankers were thrown out on either side. Thus protected, the mule drivers again cracked their whips and the column moved cautiously forward.

"Now keep yer eyes skinned," said Si to Shorty, as they trailed along through the woods and fields and over fences, on one of the flanks. "If any o' them raskils comes dodgin' 'round here let's try 'n' have the first crack at 'em, 'n' git the start o' the rest o' the boys!"

Keenly alert, with muskets loaded and capped, they

crept carefully along, poking their noses into every thicket
and peering around every building. It was clear that
there would not be anything in the nature of a surprise if
the whole line was as well taken care of as the particular
point guarded by Corporal Klegg and his faithful friend
Shorty.

"It's some like huntin' squirrels, ain't it, Shorty?" said
Si, as they forced their way through a patch of brambles.

"Wall, yes," replied Shorty; "but this 'pears to be
rayther more excitin'. Ye know squirrels doesn't shute
back at a feller like them pesky rebbles does, an' the fun 's
all on one side. I reckon ef squirrels c'd shute there
wouldn't be so much huntin' of 'em!"

In due time the Scroggs plantation was reached. A
thorough search showed that there was an abundance
of corn on the place to load the wagons, and arrangements for a sudden transfer of the property were quickly
made. A third of the force established a cordon of picket-
posts around the working party, covering all the avenues
of approach, with reserves at convenient points. The
remainder of the troops stacked arms and entered briskly
upon the work of confiscation.

Part of the harvest had already been gathered, and the
first assault was made on a well-filled corn-house—one of
a group of dilapidated outbuildings a little way from the
dwelling. "Old man" Scroggs protested with profane
vehemence, reinforced by the "old woman" and the entire
family of children. There could not well have been a more
numerous progeny in one household anywhere outside of
Utah.

The head of the family cursed and swore, and his wife
and the big girls looked as if they wanted to do the same
thing, as they wrung their hands, their eyes flashing fire;
while the small-fry stood around and sobbed with a vague
idea that some dire calamity had befallen them.

The old Kentuckian declared that he was a "Union man,"

and that he would demand of the government restitution for this outrage. It was noticed that there were no young men around as there should be, according to the economy of nature, to preserve the balance of sex in so large a family. The officer in command asked him where all his sons were.

"Wall, I kaint tell yer 'zactly *whar* they is," was the reply. "They ain't to hum jest now. I 'low they've got a right to g'way ef they want ter!"

The officer had been informed that there were several

CONFISCATION.

representatives of the Scroggs family in the rebel army. The old man's avowal of loyalty was taken for what it was worth. That it was not rated at a high figure was well attested by the appearance of the plantation a few hours later.

Meanwhile the soldiers kept right along in the duty assigned them. The corn-house was surrounded by wagons, the roof was gently lifted off, and in scarcely more time than it takes to tell the story six or eight of the wagons were heaped with the contents. The mules wagged their ears and brayed in anticipation of the supply of rations they would have when they got back to camp.

Then the force moved some distance and attacked a large field of standing corn. The stalks had been "topped," but the ears were yet ungathered. The men started in between the rows and swept through that field like a tornado, pluck-ing the ears right and left. Bags, baskets and boxes were pressed into the service, and as there were not enough of these to go around, many carried the corn to the wagons by armfuls. It did not take more than an hour to strip every ear from the field. A visitation of seven-year locusts could not have done a more thorough job.

"Fo' de Lawd boss," said an old darkey who had been roosting on the fence watching the spoilers, "I nebber seed de crap gaddered so quick since Ise bawn. You-uns all is powerful smaht, dat's shuah!"

But where were Corporal Klegg and Shorty, while all this was going on?

They had been stationed as sentinels near a house, half a mile beyond, on the pike. They were cautioned to keep a sharp lookout, and for a time they obeyed their instruc-tions to the letter. Their vigilant eyes swept the surround-ing country, and no rebel could have crept up on them with-out getting a pair of bullets from their ready muskets. They saw no signs of an enemy, and after a while it began to grow monotonous.

"Shorty," said Si, "I don't b'lieve there's any seceshers 'n these parts, 'n there ain't no use 'n us both keepin' this thing up. You jest watch awhile 'n' I'll skin around 'n' see what I kin find."

Shorty agreed to this, taking it as an order from his su-perior officer. Si threw his gun up to a "right-shoulder-shift" and started off, after again urging upon his com-panion the importance of attending strictly to his duty.

Si had not gone far till he saw, penned in a corner of the barnyard, a cow with a full udder, from which a frisky

young calf was busily engaged in extracting nourishment. A violent feeling of envy toward that calf began immediately to rage in his breast. He had not had a drink of fresh milk since he left home, and he felt that a little refreshment of that kind would be particularly gratifying to his interior department. It would strengthen him and give him new courage to stand up to the rack if they *should* happen to get into a fight.

"I say, Shorty," he called, "cummere a minnit, quick!"

Si's conscience smote him for calling Shorty from his duty and leaving the post unguarded, but the voice of the tempter was too strong for him to resist, and he determined to venture it and trust to luck. Shorty came on the run, with eyes wide open, thinking his comrade had discovered some rebels hanging around.

ROBBING THE CALF.

"Look there!" said Si, pointing to the maternal scene that has been alluded to. "Let's have some o' that. We'll git over the fence 'n' you jest hold the calf while I milk our canteens full. 'Twon't take more 'n a jiffy!"

"We ortn't to leave the post, had we?" suggested Shorty.

"Oh, there ain't no danger," Si replied; "'n', besides, you kin keep lookin' out while you're hangin' onto the calf. I was allus a good milker, 'n' I'll fill up these canteens in a couple o' minnits."

So they climbed over and leaned their muskets against the fence. Shorty seized the calf and held it with a firm grip, in spite of its struggling and bleating. The cow seemed disposed at first to resent the interference, but Si's persuasive "So, bossy!" proved effectual in calming her fears, and she stood placidly chewing her cud while Si, spurred on by a guilty conscience, milked with all his might.

The canteens were soon filled, and, without stopping to drink, Si and Shorty hurried back to their post of duty. All was quiet, and no harm had resulted from their brief absence.

"I told ye 'twould be all right," said Si. "Now we'll jest empty one o' these canteens—here, take a swig—'n' we'll carry the other to camp. It'll be jest bully ter have milk in our coffee agin!"

Then they betook themselves to duty with redoubled vigilance, to atone for their derelictions. After watching an hour without seeing anything, Si said he would take another little turn around the place.

Boldly advancing to the house, which was some distance in front of their post, he was met by a good looking young woman. To Si's ardent imagination she was like a vision of surpassing loveliness. She greeted him pleasantly—for Si was a comely youth—and if the truth must be told, he actually forgot for the moment all about his duty. When she said she would get him up a good dinner, and invited him into the house to sit while she was preparing it, he just went right along.

But his conscience began to thump so loudly that after a few minutes he told her he guessed he'd have to go, but would be delighted to return in a little while and enjoy her hospitality.

"May I bring Shorty—he's my pard—'long with me?" he timidly asked.

"Certainly!" she replied with a sweet smile; and Si went away, his nerves tingling with pleasant emotions.

"Shorty," he said as he came up to the latter, "I've struck it this time. Over to that house there's the purtiest gal I ever——"

•"Wha-a-a-a-t!" interjected Shorty, with a look of astonishment; for he knew something about the girl Si had "left
behind him," and he was surprised at his comrade's trea-
sonable utterances.

Si easily divined his thoughts, for something of the same
nature had already caused his own heart to throb in a re-
proving way.

"Of—c-c-course—I d-d-don't mean th-th-that, Shorty,"
he stammered; "but she's a nice girl, anyhow, 'n' she's gittin' up a dinner fer me 'n' you. Bet ye it'll be a tip-top lay-
out, too!"

Shorty did not feel quite at ease in his mind about leaving the post again, but Si assured him it would be all right.
The peculiar circumstances of the case had sadly warped
his judgment.

So they went to the house and were cordially greeted by
their fair young hostess, who was flying around putting
the finishing touches to the meal she had prepared for
them.

"Jiminy, don't that smell good?" said Si to Shorty in an
undertone, as his sensitive nostrils caught the savory odors
that arose from the nicely-spread board.

The young Hoosiers stood their guns on the floor in a
corner of the room, preliminary to an assault on the
edibles.

"Ugh!" exclaimed the young woman, with a coquettish
shiver, "be them awful things loaded?"

"N–no!" said Si; "they won't hurt ye if ye don't touch
'em!"

Si was learning to fib a little, and he wanted to quiet
her fears.

The boys were soon seated at the table, bountifully supplied with ham, chicken, eggs, bread and butter, honey,
and all the accessories of a well-ordered repast. They fell
to with an eagerness that was, perhaps, justified by the

long time that had elapsed since they had eaten a "square meal."

While they were thus engaged, without a thought of impending danger, the girl suddenly opened the door leading into an adjoining room. A young man—who proved to be her brother—in the uniform of a rebel officer, dashed in and presenting a cocked revolver, demanded their unconditional and immediate surrender.

They were in a tight place. But Si proved equal to the sudden and appalling dilemma. It flashed through his mind in an instant how the girl had "played it" on him. He made up his mind that he would rather be shot than be captured under such circumstances. He sprang up, and the rebel, true to his word, fired. Si dodged, and the ball only chipped a piece from his left ear. There was not time to get and use his gun. With the quickness of a cat Si sprang upon him, and

THE TABLES TURNED.

with a blow of his fist laid him sprawling upon the floor. Disarming him, he placed the revolver at his head and triumphantly exclaimed:

"Now, gaul durn ye, you're *my* prisoner. I'd like ter blow the top o' yer head off fer spilin' my dinner, but I won't do it this time. But you jest git up 'n' come 'long with me!"

With this complete mastery of the situation, Si's confidence returned, and Shorty, who had recovered himself, came to his assistance.

But at this instant their ears caught the sound of horses' hoofs galloping down the pike. Shorty's quick perception told him that it was a dash of rebel cavalrymen, and that a few minutes later escape would be impossible.

"Grab yer gun an' *git!*" he said. Si cast one ferocious glance at the terrified girl, who stood, white and speechless, contemplating the scene.

Si and Shorty dashed out of the house and started for the reserve, at the highest speed of which their legs were capable. On clattered the horses, and a few shots from the carbines of the swift-riding horsemen whistled through the air.

Six feet at a jump, with thumping hearts and bulging eyes, the fugitives almost flew over the ground, throwing quick glances back at

THE VALUE OF GOOD LEGS.

their pursuers, and then ahead, in the hope of catching a glimpse of succor.

"Shorty, if we—only git—out o' this—" but Si found he hadn't any wind to spare to finish the sentence. The reader's imagination must supply the good resolutions as to his future conduct that were floating in Si's mind at this critical juncture. He saw the awful consequences of yielding to the influence of that alluring young woman and her seductive dinner. What he had read about Adam and the trouble Eve got him into, in pretty much the same way, flashed before him. It was a good time to resolve that he wouldn't do so any more.

Shorty, long and lank, was swifter on his feet than Si. Hardtack and bacon had not yet reduced the latter's surplus flesh to a degree that enabled him to run well. Shorty kept ahead, but would not desert his comrade, slowing up for an instant now and then to give Si, who was straining to the utmost every nerve, and puffing like a locomotive on an up grade, a chance to keep within supporting distance.

The soldiers of the reserve, taking the alarm, came out at a double-quick, and were fortunately able to cover the retreat of the fugitives. The half-dozen cavalrymen, upon the appearance of so large a force, turned their horses and galloped away.

"Hello, Si," said the orderly of Company Q, "yer ear's bleedin'. What hurt ye?"

"Fell down and scratched it on a brier!" said Si, as soon as he was able to speak.

That night Si and Shorty sat on a log by the campfire, talking over the events of the day.

"Don't ye never blow on this thing," said Si. "It 'd be a cold day fer us if they'd find it out."

"There ain't no danger o' *my* tellin'," replied Shorty. "But, say, *ain't* that a 'nice' girl out there?"

"She 's a mean rebel, that 's what she is! But that was a smart trick o' hern, wa'n't it?"

"Come mighty near bein' too smart fer us!" replied Shorty. "I don't want no more sich close shaves in mine. You 'member the story of the spider 'n' the fly, don't ye? Wall, she was the spider 'n' we was two poor little fool flies!"

"Shorty," said Si, "I'd a mighty sight ruther be an angel 'n' have the daisies a-bloomin' over my grave than to ha' been tuk a pris'ner in that house. But that dinner was good, anyhow—what we got of it!"

CHAPTER XXVIII.

"IT'S purty nigh Christmas, Shorty," said Si one day in December. "Goin' ter hang up yer stockin's?"

"Stockin's be blowed!" replied Shorty. "What's the use o' doin' that here? Old Santa Claus 'll never come nigh the army. He's no fool!"

"I'm 'fraid you're 'bout right!" said Si, sadly. "But I seen Pete Jimson this mornin'. You knowed him, didn't ye? He's bin trampin' 'round an' carryin' a musket goin' on two years. He told me we'd be all right Christmas, anyhow, as the guvyment always gives the soljers a bully dinner—roast turkey, 'n' cramberry sass, 'n' eyesters, 'n' mince pie, 'n' sich. Ye know when the fellers come 'round speechifyin' ter git us to jine the army they *told* us this was the best guvyment in the world!"

"Pete Jimson was only a-stuffin' of ye!" said Shorty, with a smile of derision. "Don't ye b'lieve it, Si; fer I tell ye he's foolin' ye!"

A shade of sadness crept over Si's face, as the thought that what Shorty had said might be true clouded his bright visions of a Christmas feast.

"Wall, I dunno," said he, musingly, "mebbe that's so. But me 'n' Pete Jimson used ter go ter Sunday-school together, 'n' I wouldn't s'pose he'd lie ter me 'n that way."

"Ye'll git yer eye-teeth cut arter a while, and then ye'll

377

know more 'n ye do now!" said Shorty, with a glance of
pity at Si for his simplicity.

"Wonder 'f I'll git so I kin lie like Pete Jimson by the
time I've been in the army 's long 's he has?" observed Si.

"I reckon ye will," answered Shorty; "I guess they all
does."

For some time the 200th Indiana had been lying in
camp. That night the mail brought Si a letter from home.
His sister Maria wrote that they were filling up a big box
with lots of good things which they were going to send
him for Christmas. In the letter was a slip from Annabel,
telling Si how glad she was to have a chance to send him
something. She had made another big fruit cake, all herself, for him, and she hoped the mean "grillas" she had heard
about, whatever they were, wouldn't get it. If she really
believed they would she'd fill it with "kyen" pepper, or
"pizen," or something that would make them wish they
had let it alone.

Si told Shorty, with a good deal of emotion, about the
box he was going to get, running over a list of the "good-
ies" that would be in it, and which he would be so glad to
share with him.

"I ain't goin' ter open the box 'fore Christmas mornin',"
said Si, in joyful anticipation of the dawn of that auspi-
cious day.

"I don't much think ye will, myself," replied Shorty. "I
'low ye'll be mighty lucky 'f ye git a chance ter open that
box at all. The grillas gathers in a good deal of that trash,
and what gits past them is gobbled up by the mule-whack-
ers."

But Si had an undying faith that *his* box would get
through all right, however disastrous might be the fate of
others. As Christmas drew near he began to watch for it
daily. The regiment was camped two or three miles out
from the city. Si watched every train of wagons that
brought supplies to the camp, and whenever he got an

opportunity he sent to town to see if he could get any tidings of it. Once or twice he got a "pass" himself, and hunted the city over for that box.

The day before Christmas the brigade to which Si's regiment belonged was ordered out on a reconnoissance. It was a rainy day. The brigade went charging over the fields and tearing through the woods and thickets, sometimes on the double-quick, trying to catch a squad of rebel cavalry, and then creeping up to gather in some of the enemy's pickets. Late in the evening the brigade returned to camp. Si thought he had never been so tired before in his life. All day his drooping spirits had been cheered by the hope of finding his box when he got back. But it had not come, and he was inconsolable.

"Ef I was you I wouldn't open yer box 'fore Christmas mornin'," said Shorty, as he and Si stood around the fire, getting supper. "And what d'ye think now about Pete Jimson's turkey 'n' mince-pie?"

Si didn't say anything. His grief was too deep for utterance. He didn't care whether the spangled banner had any stars left at all or not. Wet, weary, footsore and thoroughly disgusted, he went to bed and was soon asleep, dreaming of Christmas at home, and mother, and Annabel, and turkey-stuffing, and plum-pudding.

"Hello, Si, wake up here! Merry Christmas to ye!"

It was Shorty, routing out Si, soon after daylight. As soon as Si opened his eyes he saw his stockings full of something or other, pinned to the tent just above his head. He jumped to his feet with as much eagerness as when, in his juvenile days, he used to find candy apples and jumping-jacks sticking out of his well-filled hose.

The average army stocking was wonderfully made. A new one, after being worn a couple of days, looked more like a nose-bag for a mule than anything else.

Si soon found how the boys had conspired against him. They all knew about the box which he had so anxiously expected, and which none of them believed he would get. So, after he went to sleep that night, they slyly pulled off his stockings—for Si slept with them on, as did nine-tenths of the soldiers—filled them with wormy hardtack, bacon-rinds, beef-bones, sticks, and bits of old harness, pouring in beans and rice to fill up the chinks, and pinned them to the tent above him.

The greatest mistake a soldier ever made was to lose his temper on account of a harmless joke. Si was wise enough to take it good-naturedly as he emptied the "nose-bags" and drew them on his feet.

CHRISTMAS MORNING.

It was a raw December morning, with a keen, nipping air. As Si skirmished around for his breakfast he realized that all his festive anticipations of a few days before were doomed to utter and irremediable disappointment.

"It's tough, fer Christmas, ain't it, Shorty?" said Si, as he gnawed his hardtack.

If his box would only come he might yet be happy, so to speak; but hope had given way to despair.

It was more than four weeks after that time, when the debris of the battle had been cleared away, that Si's Christmas box found its way to the front. Its contents, what was left of them, were in a condition to make angels weep. The teamsters had pried it open and rioted upon the savory dainties that loving hearts and hands had prepared for Si. A small section of Annabel's cake was left, and the ravagers, with a refinement of cruelty, had written on the paper wrapped around it:

"This is bully cake. Try it!"

Almost everything in the box had been eaten, and what remained was a hopeless ruin. Rough handling, that would have done credit to a railroad baggage-master, had broken bottles of pickles and jars of fruit, and the liquids had thoroughly baptized the edibles that the mule drivers had spared. It was a sorry mess, and Si's heart ached as he gazed upon the wreck.

The forenoon of Christmas day was dull enough. The boys were let off from drill, and spent the time chiefly in writing letters and chasing the pensive *pediculus*.

Soon after noon the sergeant-major of the 200th was seen rushing along the line of the officers' tents with orders. He had the air of a man who bore important tidings. In a few minutes it was known through the camp that the commanding general had issued orders for an ad-

THE FATE OF SI'S BOX.

vance, and the army was to be ready to move at daylight next morning. Tents, wagons, and everything that men did not choose to carry on their backs were to be left behind.

"Wonder 'f we're goin' ter have a fight this time?" Si said, with some solicitude.

"Looks that way!" replied Shorty.

The quiet of the morning was followed by the bustle and confusion of getting ready to move. There was hurrying to and fro. Feet and hands and tongues were busy. The officers made the usual fuss, and kept everybody in a stew. The orderly sergeants had their hands full, as they always did at such times. There were rations to be drawn and issued—for the men were to march with full haversacks; cartridge-boxes to be inspected and replenished; the sick to be sent to hospitals in the city; needed articles of clothing to be supplied; all camp equipage and personal baggage to be packed and sent back; frequent details of men to be made for this, that and the other duty; and all the numberless things that appertained to the beginning of a campaign.

So it was that during that Christmas afternoon and evening fifty thousand men were busily engaged in preparation. While he was hustling around Si thought how different it was from all his previous Christmases, and even from the one he had hoped to have this time. But he was fast learning to be a good soldier and take things as they came.

It was late that night when the work was finished. Then the soldiers wrapped themselves in their blankets to get a few hours of sleep before the reveille should awaken them for the march to battle.

This was the way Si Klegg and all the other soldiers of that army spent that Christmas. Si managed, as did most of the others, to snatch a few minutes to write a brief letter or two. A great mail started northward the next day. Many a poor fellow never wrote again.

The soldiers did not suffer during the night from the gripings of indigestion, in consequence of having overloaded their stomachs with turkey and mince-pie. It is unquestionably true that their abstinence from these time-honored accessories of the festive day was not voluntary, but was due to circumstances over which they had no control. While nightmares were prancing around upon the prostrate forms of their friends at home, the soldiers quietly slept, wrapped in army blankets, in their camps that fringed the far-off southern city.

Nor did they sleep any the less soundly because they were under orders to march. At four o'clock they must spring at sound of bugle and at daylight the foremost battalions must file out upon the roads leading southward. The army was soon to look into the very·eye of its antagonist, and engage it in deadly conflict.

All the arrangements for an active campaign of a great army had been carefully made. The troops were thoroughly equipped and provisioned. Long trains of wagons loaded with ammunition of all kinds, for infantry, cavalry and artillery, gave unerring indication of important events in the near future. The presumption that the enemy would be equally, or at least sufficiently, well provided in this respect was shown by the suggestive array of ambulances, stretchers, medical stores and hospital supplies. Surgeons were summoned to their regiments, and put their instruments in order for the ghastly work before them. All who could not march and fight or be otherwise useful were left behind, the army being stripped of everything that could impede its movements or impair its efficiency.

A day or two before this, Corporal Klegg, while walking just outside the camp, saw an enterprising idiot nailing·a large placard to a tree. He naturally stopped and read it. It bore this legend:

EMBALMING THE DEAD

AT LOWEST RATES.

BODIES CAREFULLY PRESERVED AND SHIPPED NORTH.

Satisfaction Guaranteed—Caskets a Specialty.

CÓFFIN & GRAVES, UNDERTAKERS.

Si read this gratifying announcement two or three **times,** as if to catch its full meaning, and then turned away with a low whistle. The man—who wore crape on his hat and looked like the head of a funeral procession—had gathered up his roll of hand-bills and was starting for another tree when Si addressed him:

"Say, Mister, who is it yer guarantees satisfaction to— the corpse? 'Cause ef yer kin make *him* feel satisfied 'n' comf'table-like it'll be a fust-rate thing."

A CHEERFUL LEGEND.

"Young man," said the undertaker, "this is a serious business, and your levity is unseemly." And he went on to explain to Si his beautiful system of embalming, as if he thought he had succeeded in robbing death of half its terrors. But Si had never for a moment imagined that he was going to be killed, and the remarks of the melancholy man did not make the impression upon him that might have been expected.

"Mebbe ef ye'd git yer gun 'n' come 'long with us," he said, "ye might have a chance ter find out yerself how yer embamin' works, 'n' what sort o' satisfaction a man feels when he's all fixed."

"I would advise you to read these," was the solemn reply; and the man handed Si a package of tracts.

"I'll hand 'em 'round ter the boys," replied Si.

The 200th Indiana had passed through the first stage

of army life and experience, with the result common to all regiments. A few months of active campaigning, without decimation by battle, always weeded out the two classes of those who were but an incumbrance to an army. There were the men of whom it might be said the spirit was willing but the flesh was weak. They were ready to do and dare, but physically unable to endure the fatigues and hardships of the service. The other class was composed of those who could march and eat well enough, but were deficient in "sand." Every company had such men at first, but they did not stay long. This inevitable shrinkage had left the 200th with five hundred or six hundred *soldiers*—men who were to fight its battles and follow its flag.

The prospect of meeting the enemy had a varying effect upon the soldiers. Many of those who at that time were entitled to be called veterans had already breasted the storm of battle. The ardor begotten of a desire to engage for the first time in the deadly fray, and to hear the whistling of bullets, the bursting of shells, and the awful roar of conflict, had given place to a courage far more enduring. The truly brave man was not the one who rushed into battle "like the unthinking horse," but rather he who knew and appreciated the danger, and yet, at the call of duty, stood willingly face to face with death. This was the feeling that pervaded the older regiments as they girded themselves for the trial that was before them.

The bulging patriotism of the new troops manifested itself in the usual way. All the blood-curdling pictures of slaughter they had ever seen, and the harrowing tales told by their veteran comrades on the march and around the camp-fire, could not stanch the overflow of their bubbling zeal. Most of them could be satisfied with nothing but an opportunity to charge up to the very muzzles of belching batteries, and to plunge their yet unstained bayonets into the quivering bodies of the foe. This frantic desire

melted away when their eyes and ears had been once
shocked by the sights and sounds of battle. Their silence
on this subject ever after was oppressive.

Corporal Klegg and Shorty were typical representatives of two extreme phases of feeling. Si was in that
condition sometimes described as "spoiling for a fight."
In imagination he saw the whole country moved with admiration for the heroic deeds of Corporal Klegg, and it was
with a feeling of glad and impatient expectancy that he
awaited the long-delayed clash of arms.

Shorty took a more conservative view of the matter.
He was some years older than Si and had lost the exuberance of youth. Prosy and calculating, with an eye to the
results that were likely to follow, he was not dazzled by
the splendor of martial glory. He was no more a coward
than Si. His "pard" would always find him at his elbow,
whatever of danger might betide, but he did not pant for
it as Si did.

The prevailing idea among the members of the 200th
Indiana was that if the rebel general only knew that their
regiment was coming he would be wise and give up without a fight. They hoped, however, that he wouldn't hear
of it, because they wanted to annihilate his army and end
the war.

"Seems to me," said Si, as he was talking it over with
Shorty, "we ought ter use 'em up purty quick. I ain't
much on figgerin', but I've worked it out 'n this way:
We've got a hunderd rounds o' catridges apiece. There's
'bout six hunderd on us, and that'll make sixty thousand
catridges. I reck'n the rebs 'll be so thick 't we kin hit a
man every crack. We kin load 'n fire once every two
minits, easy 'nuff, 'n' 'twon't take us more 'n three hours
er so to kill off the hull army. I can't see why the 200th
Injianny hadn't orter cook their goose fer 'em."

"What d'ye s'pose the rebs 'll be doin' all that time?"
said Shorty. "D'ye think they're goin' ter stan' there like

so many rows o' wooden men 'n' let us shoot 'em down 'n their tracks? Ye don't want ter fergit 't they've got guns, too, 'n' they know how to use 'em jest 's well 's we do."

Si really had not thought of this. He saw the force of Shorty's suggestion, however, and that it would be necessary for him to revise his calculation.

"Wall, I don't care how ye fix it," he said, "we're goin' ter lick 'em, anyhow! The 200th Injianny's goin' to walk right inter that town there, and we're goin' ter plant the fust flag on the court-house."

"I hope ye're right," said Shorty, "but ye can't sometimes tell. We'll know more 'bout it arter the racket 's all over."

CHAPTER XXIX.

THE 200TH INDIANA MARCHES TO BATTLE, AND SI KLEGG EXPERIENCES
THE THRILLING EMOTIONS THAT PRECEDE THE CONFLICT.

FAR and near sounded the reveille through the camps of a hundred regiments, that covered field and hillside. It was two hours before dawn, but by the dancing light of the fires the final preparations for the advance were made. Every officer and man was busy. There was no time for loitering or for sentimental meditation. Horsemen dashed hither and thither with orders, and men sprang at the word, in willing and prompt obedience. All baggage and equipage were loaded upon wagons and sent to the rear. At the appointed hour the "assembly" was sounded. Companies, and then regiments and brigades, were quickly formed. The men carried full haversacks and cartridge-boxes, with sixty additional rounds per man in their pockets. Nearly all chose to be unincumbered by their knapsacks, and left them with the baggage train. Each man had his overcoat and blanket rolled up with the ends tied together like a great doughnut, and thrown over his shoulder. The bugles sounded "Forward," and the long columns, with swinging step, filed out upon the roads and stretched away to the southward.

The seasoned veterans of '61 still availed themselves of every opportunity to "nag" the recent levies. Troops

were always "new" until they had been through a battle, and by good behavior earned the right to be called soldiers. Then the good-natured jest and gibe were heard no more.

As the 200th Indiana filed past one of the old regiments it received the inevitable fusillade:

"Hey, you paper-collar Hoosiers; had ter leave yer trunks behind, didn't ye?"

"Ben measured fer yer coff'ns yet?"

"They won't none on 'em git killed; can't git 'em up close enough!"

READY FOR BUSINESS.

"How they'll climb fer the rear 's soon 's the bullets begins ter zip!"

Si Klegg felt his angry passions rise at these imputations upon their valor. He would have resented them then and there had he not a vivid remembrance of his experience upon former occasions, under circumstances somewhat similar. So he bottled his wrath and kept his eyes fixed on his file-leader. He comforted himself with the thought that sometime *he* would be a veteran, and other new troops would appear in the field. He would square the account by taking out his revenge upon *them*.

The advance occupied three or four days. Much of the time the weather was wet, raw and dismal. There was no trouble in finding the enemy. He made himself conspicuously obnoxious day and night, stubbornly yielding to the pressure of the long lines of blue, and falling back from one position to another.

It was one of those jerky, exasperating marches that put the temper and patience of the men to the extreme test. On the pikes the columns advanced and halted alternately, reaching out a little way and then gathering themselves up, inching along like huge worms. The men, wet and weary, stood around and shivered in the chilling air. An occasional cannon shot or a sputtering fire of musketry kept all on the alert.

THEY STOP FOR NOTHING.

Between these columns the stretches of field and wood were swept by heavy lines of skirmishers, supported by brigades and divisions moving in battle array. These forded streams and plunged through dripping thickets, throwing down the fences that stood in their way. Now and then, when the enemy grew saucy and did not seem disposed to take a hint, there would be a dash, a yell, and a scamper.

In this way passed the days of holiday week. The

nights were spent in abortive attempts to sleep, lying upon the muddy ground, with sodden clothes and blankets, or dozing around the feeble fires, half-blinded by smoke. Strong picket-lines extended entirely around the army, and watchful eyes kept vigil through the slowly-dragging hours. More than once each night straggling shots were heard, and instantly all the soldiers in that vast bivouac seized their arms and sprang into line.

The 200th Indiana had its full share of duty in all its diversified forms. Si and Shorty, with soaked and muddy garments, and hands and faces begrimed with smoke and dirt, were always at their post, and in the front when the regiment had the advance. The occasional whiz of a bullet or the bursting of a shell contributed a sufficient flavor of danger to keep Si in a state of effervescent excitement.

"If them raskils 'd only quit runnin' 'n' give us a fa'r stan'-up fight!" he exclaimed, as the 200th dashed through a piece of woods, only to see the gray troopers galloping in the distance.

"Don't be in a stew, Si, 's I've told ye before," said Shorty. "I don't b'lieve ye'll have ter wait much longer 'fore ye'll git 's much 's ye kin hold. Them Johnnies is only fallin' back to jine the main army, and we're goin' ter bump agin suthin solid purty quick. Now you mind what I'm a-tellin' ye, 'n' jest hold yerself level, fer ye're goin' to have all the fightin' ye want this trip!"

But it was difficult for Si to restrain his impatience. The forward movement of the army was all too slow for him. His heart beat high with ambitious expectation, undisturbed by a thought of the danger and the awful scenes that were soon to destroy the bright illusion.

After days of creeping along and picketing and skirmishing, the army struck "something solid," as Shorty had predicted. Then another day was occupied in making the necessary dispositions for battle. Arms were cleaned and put in order. Cartridges were carefully inspected, and such as had become wet and unserviceable were cast away and replaced by others. Batteries were put in position, with the chests of limbers and caissons filled with powder, ball and fixed ammunition in all the various forms of grape, canister and shell. Hospitals were established in the rear; musicians and other non-combatants were detailed to bear the stretchers, attend the ambulances, and otherwise assist in the work of caring for the wounded; medical stores were unpacked, and medicines, instruments and countless rolls of bandages placed at hand for use. Provision trains were brought up and rations issued to the soldiers. None could tell how many days would elapse before their haversacks might again be filled. The troops rested quietly in line of battle in their designated positions, calmly awaiting the storm which was to burst on the following day. There lives no man whose heart would not at such a time beat with hope and anxious fear.

BEHIND THE RAILS.

The 200th Indiana spent the day on picket, Company Q occupying the extreme outposts at an exposed point. All the rail fences in the vicinity were quickly converted into little V-shaped barricades, behind each of which two or three men were stationed. These were a partial protection against musket balls, but none whatever against artillery.

Within one of these frail shelters lay Corporal Klegg and Shorty, watching the enemy on the hills a mile away. Eager and alert, they lay hour after hour, with ready muskets, intent upon the duty assigned them.

Si was less talkative than usual. He was, no doubt, just as anxious as ever for a fight, but he did not have so much to say about it. In fact he didn't say anything. Matters had begun to look serious, and he seemed quite content now to let them take their course, without any desire to crowd them. There was now and then an exchange of shots, although the distance rendered them harmless.

But along in the afternoon something came from the other side that did reach. A rebel battery could plainly be seen on a high piece of ground far to the front, but up to that time it had remained quiet. At last the cannoneers thought they would send over a "feeler." There was a belching of smoke, a boom and the shrill scream of a flying shell. Si's heart leaped into his throat as it came nearer and nearer with its affrighting sound. Its flight occupied only a few seconds, but it seemed to Si that it lasted till sometime in the next week.

The well-timed missile struck almost at the apex of the V and instantly exploded, tearing up the ground, shattering the rails into kindling wood, and sending the fragments flying in every direction. For a moment Si and his comrade were paralyzed by the noise and shock of the explosion. A shower of earth and splinters fell upon them, but they received no serious injury. They escaped in the same unaccountable way as did thousands of others from peril equally great.

But the unabridged dictionary does not supply any words that can adequately express the degree of panicky demoralization that for the moment took entire possession of Si and Shorty. Both of them together did not have sand enough left to stock the digestive apparatus of a chicken. Many will recall similar moments during the experience of those years. The writer enters a plea of guilty for himself on more than one occasion.

Ninety-nine men in every hundred would have done just as our Hoosier friends did. True, with the bursting of the shell and the harmless dissipation of the fragments, the danger was over, but without stopping to reason this out they acted upon the natural impulse to get away from there immediately, country or no country, and they did. Si soon came to himself, and when he realized that he

was actually scared and running away, he stopped. He knew that would never do for the "model soldier" of the 200th Indiana.

"Now, Corporal Klegg," he said to himself, "d'ye know ye're jest makin' the biggest kind of a fool o' yerself? If ye gits skeered this way fer only one o' them 'ere shells, what'll ye do in a big fight when the air 's thick with 'em?"

A HASTY EVACUATION.

"Hold on, Shorty," he shouted. "It's all over now 'n' there ain't nobody hurt. Let's go back! I don't b'lieve 'nuther o' them durned things 'll hit that place, no more 'n lightnin' strikes twice 'n the same spot."

"Course we will," replied Shorty, but his voice quivered a little. "It didn't skeer me any. I jest come 'long with ye ter keep ye f'm fallin' back too fur."

Si did not question Shorty's assertion, but he wondered if his comrade had exactly told the truth.

So they went back, rebuilt their barricade as well as they could with the fragments, and resumed their watch. But it was a long time before Si's ears ceased to ring and his heart to thump against his blouse.

In the evening the 200th was relieved by another regiment, and ordered back in rear of the main line to cook supper. Just before leaving the post Shorty gathered up an armful of the splinters that were lying upon the ground.

"What ye goin' to do with them?" asked Si.

"Take 'em back to make a fire with," replied Shorty. "Them chaps over yonder done a sort o' good turn fer us arter all!"

Darkness settled down upon the two armies that lay so near, each having accepted the other's challenge to mortal combat. Every man was intent upon what the morrow would bring forth.

The veteran soldiers had learned to give themselves over to rest and sleep under any and all circumstances, with little thought for the future. Few of the new troops on the eve of such a momentous struggle, amid the excitement of the hour, were able to calm their thoughts so that slumber came to their eyelids. Under orders to leap to their feet at the slightest alarm, the men threw themselves down without removing their shoes or even unclasping their cartridge-belts. Each had his musket beside him, and lay with ears strained to catch the smallest sound of danger.

The night was cold. There was a keen and biting air, and a covering of white frost spread itself over the blankets, as the soldiers lay upon the ground, with nothing between them and the stars above that winked responsive to their wakeful eyes.

Shorty would probably have slept fairly well if his "pard" had permitted him to do so. But Si fidgeted and shivered with the cold, turned from side to side, and kept pulling off the blanket from his dozing comrade.

"Wish ye'd lie still 'n' let a feller sleep!" growled Shorty. "Ye'll have 'nuff to do termorrer 'n' ye better keep quiet while ye've got a chance!"

"I'd like ter do it, pard," said Si, "jest ter 'commodate ye; but I'm thinkin' 'bout the fight we're going to have, 'n' 'bout mother 'n' sister Marier 'n' all the rest o' the folks. I jest can't help it, Shorty!"

"Ain't weakenin', ar' ye, Si?"

"Not by a jug-full. I ain't goin' ter do any braggin', but I tell ye I'll jest die 'n my tracks 'fore I'll show the white feather. That shell bustin' under the rails today would ha' skeered old Gin'ral Jackson hisself for a minnit, but ye know it didn't take us long ter git over it. I'm gittin' myself braced up big fer what's comin'."

"Wall," said Shorty, "you jest keep on bracin' yerself up while I git 'nother little cat-nap."

Shorty dropped off into another doze while Si lay with his eyes wide open, looking up at the stars, and wondering how he *would* act when he got into the battle. He felt that he had little to fear, provided he did not lose control of himself. Hitherto he had never imagined a bullet was going to hit him, but now that he was brought face to face with the dread reality, he could not help wondering if he would be killed or wounded; and then how badly his mother and Annabel would feel. He thought, too, of Shorty, and wondered if *he* would get through all right. He would almost as soon be hit himself as to lose Shorty. Then Si thought of all his past life, and hoped he hadn't been *very* wicked. He ran over in his mind some of the scripture verses he had learned in Sunday school when a lad, and even repeated the "Now I lay me," just to see if he had forgotten it. He promised himself that if he got out of this fight he would never crawl under the sutler's tent again, nor steal anything from the colonel's mess-chest, nor play chuck-a-luck, nor swear. As to the last he could not avoid a mental reservation, in case he was detailed again to drive a mule team. As he lay thinking over all these things, the crack of a musket on the picket-line rang out sharply in the clear night air.

"D'ye hear that, Shorty?" he said, as he nudged his comrade with his elbow.

Si and Shorty seized their guns and leaped to their feet. Whole battalions arose as if by magic, and in a moment were standing in serried lines. It was a false alarm, and after a time the soldiers lay down again to wait for the morn.

It was a weary night to Si. His thoughts would have filled a volume. He longed for the day, although his feelings were not unmingled with a dread of what that day must bring to many, and perhaps to him. He wanted the battle to come on, and yet he would be glad when it was over.

Long before the dull, gray dawn of that December morning the orderly of Company Q passed quietly along the line, here and there touching a prostrate form, and uttering words of command in those low, suppressed tones that always awakened the soundest sleeper.

"Wake up, men! Fall in promptly!"

There was no blast of bugle or twang of drum, for the solid and alert battalions of the enemy lay but a short distance away. They, too, were astir betimes, for each army was preparing to spring like a tiger upon the other.

When the orderly aroused the company Si and Shorty were quick to obey the summons. Rolling up their blankets they threw them over their shoulders, took their places in line, and were ready for the duties before them, whatever they might be. Until daylight the regiment stood in battle array. To the right and left in long lines, stretched regiments and brigades and divisions. Batteries were in position, with every man at his post. Cavalrymen and general officers and their staffs stood beside their saddled horses, ready to spring into their seats.

At length the darkness melted away and the dawn appeared. When it was fairly light the soldiers were allowed to break ranks and partake of a hasty breakfast. Orderlies and staff officers galloped hither and thither with orders for the movement soon to begin. Few of the men were able to procure the luxury of a cup of coffee, for the time was short and the command to fall in was momentarily expected. Details were sent to fill the canteens with water. This would be needed, and no other opportunity might be afforded.

Si and Shorty, sitting upon the ground with all their equipments on, ate with a keen relish their hardtack and uncooked bacon. Si's heart beat with anxious expectation when he heard now and then a distant shot, and saw on every hand the constantly increasing activity in the work of getting ready for battle.

"Wonder which side 's goin' ter pitch in first?" he said to Shorty.

"Dunno nothin' 'bout it," was the reply. "The ossifers don't tell them 't carries the muskets what they're goin' ter do. We jest have ter 'bey orders 'n' trust ter luck. Looks 's if the gin'rals was each on 'em stan'in' with a chip on his shoulder, 'n' a-darin' t'other to knock it off!"

One of the chips was soon knocked off, and it was the rebels that did it. While the dispositions were being made for an attack by the Union army, the storm burst with the suddenness of a thunderbolt. From the thick cedars away to the right there came the loud boom of artillery and the "long roll" of musketry volleys. Louder and louder grew the noise of battle, as the attack extended along the line.

"That's the music ye've been so mighty anxious to hear," said Shorty to Corporal Klegg, as the 200th Indiana stood awaiting orders to go in. "How d'ye like it?"

"I hain't got the hang o' the tune yet," replied Si; "tell ye better arter a while."

As he listened to that terrible roar—that no man who has heard it can ever forget—Si clenched his teeth and seized his musket with a firmer grip. His cheek lost for the time some of its ruddy glow, and it must not be put down to his discredit if his fingers were a little shaky. He struggled hard to conceal all symptoms of weakness. He was afraid Shorty and the rest of the boys would see his trembling hands and hear the beating of his heart.

But although Si did not realize the fact, he was secure from observation. Like himself, each of his comrades was occupied with his own thoughts and feelings, without bestowing any attention upon the mental or physical sensations of anybody else.

Si was determined to be, and he was, brave. The blanched cheek and quivering limbs were not signs of cowardice. At that moment he would have charged upon a line of bristling bayonets, or leaped over the parapet of a hostile fort, into the very smoke and fire of the enemy's guns. He was simply going through the struggle, that every soldier experienced, between his mental and physical natures. The instinct of the latter at such a time—and what old soldier does not know it?—was to seek a place of safety, without a moment's delay. To fully subdue this feeling by the power of the will was not, in most cases, as easy a matter as might be imagined by those who have never been called upon to "face the music." Some there were who never could do it.

Shorty, older and less excitable by nature, took things rather more coolly than Si. Although he had never seen a battle, he had heard and thought enough about it to have a tolerably definite idea of its character, and was therefore, in a measure prepared for it, now that it was about to become a reality to him. Si had never gone as far as that. He knew in a general way that in a great battle many men were killed, and many more were wounded, but he thought only of the excitement, and the glory of heroic deeds for his country. He had enlisted to be a soldier, and considered it essential that he must do some fighting. If his imagination had ever drawn the picture at all, it fell far short of the actual scene, as he was soon to view it.

At this time Si was passing through the most trying moments of a soldier's life. Standing in his place, holding his musket in a tightening grasp, listening to the sound of battle that came nearer and nearer, looking at the smoke that circled above the trees, he awaited, with a suspense that language cannot portray, the word of command for the 200th Indiana to engage the enemy.

The volley that reaps its ghastly harvest, the charge amidst shouts of wild excitement, the desperate struggle of brave men—these, when every nerve and fiber of mind and body is strung to its utmost tension, bring no such crucial trial as the throbbing emotions that immediately precede the clash of arms.

To Si and Shorty it was no occasion for hilarity. As months and years passed, and they became accustomed to such scenes, they would learn to be cheerful and even mirthful, on occasion, in the presence of death in its most hideous forms, but not now. These were solemn moments, when the wonted sound of laughter was hushed, and it seemed a jest would be sacrilege.

Was it for lack of manliness that Si wiped a tear or two from his cheek? Let him who would answer yea, first be sure that his *own* eyes would not moisten at such a time, as there sweeps through his mind the rushing tide of hopes and fears and patriotic devotion and thoughts of life and far-off loved ones. The brave man has a true and tender heart. Tears are neither cowardly nor unmanly.

"Shorty," said Si—and his voice was low and tremulous—"I b'lieve in the good Lord 't mother used ter teach

me ter pray to. I'm afeard you 'n' me has kinder lost
our grip on such things, 'n' don't desarve very much, but
mebbe He'll be good to both on us today. I hope He'll
give us lots of sand to stand up to 't; I keer more 'bout
that 'n I do 'bout the other. I'm willin ter die—'f I have
to—but I don't want ter be no coward. Ef ye see me with
my back to the rebs ye'll do me the biggest kind of a favor
by jest puttin' a bullet through my head. And, Shorty,

if I *should* be killed, 'n'
you git home all right,
you'll tell mother that
I didn't—"

A staff officer comes
galloping up and de-
livers a hasty message
to the colonel of the
200th. " There !" he
says, indicating with
outstretched arm the
point where the com-
bat seems to be rag-
ing with the greatest
fury. Every man in
the ranks knows what
that order is, and in-
stinctively straightens
up. Every face bears

"THERE !"

the impress of determination to obey the call of duty. The
colonel springs into the saddle and his words ring out
sharp and clear :

"Attention—Battalion !"

The order is scarcely necessary, for the soldiers have
already dressed the line and stand with the magic touch
of elbows, waiting for the next command.

"Load at will—Load !"

Hands fly to cartridge-boxes, teeth tear away the paper,

powder and ball are charged into the muzzles. See the rammers leap from their sockets, and how they ring as the bullets are rammed home! Back to their places go the rammers, and caps are put upon the nipples. All this is but the work of a moment. The regiment is ready to meet the enemy.

While the men are loading the colonel rides along the line, uttering words of encouragement and cheer. He tells them that he knows every man will do his duty, and that the flag of the 200th Indiana will come out unstained, except by the blood, if need be, of its defenders. The men shout in response.

Already the tremor of hands is gone. The pallor of face has given way to the flush of excitement. Eyes are kindling with animation.

"Battalion! Shoulder—Arms! Right—Face! Right shoulder shift—Arms! Forward—Double-quick—March!"

The colonel plunges his spurs into the flanks of his horse and dashes ahead. The soldiers follow on the run. On and on they go, toward those historic cedars upon the right, where the enemy delivered his well-nigh fatal stroke. On, through the wild confusion that always reigns supreme in the rear of an army staggering under such a blow.

Still on goes the 200th, threading its way through the struggling mass of teams smarting under the lash of yelling, half-crazed drivers; horsemen vainly striving to bring order out of chaos; and demoralized stragglers who have fled or become detached from their regiments and are seeking personal safety at the rear.

Ah! here are ambulances freighted with the mangled and dying. Others are being borne from the field upon stretchers. The men of the 200th have never looked on such scenes before. They gaze upon the pallid faces and bleeding forms of war's victims. There is an involuntary shudder, and a shrinking from the agonizing spectacle. But it is only for an instant, and they press forward.

Hurrying past them go hundreds of brave men with blood streaming from their faces, or flowing from pierced limbs and bodies, but yet able to make their way to the rear in quest of aid to stanch their wounds. How tenderly they help one another in their hour of need. See that soldier with an arm hanging broken and helpless, supporting with the other a comrade who hobbles with a shattered leg. Here is another, limping painfully, but leading carefully along one whom blood and grime and smoke have for the time made sightless.

With what glad shouts of welcome these maimed and

INTO THE BATTLE.

bleeding heroes, whose breasts are yet heaving with the emotions of the conflict, greet the fresh, stalwart men of the 200th, pushing toward the front!

"How's it goin'?" asks Si Klegg of one of them.

"Its mighty hot in there!" is the reply. "The boys are hangin' on, but they need ye *bad*. The woods is full o' Johnnies, but we're goin' to whip 'em!"

"Go for 'em!" shouts another, "Give 'em the best ye've got."

Si is beginning to pant for breath, from the long double-quick, but he had rather a cannon-ball would take off his head than that he should appear a laggard. Straining every nerve he keeps his place in the eager rush of the 200th to succor the reeling line.

On and yet on! The rattle of musketry becomes more and more distinct. They begin to smell the smoke of battle. A shell comes screaming through the air and bursts over the hurrying column. The fragments hurtle on every side. The droning buzz of well-spent bullets is heard.

"Steady, men! Steady!" exclaim the officers.

They have just reach-ed the edge of the awful storm. They begin to see the bodies of the dead, lying torn and mangled, upon the ground. They instinct-ively turn their eyes away, appalled at the sight.

"STEADY, MEN!"

It requires little effort to display magnificent courage a hundred miles away from the scene of carnage, with, perhaps, no prospect that the dis-tance will ever be less-ened between the battle-field and him who talks so grandly of capturing batteries and sweeping away the blazing battalions of the foe. It is a very different thing when a man is brought face to face with the question of keeping his feet from turning around and pointing the wrong way, as he moves into the vortex of death, amidst the deafening roar of conflict, while swift and deadly missiles fill the air, and the bodies of his fast-falling com-rades thickly strew the ground.

Still on, and the bullets begin their fatal work. Now, Corporal Klegg, we shall see what kind of stuff you are made of !

CHAPTER XXX.

Si and Shorty are Tried in the Fire and Prove to be Pure Gold.

NOW the 200th Indiana changes from its movement by the flank. Still on the double-quick the regiment forms in battle array. There is a momentary pause to dress the line, and then it moves rapidly but steadily forward. Every eye is fixed toward the front. Every face is rigid with a determination not to flinch before any danger.

More thickly fly the bullets, and more angrily they hiss through the air. The first man falls. A swift bullet strikes him squarely in the forehead and he goes down, a lifeless heap. His comrades on either side for an instant shudder and look aghast.

Who, himself mortal, and liable the next moment to meet a similar fate, can look upon such a scene without a tremor? A brave fellow-soldier, an associate from boyhood, a loved messmate, perchance a brother, presses forward by your side, facing the pitiless storm. You feel the touch of his elbow, and your own courage is strengthened by his presence and comradeship. The next moment his bleeding body lies at your feet. How your heart leaps; how keen the pang that pierces your breast! One quick glance, and you are borne along by the rushing tide that sweeps on and on. Soon your mind and heart are full of other thoughts, as you enter the whirlwind of battle, and death's sickle is busy around you reaping its fearful harvest. But when the fight is done, around the camp-fire, in the narrowing circle of the "mess," on the march, or lying wrapped in your blanket, tender memories will come to you of him who fell by your side. Nor can the thrilling emotions of that moment when he was stricken down be effaced by all the years of life's longest span!

Another falls, and another! Quick as the lightning's flash speed the missiles upon their awful errand. Soon a dozen—twenty—are missing from the ranks. As you push on, cast your eye backward for an instant and you may see them. Some are lying motionless. They will answer no more at roll-call. Others, pierced through body or limb, are writhing in pain, while the fast-flowing life-streams redden the shuddering earth. Above the roar of the conflict groans and sharp screams of agony reach the ear.

A solid cannon shot comes rushing through the air with a loud "zh-h-h-h." It plows through a file, front and rear, and two brave heroes lie in shapeless, quivering mass. A well-timed shell plunges into the ranks. It bursts with deafening sound, and half a score of men are scattered upon the ground, torn and mangled by its cruel fragments.

"Close up, men!"

The gaps are closed and the panting soldiers push forward.

This is war, in all its dreadful reality. The moving canvas has at last brought to the eyes of the 200th Indiana the picture painted in its most lurid colors.

The regiment nears the spot where the fight is raging. A little way ahead, dimly seen through the smoke that now hovers over the field, is the line of blue wavering before the storm. Bravely and well those fast thinning ranks have stood in the face of that withering blast. But their cartridge-boxes are well-nigh empty. Some have fired the last charge and have fixed bayonets, determined to die rather than yield. The enemy is preparing to launch fresh troops upon them, and without speedy succor they must be overwhelmed. Messengers have been sent in hot haste to hurry forward the promised relief. Will it arrive before the exultant foe hurls his eager battalions upon them?

"Forward, my brave men; do your utmost!" shouts the colonel of the 200th. All along the line officers and men catch the word. A loud cheer bursts from every lip as they sweep forward. It reaches the ears of the sorely-pressed men at the front, and they send back through the trembling air glad shouts of greeting.

At every step men are falling before the leaden hail. Shot and shell tear the ranks, or go crashing through the trees above and around. An instant the line wavers, then rushes over the ground now thickly strewn with the dead and the dying.

Down goes the colonel's horse, pierced by a ball. Springing to his feet the officer waves his sword and dashes ahead. The shouts of the enemy are heard, and a wild yell of defiance is sent back in response.

Twenty paces more—ten—five! Lack of ammunition has caused the fire to slacken. Encouraged by this the enemy is preparing to charge. Not a moment is to be lost. The 200th Indiana passes through the decimated ranks and stands face to face with the foe. As the colonel steps to the rear of the line he gives hasty command:

"Battalion! Ready—Aim—Fire!"

With blaze and roar five hundred muskets send a volley of bullets that causes the enemy to reel and stagger.

"Load and fire at will!"

Now it is work, desperate and furious. Every man feels that his own life may depend upon the rapidity with which he delivers his fire. Cartridges and ramrods are handled with nimble fingers. Thick and fast the bullets fly into the ranks of the enemy.

But in the onward rush of the regiment we have for the moment lost sight of Corporal Klegg and Shorty. Let us find them if we can, amidst the smoke and din and carnage, and see how they carry themselves in this trying ordeal.

There, side by side, they stand, loading and firing as coolly as if they were veterans of a hundred battles. Look upon the face of Si and you will see pictured there what it was that conquered the great rebellion. See in those flashing eyes and firmly-set lips the spirit of courage, of unyielding determination, and of patriotic devotion, even to the supreme sacrifice, if need be, of life itself. There were many boys such as he, who were giants in valiant warfare — heroes, indeed, who looked unflinchingly in the face of death on many a well-fought field.

The missiles fly around him with venomous hiss and patter against the trees, but he seems not to hear them as he rams home cartridge after cartridge and fires with careful aim. The fall of a loved comrade, struck by a fatal shot, or the

"PLUCK."

sharp cry of anguish from one who has been torn by shell or bullet, draws his attention for an instant. There is a quick, tender glance of sorrow, a word of sympathy, and again he is absorbed, with an intensity that no words can express, in the awful duty of the hour. Every nerve is at its highest tension. He has no thought for himself, but now and then he turns his eye to see if Shorty is still untouched. It has been no time for talk; but, standing together in the fiery breath of battle, they have ex-

changed now and then a word of cheer. Bound together
by ties of companionship that none but soldiers can know,
each holds the life of the other as dear as his own.

Shorty is cool and deliberate, though scarcely less active
than Si in all his movements. He has never felt any real
doubt of himself. His experience with the world all his
life had been somewhat of the "rough-and-tumble" sort,
and there had been occasions when his personal courage
was thoroughly tested. His feeling for Si was like that of
a brother, and while he had unbounded confidence in his
good intentions, he had not been without a fear that his
"pard" might be one of the many whose courage would
fail at the critical moment. Ever since they were aroused
from their bivouac he had kept an anxious eye upon him,
and it was with a keen satisfaction that he noticed his
gallant bearing. An occasional glance at the face of his
comrade was enough to assure him that he was made of
true metal.

"That feller was 'bout right when he said 'twas mighty
hot in here," says Si, as he rams a bullet into his musket,
"but I'm gittin' kinder used to it now, 'n' I don't keer fer
it a bit."

Si takes a cap from his pouch, places it upon the nipple,
and blazes away.

"Thar!" he says, "I don't like ter think 't I'm here doin'
my best to kill people, but I jest hope that bullet 'll hit the
man 't broke Bill Brown's leg a bit ago. Bill 's sittin' 'hind
that tree tryin' ter tie up his leg. I'd like ter go 'n' help
him, but we've got ter whale them Johnnies fust." And
another ball from Si's gun speeds upon its mission.

The tremor and unsteadiness that Si showed in the
morning have entirely disappeared. As he had told Shorty,
he is now "getting used to it." His tongue is once more
loosened and he finds relief from the strain upon him in
talking to Shorty in his accustomed way, still loading and
firing with unabated zeal.

"I was afraid we'd be too late gittin' here"—and Si interrupts himself to bite a cartridge—"'n' I tell ye we was jest in the nick o' time, for them boys was mighty near out o' am'nition. One on 'em told me he hadn't a catridge left."

"Take that, 'n' see how ye like it!"—and Si pulls the trigger again.

"I've emptied my box a-ready," he goes on, "'n' I'm usin' the catridges I brung 'long in my pocket. Mighty glad I've got 'em, too. I've been aimin' low, jest 's the cap'n told us, 'n' I'd orter 've hit forty or fifty of the raskils by this time. I sh'd think what's left on 'em 'd begin ter think 'bout lightin' out o' there. Mebbe we'll git a chance purty soon to give 'em the bay'net. I feel 's though I'd jest like ter charge 'em once."

"P'raps the rebs 'll do the chargin'," says Shorty, who has taken scarcely part enough in the talk to make it a conversation.

The officers had ordered the men to lie down, that they might be less exposed to the enemy's fire. But Si will not lie down.

"I'm goin' ter stan' up to it," he says to Shorty, "I kin shoot jest twicet 's fast that way 's I kin lyin' down; I ain't goin' ter git 'hind no tree, nuther. I'll let the ossifers have the trees. They 'pear ter want 'em more 'n I do. It looks 's if a man was afeard, 'n' I know I ain't."

This feeling was common to new troops in their first fight. In their minds there was an odium connected with the idea of seeking cover. It was too much like showing the white feather. But in the fullness of time they all got over this foolish notion. Experience taught them that it was the part of wisdom, and not inconsistent with the highest courage, to protect themselves when opportunity was afforded. They found that it was a good thing to interpose trees and stumps and stone walls between their bodies and the enemy, while loading their pieces.

"Ouch!" exclaims Si, as he feels a smart rap on his head, that staggers him for a moment, and a twinge of pain. "Did ye bump me with yer gun, Shorty?"

"No, I didn't touch ye, Si."

"Then I reck'n 'twas a bullet. Jest look at my knob, 'n' see 'f I'm hurt any!"

They drop upon their knees and Si whisks off his hat. There are the holes where a bullet has passed through it. Blood begins to trickle down over his face.

"Plowed a neat little furrow on yer scalp, Si, but 'tain't deep. D'ye want ter go back?"

"Not 's long 's I kin stan' up and shoot," says Si. "Guess 'f I was killed I'd ha' found it out 'fore this. Take my han'k'chief 'n' tie 'er up. That's 'bout 's cluss 's I keer to have 'em come. But Johnny Reb 'll have to do better 'n' that 'f he wants ter make me quit. I tell ye, I've come to stay, Shorty."

"Bully fer you, Si! I'm proud o' yer pluck!" says Shorty, as with gentle fingers he wipes the blood from Si's face, and ties the crimsoned handkerchief around his head.

"Now I'm all right!" says Si, as he springs to his feet and rams in another cartridge. "Shouldn't wonder 'f it 'd do me good ter let out a little blood. I'd like ter git even with that chap!" And he sights his gun in the direction from which he thought the hostile bullet had come. "I hope that'll fetch him!"

Spat! A ball strikes the stock of his musket, and knocks it into splinters.

"There goes my gun, Shorty. Seems 's if them fellers was all tryin' ter hit me. But this only strikes Uncle Sam n the pocket, 'n' I guess he kin stan' it. There's poor Andy Green 't was killed a few minnits ago. He's lyin' thar with his gun 'n his hand. I'll git that 'n' try 'n' make it do good sarvis fer him 'n' me, too!"

Si flings away his disabled piece. Bending over he tenderly disengages the musket from the clutch of the yet warm but stiffening fingers of his dead comrade. Fearing that his ammunition may be exhausted he takes from the body the cartridges that remain and puts them in his pocket. A tear gathers in his eye, but he brushes it away, and again he is by the side of Shorty, loading and firing with redoubled energy, as if to make up for the time he has lost.

A bullet skims very close to Shorty's body, cutting the strap to his haversack, and the latter falls to the ground.

"They've cut off my supplies, Si," he exclaims, as a faint smile creeps over his grim face. "But I can't stop ter fix that now!"

"Never mind!" says Si. "Jest keep blazin' away at 'em, 'n' we'll manage 'bout the grub. I'll go halvers with ye on what I've got."

Scarcely twenty minutes have passed since we found Si and Shorty so bravely fighting the foe. Events crowd rapidly upon each other at such times.

We glance along the line of the 200th Indiana. Nearly half its men and officers have been killed or wounded. The body of the lieutenant-colonel lies stiff and stark. The adjutant has been borne to the rear with a bullet through his breast. The major is still at his post, with a bleeding arm carried in a sling. The brave colonel is yet untouched. Proud of his gallant men, he passes fearlessly through the ranks, with words of commendation and cheer. Now he stops for a moment to stanch a wound, and again to place his flask to the lips of a fainting sufferer.

Captains and lieutenants have fallen on every hand. Some of the companies have lost all their officers and are commanded by sergeants. But the men who have been spared fight bravely on, with no thought of turning their backs to the enemy.

Once—twice—thrice the colors of the 200th have gone down, as those who bore them have successively fallen. They disappear but for an instant. Other ready and willing hands grasp the staff, and bear aloft the soldier's beacon. The flag, torn and rent, but glorified and beautiful, floats proudly in its place. The sight of its stripes and stars, waving amidst the smoke and blaze of battle, is a sublime inspiration. It is the very embodiment of the cause for which they are fighting and bleeding and dying—the emblem of liberty and the unity of a great Nation. The soldiers cheer as they look upon it. Brave men wounded unto death, turn their eyes to its graceful folds and faintly shout, with the last gasp of swiftly-ebbing life. Ah! you who have never stood beside your country's flag amidst such scenes as this can know little of the emotions that thrilled the throbbing heart of the patriot volunteer! He never looks upon it today that it does not recall the valor and the heroic suffering of those who followed it during those fearful years of fire and blood and death!

The steady and well-directed fire of the 200th and the other regiments of the brigade to which it belonged has held the enemy in check. There are signs of weakness in the opposing line and a charge is ordered.

"Battalion—Cease firing!" shouts the colonel of the 200th, dashing to the front. "Fix—Bayonets!"

"D'ye hear that, Shorty?" says Corporal Klegg, as he quickly responds to the command. "Now we're goin' ter go for 'em. That jest suits me!"

There is a click and a clatter for an instant, and the line bristles with points of steel.

"Close up on the center!"

The line is but half as long as when it formed in the morning.

"Charge—Bayonet! Forward—Double-quick—March!"

The men spring at the word, and sweep forward with loud shouts. A minute or two and they are looking into the very muzzles of the enemy's guns. During that brief period many more have fallen, but the rest rush on like a resistless tide. The hostile line trembles, quivers, and then, without waiting to meet the shock, breaks in confusion. The men of the 200th dash after them with wild yells, picking their way among the dead and wounded that incumber the field.

Si and Shorty engage in the charge with the utmost enthusiasm. None are farther to the front than they. One of the enemy's color-bearers stands bravely at his post, but on either hand the line is fast melting away. Swiftly leaping over the ground Si and Shorty present their bayo-

THE CHARGE OF THE 200TH INDIANA.

nets and demand surrender. There is no alternative, and the flag and its bearer are theirs.

At length the eager men are recalled from the pursuit. Back they come with glad shouts of exultation, bringing many prisoners as trophies of their valor. Whatever may have been the fate of battle elsewhere along those miles of fighting, the 200th Indiana has won its victory.

A member of Company Q, a friend of Si, is one of the last to fall, in the moment of triumph. As the regiment is ordered to withdraw Si bends over his wounded comrade.

"How d'ye feel, Bob?" he asks, with kindly sympathy, "Ar' ye hurt much?"

"Purty bad, I'm 'fraid," is the answer. "I guess that bullet busted my knee. But we licked 'em, didn't we, Si?"

"Course we did! I knew we was goin' to all the time. You're a brave boy, Bob, 'n' I ain't goin' ter leave ye lyin' here. Shorty, jest take my gun, 'n' you march our pris'ner. Let him carry his flag, 'n' I'll take Bob on my back. Here, Bob, take a swig out o' my canteen.'

A draught of water refreshes the sufferer.

"Hyar, lemme give ye a lift," says the rebel color-bearer.

"I 'low we're all human bein's if we be fightin' an' killin' each other. He's wounded an' I'm a pris'ner. We ain't none of us cowards an' we kin be friends now."

Shorty and the captive gently lift Bob and place him on Si's back.

"Grip yer arms 'round my neck 'n' hang on!" says Si; and away he goes bearing him to the rear.

A COMRADE IN DISTRESS.

The 200th is relieved by a regiment which, thrown into confusion by the attack in the early morning, has been rallied and reformed, and is again ready for battle. The 200th is ordered to the rear for rest and refreshment, and to replenish its cartridge-boxes, that it may be ready if again called into action. Its wounded are tenderly cared for, but there is no time now to bury the dead. For the present they must lie where they fell.

The day wears away. All along the line the fierce assaults of the enemy have been successfully resisted. The threatened disaster of the morning has been averted. More than a third of the men in both armies have been killed or wounded. Some companies and regiments have been for the time almost blotted out of existence.

The deepening shadows of that awful night settle down upon the bloody field—upon soldiers weary and worn, blackened by smoke and grime, but yet undismayed—upon great hospital camps filled with thousands of torn and mangled men, whose sufferings tender hearts and willing hands are striving to allay—upon other thousands of wounded who yet lie among their dead comrades, chilled by the cruel December frost. It is New Year's eve.

CHAPTER XXXI.

SCENES AFTER THE BATTLE—CALLING THE ROLL AND BURYING THE DEAD.

WHO that carried gun or sword through that fearful day can ever forget the horrors of the long night which followed? It was keenly, bitterly cold. The ground and everything upon it was whitened by a frost so heavy that it seemed almost as if snow had fallen.

Those who had met instant death upon that bloody field were more fortunate than some of their comrades who, desperately wounded, were left far out between the hostile lines, beyond the reach of succor. The biting frost supplemented the dreadful havoc of bullet and shell. Lying there under the stars, mangled, bleeding and helpless, the flickering spark of many a life went out in agony.

After the fighting of the day had ceased the commander of each army gathered his shattered battalions and established his lines for the night, in readiness to meet any emergency. The soldiers of the 200th Indiana—they had nobly earned the right to be called soldiers now—were ordered to lie upon their arms. No fires were permitted. Hardtack and raw bacon, without coffee, comprised their evening refreshment.

Like all the rest, Si Klegg and Shorty were greatly fatigued after the exertion and intense excitement of the day. In the heat of battle they had no thought of weariness, but after the fight was done, when mind and heart and body were relieved from the strain, there followed a feeling of extreme exhaustion. They lay down upon the hard, cold earth, between their blankets, and tried to sleep, but could not. The appalling events of the day were before their eyes in all their awful vividness. The hours since morning had flown as if they were but minutes. Amidst such scenes the senses take no note of time. And yet, looking back to the morning, it seemed an age. Occurrences of the previous day were but dimly remembered, as if they belonged to the half-forgotten past.

"Shorty," said Si, as they lay shivering with the cold, "wonder 'f I killed anybody today! I tried ter—ye know that—when I was in the fight, but now it's all over I don't like ter think 'bout it."

"Them raskils tried hard 'nough ter kill you 'n' me, Si," said Shorty, "'n' they come purty nigh doin' it, too. How's yer head?"

"It's a little bit sore, but that don't amount ter nothin' —only a scratch. It 'll be all right 'n a day er two. But I tell ye," continued Si, taking up the thread of his thoughts, "fightin' 's mighty tough business. I ain't much of a ph'los'pher, but I don't b'lieve all this murderin' 'n' manglin' 's right. Ef I sh'd kill a man up in Injianny I'd git hung fer it, 'n' it 'd sarve me right. When ye git down ter hard-pan I can't quite see why 'tain't jest 's cruel 'n'

wicked ter put a bullet through a man's head or shoot off
his leg in Tennessee 's 'tis 'n Injianny.''

"Ye 're a good, brave boy," said Shorty, "'n' yer gizzard
is chuck full o' sand, but ye want ter git over them squeamish notions. Them fellers begun this row, 'n' we've got
ter fight 'em till they quit. Yer idees 's right 'nuff, but
ye can't make 'em fit war times. Ye'll have ter hold 'em
a while; they'll keep."

"I s'pose that's so, Shorty. Course I ain't goin' ter
stan' with my hands 'n my pockets 'n' let a reb shoot me
down 'n my tracks 'f I kin help it. The Guvyment's got
ter be defended, but I tell ye it's mighty rough on them as
has ter do the defendin'. I understand how that is, but I
can't git it out o' my head that there's suthin out o' j'int
somewhere when people 't pertends to be civilized, 'n' some
on 'em thinks they's Christians, gits up sich a shootin'
match 's we had today, when everybody 's blowin' men's
brains out 'n' punchin' bay'nets inter their bodies. I know
when ye git a war on yer hands ye've got ter fight it out,
'n' somebody 'll have ter git hurt, but seems ter me there
ortn't ter be any war, 'cept 'mong dogs, 'n' tigers, 'n'
heathens. My notion is that there wouldn't be none,
nuther, 'f the men 't got it up was the ones that had ter
do all the marchin' 'n' fightin'. If they did screw up their
courage to try it, one day like this 'd cure 'em, I'm thinkin'.''

"I b'lieve ye, Si," replied Shorty, "but 's I said, ye've
got ter git over bein' so chicken-hearted. I ain't afeard ye
won't stan' up ter the rack, fodder or no fodder, after seein'
how ye behaved yerself today, but ye'll feel better jest ter
go in on yer nerve 'n' do 'em all the damage ye kin. That's
what ye're here fer. If ye'd been bumped around in the
world like me ye'd 've had the senterment all knocked out
o' ye same 's I have. Fact is, I couldn't hardly tell ye what
I 'listed fer, 'cause I don't know myself. I s'pose almost
every man's got some o' what they calls patri'tism, but
I'm more 'n half thinkin' 't when they distributed it 'round

I didn't git quite my sheer on it; an' it hain't growed any sence I've bin soljerin', nuther. I reck'n ye've got more on it, Si, 'n I have. I can't see 's it makes any diff'runce ter me, indivijly, whether this country 's cut in two or not. But I'm in fer 't 'n' I'm goin' ter keep peggin' away all the same 's if I was 's full o' patri'tism 's them red-hot speech-ifiers up North that goes around sloppin' over—but they're mighty keerful not to jine the army theirselves. I'm goin' ter try 'n' keep up my eend o' the barg'in, 'n' 'arn my thirteen dollars a month. There's jest one more thing I want ter say, Si. Ef either on us has got ter git killed, I hope 'twon't be you, 'cause you've got lots o' friends 't 'd feel bad. I ain't o' very much 'count, noway, 'n' I don't b'lieve anybody's eyes 'd leak over me!"

It was a singular companionship—that of Si and Shorty—their dispositions and characteristics were so different, but they had been drawn together and held in an ever-tightening clasp that only a fatal bullet could sever.

Shorty was a type of the volunteer soldier that was found in every company. All his life he had been buffeted about on a tempestuous sea. A "pilgrim and a stranger," he had few ties of kinship. His intercourse with the world had not tended to the growth and development of the finer sensibilities of human nature. His heart had not known that glowing heat of patriotic ardor that was the impelling force of so many who shouldered musket or buckled sword. He had enlisted, influenced, perhaps, in some degree by an impalpable sense of duty, but, as he told Si, hardly knowing why he did so. He cheered the flag when the others did, very much as though that were part of his duty as a soldier. And yet, notwithstanding all this, there was no man in the ranks of the 200th Indiana who would prove more patient and faithful and brave than Shorty.

Si's state of mind at this time was a natural condition. It did not indicate any weakening of his patriotic resolution to do his duty well and faithfully. It was the inevitable reaction after the intense strain of the day upon his mental and physical resources. It seemed to him, as it did to thousands and hundreds of thousands of others, that war, in the abstract, was monstrously cruel and barbarous, and to reconcile it with the teachings of his boyhood was no easy task. Many others found the same·trouble with this question that he did.

After lying for an hour Si and Shorty arose and moved about to warm, by exercise, their benumbed and stiffened limbs. They walked out a short distance to the front, where the watchful pickets were keeping guard. Si's attention was arrested by a sound that came from beyond the line.

" Hark!" he exclaimed, "d'ye hear that, Shorty?"

They listened, and there came to their ears a low moan of pain. Si's tender sympathies were instantly aroused.

"Shorty," said he, "let's see if we can't help that poor sufferin' man. He'll freeze to death 'fore mornin'. You wait here t'll I go 'n' ask the cap'n, 'n' we'll see 'f we can't bring him in. We don't know how soon we'll be wantin' somebody ter do it fer us."

"I'm with ye, Si," said Shorty. "Like as not them raskils over thar 'll fire at us. If we sh'd be killed, mebbe, if there *is* anybody up above that keeps the account, he 'll give us a credit mark for tryin' ter help a feller-bein' 't 's in misery; 'n' perhaps it 'll offset a little o' what he's got charged agin us on t'other side. Go ahead, Si, 'n' bring yer blanket with ye. I'll stay here t'll ye come."

Si hurried back to where the remnant of Company Q was lying, and made known his wish to the captain. The latter accompanied him to the colonel, who, after commending in the highest terms his gallant conduct in the battle, consented that he might carry out his desire, at the same time warning him of the danger to which he would be exposed.

Seizing his blanket Si returned to his comrade. Cautioning the pickets, so that they might not be fired upon by their friends, the two good Samaritans went upon their errand of mercy. Carefully and stealthily they picked their way—for the enemy's videttes were but a short distance off—guided by the groans that grew more distinct as they approached.

Dropping to their knees they crept over the frost-covered

ground, among the stiff and whitening forms of the slain. Over that field which a few hours before was the scene of the battle's roar and carnage, now hung the awful silence of night and death.

The object of their search lay in an open spot, beyond which, through the dim starlight, Si and Shorty could see the picket-posts, behind which they knew the hostile sentinels were watching with sleepless eyes. They could scarcely hope

"FOR GOD'S SAKE, HELP!"

to accomplish their purpose without being discovered. But they shrank not from danger. Slowly they made their way toward the sufferer.

"Oh, help, help! For God's sake won't somebody come!"

"Hello, pard!" said Si, in a suppressed tone. "Keep up

yer nerve! We're comin' arter ye, and 'll be thar 'n a minnit!"

Flat upon their faces they worked themselves along, with hand and foot, and at length reached the sufferer. There he lay upon the cold earth, a brave boy no older than Si, chilled by the frost, weak and fainting from hunger and loss of blood, in an agony of pain.

"Good Lord in Heaven bless 'em, both of 'em!" he moaned, as they crept up beside him.

The prayer of the penitent thief upon the cross was not more fervent and sincere.

"Never mind that, pard," said Si; "all we want now is ter git ye out o' this."

With tender touch they raised him gently from the ground and laid him upon the blanket. There was a blaze from one of the enemy's pickets, the sharp crack of a rifle rang out in the clear night air, and a bullet whizzed past them. They dropped upon their faces for a moment.

"Seems to me," whispered Si, "that Satan hisself wouldn't fire on us 'f he knowed what we was doin'."

After a brief pause Si and Shorty started upon their return. For the safety of their charge, as well as their own, they could not arise to their feet and bear off their burden, as they would be certain to draw the enemy's fire. Upon hands and knees they moved him along, a foot or two at a time. It was a slow and laborious task, but they toiled on patiently and perseveringly. Two or three times they were fired upon, but the balls passed harmlessly by them. Reaching cover, they were able to walk erect, and were soon within the lines. They bore the wounded soldier to the nearest hospital. There he received the care that might save a life which, but for the rescue, would have expired before the day dawned.

Si and Shorty took the cold hands of the sufferer and bade him good-by.

"I don't s'pose I'll ever see ye ag'in," said Si; "but I hope ye'll pull through all right, 'n' I b'lieve ye will. What riji-ment d'ye b'long to?"

"Hunderd 'n' seventy-fifth Michigan," was the faint reply.

"Then we're neighbors when we're to home. I live in In-jianny, 'n' I'm in the bully 200th. I s'pose you've heern tell 'bout her; she's the boss rijiment."

The wounded boy gazed into the faces of Si and Shorty with a look of unutterable gratitude. It was clearly his opinion that if all the members of the 200th were like them, the regiment might well deserve the designation Si had given it.

"If ye git well 'n' come back," continued Si, "ye must be sure 'n' hunt up me 'n' Shorty, 'cause we'll be glad ter see ye. My name's Klegg and my pard's—well I most fergot what his other name is; we jest calls him 'Shorty.' I hope ye'll find us 'live 'n' kickin' yet."

"Ye've been mighty good to me!" said the young sol-dier. "Ye've saved my life, and I'll never forget ye if I live a thousan' years. God bless ye!"

Si and Shorty went back to their post with hearts aglow with pleasure at the thought of what they had done.

The night wore slowly away. There were frequent alarms on the picket-line that kept the soldiers in constant trepidation. Regiments and brigades were being moved from one point to another, in preparation for the combat which it was expected would be renewed with the break of day. The measured footsteps of the marching battalions creaked upon the frosty ground. Few eyes were closed in sleep, and those only in short, fitful naps that gave little rest to weary bodies.

For three days the two armies lay like wounded lions, glaring and growling each at the other, with occasional fighting at one point or another on the long and tortuous line. Then, "between two days," the rebel army

> " Folded its tents like the Arabs
> And as silently stole away "

With the dawn of Sunday morning came cessation of the toil and turbulence of the week. No shot sounded on the picket-line; no cannon thundered its morning alarm. An advance of skirmishers revealed only the deserted works and camps of the enemy. Victory, so long hanging in the balance, had at last been decided for the Union arms.

As if borne upon the wind the glad tidings spread through the army. The air was rent with wild huzzas. Whole regiments united, with a fervor and zest that words cannot describe, in singing to the tune of "Old Hundred:"

> " Praise God from whom all blessings flow."

It was not prompted by any sudden ebullition of piety, but to those rejoicing hearts it seemed appropriate to the day and the occasion, and thousands of voices swelled in grand harmony till the woods rang with the inspiring sound.

For the first time in a week the soldiers, wearied and worn with marching and fighting and nightly watching, stacked arms, threw off their accouterments, built fires, and disposed themselves for needed rest and refreshment, without fear that crack of musket or scream of shell would summon them to battle.

After breakfast Company Q, of the 200th Indiana, was drawn up in line for roll-call, for the first time since the havoc of the fight. One of the lieutenants had been killed and the other wounded. Only the captain remained of the officers. The company looked a mere squad when contrasted with the full ranks with which it went so bravely into battle. There were sad faces and aching hearts as the men thought of loved comrades who had marched by their side, whose familiar touch they would feel no more.

"Call all the names," said the captain to the orderly, "and let the men answer for their comrades who are not here to speak for themselves."

"Sargeant Gibson."

"Killed; shot through the head!"

"Sargeant Wagner."

"Here!"

"Sargeant Thompson."

"Wounded in the thigh while holding the colors."

"Corporal Brown."

"Mortally wounded; died the morning after the fight!"

"Corporal Klegg."

"Here!"

Si's response was clear and full, as if he was proud to be "here." There was a perceptible tremor in his voice, however, for his heart was full of tender memories of those who had gone down before the storm.

"Private Anderson."

"Here!"

"Aultman."

"Dead! fell by my side and never spoke a word!"

"Barnes."

"Right arm torn off by a piece of shell; in hospital."

"Bowler."

"Here!"

"Connolly."

"Killed in the charge when we drove 'em!"

"Day."

"Here."

And so it went on through the list. Little wonder that the captain wept, as he stood with folded arms listening to the responses, and looking with feelings of mingled pride and grief upon what remained of his gallant company! Little wonder that tears trickled down through the dust and grime, over the faces of men strong and brave! Little wonder that lips quivered and voices trembled with emotion, and the words, in answer to the call of the orderly, found difficult utterance!

After the roll was finished the captain tried to speak a few words of compliment to his men, but heart and voice failed him. Vainly striving to control his feelings he bade the orderly dismiss the company, and turned away with streaming eyes.

Later in the day an order was issued for a detail from each company to go upon the field where the regiment fought, and discharge the last sad duty—that of gathering and burying the dead. As yet the slain of the army were lying where they fell, scattered over miles of field and copse and wood.

The orderly of Company Q called for volunteers, and the necessary number stepped promptly to the front, Si Klegg and Shorty among them. Picks, spades and stretchers were supplied, and the detachment from the 200th, in charge of an officer, started upon its mournful mission.

A suitable spot was selected and a long trench dug, seven feet wide and three feet deep. Then the mangled and stiffened corpses were borne thither upon stretchers. They were wrapped in the blankets which they had carried over their shoulders when they went into the fight, and which still encircled their lifeless bodies, reddened by the blood of those who wore them. The men laid their dead comrades side by side in the trench. Then the earth was shoveled in, and those familiar faces and forms were hidden from the eyes of the living. At the head of each was placed a bit of wood, perhaps a fragment of a cracker box, with his name, company and regiment penciled upon it for future identification. Few words were spoken during these sad rites. Hearts were too full.

"Shorty," said Si, as they marched back to the bivouac, that's the best we could do fer the poor boys, but it 'd make me feel bad ter think I was goin' ter be buried that way, hunderds o' miles from home 'n' friends, 'n' 'thout even anybody to speak a prayer. I think a man 't willin'ly gives his life fer his country as they did—an' ye know that's jest all a man *kin* do—desarves suthin better 'n that kind o' plantin', like so many pertaters in a row.''

"Ye keep gittin' sentermental, Si," replied Shorty. "That's all well 'nough, but it don't matter much what they do with ye after a bullet 's gone through yer head. I'd 's lief be buried one place 's nuther. Anyhow, it's a part

"WE CARVED NOT A LINE, WE RAISED NOT A STONE."

o' war. Ye git killed 'n' they dig a hole 'n' tumble ye in, 'n' that's all 't military glory 'mounts to!'"

That evening the word was passed around that a mail would leave the next morning, and everybody addressed himself to the work of writing brief letters to friends at home. The necessary materials were scarce, but bits of pencils were hunted up and used by one after another in turn. Messages were written on leaves torn from diaries and odd scraps of paper picked up here and there   Anybody who had postage stamps divided them around among his comrades. Uncle Sam ought to have "franked" the letters, but he didn't.

By the flickering light of a fire Si wrote—on paper that had found its way to the front as a wrapper for cartridges —a short letter to his mother, and another that ran in this way:

jan the 4 1860 3

Deer Annie I spose youve saw in the papers bout the awful fite we had. Yude better blieve we lictem too. Of course taint fer me to brag bout myself an I aint going to but ile jest say that me an Shorty was thar all the time an we dident git behind no trees nuther. I tell ye it was hottern a camp meetin. Wun bullet scraped the hare offn my hed an nuther nocked the but of my gun into slivers an nuther cut the strap of Shortys haversack thats the bag he carrys his grub in but we got out all rite. I had a idee yude be kinder glad to no i dident run and hide in a mewl wagin when the bullits began ter zip. I want yer to think as mutch of me as ye kin an I no a gurl likes a feller wat tries ter be brave an do his dewty bettern she does wun wats a coward. If enny of cumpny Q as was wownded gits hum on furlo I aint afeerd ter have ye ask em how Si klegg stood the rackit. Shorty an me capcherd a rebble flag an the man wat was carryin it. It was mity billyus an i dident bleeve ide ever see ye agin. Maby i wunt cause i spose weve got ter go threw sum more fites but ittle make me feel awfle bad if i dont fer ive thot a heap of ye durin these days. I hoap ye think bout me as offen as i do bout yu. But say Annie i doant want ter fite haf as bad as i did afore taint funny a bit. But the 200th is a bully rijiment an ime goin ter stick by her jest the saims ime goin ter stick by yu. Thares lots o things ide like to rite but i cant now as i haint enny more paper an i got this offen a packidge of catridges.

if yu luv me as i luv yu

kno nife can cut ower luv intu.

Yourn frever   SI KLEGG.

CHAPTER XXXII.

The 200th Indiana has a Protracted Turn of Fatigue Duty—Si
Wrestles with Pick and Shovel and Tries to Outflank
the Doctors.

"EVERY man must be ready tomorrow mornin' for fatigue duty!" said the orderly of Company Q, one evening. "There ain't goin' to be any playin' off, fer everybody's got to turn out!" What the nature of the duty was, or how much "fatigue" there would be in it, the orderly did not say, if, indeed, he knew.

It was always characteristic of soldiers during the first few months of their service that they wanted to know about everything that was going on or that was expected to happen. The proverbial curiosity of woman dwarfed into insignificance beside the consuming desire in the breasts of the raw soldiers, to find out what the generals were going to do next. Whenever an order was given, a volley of conundrums was fired at the officers—where were they going and what for? what was to be done, and why? The answers were generally so unsatisfactory that they knew even less about it, if possible, than before. They came gradually to realize that the whole duty of a soldier was contained in the single word "obey"—without asking any questions. They would find out soon enough whatever was necessary for them to know.

"Wonder what's up now!" said Si Klegg, as he and Shorty walked back to the tent after the company was dismissed.

"I ain't sartin," replied Shorty, "but I've an idee they're goin' ter put us to diggin'. When I was out with the detail after wood yisterdy I seen a lot o' ossifers surveyin' 'n' squintin' 'round 'n' drivin' stakes, 'n' I hearn 'em talk 'bout fortifyin'; so I shouldn't wonder 'f we was 'lected fer a job. Looks 's though spades 'd be trumps fer a while!"

Si and Shorty talked the matter over before going to sleep and made up their minds to go along the first day without any fuss and see what kind of work they had on their hands. If it proved to be heavy and continuous they could, from time to time, make judicious use of their ability to "play off."

"Guess we kin stan' it fer one day," said Si, as he rolled over, pulling the blanket from Shorty, "but I tell ye what, I ain't goin' ter make a nigger o' myself 's long 's my name 's Si Klegg. Talkin' bout niggers, there's thousands on 'em lyin' 'round doin' nothin'; why don't the Guvment make *them* do the diggin'? I ain't no statesman, but it looks ter me 's though 'f anybody 's goin' ter have any good out o' this war the niggers 'll git the most on it. Ef I had my way I'd make 'em help some way er ruther!"

"'Tain't no use ter phlosofize or argefy 'bout the war 'n' what's goin' ter come of it," replied Shorty, drawing the blanket over his lean limbs. "In the fust place you 'n' me don't know nothin' 'bout 'sich things, 'n' in the next place 'twouldn't make a diff o' bitterence 'f we did. We hain't got nothin' ter say, nohow; so don't ye bother yer head with what b'longs ter the pollytishuns. That's what they're fer. Mighty few on 'em comes down here ter git shot at. Now let's dry up 'n' go ter sleep!"

In the morning breakfast call sounded early. As the

bugle notes floated over the camp the boys joined in with the well-known words:

The order for fatigue duty seemed to have an unfavorable effect upon the health of the company. At least, in no other way could be explained the unusually large delegation that responded at sick-call. It is true the orderly had cau-

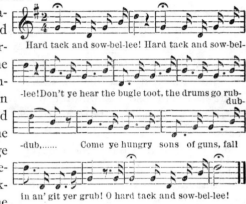

Hard tack and sow-bel-lee! Hard tack and sow-bel-lee! Don't ye hear the bugle toot, the drums go rub-dub-dub,...... Come ye hungry sons of guns, fall in an' git yer grub! O hard tack and sow-bel-lee!

THE CALL TO BREAKFAST.

tioned them about "playing off," but these men were so fast becoming veterans that they had already acquired a chronic dislike for fatigue duty, especially if it promised to be somewhat protracted. In most cases this feeling appeared to be constitutional, and the longer the men were in the service the more it grew on them.

The veteran soldier, no matter how hard the march, would go swinging along, with song and jest, and with never a word of complaint; but he drew the line at fatigue duty. That was where he "kicked." When an unsoldierly job of this kind was set before him he at once became the very incarnation of laziness. His aversion to the pick and shovel was only overcome when, amidst the zipping bullets of the enemy, he was hunting around for something with which to dig a hole to get into. At no other time could he even look upon these menial implements without a desire to organize an insurrection.

A good many of the boys didn't feel very well that morning, and helped to swell the crowd that attended the matinee at the doctor's tent. In most of the cases, however, the symptoms were not sufficiently alarming to justify the dispenser of medicines in marking them off duty.

The daily detail for guard usually provoked more or less grumbling, but on the morning in question those whose turn it was responded with a cheerfulness that under other circumstances would have been surprising. Tramping to and fro on a beat two hours out of six was preferable to degrading toil with axe or shovel. It wasn't as hard, and besides it was less compromising to the dignity of a soldier.

Shorty's surmise proved to be correct. When the customary routine of the morning was over companies were formed and marched to the color line. The regiment moved out beyond the camp to its assigned place. Here the eyes of the men were greeted by the unwelcome sight of wagons loaded with picks, shovels and axes. Each man was ordered to arm himself with one of these inoffensive implements.

It did not take long for the men to size up the job which the engineers had laid out for them. Stakes and lines running at all sorts of angles as far as the eye could reach in either direction marked the cordon of heavy earthworks that was to be built around the town.

"Now shuck yerselves an' pitch in!" said the orderly of Company Q.

Si cast a despairing look, first at the tools and then at Shorty. He appeared to be waiting to see if some special dispensation of Providence in his favor would not yet release him from the irksome duty. There was no alternative.

"Have ter come to it, Si," said Shorty, who already had a pick in his hand. "Grab a shovel 'n' let's go to work. It does seem like gittin' down ter hard-pan, but 'tain't no use growlin'."

Later in the war there were times when Si wanted a shovel to dig a rifle-pit as badly as Richard III., at the battle of Bosworth Field, wanted a horse. But he didn't feel that way now.

The men stripped off their blouses and began to dig, while the officers did the heavy standing around and "bossing" the work. Corporal Klegg was not able to divest himself of the feeling—which had shown itself on several previous occasions—that his rank, humble though it was, ought to excuse him from such plebeian toil. He even ventured to hint as much, but was informed with some emphasis that the privileges of rank in this respect only reached far enough below shoulder-straps to take in the orderly sergeants.

"I don't see no good 'n *bein'* a corporil," he muttered, as he seized a shovel and began to throw out the dirt that Shorty had loosened with his pick. "I've a great notion ter resign 'n' be a privit 'long with you, Shorty. Corporils don't git no more pay, ner no more grub, ner no more nothin' 'n anybody else does. It's jest a fraud!"

"Now, don't ye be gittin' inter a fret!" replied Shorty "I'm hopin' ter see ye up a right smart higher arter a while, but ye can't jump up all to oncet. It's jest the same 's gittin' up stairs; ye've got ter go up one step 't a time. I don't never expect ter be nothin' but a privit, myself, 'n' I don't want ter; but I'd like you to git 's high 's ye kin. Ye'll be a sargint one o' these days; 'n' then afore ye know it ye'll have sardine-boxes clapped on yer shoulders, 'n' be swingin' yer toad-stabber 'n' orderin' us fellers 'round. I'd jest be happy ter see ye doin' that, Si. When ye gits a little more 'sperience ye'll make as good 'n ossifer 's any on 'em. Ye've got more sand 'n half on 'em, now; 'n' sand 's wuth a heap more 'n book-larnin' to a soljer. I don't s'pose ye'll git ter be a gin'ral 'nless the war hangs on a good while, but I'd like ter see ye a leftenant er a cap'n."

It was rarely that any serious disturbance of Si's good temper occurred, and when it did Shorty knew how to bring him back to his usual placid state of mind. This hopeful view of Si's future served as a poultice to his injured feelings, and he was soon chattering away as cheerily as ever.

"Ye know I didn't mean nothin', Shorty," he said. "I reck'n a soljer couldn't keep hisself 'n good health 'f he didn't grumble once 'n a while. I'm ever so much 'bleeged to ye fer all ye said. I hain't no more idee o' ever bein' a real ossifer 'n I have o' flyin'. It don't look much 's though I would, either — me here a-shovelin' dirt like a Paddy on the railroad. Guess I won't git above bein' a non-commish."

"Well, ye don't want ter fergit, Si, that if this infernal rebellion 's squelched it's them as carries the muskits that 's got ter do the business. The gin'rals 'n' colonels 'n' cap'ns tells 'em what ter do, but the men 're the ones that has ter *do* it. The ossifers most allus gits the heft o' the

TALKING IT OVER.

glory, but we has ter do the shootin' 'n' diggin' jest the same."

It may be readily inferred—and old soldiers will need no averment of the fact—that Si and Shorty did not exert themselves to an excessive degree. Anybody would have known they were working by the month, and for small wages at that. An hour or two after the beginning of operations the captain of Company Q was moved to remark that a fairly industrious hen, in quest of rations for a brood of chickens, would have scratched out a larger hole in the ground that appeared as the result of the combined efforts of the corporal and his comrade.

"If hens is so smart," said Si to Shorty, "p'r'aps they'd better git some 'n' put 'em to work. I don't b'leeve they'd *live* long 'nough, though, ter do much scratchin'. They'd have ter roost mighty high."

The work done by our heroes was a fair sample of that accomplished by the other members of Company Q. They did not take kindly to the pick and shovel. Such labor was wholly at variance with all their preconceived notions of a soldier's life. A large fraction of the poetry and romance of their martial dreams had already been dissipated by the fighting and marching and picketing and bivouacking, and now to be put to shoveling dirt was an indignity that few had philosophy enough to endure with composure. So it was that mutterings were heard all along the line.

As the distance from camp was considerable, the men had brought along their haversacks, and at noon they were allowed to "knock off" for dinner. "Dinner," was the name of it; but it presented few of the attractions for a hungry man that cluster around that word. The bill of fare was not one to tempt an epicure. Eating in those days was, like a good many other things, a military necessity. It was in this spirit that the men munched the flinty crackers, anointed with the unctuous drippings from sizzling swine's flesh, and washed them down with draughts of coffee well-nigh strong enough to have floated an egg.

The time allowed for refreshments was about as long as that usually vouchsafed at a railroad eating-house. The "All aboard!" of the conductor is not more unwelcome to the ear of a famished traveler who has but half eaten his dinner than was the order to those lazy Hoosiers to resume the pick and shovel.

The hours dragged slowly along—and so did the work. No doubt a few shots on the picket-line, followed by the galloping in of a stampeded cavalryman, would have urged them to greater activity; although they had not yet learned by experimental knowledge what a very comfortable thing it was, sometimes, to have a good line of works to get behind—and the comfort and satisfaction were always in proportion to the height and thickness of the wall of dirt and logs. Thus far their ideas of fighting were confined to a square, stand-up, give-and-take, with bullet and bayonet. They had a vague notion that fortifications might come handy in certain contingencies, but on the whole they were at this time willing to take the chances in open field.

"I wouldn't mind it so much," said Si, as he looked ruefully at a well-developed blister that had already made its appearance on one of his hands, "if the Johnnies 'd only march up in front o' the works after we git 'em done and let us shoot 'em. We'd end the war purty sudden. But I don't s'pose we'll git a chance ter fight behind 'em arter we've built 'em. We'll be sure ter go scootin' off some where 'n' some other fellers, lazier 'n we be, 'll come in here 'n' git the good of 'em."

Si was about right. It was seldom, indeed, that the drums and bugles did not sound for a break-up as soon as the boys had finished a good job of intrenching. Then other troops would come along and enjoy the fruit of their labors.

To the members of the 200th Indiana the sun seemed to stand still that day. They thought it never would go down. It did reach the horizon at last, and with unspeakable relief the soldiers obeyed the order to fall in and march back to camp.

"If I ever 'list ag'in," said Si, as he washed the dust and sweat from his hands and face, Shorty supplying him with water from a canteen, "I'm goin' ter have a squar' barg'in.

I'll have it all down in black 'n' white so I'll know jest what I've got ter do. I s'posed soljers jest had ter wear nice clothes kivered with brass buttons, 'n' march 'round with the flags a-flyin' 'n' the bands a-playin' in galyant style. That's the way they all do up North, but it's a mighty sight diff'runt down here. It jest knocks a feller's notions higher 'n Gilderoy's kite!"

"Thar ye go ag'in, blowin' off yer steam," replied Shorty, as Si took the canteen and began to pour water

on his comrade's grimy hands. "I knowed a good deal 'bout it 'fore I jined the army, from what I'd read and heern, but I never told ye 'cause I didn't want ter make ye feel bad 'forehand. 'Tain't wuth while ter be fret- tin' 'bout what's ahead o' ye. Now cheer up, pard, 'n' we'll do our sheer, whether it's marchin' er fightin' er diggin'. But I tell ye, Si, we ain't goin' ter do any *more* 'n our

CAMP ABLUTIONS.

share. Ye kin jest bet yer gunboats on that."

Day after day and week after week the work went on. There was nothing but picking and shoveling dirt and cutting fagots and tying them into fascines and gabions, to be used in the embrasures and inner walls. The boys grew very tired of such plodding, uneventful toil. They wrought themselves up to the belief that they would rather tramp, and even fight a little now and then, than to wear their lives away in digging. There was nothing inspiring or exciting about it, and patriotism was at a low ebb.

The warm weather came, and still the great work was unfinished. Under the broiling sun the perspiring soldiers still kept shoveling and chopping, grumbling at the cruel fate that had overtaken them, and constantly exercising their wits to find new schemes that seemed to give promise of success in "playing off." Every man considered it his inalienable right to do this if he could. He who was most fortunate in "beating" the doctors was an object of supreme envy to all his comrades.

Si and Shorty contrived to get a day or two off now and then, nor did they seem to suffer from the smitings of conscience by reason of the means they employed to compass their ends. They did not propose to work all the time. They were going to get their share of rest, by fair means or foul—and they did.

One day Si told the orderly he wasn't able to work, but the orderly said he would have to shoulder an axe or a shovel, unless he was excused by the doctor. He went up at sick-call and made a wry face, with his hands clasped over his body in the latitude of his waistband. The doctor gave him a lot of blue-mass pills, which Si threw into the fire as soon as he got back to his quarters. Then he spent the day in learning to play seven-up. He thought this was a great idea, but he tried it once too often. The doctor "caught on," and said, the next time Si went up, that castor oil was what he needed to fetch him around. So he poured out a large dose and made him take it right then and there. This was worse than digging.

Sometimes Si would eat nothing for a day, carefully putting away his rations, however, for subsequent use. This rarely failed, with him, to make out a *prima facie* case of sickness sufficiently grave to secure an excuse from duty. Everybody in the regiment knew that when he did not eat his full quota of hardtack and bacon something was the matter. The doctor was assisted in making up his verdict by the marked effect of abstinence upon Si. It did, in fact, make him sick; but as soon as he got back to his quarters he found in his haversack a sovereign remedy. He would eat up everything in sight and be speedily restored to his normal condition.

Shorty proved to be highly gifted in the popular art of feigning sickness. He could make any doctor in Christendom believe—for a few times—that he was on the outermost verge of his mortal existence and was about to be gathered to his fathers. He was shrewd enough to know that he could not reasonably expect to play it always on the same doctor. So he would watch when a different one —the surgeon, or an assistant, or sometimes the hospital steward—was running the pill shop. If it was not the same doctor that excused him the last time, Shorty would be suddenly seized with a violent and painful illness, and generally with highly satisfactory results.

The pretended spraining of an ankle, with a little coloring matter artistically applied to the unlucky member, coupled with the judicious use of a cane or an improvised crutch, at one time secured nearly a week of release from pick and shovel. A little flour sprinkled upon the tongue gave it a coating which, once or twice, deceived the hasty glance of the doctor, and led him to believe that the patient had a clear case of fever, which gave him respite from work.

Most of the time gained by these schemes was spent by the boys of Company Q in their tents playing euchre and "old sledge." It was an unlucky day for Si and Shorty when an officer, who was nosing around the camp, stuck his head into the tent where exercises of this kind were in progress. Si had a good hand, and was just leading out with great earnestness in an effort to "ketch jack" from Shorty. Five minutes later they were on the way, under guard, to the fortifications, where they were made to buckle in for the rest of the day.

Some of the doctors whose hearts, when they entered the service, were overflowing with the milk of human kindness, had the wool pulled over their eyes at first by the flimsy deceptions to which the boys soon learned to resort to get excused from fatigue duty; but after a few months of practice they got so that they could tell a sick man when they saw him. Then they took a fiendish delight in making life a burden to the "play-offs." They poured horrible doses down their throats, and this would often be supplemented by a trick of extra duty. Human ingenuity was literally exhausted by the soldiers in their efforts to outflank the doctors. Often they achieved a temporary success, but in the long run the doctors rarely failed to come out ahead.

AN UNEXPECTED GUEST.

Si had heard a good deal about the "Articles of War," and one day, after fatigue duty was over, he borrowed the captain's "Army Regulations" to see what the articles were. He had not read far when he burst into a laugh.

"Shorty," he said, "jest listen ter this"—and he read aloud Art. 3, as follows:

Any non-commissioned officer or soldier who shall use any profane oath or execration shall, for his first offense, forfeit one-sixth of a dollar, to be deducted out of his next pay; for the second and each subsequent offense he shall forfeit a like sum and be confined for twenty-four hours; and a commissioned officer shall forfeit and pay, for each and every such offense, one dollar.

"This war must be costin' a heap o' money," continued Si, "'n' I've read 't they was gittin' a big nashnel debt. 'Pears ter me ef they 'd jest stick it to the soljers 'n' the ossifers 'cordin' ter this article o' war they 'd have money 'nuff ter pay everything 's they go 'long, 'n' not have ter be borryin' all the time 'n' givin' guvyment bonds. Wouldn't they sock it to the ossifers? It 'd cost 'em six times 's much fer the priv'lege o' sw'arin' 's it would them as carries muskits."

"I never knowed ther' was any sich reggelation 's that," replied Shorty, "'n' I don't reck'n any o' the boys ever heerd 'bout it. I shouldn't wonder ef they was layin' fer us with some sort o' skullduggery. The chapl'ins don't have much else ter do, 'n' mebbe they're keepin' tally on us, 'n' when the war's over like 'nuff Uncle Sam 'll bring in his bill fer it all to oncet."

"Ef they do" said Si, "It'll be purty rough on some on 'em. I 'low most o' the big gin'rals 'll be busted, 'n' the mule-drivers 'll owe the guvyment 'bout a million dollars apiece."

CHAPTER XXXIII.

In Which Si Serves as a Railway Train Guard and has a Call from Guerrillas.

AN unusual stir was occasioned one evening in the camp of the 200th Indiana, by an order for half the regiment, including Company Q, to be ready in an hour to go as guard for a railroad train, which was to return on the following day with supplies for the army.

"'That'll be jest fun, won't it, Shorty?" exclaimed Si Klegg, as he and his comrade hustled around, making the necessary arrangements for the trip. "Ridin' on the keers 'll be a heap better 'n hoofin' it, with a feller's bones achin' 'n' his feet smartin'. Ye know, we kin git right inter one o' the passenger-keers 'n' be reel comf'table. It'll be suthin like ter travel 'n that sort o' style. I wouldn't mind sarvin' out my time a-doin' that."

Si was in high glee at the prospect of what he thought would be in the nature of a pleasure excursion. With a light heart he stowed away some hardtack in his haversack, filled his canteen, and examined the contents of his cartridge-box.

"What do we want our blankets fer?" he said to Shorty, as he saw the latter rolling his up with the evident design of taking it along. "'Pears to me they'll only be in the way 'n' we'd better leave 'em."

"I'm goin' ter stick ter mine," replied Shorty, laughing to himself at Si's luxurious ideas, "'n' my advice to ye is ter take yourn. I'll miss my guess ef ye don't find use fer it 'fore mornin'. I'm 'fraid ye're foolin' yerself 'bout the coaches, 's they calls 'em. Mebbe we'll have 'em, but 'cordin' ter my notion it's a good deal more likely we won't."

At the signal the companies formed and marched to the train. This was composed of twenty or thirty ordinary box cars.

"D'ye see any passinger-keers hitched onto that 'ere train, Si?" asked Shorty with a broad grin.

A look of disappointment passed over Si's face as he ran his eye quickly from one end of the train to the other.

"Don't look much like it!" he replied.

Again his exuberant vision of "having a good time" was rudely dissipated. But this had happened so often that it was getting to be an old story. Fortunately for him his disposition was like a ball of India-rubber, that yields for an instant to a sudden blow and then springs at once back to its proper shape.

"Wall, Shorty," he said, "it'll be some satisfaction ter ride in them keers, if '*tis* same 's cattle."

Shorty smiled again, for he knew they would have to take passage on the "hurricane deck." The cars were filled with sick men and discouraged cavalry and artillery horses, bound for the hospitals and convalescent camps in the rear; for the army was getting rid of its incumbrances preparatory to a general advance.

"Company Q, tumble up on top o' them k'yars," shouted the orderly.

"What, hev we got ter ride up thar?" said Si, with astonishment.

"That's jest the size of it," replied Shorty. "I knowed how it 'd be. I 'low ye won't be sorry ye fotched yer blanket with ye!"

Climbing between the cars, encumbered with arms and accouterments, was not an easy task. There was a great deal of slipping and tugging and "boosting," with the full quota of yelling. Si and Shorty clambered up as best they could, and found themselves, with some twenty others, looking for soft spots on the roof of a crazy car. One of those copious dews, peculiar to the southern climate, even in midsummer, had made the top of the car slippery to the feet and cold and clammy to the touch.

"Purty scurvy place ter sleep!" exclaimed Si, as he unloaded some of his traps, flung his rolled-up blanket upon the ridge-board, and sat down upon it to think over the matter. "How does it strike *you*, Shorty?" he asked.

"Didn't spect nothin' else," replied his comrade. "P'r'aps we won't git much chance ter sleep, anyway. Like as not some o' them pesky g'rillas 'll throw us off the track 'n' capter the hull outfit."

"D'ye really b'lieve they will, Shorty?" said Si, with alarm. He had not thought of this as a possible outcome of the expedition. It might turn out to be a serious business, after all.

"Course I don't know nothin' 'bout it, Si, 'n' I don't b'lieve one way ner t'other. Sich things has bin did, 'n' they're jest 's likely ter hap'n ter us 's anybody else. Them mizzable critters is allus pitchin' on when ye least expect 'em."

As soon as the men were on board, the engine, a wheezy, old-fashioned wood-burner, gave a warning whistle and immediately pulled out into the darkness. The men spread their blankets and lay down, with their heads to the ridge and their feet in a row along either edge.

All who remember the condition of the southern railroads during the war will appreciate the night ride of those Hoosier soldiers. The track was rough and crooked, and the cars swayed from side to side, and bobbed up and down, and jolted one against another in a way that kept the more timid ones in a state of consternation lest the train should go through a bridge or pile itself in a heap at the foot of an embankment. The chances seemed to favor some sudden stoppage of that kind.

"If a feller's got ter die fer his country," said Si, as he lay holding fast to Shorty so that he might not be shaken off the car, "I'd a heap ruther a cannon ball 'd take my head off while I was chargin' a battery, or be stabbed with a bay'net in a rough-'n'-tumble scrimmage, than ter be ground all to pieces in a railroad smash-up. Thar ain't a bit o' glory dyin' that way."

As the result of the constant shaking, the prostrate forms of the men showed a continual tendency to slide off the roof. It was long before Si and Shorty dared to close their eyes, but at last, overcome by weariness, they were cradled to sleep by the swinging motion of the cars. It was only for a brief and fitful "cat-nap." Shorty awoke with a start to find that both himself and Si had slipped down until their legs were dangling over the precipice, and their heels thumping against the side of the car.

"Wake up, Si, quick, or you're a goner!" he shouted, as, recovering himself, he seized his comrade and assisted him to scramble back upon the treacherous roof. "We come mighty near bein' joggled off."

Si's heart beat furiously for a moment as he thought

"RIDING ON A RAIL" IN THE ARMY.

what a narrow escape it was, and how badly Annabel would have felt if he had tumbled off and been killed.

For the next hour they kept wide awake. Si suggested that if they only had a rope they might tie themselves to the ridge-board, but as they had none the proposition did not help them out. So they took turns at sleeping, one remain·

ing on guard to prevent accident. On talking it over they had concluded that if they were to be attacked by guerrillas it was more likely to be on the return trip, when the train would be loaded with supplies, and therefore a much greater prize to the rebel troopers.

Meanwhile the train kept on its swinging, jostling way. The engine puffed and snorted, and the smoke and cinders streamed along the top of the cars, filling the eyes and ears and blackening the faces of the soldiers. Sparks and glowing coals fell upon them in a continual shower, burning countless holes through clothes and blankets. Now and then a frantic "Ouch!" told that the fire had found its way through and was getting in its blistering work on the skin. If there was any mode of traveling productive of greater discomfort, those men had not yet experienced it. A twenty-mile march was sportive recreation by comparison.

There were the usual long delays and "waits" that characterized the chaotic management of those confiscated railroads. Two or three times large details were made to "wood up," the necessary fuel being procured by chopping fence rails. At other points the men were obliged to pump water to supply the engine.

It was morning when the train reached its destination. As Si clambered down from the car, weary and stiff, his face and hands begrimed with dirt and smoke, he would scarcely have been recognized as the jubilant youth of the evening before, elated at the prospect of soldiering in a passenger-car. He felt, and looked, as if that night had added ten years to his life. He had caught his full share of the sparks, and his overcoat appeared as if it had been used as a target by a company during a day's practice at shooting.

"Now, men, ye want to stir around lively and git yer breakfast," said the orderly, "'cause ye've got to pitch right in an' load up these here k'yars!"

Si had not reckoned on this, and he grumbled to Shorty as they limbered themselves up, washed their hands and faces, kindled a fire, and made coffee and toasted bacon. A chance to get all he wanted to eat brought him around in good shape, and he was himself again—good-natured as ever, and ready to do his part.

Beside the railroad were huge piles of stores—boxes of clothing and hardtack, casks of bacon, barrels of pickled pork, sugar, coffee and beans, great bundles of blankets, bales of hay, and sacks of corn—to supply the men and animals of the army. The men swarmed around, twenty or thirty to each car, and in scarcely more than an hour the train was loaded to its full capacity. When a cracker-box gave way or the head fell out of a sugar barrel, the men made good use of the opportunity to replenish their supplies. By the time the work was done all the haver-sacks of the detachment were filled to repletion. Corporal Klegg, in addition, stuffed all his pockets full of commis-sary stores. In the promise of an abundance for the next few days he found some compensation for the dis-comfort and labor of the trip.

As soon as the work was finished the train was ordered to start directly for "the front." The companies were formed and the somewhat ominous command "Load at will—Load!" was given. The clink of the ramrods had the sound of business. The men knew what it meant, and as they clambered again to the roofs of the cars their faces reflected the sober thoughts that were passing through their minds. There was an absence of the usual levity, as they discussed the probability of being molested by rebel cavalrymen. While engaged in loading the cars they had been repeatedly cautioned to keep a sharp lookout. Ru-mors were always more numerous and of greater size in the rear than at the front.

"Tell ye what, Shorty," said Si, as they lay on the roof of the car, "we won't have much of a show up here in a fight. The Johnnies 'll jest peck away at us 'n' we can't help ourselves. There ain't no trees er fences fer us to git behind, 'n' a feller can't even dodge 'thout tumblin' off the

LOADING UP.

keer. I don't want more'n 'n even chance, but seems like the odds was all agin us."

"We can't have things jest 's we want 'em," replied

Shorty, "'n' we've got ter make the best on it. I'm ready ter go my bottom dollar on ye, whatever comes."

The train bumped and jolted along the uneven track. Every eye that was not full of dust and cinders was strained to catch the slightest indication of any hostile band lurking about. Mile after mile was passed in safety, and every turn of the wheels seemed to lessen the danger.

As the train dashed around a sharp curve the engineer discovered a pile of logs and stones upon the track. He was a cool-headed man and knew just what to do in the emergency. It took as much nerve to be a "railroader" in the government service as it did to be a soldier. Many of those intrepid engineers and brakemen quite as often heard bullets whistle, and had their wits and their pluck taxed to the utmost to get them out of tight places.

The engineer saw at a glance that it would be impossible to plow through the obstruction. The train would inevitably be "ditched" and the alternative of fight or surrender forced upon them. Quick as a flash he determined to stop the train. There was not an instant to lose. Reversing his engine and pulling the throttle wide open, he whistled down brakes. The shriek of the whistle pierced the ears of the soldiers. Every man seized his gun and looked eagerly ahead. Crack! crack! went a dozen carbines and as many bullets went singing over the heads of the guards.

"Jest wait t'll the train stops, 'n' we git a chance to go for 'em," Si said to Shorty, who was at his side ready for anything except being captured. Just then he saw one of his comrades tying a white handkerchief to his ramrod.

"What ye doin' that fer?" said Si.

"I d-didn't know b-but we m-might have to s-s-surrender," he stammered in reply, through his white lips, dodging to get out of the way of a bullet that went whizzing ten feet above his head, "an' I jest th-thought I'd g-git this thing ready to shake at 'em an' tell 'em we g-give up afore we was all k-killed!"

"You put that 'ere wipe back into yer pocket jest 's quick 's ever ye kin!" said Si, his eyes blazing with indignation. "Ef ye don't ye'll be huntin' 'round fer a hospital mighty sudden. Company Q ain't goin' ter have no white rags stuck up here. D'ye s'pose we're goin' ter s'render? No-sir-ee-*bob!* We're goin' ter thrash the daylights out o' them fellers!"

By this time the train was nearly at a stand. On either side of the track were the cavalrymen in gray prancing about and yelling to the blue-coats to surrender, backing up the demand with their carbines and revolvers. This was an argument that had two sides, and the men of the 200th Indiana delivered a well-directed fire that caused several of them to reel from their saddles and threw the remainder into confusion, evidently suggesting to their minds the thought that possibly they had waked up the wrong passengers.

"Now, men, to the ground, quick, and at them!" shouted the officer in command.

The soldiers clambered down with all speed, many leaping from the cars in their zeal to obey the order. It was one of those critical times when a moment might decide the issue of the fight. Instinctively each man seized his bayonet, and in an instant the bright shafts of steel glistened in the sunlight.

"Forward—Double-quick—March!"

Away they went, with a yell. Horses will not stand before a determined bayonet charge. The terrified animals turned and fled, bearing away their not unwilling riders. The latter, finding that they had reckoned without their host, were only too glad to make good their retreat. Hastily reloading their pieces, the plucky Hoosiers sent their farewell compliments after the fleeing horsemen and then returned to the train.

As a general thing these predatory bands of marauders were very brave when they outnumbered their opponents four or five to one. A stout resistance, unless the odds were too great, seldom failed to drive off the assailants.

Corporal Klegg was in high feather over the result, to which he had contributed his full share. "Told ye we'd lick 'em!" he said to the comrade who, yielding to the weakness of the flesh, had made preparations to display a white flag, but who, after all, had charged in the front rank and borne himself bravely through the skirmish.

A BRUSH WITH GUERRILLAS.

"Now when ye git back ter camp," continued Si, "jest throw that hankercher into the fire, 'n' go ter the skinner 'n' git one o' some other color. The 200th Injianny hain't got no use fer anything ter make white flags of. Ef ye hain't got 'em ye won't think o' usin' 'em."

The firing had not been wholly without effect, and a few were killed and wounded on both sides. These were gathered up and placed on board, the track was speedily cleared, the men once more mounted to the roofs of the

cars, and the train sped on its way. In due time, without further molestation, it entered the lines of the great army.

Next day, at dress-parade, an order from the commanding general was read, complimenting in the highest terms the gallant conduct of the detachment.

" Tally one more fer us, " Si said to Shorty, as he sat boiling his coffee for supper.

CHAPTER XXXIV.

The Rebels Cut the "Cracker-Line" and Si is Put on Quarter Rations.

ANOTHER great engagement took place. The 200th Indiana was in the forefront of battle. Its thinned ranks and its long list of killed and wounded again bore eloquent testimony to the gallantry of its officers and men. Both Si and Shorty were so fortunate as to pass unscathed through the dreadful storm. Side by side they stood in the ranks and quailed not in the awful presence of death.

Overwhelmed by the superior force of the enemy, the Union army was compelled to give ground. Stubbornly it yielded, fighting desperately, and bravely meeting the onward sweep of the exultant foe. Lines of musketry blazed defiantly, and batteries of artillery, planted on each advantageous spot during the sullen retreat, belched forth murderous missiles.

Falling back to a chosen position the army planted itself, determined to yield no more. It had suffered a temporary reverse, but its spirit was unbroken, its courage unfaltering. All through the long night, and the next day, the uncomplaining soldiers, though wearied by days and nights of marching and fighting and sleepless watching, toiled with pick and shovel, under the constant fire of the enemy, to make their position secure.

The Confederates, jubilant over their success, mounted their heaviest cannon upon the surrounding hills and, stretching out their long arms, grasped the line of railroad which was the only source of supply for the Union army. Then they sat quietly down to wait for hunger to do what valor could not.

The soldiers and animals of the imprisoned army were immediately put on half rations and the strictest orders were issued against waste of anything that would afford sustenance to man or beast. Much of the time was passed, night and day, in the trenches. On the front line whole brigades and divisions stayed for twenty-four hours at a time in order of battle. At night part of the men lay down and slept, with their loaded muskets by their sides. while others watched. If a shot was heard on the out' posts they sprang to their feet in an instant and took their places at the works. Without shelter, drenched by frequent rains and chilled by nipping frosts, with rations meager and daily growing less, those brave, patient men, through weary weeks that lengthened into months, with unexampled intrepidity and fortitude, defied alike hunger, storm, and haughty foe.

Si Klegg had become pretty well "seasoned" during his year and more of campaigning. He had seen, for that period, a fair share of hard service; but these times that "tried" men's stomachs as well as their souls proved more serious to him than any of his prior experiences. Marching had been robbed of its terrors, the nightly vigil upon the lonely outpost had become a part of his regular duty, and he was always ready for a "whack" at the rebels in battle or skirmish. But when the enemy assailed his haversack, by cutting off his supplies, it was a grave matter, that made heavy demands upon his patience and endurance. The full army ration was just up to the measure of his needs. He had never seen the time when he could not "get away" with his daily allowance. If the reduction had been made by easy stages he might have educated his appetite to meet the exigency, but this sudden and alarming shrinkage filled him with dismay.

In this land of plenty there are few who know—as did many thousands of the soldiers—what it is to feel for weeks at a time the incessant gnawings of hunger. In all the range of human sensibilities there is no other feeling so searching and corroding as this. It clutches the very heart-strings, sours the temper, and makes a man desperate.

"Shorty," said Si to his comrade one day, as they stood in the muddy trenches, peering at the circling line of the enemy upon the adjacent hills, "durned ef I don't b'lieve we kin lick them pesky rebils. I'd a heap ruther try it than ter lie here starvin' to death. Don't ye see I'm gittin' 's thin 's a shadder?"

"I knowed it 'd be rough on ye, Si," replied Shorty, "when the ajitant read the order 't we was ter be put on half rations. I c'n git along better 'n you 'cause I allus was thin 'n' it don't take so much to keep my steam up. I reck'n ye don't weigh quite 's much 's ye did when ye jined the army, but ye're in purty good order fer soljerin' yet. Ye don't want only jest meat 'nough ter keep yer bones from tumblin' apart. I'm thinkin' it 'll be wuss yet 'fore long 'f suthin don't happen. Ye know our cracker-line 's all cut off. I 'low 't we've got ter do one o' three things—make a raise o' some fresh grub, git out o' this, er fight. I 'gree with ye, pard, that it 'd be the best way ter pitch into them gray-coats some fine mornin' 'n' jest *whale* 'em. I b'lieve we c'n do it, fer the way the boys 's feelin' these days they'd wade through a solid mile o' rebels. When the gin'ral gits 'em started next time ther' can't nothin' stop 'em."

Si was greatly edified and encouraged by Shorty's observations. He almost felt as though he wanted to march up to the commanding general and tell him how he felt about it. He was restrained by the thought that if he did he would probably be put on extra duty for a week.

While they were talking the general and his numerous staff in gorgeous uniforms, and with an overpowering display of epaulets and gold lace, came riding along the lines on a tour of inspection. The boys saluted by presenting arms. Then the general alighted from his horse, examined

CHEERS FOR THE GENERAL.

the works, and talked cheerily to the soldiers. He was evidently in a pleasant frame of mind and Si felt emboldened to speak. He always had been somewhat deficient in the sentiment of reverential awe with which the soldiers were wont to regard those high in command.

"Gin'ral," he said—and the smile on the face of the commander encouraged him to proceed—"ef ye'll give us a chance one o' these days 'n' let us go fer them fellers over yonder we'll warm their jackets fer 'em so they won't fergit it right away. The thing sort o' flashed 'n the pan the last time, but whenever ye says the word, Gin'ral, we'll make 'em think the day o' reck'nin' 's come. All the boys feels that way."

"That's the right kind of talk, my boy," said the general, evidently impressed with Si's earnestness. "I do not doubt that you mean every word of it and that you will do your full share the next time we meet them; and you won't have to wait a great while, either."

This declaration was received with great enthusiasm. A wave of cheers swept either way along the line until it was lost in the distance.

"Ef I ain't presumin' too much, Gin'ral," said Si, touching his hat respectfully, "I'd jest like ter say that the sooner ye turn us loose the better it'll suit us; 'cause I c'n tell ye fer a fact 't we've got ter scare up more grub, some way er other. I think it 'd be a good idee 'f we could trade off some o' the shoulder-straps 'n' brass buttons in this 'ere army fer hardtack 'n' sowbelly."

"I don't know but you're about right!" said the general, laughing heartily as he mounted his horse and galloped away.

"I'd expect ter be tied up by the thumbs with a bay'net 'n my jaws 'f I sh'd talk ter the gin'ral like that!" said Shorty, as the staff went clattering down the line. "I wouldn't ha' da'st ter speak that way!"

"Mebbe I did put my foot in it," said Si, "but I seen 't he was good-natered, 'n' I thought 's how he'd take a little joke, even f'm a corporil."

"Ye wants ter be mighty keerful 'bout jokin' with the gin'rals, Si, 'cause it's ticklish business. There's a few on em' 't 'll stan' it, but four out o' five 'd have ye strung up 'n a jiffy. I don't say 't my advice 's wuth much, but 'f I was you I wouldn't try it on ag'in!"

Si was a true representative of the volunteer soldier. When he entered the service he took the oath with a mental reservation that he would not, except in so far as he could not help himself, surrender his independence and his individuality. He couldn't help being Si Klegg in the army just as much as at home, subject only to the laws of war and the "Regulations." His thoughts were always active and his tongue ready to give them utterance. Sometimes it would have been better had he left things unsaid; but his gallantry in battle, his faithfulness in the discharge of every duty, and his general good conduct as a soldier, fully atoned for his guileless violation, now and then, of the proprieties of military intercourse. If a soldier committed a flagrant offense it could not be condoned without an entire subversion of discipline, so indispensable to the efficiency of an army; but his minor peccadilloes, not prompted by vicious motives, were overshadowed, in the eyes of most officers, by exemplary conduct in battle.

The days and weeks wore slowly away to the soldiers of the beleaguered army. The subsistence of men and animals became a question of the gravest import. The enemy clung tenaciously to the railroad, and no trains could pass the frowning batteries and the phalanx of gleaming muskets. Desperate efforts were made to reach the army with supplies by means of wagons over the mountains, for the rear was yet open, but the enemy's cavalry swarmed in the passes, and few of the vehicles reached the famishing soldiers. A large part of the rations thus sent only served to replenish Confederate haversacks.

Si's heart sank to a point a few degrees lower than it had ever before reached, when an order was read one day directing that the troops be put upon quarter rations. The general in issuing the order sought to mitigate its severity by expressing his regret that such a measure had been found necessary. He exhorted the soldiers to bear their trials with fortitude, and assured them that relief was near at hand.

"That kind o' talk 's all well 'nuff," said Si, when he and Shorty were condoling together over the hard times indeed that had fallen to their lot. "Of course the gin'ral had ter say *suthin*, but it don't go very fur tor'd fillin' up a stomach 't hain't got nothin' in it. I don't like ter think o' peterin' out, Shorty, but it kind o' looks that way. I've been runnin' down ever since they cut our rations in two, 'n' now they've quartered 'em I reck'n I'll go on a gallop."

"Ye mustn't git down in the mouth, Si," replied his faithful companion. "It's tough, but we're goin' ter pull out o' this pinch. Ye've allus kep' yerself braced up so well 't I don't b'lieve ye'll weaken now. Every body has their dark days once 'n a while, out o' the army 's well 's in it. It does seem 's though the soljers gits more 'n their sheer on 'em, but there's nothin' like keepin' up yer nerve.

Spit on yer hands, Si, 'n' take a fresh grip."

"Don't ye be afeard o' my peggin' out, Shorty. Ye know I ain't in arnest when I talk that way. I can't help gittin' the blues sometimes, but I never lets 'em hang on long. I'm goin' ter keep knockin' 'round jest 's long 's I kin, 'n' 'f it comes to

CONDOLENCE.

the wust, 'n' I can't do no more, they c'n set me up fer a dummy ter scare the Johnnies. I've heerd 'bout dummies 'n' wooden cannons 't was jest 's good 's the reel thing 's long 's t'other fellers didn't know they was a fraud."

Still the days and nights dragged on. Hunger, grim and gaunt, began to leave its marks upon the faces of the soldiers. Their hollow eyes and shrunken cheeks attested the gradual impairment of their bodily strength. Men cannot long maintain their wonted vigor on quarter rations. There was no abatement of the duty that the emergency required. By day the troops filled the trenches, and by night a thousand sleepless eyes watched at every point the flushed and vigilant foe. Very, very long were those midnight hours, midst storm and darkness, on the dreary outposts and along the well-trodden beats around the inner lines.

Ye who around peaceful firesides enjoy the fruits of that four years' struggle know little of the fearful cost!

The dauntless spirit of the army was unbroken. No word of complaint was heard. When privation and hardship were unavoidable the sound of murmuring was hushed. It was when things might have been better, and the hard lot of the soldiers was made harder still by ignorance or mismanagement, that grumbling and cursing went up in loud and discordant chorus.

It was a wise order that the general issued when he directed that the attenuated rations should be issued daily. If issued once in three days, as was the usual custom, there were few who would not, impelled by the cravings of hunger, consume their scanty allowance by the end of the first or second day, and have absolutely nothing until the next issue.

It will not be difficult to understand the value of this system in such cases as that of Si Klegg. As long as he had anything in his haversack he could not help eating it. Up to this time he and Shorty had continued to "pool" their supplies, and eat their scanty meals together, out of the common stock. It was no doubt true that this arrangement was more advantageous to Si than to his comrade. He did not intend to eat more than his share, but such was the fact. When in the enjoyment of Uncle Sam's full bounty of hardtack and its concomitants it made no difference, as there was enough; but at this time the question of equity was a serious one, that could not well be ignored. Si was conscious of his weakness, and that he might not defraud his comrade he proposed that until the "cracker line" was opened again each should take his own pittance for himself. Shorty demurred, in the kindness of his heart, but Si insisted that it should be so, and so it was.

The same plan was generally adopted among the soldiers. For the time "messes" were almost unknown. The orderly divided the rations *pro rata*, by careful measurement, to the various squads, and they were again apportioned to each man. The few crackers were evenly distributed; the meat was cut into little blocks with mathematical precision; sugar and rice were doled out with spoons; coffee, most precious of all, became so scarce, and the rations so small, that the grains were scrupulously counted off to each man, that he might receive his full share. Much of the hardtack was mouldy or worm-eaten; and the rancid bacon was bored through and through with maggots that, to the last moment, disputed the claim of the soldier to the repulsive morsel from which, under other circumstances, his stomach would have revolted.

Everything within the lines that could eke out the stinted fare had long since disappeared. In front were the bristling battalions of the enemy. The barren hills in the rear, separated from the army by the wide river, had been scoured by the cavalry of both armies, and nothing in the way of forage for man or beast remained. Many of the animals died of starvation. Horses and mules on the verge of dissolution were killed by the desperate soldiers, and their almost meatless bones were boiled and scraped as clean as if bleached by sun and storm. Kernels of corn were picked from the dung-heaps and eaten with avidity. With magnificent heroism the men endured this crucial test of their patriotism and fidelity. Day and night they went through the round of arduous duty, now and then exchanging defiant shots with the hostile pickets; day and night hunger gnawed more and more fiercely at their vitals; day and night they grew weaker and fainter, and longed and prayed for relief. The hospitals were filled to overflowing with those who could no longer endure the strain. Doctors and nurses sought in vain to relieve their suffering. It was food they needed, and the supply was all too small to restore those famished bodies. Death was busy, and every day the solemn processions moved out to the populous city of the dead. The scenes in that suffering army were only exceeded by those in the ghastly prison stockades of the South.

Si's strong constitution and indomitable pluck carried him through. He lost a good many pounds of flesh, and spent a large part of his leisure time in trying to figure out how long he would be able to stand it, but not once did he join the squad that each morning responded to sick-call, nor did he miss an hour's duty.

"I've got some bully news, Shorty," said Si one day.

"What's up now?" asked Shorty.

"I heerd 'em say that over yonder a few miles the country 's jest alive with soljers that 's come down ter give us a lift. I don't know whar they's from, ner I don't keer, but they're old vet'rans 'n' there's lots on 'em. I reck'n we'll git some grub purty quick, 'n' then won't we make them Johnnies hunt their holes?"

Not for weeks had so genuine a smile played over Si's wasted face. The welcome news had wrought him up to a high state of excitement over the double prospect of once more having his appetite satisfied, and of getting another opportunity to "go for" the rebels and get even with them for cutting off his supplies. It would not be easy to say which afforded him the greatest satisfaction.

"I hope it's true," said Shorty, "but I'll bet you a day's ration o' hardtack that it's only 'nother o' them 'grape-vines.' Ye know we've been hearin' that sort o' yarns every few days fer a month, 'n' they didn't 'mount t' nothin'. Ye can't make me b'lieve it t'll I sees 'em 'th my own eyes."

"Grape-vine dispatches" was the name given to the

wild, sensational rumors that were always circulating through the army. They grew rapidly and enormously as they passed from mouth to mouth and from one regiment to another. Important war news was usually made known to the soldiers through orders from headquarters. Even these official bulletins often appeared to have been written by Baron Munchausen.

"Thar goes some o' the new chaps, now," said Si, as a group of healthy officers and orderlies dashed by. "I kin tell by their looks; they're's fat's pigs. D'ye s'pose they'd ha' been that way 'f they'd been *here* fer a month back livin'—er rather dyin'—on starvation fare? No-sir-ee!"

Shorty was forced to admit the plausibility of Si's theory, conceding that there might, after all, be some foundation for his exuberance of spirit.

Too-o-o-o-t! Too-o-o-o-t! It was the whistle of a locomotive.

"D'ye hear that? What 'd I tell ye?" exclaimed Si, jumping to his feet, swinging his cap, and beginning to yell with all the strength he could command. Although it lacked some of the vigor of other days, when haversacks were full, no yell that had ever before escaped his lips seemed so to come from the depths of his inmost soul.

"Hooray fer the bullgine! Hip! Hip! Hooray fer the hardtack! Whoop—Wh-o-o-o-o-oop! Ki-yi! Tiger-r-r-r!"

If any one is disposed to think that Si's tempestuous enthusiasm was inappropriate to the occasion, let him withhold his judgment until he has "been there."

The effect of that longed-for and prayed-for whistle upon the army was like that of a shock from a galvanic battery. In an instant everybody, from the generals down, was yelling and shouting and cheering. It was as if bedlam itself had been let loose in all the camps. The noise would have drowned the screams of a hundred locomotives. Men danced and sang and laughed until the tears streamed

down their hunger-pinched faces. Si Klegg was no more
of a lunatic than all the rest.

Succor had come at last. Large reinforcements for the
besieged and starving army, ordered thither from other
departments, had arrived. These swiftly-moving columns
had brushed away the force of the enemy that occupied
the railroad, and the "cracker-line" was open once more.
Close upon their heels came long trains of cars freighted
with food, clothing, forage, and other munitions of war.
As the cars rolled into the town the soldiers yelled again,
and kept yelling, until they could yell no longer.

REINFORCEMENTS.

Si told Shorty that
although his most
pressing immediate
need was provisions,
he hoped they had
not forgotten to bring
along plenty of pow-
der and lead so that
the soldiers might take
their revenge upon the
rebels who had re-
duced them to such
dire extremity and
gloated over their
woe.

As some of the fresh troops marched in, bearing aloft
their faded flags, that had been carried through many a
storm of battle on distant fields, they were greeted with
such shouts as do not often fall upon the ear of man. Responsive cheers were heartily given while banners waved
and hats were flung high in air.

It took little time to unload the cars. For this duty
details were made from the newly-arrived troops. Strong
arms and willing hands quickly heaped the wagons that
were provided to convey the boxes and barrels of supplies

to the camps. Soldiers never worked with more alacrity than when exerting themselves for the relief of suffering comrades. The mule-drivers cracked their whips and drove rapidly to the various brigades.

"Volunteers, fall in to draw rations!" shouted the orderly of Company Q. The entire company responded, to a man, with another wild yell.

THE RUSH FOR RATIONS.

For once red-tape was thrown aside, and there was no systematic "issue," according to regulations, of so many ounces per man. Squads from the different regiments were in waiting, and as the contents of the wagons were dumped upon the ground some seized boxes of hardtack, and "slabs" of bacon, while others knocked in the heads of barrels, filled camp-kettles and horse-buckets with coffee and sugar, and away they went. The cracker boxes were quickly "busted" and the ravenous soldiers were told to help themselves.

"Thar!" exclaimed Si, as he and Shorty flung down a box of hardtack with such force as to break it open, "them rebils thought they had a purty good hand, but we've made 'high, low, Jack' a-ready 'n' in a day er two we'll give 'em a lively tussle fer the 'game.' We've jest got the keerds ter do it with now!"

While Si was indulging this patriotic outburst he had stuffed his pockets full of hardtack and slashed off a liberal supply of bacon. Shorty in the meantime had filled two tin cans with sugar and coffee, and they at once set about active preparations for the first "square meal" they had had in many a day. With a cracker and a slice of raw bacon, from which they took alternate mouthfuls, in one hand, they kindled a fire with pieces of the box, and in a few minutes had a quart or two of steaming coffee. Each man preferred to make his own, as this could be done so much more quickly than to boil a camp-kettle, with a supply for the company.

"*Don't* that coffee taste good, Shorty?" said Si, as he quaffed the fragrant elixir from an old cup that was black with long usage. "An' them hardtack, I don't keer 'f they was baked B. C., they goes right to the spot."

Shorty attended strictly to the business in hand, leaving most of the talking to Si, who could talk and eat at the same time without prejudice to either. It took a good while to fill the vacuum that had so long existed under their blouses. At length they could eat no more. Si arose with a feeling of internal comfort to which he had long been a stranger.

"Look at them britches, Shorty," he said, with a broad smile of satisfaction, as he tenderly placed his hand where his body was distended by the large deposit of commissary supplies, "this 's the fust time 'n a month 't I've come anywheres nigh a-fillin' of 'em. They've been flappin' 'round me 's if I was a scarecrow stuck up 'n a cornfield. I'd a-had ter take a reef in 'em 'f the grub hadn't come. My legs 'n' arms 's purty thin 'n' I reck'n my face 's a leetle peaked, but 'twon't take me long ter fill 'em out 'f they keep the cracker-line open. I hain't had no glas's ter look at myself lately, 'n' I'm glad on it, but I c'd feel the bones stickin' out."

There was feasting all through the camps. The consumption of rations exceeded anything that had ever before been known in the history of that army. Men on duty were not forgotten by their comrades, who supplied them liberally with food and flagons of coffee.

The next morning it was Company Q's turn to go on picket. With plenty of rations in their haversacks, the men marched with light step to their posts of duty. Si was stationed on the bank of a stream, on the opposite side of which were the rebel pickets. By tacit agreement a spirit of comity prevailed along the outposts, and the sentinels refrained from firing at one another, so long as no active military operations were in progress. The shooting of a picket under such circumstances was barbarous. It could have no possible effect upon the result of a campaign, and was simply murder, without the excuse that actual conflict gives to man to kill his fellow. This principle was generally recognized on both sides during periods of inaction, and rarely was it violated.

The two or three men who were with Si had scarcely more than disposed themselves behind the little barricade —built for a protection in case the other fellows *should* break the implied contract—when a call from the other bank was heard.*

* The dialog which follows, between Si and the Confederate, is substantially the same as the writer listened to one day in 1863. It is as nearly a reproduction as memory can recall. It illustrates the state of

"Hello, Yank!"

"Hello, Johnny!" responded Si.

"I 'low you-all ain't goin' fer to shoot a feller this mornin,' ar' ye?"

"No, not 'nless you goes to pepperin' *us*. Ef you begins it ye'd better look out, fer we've got some fresh catridges —sure pop every time!"

"All right, Yank, that's a go. Lay down yer shootin' iron 'n' come outen yer hole. Squat down on the bank 'n' less talk it over."

"HELLO, JOHNNY!"—"HELLO, YANK!"

In such cases a soldier's word could be taken with safety, whether he wore the blue or the gray. Si was in good spirits, and in the humor for a little chaffing. He at once went out and sat down at the edge of the stream, which was not wide, and a Confederate soldier, unkempt and unshaven, clad in "butternut," came out on the other side. The latter opened the interview:

"Got plenty o' grub now, hain't ye?"

"Bet yer life!" said Si.

"Been pinched right smart 'long back, I reck'n."

"Wall, we could ha' et more 'f we'd had it, but we man-

feeling that under such conditions existed between men who at other times sought to take one another's life in the fierce conflict of battle. It was one of the anomalies of the war.

aged to wiggle through. I think it was mighty mean of you fellers ter cut our cracker-line 'n' keep it cut so long. We don't mind bein' short a day er two once 'n a while; it jest gives us a good appetite fer army grub. But ye spread it on most too thick this time, pard!''

"Oh, it's all fair 'n war, ye know; we-uns 'lowed ter squeeze you-all t'll ye'd have ter cave in er climb out o' that. We had ye foul, 'n' we'd ha' done it 'f ye hadn't brung down them other Yanks to help ye out. I heerd the gin'ral say myself 't ye couldn't stan' it much longer. I reck'n it sort o' sickened him when he heerd the ke-yars a-tootin' yistuday. Some o' the boys was sayin' that you-all was gittin' reinforced big, 'n' when the whistles blowed we knowed the jig was up. But all the same we're goin' ter git a twist on ye one o' these days.''

"Don't be too sartin o' that," said Si. "The boys 's purty mad 'cause ye cut off their s'plies 'n' ye hain't seen no sich fightin' yet 'n this 'ere war 's they'll show ye nex' time they gits a hackle at ye. We're goin' right through ye.''

"Wall, now, 'f I railly b'lieved that I'd think 'bout startin' now! But say, don't you Yanks do a heap o' blowin'?''

"Mebbe we does, but we allus gits thar arter a while. Ye know that, yerself. Ye don't do jest 's we want ye ter sometimes, but ye keeps backin' up all the time.''

"We've only jest been drawin' ye on. We've got ye right whar we want ye, now, 'n' we ain't goin' ter git back no furder. You put that 'n yer pipe 'n' smoke it. But I'd like ter know what you-all come down here ter fight us fer, anyway, 'n' tryin' ter steal our niggers. What good 'll they do ye when ye git 'em?''

"Now, pard, ye can't git me inter no argyment 'bout that, 'cause I ain't no politician. All I know 'n' all I want ter know is, that you rebels 's fightin' agin the flag o' yer country, 'n' anybody 't does that 's goin' ter git walloped mighty bad. Abe Lincoln didn't set yer niggers free t'll arter he'd gi'n ye fa'r warnin'. Ye mout a-had 'em yet 'f ye'd laid down yer arms 'n' behaved yerselves. Now ye've got ter take the consekences."

"That's all right, Yank. You're on one side 'n' I'm on t'other. We both thinks we's right. Ther' didn't nary one on us have anything ter do 'th gittin' up this war. Them as did stays ter home 'n' don't do no fightin' 'cept with their chins. You 'n' me don't want ter have no hard feelin's, 'cause we kaint help it. Our cussin' 'n' 'discussin' don't 'mount to nothin', nohow. Say, ye don't want ter sling over a hardtack, do ye? We don't have none only what we gobbles f'm you-uns, 'n' I'm gittin' dog-goned tired o' livin' on corn-dodgers!"

"Wall I declar', Johnny, ef ye hain't got more cheek 'n a mule, arter cuttin' off our rations so 't we didn't git but one cracker a day, 'n' mouldy 'n' full o' worms at that. Ef a bullet ever hits ye 'n the face 'twon't hurt ye any. The hide on it 's thicker 'n a 'noceros. I can't spar' 'em very well now 'cause I've been empty fer a good while 'n' I hain't got filled up yet. But ther' ain't nothin' mean 'bout me. What ye got ter trade fer one?"

"Nothin' but terbacker. I'll throw ye a hunk o' that."

"I don't chaw!" said Si.

"Ye don't! What kind of a soljer ar' ye 'n' don't chaw terbacker?"

"Some likes it 'n' some don't, 'n' I hap'n ter be one o' them as don't. But ye may toss 'er over; my pard, Shorty, he chaws 'nuff fer both on us, 'n' he'll be glad ter git it. Terbacker 's bin mighty skeerce, 'n' he's been doin' some tall growlin'."

"Look out, here she comes!"

The Confederate threw over a good-sized lump of "twist," and Si sent a 4-inch hardtack sailing through the air.

"I'm bleeged ter ye, Yank. If ye ever git 'n front o' my gun I hope it'll miss fire, 'n' 'f I ever take ye pris'ner I'll treat ye tip-top. I'd like powerful bad ter have some coffee 'n' some salt. Ye hain't got a leetle ye kin tie up 'n a rag 'n' throw over, have ye?"

"'Pon my word I hain't, pard, ner I hain't got no rag less I tear off a piece o' my shirt. I guess ye'll have ter wait t'll some other day. I reck'n we'd better dry up now er the ossifers 'll git after us. Good-by, Johnny."

"Good-by, Yank."

CHAPTER XXXV.

CORPORAL KLEGG BEARS THE FLAG OF THE 200TH TO VICTORY AND IS WOUNDED.

"SI, are ye hungry fer 'nother fight?" asked Shorty a few evenings later, as he sat by the fire, frying-pan in hand, carefully preparing a mess of "lobscouse" for supper.

"Wall," replied Si, "I dunno 's I've ever felt 's though I was reely starvin' fer a battle sence that fust big one we had. That sorter took the edge off'n my appetite fer fightin', 'n' I reck'n it worked the same way with most o' the boys, 'cause they don't say nothin' more 'bout hankerin' arter it. I heern more o' that sort o' talk in one hour, right away arter we j'ined the army, when we was trampin' 'round the country tryin' ter find the Johnnies, than I does now in a hull month o' Sundays. Ye know 'tain't nat'ral ter walk right up whar ye're likely ter git killed the next minnit. When a feller 's heerd the bullets a-buzzin' 'n' the shells a-bustin' right smart fer *once*, he can't very well help feelin' 's though he'd had 'nuff. Ther' don't nobody like ter have holes 'n his hide 'f he c'n git out of it. Ther' 's a few o' the boys 't allus manages to wiggle

out o' goin' inter a fight, 'n' I don't blame 'em 's much 's I
used ter, 'cause I know how I feels myself.   Course I don't
think s' much 'bout it arter I'm in 'n' gits purty well excited, but I tell ye, Shorty, every time I begin ter hear them
pesky things a-zippin', I'd a heap ruther be hoein' corn
'long 'th dad."

"I hain't never seen ye act 's though ye felt that way,"
said Shorty.

"It's the fust time I've ever told ye 'bout it, 'n' I s'pose
ye've allus thought I was brave 's a lion, but I ain't.   When
we're goin' inter a fight, seems 's if ther' was *two* Si Kleggs.
One on 'em wants ter run mighty bad, 'n' ef I sh'd do 's
he says I'd more 'n scoot out o' thar, every time.   But I
know we can't never lick the rebils that way, 'n' so I jest
says to that other Si, 'Now ye've *got* ter face the music,
'n' I won't have no more o' yer white-livered nonsense.
Ye can't git out of it, 'cause ef ye try I'll jest blow yer
brains out, ef ye've got any.'   That settles it 'n' I don't
have no more trouble t'll the next time, 'n' then it's the
same thing over ag'in.   'Pears like I never could make
t'other feller—I mean the one 't ain't *me*—behave hisself.   I reck'n 't sometimes the wrong part 's the biggest,
'n' that's what's the matter 'th a few o' the boys.   They's
made that way 'n' they can't help it.   Ye *know* how I
hates a coward—I mean one o' them critters that's so
a-purpose, 'cause he don't *want* ter be nothin' else—but some
o' them as hain't got the sand I'm sorry fer.   They don't
mean ter do it but that t'other feller jest carries 'em right
off.   My sand 'd ha' run out 'fore this 'f I'd ha' *let* it.   There
was that poor fellow 't they court-martialed and shot
t'other day fer flingin' away his gun 'n' runnin' in that
last fight.   I don't reck'n ye've fergot it— I know I shan't
right away—our bein' drawed up 'n a holler square while
the detail o' soljers riddled him 'th bullets.   I s'pose
they've got ter have sich things in war, but I tell ye the
shootin' o' that boy 'n cold blood was the hardest thing

I've looked at sence I've been soljerin'. I couldn't help thinkin' 't might ha' been *me*, 'f I'd weakened a leetle bit that day o' the battle. Pity they couldn't ha' shot jest that part that made him run, 'n' there 'd been 'nuff on him left ter make a fust-rate soljer. I'm glad he didn't b'long ter Company Q, 'n' I'm gladder yet 't I wasn't one o' them as had ter shoot him. I'd ruther fight rebils fer a month hand-runnin' 'n ter ha' done that. It'd be a fust-rate notion 'f they c'd diskiver some way ter tell them as has got sand, when they're 'xaminin' 'em fer 'listin', and then bounce all them that's short. It 'd be better'n waitin' ter find out by tryin', after feedin' 'n' clothin' 'em so long. I'm afeard it 'd ha' been a tight squeak 'th me 'f they'd had a machine o' that kind the time the doctor made me peel myself."

"Look out, thar, pard," said Shorty, "ye're lettin' the coffee bile over while ye're a-speechifyin'. S'posin' ye give us a rest now 'n' less eat supper. This 'ere stuff 's done."

"Ye was wound up fer keeps, wa'n't ye, Si; I thought ye'd never run down!" continued Shorty, as they filled their cups with coffee, and made a simultaneous attack upon the heap of "lobscouse" which Shorty had emptied upon a tin plate that looked as if it had been dug out of the ruins of Babylon. "I didn't s'pose ye *had* s' much phlos'phy inside yer clothes. Lemme tell ye, Si, 'tain't nothin' agin a man ter be afeard, pervidin' he don't let it git away with him. That's the kind of a man you be, 'n' I tries hard ter be that way myself. 'Cordin' ter my notion it's a brave man 't *knows* how unhealthy 'tis 'mong the bullets 'n' shells but has got the spunk ter go right up into 'em when the orders says so. That's the kind o' men 't makes stayers. The gin'rals goes 'long 'th the boys—that is some on 'em does—but I tell ye they don't love them whizzin' things no more 'n you 'n' me does. But 's I was sayin' Si, I shouldn't be s'prised 'f we had a big scrimmage termorrer er nex' day."

"Well, I'm ready!" said Si, with quiet soberness.

It was rarely that the men knew, save from their own intuitions, when a battle was about to take place. Sometimes a fight was brought on suddenly and unexpectedly even to those in command. It was no doubt best that a soldier should not know beforehand that he was to engage the enemy. He was, perhaps, not always fully prepared to die, from a theological point of view, and yet he must be ready—and willing—to meet death at any moment. The uncertainty of life, even under the most favorable conditions, was vastly increased in the army. Looking back to those awful years, when companies and regiments were almost annihilated by successive fiery tempests, memory recalls with amazement the stoical indifference to which the soldier schooled himself. He came to look unmoved upon the ghastliest scenes, and in the excitement of battle the peril to his own life was scarcely remembered.

When deliberate preparations were made for battle, the signs of the impending conflict were clear enough to those who kept eyes and ears open. Shorty had noticed these indications for a day or two and had readily formed the opinion he expressed to Si. It proved to be correct; nor had they long to wait. Even while they were talking the Union forces were moving on the extreme right and left to "feel of" the enemy.

"Jest listen at that!" said Shorty, as a sharp rattle of musketry was heard in the distance, soon followed by the booming of artillery. "They're ticklin' 'em on the flanks to stir 'em up. You see 'f we don't git orders t'night that means business!"

"We're goin' ter make them Johnnies skedaddle this time," said Si, as he jumped at the sound of the guns and began to put on his accouterments. "We're goin' ter git even with 'em fer keepin' our haversacks empty so long."

Moved by a common impulse the men, without waiting

for orders, seized their arms and fell into line, to be ready for whatever might happen.

Si took a "deck" of cards from his blouse pocket and gave them a fling, scattering them far and near upon the ground.

"What ye doin' that fer?" asked Shorty, who had none of the sentiment that prompted the action.

Indeed, when called upon to give a reason Si was unable to reply in a manner satisfactory even to himself, so he simply said he didn't know.

"If ye'd kep' 'em in yer pocket 'n' a bullet sh'd hit ye thar them keerds mout ha' saved yer life," said Shorty, who looked at the matter in a practical way.

Even this suggestion failed to impress Si and he made no attempt to gather them up. He told Shorty that they were about worn out, anyway, and after the fight was over he would buy a new pack

A MISDEAL.

from the sutler. He was afraid his comrade would laugh at him if he should tell him that he did not want to be killed with cards in his pocket.

Like thousands of other good boys, Si did not know the difference between an ace and a ten-spot when he went to the army. He had never turned truant when his father set him to digging potatoes, by stealing away to a neighbor's barn and playing seven-up in the hay-mow. He never gambled in the army, save when, only once, he was beguiled from the path of virtue by the seductive allure ments of "chuck-a-luck;" but he learned to play cards purely as a diversion, to while away the tedious hours. On this ground he satisfied his conscience; yet he never came to consider a pack of cards as a means of grace.

Si was not the only soldier to whose mind the sound of guns brought such feelings. Often the ground in rear of a line moving to battle was as thickly strewn with well-worn cards as if they had snowed down. Many of the boys waited until they were sure there was going to be a fight, only flinging away their cards when there was no longer a reasonable doubt on that score. It was a good thing for the sutlers. After a battle, trade was lively in this article of merchandise.

But there was really no occasion for Si to throw away his cards so soon, for the 200th Indiana was not called upon to do any fighting that night. As darkness settled down over the armies the firing on the flanks ceased. The pickets were reinforced and doubly cautioned to be vigilant. All through the camp orders were given for the men to lie upon their arms. Muskets and accouterments were carefully inspected, cartridge-boxes filled, and extra rounds issued to each man. Haversacks and canteens were replenished, brief letters were hastily written to far-away northern homes, and the army lay down to rest.

There were always some who had, or thought they had, presentiments of death just before going into a battle, and it was their habit to place money, watches and other valuables in the possession of comrades who, they seemed to think, would be more fortunate, although in every respect as likely to fall as themselves. They did not on this account shrink from danger. Indeed there was no more sublime courage than that which carried a soldier with unfaltering step into the enemy's fire when he believed he was marching to his death. It is not probable that those whose minds were clouded by presentiments suffered

any greater ratio of mortality than those who were free
from such forebodings.*

There was another class the opposite of these, who did
not believe—at least they said they didn't—that any missiles had been or could be made that would hit them. There
were many times when to be fully persuaded of this would
have been extremely comforting. The truth is, however,
that the cruel bullets of the enemy made sad havoc with
these pleasing hallucinations. But when a man was possessed of this belief it was easier for him to be brave than
for his comrade who was continually standing in a cemetery and looking into an open grave.

Si Klegg did not belong to either of these classes. His
mind was not shadowed by constant visions of death,
nor did he delude himself with the belief that he bore a
charmed life. In common with most of the soldiers, his
first battle had given him a full realization of the danger,
but he was ever ready and willing to meet it at the call
of duty. It was this spirit of entire self-abnegation
that made a man a soldier, with all that the word
implies.

Long before daylight the army was up and in line
of battle, standing at arms in the trenches. The men,
elbow to elbow, grasped their muskets more firmly as a
shot was heard now and then on the picket line. They
heeded not the damp and chilling air as they peered with
eager eyes into the darkness, to catch the first sign of the
enemy's possible approach. Along the lines of the besiegers,

---

* The writer was twice made the custodian of the effects of a comrade
who was always sure he would be killed. The third time he had a pre-
sentiment that the writer would be killed, too, and put his watch and
money into the hands of another. The latter was taken prisoner and
the valuables were "gobbled" by his captors. After that the comrade
had no more presentiments and acted as his own treasurer. He went
through every battle in which the regiment participated and was not
even touched.

upon the hills and ridges, the vigilant foe was watching. No fires gleamed on the crests. In the darkness and silence the two armies waited for the dawn that should usher in another bloody day.

"Shorty," said Si in a low voice, as the first faint light revealed the neighboring heights, crowned with earth-works and bristling with cannon, "ef we don't make them fellers git off'n thar today I ain't no good at guessin'. They've been a-havin' things purty much 's they wanted 'em fer a while back, 'n' now it's *our* turn. All we wants is fer the gin'rals ter jest give us a chance."

"We'll wait 'n' see," replied Shorty. "'Twon't be no easy job, I c'n tell ye, ter go up them hills 't they've been fortifyin' all the time we've been lyin' here, 'n' the Johnnies swarmin' 'n the works 'n' pourin' down bullets 'n' grape. We'll try it ef the gin'ral says so, but I hain't no longin' arter that sort o' thing. Ther' 'll be a good many on us 't won't git ter the top!"

Si did not answer, but stood, with serious face, looking earnestly toward the heights on which lay the hostile army, as if calculating the probable result of a mighty rush upon the foe.

"Half an hour for breakfast!"

The daylight had fully come, and one wing of each regiment at a time was directed to retire a short distance for the morning meal.

"Eat hearty, boys," said the orderly of Company Q. "Looks like we'd got business on hand, an' we may not git 'nother chance 'fore night."

Hastily, but quietly, coffee was made, and bacon toasted on sticks and ramrods. The men sat down in little groups, drawing crackers from their haversacks, and with keen appetites proceeded to strengthen themselves for the duties of the day.

"I wonder how many of Company Q 'll be makin' coffee tomorrow mornin'!" said one of the boys. Although

nothing was known of the contemplated movement except by inference, it was well understood that a great battle was pending.

"Now, pard, don't go ter talkin' that way," said Si, "'cause it makes a feller feel kind o' streaked, 'n' 't don't do no good, nohow. Soljers has ter fight er they wouldn't *be* soljers; 'n' some on 'em has ter git killed. Like'y 'nuff it'll come 'round ter my turn today, but what's the good o' stewin' 'bout it? Comp'ny Q 's goin' ter git thar 'f any on 'em does, 'n' I calkerlate to be up 'mong the boys 'nless suthin stops me. The 200th Injianny hain't done nothin' yet ter be 'shamed of, 'n' I don't b'lieve she will when we go fer them raskils 't cut our cracker-line."

Si's words of cheer and hope were not without their effect, and the dismal inquiry suggested by

BREAKFAST BEFORE THE FIGHT.

his comrade was not pursued.

Before they had finished their breakfast every ear was startled by the boom of cannon, with sharp successive volleys of musketry two or three miles to the right and left. The movement had begun simultaneously on both flanks.

"Thar goes the music!" exclaimed Shorty. "Choose yer pardners fer the dance!"

"I jest hope we c'n make them rebils sashay ter the

rear!" said Si, as he poured down the last of his coffee and seized his musket.

To the right and left the firing each moment grew heavier, telling that the storm had burst. The men hurried back to their places at the front, and stood with every nerve and sense strained to the utmost. Nothing could surpass the intensity of eargerness with which they watched for tidings of the conflict.

"How 's it goin'?" was asked by a hundred voices of an orderly who went dashing by.

"They say we're drivin' 'em!" was the answer.

"I knowed it!" said Si, as he swung his hat and joined in the yelling that followed this announcement. Whether true or not it raised the spirits of the soldiers to a high pitch.

Si yelled and shouted whenever he saw or heard anything that stirred his emotions. He had never before felt so strong a personal interest in any battle. Aside from his devotion to his bleeding and distracted country, his sufferings from hunger, during the weary weeks, for which the rebels were responsible, were to be avenged.

"Now they're goin' fer 'em!" he shouted, when the sharp firing indicated hot work. "Give 'em —" In his excitement Si came very near uttering a word that always seemed to fit in such cases—the "Revised Version" had not yet softened it into "gehenna" or "sheol"—but remembering the teachings of his early youth and switching off his tongue just in time, he only said: "Give 'em Hail Columbia!" This was patriotic, and on the whole satisfactory as an expression of his feelings.

Now the order was passed along the line to be prepared for an advance at a moment's notice. There was little occasion for this, as every man in that impatient army was ready and eager to go forward at the word of command. The increased roar of artillery and the sharp rattle of musketry told of fierce fighting on the flanks. As the direction of the sound indicated the steady advance of the Union forces, cheer after cheer swept through the compact battalions that formed the center.

"Look there, boys, *quick !* ' exclaimed Si, his eyes flashing with excitement, as he pointed to the loftiest height that had been long occupied by the besieging host.

In an instant all eyes were fixed upon the point. The scene was one to make the blood leap through a soldier's veins. On the summit could be seen the smoke of battle and the rebels giving way before the victorious blue-coats. Flags were dimly discerned that the soldiers knew were the stars and stripes. Forty thousand men looked upon the glorious spectacle, and forty thousand voices joined in a shout of gladness that rolled in billows along the lines, filling the air with its mighty volume, and echoing from the surrounding hills.

Now is the time for a general advance. Never were soldiers in fitter mood for deeds of supremest valor.

A bugle sounds at army headquarters. Through all the divisions and brigades men who have long stood waiting for this signal raise their bugles to their lips and the shrill notes ring out upon the air.

"Forward!" is the word. It is the only thought in the breast of every soldier. The men leap over the works, and the long line, with flags waving and muskets flashing in the sunlight, moves steadily and grandly on.

" Battalion—Double-quick—March!" shouts the colonel of the 200th Indiana. The regiment, in prompt obedience, advances rapidly until the proper distance is reached, when it is hastily deployed into a heavy skirmish-line, covering the brigade front.

Half a mile away are the enemy's pickets. Beyond, skirting the foot of the range of hills, are the rifle-pits, behind which, with loaded muskets, the rebels are awaiting the onset. The high ridge is surmounted by works that many thousands of men have been weeks in building. A hundred cannon, double-shotted, peer angrily through the embrasures. Behind them, swarming in the trenches, is the main body of the Confederate army.

"Halt—lie down!"

Half the distance to the enemy's pickets has been traversed. The final disposition of the troops is not fully made and a brief halt is necessary. The men of the 200th throw themselves flat upon the ground.

The bullets from the enemy's guns are already singing through the air. Now there are flashes of flame and puffs

HUGGING THE GROUND.

of smoke on the crest of the ridge. The rebel artillery has opened with ominous roar. Shells come screaming through the air, and, bursting with terrifying crack, send their ragged fragments whizzing among the prostrate soldiers.

"Steady, men, steady!"

Few things that ever fall to the lot of man are more severely trying than to lie, idle and helpless, under an artillery fire. At such a time the stoutest heart quails and the steadiest nerves twinge. The inexperienced reader may think this ought not so to be, particularly after he is informed that long-range artillery firing rarely sheds any blood. But let him not form a theoretical opinion as to how soldiers ought to demean themselves under such circumstances. If his life passes without bringing to him an opportunity to lie and quietly enjoy himself in reading or smoking or sleeping while shells are bursting and tearing up the earth around him, let him be satisfied to accept the unanimous verdict of those who have learned from actual experience and observation.

Si wriggled uneasily and fairly ground his nose into the dirt as the swiftly-flying missiles hurtled about him. When one of them struck uncomfortably near and sprinkled him with earth, he was for the moment on the verge of demor-alization. It was not that he was "afraid," but he did not relish the idea of being under fire without any chance to shoot back.

"I'd a mighty sight ruther go ahead," he said to Shorty, "'n' pitch inter them fellers than ter lay here like a log while they're heavin' their old iron 'round so promisc'us like. I sh'd think they mout ha' got things fixed 'fore we started so 's we wouldn't have ter stop arter we got up in range o' them pesky guns."

It was not to be expected that Si could comprehend all these mysterious ways. Such things often happened.

The artillery fire was not wholly ineffectual. Some of the fragments did their ghastly work, and here and there lay a comrade, mangled, quivering and bleeding—dead or writhing in pain.

A staff officer dashes up and says that all is ready.

"Attention—Battalion!" shouts the colonel of the 200th. Every man springs to his feet, impatient for the charge. "Men, I don't want you to stop till you get those rifle-pits. Don't halt to fire, but jump right into 'em with cold steel. Fix—Bayonets! Go!"

Now the soldiers are themselves again. There is no shrinking nor dodging, though faster and thicker come the bullets and shrieking shells.

In the onward rush the alignment of the regiment is broken. The more eager ones dash forward, regardless of company formations, intent only upon reaching the enemy.

They know that when such a job is in hand "'twere well 'twere done quickly." Others do not get over the ground quite so rapidly. Perhaps they are not less brave than those who are forging ahead, but they do not see the use of being in such a hurry. Then, some men can run faster than others—when they want to.

Si's legs are nimble and he is among the foremost, with the faithful Shorty at his side. On they go with flying feet, unmindful of the spiteful zip of bullets or the shells that burst above them. Now and then a comrade falls, but none can stay to staunch his wound or receive his last words.

The enemy's pickets are powerless to check the onward sweep. Some break for the rifle-pits, others stand to their posts until, overwhelmed by the tide, they yield themselves prisoners.

YIELDING TO THE INEVITABLE.

In front of Si and Shorty is a fortified post occupied by two plucky rebels who are determined to hold the fort to the last extremity. The shouts of the charging troops are answered with loud yells of defiance.

"Flank 'em, pard," says Shorty.

Si dashes one way and Shorty the other, and in an instant their bayonets are at the breasts of the little garrison.

"S'render, will ye?" yells Si.

There is no escape, and they throw up their hands in token of submission.

"Now you git back ter the rear, lively. We're goin' fer some more o' you fellers 't cut off our s'plies. Come on, Shorty!"

Away go the "Johnnies," while Si and Shorty join the grand sweep for the rifle-pits. Here the struggle is short but fierce. For a few minutes there is a stubborn resistance. The rushing tide flows over the embankment and down into the very trenches. Men plunge with their bayonets and beat one another with the butts of their guns, their voices mingling in wild yells and imprecations and sharp cries of pain.

Not long can such a scene continue. The rebels abandon the hopeless contest. Many surrender and others fly. The dead and wounded—blue and gray—are thickly mingled.

There is a brief halt, while all along the line the air resounds with the shouts of triumph. The objective point of the order to advance has been reached. Shall the men stop here? There are no orders to go further.

The pause has given them breath, and now, animated by a single thought, the impetuous soldiers again dash forward with a yell. On they go, up the steep side of the ridge, in the face of a hail-storm of bullets and canister from the enemy on the crest. Can mortal man breast this fiery tornado and live?

Men fall by scores and hundreds before the deadly blast, but still on and up sweeps the audacious line. Shells are lighted by hand and tossed over the works, to roll down and make havoc among the assailants. Here and there the soldiers waver, but it is only for an instant, and again they push for the summit.

How fares the 200th Indiana? It has kept its place at the front, and its fast melting ranks are far up the rugged height. The color-bearer falls dead. Another carries the banner aloft, but in a moment he, too, is shot down.

Now Corporal Klegg slings his gun over his shoulder and

snatches up the blood-stained staff. With a royal will he waves the flag, shouts to his comrades to follow, and fairly leaps toward the crest. A missile strikes his arm and for a moment there is a keen sensation of pain. But he stops not—heeds it not.

The standard is riddled by bullets, but it waves farther up the hill than any other. It will not lose its place so long as Corporal Klegg is able to bear it. Inspired by his example, the men of the 200th who have not been stricken down follow close after. Behind them, and far to the right and left, thousands of brave men are crowding upward.

The 200th reaches the top with a loud shout as Si plants its flag on the rebel parapet. The men climb over in the very faces of the rebels. The latter, dazed by the audacity of the charge, are seized with a panic and break in confusion. It is folly to fight against men who can go up that ridge in the teeth of such a fire.

The day was grandly won. Prisoners and cannon in large numbers were taken. With yells and shouts the men pursued the fleeing enemy until exhaustion compelled them to halt.

Si was rejoiced that Shorty had not been touched. They embraced each other and tears of gladness flowed down their cheeks.

The colonel came up to Si, shook his hand warmly, and complimented him in the highest terms for his gallantry. "I am proud to command such men," he said. Noticing blood on Si's arm, the colonel asked him if he was badly hurt.

"Wall, I declar'," replied Si, "I'd fergot all 'bout that. I felt it comin' up the hill, but we was too busy fer me ter bother with it then. I reck'n 'tain't nothin' very serus."

The clothing upon the arm was saturated with blood, and a hasty examination showed a serious wound.

"You've behaved like a hero, my boy," said the colonel.

"but you must go at once to the hospital and have your wound cared for."

Si had always dreaded the word "hospital," but there was no choice, and he consented to go. As he turned away he said to the colonel:

"I rayther guess we got even with them rebils for shuttin' off our hardtack!"

CHAPTER XXXVI.

SI SPENDS A NIGHT IN THE FIELD HOSPITAL AND SEES SOME OF THE HORRORS OF WAR.

SI spent the night as a patient in the field hospital. When he reached that place he was met by the surgeon of the 200th Indiana who had been detailed for duty there. Everybody in the regiment, from colonel to mule-driver, knew Corporal Klegg.

"Well, Si, they've winged you, too, have they?"

"I had ter take my turn gittin' hit. I'm thankful 'tain't no wuss." And Si laughed good-naturedly as he looked at his arm.

"Say, Doc," he continued, with that easy familiarity that characterized his intercourse with high and low, "this ain't nothin' but a scratch. You jest tie it up in a rag 'n' let me go back with the boys. That's a bully old musket I've got, 'n' if there's any more fightin' goin' on I want ter keep her blazin' away. I'd like ter pay up the raskils fer pluggin' me."

"You're a good boy, Si," replied the kind-hearted surgeon, "and the 200th Indiana is proud of you, but you had better take my advice and lay up a while for repairs. You will come out all right, but your arm will be sorer than you think. You have been a good, faithful soldier, and I guess we had better send you home for a few days."

Home! The word touched a tender chord in Si's heart. Tears moistened his eyes in an instant, as before them came a vision of that "dearest spot on earth," and thoughts of father, mother, sister and the one that made his slippers. How many long months—years they seemed —had passed since that tearful parting, the day the company left for the war. His lips quivered and his voice trembled as he said:

"I'd like ter be to home fer a bit, more 'n I can tell ye, Doctor. It 'd be almost 's good 's goin' ter Heaven. But I don't like ter go back on the old rijiment. Ef I knowed the boys wouldn't be doin' nothin' while I was gone I wouldn't keer so much, but I shouldn't never git over it to have the 200th Injianny gittin' any more glory 'n' me not there to do my sheer."

"There's no danger that you will not do your part, Corporal. What we want now is to get your arm cured up. You'll get well in half the time at home. And I guess you won't object to having something good to eat for a change. You'll come back as fresh as a pippin."

During the conversation the surgeon had carefully cut away the blood-soaked garments and made an examination of the wound. It was an ugly hurt. The rough, cruel iron had torn away and mangled the flesh down to the bone.

"I didn't know 'twas so bad," said Si, as he surveyed the injured part. "I didn't feel nothin' but a thump when that thing struck me. I reck'n I was a leetle excited 'bout gittin' ter the top o' that hill 's soon 's any other feller did, 'n' I couldn't think o' nothin' else."

"I heard all about how you got there," said the surgeon. "Now don't let this knife frighten you, Si. That piece of shell made bad work and I'll have to do a little cutting to get it in shape so that it will heal."

"All right, Doctor, slash away; only so ye don't cut my arm off; I can't spar' that, nohow. I know some o' the boys has ter, but I'm goin' ter keep mine hangin' to me 'slong 's I kin. 'Pears ter me it 'd be a great scheme 'f they c'd raise a crop o' men fer soljers with three or four arms 'n' legs apiece. Then a feller mout let some on 'em go 'n' have 'nuff left so he c'd git along. No, Doc, I don't want no chloryform ner nothin'. I'll jest see 'f I've got 's much spunk 's I think I hev." And as the surgeon began operations

IN THE SURGEON'S CARE.

Si clenched his fists and his teeth. The surgeon trimmed off the ragged fragments of flesh, washed the wound tenderly, and bound it up with soothing remedies.

"There, my boy," he said, as he fastened the bandage, "that's the best I can do for you now. You are in good health and spirits, and nature will do wonders for you. Many a poor fellow dies just because he gets down in the mouth."

Who that marched and fought and endured does not know that a lightsome, plucky spirit was a perennial fountain of life and health. Fortunate indeed was he who possessed it, and could meet with cheerfulness the privations and dangers and sufferings incident to a soldier's life. Nothing but the piercing of a vital part could kill such a one. He would fight off the grim monster and recover from frightful wounds, while his gloomy and desponding comrade, who had received but a mere scratch in comparison, would pine away and die. There were those who could be cheerful and laugh and even jest while enduring unspeakable agony of body and in the immediate presence of death. Such men were worth more to their fellow-sufferers than a whole college of surgeons. The warmth of a few genial natures would diffuse itself through a regiment while on the weary march, in fierce heat or drenching storm or winter's cold, or suffering for want of food, and drive away the "blues"—the soldier's greatest enemy—from hundreds of aching hearts. Such a one was Si Klegg. His droll ways and cheery nature were a well-spring of happiness and health to himself and a perpetual blessing to those around him.

The surgeon arranged a sling in which to carry the wounded arm, and Si began to look about to see if he could render assistance in alleviating the sufferings of others. He had never before seen the awful picture of war presented by a field hospital just after a battle.

The horrors of the conflict of arms, and the deadly work of hissing bullet and screaming shell are not realized by the participant, when every nerve is strained to its utmost; when every thought and emotion is dominated by the one overmastering passion of the struggle for victory; when the eye looks only toward the foe, and the ear hears not, amidst the roar of musket and cannon, the cry of agony and the moan of expiring life. It is when the calm succeeds the storm, and the ghastly harvest is garnered in the hospitals, where, amidst the dead and the dying, the probe and knife and saw, plied by a hundred skillful hands, are busy during all the dragging hours of the night; while on every hand are heard the screams and groans that pain extorts from the bravest hearts—it is then, and then only, that there comes a full realization of the hideous barbarity of war.

Si's sympathies were deeply stirred. His own wound was becoming painful, but he scarcely felt it as the stream of sympathy flowed out toward those whose wounds were so much more severe than his own. All about him they lay, on cots and on the hard earth. The great hospital tents were filled, and mangled and bleeding men covered the ground without. Huge fires were burning at frequent intervals to aid the attendants in their work, and to take away the chill from the damp night air. The glare of the flames lighted up the dreadful scene. The surgeons and their assistants moved about with instruments and rolls

THE FIELD HOSPITAL.

of bandages and cordials. There were amputating tables —some built of rough poles laid side by side, the ends resting upon cross-pieces supported by forked sticks driven firmly into the ground—to which, one after another, were borne those whose limbs were so shattered by the battle's missiles that they could not be saved. Around them stood the operators, with hands and arms bared and bloody, intent upon their horrid work.

Here a hand has been torn by a bullet. Bone and muscle and tendon are crushed and severed. It has pulled trigger for the last time. If it could heal at all it would be but ragged and shapeless, and it were better off. A cloth saturated with chloroform is held to the nostrils, and in a moment the wounded man is unconscious. There is a quick movement of knife and saw, the arteries are closed, the skin is sewed over the quivering flesh, dressings are applied, and the soldier awakes to find that he is crippled forever.

He gives place to the next—a brave lad, pale and faint from loss of blood. A rough fragment of shell has crushed his foot, to the ankle, into a shapeless mass. There is nothing to do but to cut it off. Again the chloroform, the knife, the saw, the needle and the bandages. Five minutes suffice for the operation, and the boy opens his eyes to find that he must hobble through life upon crutches.

Here is a man with a shattered right arm. He pleads piteously with the surgeons to save it. They tell him it is impossible, and their judgment must direct. He refuses to breathe the stupefying anæsthetic, and with his other hand he pushes away the cloth that an attendant attempts to throw over his face.

"I don't want none o' that!" he says. "I've got the nerve to stand it, and I'd rather have my eyes open and see what's going on. Saw away, Doctor, if you've got to!"

While the gleaming instruments sever bone and flesh he sings in a clear, steady voice,

"Yes, we'll rally 'round the flag, boys, rally once again!"

Men who lie upon the ground writhing with pain, wounded even unto death, catch the spirit of the brave sufferer. Here one joins in the song with tremulous voice; there another greets with a feeble huzza the cheerful, patriotic sacrifice. The surgeons are accustomed to scenes of suffering and death, but their hearts are touched and their eyes moisten. In a few minutes only a stump remains.

Here comes one borne upon a blanket. Handle him tenderly! A bullet has plowed its cruel way through his thigh. It is a desperate case. Amputations so near the body are accompanied with extreme danger. He is an officer, who fell at the head of his company as he led his brave men over the crest of the ridge. The surgeons hold a hurried consultation. The bone of the limb has been pierced and shivered. The doctors shake their heads dubiously. They tell the patient that his only chance of life lies in the knife, and that the operation is likely to result fatally.

"There is but one choice to make," he says. "Proceed!"

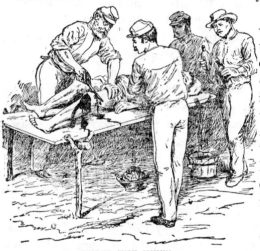

UNDER THE KNIFE.

Ten — fifteen — twenty minutes, for the operation is a serious one, and he is carried from the table, weak and exhausted. There is little hope that his eyes will see the morrow's sun.

A man with one of his legs crushed and mangled is brought upon a stretcher. The overpowering pain has for the time dethroned his reason. He utters piercing shrieks and yells, and resists with mad fury those who lift him to the table. A cloth saturated with chloroform is held over his face and in a moment he lies as one dead. Quickly the knife and saw do their work, a dash of water restores him to consciousness, and he is borne away to make room for another.

And so, hour after hour, the ghastly work goes on, amidst screams and groans and sighs that are wrenched from unwilling lips. There are men with mutilated faces

—an eye gone, an ear torn off, a jaw crushed to fragments. Charging through that leaden hail, necks and
shoulders were torn by hissing balls. Here are men with
pierced lungs—men through whose bodies in every part,
bullets have passed. Many of those thus stricken down
lie where they fell, on the rugged side of yonder ridge or
beside the cannon that belched from its summit. These
yet survive their awful wounds. A few—here and there
one among them—will recover in a measure, and will live
through years of suffering, and yet every moment in the
presence of death. To the rest, upon whom the surgeons
exhaust their skill in the hopeless effort to give relief, the
final muster-out will come in a few hours or days or weeks.

Far into the night the wounded continue to arrive from
the battle-field, borne upon stretchers or blankets or carried
in the succoring arms of their comrades. They are chilled
by the dews, and their reddened garments are as if starched
by the stiffening blood that has flowed from their wounds.
One by one they pass under the hand of the surgeons and
are laid in rows upon the ground, where the nurses can
serve them with food and water and remedies to allay
their pain.

One needs not to be told to tread with gentle feet as he
passes through the tents and between the long lines of
prostrate forms without. Death is all around. Here,
there and yonder the breath comes feebly, and the heart
beats more faintly with each passing moment. Ever and
anon the flickering spark of life goes out in a breast that
a few hours ago was bared to the battle-storm. The dead
are removed from among the living. Here lie their pulseless forms, each covered with a blanket. Tomorrow the
spade will perform its sad office. A long trench will be
dug and they will be laid in, side by side, without shroud
or coffin, and the earth will be heaped above them. At
roll-call their comrades will answer "Dead!" They have
made the supreme sacrifice for country's sake.

Willing hearts and hands find plenty to do in attending to the needs of the patient sufferers. Men who bear arms cannot be spared for this. Their post of duty is at the front. Here is work for the non-combatants—chaplains, musicians, clerks and others. Their duty in time of action is to bear the wounded from the field and care for their wants, under the direction of the surgeons. Many of the injured who are not wholly disabled render such service as they can to their more severely wounded comrades.

One of the most active and efficient among these was Corporal Klegg. Giving little heed to his own wound, hour after hour he passed from one to another, performing his kindly offices. There were many from his regiment, and to them he naturally devoted his efforts. His pleasant face and words of encouragement brought cheer to many a sad heart.

"Hello, Si!"

It was a familiar voice, that Si would have recognized among a thousand. Turning quickly around he looked into the glad face of his friend Shorty.

"I declar', old pard, I'm glad to see ye," he exclaimed, and his manner left no room to doubt the sincerity of his words. "Whar 'd ye come from, Shorty? Seems 's though I hadn't seen ye fer a dog's age. Whar's the rijiment at? Did ye have any more fightin' arter I left ye?"

"I kin answer yer questions better, Si, ef ye'll fire 'em one 't a time, and not shoot off a hull volley of 'em to oncet," said Shorty with a laugh. "I s'pose ye warn't expectin' ter see me, but I couldn't stan' it 'thout findin' out how bad ye was hurt, 'n' how ye was gittin' 'long. 'Tain't more 'n a couple o' miles to whar the rijiment 's lyin'. Ther' ain't no scrimmagin' goin' on; I reck'n the Johnnies got 'nuff today to last 'em over night. I axed the cap'n 'f I mout hunt ye up 'n' he said he didn't have no 'bjections pervidin' the colonel was willin'. I made bold to ax him 'cause I knowed he allus had a warm side fer ye, 'n' I didn't b'lieve he'd think any less on ye fer carryin' the flag o' the old 200th Injianny up to the top o' that blazin' ridge. Jest 's soon 's I told him what I wanted he said right away, the colonel did: 'Certingly, my man, 'n' when ye git back' says he, 'come straight ter my tent 'n' tell me how badly Corp'ral Klegg 's wounded. He's a brave fellow, is Klegg.' That's jest what he said, Si. Then he give me a pass 't he writ with his own fingers, so nobody wouldn't pick me up fer a straggler, slinkin' back ter the rear. I had a hard time findin' the right

place, but I stuck to it 'n' here I am, yer most 'umble sarvint. Now how's yer arm? That's the fust question I've got ter ax *you!*"

Shorty's tongue was much like Si's in its tendency to run on, when once it got fairly started. By this time, however, Si was getting well wound up, and was impatient for his turn. He will be readily pardoned for the undisguised pleas-

THE TWO "PARDS."

ure with which he had listened to Shorty's recital of what the colonel said.

"Ther' ain't very much the matter o' my arm, Shorty," he replied. "I tried 's hard 's ever I could ter have the doctor tie it up 'n' lemme go back ter the comp'ny, but he wouldn't do it, nohow. He said I'd have ter lay up fer a while and he guessed he'd send me hum. P'r'aps ye c'n form some kind of an idee how glad I'd be ter go, 'n' yet I tell ye I'd ruther stay 'long with you 'n' the rest o' Company Q. I don't want the 200th Injianny ter do anything 'thout I'm thar ter help do it. Ef I do go, the boys ner the colonel won't think I'm playin' off, will they, Shorty? Ef I thought they'd feel that way I wouldn't budge an inch fer all the doctors this side o' Texas."

"Course they won't, Si; ye needn't be noways 'fraid o' that. They've seen ye stan' up to the rack often 'nuff ter know better 'n that. I 'low ther' 's lots on 'em as wishes their gizzards was as full o' sand as yourn. Ye've arned a furlough, 'f anybody ever did, 'n' I'm glad ye're goin' ter git one. It'll be kind o' lonesome 'thout ye, Si, 'n' I'll be watchin' fer ye to come back. I shan't take no other pard under my blanket. That's *your* place, 'n' I'll keep bachelor's hall t'll ye come."

Si and Shorty were really so delighted to see each other that for the moment they gave no heed to their surroundings. During their conversation they had walked a little way from the hospital; but what their eyes saw and their ears heard soon brought them to speak of what was around them.

"I'm 'fraid Company Q 'n' the rest o' the rijiment got cut up purty bad, didn't they?" asked Si. "Ye know," he continued, "we didn't have no time ter look back 'n' see who er how many o' the boys went down; 'n' ye know arter we'd got thar 'n' the rebs was runnin' every which way, the colonel jest made me come back ter the hospital. A good deal o' blood was runnin' out 'n' made my arm look wuss 'n it reely was. I'm ever so glad you didn't git hit, Shorty."

"Like enough it'll be me next time," replied his comrade. "I'd ruther keep a whole hide, but a feller can't expect to be that lucky when the bullets is flyin' so thick. The wonder is 't anybody gits through 'thout bein' 's full o' holes 's a sieve."

"It does seem that way when ye stop ter think 'bout it," said Si, "but how 'd the rijiment come out?"

"The boys is thinned out a good deal. The line ain't more 'n half 's long 's 'twas when we started fer the ridge. I 'xpect there 's a good many lyin' up thar on the hill, fer we hain't had no chance ter bury 'em yet. I s'pose 'f we don't have ter fight some more we'll do that in the mornin'. I don't know all of Company Q that 's killed, but it was a heart-breakin' roll-call 't we had tonight. Some o' the wounded 's here, ain't they?"

"Yes, plenty on 'em," said Si. "I know you ain't so chicken-hearted 's I am, but I can't keep the tears f'm comin' in my eyes when I see how the poor boys is sufferin'. Some on 'em 'll be glad ter see ye, Shorty."

They passed among the wounded men and spoke words of greeting to their comrades. Shorty had been cautioned that he must not be long absent and felt that he must return to his regiment. It might be called upon to move at any moment. Before leaving he asked the surgeon about his comrade's wound, telling him that the colonel was solicitous about him.

"Si is a noble boy," said the surgeon.

"Yes," replied Shorty, "he's my pard, 'n' they don't *make* no better soldiers 'n him."

"We all know that," said the doctor. "You may tell the colonel that Si has a bad arm and we're going to furlough him. He'll come back in a few weeks as good as ever. Do you know that ever since I dressed his wound and got his arm into a sling he has been working hard helping to take care of these poor fellows?"

"Jest like him!" said Shorty.

The latter rejoined his comrade and told him that he must say good-by.

"Now, Si," he said, "when ye start back ye mus'n't let 'em load ye down as they did t'other time. Tell 'em to keep all the good things t'll ye gits hum ter stay. I don't s'pose ther's anybody up thar 't cares a pinch o' snuff 'bout me, but 'f ye sh'd happen to hear 'em axin, ye c'n tell 'em I'm a stayer. Good-by!"

"Good-by, Shorty! Tell the boys that I'll give a good report of 'em, 'n' fer 'em ter keep my place fer me, 'cause 'twon't be long t'll I'll want it."

Shorty vanished in the darkness, and Si returned to his self-imposed work.

There was one of his boyhood companions, a member of Company Q, who lay desperately wounded. A bullet had entered his breast and passed entirely through his body. The surgeon had dressed his wound, but it was apparent that he had little expectation of being able to do more than afford temporary relief. When Si asked the doctor about his comrade, he shook his head and told him that there was but one chance in a hundred that he would live beyond a few hours.

"We'll do all we can for him, Si," said the surgeon, "but there isn't much hope. If you can cheer him up it will do him more good than medicine."

Si's heart went out in sympathy for his friend. He devoted himself assiduously to doing all in his power to relieve his suffering. He almost forgot that one of his own arms was lying helpless in a sling.

"Cheer up, Tom," he said, as he placed a canteen of fresh water to his lips. "Ther' ain't no use denyin' 't ye've got a bad hurt, 'n' if my bein' sorry fer ye 'd do any good ye wouldn't be long gittin' out o' this. Ye must keep yer spirits up; that'll do more fer ye 'n anything else. Men gits well sometimes after the doctors has give 'em up, jest 'cause they says they will. The doctor told me ye had a chance, 'n' I want ter see ye make the most on it. It was mighty hot up on that ridge, but didn't we go fer 'em? I tell ye ther' ain't nobody needs ter be 'shamed 'cause he b'longs ter the 200th Injianny. Here, Tom, take a sip o' this." And Si gave him a spoonful or two of brandy which the surgeon had left with him for that purpose.

"As I was sayin'," he went on, "ther' ain't none o' them rijiments any better 'n ourn, ef some on 'em *has* been goin' it longer 'n we have. Ye mind how them old soljers used ter poke all sorts o' fun at us when we fust come out? Mebbe ye've noticed lately 't they don't do it no more. I reck'n it's 'cause we've showed 'em 't we've got jest 's much grit 's they have. Ye behaved like a hero today, Tom, 'n' yer folks 'll be proud o' ye when they hears 'bout it. Now cheer up, 'n' ye'll beat the doctors yet, 'n' git home to tell 'em how bravely ye went up that hill."

Si rattled on without expecting any reply or giving his comrade any opportunity to talk if he had wanted to. Tom lay with closed eyes, breathing heavily. Now and then a half-suppressed groan escaped his lips. At length he spoke, in feeble tones. Si bent over him to catch his words.

"You're good to me, Si," he said. "I can't tell ye—how thankful I am to ye. It's the next thing to havin'—mother or—sister. Seems to me almost as if I—might have a show if *they* were here. I feel as though the touch—of their hands would ease this awful pain. It hurts more and more an'—I'm gittin' weaker all the time. I'm afeard, pard, I can't—hold out much longer."

"I don't like ter hear ye say that, Tom, 'cause I b'lieve ye're goin' ter pull through. Ye'll feel better tomorrow."

"Tomorrow—tomorrow," said Tom in a whisper, as if his thoughts sprang unbidden to his lips, "what—where will I be?"

"Tom," said Si, "ye mustn't talk that way. I hope God 'll let you git well fer the sake o' yer mother. It 'd break her heart ef ye shouldn't. But ye'd better let me do the talkin' fer both on us. You lie 's quiet 's ye kin 'n' mebbe that pain won't be quite so bad. I wish I c'd help ye b'ar it. You've got more 'n yer sheer."

At this moment one whose suffering had just ended was carried by to be laid in the fast lengthening line of the dead. Tom opened his eyes for an instant and caught a glimpse of the body and those who bore it away with solemn tread. His eyes closed again, and an involuntary shudder passed over him. Si, who was holding one of his comrade's hands in his, felt the tremor. He knew what had caused it.

"Si," said Tom, in a low voice of unutterable sadness, "you saw 'em—go by just now—didn't ye?"

Si did not reply.

"They'll carry me out—like that—an' it can't be—very long. Perhaps they'll have to—take me next!"

The surgeon stopped, while making his round, to see if aught could be done to stay the hand of death. He felt the feeble pulse, and laid his hand upon the clammy brow. Si looked at him inquiringly, but the doctor shook his head. There was no need of words. Si knew, as he had feared, that his friend would ere long be beyond the reach of pain.

"Tom," he said gently, with a soft pressure upon the hand that lay within his own.

The flickering firelight played upon the face of the dying soldier, who looked full upon the faithful watcher as he asked:

"Did—the doctor say—I was—any better?"

Si turned away his head, that his comrade might not see the tears that dimmed his eyes.

"He didn't say nothin', Tom!"

The wounded man summoned all his fast wasting strength to communicate to his companion the thoughts that had been running through his mind.

"I knew it—would be so," he said. "I've felt it comin' ever since they—brought me down from that hill where—we fought so hard. I hoped it mightn't be that way—not 'cause I ain't willin' to—give up my—my life as so many others do but—for the sake of them that 'll feel bad when they hear I'm—dead. I'd rather have lived to go back to 'em. But it's—all right. It may as well be me—as anybody else. Most of the boys has got—mothers an' sisters. You'll get—home in a few days an' I'm glad of it. I'm glad ye didn't—git hit no harder 'n ye did."

"It 'd make me happier 'n ye can think, Tom, ef you could only go 'long with me."

"It 'd have to be in a—coffin, an' they don't have any coffins here. Let me talk for a few minutes, Si—while I've got strength, for there's one or two things—I'd like to say before I go. You can tell 'em whether I done my duty or not—how I was lookin' right into the muzzles of the rebel guns when that—ball struck me. You was right there, too. An' be sure an' tell 'em that—we drove the rebels off that ridge an' captured the cannon. I b'lieve it 'll comfort 'em some to know—I wasn't a coward. Here's my watch; I'd like ye to take that home an'—give it to father. I haven't got anything good enough to send to—mother; but here's some money left from last time we was paid off. Give that to her an' tell her—to buy a ring or something she can always keep. You'll remember all I tell ye—won't ye, Si?"

"Of course—I will, Tom—every word," said Si, in broken tones, struggling with his emotions. "An' I'll tell 'em—"

"Wait a minute, Si; I ain't quite through yet. My time 's short. I can't get my breath—much longer. I want *you* to take this pocket-knife. It's all I've got to give ye. You deserve something better, but it 'll do to remember —yer old comrade by. And, Si, there's one thing more. This—locket I've always wore. Perhaps ye've got one yerself, an' if ye have ye know what a blessin' this has been to me. I don't need to tell ye who gave it to me—the day we left home. You'll know as soon as ye see the picture in it. I want you to give it back to—to her, Si, an' tell her, if ye think it's true, that she needn't be 'shamed of the boy 't carried it on the march and—into the battle. I see red stains on it. You needn't—rub 'em off. Mebbe she'd rather have it that way, 'cause—it shows 't I was up in front. Tell her I was thinkin' about her at—the last minute, while I was bein'—mustered out. An' when ye git well an' come back to the regiment, Si, I want ye to—tell the boys of Company Q good-by for me. Perhaps some of 'em 'll be a bit sorry 'cause—I had to leave 'em—this way. Tell the capt'n—"

The effort to talk had been too much. There was a spasm of pain, for the pang had reached at last the very source of life. The weary eyelids closed and there was a labored struggle for breath. Si pressed the nerveless hand of his comrade and felt the weakening pulse.

The surgeon passed that way and Si beckoned him. A glance told him that the end was very near.

"*Can't* you do some·thing for him, Doc-

DEATH OF POOR TOM.

tor?" said Si, in a low voice, choked with smothered sobs.

"I would do it most gladly if it were possible, but he is beyond human power."

Once more, for an instant, the eyes opened, glowing with a wild, strange light. In the last moments the mind wandered.

"Come on—boys—right up—the ridge—there's our flag —we'll get—the guns!"

At the instant of dissolution there was a flash of consciousness, and the quivering lips parted.

"Good-by—pard! Good-by—Doctor!"

Very still he lay, and a restful look fell upon the whitening face. The surgeon's fingers touched the pulseless wrist.

"Poor, brave Tom is discharged," he said, as he brushed a tear from his eye. "You cannot do anything more for him, Si."

By the light of the gleaming fires they bore away the body and placed it beside those lying cold and motionless under the sheltering trees. Si walked sadly after—a solitary mourner. He tenderly folded the hands across the quiet breast, drew the blanket over the face of his dead friend and pressed it gently around the inanimate form, as if to guard him from the chilling dews while he slept.

And still went up to heaven that agonizing chorus of moans and cries; still moved about, hither and thither, the ministers of relief, intent upon their work of mercy; still one and then another was carried to the place appointed for the dead. Over all the firelight shed its sympathetic glow; while above and beyond was the deep darkness of midnight, as if it would hide the awful scene of suffering and death.

CHAPTER XXXVII.

IT was long after midnight when Corporal Klegg, exhausted with the labor and excitement of the day and night, wrapped a blanket around him and lay down upon the ground, in the hope of getting needed rest. It was but little that he slept, however. He had felt and seen and heard enough to keep his thoughts occupied a lifetime. The scenes he had witnessed were yet vivid before his eyes, his mind was busy recounting the incidents of battle and hospital, with occasional pictures of home and friends, and his nerves were yet strung to so high a pitch that even his fatigue was not sufficient to quiet them. His wounded arm was becoming more and more painful, and he was just beginning to realize that he was badly hurt. His resting-place was under a tree a short distance from the hospital, whither he had gone that his ears might not be pained by the cries and moans of the suffering hundreds. He tossed about uneasily, dozing fitfully, and now and then starting up, affrighted by the distorted visions that disturbed his unquiet slumber.

He was glad when daylight came. The chirping of the birds in the trees seemed a mockery, as he thought of the pain and woe and death that were so near. He got up and went to see how his comrades were faring. Several more of them had died, while others were apparently doing as well as their wounds would permit. For each of these Si had a pleasant greeting and words of sympathy and encouragement.

Early in the day a long train of ambulances drew up at the field hospital, to convey to the rear such of the wounded as could be moved. They were to be distributed among the permanent hospitals, where they could receive better care than was possible in the field; and the army at the front would be relieved of the incumbrance. As fast as they were able to go large numbers of the wounded would be furloughed to their homes, where their recovery would be much more certain and rapid.

The vehicles were soon loaded and started upon their journey. Si said he would take it afoot and let some one ride who was less able to walk than he. After a farewell word to those of his comrades who remained behind, he trudged off in rear of the train, with a few hardtack in his pocket to eat by the way, and a canteen of water at his side. The distance to be traveled was but a few miles.

The surgeon of the 200th Indiana was one of those detailed to accompany the ambulances. As he rode slowly along he accosted Si:

"I'm glad to see you doing so nicely, Corporal. I have something to tell you that I think may please you. This morning I made application for immediate furloughs for half a dozen of the regiment, and yours was one of the names. The man I sent will take the application right through brigade, division and corps headquarters to the general commanding the army; and if the red tape doesn't get kinked anywhere I think you will get your furlough tonight. If it comes you can start home as soon as you have a mind to."

"I'm ever so much 'bleeged to ye, Doctor," said Si. "As I was tellin' ye last night, I'd a heap ruther stay by the rijiment 'f I c'd do any good, but it looks 's though I wouldn't be wuth nothin' ter handle a gun fer a while, 'n'

I s'pose I mout 's well git out o' the way. 'Tain't 'cause I
don't want ter go home, fer ther' never *was* anybody
gladder to go 'n I'll be. D'ye think I c'n make a raise o'
some clothes when we git ter town. These old duds looks
purty hard, 'n I don't like ter go home lookin' like a scarecrow. I flung away my knapsack, so 's I c'd git 'long
faster, when we was chargin' up that ridge yisterdy, 'n'

THE AMBULANCE TRAIN.

I hain't got a stitch o' nothin' 'ceptin' what I'm wearin'.
I'd like ter look sort o' scrumptious like."

"We'll fix it so that you can draw a new suit, Si, and
send you home in fine style. I'll just say to you that I
haven't the least doubt that you'll get the furlough. I
wrote that you were the man that planted the flag on the
works. The colonel of the 200th will give it a good send-

off, and I'll miss my guess if the general doesn't set the clerk to making out the papers in a hurry."

Si had been thinking that he ought to write a letter to his mother and one to Annabel. They would know of the battle and be anxious to hear from him. Now that there was a prospect of a furlough he thought it would be a nice thing to surprise them all. Should he be so fortunate as to start at once, he would be likely to reach home as soon as a letter. So he made up his mind not to send any word that he was coming.

Before the slowly moving train of ambulances reached its destination a galloping horseman overtook the party. It was an orderly bearing the furloughs that had been asked for.

"Here you are, Si," said the surgeon, handing him one of those documents that a soldier so often wished for but so rarely got. "You deserve to have a good time and I hope you will."

"Thankee, Doctor," said Si. He could not say more than that. For the first time he knew that he was going home. Up to this moment it had been only a dim unreality. He had so fully identified himself with the 200th Indiana, and so completely given himself up to the discharge of his whole duty as a soldier, that he had been perfectly sincere in the expression of his preference to remain with the regiment. It had been deemed best that he should go, and now a flood of tender thoughts rushed upon him. There were symptoms that his emotions would get the mastery for the moment, and he dropped back a little till he should recover his composure. As he came to a full realization of the privilege he was to enjoy, a happiness filled his heart that he had not felt for many a month.

When the town was reached and the wounded had been temporarily cared for, the surgeon made the necessary arrangements to enable Si to "draw" some clothing, and the latter was soon arrayed in an entire new outfit, from sole to crown.

"I don't suppose," said the doctor with a suggestive wink, "that you care to take your old clothes home, do you?'

"Not much!" said Si. "If mother sh'd examine 'em with her specs on she'd go crazy. I'll jest burn 'em up. That's all they 's fit fer."

Si learned, upon inquiry, that a train would leave that evening and he told the surgeon he believed he would start right off.

"You had better get a good sleep and go in the morning," said the doctor. "You need the rest and you'll have a hard time of it bumping around in those rough cars all night."

"I won't mind that a bit," replied Si, "'s long 's I'm goin' to'rd God's country. It 'll give me that much more time to hum. It's a chance a feller don't have very often, 'n' I'm goin' ter git all ther' is in it."

The surgeon admitted the force of this reasoning and made no further objection. Carefully dressing Si's wound, he gave him a liberal supply of such things as it was likely to need during the long journey. He told him that anybody would help him whenever he wanted to change the dressing of his arm. Then he replenished Si's haversack and bade him a warm good-by.

The train was composed of empty freight cars that had come down loaded with supplies for the army. The only passengers were the usual detail of guards and a few furloughed men and officers who, like Corporal Klegg, were impatient to be off. The severely wounded who had come in the ambulances would rest till the following day and then be loaded in cars of the same kind and sent northward.

Si and a dozen others, mostly wounded men, were assigned to a car, and by assisting one another they managed, after much effort, to clamber in. The car had been used, at no remote period, for the transportation of cattle, and little had been done in the way of disinfection. An over-fastidious person might have been disposed to grumble at such unsavory accommodations; but Si Klegg, with a furlough in his blouse pocket and his face turned homeward, was as happy while breathing the noxious odors of that cattle-car as if his nostrils were being tickled by the "spicy breezes" that

"Blow soft o'er Ceylon's isle."

Just before the train started, a man—whose bearing justified the belief that he already had a title, in fee simple, to a good part of the earth, and wanted the rest— jumped into the car and bustled around among the soldiers. With notebook and pencil in hand, he took down the name and regiment of each, and the nature of his wound.

"What's *your* name, young fellow?" he said, with a patronizing air.

"My name's Si Klegg, sir."

THE WAR CORRESPONDENT.

"What! Corporal Si Klegg, of the 200th Indiana?"

"Bet yer life I'm him."

"What! The man that so grandly bore aloft, amidst the awful carnage, the star-bespangled emblem of liberty and equal rights and planted it on the ramparts of treason, while the roar and smoke of battle filled the circumambient air?

"I'd like ter have ye say that over ag'in, Mister," said Si. "I can't understand yer hifalutin' talk. I'm Si Klegg, of the 200th Injianny, bein' as how ye wants ter know so bad."

"Excuse my big words. I haven't got fairly cooled off from the excitement of yesterday, and for the moment I thought I was writing dispatches. I'm glad to see you, Corporal. I've heard all about you, but they told me you were dead." Then he said in an undertone as if thinking aloud: "By Jove! I'll scoop the boys on this. It'll make a splendid item!"

"Make a what, did ye say?" asked Si, wondering what it all meant.

But he was gone. Si did not know that he was a newspaper man.

The journey was tedious, like all southern railroading in war times, but Si was happy in knowing that every revolution of the clattering wheels brought him nearer to "Injianny" which to him was but another name for Paradise. Everywhere he found kind and ready hands to bind up his wound and minister to his wants.

Si was amazed to find that through the instrumentality of the telegraph and the newspapers his fame was already being spread abroad. He was wholly unconscious of having done anything that was especially meritorious, but his gallant conduct at the storming of the ridge, in bearing the colors of the 200th Indiana to the crest, had been highly commended by the officers, and had reached the ears of the reliable war correspondents of the excellent family journals. His deeds were described in the telegraphic dispatches, so that at the very time he was tramping along behind the ambulances, with his arm in a sling, thousands of people at the north were reading about what he did, besides a good deal that he didn't do; for the average war correspondent was gifted with a fervid imagination that never failed to supply all the details when authentic information was meager. It was rumored that Corporal Klegg had been wounded, but in the chaos at the front no one could tell how severely, or whether he was even alive or not. So the newspaper men reported him in all the various stages of mutilation and dismemberment. Some of them added to the pathos of their narratives by setting forth that he was killed just after he had planted the flag on the summit.

At the first city that was reached, after the all-night ride, the newsboys swarmed around the train crying:

"'Ere's yer mornin' papers! Latest news from the big battle! All 'bout Corp'ral Si Klegg!"

"Wha-a-a-t!" exclaimed Si, unconsciously, as he heard the clamor of the oft-repeated cry. He rubbed his eyes to be certain that he was awake, and pulled his ears to assure himself that they were still there and performing their legitimate functions. Then turning to one of his fellow-passengers he said:

"Who d'ye s'pose all this 'ere fuss 's 'bout? I hain't never heerd o' no other Corporil Si Klegg 'ceptin' me, but I hain't done nothin' ter have the papers blowin' me up! I reck'n it's some other feller, but I hope he hain't done nothin' ter make me 'shamed o' the name! I'm goin' ter find out. Here, you young rascal, gimme a paper!" and Si handed the boy a 10-cent scrip in payment.

"I guess you'll find they've got you into the papers, sure enough!" said the comrade to whom Si had addressed his somewhat explosive remarks.

All the chance occupants of the car were entire strangers to Si when he boarded the train the night before. No two of them belonged to the same regiment. But there was not one whose acquaintance he had not made before midnight.

Si found in the paper a long account of the battle and a

liberal paragraph devoted to "Corporal Si Klegg, of the 200th Indiana."

"Wall, I swow," he exclaimed, looking up from the paper, "'f that don't beat the Jews. I'll make an affidavy that ther' ain't no other Si Klegg in the 200th Injianny." And then he thought: "What 'd mother, 'n' sister Marier, 'n' Annabel say 'f they sh'd see that!"

The closing lines of the paragraph were as follows:

Our readers will be pleased to learn that the report that Corporal Josiah Klegg of the 200th Indiana was killed, published in our issue of yesterday, proves to have been a mistake. The gallant young soldier was severely wounded, but when seen last night by our able and discriminating correspondent he was as frisky as a spring lamb. Our special telegraphic dispatches convey the gratifying intelligence that Corporal Klegg was yesterday granted a furlough by the general commanding the army, and left last night by rail for his home in Indiana. He will arrive in our city this morning. All our readers will join us in the hope that he may "live long and prosper."

It was not often that Si was unable to find some kind of language to express his feelings when unexpected things happened, but this was one of those exigencies when his usual volubility of tongue failed him. He stared blankly around, without uttering a word, to the great enjoyment of his companions. He finally managed to say that he was completely "kerflummuxed." It is no doubt true that the dictionary, from A to Z, could not afford a word more suitable than this to express his mental condition at that moment.

Then he gave a sudden start as a thought flashed through his mind. What if the papers in the north should publish the report that he was killed, and *they* should see it!

As soon as it became known that a train with wounded had arrived from the front, there came a delegation of men and women from the Sanitary Commission, bringing gallons of hot coffee and baskets of sandwiches and boiled eggs and all manner of delicacies. Some of the ladies began at once to inquire for Corporal Klegg, whose name had appeared so conspicuously in the head-lines of the morning papers.

"Here he is," exclaimed Si's traveling companions. In vain he protested and shrank into a dark corner of the car as half a dozen ladies demanded that he come forth. His comrades at length surrounded him and forced him to the door, where he was greeted with boisterous enthusiasm.

"Just look at him; he's only a boy!"

"I'd like to be his mother! Wouldn't I be proud of him?"

SI FINDS HIMSELF FAMOUS.

"I do hope his folks didn't hear that awful story that he was dead!"

Si thought it was about as bad as being under the fire of the rebels. He blushed to the roots of his hair when a matronly dame manifested a desire to "kiss him for his mother." It had been a long time since any female, old or young, had kissed him, either "for his mother" or on her own account. Pleasant as would be the touch of the soft lips of woman, he gently but firmly declined the vicarious salute. He said he hoped to be at home in a day or two, and he had reason to believe his mother would be glad to do it for herself.

It was indeed a feast that Si and his comrades enjoyed. The daintiest morsels were spread before them with a profusion that was bewildering to soldiers who had been at the front for a year, living on army rations. Not less startling to the ladies must have been the almost unlimited stowage capacity which the men exhibited.

The visitors brought with them various appliances for the relief of injured limbs. There were crutches for the lame, and ingenious devices to support wounded arms. One of the latter was given to Si, and a most comfortable and convenient thing it was—a sort of trough in which to lay the arm, suspended by straps that went around the neck. These contrivances were freely bestowed upon all to the nature of whose wounds they were suited.

The all-pervading newspaper reporter was there, armed with pencil and note-book, to "interview" Si and "write him up." Si was well-nigh dazed at finding himself the object of so much attention. He could not understand why so great a "fuss," as he called it, was made over him. At first he did not take kindly to the newspaper man. The latter, however, by that persistence so characteristic of the profession, at last succeeded in getting Si's tongue unloosed, and he rattled off, in his quaint, ingenuous way, the story of how the flag of the 200th Indiana came to be the first that floated amidst the flame and smoke on the crest of the ridge. He told it in simple words, without the least attempt at self-glorification. He was proud of his regiment and of himself, not as an individual, but as one of its members. So far as he was concerned he had done nothing more than what he enlisted to do, and what might be expected of him. He did not even ask the reporter to send him a marked copy of the paper.

CHAPTER XXXVIII.

FARMER KLEGG was husking corn when a neighbor, who also had a son in Company Q, came galloping down the road leading from the village. Tying his horse to the fence he climbed over, approached with rapid steps, and accosted him. The earnest tones with which he spoke betokened the gravity of the message he brought.

"Neighbor Klegg," he said, "I had to go to town this mornin' to git the old mare shod, an' I heerd they had another great battle yesterday. I tried to find out suthin definite for I couldn't help feelin' anxious 'bout my Tom. All anybody knew was that our men druv the rebils, capturin' a hull lot o' their cannons an' I don't know how many thousan' pris'ners. What consarns you an' me most is that the 200th Indiana was in the thickest on 't and was cut up terrible. I couldn't git no names yet tellin' who 's killed an' who ain't, but I thought you an' some o' the rest o' the people hereabout would like to know there had been a fight that our boys was in, an' so I jumped on the hoss an' come on a dead run."

The first glance into the face of his friend had told Farmer Klegg the serious character of the hasty visit. Dropping a half-husked ear he stood listening intently to the startling words.

"I must go an' tell mother!" he said gently, and his lips quivered as he spoke. "Then I'll go to town an' see if I can hear any of the particklers. They said the 200th was badly cut up, did they?" he continued, as they walked toward the road.

"That's what they told me," replied his companion.

"If that's true a good many of Company Q must ha' got hurt, 'cause I don't believe any on 'em was furder in front than our boys. Ye know, neighbor, it's most always the brave ones that gets hit. 'Tain't them as is skulkin' back in the rear. If a man is killed or wounded, it stands to reason that he was somewheres 'round where he ought to be. It 'd be purty hard to see my boy's name in one o' the long lists the newspapers print after every big battle, but even that wouldn't be so hard as to have it said that Si wa'n't no good. If I only know that he done his duty like a brave soldier I'll try and—"

The patriotic old man left the sentence unfin-

NEWS FOR FARMER KLEGG.

ished. Something came into his throat that choked his utterance. He drew his rough sleeve across his brown face.

"I agree with ye, Mr. Klegg," said the other. "That's jest the way I feel about Tom. I'd rather know he was dead than to hear he'd showed the white feather. But from all accounts we've had I don't think either on 'em is a boy to be 'shamed of."

At the road they shook hands and parted, with dimmed eyes, and voices tremulous with anxiety and foreboding for the absent ones. One turned his steps toward the house and the other remounted his horse and rode away.

Farmer Klegg's wife had seen the neighbor ride past at furious pace. She had watched him as he alighted from his horse and joined her husband in the field. She knew, with the keen instinct of a mother, that something unusual had transpired, and that it concerned her boy. She stood in the open door and did not take her eyes from them during the brief interview. The instant they separated she drew her apron over her head and walked rapidly with beating heart to meet her husband. His head was bowed and he was not conscious of her approach until she was near him.

"Father," she said—and words and tears came together —"is it bad news? Si is not—dead?"

He opened his strong arms and clasped them about his wife as she fell, weeping, upon his breast.

"There—there—mother! Don't!" he said, with the utmost tenderness, and with a mighty effort to control his own emotions, as he laid his hand softly upon her forehead and moistened cheek. "'There's sad news for a good many people; I pray the good Father above that it may not prove so to us, dear. The army that our boy is in has had another battle and the report is that the 200th Indiana was in the thickest of it and was badly cut up."

"And—tell me quick," she sobbed—and her breath came fast as she looked into his face with her tearful eyes— "what did—he say—about our Si?"

"Not a word, mother. I tell you truly." He cast upon her a look that is only born of the affection of half a lifetime. "I have heard nothing beyond what I have told you. We may hope that all is well with *him*, and now we will be thankful for that privilege. Cheer up, wife; it'll all come out right."

The fact that nothing was known as to how Si had fared in the battle brought to the mother a sense of relief.

"I will drive to town," said Mr. Klegg, "and see if I can hear anything more. Be brave and patient till I come back."

"I will go with you," she answered, quietly, "I could not endure it to wait for you. And let us go at once."

"Perhaps it may not turn out to be so bad," he said, as they walked to the house. "The first reports are always the worst."

"You know," said his wife, "there isn't hardly a minute, day nor night, when I ain't thinkin' or dreamin' of Si. I've never thought it possible that anything could happen to him. These are times when people have to make sacrifices, but it seems as if for us to give up our only son, and he so good a boy as Si, is too much for the country to ask of us."

"Now, mother, get your things on," he said, as they reached the house. "I'll have the buggy ready in a few minutes."

Little was said during the drive to the village. The hearts of both were throbbing with anxiety for tidings from the absent one.

The village was thronged with people on like errands. The news of the battle had spread, as if borne upon the wings of the morning, through the region round about, and the friends of Company Q gathered from all directions. The men at the front knew little of the unutterable longings, the prayers, the fears, the yearning hopes of those at home who loved them.

Farmer Klegg thought it best to leave his wife at the house of a friend, while he hastened to the postoffice and railway station in quest of news.

"Hurry," she said, "and come back to me as soon as you can, for you *know* how much I want to hear from Si."

"You had no need to tell me that," he replied, with an

affectionate look into her face. "As soon as I can learn anything I will come to you."

A short time before he arrived the morning papers from a neighboring city had reached the village. They were seized with the utmost avidity, and the long columns that told of the great victory were read with an intensity of interest that no language can portray. It was too soon for the heart-breaking lists of the dead and the mangled. For these the agony of suspense—scarcely less hard to bear than the pang of finding the name of a loved one among those of the heroic slain—must continue another day, perhaps many days. Now the moans of the wounded and the sound of pick and shovel in the burial trenches are drowned in the shouts of triumph. When the echoes of the wild huzzas have died away, then will come to aching hearts that cannot be comforted, a realization of how great a price was paid for the victory.

Though the first hastily prepared report of the battle is barren of the details so eagerly sought, there is yet enough to absorb the thoughts and stir to their profoundest depths the hearts of these people. Such gallantry as that displayed by the 200th Indiana could not pass unnoticed, even in the furious hurly-burly of the fight. As they read how it led the charge up to the very mouths of the belching guns, and how its ranks were thinned as it grandly breasted the fierce and deadly blast from musket and cannon, they know that Company Q was there and many of its brave men must have fallen. Instinctively they look into one another's faces as if to ask, Is it *my* son? *my* father? *my* brother? *my* husband? Oh that one might be found who can answer, and put an end to these awful forebodings! It were better to know the worst.

Then a wave of patriotic rejoicing sweeps over that gathering, and before it even the fear and dread and love give way for the moment. Men and women, old and young, with tearful eyes, swing their hats, wave their kerchiefs, and unite their tremulous voices in a shout for those who so nobly obeyed the call of duty. They are proud of their sons and brothers, even though their mangled bodies lie stark and stiffened on the field their valor helped to win.

But there was one thing in the newspaper report that pierced like an arrow the hearts of that company. Their pulses quickened as they read how Corporal Klegg of Company Q had borne the flag of the 200th Indiana up the rugged hill and planted it upon the flaming crest, and then—that he was killed. For more than two years they had been reading of battles with their awful scenes of slaughter. They were becoming familiar with death, but this brought it near to them. Strong men shuddered and women wept as they heard the sorrowful tidings. On every hand were heard the most sincere expressions of grief for "Poor Si."

Farmer Klegg, in his eager quest for news, walked rapidly toward the railway station.

"There comes Si's father!" said one. "Poor man, what a blow it will be to him!"

"True enough," said another, "and tomorrow the blow may fall on you and me."

A moment later Mr. Klegg, flushed with anxiety, joined the throng. He saw at a glance the unwonted excitement, the sad, earnest faces, the crumpled newspapers; he heard the hum of many voices, talking in hushed tones. He knew that information of some kind had been received. He needed not to ask what it was about. There was but one subject, and that filled all minds and hearts. As he glanced quickly into the faces of his friends and neighbors he saw looks of pity, and seemed as if by intuition to divine their meaning.

"What news from—the battle?" he asked, hesitatingly, and yet with breathless longing.

"It was a splendid victory. The 200th Indiana covered itself with glory. We can all be proud of Company Q."

"Yes," he answered, nervously, "I wasn't afraid of their flinchin', but did you hear anything about my—about any of the boys?"

A sad silence fell like a pall over the crowd. Hearts that were racked with alternate hopes and fears for their own dear ones, ached for him, yet none could break to him the tidings.

"The paper says Si was—badly hurt!" said one, timidly.

"Let me see it! Give me the paper!" he exclaimed, as with trembling hands he drew his glasses from his pocket and put them on.

A paper was handed him. He looked for an instant at the startling head lines, and then his eye wandered up and down the long columns. Tears stole down the cheeks of those around as they watched him.

"Will some one show me where it tells about my boy?" he asked, struggling to suppress his emotions.

A finger was laid upon the paragraph. With what passionate eagerness he scanned it. When he reached the fateful words that told him his brave boy was among the slain the paper dropped from his tremulous grasp, the color left his face, and with his hand pressed to his forehead and his eyes closed, he stood for a moment like a statue, the embodiment of paternal grief. In such a presence the people stood in silent compassion.

"Dead? Si dead?" he said at length, in a choking voice, as if thinking aloud, and unconscious of his surroundings. "God help your poor mother! How can I tell her! And yet I must go to her at once!"

Then there came to him thoughts of the heroic manliness of his son, and in the noble spirit of patriotic sacrifice he said in tender tones:

"But Si did his duty bravely and died like a true soldier! Better dead—a hero, than living—a coward! Si was a good and dutiful boy. It is very hard to think of him—so! Oh, if I could only believe it is not true! I would gladly give my own life if it could bring Si back to his mother." Then he added, as if ashamed of his weakness, even under such a crushing burden of sorrow: "May God give me strength to show myself worthy of such a son. Ten thousand fathers, whose sons were as dear to them as was mine to me, have been called to lay them upon the altar; why should not I?"

An involuntary cheer went up in honor of the old farmer's brave spirit. The people crowded around him with streaming eyes and in turn grasped his hand and spoke words of sympathy. He heard them, but the kindly utterances seemed almost meaningless.

"Neighbors and friends," he said, "I thank you all. This nation is going to be saved, and if it's necessary I'm ready to shoulder a gun and take Si's place. I haven't felt the war before. My share of the burden has been laid on me at last, and I'm willing to bear it. The war is going to end right as sure as there's a God in heaven, and when it's over the country will be all the dearer to us for the sacrifices we have made to save it."

The first great shock was over. It was well for Farmer Klegg that he had recovered himself before facing the ordeal of communicating the intelligence to his wife.

"Si's mother is waiting for me," he said. "May the good Lord give her the same strength that he has given me."

His steps were unconsciously slow as he walked back to the house where he had left her half an hour before, and where he knew she was awaiting his coming with all the yearning solicitude that a mother's heart can know. He prayed for help, feeling his need of every assistance, human and divine, to meet the sorest trial of his life.

Every moment since he left her she had been sitting with her face at the window-pane, gazing wistfully down the street whence he had gone. Minutes seemed hours as she watched for his return. When he came in sight her heart gave a great bound. Springing to her feet she flew to meet him at the gate.

As he approached, with his eyes fixed upon the ground, a subtle instinct told him she was there. He felt her presence; and her appealing look, though he saw it not, thrilled his inmost soul, but he could not lift his eyes to hers.

"Husband?"

He looked up. She read it in his face as plainly as if the printed words had been stamped upon his moist cheek and quivering lip. With a quick gasp and a convulsive cry she flung herself upon his breast. She would have fallen but for his enfolding embrace.

"I will help you to bear it, mother," he said tenderly. "Let us go into the house."

Lifting the fainting woman in his strong arms he bore her across the threshold. Laying her upon a sofa he kissed her white lips and took her hand between his own. Large hands were his, browned and calloused by two score years of toil, but to her there was no touch on earth so soft as their tender, loving pressure. Kind-hearted friends gathered around and proffered their services, but he waved them aside.

"Leave her to me—and God," he said.

He softly smoothed her hair with his hand, and spoke to her in endearing words. A flood of tears came, and brought relief to the overburdened heart.

"Mother," he said, when calmness came, after the paroxysm had subsided, "Si carried the flag of the regiment up the ridge ahead of all the others, right into the blaze of the rebel guns. I read it in the paper. It was just after he got to the top and victory was close by that he was—that he fell. There never was a braver, nobler boy, nor one who did his duty better. It will be a great comfort to us. mother, to think of this, and to remember what a good son he has always been to us. It isn't everybody that *has* such boys to give when the country needs them."

Strength of body and mind came slowly but surely back to the stricken mother, and with it came that matchless spirit of devotion that nerved the women of the whole country, north and south, during those four years of fire and blood.

"My dear husband," she said quietly, "it is God's will, and I submit. But I cannot talk of it now. We will go home if you are ready."

Almost in silence, with brave though bursting hearts, they rode to the home that would be so desolate now. The light of *his* presence would never dispel the darkness.

During the few hours of their absence the daughter had done little but strain her eyes along the road by which they would return. Nor was she alone. Is it any wonder that Annabel, learning that the farmer and his wife had gone to the village, should put on her bonnet and go over to see if Maria had any news from *him ;* and then to wait and watch with her?

There were two more bleeding hearts when Farmer Klegg and his wife came. There were bitter tears and convulsive sobs as the dreadful words, like keenly-barbed shafts, did their cruel work.

The next morning Mr. Klegg drove again to the village. All his farm work was forgotten except such periodical duties as necessity required. He was waiting at the railway station long before the train was due that would bring the daily papers with later accounts of the battle. Others, too, were there, by scores, anxious for tidings from "the front." On all sides were heard words of sympathy for Farmer Klegg, in the great sorrow that had befallen him.

When the train dashed up a hundred eager hands were outstretched for the newspapers. In a moment Mr. Klegg had secured one, and withdrawing a little way from the crush he opened it. Instantly his eye caught, among the flaming head-lines:

"BRAVE CORPORAL KLEGG NOT KILLED."

Si's preëminent gallantry, coupled with the fact that the 200th Indiana was from that part of the state, had made him a conspicuous object of interest.

Farmer Klegg's heart seemed almost to burst from his body as he read it again, to assure himself that he was not mistaken. The sudden revulsion of feeling, the overwhelming joy, swept entirely away for the moment the staid dignity of his usual mien. Swinging his hat in one hand and his newspaper in the other he leaped into the air with a great shout. Then he looked again at the blessed words,

"MY BOY IS NOT DEAD!"

and as the happy tears trickled down his cheeks he reverently turned his eyes upward and, with an intensity of pathos, breathed the words:

"Father in Heaven, I thank Thee!"

Under other circumstances those who stood by would have thought him bereft of reason; but other quick eyes had read the tidings, and none wondered at the overflow of his feelings.

He gave no heed to those who gathered about him. He waited not to read the dispatches. His only thought was of mother and sister, who were sitting in the shadow of death, while grief was gnawing at their heart-strings. Dashing through the crowd he went upon a run, nor stopped until he reached his buggy.

"What is it, Neighbor Klegg?" asked a friend whom he passed in the street.

"*My boy is not dead!*" he answered without pausing in his flight.

The strap by which the horse was tied had perversely drawn itself into a hard knot. Without waiting to untie it he quickly drew out his knife, cut the strap, leaped into the seat, seized the reins, and began to apply the whip to the horse's back and sides.

"Now, git up, Doll!" he shouted. "Travel for your life! Ye never carried such news before. G'lang, there, why don't ye!"

The mare was at a gallop, but it seemed to him a snail's pace, in his impetuous haste. Again and again the lash descended upon the astonished beast. Goaded to desperation, the faithful animal seemed at length to realize that it was an extraordinary emergency and fairly flew along the road. The fast-clattering hoofs startled the people in their houses, and they looked with wondering eyes upon a thing so strange for Farmer Klegg. Other vehicles, as he approached at furious pace, drew off the road as if to escape from a runaway. But he leaned forward and unconsciously plied his whip, urging his steed to still greater efforts. Men who recognized him tried to speak to him as he went whirling by.

"Don't stop me!" he exclaimed. "My boy is alive!"

The farmer's wife and daughter had mechanically performed such simple household duties as could not be left undone. Then, with pale faces and tearful eyes, they watched for his return.

"There he comes, mother; and see how he drives! Oh, can it be possible that—"

Both run out to the gate. Maria does not finish the sentence she began; she dares not suggest a hope only to see it dashed to pieces, and themselves plunged into even a lower depth of grief.

Rapidly he draws near. His hat has fallen off and his thin, gray hair is streaming in disorder about his head.

"Mother!" he shouts, as he draws rein upon the panting horse, "our boy is not dead! He —is—not—dead!" And the tears start afresh as he exclaims, "Praise God from whom all blessings flow!"

He springs from the buggy and in an instant father, mother, daughter, are clasped in one another's arms, mingling their glad tears for him that "was dead and is alive again."

FARMER KLEGG'S DRIVE.

"Come into the house, dears," said Farmer Klegg. "I've got a newspaper that tells about it. I didn't stop to read it. I saw it in big letters that Si wasn't killed and that was enough for me to know till I could come home and tell you. If I've killed old Doll, she couldn't die in a better cause."

He tried to read, but his misty eyes refused to perform their office.

"Read it, daughter!" he said, handing her the paper,

"there's something wrong with my specs, and I can't see through 'em!"

And while their hearts throbbed, and the light of their smiles seemed to make rainbows in their tears, Maria read how Si had been wounded as he bore the flag into the flame and smoke of the enemy's guns. How badly he was hurt the report did not say, and there were tender longings to know all; but their son and brother was not dead, and this knowledge came to them like a sweet benediction from heaven.

"God will not let him die!" said the farmer's wife.

"Amen!" exclaimed Farmer Klegg.

A few minutes later Maria put on her bonnet, slipped noiselessly out of the house and went with hurrying feet to tell Annabel the glad news. They wept together in the fullness of their joy.

CHAPTER XXXIX.

CORPORAL KLEGG REACHES HOME AND THERE IS HAPPINESS ALL AROUND.

"HELLO, Si!"

This cordial and hearty greeting fell upon Corporal Klegg's ears as he alighted from the train two days later. His face was recognized by a dozen in the crowd, the instant it emerged from the door of the car, and a chorus of voices uttering these words of welcome was the introductory overture to the tumultuous reception that awaited him. It was purely spontaneous, for not even Farmer Klegg had any intimation of his coming.

The daily throng of people in quest of news from the battle was unabated. Many of them were the same persons, who had come day after day in the hope of hearing from those who were near and dear. Business and all the ordinary concerns of life were almost forgotten in the one engrossing theme of thought and conversation.

As Si descended the steps of the car, with one arm in a sling, he glanced hastily around upon the eager faces, with a glad smile and a cheery "Hello!"

"Three cheers for Si Klegg!" shouted an enthusiastic admirer of the gallant young soldier, and they were given with royal good will.

He was instantly surrounded by scores of people, jostling and crowding one another in their desire to take him by the hand and ply him with questions.

"I'll have ter ax ye ter be a leetle keerful," he said, as they thronged about him, "fer that arm's consid'ably dam-idged 'n' it's sorer 'n' any bile ye ever seed."

This word of caution had the desired effect,

"HELLO, SI!"

and care was taken that he should have plenty of "sea room" on that side.

Si was furiously bombarded with words of commendation and inquiries from everyone. The whole community was proud of him. The people said that if they had known he was coming they would have turned out the brass band that he might be received in a fitting manner. A dozen at the same time were asking eager questions concerning other members of Company Q, for as yet but few details of the casualties had reached the village. It would have kept his tongue busy for hours to answer all the questions that were put to him in five minutes.

For a time it was impossible for Si to make his way through the crowd; but he looked wistfully about, if perchance he might see the face of his father or mother or sister Maria. He even thought it barely possible that Annabel might happen to be there. *One* of his arms was still in serviceable condition, and he was sure it would be able to do extra duty, to make up for the other, that must be but an idle witness of the proceedings. His heart and head were so full of these things, and of home and the dear ones there, that he heard little of the confused babble of the crowd around him.

An old man came up in breathless haste and began to push his way through the throng.

"Let me see Si!" he exclaimed, while tears of joy trickled down his cheeks. All recognized his right, and the crowd gave way on either side that he might pass.

"Oh, my boy!"

"Father!"

Farmer Klegg clasped his arms about the neck of his son and long held him in a joyful embrace. The eyes of the bystanders moistened in glad sympathy. Many who looked upon the happy meeting longed, with an unspeakable yearning, to fold *their* sons and brothers to their hearts.

"Let us go home," said Mr. Klegg, leading the way. "There's a couple o' women there as 'd e'ena'most go crazy 'f they knowed ye'd come. I've got the old mar' here an' it won't take long to drive out. She's got used to goin' back and forrard 'tween here an' the farm, these last few days. I reck'n I don't need to tell ye why I've been comin' to town every mornin', as fast as Doll's feet could fly!"

"I don't know, 'nless ye was bringin' yer farm truck to

market," replied Si, as they walked rapidly away, "but I can't see what ye druv so fast fer; ye allus told me to be easy with the hosses. Was ye hurryin' 'cause ye was afeared prices 'd drap?"

"My dear boy, can't you think how we felt when we got news of the battle, and knew Company Q was in it. An' it was a good deal worse 'n that, Si, for we heard you was killed. I read it myself in the newspaper. I ain't goin' to tell ye what a cruel blow it was to yer mother an' sister. Ye can git some kind of an idee if ye'll observe how glad they are to see ye. It was like a camp-meetin' at our house the next day when I got back from town with the news that ye wasn't dead. An' every day since I hain't done much else besides tryin' to find out how bad ye was hurt an' where ye was. I told mother this mornin' that I'd 'bout made up my mind to take the keers an' go down there an' see 'f I couldn't hunt ye up an' bring ye home. An' here ye are, bless yer heart, lookin' jest like ye always did, 'cept that ye're a little tanned an' weather-beaten, which ain't noways strange considerin' the way ye've been livin'. An' how's yer poor arm? an' won't ye be glad to have mother dress it for ye? I read in the paper how ye behaved yerself in the fight; an' mother an' me was proud that you was our boy, even when we thought ye was dead."

From the overflowing heart of the farmer came a rush of happy thoughts, which almost insensibly bubbled forth in words. He talked, scarcely conscious of what he was saying, only knowing that he was once more speaking, face to face, with his boy.

"I didn't think ye was worryin' so 'bout me," said Si. "I might ha' telegrafted ye a couple o' days ago 't I was all right 'n' was comin' home, but I thought it'd be kind o' nice to s'prise ye like. The fust noosepaper I seen arter I started, had a long lingo 'bout Si Klegg, 'n' I thought it must be there was some other feller 'd got my name, but everybody said it was me. I couldn't see what they wanted to put sich a piece in the paper fer. Ef I'd had my way I wouldn't ha' come home fer *this*, but the doctor told me I *had* ter. Ye mus'n't think 'twas cause I didn't keer ter see ye, but I didn't want ter go back on the old rijiment. I didn't know *'twould* feel so good ter git hum. Can't we git over the ground a leetle faster?"

They were now well on their way. Si looked at once familiar objects with as much interest as if his absence had been ten times as long. Indeed, he had lived so much since he went to the war, that it seemed like half a score of years instead of one. So completely had the new life absorbed his very being that memory gave him only faint glimpses of his boyhood days, though they were but such a little while ago. Now the old scenes were before him, and for the time he was not a soldier, but again the simple-hearted farmer's boy.

At home wife and daughter were watching for Farmer Klegg's return, as they had done every day since the news of the battle.

"Father is coming!" said Maria, whose keen eye recognized him while he was yet a great way off. "There's somebody riding with him, dressed in soldier clothes. *Oh, mother, it's Si!*"

With beating hearts and quickening pulses they flew to the door and out through the gate. With rapid steps they hurried down the road to meet them. They clapped their hands and waved they kerchiefs, while Si swung his hat and shouted, and Farmer Klegg stung the mare's foaming flanks with his whip.

A moment later Si clambered out of the buggy, as fast as his wounded arm would permit, and was received into the welcoming embrace of mother and sister.

"My dear, brave boy!" said his mother, folding him to her bosom, and smiling through her tears. "My life has never known a greater happiness than this. I believe I know something of how that poor widow felt when Christ raised her son from the dead. Did you know he was coming, father? Why didn't you tell me?"

"Mother," replied Mr. Klegg, "do you suppose I would have kept back such a joy from you if I had known it? I was just as much surprised as you was. I hadn't the faintest idee he was comin' till they told me in town, as I was hurryin' to the depot, that Si had jest got off the train. An' didn't I make the crowd get out of the way an' let me through till I had him in these arms?"

HOME!

"It was this way, mother," said Si, "I didn't know myself 't I was comin' t'll jest 'fore I started. While the doctor was tyin' my arm up in a rag he told me he'd get a furlough fer me, 'n' I'd got ter come home 'n' repair damidges. If I'd thought ye was all a-frettin' 'bout me I mout ha' sent ye a what-d'ye-call-it — I mean a tellygram, but I was stupid 'nuff not to think on it. I 'lowed mebbe ye'd be gladder ter see me 'f I sort o' bounced in on ye 'thout lettin' ye know nothin' 'bout it. I don't wonder at yer worryin' since father told me ye heerd I was killed. I seen suthin 'bout it in the paper, myself, but I didn't think it had ter be true jest 'cause the noosepaper said so. I didn't b'lieve it, 'n' I didn't s'pose you would ef ye sh'd happen ter see it. But it's all right anyway, mother. I'm here, 's sound 's a hardtack, 'ceptin' where the Johnny rebs chipped off a piece, 'n' that won't be long gittin' well now 't I've got you 'n' Marier to do the nussin'. But say, mother, have ye got any pie?"

"Why, bless ye, Si, of course I have, an' if i'd known you was comin' I'd 'a' had a dozen ready baked for ye. I'd ought to thought o' yer bein' hungry, but I couldn't think o' nothin' only that you was here."

They had already reached the house and there were not four happier hearts in the world than theirs, as they crossed the threshold. Si's mother inquired with tender solicitude if his arm did not need attention.

"We've been makin' bandages and scrapin' lint to send down to the hospitals," she said, "and I've got plenty of 'em. Who'd ha' thought I was gettin' 'em ready to use on my own boy!"

Si thanked his mother, but assured her that his stomach was just then in much greater need of her kindly ministrations than was his arm. Remembering the perennial vigor of his appetite, she bestirred herself with a zeal befitting the occasion.

"Look around a bit, Si," she said, "an' see if things is nat'ral. I'll have a good snack ready for ye right quick."

Si wandered about the house and farmyard in a transport of delight, as everywhere his eye met objects that had been familiar to him from his earliest remembrance. Every article in the house looked just as it used to, only tenfold more charming, and the well polished furniture seemed to shine with a smile of welcome. Out by the barn Old Spot and Muley rolled their big eyes and lowed as if in recognition; the speckled hen and the lordly rooster cocked their heads and winked as much as to say "How are ye, Si;" the sheep came galloping up at his call; and even the swine lifted their snouts and grunted a greeting that was evidently sincere, whatever it may have lacked in melody.

Si was half inclined to draw the line at the pigs. After

his diet of the past year he felt that he never wanted to see another pig as long as he lived.

"Great Cæsar!" he exclaimed, as he peered over into the sty, "I wonder how many more bar'ls o' pork 'n' flitches o' bacon I've got ter swaller 'fore this 'ere rebellion 's squelched! But it *does* taste good 'long 'th the hardtack when a feller's reel hungry. I don't see how they c'd run a war 'thout hogs any more 'n 'thout soljers."

"Come, Si!"

His soliloquy was abruptly ended by his mother calling him to the meal that had been prepared. How sweetly her voice sounded in his ears; and with what alacrity did he obey the welcome summons. The combined efforts of mother and sister had produced a royal feast. Exhaustive drafts had been made upon the family larder, and the table was spread with everything that appetite could wish.

SI'S BARNYARD WELCOME.

"I'm sorry I hain't got nothin' better for ye, Si, "remarked his mother, in an apologetic way—as the skillful housewife always does when she is conscious that her culinary efforts have been more than usually successful.

"'*Tis* too bad, mother, I feel sorry 'bout it, myself," said Si, as he began the attack upon a quarter section of pie. "But reely," he continued, "ye don't mean it, fer this is jest boss. Ye'd think same 's I do 'f ye'd been tryin' ter live on the kind o' grub we have down in Comp'ny Q. Ye wouldn't have a tooth left in yer jaws. I tell ye what 'tis, mother, that feller's head was level 't writ that song 'bout 'Ther' ain't no place like home.' The boys sings it a good deal down in Dixie, 'n' 'tain't no nonsense, nuther."

Si's talk was not continuous. It was as natural for his tongue to go rattling on as it was for him to eat whenever he had a good chance. At this time both impulses were strong and he gratified them by turns. The happy combination was not more satisfactory to himself than to his mother and Maria, who sat upon either side listening to his chatter and enjoying almost as much as he did the keen relish and the rapidity with which he disposed of the edibles. His ability to wait upon himself was sadly crippled, but this lack was fully supplied by his faithful attendants, who anticipated his every want, and prepared his food in convenient shape for conveyance to his mouth.

"Wish Shorty was here so he c'd have a squar' meal fer once," he continued, as he poured a liberal "ration" of rich cream into his third cup of coffee. "I'd like ter send a gallon er two o' this stuff down to the boys o' Comp'ny Q—what there is left of 'em, fer they got cut up awful when we went up the ridge. But I ain't goin' ter talk 'bout that now, fer it makes me feel bad jest ter think on it. Ye don't know Shorty, do ye? P'r'aps ye don't understand how every soljer 's got a pard. Shorty 's mine, and ther' ain't a man 'n the rijiment that's got 's good a pard 's I have. He ain't so mighty scrumptious lookin', but he's what some folks calls a 'singed cat'—he's a heap better 'n he looks. I couldn't git 'long 'thout Shorty, nohow. An' the best thing 'bout him is he's got sand 'nuff fer him and me both."

"What in the world do soldiers want to carry sand for?" asked Maria. "I should think they'd have load enough without that, an' I can't see what good it can do 'em."

"Oh, I don't mean 't Shorty er any o' the boys lugs gravel 'round with 'em all the time," said Si, amused at his sister's literal interpretation. "It's jest a way we has o' talkin' in the army. P'r'aps *you'd* call it 'nerve' er 'spunk' er 'grit,' but we calls it 'sand,' 'n' I don't b'lieve there's any place in the wide world where a feller needs so much on it, 'n' fust quality, too, 's in the army. When the boys says a feller hain't got no sand, that means he's no 'count. Now I guess ye understand what 'sand' is, don't ye?"

Maria readily admitted that his explanation was clear and ample.

"Si," said his mother—and a tear glistened in her eye as she looked into his face, with maternal love and pride— "I'm glad *you've* got what you call 'sand.' I shouldn't like to have ye one of the other kind ye was tellin' 'bout."

"Well, mother, I jest *had* to have it, 'cause I wasn't goin' ter do nothin' 't 'd make ye 'shamed o' me. I've had 'nuff ter last me this fur, but I tell ye it purty nigh gi'n out sometimes. 'Tain't safe ter brag any, fer I've seen fellers 't you'd think to hear 'em talk they had sand 'nuff ter stock up a hull rijiment; 'n' when it come ter the pinch they didn't have no more 'n ther' is in the gizzard of a chicken what's jest hatched. Ye can't most always tell t'll ye see a man in a tight place. Mebbe *my* sand 'll run out some day, but I don't b'lieve 'twill. If it does it'll be time fer Si Klegg ter turn up his toes."

When Si had eaten all he could hold, his mother and sister gave their attention to his arm. As they unwound the bandages with gentle fingers and disclosed the ugly gap that had been torn in the flesh by the cruel missile, the tenderest and most emphatic expressions of sympathy and commiseration escaped from their lips. They were unanimous in the opinion that it was "awful."

"Fiddlesticks!" said Si, "that ain't nothin' 't all—jest a mere scratch—compared ter what hunderds o' the boys got. If you'd been where I was the night arter the fight you'd ha' thought I was mighty lucky ter git off with that, sayin' nothin' 'bout all them that was killed."

While they washed and dressed his wound, Si drew a graphic picture of the scenes he had witnessed at the field hospital. They had read of such things in the newspapers, but they had never seemed *real* to them before. There were many involuntary shudderings and exclamations of horror during the recital.

Si's wound was already beginning to heal, and his healthy condition was favorable to speedy recovery.

"That's fust rate!" he said, after his arm was nicely wrapped in clean, white bandages. "I wish the poor boys a-sufferin' down there had 's good nusses as you be. I want ye ter do yer level best on me 'n' git me cured up so I kin go back. My musket 's waitin' fer me."

His mother and sister looked sadly at each other, but made no reply.

"Si," said Maria, after she had assisted her mother to clear away the "things," "I'm goin' to run over and tell Annie that you've come, and that I guess you'll call 'round this evening. She'll be *most* as glad to see ye as *I* was."

"D'ye reely mean that, Marier?" and the rich color mantled Si's brown cheek as he spoke.

"Of course I do," replied Maria. "I thought her poor little heart was clean broke when the awful news came that you was killed. You jest wait and see, Si—if you can muster up courage enough to go over there."

"I was thinkin'—that is—I mean—I was goin' ter ax ye 'bout her, soon 's I got a chance," and Si's face kept growing redder.

"What a goosey you are, to be sure," said his sister, roguishly. "*Ain't* you a brave soldier, talkin' so much about 'sand' an' chargin' batteries an' capturin' flags, an' ye dassent go to see a pretty little girl like Annabel!''

Si did not reply to this sally, for he was painfully conscious that what she said was true. He felt that it would take more "sand" to go and see Annie than it did to carry the colors of the 200th Indiana up the blazing ridge.

"You may tell—Annie—that I'll be 'round this evenin'!" he said at length.

Then he put on his hat and went out back of the house to think. He wanted, more than anything else in the world, to go right along with Maria. If the house of Annabel's father had been full of armed rebels, he would not have hesitated a moment; as it was, he concluded to wait till the friendly darkness would cover his movements. If he should go now the eyes of the whole world would be upon him.

Si watched eagerly for his sister's return, though it was, of course, wholly accidental that he happened to be standing at the front gate when she came.

"What did—she say?" he asked.

"I ain't goin' to tell you nothin' 'bout it," she replied. "It spiles such things to have 'em go drizzlin' at second-hand from somebody else's tongue. She ain't half as 'fraid of you, Si, as you be of her. She tried to hide from me the tears that come into her eyes when I told her you was here. Now don't keep askin' questions, for I shan't tell ye no more, only jest that ye needn't be noways afeard that ye'll find yerself locked out when ye go there."

During the remainder of the day Si strolled over the farm and talked with his father, who was busy in bringing up the arrears of his work.

"It's precious little I've done fer nigh a week," said Farmer Klegg, "'cept drivin' to town arter news, an' things is badly behind. I reck'n it's purty much the same with a good many o' the neighbors that has boys in Company Q."

"Wish 't I c'd help ye, father," said Si, "but I can't arn my board jest now."

"Si," replied his father, "all I want o' you is jest to stan' 'round where I can look at ye. It's a powerful blessin' to these old eyes o' mine!"

In the few hours since his return, Si had come to realize, more than during all the long months of his absence, how tender the affection and solicitude, how grievous the corroding anxiety, of those who watched and waited and prayed at home.

After supper Si fixed himself up, with the help of his sister, put on his hat and went out. No one asked him where he was going, but his mother and Maria exchanged smiles as he remarked, with averted face, that he wouldn't be gone a great while.

His heart beat furiously as he drew near to the house where Annabel lived. Perhaps its unusual agitation was due to his rapid walk to get there. Be this as it may, he found it necessary to pause a moment and make an effort to compose himself. Then he rapped timidly on the door, as if he were afraid of alarming the whole community. In fact, like Poe's fantastic raven, "so gently he came tapping" that neither the good farmer, who sat reading aloud the latest war news, nor his wife, who was listening while she mended the family hose, heard it. Old people do not always hear very well.

But there was one whose quick ears caught the sound, just as though they had been listening for it. As Annabel rose to answer the summons, her heart was galloping not less rapidly than was the one beneath the blouse of the young soldier standing without—and she had not been doing anything that might cause such vigorous pulsations. Very softly she lifted the latch and opened the door.

"Si!"

"Annie!"

There was no need for elaborate phrases of greeting.

A whole lexicon could not have expressed more. Obeying her first impulse she threw her soft, round arms about his neck, while he made most efficient use of the one arm at his command. At no time since his hurt had he felt so sorely the need of two good ones. But then, if he had not been wounded he would not have had the privilege of see= ing Annabel, and half of *such* a loaf was a good deal better than no bread at all. So he was comforted.

Up to this time the interview had been so much in the nature of a pantomime that Annabel's father and mother did not know that it was going on. The farmer read on and his wife stitched away with her darning.

An instant later there was a sound that the farmer and his wife *did* hear. Si, in his ardor, did not properly gauge the smack he bestowed upon the girl who was trembling in his embrace. It made the farmer drop his paper, and his wife start so that she pierced her finger with the needle. Both greeted Si with effusive cordiality.

Fully aware of the childish partiality of Si and Annabel for each other, they had naturally watched his conduct in the army with something more than a mere neighborly interest. He had often been the subject of conversation, and Annabel knew that the faultless manner in which he had acquitted himself had won for him a warm place in their hearts. Nor did they seek to repress her growing fondness for a lad who had passed so honorably through the fiercest test of true manliness. Under these favoring influences the coy sensitiveness which she felt at first had been, in a measure, gradually dissipated. So it was that at this time the presence of the " old folks "—usually considered a discouraging feature of such an occasion—caused no embarrassment to Annabel; while the warmth of his reception at once put Si at his ease.

For an hour his tongue was kept busy answering the multitude of questions from the farmer and his wife about the great battle, the neighborhood boys in Company Q, his wound, and his soldier life in general. There was now and then a word from Annabel, though she was mostly content to sit and listen. Si was supremely happy in the sunshine of her presence. Between their eyes there seemed to be a telegraphic communication, the result of which was mutually satisfying.

"I s'pose ye won't go back to the army, now ye've got hurt so bad," said her father. Annabel glanced quickly at him, as if to read his answer before it was uttered.

"Of course I will," he replied, "'n' I shan't be a great while gittin' over this pin scratch. As long 's ther' *is* any Company Q I'm goin' ter stay with the boys, 'nless I ketch it a good deal wuss 'n this!"

Annabel's eyes dropped to the floor, for the thought of his plunging again into battle was painful to her. She could not but admire his pluck, however, and his spirited answer raised him another peg in the estimation of her parents.

When Si said he "guessed it was time for him to go" the farmer and his wife expressed the hope that they might see him often during his stay, and he mentally resolved that this hope should not be disappointed.

CHAPTER XL.

SI GETS A BIG LETTER FROM THE GOVERNOR, ANSWERS IT, AND REJOINS HIS REGIMENT.

FOR days Si was besieged by those who wished to inquire after their friends in Company Q. There were some sad interviews, as he told of one that was killed and another that was wounded in the battle. One of the first to call was the neighbor who brought the news that day to Mr. Klegg, and whose son Tom died of his wounds at the field hospital. Si had carefully brought home the ar-

ticles Tom intrusted to his care, and delivered them to the
heart-broken father. In reply to the latter's inquiries, Si
described the death scene in a simple, earnest way that
brought tears to the eyes of all who heard it.

Si's furlough was for thirty days, with an assurance
that it would be extended if he was not able to return to
duty at the expiration of that time. Although the days
passed like a happy dream, before the time was half gone
he began to grow impatient. His arm was doing nicely,
but the healing process, necessarily slow, was by no means
fast enough for him. Every time his wound was dressed
he examined it with a critical eye, and calculated the
chances on his being able to start back at the end of his
thirty days. He finally made up his mind that he would
go, whether his arm was well or not. He was sure that
he could make himself useful at the front in some way,
and he longed to be once more in his place among his
comrades.

"Si," said his mother one day, as he sat eating a freshly-
baked mince-pie, "ye can't think what a comfort it's been
to me to think of yer havin' that nice warm quilt I gave
ye when ye went away. There hasn't been a single night
when it was cold an' stormy that it hain't come to my
mind what a blessin' to ye it was that ye had it. I reck'n
ye've slep' a good deal comfortabler than the poor fellows
that don't have nothin' but their army blankets—an' some
o' them, I hear, is awful shoddy. I s'pose there's lots o'
the soldiers that hasn't got mothers to give 'em warm
quilts."

Si was in a tight place and did not know what to say.
He had often thought of that quilt, since it met its cruel
fate at one of the halts during the first day's march.
Whenever he recalled the circumstance it caused a shock
to his feelings to think how glad he was to get rid of
it, to ease his aching shoulders; and it is not to be wondered at that he had never had the courage to tell his

mother, in any of his letters, what had become of it. He was sure that if he did she would never forgive him. Now he was in a sad quandary. Something *had* to be said, and he racked his brain to find a way out of the woods. As he did not reply with his usual readiness his mother ventured the remark that maybe it was getting pretty well used up by this time. Si was quick to make the most of the opportunity thus offered, and he promptly answered that he believed it was "about gone up."

"Well, it's all right," said his mother. "I was hopin' ye might bring it home with ye when ye was through soldierin', for I worked many an hour to make it, but I don't care if ye've wore it out, seein' it's done ye so much good."

Then Si concluded he had better tell her the whole story. While he was about it he told her what became of most of the other pretty things with which they equipped him for the war.

"I tell ye what, mother," he said, "it went mightily agin the grain ter do it, but 'f I hadn't I'd ha' been dead long ago. I'd jest like to seen *you* tryin ter tote the load 't I did. No, I don't mean that, nuther, fer I wouldn't fer the world have ye suffer 's I did that fust day we marched. My knapsack seemed like 't was 's big 'n' 's heavy 's a load o' hay, 'n' my gun like a saw-log, 'n' the catridge-box 'n' canteen 'n' haversack all a-pullin' 'n' grindin', 'n' me a-sweatin' t'll I was 's wet 's a drownded rat, 'n' every bone 'n my body achin', 'n' my feet all kivered with big blisters—I tell ye, mother, ef it *had* been you, you 'd ha' flung them traps away long 'fore I did. I stuck to 'em 's long 's I could, 'n' Shorty all the time a-tellin' me to git shet of 'em."

Si's mother listened with some surprise. She had read about the suffering of the soldiers on the march, but she had never realized it before. Si had said very little about it in his brief and rather infrequent letters, for he wished to avoid increasing his mother's solicitude by letting her know what hardships they were compelled to endure.

"Well, I declare," she exclaimed, "how foolish we was, and didn't know it! We thought them things was jest what ye wanted. Of course ye did right, Si. Ye oughtn't to tried to carry 'em at all. I'm glad ye told me, 'cause I was gettin' a lot more things ready for ye when ye go back—which Heaven knows I wish ye didn't have to—an' now I 'low ye won't want 'em."

"No, mother! I'm ever so much 'bleeged to ye, but a soldier's better off 'f he hain't got but mighty little 'sides what the guvyment gives him. We thought we knowed it all, but it didn't take long ter find out 't we didn't know nothin'. We don't mind the marchin' now, fer we've got broke in—'ceptin' once 'n a while when they crowds us extry hard—but ye'll have ter 'xcuse me f'm tryin' ter make a pack-mule o' myself ag'in. I b'lieve I know when I've got 'nuff. I guess I ought ter have a new fine-tooth comb, but I don't think o' nothin' else."

Si was a little more diplomatic in explaining these things to Annabel. In fact he had hung on to the keepsakes she had given him with a tenacity that was the strongest possible evidence of his regard for her. One by one they had succumbed to the inevitable, and through the accidents of campaigning had gone to swell the long list of casualties. All he had left was the locket he wore around his neck. This had escaped the general wreck, though in a badly tarnished and battered condition. The slippers he had carried for months, braving the rude jests and gibes which they never failed to elicit from his comrades. They were like a poultice to his feet after a day's march, though there was usually so much camp duty to be done that it was only now and then that he had a chance to put them on. One evening he went to sleep with his feet so close to the fire that the heat warped and twisted the soles into wrinkles and scorched the uppers so that they were no longer either useful or ornamental. This catastrophe was very depressing to Si, but time gradually softened the poignancy of his grief. In one of his interviews with Annabel he told her how much her kind remembrances had done to assuage the sorrows and discomforts of army life. She thought the slippers must be about worn out, and said she would make a new pair for him, but he tenderly dissuaded her by the assurance that he wouldn't need any more.

One day Si's old Sunday-school teacher, who armed him with the big knife, called to see him. This excellent man had an idea that the brilliant individual record his former pupil had made—of which he was so proud—and the halo of glory that surrounded the name of the 200th Indiana, were chiefly due to the ghastly havoc of that devastating weapon, as Si hewed his way toward the heart of the Southern Confederacy. He asked Si about it, and the answer he received caused him great heaviness of heart. Si told him frankly that the knife had not created any need of orphan asylums, nor made any women widows. It had not been without its uses in camp. It was a good thing to chop off the heads of confiscated chickens, and did general utility service as a butcher-knife until its edge was gone. Then its usefulness waned, as grindstones were not issued to the army. Finally he broke it while trying to pry open a sugar barrel, one dark night when he was on guard over a pile of commissary stores. Thus ended the picturesque romance of that knife, as an implement for the rapid extirpation of the human race.

Kind-hearted old ladies from all the region round about called at the Klegg farmhouse. Not one of them would be satisfied until she had seen Si's sore arm, and the profoundly sympathetic "m-m-m's" and "a-a-ah's" made him laugh in spite of himself. They wanted to see how a wound looked. Each of them suggested a healing emollient that always "worked like a charm," and could not fail to "bring him 'round" in short order. No two of these remedial prescriptions were alike, but each was a sovereign balm, better than anything in the *materia medica* of the doctors. The faith of these noble women in the efficacy of their respective remedies was unbounded, based upon forty or fifty years of domestic experience. Si was so anxious to get well that he wanted Nature supplied with all possible accessories that might aid her in the work of restoration.

One of these good Samaritans extolled the virtues of "goose-grease"—it was "powerful soothin'." She'd send Betsey over with a bottle, right away. Si's arm was copiously anointed with it, and the next morning he said he believed it was a good thing.

Then came another matron who inquired with the tenderest solicitude what he was doing for his wound. When informed of the application that was being made she held up her hands in astonishment.

"The very wust thing ye could put on it," she exclaimed. "I know who 'twas reckimended that stuff; it was Widder Pottleby. She uses goose-grease fer everything, from headache down to a stubbed toe. When folks gits well in spite of it she thinks it's that as does it. The best eintment in the world is mutton taller from a Southdown lamb killed at the full o' the moon, mixed ekal parts with cream from a three-year-old Alderney heifer. I've been experimentin' with all the different kinds o' sheep an' cattle an' these mixes the best. I jest made up a fresh lot t'other day an' I'll send ye some."

Then the goose-grease was carefully rubbed off and the new unguent was applied, only to give place, the next day, to some other homely specific. Every known variety of salve, ointment, "ile," poultice, plaster, liniment and cataplasm was urged, and, as the result of this universal sympathy, the mantels and window-sills of the house were covered with bottles and boxes, enough to stock a brigade hospital. Si's faith in them was badly shaken by the dis agreements of the numerous woman-doctors, and at length he wisely concluded that he would get along better without any of them. He thought his arm would get well quicker "itself," an opinion that was fully justified by the outcome.

During the whole of Si's stay there was unabated activity in the kitchen. His mother and sister exerted themselves with a zeal that never for an instant flagged, to satisfy his appetite with everything that their combined skill could produce. He had unrestricted license to forage at will in the pantry and the various cupboards which were used for the storage of pastry and delicacies. It is hardly necessary to say that he made the most of so choice an opportunity, and as a result of his riotous living he fattened rapidly, fully recovering from the shrinkage of flesh that was the natural consequence of his hard field service.

SI AT THE CORNER GROCERY.

He went often to the village, where everybody met him with warm greetings. The blushing maidens smiled sweetly upon him, as he promenaded the streets, and the small boys regarded him as a more conspicuous figure in the world's history than Napoleon Bonaparte, or Alexander the Great. Whenever he dropped into the corner grocery he was compelled to tell, over and over again, the story of the battle, for the edification of the loungers who sat around on the barrels and crippled chairs. The grocery was the village "clearing-house" for news of all kinds.

Here weighty problems of war and statesmanship were solved, brilliant campaigns carried on, fierce battles fought over, and unmistakable conclusions reached as to how the war ought to be conducted. The listener could not but realize what the country had suffered because these rustic patriots had not been chosen to lead the impatient armies, and pilot the ship of state over the tempestuous sea.

Si and Annabel got on famously. He was a frequent visitor, basking in the smiles of the red-cheeked lass. Although no word passed between them on the subject, it required no extraordinary gift of prophecy to foretell that by and by, when the cruel war was over, the parson would be called in.

A day or two before Si left for the front there came to the post-office an envelope about a foot long, addressed in a large, bold hand, "Lieutenant Josiah Klegg." The post-mark showed that it was from the capital of the state. The village postmaster served as a kind of substitute for a daily newspaper. He was the great disseminator of neighborhood news and gossip, much of which he obtained by guessing at the contents of the letters that passed through his hands. All these he examined and speculated upon with a skill only acquired by long practice. Si's big letter, with its impressive superscription, riveted his attention, and before it was called for half the people in the village knew all about it.

Si drove into town that day, and the first person he met told him there was an important letter at the post-office for him. Before he reached the office half a dozen others had imparted the same information.

"Hello, Lieutenant," said the smiling postmaster, as Si appeared at the threshold, "I've got a letter for you."

"That's what everybody's been a-tellin' me," said Si. "But what ye talkin' that way ter me fer? I ain't no lef-tenant!"

"I have an idea that the man who wrote your letter

knows more about that than you do, Si. Of course I don't know what 's in it, but folks think I'm pretty good at guessin'. I 'low it 's from the governor."

With feelings of mingled awe and bewilderment Si took the ponderous missive. He turned it over and over, wondering what its contents could be. He was a little piqued at the burning impatience of the postmaster to have him open it, and intimated that it was *his* letter, and he would wait until he was ready. When his agitation had subsided he went out into the adjacent wagon-shed, and after assuring himself that no one was looking at him, he carefully tore open the envelope. With trembling fingers he drew out an imposing document, with a big red seal and bearing the signature of the governor. He read with amazement that Josiah Klegg had been appointed a second lieutenant in the 200th Indiana. Accompanying it was a personal

A LETTER FROM THE GOVERNOR.

letter in which the governor told him that he had been promoted in recognition of his conspicuous gallantry in the recent battle, which had been so honorable to himself, his regiment and his state.

Impelled by curiosity the postmaster hunted up Si and found him in a half dazed condition, scratching his head and trying to comprehend it all.

"Well, Si," he said, "didn't I guess it about right?"

"I'm jest teetotally flabbergasted," replied Si. "Ef I knowed of any other Josier Klegg I sh'd think it meant him, but 'pears 's though I'm the feller the guv'ner 's after."

"Let me be the first to congratulate you, Si—excuse me, I mean Lieutenant Klegg," said the postmaster. "You have nobly earned your promotion and we are all proud of you. I'm going to start a subscription to buy you a sword."

But Si was already off and scarcely heard the old gentleman's words. He was thinking only of the good people at home and how glad they would be to learn the news. It sounded strangely to hear people whom he met address him as "Lieutenant"—for the gossip of the postmaster had come to be universally believed.

Si drove rapidly homeward. All the way he was thinking of his promotion—as unexpected to him as would have been a stroke of lightning. How nice it would be to wear shoulder-straps, and swing a "cheese-knife." How proud of him his mother and sister Maria would be, and how happy he hoped it would make Annabel. Then it flashed across his mind that if he was an officer he could not have Shorty for his "pard" any longer, and that outweighed all other considerations. He wouldn't be an officer.

Si's face flushed with pardonable pride as he unfolded the commission before the astonished eyes at the farmhouse. His declaration that he would not accept it was received with the greatest surprise. Maria told him he ought to be a brigadier-general. At first every effort was made to dissuade him from declining his promotion, but without avail.

"Well," said his mother, at length, "Si knows best. It's jest as much honor to have had the commission sent to him, an' if he don't want it I s'pose he'll have to send it back."

Si sat down and wrote to the governor. It was the most momentous undertaking in the way of writing a letter he had ever attempted. After a dozen fresh starts he succeeded in conveying his message. He wrote:

Mr. Guvner

Deer frend. i rite these few lines hopin you are enjoyin the blessins of good helth. i wasent expectin a letter from you speshly such a kind of one as i got today. Ime ever so much bleeged to ye Mr. Guvner fer sendin me that commishn but i very respectively incline. In the fust place i aint fit to be no ossifer i dont no enuff cause ime jest nothin but a boy and haint never had much larnin. I can git long faster puttin down the rebelyun, that is helpin do it yew no what I meen, with my muskit than i can with a sord. Ive got used to my gun but I dont no nothin bout a sord an I never seen a sord hurt nobody nuther. Ef the army was all ossifers thout nobody to carry muskits the war woodent be over in a thowsan years. Course we needs to have ossifers an weve got some bully ones in the 200th ridgment. When ye want to make a new lot of em ye wont have no trubble a findin plenty thats bettern me an they wants sholeder straps wussen I do. But I haint toled ye the biggest reeson why i send ye this dockyment. Its cause I cant go back on Shorty. Mebbe ye dont no Shorty but hes my pard an hes the boss soljer. Ef ye cood make him fust lewtenant i woodent mind bein seckond an then we cood bunk together sames we allus has. Hes nothin but a privit so i spose ye cant do it an ide ruther be jest Corporil Klegg ef its all the saim to you.

Yer umbel sarvent

Josiah Klegg

P S pleese exkuse bad ritin an spellin.

When Si's furlough expired his wound was not fully healed. His friends had urged him to have his leave renewed but he was impatient to return and would not listen to their advice. Tearful farewells were spoken, and with a handful of trifling remembrances—instead of the wheelbarrow-load with which he started out before—he boarded the train and went whirling away. He was not wholly unincumbered, however, for the mothers and sisters of his company comrades had intrusted to his care for them many tokens of affection; besides surcharging him, to the very muzzle, with a hundred verbal messages, not one in ten of which he could possibly remember.

When Si reached the camp of the 200th Indiana, still carrying his arm in a sling, he received an effusive welcome.

"P'r'aps I can't do much 'th my gun fer a while yit," he said to Shorty, whom he was overjoyed to meet, "but I couldn't stan' it no longer, 'n' I reck'n I kin find suthin ter do. Ef we git inter a fight I kin bite catridges 's fast 's half a dozen on ye kin shoot."

After they had gone to bed that night Si told his comrade about the commission he had received from the governor.

Shorty threw off the blanket and jumped to his feet with a shout of delight.

"Pard," he said, "I'm gladder 'n I kin tell ye, 'cause I know how well ye desarve it. The guv'ner's head was level when he done that. I'll be mighty proud on ye, seein' ye rigged up like 'n ossifer. I s'pose ye got a gorjus outfit. Why didn't ye put on yer leftenant's traps so the boys could see ye was some punkins?"

Si knew there was no sham in Shorty's words, and on his account almost regretted that he had declined the promotion.

"Shorty," he said after a moment, "I'm 'feard ye won't like it, but I didn't keep the commishn. I jest sent it back ter the guv'ner."

"What!" exclaimed his pard in amazement. "Sent it back! Ef you ain't the biggest—"

"Hol' on, pard," interrupted Si. "I know what ye're goin' ter say. Mebbe I am, but wait t'll ye hear the hull thing. It was jest 'cause I couldn't go back on you, Shorty. I knowed I'd have ter take my grub 'long 'th ossifers 'n' I couldn't have ye fer my pard no more. Seemed ter me I wouldn't 'mount ter shucks 'thout you, 'n' that settled it. I writ the guv'ner 't ef he'd make you fust leftenant 'n' me second I'd call it a go."

"Si," said Shorty, after giving expression to his surprise in a long, low whistle, "I kin tell ye one thing; ye wouldn't ha' sent that thing back ef *I'd* been thar!"

CHAPTER XLI.

"SI," said Shorty, one cold night in January, "how d' ye feel 'bout reinlistin' fer three years more?"

The 200th Indiana was a long way from its base of supplies, engaged in an arduous campaign. For many days the soldiers had been without tents. At this time they were bivouacking in the woods, with no shelter save such as they had made of sticks, boughs of pine and balsam, and a few rails and boards that were picked up by scouring that desolate region. It was snowing heavily and the biting blasts of midwinter howled among the trees. The men heaped high the blazing fires and hovered closely around them, grimy with smoke and shivering with cold. It was a wild, rough night, that made a soldier think of home in spite of himself.

Si was standing before the fire, his front and rear freezing and toasting alternately as he turned himself around at frequent intervals. The smoke, whirled about in every direction by the wind, caused a copious and involuntary shedding of tears, and steam ascended from his garments, wet by the melting snow. It may be doubted whether his mother or sister Maria or even Annabel could have identified him, in that dismal group.

"What's that ye're sayin'?" he asked, in reply to Shorty's remark. A general interest in the subject was manifested by his comrades, who formed a circle around the fire.

"I was only axin' ye," said Shorty, "how ye'd like ter put yer name down 'n' be swored in fer three years longer o' this sort o' thing. I was over to the 199th Michigan this afternoon 'n' I heerd the boys say the guvyment wants all the old soljers ter reinlist. I reck'n f'm the way you fellers seems ter be enj'yin' yerselves tonight ye'll all on ye jest go a-tumblin' up ter the 'cruitin' office—in a horn."

"What's the idee o' their talkin' that way," said Si, "'s long 's we've got a good bit ter sarve yet 'fore our fust three years is up? I sh'd think ther' 'd be time 'nuff *then* ter talk 'bout goin' in ag'in."

"I don't quite git the hang o' the scheme myself," replied Shorty, "but 's near 's I c'd make out this 's the way on 't. Ther' don't nobody know how long this 'ere re-bellyun 's goin' ter last. Don't seem 's

A MOMENTOUS QUESTION.

if we'd made much headway yet puttin' on it down. Looks 's if the war wouldn't quit t'll all the men 's killed off 'n' ther' ain't no people left 'cept the women. Then mebbe *they* 'll pitch in 'n' keep it up. 'Twouldn't be s'prisin', f'm the way some o' the secesh women talks down here. They're good at fightin' 'th their chins. But ye see what the guvyment wants is ter git the dead wood on these old rijiments. Ye know most o' the fellers that's left in 'em has got purty tollable tough. They ain't none o' yer spring chickens. They've got used ter the army grub 'n' the hard marchin' 'n' lyin' 'round 'n the mud 'n' they kin stan' it; 'n' when 't comes ter fightin' most on 'em 's got the best kind o' grit. 'Sides that they've got the hull business larned 'n' they allus knows jest 's well 's the gin'rals what 's got ter be did, 'n' they wades right in. When it comes ter reel red-hot campaignin', a hunnerd sich soljers is better 'n five hunnerd tenderfoots. Ye recolleck 't *we* wa'n't good fer much that fust day we marched, 'n' it's jest so 'th all on 'em when they're green. It takes a long time ter make soljers outen such fellers, 'n' a good many on 'em dies in the makin'. Now 't the guvyment 's got a purty fa'r lot o' the fust-class article it wants ter freeze to 'em."

"It's bully weather fer doin' that!" said Si. "I guess them big ossifers 'n Washington 'd think so ef they was here 'bout now."

"Wall, that's the idee," continued Shorty. "Ther''s got ter be a heap o' hard fightin' 'fore this thing 's over, 'n' they want soljers 't they kin bet on every time."

The members of Company Q had listened attentively to Shorty's remarks on the situation. The subject of re-enlisting had never entered their heads before. The time and circumstances did not seem propitious for such a suggestion. Hardships never came singly in the army. It was during the trying campaigns, when the men were footsore and weary, bivouacking without tents and exposed to the rigor of the storms which always came at such times, that rations were short and hunger was added to the aggregation of human woes. It was so at this time with the 200th Indiana; and as the men stood around the fires, in the driving snow, wet, shivering and famished, it would have been but natural if they had felt like mobbing a man who should come among them to urge them to re-enlist.

Corporal Klegg was the first to speak, as Shorty stopped to breathe. "Wall, boys," he said, plowing his fists into his eyes and ducking his head to escape a fresh cloud of smoke, "I dunno how the rest on ye feels 'bout reinlistin', but ef they wants me ter jine ag'in I'm ready ter do it."

"I'd go with ye, Si, ef I was a nat'ral born fool!" said a lank Hoosier, one of the constitutional grumblers of the company.

"Look a-here, pard, ye don't want ter go to insiniwatin' 'round like that, 'cause I ain't no fool! *You* don't have ter reinlist 'cause I do. I hain't axed ye ter jine. Ye kin do jest 's ye likes, but when I tuk a gun on my shoulder I calkylated ter stay t'll arter the benediction. I never was in the habit o' goin' out t'll meetin' was dismissed."

"That's all right, Si; ye needn't spunk up about it. If ye want three years more o' soljerin' I hain't no 'bjections, 'n' 'twouldn't make no difference 'f I had. But I b'lieve I know when I've got enough, 'n' by the time my three years is up I'll be 's full 's I kin hold."

"That's my ticket," said another. "They don't ketch me fer any more o' this. I'm goin' ter stay 's long 's I agreed ter, 'f I don't git killed, 'n' then I'm goin' ter quit 'n' give s'mother feller a chance ter lug my traps a while. The woods up in Injianny is full o' men 't hain't 'listed yet, 'n' I'd like ter see 'em take their turn. No, I thank ye; I don't want no more on it 'n mine. If any on ye reinlists 'twon't be long t'll ye 'll be kickin' yerselves fer doin' it."

And so the talk went on. At first it seemed that Si was the only member of Company Q who was willing to enlist for another term. At length one of the boys asked Shorty, who had taken no further part in the discussion, what he was going to do about it.

"Wall," he replied, "it don't make much diff'runce ter me. I hadn't reely made up my mind what ter do t'll I heerd Si say he'd reinlist, 'n' that settled me. I ain't goin' back on my pard. The 'cruitin ossifer 'd be sartin of a pair ef he sh'd start in tonight. I didn't quite git through tellin' ye 'bout the business. They say 't every man 't reinlists 'll git a bounty of four hunnerd dollars."

"How much did ye say?" asked Si, opening his eyes very wide.

"Four hunnerd dollars!"

"Jiminy, but that's a pile o' money—more 'n I ever seed 'n my life to oncet. Lemme see; that's purty nigh 's much 's a feller gits fer three years o' soljerin'. I s'pose they keeps payin' the reg'lar wages jest the same?"

"Course they does!" replied Shorty. "The four hunnerd 's extry."

This information gave a new interest to the subject, and had the immediate effect to modify somewhat the general feeling. A disposition was manifested to at least give the matter a fair consideration.

"It'll be kind o' nice ter have them four hunnerd dollars!" said Si, "but I tell ye what 'tis, money ain't no objick. All the gold 'n Californy wouldn't hire me ter go through three years o' this thing, same 's I'd hire out ter hoe corn er chop wood." Si could say this with good grace, as he had de- clared his willingness to re-enlist before he had heard any- thing of the bounty.

"Right ye are," said one of his comrades. "Money ain't much account to a feller arter he's planted two foot under ground; ner it don't pay fer havin' his arms 'n' legs sawed off. The bounty 's only the sugar they're coatin' the pill with so we 'll swaller it. Fer 's I'm consarned I'm goin' ter 'pass.'"

"Ther' 's jest one thing more, boys," said Shorty, after they had spent some time in discussing the financial phase of the question. "All them as reinlists gits a thirty-day furlough right away, 'n' the guvment takes 'em home 'n' brings 'em back ag'in, free gratis. I'll miss my guess 'f *that* don't fetch some on ye!"

That magic word "home"—how it thrilled the hearts of those war-worn and weather-beaten soldiers! The tenderest chords vibrated at its touch. Shorty was right in his surmise that this would "fetch" many of them. The thought of spending a whole month in "God's country," with mothers and wives and sisters and sweethearts, eating three "square," Christian meals a day, and sleeping under a roof, in a good bed, was something that few could withstand. The desire to re-enlist at once, under such conditions, spread through Company Q like the measles. They would stand by the old flag till the last rebel had laid down his arms—of course they would!

There was little opportunity for sleep that night in the cheerless quarters, swept by the wintry blasts and half filled with the drifting snow. Nowhere except close to the fires could be found the slightest approach to comfort. Far into the slowly-creeping hours the boys shivered and smoked and talked, with chattering teeth, about going home, and what they would have to eat when they got there. Before they turned in for the night most of them had reached the point of being actually afraid the chance to re-enlist would not be offered them. There were still a few who stoutly resisted the blandishments of bounty and furlough, avowing their unalterable determination to repel all such beguiling influences, which, they said, were only bait to catch gudgeons. They did not propose to bite again, for they knew by experience how keen the hook was.

"Three years o' this kind o' sarvis," said one of them, "is my sheer. When all the chaps that's stayin' to hum has done that much, 'n' it comes my turn ag'in, mebbe I'll give 'er another whirl, but I don't want no more on it this time, ef the court knows herself, and she thinks she does. Them's my sentiments, 'n' I don't keer who knows 'em."

"You jest wait t'll ye see Comp'ny Q gittin' ready ter go home, 'n' ye won't feel quite so cranky!" said Si, who was getting much warmed up over the project.

It is true Si had been home once, to nurse his wound, but

he was more than ready to go again. He told the boys that he hoped the army would not move while they were away, for he wanted the 200th Indiana to have a hand in everything that was going on. It is possible that some were not quite so anxious on this point as he was. Indeed there is little doubt that, albeit they were proud of the regiment and of their part in winning its honor and fame, they would be resigned to the dispensations of Providence if it should happen that a great battle were to take place during their absence. This was not an unnatural feeling, for there were few who wore either the blue or the gray that did not crave fighting less and less, the more they had of it.

At length, when the animated debate had exhausted the subject, and each man seemed to have fully made up his mind what he would do in the premises, they disposed themselves as best they could for rest. Some crept into their dreary "shebangs," wrapping themselves tightly in their blankets and overcoats. Others stretched out upon the wet ground, as near to the fire as they could and yet be safe from absolute cremation. It was but a choice of two evils, either of which was bad enough.

Si and Shorty calculated the chances for sleep and concluded to try the fire. Spreading a poncho and a blanket in the slush, they laid themselves down with a single blanket over them and a log for a pillow. The capes of their overcoats were drawn over their faces and tucked around their heads, to protect them from the wind and snow and stifling smoke.

Si finally went to sleep and dreamed he was eating a pie as large as a wagon wheel, when he was awakened by the warmth of a large coal that the snapping fire had landed upon his blanket, and which was rapidly burning its way through to his body. He sprang up with unusual agility, and for the moment resolved himself into a fire department. A hasty application of snow proved effectual, and he then went to poking up the fire, which sent a shower of sparks and a scorching blast over the forms that covered the ground. After heaping on a fresh supply of fuel he went around and put out the sparks and embers that had fallen upon his sleeping comrades, and again snuggled down by the side of Shorty. Scarcely anybody lay for an hour during the remainder of the night without getting up to extinguish his smoking garments and to stir the fire.

The reveille sounded at dawn, but the bugler did not blow with his usual artistic excellence. His notes came in a feeble, discouraged way, telling plainly that he, too, had passed a sorry night. Everybody was glad that it was time to get up, and rejoiced to see the daylight again. It was a forlorn company that straggled into line in response to the "Fall in for roll-call," of the orderly. They answered "Here!" in tones which, while fully establishing the fact of their presence, betrayed a wish that they were anywhere else.

The first duty was to examine the arms and put them in order, for such a night was apt to have a disabling effect upon muskets as well as men. It is true there seemed little probability that there would be immediate occasion to use them, for no doubt the "Johnnies," too, wherever they might be, were moping around smoking and spluttering fires, as solemn and lugubrious as so many undertakers. But it was better to be ready a thousand times when the rebels did not come than to be unready once when they did. So the boys wiped their guns with their ragged blouses, swabbed out the barrels, picked open the nipples and snapped caps to be sure they would "go" if they should want them to.

The scanty breakfast—consisting of pale coffee, from "grounds" that had been repeatedly boiled over, a few fragmentary, water-soaked hardtack, and a rind of bacon —was quickly disposed of. The regiment was not to move

that day, and the boys expected to be ordered out for drill
in the snow, but for some reason the officers forgot it.
This was an oversight that did not often occur.

The topic of conversation the evening before was still
uppermost in the minds of the members of Company Q,
and all were eager to know whether what Shorty had told
them was true, or was only another "grapevine." Their
desire for official information was soon gratified. The
company was ordered to fall in again, and the commanding officer read the order from Washington regarding veteran re-enlistments. The terms and conditions were the
same as Shorty had heard, except that a number was fixed
as the minimum who must re-enlist in a regiment to entitle
it to recognition as a "veteran" organization. It was
further announced that, as all could not be furloughed at
the same time without manifest injury to the service, the
regiment in each brigade which first presented the requisite
number of re-enlisted men should be the first to go.

When the officer had finished Corporal Klegg swung his
hat and led off with a yell, in which all the company joined
except those who had thus far been proof against the con-
tagion. But their wistful eyes showed that they were
already contemplating a motion to reconsider.

The veteran roll was opened at once. In matters of
this kind there is nothing like striking while the iron is
hot. Certainly no more favorable degree of heat could be
expected than that which at this moment warmed into
activity the emotions of Company Q. There was no table
or desk or tent in the whole bivouac, but a folded poncho
was laid across a log near one of the fires, a paper ready
for signatures was placed upon it, a pen and a pocket ink-
stand were produced, and the recruiting office was complete.

Si Klegg was promptly at hand to take the pen and be
the first to sign the roll. His fingers were stiffened by the
cold, and he had a hard job of it, but in course of time

his picturesque autograph adorned the page. Others followed in quick succession, and three-quarters of the company were ready to be mustered as veterans as soon as their names could be written.

Then the work dragged a little. Those who had so firmly resisted all overtures were seen standing around uneasily, holding silent communion with themselves. The impulsive ones, who had responded so readily, were desirous that every man in the company should sign the roll, and plied their obdurate comrades with persuasive words.

Is it any wonder that they hesitated? Was it not rather a wonder that any should consent to bind himself to three years more of such hardship and suffering? The life of a soldier had long since been stripped of all its fascinating show and tinsel. Fiction and romance had given place to the stern and ghastly reality. The history

SI STARTS THE VETERAN ROLL.

of the war records no grander heroism than that displayed by the re-enlistment of two hundred thousand men. It was a critical time. The government needed those tried and trusty battalions, and the securing of them was its salvation.

It was not cowardice that held back the few. None had been better soldiers than they; and when the slow leaven should do its work none would be more brave, patient and faithful in the dim, uncertain future. They were of those who do not yield quickly to an impulse, but when their minds are made up cast no regretful glance behind.

"Wall, boys, I'm with ye!" exclaimed, at length, the leader of the opposition, who the night before had declared his fixed determination not to re-enlist. "Tain't none o' yer coaxin' that 's done it nuther. I've been thinkin' it all over 'n' I've made up my mind that it's the c'rect thing fer us to do to see this thing through. I hope that if there 's a God in heaven he won't let this cussed war last three years longer, but I'm goin' to stay by the 200th Injianny as long as there 's anybody left to carry the flag."

This patriotic outburst was greeted with uproarious cheers. The boys yelled with delight as the sturdy soldier deliberately marched up and with a firm hand signed his name to the roll. This important accession to the ranks gave a new impetus to the work of "veteranizing" Company Q. The opposition was thoroughly demoralized, and those who had denounced the scheme now scrambled in their haste to get hold of the pen. Some of them said they had intended all the time to re-enlist, but they didn't see the use of rushing things. In a few minutes the last man had put his name to the roll; and then there went up a cheer that would have gladdened the heart of "Father Abraham," could he have heard it as it re-echoed through the bleak and dreary woods. With an army of such men, victory was but a question of time.

The captain of Company Q was the first to report at regimental headquarters, and the colonel sent his compliments to the men for their prompt and emphatic response to the call of duty. Each of the other companies had the same experience in the process of patriotic evangelization. Many were ready to sign the rolls at once, while others gave to the subject grave and careful thought. A few refused to the last to be persuaded. But before night the figures showed that the minimum line had been passed, and the 200th Indiana was ready to be mustered in as a veteran regiment. The fact was immediately communicated to the general commanding the brigade, who at once ordered that it should be the first to enjoy its furlough. It was directed to start on the following day.

The men received the tidings of their good fortune with glad shouts, again and again repeated. When the mustering officer came over to catch and string the fish that had been "biting" so freely at the bait, they hurried into line; and when the oath was administered they thrust their right arms up to their full length, evidently determined to make the ceremony as binding as possible. They had swallowed bait, hook and bob.

"Say, Shorty," asked Si, after the prescribed forms had been duly observed, "what 'd the must'rin' ossifer mean when he said 'fer three years er durin' the war'? S'posin' the war hangs on forty er fifty years; are we stuck fer the hull business?"

"'Durin' the war' sounds a leetle like that," replied his comrade, "but it means suthin else. I axed the cap'n today 'n' he said the guvyment couldn't hold us longer 'n three years 'thout we reinlisted ag'in. I reck'n ther' won't be more 'n a corporal's guard left o' the 200th Injianny by the time we've been through three years more o' such sarvis 's we've been havin'."

"It don't make no partickler diff'runce ter me, nohow," said Si, "fer I'm goin' ter stay t'll the eend—either of the war er of *me*—but I was jest a bit curus to know what 'durin' the war' meant."

"I'll tell ye what they put that in fer," said Shorty. "It's so 't ef the war sh'd happen ter wind up 'fore yer three years 's out, 'n' the guvyment don't want ye no longer, ye'll *haf* ter quit 'n' go home. Don't ye see 't ef the guvyment agreed ter keep ye three years, war er no war, it 'd be 'bleeged ter do it, pervidin' ye wanted ter stay 'n' hold it ter the barg'in."

Si burst into a paroxysm of laughter, so loud and long

continued that his comrade feared he would go into a fit.

"What on airth ails ye?" asked Shorty.

"Ye struck my funny-bone, pard," replied Si, as soon as he could speak, "with that idee 't we 'd all want ter keep right on soljerin' arter they gits this fuss settled. This 'ere sloshin' 'round, 'thout no tents ner no grub ner nuthin' 'cept fightin'—we've had plenty o' that—them big fellers must think it's a heap more fun 'n sleepin' under the kivers to hum, 'n' sittin' down to a fust-class lay-out mornin', noon 'n' night, 'n' hearin' a blessin' axed 'fore eatin'. *That* wouldn't be no good here, 'cause ther' ain't nothin' ter ax a blessin' *on*. The guvyment thinks we're all a lot o' idjuts, er else *it's* a mighty big durned fool ter s'pose ther''s any danger 't we'll want ter stay arter the rebils is licked." And Si laughed again till the tears flowed down his grimy cheeks.

Not since the night the regiment left Indiana to take the field had so great hilarity prevailed in the ranks of the 200th. The men danced and sung and laughed and shouted in such a tumultuous way that an ignorant looker-on would have imagined that they were bereft of reason. One more night in the comfortless bivouac and they would turn their faces toward home. As the darkness settled down it seemed to them that never had fires blazed with such a cheerful glow. The bitter blasts had lost their sting, and before the eyes of the glad soldiers appeared only visions of happy scenes and a brief respite from toilsome march and lonely picket—from hunger and cold and wretchedness. There was no thought of the toil and danger and pain that would come afterward.

Si had observed with some concern that his pard did not fully share in the general rejoicing. While trying to imagine the cause of this, it came to him that Shorty had no home to go to—no loving friends to clasp their arms about him and weep for joy at his coming. He instantly decided what he would do.

"Shorty," he said, as he sat on a log before the fire, "whar ye goin' ter spend yer furlough?"

For a moment Shorty did not reply. There was a sad look in his face that touched the sympathetic chords of Si's heart.

"I can't jest tell ye what I *will* do with myself," he said at length. "Ye know, Si, 't things ain't divided round equil 'n this world. Some has homes 'n' friends 'n' all that, 'n' I'm glad fer ye, pard, 't ye're one on 'em. Then, ag'in, there's others 't hain't, but goes driftin' 'bout like a boat 'fore the wind 'thout no rudder. I'm one o' *them*, 'n' p'r'aps it's jest as well that way. I reck'n I don't desarve ter have friends 'n' relations 'n' a place ter go to 't I c'd call home, er else I'd had 'em. It 'd be kind o' soothin' ter sich 's me to b'lieve ther' 's a place arter we git through livin' here, whar things 's evened up. Ye mustn't think, Si, 't I'm grumblin' 'cause I ain't fixed like the rest on ye; er 't I've got the blues, fer I hain't, no more 'n I often gits 'em. I reck'n 'tain't only nat'ral ter feel sort o' solemncholy when all the boys is lookin' forrard ter sich a good time 'n' ther' ain't nobody on earth 't keers a picayune whether I'm dead er 'live."

"Don't ye say that, pard," said Si in a voice full of earnest sympathy, "fer ye know 't *I* care a heap. Ef ye was my own brother I couldn't think more on ye!"

"Wall I'm right glad ef ye do, but I guess ye're the only one. I tell ye Si"—and Shorty's lips quivered with emotions that had not often been awakened in his starved heart—"it's been a Heaven's blessin' ter me 't I ever knowed ye. Blessin's has been rayther skurce, 'n' when I git one o' the ginowine article it looks big to me. Fact is I'd 'bout 's soon stay here 's ter go up t' Injianny 'n' lie 'round loose like a wagrant."

"Shorty," said Si, looking squarely into the face of his friend, "*I* kin tell ye whar ye're goin' ter spend yer month off, 'n' ye'll have a good time, too!"

"Then ye're smarter 'n' I am" replied Shorty, with a look of surprise and inquiry.

"Would ye like ter know? Ye're goin' hum 'long 'th me. I want ye ter see father 'n' mother 'n' sister Maria 'n' An—Annie—that's all right 'th you, Shorty, 'cause she's a nice gal 'n' she'll be glad ter see ye. I've writ to her 'n' all the rest on 'em 'bout ye, lots o' times. Now ye needn't go ter puckerin' up yer mouth ter say ye won't go, 'cause I'll go ter the colonel 'n' have him detail a guard ter *make* ye!"

The first tears that had moistened Shorty's eyes for many a year glistened in the firelight as he said, warmly grasping the hand of his comrade:

"Si, when I fust got yer idee I thought ter myself 't I wouldn't accept yer invite, fer I didn't s'pose yer folks keered anything 'bout me 'n' I didn't want ter be spongin' on 'em; but I b'lieve ye was 'n arnest when ye axed me, 'n' I'm goin' with ye. I don't 'low ter stay thar all the time, 'cause 'twɵn't take 'em long ter git tired o' me. I'm ever so much 'bleeged to ye, pard."

So this matter was satisfactorily arranged. Si was overjoyed at the thought of having his comrade go home with him; and the prospect of spending his holiday as a guest in somebody's home threw a ray of sunshine across the clouded pathway of Shorty's life.

The boys cared little whether they slept at all that night. Some of them tried to, but most of them huddled around the fires, in merry mood, with song and shout and mutual congratulations. Under the circumstances the strict camp regulations were relaxed, and the soldiers of the 200th were permitted to do about as they pleased.

In accordance with the unanimous desire of the men it was determined to start at an early hour in the morning, as the regiment had to march two or three days to reach a point where railroad transportation would be provided. Breakfast—such as it was—was eaten before daylight, and five minutes later they were ready to fall in, for they had no packing to do except to roll up their blankets. When the bugle sounded and the colonel mounted his horse, the boys set up a wild yell and hurried into line.

It was a trying moment for the "non-veterans," who, having declined to re-enlist, were to remain, temporarily assigned to a comparatively new regiment of the brigade, whose length of service was not sufficient to entitle it to the inestimable privilege of re-enlistment. The members of the little squad gazed sadly upon the preparations of their comrades to start homeward. Sallies of army wit, some of them keen and pungent, were aimed at the forlorn group. A few of the more stout-hearted kept up their "nerve" and shouted back that *their* turn to laugh would come after a few months, when they would go home to stay. But about half of them couldn't stand it any longer. They held a brief council of war and sent a delegate to the colonel to ask if they might yet be saved, or whether the day of grace was past. The colonel directed that an officer be detailed to have them mustered at once, and by a rapid march overtake the column. The conversion of these men at the eleventh hour was received by the regiment with tempestuous shouts.

At this moment every ear was startled by half a dozen shots on the picket-line, a mile away. Then the sound of drums and bugles was heard, regiments were hastily formed, and staff officers and orderlies galloped hither and thither with orders. The men of the 200th Indiana grasped their muskets more firmly and looked inquiringly into one another's faces. Was it an attack of the enemy? Must they go into battle at this most unwelcome moment? Were some of them to get their eternal furloughs, or be borne away on stretchers?

"Ef it don't make any diff'runce ter the Johnnies," said Si to Shorty, "it 'd be my ch'ice ter have 'em wait t'll we git back, 'n' then we'll give 'em all the fightin' they want

—we'll jest fill 'em up. 'Course we ain't goin' ter run away long 's ther' 's any shootin' goin' on, 'n' we'll do all we kin ter arn our furlough 'f we *haf* ter, but it *does* go a leetle agin the grain this mornin'."

The colonel made a speech to the boys, telling them he knew they didn't feel like fighting just then, and he did not blame them. "I feel a little that way myself," he said, "but if we are needed I know you will show them that you are worthy to be called veterans, and add new luster to the good name of the 200th Indiana."

The boys swung their hats and cheered lustily. The colonel needed no further assurance of their fidelity.

But they were spared the test. The firing ceased and an aide, who had been dispatched to the front at the first alarm, returned with the intelligence that it was only the half-starved pickets firing at some pigs which came within range of their muskets. The loud profanity of the general and the colonels was drowned by the shouts of the soldiers. High above all others was heard the mighty yell of the 200th Indiana.

The men of the other regiments crowded around the happy Hoosiers to bid them good-by and God-speed, and to fire a few parting shots.

"You fellers got the start of us by gittin' thar first, but we're all comin'."

"I reck'n ye're purty empty in the stumick, same 's we are, but when ye git up inter God's country don't eat every thing up. Tell the folks to save suthin fer the rest on us."

"Better peel off them old duds 'fore ye git home er yer gals won't know ye. They'll take ye fer a lot o' wagabonds."

The band at brigade headquarters played "The Girl I Left Behind Me," and then "Home, Sweet Home," as the 200th Indiana went swinging away on its "veteran furlough." The steps of those eager feet were longer than the regulation twenty-eight inches.

The distance to be marched would usually have taken three days; the homeward-bound regiment covered it in two; and no complaint was heard of aches or blisters. The fear that the time consumed in traveling would be taken out of the furlough, was quieted by the assurance of the officers that the full thirty days would be given after the regiment reached Indiana.

There was a day or two of impatient waiting when the railroad was reached, but at length a motley train of flat, box and odorous cattle cars was provided, and the men, not forgetting to yell, swarmed in and upon them. They were not disposed to be hypercritical about their accommodations.

When the first depot of supplies was reached they drew entire new outfits of clothing, from hats to hose. But for their weather-beaten faces, they might have been mistaken for new troops. The practiced eye, however, could easily detect the firm, confident step and soldierly bearing that told of long service.

ON THE WAY TO "GOD'S COUNTRY."

Wherever opportunity offered, during the homeward journey, extraordinary demands were made upon the hotels, restaurants, barber-shops and bath-houses. The effect of these various regenerating agencies was to so transform the men of the 200th Indiana into the semblance of civilized beings that their comrades, who were still crowding around the smoking fires in the forest bivouac, would have thought they belonged to another planet. Scraggly beards were shaved off; long mustaches were trimmed and waxed; heads were shorn of luxuriant crops of hair, and what remained was neatly combed and perfumed; collars and neckties were put on; and many indulged in the luxury of white shirts. Part of the bounty had been paid in advance, and money was lavishly spent. Expense was no consideration when anything was wanted.

A little more than a week from the day the regiment left the front Company Q reached home. Si Klegg had hoped to surprise his parents and sister and Annabel, but, as before, the telegraph had upset his plans. The news that the company would arrive spread through all that region, and the boys were received with great effusion of tears and cheers by a multitude of people.

In a moment Si was imprisoned in the arms of his mother and sister. When they released him he greeted Annabel, who was blushing like a peony, with a smack as loud as a pistol shot. He didn't care now who heard it. Then he presented Shorty all around, and "Si's pard" received abundant assurance that he was welcome.

Those were "red letter" days. Farmer Klegg's good wife and daughter cooked and cooked, and Si and Shorty ate and ate. Si frequently strolled over to the neighbor's house, and he and Annabel were unanimous in their opinion as to what they would do "when Johnny comes marching home." Shorty did not carry out his intention to stay only a few days. The proposition to go elsewhere was received with such disfavor by all the members of the family, including "sister Marier," that he was forced to yield, and passed the entire month at the hospitable home. Si even indulged the hope that Shorty and Maria might take a mutual "shine" to each other, but in this he was doomed to disappointment, so far, at least, as outward appearances were concerned. Shorty never got any further than to remark confidentially to Si that she was "a nice girl."

Si had feared that his mother and the rest would reproach him for re-enlisting, but the Spartan spirit was stronger than ever in their breasts, and they lavished upon him only words of love and prayer and blessing.

The happy days passed swiftly, and yet Si and Shorty grew impatient to return. It was with cheerful hearts that they said adieus and went whirling away to the place of rendezvous. The men were prompt to report, and when the regiment was drawn up to take the train a distinguished citizen, in behalf of admiring friends, presented to it a new stand of colors, with a burst of sanguinary eloquence. Then, amidst the shouts of the multitude, the 200th Indiana started again for the field of glory.

The soldiers knew, by long experience, just what they wanted and what they did not want. They had all improved the opportunity to fit themselves out with small coffee-pots and frying-pans, and a few other articles of necessity and convenience; but all the ill-judged though kindly efforts of mothers and sisters and sweethearts to load them down as they did when they first went to the war, were mildly but firmly resisted. The most important investment made by Si and Shorty was in providing themselves with Henry repeating rifles—sixteen-shooters—and a bountiful supply of ammunition.

" I reck'n them 'll make the Johnnies feel tired," remarked Si.

CHAPTER XLII.

"SAY, Shorty, what kind o' contrivance is a shelter tent?"

This inquiry was occasioned by an order from the commanding general, which had just been read to the 200th Indiana on dress-parade, to the effect that the army would move on the following day. A protracted campaign was expected, and all company baggage would be sent to the rear. Tents were included in the order, and everything else except what the men—and officers below the rank of colonel—could carry on their backs. Although the order did not say so in words, there was good reason to believe that the soldiers would bid a last farewell to their comfortable canvas dwellings, for in their place shelter tents— whatever they were—would be issued immediately, and the army must strip itself down to the lightest marching order possible.

Si never had heard of a shelter tent before, and he naturally wanted to know what it was. Shorty was not able to throw any light on the subject, and further inquiry developed a dense and universal ignorance. In fact everybody in Company Q was trying as hard to find out as Si was. They asked the captain and he didn't know—at least he said he didn't, and as the officers were never known to tell fibs, what he said was probably true.

574

In 1861 most of the troops, on taking the field, were furnished with the "Sibley" tent. This was a spacious pavilion, large enough for a good-sized circus to show in. When pitched it was a perfect cone in shape, the apex be ing fully twelve feet from the ground. The foot of the center-pole rested upon an iron tripod, the limbs of which straddled out like those of a "daddy-longlegs," covering a great amount of territory. This tripod, with sprawling feet, seemed to have been invented expressly for the soldiers to stumble over when moving about at night. It was admirably adapted to this purpose.

The writer remembers a burly fellow of his mess coming in at midnight after a trick of duty. The tripod caught him on the shin and threw him heavily across the feet of three or four of his messmates. A stenographic report of the remarks that were made would not be good Sunday reading. Leaping to his feet in a raging condition, the soldier sought to wreak his vengeance upon the tripod. Seizing one of the legs he gave it a tremendous "yank" which threw out the center-pole, and the tent came down flat upon the baker's dozen of prostrate forms. The pole in its promiscuous descent struck the head of one of the boys and raised a protuberance that lasted him a fortnight. There were three or four nationalities represented in the mess, and for some minutes a spirited conversation was carried on in as many different languages. Nearly the whole company turned out to see what the riot was about. The captain came on the run, looking like a ghost in his white underclothing, evidently thinking an insurrection had broken out. At length, when their wrath had somewhat abated, the boys fell to and put up the tent. To the credit of the shelter-tent may be placed the fact that after it was in use no catastrophe of this kind was possible.

Five or six Sibley tents were supplied to a company, and the men were packed like sardines in a box, from fifteen to eighteen in each. At night they lay with their feet mixed

up with those of the tripod around the center, while
their bodies radiated outward to all points of the
compass, like the spokes of a wagon wheel, their heads
fringing the outer rim. Each man's knapsack marked the
particular section of ground that belonged to him. Before
the messes began to be thinned out by the casualties of
war, the men slept like a great circular row of spoons, and
if one wanted to turn over to give the bones on the other
side a chance, it was difficult to do so without creating a
serious disturbance in the harmony of the formation. So
he would yell out the order to "flop" and all would go
over together, reversing the spoon along the whole line.

The Sibley tents were cumbrous things to handle, and
enormously bulky. A regiment with sixty of them, and all
other baggage in proportion, required a train of wagons
sufficient to transport a menagerie. The lumbering vehicles, crammed to the top of the bows, with camp-kettles,
knapsacks, and odds and ends of all kinds hung on at
every available point, made a picturesque and imposing
parade as they filed out upon the road.

But the Sibley tent had to "go." The armies grew rapidly, and it became a grave question whether there were in
the country enough mules available to haul Sibleys for a
million men. The second year of the war the shrinkage
began. In the writer's experience there was a disastrous
collapse that was sudden and complete. Caught in a tight
place, the tents and baggage of three or four brigades were
burned that they might not fall into the hands of the enemy.
They made a splendid fire, but the hearts of the houseless
tramps sank as they saw them disappear in that great
holocaust. During the twelve weeks that followed, of almost constant marching—amidst the chilling rains of fall
and winter, often bivouacking in cultivated fields, with mud
over shoe-tops—those men did not once sleep under the
friendly cover of a tent.

To justify the writer in giving his own recollections of

the Sibley tent, he puts in evidence the fact that Si Klegg did not shoulder a musket until after the reducing process was well advanced. The Sibley had wholly disappeared from the field, and was only used where troops were permanently stationed.

After the Sibley came the "A" or "Wedge" tent—the shape of which is, perhaps, indicated clearly enough by its name—and the "Bell" tent, which was much like it, except that it swelled out at each end, increasing its capacity. Five or six men could be comfortably domiciled in the A tent, and from eight to ten in the Bell. A year or so later the quartermaster gave the thumb-screw another turn and squeezed out the unique shelter tent, which was as near the point of none at all as it was possible to reach.

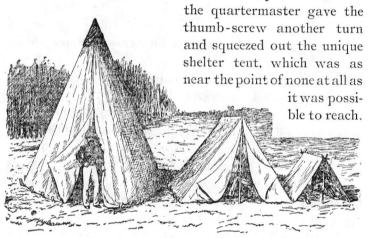

THE SHRINKAGE OF THE TENT.

Early in the morning the members of the 200th Indiana received their shelter tents. To each man was given a piece of stout cotton cloth, about six feet long and four feet wide. Along one edge half of them had a row of buttons, and the other half had button-holes to correspond. It took two— one of each kind—to make a tent, in which two men were to live and move and have their being.

In the scramble to get possession of the newest thing in war—this masterpiece of military invention—the halves were distributed in the most miscellaneous way, without any reference to the buttons and button-holes. It will be easily understood that it was indispensable for two men to "go snacks" on the tent business, and that "pards" must have two pieces that would go together.

Si and Shorty found themselves each with a section that was decorated with a row of buttons. They had not yet been enlightened as to the manner in which a beneficent government intended they should be used.

"Well I'll be dog-goned, ef that thing don't *git* me!" exclaimed Si, after he had thoroughly inspected this work of genius, turning it over and around and eyeing it from every possible point of view, longitudinally, transversely and diagonally. "That's the queerest thing fer a tent I ever heern tell of. Got any idee how the old thing works, Shorty?"

The latter had also been wrestling with the problem, and his mental processes seemed to have been rather more successful than those of his comrade. He told Si that he believed he could see through the scheme. Inquiring around among the other members of Company Q, all of whom were similarly engaged, he found that part of the pieces had holes where his own and Si's had buttons. Bringing his reasoning faculties into play he was not long in reaching a satisfactory conclusion.

"I'll tell ye, Si," he said, "ourn don't fit 'cause they've got all buttons. That's what's the dif-*fu*-culty. Part on 'em 's got button-holes, 'n' one on us 'll have ter trade with some feller that's got more holes 'n he knows what ter do with, 'n' then we'll see 'f we can't make 'em jine!"

A little inquiry developed the same confusion on all sides. There was a general effort to secure a proper adjustment of the pieces, and exchanges were quickly and cheerfully made.

"Thar!" exclaimed Shorty, "you begin on that side 'n' let's button 'er up 'n' see what she looks like!"

In a minute their nimble fingers had connected the two pieces.

"Wall," said Si, "I don't see nothin' yet 't looks like a tent." And his curious eye critically surveyed the cloth that lay spread out upon the ground.

"Jest you wait a bit, 'n' I'll show ye a trick," said his comrade. "We'll try 'n' find out how she goes 'fore we start this mornin', so we'll know whether we're goin' ter have anything ter sleep under t'night. You hunt up a couple o' forked stakes 'bout 's high 's yer bread-basket, 'n' I'll squint 'round fer a ridge-pole."

Si was not long in finding his part of the outfit, and Shorty soon appeared with a stick an inch in diameter and six or seven feet long. They forced the stakes a little way into the ground and put the ridge-pole in place.

"Now stretch 'er over," said Shorty, "'n' we'll have a tent 'fore ye know it."

Suiting the action to the word they threw the cloth across the pole and pulled it out each way at the bottom, fastening it to the ground by pegs driven through the loops of stout twine provided for that purpose.

"Thar, what does *that* look like?" observed Shorty, as he cast an admiring glance upon the imposing structure.

"Looks to me more like a chicken-coop er a dog-kennel 'n it does like a house fer two men ter live in," said Si.

It could not be denied that there was force in Si's remark. It was three feet high to the ridge, and the "spread" at the bottom was about four feet.

"Git down on yer marrow bones 'n' crawl in," said Shorty, himself setting the example. They went in on their hands and knees and squatted upon the ground. Their heads rubbed against the sloping sides.

"Beats all creation, don't it Shorty? Ef we had the man here 't built that thing we'd toss him 'n a blanket t'll he couldn't tell which eend his head was on; 'n' then we'd set the fifes ter playin' the Rogue's March 'n' ride him out o' camp on a rail."

This expression of opinion seemed to meet with universal approval from the rest of the company, as they gathered around for the purpose of inspection. If the inventor of the concern had made his appearance at that moment, had he succeeded in making his escape at all from the avenging fury of those exasperated Hoosiers, it would have been in a badly disabled condition. Taunts and scoffs and jeers, and words of harsher sound, were hurled at that poor little tent. It is safe to say that no new thing ever produced on this or any other continent was greeted with such a torrent of ridicule and vituperation. Some of the boys crowed and clucked after the manner of fowls, while others whistled at Si and Shorty as if to call out the dogs from their kennel. It was immediately christened the "pup" tent, and till the end of the war it was known only by that name, through all the armies, from the Potomac to the Rio Grande. Often the

THE "PUP" TENT.

ridicule conveyed by this name was intensified by putting in another letter and making it "purp."

There were many names, words and phrases in the free-and-easy language of the soldiers that were universal. It seemed as though some of them had their origin spontaneously, and at the same time, in armies hundreds of miles apart; or, starting at one point, they were carried upon the winds to the remotest camps. Wherever the flag floated, the staff of army life was called "hardtack." Its adjunct, bacon, was known by that name only on the requisitions and books of the commissaries. An officer's shoulder-straps were "sardine-boxes" and his sword was a "toad-stabber" or "cheese-knife." A brigade commander was a "jigadier-brindle;" camp rumors were "grapevines;" marching was "hoofing it;" troops permanently stationed in the rear were known as "feather-bed soldiers;" and raw recruits were "fresh-fish." Among scores of expressions, many of them devoid of sense or meaning except as they were used by the soldiers, were "Grab a root;" "Hain't got the sand;" "Git thar', Eli;" "Here's yer mule;" "Same old rijiment only we've drawed new clothes;" "Go for 'em;" "Hunt yer holes;" "Bully fer you." The word "bully"—more expressive than elegant—entered largely into the army vernacular; it seemed to "fit" almost anywhere.

Since the war there have been a score of widely different explanations of the origin of "Grab a root!" It was heard in every regiment, and its application was widely diversified. If a comrade on foot made a mis-step, or an accident of any kind befell one who was mounted, a hundred men would yell "Grab a root!" The boys usually took great satisfaction in shouting it in the ears of a gay and dashing staff officer, who might be galloping along the flank of a moving column, or between the blue lines on either side of the road during a "rest." If he chanced to be an unskillful rider, and bumped about in his saddle, he was vociferously exhorted to "grab a root." The theory of the yelling soldiers seemed to be that if he would do this he might be able to save himself from tumbling off his horse. The helpless officer usually looked as if he would like to "grab" a whole armful of good-sized "roots" and fling them at the heads of his tormentors. The boys did not often try it on a general—unless it was night, and pretty dark.

The soldiers of the 200th Indiana loaded upon the wagons the tents that had so long sheltered them, and they never saw them again. The order said they would be sent to the rear "for the present," but the boys learned in course of time just what that meant. Henceforward the "pup" tent was to be their only protection from sun and storm.

When the call was sounded for the regiment to fall in and take the road, Si and Shorty found that it did not require more than two minutes to "strike" their little tent, detach the halves, and roll them up ready for transportation. Each half weighed scarcely more than two pounds and its addition to the soldier's load was barely appreciable.

By this time Si had reached that stage in his army career when he could wholly dispense with a knapsack. Shorty had parted company with his some time before, and Si had been thinking for a good while about cutting loose from this incumbrance. All the sentimental notions, of which his head was so full when he started out, had entirely vanished. With them had disappeared the last vestige of everything that was not a necessity, save only Annabel's well-worn locket—which had a permanent resting place near the spot where he imagined his heart to be located—and two or three trifling keepsakes that he stowed away in the pockets of his blouse and trousers. His knapsack was about worn out, anyway, and he concluded it was not worth while to draw another. His "dress coat," in which he used to feel so grand at Sunday morning inspection and evening parade, had long since gone to join "the innumerable caravan" of things which, at first considered indispensable, came to be only a useless burden. In fact he did not have anything to carry in his knapsack worth speaking of. Sometimes he had an extra shirt or pair of drawers and sometimes he didn't. He was equally well and comfortable and happy, whether he had or had not a reserve supply of these articles. When he had no clothes except those he wore, he found abundant compensation for his poverty in the fact that his load was so much the lighter. When his shirt gave abundant evidence that its days of usefulness were past he would draw a new one, put it on, and throw the old one away.

In short, Si had now "learned his trade." Some had proved more apt pupils than he, for he had been loth to cast away his cherished idols; but at last he had mastered his lesson. Little by little he had found that there was a great deal besides knowing how to load a gun and push a bayonet that was necessary to make a toughened and thoroughly efficient soldier—one who could be depended upon not only to charge up to the mouths of blazing cannon, but to march twenty-five miles a day and do picket duty at night, on half rations, in all kinds of weather, for weeks at a stretch. Such men there were, by tens of thousands, whom nothing but the deadly missiles of war could kill.

So when Si, that morning, rolled up his overcoat and half of a pup tent inside his blanket, tied the ends together, threw it over his shoulder, and marched off at a swinging gait, he was justly entitled to be classed as a veteran—a soldier, in the fullest significance of the word. He was one of the happy-go-lucky sort, who took things as they came and never had "the blues." To him the rain did not seem so wet, nor the sun so hot, nor the "tack" so hard, nor the miles so long, nor his "traps" so much as if they weighed a hundred ounces to the pound, as they did to those less buoyant and elastic in spirit than he. Blisters came less often than formerly upon his now calloused feet; when they did, he would tramp along just the same. He had "got used to it."

"They're gittin' things down ter a purty fine p'int, ain't they, Shorty," he said, as he trudged along, "makin' us lug our houses on our backs, 'sides the muskits 'n' am'nition 'n' groceries 'n' bed'n. I don't see 's they c'n crowd us any furder 'nless they makes us tote the ossifers' duds.

Mebbe they'll pile onto us the hay 'n' corn ter feed the hosses. It's bin gittin' wuss 'n' wuss ever since we fust started out, but I can't 'magine what it'll be next. P'r'aps arter we've marched the mules to death they'll hitch *us* ter the waggins. I reck'n that wouldn't be much wuss 'n some things we *have* had ter do. D'ye s'pose ye'd ha' 'listed, Shorty, ef ye'd ha' knowed all 't ye had to go through?"

"Would *you*, Si?"

"I — b'lieve — I — would," he replied, speaking slowly and thoughtfully. "I *know* I would," he added, "but mebbe I wouldn't ha' been quite so fierce 's I was fer gittin' in. I didn't s'pose ther' was very much reel solid fun 'n goin' to war, 'n' I hain't found no reason yet ter change my notion. Ther' is a leetle bit, now 'n' then, 'n' ye know I've allus tried ter git all ther' was goin'. But ye didn't answer my question yet."

SI AS A VETERAN.

"Oh, 'twouldn't ha' mattered much ter me," replied Shorty. "I 'low 't I went in with my eyes opened wider 'n yourn was. Ye know I'd had a tetch on it in the three months' sarvice, though that wa'n't a patchin' ter what I've struck since I j'ined this 'ere rijiment. I 'xpected hard knocks 'n' I've got 'em, so I ain't noways dis'p'inted. But I tell ye what 'tis, Si, I b'lieve there's more 'n one man dead that 'd bin livin' yet if he'd had sich a feller 's you be fer a pard. It makes a heap more diff'runce 'n ye think whether a man 's down in the mouth all the time er not. Ye've been wuth more ter me 'n forty-'leven doctors. I hain't never tuk no medicine 'cept when I was playin' off, 'n' I don't 'ntend ter 'f I c'n help it."

Every day were more firmly cemented the ties that bound together Si and Shorty. Each knew the other's true, manly worth, and the hardships and dangers shared and the sufferings endured had so united them that in their thoughts and feelings, their devotion to duty and to each other, their hearts were as one. They were friends of the kind that "sticketh closer than a brother," and would have faced for each other any peril, however great.

As the army halted, toward evening, the great bivouac presented a scene of unwonted activity. There was a general rush to put up the new tents. The adjacent woods literally swarmed with men in quest of forked sticks and poles, the demand for which quite exhausted the supply. Then in a few minutes, as if by magic, the little patches of white cloth dotted field and hillside, far and near. For fifty thousand men there were twenty-five thousand of them. It was almost as if an untimely snow-storm had whitened the earth.

With a mixture of mirth and profanity, the men crept into and took possession of their novel quarters. An army on its knees would have been, under certain conditions, a most gratifying spectacle to the chaplains, but it is to be feared that the universal posture at this time afforded them little spiritual encouragement. The language generally used did not indicate that the army was engaged in evening devotions. The men scrambled around and "made down" the beds. Such as could get an armful of straw counted themselves fortunate, while others made mattresses of boughs or bushes.

After supper they stretched out their weary limbs to rest. They made the night hideous with their yells and cat-calls and barkings, as if they imagined themselves transformed into the various species of domestic animals that might be supposed to inhabit such dwellings. They made the quartermaster, who supplied them with the pup-tents, wish that he had never been born. The commanding general, who issued the order for the quartermaster to do it, came in for his full share of attention.

Occasions were not infrequent when whole regiments and brigades, utterly disregarding the sanctity of rank, filled the air with yells and shouts and gibes aimed directly at certain officers, often in high command, on account of some order or action that was distasteful to the men. Dark nights were usually taken advantage of for such performances, when it was impossible to identify individual offenders. If an officer tried to "catch" anybody at it, he found himself attempting the biggest job of his life. Hearing the derisive shouts in a company on one flank of the regiment, he would hasten thither only to find the men snoring as if asleep. Then there would be an outbreak on the other flank and away he would go in that direction, with no better success than before.

As a rule, officers paid little attention to this badinage, as long as it was harmless, permitting the boys to have their fun. They knew that it meant nothing, and that those who yelled the loudest and said the most irreverent things, would, on the morrow, at their command, leap into the very jaws of death. None knew as well as the generals how much the efficiency of an army was enhanced by keeping the soldiers in good spirits.

Sometimes the shafts of ridicule were so keenly pointed and fired with such unerring and persistent aim, that their stings became unendurable, and the goaded officers would charge around in a furious rage, threatening the offenders with the most awful and tremendous punishments. Usually the boys made life a burden to such an officer to the end of the war, if he remained in the service so long.

Here and there was a "West Pointer," whose punctilious ideas of the respect due to epaulettes and gold-lace would not permit him under any circumstances to "take a joke" that came from the rank and file. If he chanced to be the beneficiary of the vocal "shivaree" (as they call it in the west)—and he was quite as likely as any one to be the target of the wild volunteers—a storm was pretty certain to follow. That officer was fortunate who could act the part of wisdom, and laugh with the rest at the rude and noisy jests of the soldiers, as they rolled about in their pup tents or stumbled along through the tedious hours of a night march, even though their words might cut to the quick. The only sure and speedy way to put an end to the "racket" was to pay no attention to it. If the men found that an officer was "bored" he was likely to be assailed again and again, with redoubled vigor.

A very common and effective method that was popular among the troops—probably less so among the helpless victims—was for a stout-lunged soldier to shout at the top of his voice a question touching upon some foible or peccadillo of an officer. Another stentorian patriot, perhaps at some distant point in the regiment, would answer by yelling out the name of the officer in a tone that could be heard half a mile. This colloquial exercise was not unlike that carried on between the "interlocutor" and "end-men" of a minstrel troupe. Those among the officers who could conceal from the boys their weak spots—for all were human, and many very much so—were smarter men than the average. All these things were carefully treasured up in the memories of the soldiers, and every now and then, when the conditions were favorable, and the boys were in the right humor, there came a "snap" of very cold weather for those unlucky officers.

On the night in question the soldiers of the 200th Indiana, after they had exhausted their rage and wit upon the pup-tent and the hapless quartermaster, took up the catechism, in the manner described.

"Who stole the ham?" shouted an anxious inquirer.

"Captain Smith!" was the answer, loud and clear.

"Who got behind a tree at Stone River?"—from another voice.

"*Lef*-tenant Brown!"

"Who gobbled the lone widow's chickens?"

"Capting-g-g Jones!"

"Who drank too much applejack?"

"Major Robinson!"

"Who got sick at Mission Ridge?"

"Lieutenant Johnsing!"

"Who tried to run the guards and got nabbed?"

"Colonel Williams!"

"Who stole the black bottle from the sutler?"

"Lieutenant Duzenberry!"

"Who played off to ride in the ambulance?"

"Captain Smart!"

"Say boys, ther' won't be no fightin' tomorrow."

"Why?"

"'Cause Capt'n Dodgit 's up with the ridgment."

So it went, until the entire list had been exhausted, for there were few officers concerning whom something had not been put in pickle for such occasions. A few impetuous victims made matters infinitely worse by prancing around in a high state of excitement, threatening their relentless tormentors with sword and pistol; but they did not shoot or "prod" anybody—the boys knew they wouldn't—and their impotent wrath expended itself in vain; the odds against them were too great. The sound of the "taps," that always brought quiet to the camp, came like a balm to their wounded spirits.

Such was the advent of the pup-tent in the 200th Indiana —and in hundreds of other regiments. It marked a new epoch in the increasingly active campaigns of the great armies. These were now mobilized to a degree that had at no previous time been reached, being almost wholly freed from the enormous quantities of baggage that in the earlier years of the war incumbered their movements with immense trains. Wagons were scarcely needed except for transporting supplies of food, clothing, ammunition and hospital stores.

As for the soldiers, their aversion to the shelter tent soon disappeared. Before many months elapsed they had come to regard it as an unmixed blessing. Under the former regime, when the army was in motion the wagons were often in the rear for days and weeks together, and the soldiers were compelled to brave the weather, wholly unprotected, save by such imperfect shelters as could be improvised. The despised and much-reviled pup-tent proved to be the one thing needful. What a man carried on his back he was always sure of, and this was the only kind of transportation that he could depend upon.

After the soldiers began to take more kindly to their new quarters, straitened though they were, they would as soon have thought of campaigning without their blankets as without their pup tents. They came to be exceedingly dexterous in pitching them. A few minutes only was required, whenever and wherever the army stopped. If no woods were at hand to supply the convenient forked sticks, rails and boards were split, or pieces of cracker boxes pressed into the service—anything with a small notch cut in one end in which the ridge-pole could rest would answer the purpose. If other sources of supply failed the soldier could always fall back on his musket. Two "pards" would "fix" their bayonets and thrust them into the ground, one at each end of the tent, catch the edges of the cloth between the nipples and the hammers of the inverted guns, and the dwelling was ready for occupancy. In such a case no ridge-pole was necessary. At the signal to strike tents they would disappear almost in an instant, as if the camp were swept by a tornado.

Under ordinary conditions of weather they furnished comfortable shelter. True, a hard rain would beat through them, and trickle in baptismal streams over the inmates; a furious wind would sometimes play sad havoc with the fragile structures, tearing them from their fastenings and sending them flying through the air in wild confusion. A visitation of this kind at night, with the accompaniment of a copious rain, was somewhat calamitous in its effects upon both the comfort and the tempers of those so rudely unhoused; but it was only an incident in the soldier's life that passed away with the morrow's sunshine.

One edition of the pup tent was provided with a three-cornered piece of cloth, which, after the tent was pitched, was quickly joined on with buttons and entirely closed one end, contributing much to the well-being of the dwellers within. In many of those issued to the troops this convenient part was wanting, and the lack was supplied, as far as possible, by a rubber blanket, or a chance piece of cloth picked up with this end—that is, the end of the pup-tent—in view. Sometimes a night raid among the mule-drivers would yield a very serviceable fragment ruthlessly cut from a wagon-cover.

Next to the hardtack and the "grayback," no feature of army life will dwell longer or more vividly in the memories of the veterans of the war than the Pup Tent.

CHAPTER XLIII.

THE campaign of 1864 was unlike any that preceded it. Up to that time the grand divisions of the Union army had moved spasmodically, and without concert of action, each plunging forward with music and banners, and then rushing back again, as the enemy, on his shorter interior lines, concentrated his forces at the point assailed. This policy seemed likely, as shown by the experience of three years, to prolong the struggle indefinitely. Now and then a town of little or no importance to either side was wrested from the enemy and its capture was announced by the newspapers in hysterical head-lines. When the people at the North read that Culpeper Court-house, or Corinth, or Little Rock had been taken, perhaps without anybody being hurt, they fondly believed that the Gibraltar of the South had fallen, the back-bone of the rebellion was at last broken, and nothing now remained to be done but to appoint a receiver to wind up the affairs of the so-called Southern Confederacy. So they shouted themselves hoarse and made congratulatory speeches, amidst the blare of bands, the ringing of bells, and the combustion of powder. But the rebel armies generally got away when they wanted to, and turned up at unexpected times and places, as pugnacious as ever.

At length a great light dawned upon those in authority. The important discovery was made that marching triumphantly into decayed and deserted towns, and impressively

591

planting the stars and stripes on empty court-houses, would never end the war, so long as the military power of the enemy remained unbroken. By this time "the wayfaring man though a fool" could comprehend the truth that the rebellion was not to be crushed by sounding official proclamations, nor by fervid rhetorical emanations from the brains of valorous "On-to-Richmond" editors. It could only be accomplished by the persistent use of powder and lead, and an occasional prod with the bayonet. Without taking issue upon the pleasing and poetic proposition that "the pen is mightier than the sword," it may confidently be asserted that for the job in question the musket outranked the pen as much as a resplendent major-general did a high private in the rear rank.

So it was that in 1864 came the long, persistent "tug" of the war. East and west the Union forces moved simultaneously, with unity of purpose and action—fighting the rebel armies whenever and wherever they could be found. There was to be no more "sparring for wind," but a mighty clinch and a "rough-and-tumble" for the mastery. The fiction of superior valor or military prowess on either side had been exploded. At the worst it was believed that the rebels could be beaten in the end, dearly-bought though the victory might be, by the same process that is sometimes employed in playing at "checkers." Having secured a slight numerical advantage over his adversary the player deliberately proceeds to "man him down," giving a life for each one he takes, and thus vanquishes him at last. This is the game that was played during the last and bloodiest year of the war, and it succeeded. More men were killed and wounded by lead and iron in the desperate grapple from April, 1864, to April, 1865, than during the previous three years. Better so, with all the sickening scenes of carnage, than to have had the struggle prolonged and thrice the number borne to their graves from a hundred hospitals and prisons during the slowly-dragging years. The price paid was a high one, but the economy of the purchase cannot be questioned.

The rank and file of the Union armies cheerfully accepted the new order of things. In fact, the idea that this was the way to put down the rebellion took possession of the minds of the soldiers long before it reached headquarters. Bravely, patiently and without complaint they faced the enemy's guns day after day, through weeks and months, and willingly made the awful sacrifice that was demanded. Surely no less can be said of the men of the Confederate armies, in their gallant and yet hopeless struggle. The pages of history bear no record of grander heroism and fortitude than were shown by American soldiers, North and South, during the last year of our civil war.

"Looks ter me, Shorty," said Si, the first night of the great campaign, "the way we're startin' out this time, 's though we wa'n't goin' ter fool with the rebils no longer. When we only whip 'em once 'n a while they don't stay whipped wuth a continental. We've got ter jest keep lickin' on 'em—git 'em on the run 'n' make 'em go t'll they're tired. I hain't got no military eddication, but I b'lieve ther' ain't no other way ter squush this rebellion. Ef the gin'rals had axed me I'd ha' told 'em so long ago. Course I don't know what they're goin' ter do, but I've got 'n idee they'll keep us a-humpin' fer a while."

"Does seem kind o' that way," replied Shorty. "I figger it out 't ther's got ter be 'bout so much shootin' 'n' bein' shot ter do the business, 'n' it'll be a heap better ter keep peckin' away 'thout givin' 'em no chance ter rest t'll we wind the thing up. One o' the boys was sayin' 't he seed a noosepaper today 't told how all the armies was gittin' ready ter move, 'n' I reck'n they're goin' ter shake up the Johnnies purty lively. I've got the same notion 't you have, Si, 'n' ef I kin see through a ladder we'll have livelier music 'n' more on it 'n we've heerd afore."

Being unanimous in their verdict upon the outlook for

the immediate future, there was no chance for argument; so they crawled into their dog-tent and went to sleep.

Two hours before daylight they were aroused to stand at arms until dawn. For months this enforced habit of rising at an exasperating hour was continued. So far as the soldiers were concerned, Ben Franklin's proverb was without force, as "early to rise" made them neither "healthy," "wealthy"—at thirteen dollars a month—nor "wise."

The enemy was within easy reach, and there was no trouble in finding him that day. He was full of fight and stubbornly resisted the advance. Then was begun the bloody struggle that, through weary weeks and months, put to the severest test that mind can conceive the valor and endurance of the well-tried soldiers of both armies. Skirmishing was incessant, and bri-

NOT TO BE CAUGHT NAPPING.

gades, divisions and corps often met in the dreadful shock of battle. The whiz of bullet and scream of shell became so familiar to the ear that they were almost robbed of their terrors. So long as a soldier was not hit he regarded with a stoical indifference to self the work of death that was constantly going on around him. The senses became calloused. The killing and mangling of fellow-beings was the every-day vocation. Men engaged in it with no more compunction than if they were hunting game. The finer feelings were seared and deadened by the fiery breath of war.

Day after day the soldiers marched and dug rifle-pits and built long, tortuous lines of intrenchments, under the fierce midsummer sun—today charging the enemy in open field, and tomorrow by a flank movement forcing him to abandon his chosen position. They lay behind works, looking into the very muzzles of hostile muskets and cannon. At times the lines were so near together that there was no room for pickets. Whole brigades glared upon one another with sleepless eyes, by day and by night. If a head or body were exposed, though but for an instant, on either side, a hundred rifles cracked and a hundred bullets sped on their errand. Every hour death reaped its fearful harvest. Men were buried beside the trenches in which they fell. Surgeons lay behind the breastworks to care for the wounded, who could only be borne to the rear under cover of the darkness.

Officers and soldiers slept in their clothes, with swords and muskets in their hands. Rarely a night passed without an alarm. An exchange of shots on the picket-line always awoke the soundest sleeper, and in half a minute he was standing in his place at the works. Often the men lay down in two long lines and had but to spring up to be in order of battle. At crack of musket and whistle of bullet, ten thousand—twenty thousand—fifty thousand soldiers rose as if by magic, grasping their trusty weapons. It was no uncommon thing for this to occur twice or thrice in a night. At no time, sleeping or waking, was a soldier where he could not seize his musket and be ready in an instant for any duty.

Even the privates became skilled in the arts of war. The general movements were directed by those in command, but so far as the details were concerned the soldiers knew as well as the officers what to do and how to do it. They no longer deemed it a mark of cowardice to take advantage of any cover that opportunity offered. On the contrary, the man who did *not* do this was set down as a fool. Skirmishers dodged from tree to tree, now crouching behind a stump or log for a shot and then dashing ahead; now creeping along a fence or wall and then taking the double-quick across a field or "open"—in every possible way shielding themselves from the fire of the enemy, but always pushing forward and shrinking from no necessary danger.

Whenever pickets were stationed there was not a moment of rest until a little fortification had been thrown up at each post that would stop musket balls. Rails, logs, stones, were hastily piled, and with bayonets, tin-cups and plates, or anything that would scratch up the ground, holes were dug and the dirt was used to strengthen the work. Back at the main line all hands were busy, each regiment covering its front with a strong intrenchment. Assaults were made by the enemy with scarcely a moment's warning, and the men toiled with their guns slung over their shoulders. Often when the work of intrenching was but half done the sharp crack of muskets, the zip and patter of bullets and the wild rebel yell sent the soldiers scampering into line to meet the onset. After repulsing the enemy a counter-charge was likely to follow, and the instant a halt was ordered the men fell to and in an incredibly brief time would have another long line of works, behind which they eagerly watched for the foe. A few axes, picks and shovels were carried by each regiment, and for hasty intrenching were invaluable. During the early years of the war these menial implements had been regarded with ineffable scorn and contempt. In 1864 a shovel was as indispensable as a coffee-pot. Frequently, as the troops changed their positions, two or three heavy lines of works, miles in length, were thrown up in a day. Weariness and hunger were not thought of until the fortifying was done. Then, with their muskets in hand or slung upon their backs, the soldiers would quickly start their little fires for making coffee and toasting bacon.

The supply of rations during such a campaign was somewhat precarious. To feed an army of a hundred thousand men and thirty thousand animals, and keep it in ammunition and other things needful, required at least one hundred and thirty car loads, of ten tons each, per day.* These had to be transported a long distance over a single line of railroad every mile of which must be guarded. It was the constant effort—often successful—of the enemy's cavalry to "cut the cracker-line," by making wide detours around the Union army and by sudden dashes tearing up the railroad, burning bridges and blowing up culverts. These interruptions occasionally made it necessary for the soldiers to be put on half rations.

In that wonderful army were multitudes representing all the learned professions and mechanical trades. Men carried swords and muskets who could preach a sermon, argue a case at law, amputate a leg or edit a newspaper. There were soldiers who could build a bridge, put up and operate a telegraph line, or make anything, from a watch to a locomotive. To provide for contingencies a corps of engineers and mechanics was organized, whose special duty it was to repair the ravages of the Confederate raiders and keep intact the slender thread of communication between the great army in the field and its remote base of supplies. So promptly and efficiently was this important service performed that when a shortage in the supply of hardtack and bacon told the army that there was another break, it was rarely more than two or three days till the whistle of the locomotive, as it went puffing up to the front, set the soldiers to yelling like lunatics.

* Sherman's Memoirs. Vol. II, p. 11.

This was the way the soldiers lived and marched and fought during that bloody year, that filled so many graves, but conquered the rebellion. It was not, as before, an occasional battle, with long intervals of "all quiet on the Potomac," the Tennessee and the Mississippi—when the soldiers spent their time in lying idly under the trees or building forts and breastworks far in the rear—when if the hostile armies moved at all it was in the effort to keep out of each other's way and avoid a collision. It was a continuous fight, month after month. No man, on opening his eyes in the morning, was secure in the belief that before night he would not be dead and buried, or a subject for the knife and saw of the surgeon. Not an hour—a moment—of life was assured. The impressive truth that "In the midst of life we are in death" has no such meaning to those dwelling under peaceful skies as it had to the brave, patient thousands who spent the long days and nights on the outposts and in the trenches, amidst blazing muskets and belching cannon.

It was upon this life that Si entered that pleasant May morning. Company Q of the 200th Indiana was on the skirmish-line and had not advanced far till it found enough in front to engage its undivided attention. The rebel pickets, as if they realized the aggressive spirit that was henceforth to animate the opposing army and were determined to follow suit, stubbornly contested the advance and yielded nothing except on compulsion. But the day had gone by when a spasmodic fusillade on the skirmish-line would cause the Union army to halt, establish and fortify its position, and wait to be attacked. "Go right for 'em, boys!" was the word passed along the line, and they went.

"This is business!" said Si to Shorty, as they darted from one tree to another, stopping for a moment to fire whenever they could see a "butternut" to shoot at. "We

ain't goin' ter have no more nonsense with them fellers.
We're jest goin' in ter win now."

Behind the skirmishers marched the compact battalions,
with steady step and the touch of elbows that always
gave the soldier confidence. Each man knew that he could
trust his comrades, upon the right and upon the left. They
had long marched and fought side by side. The leaders of
that army needed no assurance that those well-seasoned
regiments and brigades and divisions would be equal to

ON THE SKIRMISH LINE.

every demand that might be made upon them. It took
three years to create such an army, but when that veteran
host moved forward, with perfect mutual confidence between the soldiers and their commanders, it was invincible.

During its march the army reached a river, broad and
deep. All bridges over it had been destroyed by the re-
treating enemy. Two years earlier the army would have
halted for a week while the means for crossing were being
provided. Now it was not so.

"How we goin' ter git any furder?" exclaims Si, as he

and Shorty arrive at the bank and drop behind a log to escape the bullets that come singing over. "I'm 'feard we wouldn't make much headway swimmin' 'th all these traps on. Looks 's though we'd have ter knock off fer today."

"Wait a little while 'n' see," replies Shorty. "There's more 'n one way ter skin a cat."

One of the generals, accompanied by a staff officer or two, rides up. When within range of the hostile muskets he dismounts and gliding from one tree to another advances to the stream.

"The gin'rals dodges same 's we do, don't they, Shorty?" says Si.

"Course they does. They can't help it no more 'n you 'n' me kin. It's the sensiblest thing a feller kin do some times."

A single glance tells the officer what is to be done, and he scurries back to the rear. When it is necessary he will face without flinching a sheet of flame, though he fall before it, but now he does well to avoid the flying bullets.

"Pontoniers to the front!"

Away gallops one of the staff to bring up the train of wagons bearing the pontons—or pontoons as they were universally called. The "pongtong" of the Frenchman was not suited to the vocal organs of the American soldier.

The enemy on the farther bank shows his teeth and is making ominous preparations to dispute the passage of the river. On this side batteries are ordered into position to cover the laying of the bridge. A brigade is advanced to the river, where the men quickly throw up a barricade of logs, rails and earth. There is brisk firing from both sides. Neither force can advance upon the other, and it is simply a question which has the greater "nerve" and steadiness to endure the fire of its adversary.

Meantime a thousand men with axes are clearing a road to the point chosen as the most favorable for the bridge.

With a celerity little less than marvelous they fell trees, roll away logs, and open a pathway. Here comes the pontoon train, and the soldiers set up a mighty shout as the reeking mules plunge forward under stinging lash and maddening yell. With them come the pontoniers, at a double-quick, responding lustily to the vociferous greetings of their comrades. Here and there a mule falls, struck by a bullet that comes flying over, but ready knives slash the harness and cut him loose, and the rest dash furiously on.

Now batteries open and muskets blaze along both the river banks. The pontoniers stack arms and strip off their accouterments that they may work without incumbrance. They cannot stop to use their muskets and must go through the ordeal of being under fire without being able to return it. There is no more trying position in which soldiers can be placed. They must work rapidly, for every moment brings sacrifice of life and limb. The covering force redoubles its fire as the pontoniers spring to the pontoons and lift them from the wheels. The boats—frames of wood covered with heavy oiled canvas—are borne to the brink of the stream. One by one they are launched and floated to their positions. The connecting timbers are speedily put in—for every stick has been fitted to its place. A hundred men complete the work, as each successive boat is secured, by laying the planking of the roadway, soon to resound with the tread of those eager battalions. Long ropes, stretched diagonally to the shore above, prevent the bridge from being carried down by the current.

All this time cannon are hurling shot, shell and canister, and the air seems filled with hissing bullets. Much of the enemy's fire is directed at the pontoniers. Many of these are stricken down and lie helpless in the boats, or fall into the water and are borne away by the tide. Some are dead when they fall; others, disabled by cruel wounds, perish in the stream. But war and death are inseparable.

The work must not stop for an instant, and for every brave pontonier that falls a score of willing volunteers are ready to seize the plank or the oar that has dropped from his grasp.

Imagination cannot picture a scene of wilder uproar and confusion. The noise of artillery and musketry is incessant, to which are added the yells of the excited men, for it is not easy to "keep cool" with such surroundings. Officers shout their orders in vain; no words can be heard in the awful din. But it matters little, for those trained sol-

LAYING A PONTOON BRIDGE UNDER FIRE.

diers not only know what to do but they have the magnificent heroism to do it, and amidst the roar and crash, the wild shout and the scream of pain, the work goes steadily and surely on.

Down on the fast-lengthening bridge are Si and Shorty, working with might and main, unmindful of the bullets that patter around them and bury themselves in the planks they carry. They are among those who so promptly volunteered to fill the places made vacant, and none are more active and efficient than they. It is a new sphere of labor and a new test of courage, but there is not a thought of quailing.

Now the bridge stretches almost to the farther shore, and the water is but hip deep.

"Fall in 200th Indiana! Forward—Double-quick—March!"

The brave colonel dashes ahead and the men follow with a yell. Their swift feet clatter upon the planks and the floating bridge sways and throbs under their tread. Fast and furious is the fire of the Union batteries to cover the perilous passage. Unmindful of the bullets that are thinning the ranks the men push on, leap into the water and scramble up the bank. No human power can stay their progress. They throw themselves upon the enemy and break his line. Another regiment has followed, and another. To right and left they charge the hostile force, which yields before the onslaught and flees in dismay. The crossing is secured. The bridge is quickly finished, and for hours it quivers beneath the marching feet of endless brigades and divisions, and the rumbling wheels of artillery and wagons freighted with material to supply all the enginery of war.

Thus the barrier was passed, and the eyes of the enemy were opened to the spirit that animated and nerved the Union army during that final struggle—a spirit that found true expression in those historic words of the great Captain, which were an inspiration to the soldiers and to the patient, praying millions at home: "I propose to fight it out on this line if it takes all summer."

Day after day the campaign went on. Week after week the soldiers marched with their faces to the foe, or stood in the trenches with loaded muskets. Behind the fortified lines they dug "gopher-holes" in which they slept, to avoid the plunging shot from the enemy's cannon. Time and again they flanked him out of his chosen positions in the mountain fastnesses, and forced him across deep and

rapid rivers. When a halted column was called to "attention" the men sprang to their places, singing to the
strains of the bugle:

Every hour the
work of death was
going on at some
point in the long and
sinuous line. Rail-
way trains which
brought supplies for

I know you are ti-red but still you must go;

Down to At-lan - ta to   see the big show.

"ATTENTION!"

the army returned freighted with the dead and the dying,
and with prisoners taken from the enemy. On and still
on pressed the resolute army; patiently and cheerfully the soldiers discharged every duty and faced every
danger.

The enemy, maddened and desperate, vainly sought to
stay the advance of the victorious legions. Brigades and
divisions defiantly hurled themselves against the Union
intrenchments, and pounced with the utmost fury upon
marching columns. The long track of the armies was
one great battle-field. Everywhere the trees were scarred
and riven by the missiles from musket and cannon, and
the reddened earth became a place of burial for brave men.

CHAPTER XLIV.

An Unexpected Calamity Befalls Corporal Klegg and his Comrade.

IT was a hot midsummer day. The 200th Indiana was
in the front line and Company Q was on picket. Si
and Shorty lay in a rifle-pit which they had dug where
they were stationed, the night before. Under cover of the

darkness they had strongly intrenched themselves, crown·
ing the work with a small "head-log." It took them till
midnight to finish it, but they were amply repaid for their
labor in knowing that they were well fixed for the next
day, provided the army did not advance. With the confidence inspired by their repeating rifles, they knew that no
mere skirmish-line of the enemy could drive them from
their position. Shorty named it "Fort Klegg." During
the rest of the night they kept vigil, with eyes and ears,
their trusty rifles in hand for instant use. Now and then
one of them slept for a few minutes, but was quick to
spring at the lightest touch of his watchful comrade. In
all that long line of videttes, miles in extent, no eyes were
more keenly alert than those which peered over the parapet of Fort Klegg.

Daylight came, and the crickets chirruped in the grass
and the birds twittered and sang in the trees. The thirsty
rays of the morning sun drank up the dew that sparkled
for a moment and then was gone. The muskets along the
hostile lines were silent. The discordant sounds of war
were hushed in the strange, oppressive quiet that often
preceded the bursting storm. The army did not move, and
the pickets were cautioned to the utmost watchfulness.
It was deemed probable that the enemy would attack, for
his position was so menaced that he must either fight or
abandon it.

Si and Shorty, in turn, ate their breakfast of hardtack
and raw bacon, washing it down with the tasteless water
that had been in their canteens since the previous day; for
no fires could be lighted on the outposts. An hour passed
—and another—and another. Still they kept their eyes to
the front, watching for the first sign of the expected attack. The sun climbed toward the zenith and beat down
with scorching fierceness.

"I b'lieve I'm beginnin' ter fry!" said Si, as he lay sweltering in the hot, dry air, with the perspiration flowing in

rivulets from every part of his body. "I kin jest hear the grease a-sizzlin' out o' me. I reck'n it's a good thing fer me 't I ain't so fat 's I was when I 'listed er I'd melt 'n' run off in a stream. Purty hot, ain't it?"

"Ye're mighty right!" replied Shorty. "Ef I'm any good at guessin' we'll have it a diff'runt kind o' hot 'fore night. I'll bet the Johnnies 's up to suthin' 'n' 'tain't no tomfoolery, nuther, er they wouldn't be so quiet 's they've been this mornin'."

"Thar they come, now, Shorty!" suddenly exclaims Si, as he thrusts the muzzle of his rifle through the crevice below the head-log, draws up the hammer, and places his finger on the trigger. "Look at the raskils pilin' over that stun wall 'n' leggin' it this way. Seems 's if they was comin' mighty thick. Let's hold on t'll they git a leetle furder 'n' then we'll pepper 'em. Our guns 's got sixteen shots apiece, 'n' we'll make 'em think we're a hull rijiment. Ain't I glad we bought these 'ere Henrys! They're jest the boss guns."

FORT KLEGG.

Si chatters away, scarcely knowing what he says. The rebels are half a mile distant, at the edge of a large field. With their muskets at a "trail" they take the double-quick and make their way rapidly toward the Union pickets. Behind the heavy line of skirmishers come the solid battalions massed for a furious assault.

"We don't want ter stay here too long," suggests

Shorty, "'cause ye know we can't fight the hull rebel army; 'n' 'sides that our fellers back 't the works can't open on 'em—leastways they won't want ter—till arter we gits back."

Shorty is the cooler of the two, and takes in the whole situation. Si only thinks of making the most of his opportunity—for rarely had so good a one been offered him—to use his repeating rifle to advantage.

"That's all right, Shorty; we'll have lots o' time ter git back arter we've guv 'em our sixteen pills apiece. They look kinder sick 'n' I 'low our medis'n' 'll do 'em good. They're comin' so thick 't we can't miss 'em 'n' we'll jest have a picnic!"

"You're my commandin' ossifer, Si, 'n' I'm goin' ter stay t'll you says the word. But we'll hafter git up 'n' dust when we do start."

On and on come the soldiers in gray. Those in the advance are half-way across the intervening space, and are fast nearing the chain of rifle-pits. With eyes almost bursting from their sockets, Si watches their approach. His heart throbs wildly; the hot blood leaps through his veins; his cheek is aflame with the fervid glow of excitement. The impatient pickets on the right and left begin the fire.

"Now sock it to 'em, Shorty," exclaims Si, as he glances quickly along the barrel of his rifle and a bullet speeds from Fort Klegg.

As they encounter the fire from the outposts the rebels, not pausing to use their muskets, bend their heads to the storm, quicken their steps, and break forth in a mad yell.

The hands of Si and Shorty fly nimbly as they work their repeaters to their utmost capacity. Fast speed the deadly missiles. Every one seems to take effect in that charging mass, at rapidly shortening range. Now the rebels are so near that Si can see the very white of their eyes.

"Plug it into 'em!" he shouts. "We're droppin' 'em right 'n' left." And he works with redoubled ardor till the last shot in his magazine has been fired. "Now, Shorty, let's climb out o' this!"

Si has been too brave, and has permitted his zeal to out-run his judgment. He has thought of nothing but doing the greatest possible execution, and does not know that on the right and left the pickets wisely fell back to the main line after the first volley into the face of the foe. The rapid and persistent fire from Fort Klegg has checked somewhat the advance in its immediate front, but on both flanks the rebels have swept on and are swarming in the rear of the little fortification that has been so gallantly defended.

As Si and Shorty turn to retreat they are amazed to find themselves covered by half a dozen muskets, with loud demands for immediate and unconditional sur-render. At the same instant men in gray, with gleam-ing bayonets, storm the now silent work, leap over the head-log, and close in upon the hapless garrison.

Breathless and dumfounded, Si is for the instant speech-less. It is one of those critical moments which admit of no delay. Something must be said or done instantly or it will be the last of Corporal Klegg and his faithful pard. Shorty comprehends the emergency, and sees at a glance that there is but one thing that the bravest man can do under such circumstances. He throws up his hand in token of surrender, and he and Si are in the hands of the Philis-tines.

Si had not yet recovered his senses. The scenes had been shifted so suddenly that he was bewildered. He could not comprehend that he was really a prisoner. Never in all his service as a soldier had the thought of surrender once en-tered his mind.

Half a dozen Confederates sprang forward, each of them eager to secure such a prize as a Henry rifle.

"You jest leggo that ar gun, will ye!" said Si with emphasis, as one of them seized his weapon and tried to wrest it from his grasp. "*I* hain't s'rendered yet, 'n' ef ye'll jest gimme two minutes ter load up my rifle I'll fight the hull on ye!"

Si's face fairly blazed in the intensity of his indignation and wrath. Prudence was not one of his cardinal virtues, and at that instant, if he could have refilled his magazine with cartridges he would have defied a regiment of graycoats.

"Steady, thar, my boy!" exclaimed Shorty. "Ye can't help yerself 'n' ye've got ter cave."

"I'll bring him to Limerick!" said a burly Confederate, as he placed the muzzle of his musket to Si's head.

COMPELLED TO SURRENDER.

"Now drap that thar gun 'n' hold up yer hands right quick, you Yank, er ye'll be a dead man 'n three seconds!"

"Don't shoot, Johnny," pleaded Shorty. "Let up on him 'n' I'll bring him 'round. Ye see he ain't nothin' but a boy, but he's chuck full o' sand. He's got steam up purty high, but he'll git blowed off d'reckly 'n' then he'll cool down. 'Twon't do ye no good ter kill him."

By this time Si had yielded to the inevitable. Looking into the muzzle of that loaded musket, he wisely determined not to pursue the argument. The other fellow "had the drop on him," and he gave a signal of capitulation. His feelings overcame him as he saw his beloved rifle, that had served him so well, pass into the hands of an enemy, and tears of sorrow and vexation streamed down his face.

"Git right out o' this, Yanks!" said one of the rebels, who had been directed to march the prisoners to the rear. "Ye hain't got no time ter stan' here snivelin'. Now travel!"

Under the persuasive influence of a glistening bayonet Si and Shorty moved off in the direction indicated.

"Looks 's though it had cost 'em suthin ter capcher you 'n' me!" said Shorty to his comrade in an undertone, pointing to a dozen or fifteen of the enemy who were lying dead or wounded within the range of Fort Klegg. It was evident that most of their shots had taken effect.

"I'd ruther I hadn't seen 'em," said Si, "'cause it makes me feel bad, arter all, ter *know* I've killed any on 'em, even ef they *is* rebels. Ye know they're all human bein's 'n' I can't git it outen my head 't it's jest 'bout the size o' murder. Mostly when we're in a big fight, 'n' all on 'em 's bangin' away, a feller don't know whether he hits anybody er not; but ther' ain't no chance ter feel that way 'bout this 'ere scrimmage we had. Mebbe *you* killed 'em all, Shorty."

"I don't keer 'f you think so, Si. I ain't so squeamish 's you be, 'n' I kin stan' it. The faster they 's killed off the quicker it'll wind up the job."

"I s'pose ther' ain't no denyin' that, Shorty, but—I don't reck'n God meant ter have me fer a soljer, er he 'd ha' made me diff'runt."

"I don't see how he could ha' done a better job ef he'd made ye to order!" replied Shorty.

They walked over the field at a moderate pace. The "Johnny" appeared to be satisfied with his detail to march them back, and was seemingly in no hurry to finish the duty. Possibly he indulged the hope that the fight would be over before he should rejoin his regiment. Little wonder if he did.

Generally speaking, there was no feeling of personal enmity between the soldiers of the Union and Confederate armies. They learned thoroughly to respect one another for their courage and fighting qualities, and war did not make them savages or wild beasts. The instincts of humanity may have been deadened in some cases, but in others they were made more keen by the sight of human suffering, and rarely, indeed, did they wholly disappear. Even in the fiercest heat of battle, it was not often that soldiers on either side indulged in wanton killing. No doubt life was sometimes taken in a way that was simply atrocious murder ; for it would be strange if among two or three millions of men, leading a life that, at its best, had a tendency to arouse the basest passions, there were not some to whom the quality of mercy was unknown. Every year hundreds of crimes, equally revolting, are committed by men whose breasts are not inflamed by the fires of war. As a rule, when a man was wounded or a prisoner he was no longer an enemy. The last cracker and the last drop in the canteen would be freely shared with a suffering foeman. It will be understood that these observations are intended to apply to the soldiers in the field, who marched and fought, giving and taking hard blows. Such were the characteristics of these men, on both sides, with few exceptions.

"You-uns fout mighty well 'hind that thar breastwork o' yourn," said the guard, by way of scraping up an acquaintance with his prisoners.

"We made it 's warm fer ye 's we could," replied Si. His temperature had fallen several degrees, and his tongue was getting into its normal condition.

"When we was chargin' up thar ye made us b'lieve thar

was a hull comp'ny, with them dog-goned guns o' yourn, 't ye loads up on Sunday 'n' then shoots 'em all the week. What sort o' killin' machines be they, anyway? I've heern tell on 'em but I never seen one afore."

"Pard," said Si, "I didn't git that rifle f'm the guvyment. She b'longs ter me, 'cause I bought her 'th my own money 't I arned a-hoofin' it 'n' fightin' rebs. Ef she was Uncle Sam's property it 'd be all right fer ye ter hang on to her, but bein' 'tain't ye ought ter give her back."

The guard was carrying the two Henry rifles on his shoulder. The Confederates did not know how to use them, nor would they be of any service without a supply of ammunition made especially for them. The rebel soldier did not coincide with Si's views on the question of ownership. He held to the idea, almost universally prevalent in both armies, that under any and all circumstances, without regard to the claims of friend or foe, anything belonged to whoever had it. Possession was more than "nine points in law"—it was the law itself.

"I 'low ter have one o' them guns, myself," said the guard. "When we git back a leetle furder I'll ax ye to shell out what catridges ye got, 'n' then ye'll have ter show me how the old thing works."

This put a thought into Si's head, and he nudged Shorty suggestively with his elbow as he said:

"I'll tell ye what I'll do, Johnny, 'n' less see 'f we can't make a barg'in. I'll give ye my repeater 'n' all the catridges both on us 's got, 'n' show ye how ter shoot 'em, ef ye'll shet yer eyes fer jest two minutes. I'll do 's much sometime fer you."

"Ye'd like ter git away, wouldn't ye? I'd git myself in a purty pickle. I'd hate ter do it, but ef ye try any monkey-shines 'th me I'll put a bullet through ye. I reck'n I've got a tollable sure thing on this 'ere gun 'n' yer am'nition."

Shorty smiled at his comrade's offer to negotiate for

freedom. Although he had given no hint to Si he had several times carefully swept the field with his eye, and calculated the possibilities of escape. He was ready to take any hazard, and knew well enough that he could depend upon Si. But the stragglers and army followers were too numerous in all directions to allow the slightest hope of success. The impatient captives could only bide their time, trusting that an opportunity might be offered.

But no opening was presented, and Si and Shorty were delivered into the custody of an officer whose duty it was to receive prisoners, and who had at command an ample force to guard them securely. Before leaving them their escort relieved Si and Shorty of the ammunition for their rifles, and required them, at the point of the bayonet, to instruct him in the use of the weapons. Si groaned in spirit at the thought of their guns being aimed, perhaps, at his own comrades of the 200th Indiana.

All this time had been borne to their ears the roar of battle. The rapid boom of artillery and the sharp, rolling volleys of musketry told of hard fighting. The rebel wounded streamed to the rear or were borne back upon stretchers. Both Si and Shorty were eager to know the result.

"How's it goin'?" Si asked of a Confederate soldier who came limping back with a bullet hole through his leg.

"Bully fer our side!" was the reply. "We've only been fallin' back ter draw ye on, 'n' you-all 's goin' ter git the gosh-durnedest lickin' today ye ever heern tell on."

Si ventured to remark that he didn't believe it. A few minutes later there was abundant evidence that his faith in the 200th Indiana and the other regiments guarding the point assailed was well grounded. Stragglers in an advanced stage of demoralization were seen emerging from the woods and making their way across the field at the highest attainable speed. Thicker and faster they came, and soon a disordered swarm of Confederate troops was struggling to the rear. The assault had failed. The conflict was short, sharp and decisive. The air resounded with the mad yells and curses of the defeated soldiers, while in the distance could be heard the triumphant shouts of the "Yankees," as they pressed closely upon the heels of the fleeing foe.

"Jest look at the Johnnies, Shorty," said Si, as he and his comrade stood, excited and breathless, watching the tide of fugitives as it swept toward them. "List'n at our fellers a-yellin'! I knowed they'd lick the raskils. Can't ye hear the boys o' Comp'ny Q hollerin'? Don't I wish 't I was thar 'th my rifle? Who-o-o-o-p!"

Si started to yell, but was checked by Shorty.

"Better load down yer safety-valve, Si, 'n' not be shootin' off yer mouth too much. These rebils 'll come back purty mad 'cause they didn't git thar, 'n' ef ye go ter yellin' 'n' prancin' 'round, like as not one on 'em 'll be mean 'nough to punch ye with his bay'net. I feel like hollerin' myself, but thar *is* times when the best thing a feller kin do is ter hold in, 'n' this 's one on 'em."

Around them everything was in the wildest confusion. Other troops were being hurried up to cover the retreat of the regiments that had melted into a disordered mass, for the moment uncontrolled and uncontrollable. Staff officers and orderlies dashed madly about with orders for the emergency. The little squad of prisoners—for there were others besides Si and Shorty—seemed to be forgotten.

"Shorty," said his comrade in a low voice, "wouldn't ther' be a livin' chance fer us ter git out o' this. The Johnnies 'pears ter have 'bout 's much business on hand 's they kin 'tend to, 'thout botherin' the'r heads 'th us. Ef ye want ter try it I'm ready."

"I've been thinkin' 'bout it, Si, 'n' I'm keepin' my eye skinned fer an openin'. You leave it ter me, 'n' when I poke ye 'n the ribs you foller me 's tight 's ever ye kin, 'n' we'll break fer the timber. I reck'n they'll send a few bul-

lets chasin' arter us, but I'd ruther take the chances o' gittin' hit than ter be lugged off ter one o' them prisons we've
heern so much 'bout. Now watch out!"

More wild grew the tumult around them as the receding
wave of battle tossed about the debris of the shattered
column. Nearer and nearer came the shouts of the Union
soldiers, rapidly advancing in a determined counter-charge.
The disorganized Confederates rushed frantically about,
each bent on seeking his own safety, while the officers vainly
strove to rally and re-
form their broken bat-
talions. It was one of
those panics that at
times demoralized the
bravest men.

" Now!" whispered
Shorty, as he touched
Si with his hand, and
they darted away
through the hurry-
ing throng of men
in gray. It was a
desperate chance, but
Shorty hoped that
they might make their
way through the rush
and whirl and reach
the Union lines.

A FRUITLESS DASH.

"Stop them Yanks!" shouted the guards from whom
they had escaped.

An instant later Shorty was felled to the ground by a
blow upon the head from the butt of a musket. Si stopped
to look after his comrade, and they were at once over-
powered. Shorty was stunned for a moment, but not
seriously hurt. He was half dragged along, and he and Si
were again in the custody of the guards.

"What are these Yanks doing here?" shouted an officer who came galloping up. "Why don't you take 'em to the rear. Be lively about it! They're all we've got to show for this day's work, and we can't afford to lose 'em!"

Away they went, urged to the double-quick by the bayonets of the guards behind them. On came the solid lines of a fresh Confederate division that had been ordered to the breach, marching with brave and confident step. It checked the advance of the Union troops, and served as a wall, behind which the fragments of the regiments that had been torn and broken by the fruitless assault were rallied around their colors, and a semblance of order was restored.

In such a campaign, with its daily recurring attacks and flank movements, prisoners were not long kept at the front of either army. They were an incumbrance to active movements, and there was liability of escape or recapture. For these reasons they were hurried to the rear.

Nightfall found Si and Shorty and their companions in captivity miles away from the place where they had fallen into the hands of the enemy. Shorty was not disabled by the blow he had received, though there was a lump on his head as large as a door-knob.

When they went into bivouac for the night Si naturally began to inquire about rations. Nothing remained in his haversack except a few broken bits of hardtack. He had painful misgivings on this score, for he had heard that the Southern Confederacy did not provide a sumptuous bill of fare for its prisoners of war; and that in quantity it was not up to the demands of the average human stomach.

Si waited a reasonable time, with as much patience as he could command, and then, there being no visible signs of a banquet, he concluded to put out a feeler.

"Say, pard," he said to one of the guards, "how long 'fore supper 's goin' ter be ready? I'm gittin' mighty hungry."

"I'll take yer order. What'll ye have—eyester stew, roast beef, roast turkey, spring lamb 'n' peas, er pork 'n' apple-sass—anything you-all want; we keeps a reg'lar hotel here," and the guard laughed heartily at his tantalizing humor.

"I guess ye're jokin', Johnny," replied Si, "but I ain't a bit pertickler, only so it's suthin t' eat 'n' plenty on it."

"Wall I kin tell ye, Yank, 't ye won't git nothin' t'night. We hain't got no more 'n jest 'nough ter go 'round fer we-uns, 'n' desp'rut poor stuff 't that. You-all gits right smart better grub 'n we does, 'n' I 'low ye'll have ter come down a peg er two 'n' yer eatin' fer a bit. Got any coffee?"

"I'm purty nigh busted on coffee. Ef I'd knowed I was goin' ter be snatched bald-headed I'd ha' laid in a s'ply. I hain't got more 'n 'nuff fer a couple o' drawin's. 'Twon't last no longer 'n termorrer."

"I'm 'feard 'twon't last ye that long, pard, 'cause *I* want it right now, powerful bad. It's so long sence I had a swig o' coffee 't I've fergot what 't tastes like."

"Wha-a-a-t!" said Si, "ye ain't goin' fer to take that, ar' ye?"

"That's 'bout the bigness on it. You heerd what I said, 'n' I'll trouble ye to fork it over."

Si's anger rose at the thought of such an indignity. He cast an appealing look at Shorty, as if to ask what he had better do about it.

"Let 'em have it, Si," said his comrade. "You 'n' me made a good squar' fight today, but we got everlastin'ly whipped 'n' ther' ain't no way but ter take the consekences. They've got ye foul, pard, 'n' ye can't help yerself."

It went against the grain with Si to give up his coffee, but the gentle, suggestive prod of a bayonet quickened his movements, and he surrendered to the Confederate the rag in which it was tied. A similar requisition was made on Shorty, which was honored without a murmur.

"I'd like ter kick, too," he said to Si, "but 'tain't no use.

It'll only make things wuss, 'n' I'm goin' ter grin 'n' b'ar it."

He found an opportunity to whisper in Si's ear that he was going to watch very sharp for a chance to get away.

"Some o' the boys what gits capchered does make the riffle," he said, "'n' ef they kin we kin."

The thought of escape was uppermost in Si's mind, and served to assuage the grief and chagrin he felt at being a prisoner. The startling and rapid events of the day had left him little time for reflection upon the fate that had befallen him, but he had determined to make the best of it, and was cheered by the belief that he and Shorty would contrive some way to regain their liberty. They had tried once and failed but this only made him the more eager for another effort.

"Hello, Johnny," he said, as he saw the despoiler of his haversack making a kettle of coffee at a fire near by, "would 't be any more 'n fa'r ter give me a few swallers o' that coffee?"

"Ye kin have all 't 's left arter we-uns gits filled up. Ye hadn't better calkilate on gittin' much, fer we don't git sich a chance 's this only purty durned seldom. You-uns has dead loads o' coffee, 'n' 'twon't hurt ye ter go 'thout fer a while. We hain't had nothin' fer a year but chickery 'n' baked peas 'n' sich."

Si and Shorty turned their haversacks inside out and devoured the last crumb they contained. The prospect before them was such as to fill their minds with consternation. This feeling was intensified when, after the guards had drained the coffee-kettle, one of them came up to Si and said, with an imperious air:

"You Yank, come up out o' them shoes!"

"What's that ye say?"

"I 'lowed I was talkin' plain 'nough fer ye ter understand. I want ye ter take off them shoes!"

"What fer? I don't feel like turnin' in yet."

"'Cause *I want 'em!*" said the Confederate, with emphasis.

"Now, pard, ye oughtn't ter rob a feller that way jest 'cause ye got the whip-row on 'im. I wouldn't do that way to you ef the boot was on t'other leg. I only jest drawed them gunboats a few days ago, 'n' I can't git 'long 'thout 'em, nohow."

"I seen they was purty nigh new, 'n' that's why I want 'em. I reck'n they're 'bout my size. I'm only goin' ter trade with ye. I'll give ye mine fer 'em, 'n' ye know a even exchange ain't no robbery. Ther' ain't nothin' mean 'bout me."

"But yourn ain't—"

"We ain't gwine ter have no argyment. Thar ain't nothin' ter be said on your side. I want them shoes 'n' I'm goin' ter have 'em, 'n' that settles it. I know mine ain't quite 's good 's yourn, but you kin w'ar 'em jest 's well 's I kin. Now shuck them hoofs, 'n' ye don't wan't ter be all night doin' it, nuther."

The impatient voice of the guard and his menacing posture, left no room for doubt that the debate was closed. The motion to exchange was carried, for although it was a tie as between Si and "Johnny," the latter's loaded musket and fixed bayonet had the casting vote, and another victory was scored for the Southern Confederacy.

While Si was untying his shoes some things came into his mind that he would have liked to say, but on the whole he thought he wouldn't.

"Them socks o' yourn 's purty fa'r," said the rebel, "better skin 'em off while ye're 'bout it. I'll have ter borry *them*, 'cause I hain't got none ter give ye fer 'em."

Si cast a despairing look at Shorty, and then proceeded to take off the dainty hose with which the government had provided him.

"Thar," said the guard, when his feet were encased in his newly acquired property, "that feels better. Now you kin put *them* on ef ye want ter. Ef ye don't I reck'n ye'll have ter go bar'fut, same 's we does sometimes."

"Them" were a pair of nondescript articles which, like the earth before the work of creation was finished, were "without form and void." They showed some symptoms of having been once intended to serve as shoes. They were of the rudest manufacture. Army service had made sad havoc with them and they were in the last stages of dilapidation and decay.

"'Fore I'd fight fer a guvyment 't didn't do no better by me 'n that!" said Si, as he eyed them contemptuously.

"Look a-hyar, Yank, you don't want fer to talk like that; 'twon't be healthy fer ye. We've got you-uns durned nigh licked, 'n' we don't 'low ter go 'th bar' feet 'n' empty stummicks much longer. But we don't want none o' yer insiniwations!"

Si thrust his stockingless feet into the mouths of those Confederate shoes, making wry faces as he noted the holes and gaping seams.

"Ye'd better tie these yere strings 'round yer feet ter hold them shoes on!" said the guard. "I've been a-doin' that fer a month back."

After Si had acted upon this suggestion he could not help laughing, in spite of himself, at the grotesque appearance of his feet. He expressed the hope that he would not have to do much marching in those shoes.

"We're goin' ter put ye on the keers termorrer," replied the guard, "'n' run ye off down south, whar ye won't have no chance ter git away. Them old shoes *is* purty nigh played out. They ain't no good fer marchin', but they 'll do 's well 's any fer ridin' on the railroad. By the way, Yank, I b'lieve I'll swap hats with ye. I know yourn 's better 'n mine; ef 'twasn't I don't reck'n I'd want ter trade."

Si cast a glance of decided disapproval at the rebel soldier's hat, which was faded and worn and battered.

While he was considering the advisability of opening a discussion his hat was lifted from his head by the guard, who offered his own in exchange. It was a fitting companion for the shapeless things that adorned Si's lower extremities.

"Now, pard," said Si, "ef ther's anything else 't ye want I'll thank ye ter say what 'tis right now, 'n' less have this tradin' business done with. I've got rayther the wust o' the barg'in so fur, but I like ter be accommerdatin'. Mebbe ye'd like ter have my shirt!"

Si nursed with much satisfaction the thought of getting his shirt upon the back of his persecutor. It would be a prime opportunity to revenge himself. Weeks of hard campaigning and lying in the trenches found his nether garment in a condition of unusual animation. The Confederate had a kind of fellow-feeling on this point, and he replied:

"I don't b'lieve I keer fer a dicker o' that sort, unsight 'n' unseen; its too resky. Mine's bad 'nuff, 'n' I 'low I hadn't better take no chances on gittin' suthin a heap wuss. I don't want no more graybacks, but ef ye got any greenbacks ye better be a-shellin' on 'em out."

"I've got ye thar, Johnny," replied Si with a triumphant smile. "We hain't seen no money in a dog's age. Paymasters's mighty skurce whar the bullets 's zippin' 'round. The climate don't agree with 'em!"

"Like 's not ye're lyin' to me, Yank, 'n' ef ye'll scuse me I'll jest see 'f ye've got any cash in yer clothes."

"Ye're a spreadin' of it on purty thick," said Si, but he submitted meekly to the search, knowing that the result would be a full vindication of his veracity.

"Thar, what'd I tell ye," he said, when the rebel had explored all his pockets and carefully examined his clothing to be sure that there was none concealed under the lining. "P'r'aps ye'll b'lieve me next time!"

"That's all right ef ye hain't got none; but this yere 's

a purty good jack-knife. I'm needin' one, 'n' I'll jest take it 'n' we'll call it squar'. I'm much 'bleeged to ye."

Shorty's meager supply of goods and chattels had been subjected to a similar process, and sundry articles had gone to replenish the wardrobe of another of the guards. Both Si and Shorty found themselves in decidedly reduced circumstances. They were thankful that the ravage of the Confederates had spared their blankets.

"We'll let ye keep them," said one, "I reck'n ye'll need 'em when ye git down in the pen."

"Lemme see!" said the sergeant in charge of the guards to Si and Shorty, as they were spreading down their blankets by the fire, "ye're the chaps 't tried so hard ter git away today, ain't ye? I'll give ye fa'r warnin' 't I ain't goin' ter have ye playin' any o' yer Yankee tricks on me. Ef ye'll give me yer word, 'pon honor, 't ye won't

A ONE-SIDED BARGAIN.

cut up no capers t'night that'll settle it. Ef ye won't I'll have ter tie ye up, cause I'm 'sponsible fer you-all 'n' I'm goin' ter make a sure thing on 't."

"We sha'n't promise nothin'," replied Shorty. "A feller what's a pris'ner 's got a right ter git away ef he kin. It's your business ter see 't he don't. 'Tain't reggelations for ye to go ter tyin' on us up, nuther, same 's ef we was thieves 'n' cut-throats. Ye ought ter git some han'cuffs ter clap onter pris'ners when ye capchers 'em!'"

"I don't keer whether it's 'cordin' ter Hoyle er not; it's goin' ter be did 'nless ye'll gimme yer word."

"Nary time! Go ahead with yer tyin'!"

Shorty saw by the flickering firelight that Si's face was ablaze with indignation. It would be just like him to fight the entire squad, with such primitive weapons as nature had supplied. Shorty found opportunity to whisper in his comrade's ear:

"Don't make any fuss, Si; do jest 's I tell ye!"

The sergeant produced some pieces of stout rope and with the help of two or three of the guards tied together Shorty's hands and then his feet. Si's breast heaved and his eyes flashed, but remembering Shorty's admonition he checked his volcanic tendencies, by a mighty effort, and when his turn came to be bound he submitted without a word. But his thoughts were raging.

"Thar," said the sergeant, when the work was finished, "I 'low ye won't git very fur away 'fore mornin'. Ef ye'd 'have yerselves 'n' act sort o' decent we'd treat ye white, but we b'ar down hard on them as tries ter give us the slip."

"That's all right, pard," replied Shorty, "ef ye'll jest kiver us up 'th that thar blanket."

The sergeant spread the blanket over the captive Hoosiers, as they lay utterly helpless, bound hand and foot. The hearts of their fellow prisoners revolted at the scene, but it would have been worse than useless to remonstrate. They disposed themselves upon the ground for the night, and the guards were divided into reliefs, part of them to sleep while the rest paced to and fro around the motley bivouac.

Si's thoughts ran over the events of the day. It was the first chance he had had to think since the Confederate host swept over Fort Klegg. He tried hard to reconcile himself to his condition as a prisoner of war, but the more he tried the more marked was his failure. How his mother and sister Maria and pretty Annabel would feel if they knew his situation. And then to think of Company Q and the rest of the 200th Indiana marching on without him. There he was, tied up like a miscreant, surrounded by rebel bayonets, and his cherished rifle in the hands of a foeman. It was too much for Si, and his goaded feelings found relief in a torrent of tears. His comrade's mind was busy as well, but it took a more practical turn and dwelt only upon the possibilities of escape.

"Ye feel kinder leaky, don't ye, pard?" he said, scarcely above a whisper, when Si began to overflow. "I thought it 'd hit ye in yer weak spot. I don't blame ye fer takin' on, but ye wants ter cheer up, 'cause we're goin' ter git out o' this sometime. P'r'aps 'twon't be t'night, ner t'morrer, ner next day, ner next week, but ef we keep our eyes peeled we'll see a hole *sometime*'t we kin git through. I know ye'll brace up, Si, fer ye allus does. We're in a tight place, but a bar'l o' tears won't help git us out."

"Yer head 's level, Shorty," repied Si, as soon as he could command his feelings. "I ax yer parding. I didn't mean ter act like a baby, but I jest couldn't help it. I tell ye what, Shorty," he continued, after communing with himself for a moment, "I'd like ter be Samson, 't I used ter read 'bout 'n the Bible, fer jest five minnits. I'd bust these tarnal ropes, 'n' then I'd take the jaw-bone of a mule, same 's he did, 'n' I'd lay out these raskils."

"That 'd be a fust-rate scheme ef it 'd work, but I don't b'lieve 't's wuth while fer ye ter try it on. We ain't both on us 's much 's Samson's little finger jest now."

The captives were tied at the wrists but their fingers were measurably free. After a little time Shorty began to pick at the rope that bound Si's arms. He worked very carefully, under the blanket, and for a long time the tightly drawn knots baffled his efforts. He finally succeeded in loosening the cord, and Si found, to his great joy, that his hands were free. Then he proceeded to untie his comrade.

"Be mighty keerful," said Shorty, "'n' keep the blanket still. I heern the sargeant tell the guards ter keep a sharp eye on us."

Si's patient labor was at last rewarded and Shorty's arms were no longer confined. To free their feet was a more difficult task, as they could not be reached without a disturbance of position that would be likely to attract attention.

"Double yerself up like a jack-knife, Si," whispered Shorty. "Git yer feet 's fur this way 's ye kin; but do it slow—'n inch 't a time—so them fellers won't s'pect nothin'."

Very carefully, little by little, Si drew up his knees until they almost touched his chin. Shorty's arms were pretty long, and by hitching himself down he managed to reach the cord.

"I wish 't I had my knife 't that raskil stole from me," said Si, "'n' we'd make a quick job on 't."

"Mine 'd do jest 's well 'f I had it," replied Shorty, "but one o' them fellers 's got it. You hol' still a bit 'n' I'll fetch it."

The knots were stubborn but they yielded to Shorty's dexterous fingers. It took half an hour for Si to get himself straightened out and Shorty to pull his feet up where Si could reach them. At length the last cord was loosed, and they had not been detected.

"Now, Si," said Shorty, "ef ye say so we'll try 'n' make a break. The rest o' the pris'ners 's all sleepin', 'n' so 's the guard reliefs. Them 't 's on the beats 's purty well tuckered out, 'n' they're set'n down 'n' noddin'. They think we're all tied up. Ef we try it 'n' they see us, course they'll shoot 'n' the old scratch 'll be ter pay. It's mighty

ticklish business, Si, 'n' I don't ax ye ter take the chance
o' dodgin' the bullets 'nless ye wants ter."

"I'll jest jump at it, pard," said Si, who had listened with
intense eagerness. "When ye're ready gimme a hint 'n'
I'll foller ye wherever ye go."

They lay quiet for an hour, and then Shorty very carefully raised his head and peered around. It was long past
midnight. There was no moon, and the dim light of the
twinkling stars scarcely penetrated the foliage of the trees
to relieve the darkness of the forest. The fire burned
dimly and the forms of friend and foe lay motionless in
slumber. Even the sentries had yielded to fatigue and
were dozing in forbidden dalliance with the drowsy god.
It seemed possible for the two captives to dash past the
sleepy guards and in an instant be lost to sight in the dark
wood.

"Shall we try it, Si?" he asked, after he had explained
the condition of affairs to his comrade.

"Yes!" was the whispered reply, and Si's heart throbbed
violently at the thought of another bold dash for liberty.
"Shall we take 'long our blankets?"

"I reck'n not," said Shorty; "they'd bother us runnin'.
We'll leave 'em fer bail. Come on, quick!"

Springing to their feet they leaped over their sleeping
comrades and bounded away like deer into the darkness.
Their movement made little noise, but it was enough to
arouse one of the guards to a consciousness that something was out of joint. Starting up and looking wildly
about he saw the disarranged blankets where Si and
Shorty had been lying. Then his eye caught the fast receding forms of the fugitives. Before he could bring his
musket to his shoulder they were out of sight among the
trees.

Yelling "Halt, there!" at the top of his voice he sent a
bullet whistling after them. In an instant everybody was
on his feet and the little bivouac was a scene of the wildest

uproar. The sergeant cursed the guards who had permitted the prisoners to escape, and while they were mak· ing up their minds what to do, Si and Shorty were speeding away at a pace that defied successful pursuit.

Obedient to the command of the sergeant, two or three of the guards dashed after the runaways. More could not be spared, as it was necessary to watch the rest of the prisoners and prevent a further deliverance. The irate sergeant ordered his men to look to their arms, and to shoot down instantly any who might attempt to escape.

The pursuers had a bootless chase. They beat about in a frantic way among the trees and through the bushes, yelling and firing their pieces. All this evinced their zeal in the search, but did no harm to Si and Shorty. The latter had taken a circuitous route and, once fairly away in the darkness, had no difficulty in completely baffling their enemies.

CHAPTER XLV.

IN WHICH SI AND SHORTY EXPERIENCE MANY VICISSITUDES, BUT THEIR PLUCK BRINGS THEM THROUGH.

BY the time Si and Shorty had reached a safe distance they were thoroughly "blown," and crept into a thicket to recover breath and to consult regarding future movements. Thus far they had scarcely spoken since they began their flight, intent only on putting as much distance as possible between themselves and their misguided fellow-citizens in "butternut."

"Purty good job, that," said Si, as he lay panting on the ground, scarcely daring to speak above a whisper. "I never made that many tracks so quick afore in *my* life."

"We've made a good start, Si," replied Shorty, "but ye mus'n't crow t'll ye're out o' the woods. Gittin' away was easy 'nough arter we got clear o' the guards. We sha'n't have no trouble t'night; the rub 'll be when 't comes daylight. I'm all twisted up 'n these woods, 'n' I hain't no idee what d'rection we'd orter go ter find our fellers. Ef we knew which way 'n' could go straight thar 'twouldn't take long, but ye know we can't go plumb through the rebel army. We've got ter work 'round one eend o' their line, some way er ruther. 'Twon't be no soft snap, I kin tell ye. I 'low we can't do better 'n ter stay here t'll it's light so we kin git our bearin's. I ain't afeard o' them raskils findin' us 's long 's it's pitch dark; 'n' mebbe they won't make much fuss 'bout it nohow, fer they won't want ter own up 't they let us git away so easy. 'N' they thought they had us so *dead* with them pesky ropes!"

They remained in their place of concealment, considei ing what they should do when daylight came, and trying to decide upon the best possible course of action. There was little fear that they would be molested by any of the squad from which they had escaped. The guards had a lot of prisoners on their hands, and would think it useless to search for the two fugitives, supposing them to be miles away.

With the first appearance of dawn, Shorty began to cast about for the purpose of reconnoitering.

"We've got ter find out how the land lays," he said to his companion, "'fore we kin tell what 't's best ter do. We ain't goin' ter run foul o' the rebs ef we kin help it."

The increasing light revealed open ground at no great distance. Si and Shorty moved cautiously toward the edge of the wood.

"Thar," said Shorty, "I'm goin' ter shin up this tree 'n' squint 'round a bit. You watch out sharp fer any o' the

Johnnies 't mout be a-loafin' here'bouts. Whistle ef ye see any on 'em."

Shorty was a nimble climber and was soon among the top limbs of a tree that commanded a good view of the surrounding country. It scarcely need be said that Si kept a sharp lookout in all directions. Three or four miles away Shorty saw a long line of smoke, evidently from the breakfast fires of the Confederate army. There were none of the enemy in sight in the immediate vicinity, but in the distance he could see what seemed to be an encampment.

When he had finished his observations he descended and hurriedly told Si what he had seen. Their only hope of success lay in attempting a wide detour around one of the enemy's flanks, and thus reaching the Union lines. Such a journey was perilous in the extreme, fraught with danger at every step, and it was not without misgivings that they entered upon it.

"Mebbe it'll take us a week to git 'round, ef we ain't gobbled up," said Shorty, as he led the way in the direction upon which he had decided. "But we're *in* this scrape 'n' that's the only way out. The chances is 't we'll git nabbed er shot. We hain't got nothin' ter fight with ner nothin' to eat, but we'll try 'n' pull through somehow. Ye must keep yer nerve up, Si, 'cause ye're likely ter have use fer all ye've got any minnit."

"What we goin' ter do fer grub?" asked Si, for to him this question was always a living issue. Both were becoming painfully conscious that they had had no breakfast—indeed, had eaten nothing since their cold "snack" behind the friendly intrenchments of Fort Klegg.

"Men kin go 'thout eatin' a good while when they *has* ter," replied Shorty. Then, feeling that this would be but cold comfort for Si, he added: "But I reck'n we kin scratch up suthin ter bite at, ef 'tain't nothin' more'n a ear o' corn now 'n' then. Ef I ain't mistaken we'll have ter keep hid purty much durin' the daytime, 'n' go feelin' our way 'round at night. I'll jest tell ye, pard, we'll do the best we kin. Ef we gits cotched we can't help it, 'n' we'll wait fer the next chance 'n' try ag'in. Ther's nothin' like stickin' to it."

They proceeded for a time with great caution, keeping in the woods and thick underbrush wherever practicable, and when in open country creeping along walls and fences. It was their intention as soon as they began to see signs of the enemy to conceal themselves for the remainder of the day. It was not possible for them to go a great distance in the necessary direction without peril, as on all the main roads leading toward the Confederate "front," cavalrymen, stragglers and forage wagons were continually passing and repassing. Approaching one of these thoroughfares, which they dared not attempt to cross by daylight, they determined to find a hiding-place and remain till night.

They had quenched their thirst from an occasional pool of stagnant water, but their stomachs were in a state of violent rebellion over the scarcity of provisions. They had passed a cornfield or two, but every ear had been plucked. Famine stared them in the face, with no prospect of relief. To approach a house in quest of food would be madness, and an attempt to forage by daylight would be scarcely less dangerous.

"What ar' we goin' ter do, Shorty?" said Si, who leaned heavily upon his comrade for counsel. It was a sad plight in which he found himself, and he mourned as those without hope.

"It does look a leetle streaked," replied Shorty, gravely. "I can't see very fur ahead, but 'tain't often a feller gits inter sich a fix 't ther' ain't a way out ef he kin only find it."

A cloud of dust in the distance betokened the approach of a body of horsemen, and the ears of the wanderers soon caught the sound of hoofs clattering on the pike. Immediate concealment was necessary. They glanced quickly around but no friendly cover presented itself.

"Climb that thar tree," said Shorty. "Be spry, 'n' I'll foller ye!"

Two or three minutes later Si and Shorty were high among the branches, where they hoped that in any event the leaves would hide them from view. Nearer and nearer came the Confederate troopers. The anxious Hoosiers peered through the foliage, hoping the cavalcade would pass, and they might safely descend. They grew suddenly pale, and could only look at each other in blank dismay, when the head of the galloping column turned into the wood and approached them. Men yelled, horses neighed and sabers clanked as the officer in command ordered a halt. Under and far around the tree from which the unhappy fugitives looked down upon the unwelcome scene, the cavalrymen in gray and butternut picketed their horses, "baiting" them with bundles of forage that each carried strapped to the saddle. Then with rude jest and laugh, and snatches of "Dixie" and "Bonnie Blue Flag," the men disposed themselves upon the ground for rest and refreshment. They were in high feather, which seemed to be due in a great measure to the fact that they had a bountiful supply of coffee, salt, hardtack and other articles that did not usually enter into the Confederate *menu*. The festive spirit that prevailed was explained by their conversation, from which Si and Shorty learned that they had just returned from a successful raid in the rear of the Union army, where they had captured one of the corps supply trains, well laden with commissary stores.

With wistful eye and yearning stomach, Corporal Klegg looked upon the active preparations for the festivities. He wanted some of that coffee and hardtack, and wanted it "*bad*." Some of the raiders had cans, bottles, boxes and other "loot" that had evidently been taken from a sutler. Si found for the moment a little satisfaction in the thought that possibly it was the "skinner" of the 200th Indiana who had been "cleaned out."

But how long would the rebels stay there? This was the most important question to the young patriots roosting on the limbs of that tree. They might be off in an hour and they might go into bivouac for a week. Si and Shorty could readily foresee that in a day or two, at most, starvation would compel them to surrender themselves if their visitors remained.

"TREED."

"It's hard lines, pard," said Shorty, in a scarcely audible whisper, as he gazed sympathetically into the woe-begone face of his comrade.

"How *kin* we git out o' this? It's the tightest pinch yet," replied Si, who had such unbounded faith in Shorty's mental resources that it was not without confidence that he appealed to him even in this extremity.

"I don't like ter own up 't I'm beat," said his comrade, "but I'm 'feared the jig 's up, ef them scalawags don't pull out o' thar. Seems 's ef fate 's agin us. We can't do nothin' only jest wait, 'n' mebbe suthin 'll turn up ter let us out."

Hour after hour passed, and the troopers gave no sign of departure. They built shelters of rails and brush, as if for a protracted stay, and Si regarded this hopefully. He knew that whenever the 200th Indiana did that, marching orders quickly followed, and he thought perhaps it might be the same way with the "Johnnies." The soldiers cut down some of the trees to supply themselves with materials. Si and Shorty united in a fervent prayer that the axe would not be laid to the tree in which they were quartered. That prayer was answered.

During the remainder of the day the Confederates lay around, feasting and sleeping and chatting and smoking their cob pipes. The "treed" refugees could hear nothing that indicated a purpose to march, which alone would relieve them from their predicament.

The condition of Si and Shorty was fast approaching the limit of endurance. Their hunger was growing furious, and their cramped positions became hourly more painful. Haunted by the constant fear of discovery, they dared not move hand or foot. They spoke but seldom, and only in faint and stifled tones. Escape seemed hopeless, and more than once they were on the point of making their presence known and opening up negotiations for an honorable surrender. But still they waited and hoped against hope. Both were more than willing to take any desperate chance to regain their liberty, but there was nothing that afforded the slightest encouragement to attempt it.

Si tried in vain to devise some way of escape. He could not think of anything except something to eat. The sight of the riotous raiders feasting sumptuously upon their spoils, and the fragrance of the steaming coffee that seemed to be wafted upward to tantalize his nostrils, were maddening. It was plain that Si could not stand it much longer. Shorty kept his wits at work upon schemes for deliverance. One after another was carefully weighed and rejected as impracticable. At length a thought came to him, like an inspiration. By careful nursing it soon developed into a plan that he believed was feasible; it was worth trying, anyway. When darkness settled upon the wood, lessening the chances of discovery, and the "Johnnies" were noisily engaged in making shift for the night, Shorty unfolded his project to his comrade. He had little doubt that Si would be ready to do anything he might suggest.

"Si," he whisper d, "do ye want ter try makin' a break?"

"Ye kin jest bet I do. Ef ye've got a way thunk up 't 'll git us out o' this mess I'll give ye all the money 't I git nex' pay-day. I'm beginnin' ter feel 's though I was on my last legs, 'n' ef ther 's any show fer gittin' away we've *got* ter try it on. How'll we do it?"

"You give yer tongue a rest, pard, 'n' I'll tell ye. These chaps down here, ef I ain't mistook, 's nigh played out. Been a-goin' it purty stiddy, day 'n' night, I reck'n. Ye know they've been pitchin' inter the grub 's ef they hadn't had nothin' t'eat fer a month, 'n' they'll sleep mighty sound ternight. Bein' 's they're way back 'n the rear o' the rebil army I don't guess they'll put any guards on, 'n' ef they does I 'low they'll sleep 'long 'th the rest. They hain't no idee o' Yanks a-drappin' out o' the trees. Now arter they all gits ter snorin' we'll slide down 'thout makin' no fuss 'n' jest drap f'm them lowest limbs. Mebbe ye've observed 't ther' 's some o' the hosses 't ain't tied, but 's stan'in' 'round kind o' car'less like. 'Twon't take us but a jiffy ter climb onter a couple on 'em 'n' skedaddle. A good many o' them seceshers 's full o' suthin 't 'll keep 'em sleepin' 'n' I don't b'lieve any on 'em 'll git waked up quick 'nuff ter head us off. Ef they shoots let 'em bang away; them one-hoss guns 't the critter soljers lugs 'round don't 'mount ter much fer hittin' a body. Ar' ye in fer it, Si?"

This question was wholly unnecessary. Of course he was "in for" anything that offered a chance of escape.

Around blazing heaps the rough-riders lounged lazily, eating and washing it down with tipple, of which they had an abundant supply. With no danger near, discipline was relaxed after their hard service, and they were permitted to do pretty much as they pleased. The smoke of the fires at times enveloped Si and Shorty, and as they sat watching and waiting, many a cough and sneeze that would have been fatal was determinedly throttled in its incipient stage.

"Now 's our time," said Shorty at length. The fires had burned low and the weary, surfeited and tipsy troopers were lying about—some wrapped in their ragged blankets, while others had simply wilted under the influence of the warmth and the potations in which they had indulged, and lay in grotesque postures. All were in a heavy sleep.

"Now be keerful, pard," said Shorty, as he led the descent, slowly and noiselessly. In a few minutes they had reached the lowest limbs, where they paused to get breath and to reconnoiter for the dash, by the dim light of the smoldering embers.

"Pick out yer hoss, 'n' go fer him like lightnin' jest 's soon 's ever ye hit the ground. You take that 'ere spotted one 't looks like a circus hoss, 'n' I'll go fer the white-face sorrel. Now, ready—go !"

Nimbly swinging themselves down by their hands, they dropped a few feet to the ground. A Confederate lying near was half awakened by the noise and rose upon his elbow. None other of the sleepers had been aroused.

"Make a sound 'n' I'll blow yer brains out!" said Shorty in a hoarse whisper. The startled trooper thought it wise to take care of what brains he had.

In an instant the fugitives were upon the backs of the horses. Shorty dashed away in the direction he had chosen as the most favorable, urging his steed to a gallop as he picked his way through the bivouac. Si followed, a good second in the race. The straps around the necks of the horses sufficed to guide them in their course.

The commotion set the picketed horses to neighing and

stamping; and the cavalier who was cowed by Shorty's threat, thought he might now let off a yell without danger of losing his brains. A great uproar followed, but the daring riders were lost in the darkness.

Si and Shorty dashed on, they knew not whither, thinking only of getting away from the hostile bivouac. They dared not take the road, which would doubtless be picketed by the enemy. They at length determined to abandon the horses that had done them such good service, as

ANOTHER BREAK.

without them they were less likely to be discovered. After getting their bearings as well as they could they pressed forward on foot, through field and forest. Shorty believed, as nearly as he could judge the distance, that if they could continue their course unmolested till dawn and conceal themselves the next day, one more night, if fortune still smiled upon them, would enable them to pass around the enemy's flank and reach the Union lines. They succeeded in finding a few ears of corn, which they ate raw and partially allayed the pangs of hunger. With every step Si's spirits rose, as hope gradually blossomed into full belief that the hour of deliverance was near.

"We'd *orter* make the riffle this time," he said to Shorty, as they lay in a clump of bushes for a short rest, "fer I

can't help feelin' 's though we've tried hard 'nuff ter desarve it. "You 'n' me 've arned our liberty, 'n' it 'll be
purty hard ter slip up arter all we've been through. I
don't b'lieve we will, nuther."

All went well until just before day, when, emerging from
a thicket in the dim starlight, they were startled by the
challenge, "Who comes thar?" and before they had time
to think they were covered by half a dozen muskets, at
such short range that it would have been madness to
attempt escape. Wandering too near the enemy's lines,
they had walked right into a Confederate outpost. Confused and terror-stricken, Si was speechless, and made no
effort to reply to the challenge. Had he done so his stam-
mering words would instantly have betrayed them. In
this new and alarming crisis he could only turn appealingly to his companion.

"*Who comes thar?*" and the musket-locks clicked omin-
ously as the hammers were drawn up.

"Friends!" answered Shorty, without a perceptible
tremor in his voice. His quick thoughts had suggested
to him a subterfuge as the only possible way out of the
dilemma. His faith in its success was extremely shadowy,
but the remembrance of previous deliverances encouraged
him to make the trial.

"Advance 'n' give the countersign!"

"Sorry I can't acommerdate ye," replied Shorty, "but
me 'n' my pard 's jest been out skylarkin' 'round 'n' we
got left outside. It'll be all right ef ye let us in; we wants
ter git ter the rijiment 'fore roll-call. I reck'n ye've been
thar yerself."

"What ridgment d' you-all b'long to?"

"Forty-fifth Alabamy."

"What comp'ny?"

"Comp'ny D!"

"Who 's yer capting?"

"Smith!" Shorty thought this name would be more likely to hit the mark than any other.

"Now jest look-a-hyar! Ye needn't stan' thar lyin' no mo'. I b'long ter the Fawty-fifth Alabam myself 'n' this yer's Comp'ny D. Ye kain't come that air trick. Ye hain't got the right kind o' clothes on, nuther. I b'lieve ye're ornery Yanks, 'n' dog my skin ef we don't settle yer hash right now."

There was but one thing to do, and Shorty waved his hand in token of surrender. "The trick 's yourn, pard," he said. "Ye've got all the trumps 'n' ther' ain't no use tryin' ter play the game out."

Once more Si and Shorty were in the toils, and despairingly sat down upon a log. Si ventured to speak of his famished condition, and one of them gave him a section of musty corn "pone." No piece of pie from his mother's cupboard had ever been so welcome. In reply to the questions of their captors, Shorty told the story of their recent adventures.

"'Pears like ye're mighty slip'ry chaps," said one, "but I 'low ye won't git away *this* time."

As soon as it was fully light they were marched under a formidable escort with fixed bayonets, and delivered to an officer. Early in the day they were started southward, with a squad of other prisoners, strongly guarded. At the nearest railway station they boarded a train and went whirling away. Poor Si was again plunged into the lowest depths of woe.

Hours and hours the train sped on. Si would have abandoned himself to utter despair but for an occasional word of encouragement from Shorty. At last they reached their destination and were turned loose in a great "bullpen," where were many thousands of their unfortunate fellows.

What pen can adequately portray the scenes of human suffering and wretchedness that everywhere met the eyes of the new comers, as they wandered, dazed and bewildered, among the multitude of starving, half-naked captives! Pale, gaunt and haggard, wasted by disease and hunger, their scanty garments in rags, many without shelter from the weather—they gave ghastly evidence of "man's inhumanity to man." Language is feeble, and words seem to have lost their meaning, when attempt is made to depict the long, bitter agony of body and mind and heart that often made death a welcome relief, in that hell upon earth.

As Si and Shorty roamed through the prison hundreds of poor wretches crowded around them, inquiring with intensest eagerness concerning the progress of the war and the prospect of its continuance; and above all else whether anything was being done toward an exchange of prisoners. Exchange!—this was the *ignis-fatuus* that was ever before the eye of the prisoner. Time and time again its fitful light awakened hope and expectation in the sorrowing heart, only to disappear in darkness more dense and comfortless than before. Thousands of brave, patient men, in whose memories dwell the horrid specters of those prisons, never can be convinced that the United States Government was not culpably responsible for a vast amount of suffering and death, by its failure to agree with the Confederate authorities upon terms for an exchange of prisoners.

Si's tender heart was profoundly moved. He saw emaciated men struggling around the slender fires to cook their meager rations of meal, or scraping bare beef bones to the last vestige of nutriment. He saw them huddling under tattered blankets to shield them from the fierce noonday heat, or creeping like burrowing beasts into their holes in the ground. He saw his fellow-soldiers, with hollow eyes, weak and helpless and devoured by vermin, borne on stretchers to the overflowing hospitals. He saw wagons heaped like butchers' carts in the shambles with skeleton corpses, driven to the vast potter's field, where the eye grew weary and the heart sick at sight of the endless rows of graves. He heard the crack of musket and the whistle of bullet as it sped with unerring aim to strike down a demented wretch who, crazed by his sufferings, had unwittingly crossed the barbarous "dead-line." He heard the shrieks and curses of those whose gnawing misery had bereft them of moral volition and made them brutes. He heard the groans of despair from men who had lived this hideous, corroding life through many long, wretched months, and in whose hearts scarce a flickering spark of hope remained. Even the harrowing sights and sounds of the battle and the field hospital were not so sickening and abhorrent as these.

"Shorty," said Si that night, as they lay together, out under the pitying stars, "we've got ter git out o' here er die a-tryin'. I axed one o' the boys 'bout it 'n' he said a good many on 'em tries it but they mostly gits shot er ketched by the bloodhounds the rebils turns loose on 'em. A few gits away, 'n' I reck'n we kin do 't 'f anybody else kin. We got tripped up two er three times when we tried it on, but I'm 'n favor o' keepin' at it 'n' ther's no tellin' but we'll git thar next time. Anyhow I'd a mighty sight ruther be shot 'n ter stay here 'n' starve ter death er be et up by the graybacks."

"I hain't said nothin' to ye," replied Shorty, "'cause I didn't see no chance yit, but I've kep' on thinkin' 'bout gittin' away every minnit sence we walked inter the arms o' them Johnnies t'other mornin'. Arter what I've seen here I'm fiercer 'n ever. You jest keep shady, Si, 'n' I'll tip ye a wink soon 's I see the ghost of a show."

The next day the newly arrived prisoners were visited by a Confederate officer, with smooth tongue and persuasive address, who asked them if they would like to get out of prison. All were eager to know how they might be restored to liberty, for after the scenes they had witnessed the dark cloud of despair was already hovering over them.

"Course we 'd be glad ter git out," said Si, "ef ye'll only jest tell us how ter do it."

"It is a very simple thing," replied the officer, "just enlist in the Confederate army. Our cause is certain to succeed, and we will do well by you. Here is a roll if you would like to sign it."

"Cap," said Si, and his eyes flashed with indignation, "what do ye take us fer? I kin tell ye that ye're barkin' up the wrong tree. Ye kin roll up that paper 'n' put it 'r yer pocket, fer ther' ain't nobody 'n this crowd that 'll sign it. Leastwise *I* won't; I'll die a hunderd times 'fore I'll do sich a thing. I know my pard won't, nuther, will ye, Shorty?"

"No-sir-ee-*bob!*" was the terse response of his comrade. The emphasis he placed upon the "bob" was the strongest possible evidence of his loyalty.

There was perfect unanimity of sentiment in the party, and the officer retired without having secured any recruits to fight against the flag of their country. The starving prisoners gathered around, waved their skinny hands, and greeted them with approving cheers and shouts of "Bully for the fresh fish!" This term was universally applied to new arrivals of prisoners.

Ah, no! all these have long suffered for their patriotism, and yonder lie thousands who were faithful and true to the last feeble gasp of expiring life; and Corporal Klegg and his comrade are not the ones to betray their country, upon whose altar they have laid their all!

We need not enter into the details of their daily prison life. The exceeding meagerness and wretched quality of the food were a constant and powerful spur to Si in his efforts to devise some way of escape. Scarcely an hour passed that he did not propose to his comrade some plan that Shorty's better judgment condemned as impracticable. The latter was fully vested with the veto power, and most of Si's relief measures were promptly disposed of in this way.

Shorty counseled patience, but Si grew restive **at the** delay. More than once Shorty directed his attention to the cordon of watchful sentinels, clad in gray, with loaded muskets, around the stockade; the body of troops without, quick to respond to the slightest alarm; and the artillery, with shotted guns, planted upon the adjacent hills. The frequent attempts to escape, by tunnels and otherwise, had served to heighten the vigilance of the guards.

"We don't want ter make a break," said Shorty, "'less

we've got a livin' chance. Ef we try it 'n' git cotched, that'll be the end on 't. I 'low they'll chuck us in where we'll have ter stay fer a while."

Two or three weeks later, when a detail was made to go with wagons for wood, Shorty volunteered the services of himself and his comrade. They were yet vigorous, and

IN THE PRISON-PEN.

better able to do the work than others. Si gladly consented, casting a quick, inquiring glance at Shorty, which the latter readily interpreted. "Look sharp, Si," he said, "'n' watch me cluss, but be keerful 'bout lettin' on!"

The detail, accompanied by a detachment of rebel soldiers, went to the forest, half a mile from the stockade. The prisoners were so docile and industrious that their attendants were in a measure thrown off their guard and loitered carelessly about. Shorty and Si started for a stick that lay a few steps beyond the guards.

"Do ye want ter try it, Si?" asked Shorty in a whisper. "Ye know these rebil guns has all got bullets in 'em!"

"Go it!" was the reply.

As they stooped to lift the log, Shorty glanced quickly at the guards, and saw that none were watching with especial attention.

"Now, git—fer yer life!" he said in a low tone.

"Both bounded away, and so quick were their movements, and so noiseless their steps upon the yielding earth, that they were a dozen paces away among the thick trees before their flight was discovered.

"Halt, there, you Yanks!" yelled one of the guards, as he drew up his musket and fired wildly, the ball whistling among the tree-tops. Crack—crack—and a dozen illy-directed missiles were sent after the fugitives, who were now rods away and going six feet at a step. The bullets pattered against the trees, two or three of them zipping unpleasantly near, but neither of the swiftly flying Hoosiers was touched.

"Ef they stop ter load we kin git out o' range," said Shorty, to encourage his panting comrade, "'n' ef they tries ter chase us 'th the'r traps on we kin outrun 'em. Leg it, Si; put in yer best licks!"

Si needed no urging. He leaped over the ground like a deer, with a burst of speed that surprised himself and fairly challenged the longer and usually more active legs of Shorty.

A few of the guards threw down their muskets and started in pursuit. Those who remained had their hands full of business immediately. Quick to seize an opportunity, as soon as the thoughtless guards had discharged their muskets, one of the prisoners shouted "Come on, boys, here's our chance!" and away they all went, scattering in every direction. This was highly favorable for Si and Shorty, who by this time were out of sight in the woods. The demoralized guards—terror-stricken at thought of the punishment they would incur for having permitted a "delivery"—charged around with frantic yells in the vain effort to stop the runaways. Meanwhile the sound of the firing had alarmed the forces at the prison and a few minutes later a squadron of cavalry was on the gallop to join in the chase.

Si and Shorty had no difficulty in outstripping their pursuers, who were incumbered by their accouterments, and

IN THE SWAMP.

for the moment they were free. They knew they would be hunted by men and horses and fierce dogs, and they sped on, that they might get as much the start as possible. If they could baffle their enemies until night there would be hope.

An hour—two hours — passed, and they were miles from the loathsome prison. Carefully avoiding the highways and habitations of man, they threaded their way through forest and copse. At length they thought they heard the distant baying of the hounds upon their track. Fortunately one of those great swamps so often met with in the south was near. With stick in hand to feel their way they plunged in and made for its darkest recesses, the foul, slimy water at times reaching to their waists. For another hour they floundered on and then, as they seemed to be nearing the farther side of the morass, Shorty advised concealment till night. They crept into a dense clump of bushes and rank swamp grass. Standing knee deep in water, they waited through the closing hours of the day for the darkness.

Little breath had been wasted in talk during their flight. Now they were free to canvass the situation and decide upon their course. There was not much argument or difference of opinion, for Shorty's judgment had so rarely proved at fault that it was never called in question by his confiding comrade. Shorty had never studied astronomy from the books, but he thought he knew enough about the moon and the stars to be able to shape the long and perilous journey which they had so auspiciously begun. Their hearts sank as they thought of the many miles that they must traverse by night. But they cheered each other and stoutly nerved themselves for the trial.

It will suffice for this veracious chronicle to say that Si and Shorty were among the few who succeeded in running the fearful gauntlet. They traveled by night, resting during the daytime in swamps and brakes and thickets, sleeping and watching each in turn. They subsisted upon corn, which was then in kernel, raw vegetables which they found here and there, and an occasional meal that tasted "sweeter than honey and the honeycomb," in the humble cabin of a friendly negro. Thus they pressed forward, for many days and nights. The worthless shoes given them in exchange the day of their first capture gave out entirely. With feet bare and bleeding, their clothes torn by thorns and brambles, chilled by the nightly dews, beaten by sun and storm, and often enduring the pangs of hunger, they pushed on toward the goal. When at last they entered the lines of the Union army, Si's long pent-up feelings found relief in a succession of wild yells that came near stampeding a whole brigade. Such an overwhelming happiness had not filled his heart since the day he first put on a uniform as a recruit of Company Q.

The two vagabonds were received with a salvo of cheers by their comrades of the 200th Indiana. They had long since been given up for dead. The men crowded around them to hear the story of their adventures.

RETURN OF THE VAGABONDS.

"I'll tell ye all 'bout it arter a while," said Si, "but ye'll have ter jest wait t'll I git filled up with hardtack 'n' sowbelly. I'm holler clear down ter my toes!"

All the haversacks in the company were at once placed at the disposal of the returned fugitives, and nothing was thought of until their hunger had been satisfied.

Then the orderly took them to the quartermaster, who fitted them out from top to toe with new clothes. In the important matter of a shirt, Si was careful to draw one that was about four sizes too large for him. He knew it would shrink to the right proportions the first time he washed it. The first army shirt Si had, shortened up so much after a washing that it looked more like a vest than a shirt.

CHAPTER XLVI.

Sɪ ᴀɴᴅ Sʜᴏʀᴛʏ Tᴀᴋᴇ Sᴡᴇᴇᴛ Rᴇᴠᴇɴɢᴇ Uᴘᴏɴ ᴛʜᴇ Eɴᴇᴍʏ—Cᴏʀᴘᴏʀᴀʟ
Kʟᴇɢɢ Mᴇᴇᴛs ᴡɪᴛʜ ᴀ Sᴏʀᴇ Bᴇʀᴇᴀᴠᴇᴍᴇɴᴛ.

ONE day the corps to which the 200th Indiana belonged, flanked by a heavy force of cavalry, was dispatched on a rapid detour to the enemy's rear, to strike the railroad which was his chief source of supply. To favor the movement the main body of the Union army closely pressed the Confederate lines at all points, making it impossible for the latter to detach any considerable body to operate against the raiders.

Imposing and noisy "demonstrations," as they were called, to hold the attention of the enemy and mask the real movement elsewhere, were prominent in the strategy of this campaign, and of frequent occurrence on both sides. Sometimes only a brigade or division, at other times a corps or half the army, engaged in the spasmodic effort to deceive "the other fellows." The troops charged with this duty were bountifully supplied with ammunition, often a hundred rounds or more per man, and marched to the line of fortified outposts. Here, for hours at a time, they did nothing but load their muskets and blaze away into the woods toward the enemy—and yell. Often a battery or two of artillery contributed to the frightful din, sending shot and shell plunging through the trees. It was great sport for the boys, as they, in imagination, mowed down the rebels by hundreds, without danger

647

to themselves. After one of these ebullitions the trees in front, which were the only sufferers, were a sight to behold. Not one of them but was slivered and scarred for a distance of fifty feet from the ground. Twenty or thirty men would select a tree perhaps a foot in diameter as a particular target and actually cut it down with their bullets. At these times the men worked themselves up almost to the excitement of actual battle. At night they were hoarse from yelling, and as much exhausted as if they had been fighting all day. These theatrical performances were intended to distract the enemy and, if possible, induce him to weaken the point really to be assailed, by withdrawing from it troops to reinforce the line where the stunning hullaballoo indicated a probable assault. If he did this the "demonstration" was considered a success, and the tons of lead and iron so promiscuously scattered about were not wasted.

While one of these terrifying fusillades was in progress the corps alluded to, by a rapid march, brushing away the enemy's cavalry which hovered around, reached the railroad that was its objective point. The men had been crowded to the utmost and were much wearied, but there was not a moment for rest. The success of the expedition and the safety of the command depended upon the greatest celerity of movement. The cavalry was sent out in all directions to watch the enemy. Half the infantry was advantageously posted, throwing up hasty intrenchments, to cover the other half, which entered at once and with zest upon the work of destruction.

The cutting of railroads was, from the outbreak of the war, encouraged on both sides, and by this time had developed into an important military industry. Various implements and appliances, to facilitate the havoc and make it as effectual as possible, were part of the equipment of every army.

"Now we're goin' ter have some fun, Shorty!" exclaimed

Si, as the 200th Indiana stacked arms beside the track and the specific duty to be performed became apparent to all. "I hain't never fergot the time the Johnnies cut *our* cracker-line, 'n' I've allus been hopin' we'd git a chance ter pay 'em back. 'Sides that you 'n' me 's got a pertickler spite agin this 'ere railroad, 'cause it's the one 't tuk us down ter that measly place 't we had sich a time gittin' 'way from. I've got a fust-rate stummick fer pitchin' inter this job!"

Five thousand men were thickly distributed on both

DESTROYING A RAILROAD.

sides of the road for a mile. They did not lay off their accouterments, and their muskets were within grasp, should there be occasion to stop work and go to fighting. Axes, sledge-hammers, levers and "claws" were plentifully supplied. A few spikes were quickly drawn at intervals of two or three hundred yards. Then the men laid hold of the rails on one side, gave a mighty yell, and in an instant the track was turned over into the ditch. Vigorous blows with the sledges rapidly detached the ties from the rails. Meanwhile others had started a hundred fires all along the line. Upon these the ties were loosely piled, with quantities of fence rails and dry limbs and brush to feed the flames. The long, clumsy iron rails were picked up, with a dozen men to each, as if they were feathers, and laid across the blazing heaps. In half an hour they were at a red heat, for six or eight feet in the middle. Then came the final process by which the devastation was made complete. With grappling-irons, made for the purpose, the rails were twisted two or three times around, as Si had often seen his mother twist doughnuts. The still glowing rails were then bent entirely around the trunks of standing trees, where they were left to cool.

It was a scene of wild and furious tumult, never to be forgotten—the yelling, scrambling, sweating men, their faces begrimed with dust and smoke, lifting, prying, pounding and chopping, the shouts of the officers directing the operations and urging up the laggards, and the blazing, crackling fires, stretching far along the track on either side. A few hours sufficed to utterly destroy miles of the road—the ties in ashes and the twisted, shapeless rails transformed into rings encircling the trees.

When an undertaking of this kind was thoroughly carried out it caused, in many cases, serious embarrassment to the Confederate army. The vast mineral resources of the south were then almost entirely undeveloped. Before the war all iron for railroads in that section was obtained from the north or imported from Europe. The south had no means to make good the wear of constant use and the ravage of war. If rails were merely heated and bent it was possible to straighten them so that they might be relaid, but when they were fantastically twisted by the grappling-irons of well equipped raiders, they were made valueless except as they might command the market price for "old iron." The frequent raids upon the lines of supply of the Union army, though annoying, were far less disastrous than was the destruction of railroads to the enemy. The government kept at all desirable points abundant supplies of rails, ties, spikes, etc., and the engineer corps repaired the breaks with a rapidity that was amazing. Not infrequently this was done under fire, the men toiling with their muskets slung over their backs, part of them keeping back the enemy while the others pushed forward the work. There seemed to be nothing impossible to the intelligent soldiers of the Union army.

Railroads were invaluable for the speedy transportation of troops and supplies. At times, when extraordinary facilities were needed—as when two corps were sent from the Army of the Potomac to reinforce the Army of the Cumberland at Chattanooga—the government took possession of the necessary roads with all their rolling-stock, and as many engines and cars of other roads as could be used; and for the time all private business had to give way. The southern roads, in the territory occupied by the Union army, were in many cases laid with new rails, the gauge being changed when necessary, and stocked with engines and cars owned by the government. These were all designated "U. S. M. R. Rds."—United States Military Railroads. During the last year of the war the military railway service reached the height of efficiency. Plenty of engineers, conductors and trainmen were found, who took their lives in their hands as truly as did the soldiers who marched to battle.

While the 200th Indiana and the other wreckers were engaged in their work, they were more than once called into line with loaded muskets by sharp firing on the outposts, where there was constant skirmishing with the enemy's cavalry. At length a horseman came galloping in with the intelligence that a large body of Confederate infantry was approaching with rapid strides. The bugles sounded the "fall in" and away went the Union force, leaving the road for miles a smoking ruin. Through the night, stumbling along in the darkness, the men pushed on, harassed in front, flank and rear by the rebel riders. Morning found the corps safely back in its place behind the great line of intrenchments.

Si and Shorty ate their hardtack and bacon that day with keen enjoyment. Nothing since the regiment left Indiana had given them so much satisfaction as the opportunity to wreak their vengeance upon that railroad.

During the next few days the zipping bullets that came in a constant shower from the rebel side seemed to be more than usually spiteful. They hissed angrily through the air, and pelted the "head-log" that surmounted every field-work. This log—usually ten or twelve inches in diameter —was laid along the top of the work, resting upon blocks, leaving a crevice two or three inches wide through which the gun was thrust for firing, the log affording good protection to the heads of the soldiers. Of course some bullets found their way through the crevice and did fatal execution, but many lives were saved by the "head-log."

After one of the fierce engagements that were of such frequent occurrence during those bloody days, Si Klegg and Shorty were on the picket line. A small body of Confederates appeared in the edge of the timber skirting a field, waving a white cloth.

"Be they goin' ter s'render?" asked Si. "I sh'd think they'd be gittin' tired 'n' wantin' ter quit!"

"I reck'n not," replied Shorty. "Looks ter me like a flag o' truce."

This it proved to be. The proper officer being summoned to receive the message, a request from the Confederate commander was delivered for a cessation of hostilities for two hours, to bury the dead. The bodies lay between the lines, and among them were some of the desperately wounded, inaccessible from either side so long as the firing was continued.

The truce was agreed to, and the necessary orders were at once sent along the lines. Gladly the combatants laid

down their arms and threw off their accouterments. The deadly crack of musket and whiz of bullet ceased and there came a brief season of quiet that was like a glimpse of heaven to the soldiers, weary of war. Large burial parties were detailed from each army, for the valor of both was attested by the corpses that lay upon that field, fast blackening in the sun. Some with picks and shovels dug long trenches, in which were laid, side by side, the comrades who never again would fall in for roll-call or battle charge. Others tenderly lifted the wounded upon stretchers and bore them away. As far as possible the dead were identified and the resting place of
each was marked by a
roughly-carved head-
board. No prayers
were said ; there was
no hearse with nod-
ding plumes, no toll-
ing of funeral bells;
no loved ones to weep
over the fallen brave.
One by one, with per-
haps not so much as a
blanket for a winding-
sheet, they were cov-
ered with the earth

UNDER A TRUCE.

which, a few hours before, they had trodden in the awful struggle.

Officers and men not engaged in the duty of interment, leaving behind them the implements of death, mingled freely between the lines, none, of course, passing the intrenchments of the other side. Soldiers in blue and in gray chatted as if they had been lifelong friends instead of deadly enemies, whose only thought and act, day after day, was to take life. The fast-filling graves around them did not repress the laugh and jest that to one less calloused to such scenes would appear sacrilege. Personally these men were not foes, and they were alike brave in defense of what they believed to be the right. Save an occasional good-natured boast or rally in the way of badinage, little was said about the principles involved in the war or the conduct of the desperate campaign in which they were engaged. They bartered coffee and salt for tobacco, and cordially united in expressing the hope that the war would soon end. Each was equally persistent in declaring that there was but one way in which it must and should end, and that was by the complete success of his side.

Officers lounged about in little groups, talking of more weighty matters, and passing the flask from one to another in the most sociable manner.

Two hours—the last body has been buried and the mangled sufferers have been carried within the respective lines. A bugle blast gives notice "to whom it may concern"—and it concerns them all—that the truce is ended. The soldiers of the opposing armies shake hands, speak kind words of parting, and soon disappear behind the intrenchments. No one has feared to go unarmed among his enemies, for lost to honor indeed is that soldier who would violate the faith of a truce. Few graver offenses are known to military law.

Now the dove of peace, whose white wings for a little time have fluttered above the hostile legions, flies sadly away, as the soldiers buckle on again their warlike trappings and seize their muskets. There is a blazing line beneath the head-logs and the killing and maiming goes on as before. Perhaps at the first shot one may send a hissing bullet through the brain of him whose hand but a moment ago he took in friendly parting. Such is war!

Night falls, and once more the din is hushed. A band of the Union army—for the music has not all been sent to the rear—goes to the trenches and plays "The Star Spangled Banner." The soldiers wave their caps and fill the air with a tremendous chorus of shouts and cheers. All is quiet "over the way" until the echoes have ceased, and then a Confederate band strikes up the lively cadences of "Dixie," and it is *their* turn to yell. The "Johnnies" make the most of the opportunity, striving to dwarf the Union cheers by the volume of sound that comes from their lusty lungs. All is still again, and the stirring strains of the "Red, White and Blue" are heard. This arouses afresh the patriotic ardor of the Union soldiers and they shout louder and longer than before. Then upon the other side is heard the "Bonnie Blue Flag," and the men in gray, who have sung it a thousand times in camp and on the march, almost split their throats with responsive yells. The next number in the impromptu program is "John Brown's Body," which the band plays defiantly. When it is finished thousands of blue-coated soldiers join in singing, with all the power they can command:

> "We'll hang Jeff Davis on a sour-apple tree."

This has an inflammatory effect, and the crack of muskets and sputtering volley of bullets clearly show the disfavor with which half the audience receives this selection. The balls go high, as if only intended to evince disapproval. The singers seize their guns and send back a hailstorm of lead in reply.

"Say, Johnny," shouts one at the top of his voice—for the strongly fortified lines are so near that his words can reach—"That makes us squar'. Now let up on shootin' and don't spile the concert!"

"All right, Yank," was the reply, "but yer don't want ter be givin' us no more o' that dog-goned slush. We didn't 'low to hit ye, but ef ye sing that ag'in we'll aim low next time!"

The Confederate band responds with "My Maryland," and the soldiers sing:

> "The despot's heel is on thy shore,
> Maryland, my Maryland."

After the rebels have yelled sufficiently over this popular southern song, peace and good feeling are restored by the tender chords of "Annie Laurie" from the band in the Union trenches. The other meets it, in the same spirit, with "Auld Lang Syne," and the men of both armies cheer. Then follow, the bands playing alternately, "Bowld Soger Boy," "Comin' thro' the Rye," "When Johnny Comes Marching Home," "Old Kentucky Home," "Way Down upon the Suwanee Riber" and "Nellie Gray." "Music hath charms" to soften even the asperities of "grim visaged war," and thousands of hearts are moved as both bands unite in "Home, Sweet Home." But for the darkness we might see many a swarthy and battle-scarred veteran dash away a tear with the rough sleeve of his blouse. With tender, passionate thoughts of far-off loved ones the soldiers stretch themselves upon the ground, their muskets beside them, save those who are to keep vigil at the works and upon the lonely outposts.

There came a day when the soldiers of the 200th Indiana looked for the last time into the blazing muzzles of the rebel guns. The long campaign—and the war in that department of the army—closed with a defeat of the enemy, so crushing and overwhelming that recovery from the blow was impossible.

When the dispositions were made for the last grand assault upon the Confederate lines, the duty of carrying a strong fort at an important point was assigned to the brigade to which the 200th Indiana belonged. While waiting for the final word of command the troops lay down in line, covered by their intrenchments. The cannon that had long been bellowing through the embrasures of the fort were silent, and those who manned them seemed to be gathering strength to meet the expected shock. No sound of musket was heard, except an occasional exchange of shots on the picket-line. It was the calm before the bursting of the storm.

Only a fragment of the 200th remained. Of the thousand men with which it took the field, scarcely a hundred were now in its ranks. Of these many bore the honorable scars of battle. The graves of its dead thickly dotted the fiery and devious path it had so painfully traveled. Hundreds, disabled by wounds and wasting disease, no longer answered to their names at roll-call. The regiment had done its duty faithfully and well. Often tried in war's fiercest crucible, its name had never been tarnished by dishonor. Its record was without spot, and its shrunken line was a silent yet most eloquent testimonial to its valor.

The dauntless heroes looked gravely into one another's faces as they lay there, ready as ever to leap into the vortex of the conflict, with ears strained to catch the order to advance. There was an undefined feeling that the end was near at hand. To pass safely through the years of blood and fall at the last, in the hour of victory, seemed a cruel fate. Yet to many of those soon to face the belching guns of the fort but a few minutes of life remained. Who would go down before the crimson sickle that was again to be thrust into the thinned ranks? Who would once more come out unscathed, and still live to maintain the honor of that faded and riven flag?

"Shorty," said Si, "I can't help feelin' 't I'll be mighty glad when the war 's over. Ye know well 'nuff I don't mean 't I want ter quit till *'tis* over; but 'pears ter me 's though everybody, north 'n' south, them 't 's soljerin' 'n' them 't 's to hum, must be gittin' 'bout 's much on it 's they kin stand. I know 't what I've had 'll last me 'f I sh'd live ter be 's old 's Methuzelum."

"Mebbe ye hain't fergot," replied Shorty, "what I used ter say to ye 'long at fust, when ye was so fierce ter git inter a fight. Ye know I told ye 't ye'd git filled up 'fore ye got through. War 's mighty satisfyin'—a leetle on 't goes a good ways—'n' 't don't take long ter kinder use up

a feller's hankerin' arter it. I reck'n ye'll think more o'
yer home, when ye git thar, 'n ye ever did afore."

"*You've* got ter go home 'long 'th me when we gits discharged. It sort o' runs 'n my head 't the rebils is losin'
the'r grip 'n' they 'll let go one o' these days. I want ye
ter come ter the old farm 'n' stay jest 's long 's ever ye're a
mind ter. Ye know I'm yer s'perior ossifer 'n' when I tells
ye ter do a thing ye have ter do it. But I'll be glad when
this fight terday 's over."

"It'll be time 'nough when the war does peter out ter
figger on what we're goin' ter do then," replied Shorty.
"We ain't out o' the woods yet, 'n' mebbe—"

A bugle blast, sharp and clear, brings every man to his
feet.

"Now, my brave men," shouts the colonel, "we're going
into that fort; follow me!"

The soldiers leap over their intrenchments and with loud
cheers dash forward. There is not a straggler; all such
have long since disappeared from the ranks of the 200th.

Those within the fort send up a defiant yell. The guns
have been double-shotted, and at each stands a man with
the lanyard in his hand. As the assailants come within
range there is a roar that makes the earth tremble. Volumes of flame and smoke burst from the embrasures and
a tempest of canister sweeps the charging line. Before
that withering blast many a gallant hero falls. The
ground is thickly strewn with the dead and wounded.

"Forward!"

No need to give command, for save those who are stricken
down not a man falters. Muskets blaze along the hostile
line and bullets sing their death-song. Fast as men can
reload, cannon and musket send forth their fiery breath.

The 200th Indiana leads the brigade in the onward
rush. Comrades fall at every step. Each instant of time
is precious, for in a few minutes none will be left. The
ranks are thin and ragged but they sweep on with no

thought but of the goal. Close upon the heels of the 200th press those of the other regiments whom the storm of missiles has spared, vying with one another to first scale the wall of the fort. Often a flag goes down as its bearer falls, but it is instantly seized and borne proudly aloft, as the men, with loud shouts, fairly leap along the ground. Blood is streaming from some who, wounded but not disabled, push on with their brave comrades.

Now they reach the abattis of stakes and brushwood. Some have brought axes, and under the withering fire from the fort they cut and slash, while their comrades at intervals wrench away the obstructions. Through the gaps they rush, and down into the deep trench that surrounds the fortification. Now they are below the range of the enemy's guns, but shells with hissing fuses are tossed over the parapet to burst among the panting, struggling soldiers in the ditch. The assailants cannot stop here. Retreat or surrender they will not; but is it possible for them to advance further?

Quick as thought some mount the shoulders of others and clamber upon the bank. Then these seize their comrades by the hands and pull them up. One more dash and the question of success or failure will in a moment be solved. They sweep up the steep side of the fort. Some, pierced by angry bullets, roll down among those who lie mangled, dead or dying, in the ditch below.

Has Corporal Klegg escaped the bloody havoc of the conflict? Has he been found wanting in this supreme test of human courage? Ah, there he is, among the foremost, far up the blood-stained slope. His garments have been torn by the swift missiles and his hat is gone. As he nears the crest he turns for an instant and shouts a word of encouragement to those who are toiling up the bank. Not one is less brave than he among all the officers and men in that devoted band.

At the same instant a score gain the summit and leap

into the very arms of the foe. A moment, and fifty—a hundred more, have followed, and the reserves are swarming over the crest. Muskets are discharged with deadly effect and cruel bayonets are plunged into quivering bodies. Shouts, groans and mad yells and curses are commingled in hideous uproar.

The onslaught is irresistible. The Confederates fling down their arms and yield themselves prisoners or seek to escape by flight. With wild shouts of triumph the victorious soldiers pursue the fleeing enemy. At other points the long Confederate line has been broken and the entire hostile army is in complete rout. Dozens of cannon and battle-flags are taken, and prisoners by hundreds and thousands. The triumphant soldiers, with prodigious yells, keep up the pursuit until many fall to the ground in utter exhaustion.

After entering the fort Si had missed his faithful comrade, but in the all-absorbing rush and excitement there had been no opportunity to look for him or inquire after his welfare. Shorty was at his side when the 200th Indiana charged over the open ground and up to the abattis. He was sure that they must have been separated in the wild confusion, and that he would find his pard when the fight was over. As soon as the regiment halted Si began to look about and to ask, with constantly increasing anxiety, for tidings of his friend. No one knew what had become of Shorty.

A detail was sent back to the fort to look after the dead and wounded. Si eagerly volunteered for this duty, that he might search for his friend who, if a brother, could not have been more dear to him. He felt a keen pang at the thought that perhaps the one who had so long been his constant companion was lying—dead, or wounded and suffering. No; it could not, it *must* not be! How his heart throbbed as his hurrying feet neared the scene of the dreadful struggle!

Within the fort lay bodies of friend and foe, where they had fallen in the strife for the mastery. Si went from one to another of those clad in blue, looking upon the distorted and discolored features, now and then gently turning one that lay with face hidden. Here and there he recognized, with tear-dimmed eyes, a brave comrade who had gone down before the blast of death, but the one he sought was not there.

"Won't somebody give me a drink of water!"

It was a brave boy of Company Q, who lay with a shattered leg, beside one of the guns. Si dropped upon his knees and placed his canteen to the parched lips.

"Thank ye, Si," said the sufferer, "that makes me feel better. Didn't we go for 'em?"

"We did, fer a fact!" replied Si, as he picked up a blanket and placed it under the head of his comrade. "Jest be quiet a bit 'n' we'll take care on ye. But—do ye know anything 'bout—Shorty? I hain't seen him—sence the fight."

"I can't tell ye where he is. He helped me to climb out o' the ditch, an' that 's the last I seen of him. I hope, fer your sake, pard, he didn't git hurt."

Si passed over the wall of the fort and down the slope, examining the motionless forms that lay about, but he did not find the missing one. The pain that was growing in his heart found relief for an instant in the thought that Shorty might be a prisoner. But he remembered that in such a fight it was scarcely possible for them to lose by capture, and the burden of anxious fear lay heavy upon him as he leaped into the ditch to continue the sad search.

The dead and the desperately wounded lay thickly here. The earth was crimsoned by the streams that had flowed from heroes' veins. Si had not long to look. There are many survivors of the war who can appreciate—for such arrows pierced *their* hearts—the bitter anguish that thrilled him as his eyes fell upon the face and form of his prostrate comrade. There was no sound nor movement to give sign of life. The clothing was reddened with blood.

"Shorty!" he said, convulsively, as he knelt beside him, clasping in one of his own the nerveless hand that lay across the breast, and with the other pressing the clammy forehead. "Shorty!" he repeated, in tremulous tones that conveyed a wealth of tenderness and affection, "can't ye speak a word to me, pard? Can't ye jest open yer eyes 'n' look at me?" Tears flowed unchecked down the face of Si, as he pressed the unresponsing hand, and gently smoothed the face of his comrade The feebly fluttering pulse told that the spark of life had not yet gone out.

The warm, tender touch revived the dying soldier. He opened his eyes, already dimmed by the film of death. He gazed into the face of Si and a faint smile of recognition lighted up the pallor upon brow and cheek. His lips moved as if he would speak, but no sound reached Si's straining ear.

"Dear Shorty"—and Si's words came heavily as the tears flowed afresh—"ye mustn't die! Don't leave me, pard! Here, take a drink out o' my canteen."

"Si," said Shorty, in a slow, feeble whisper, "did—we—get—the—fort?"

"Course we did," replied Si, "I knew we would when we started fer it. Now I want ye ter cheer up 'n' we'll git ye out o' here. Ye've *got* ter git well o' this!"

His comrade had recognized and spoken to him, and Si's heart throbbed with a brief happiness, born of the hope that Shorty would not die. But even then the eyes had closed to open not again, and the pulse was forever still. It was some minutes before Si could believe that Shorty was dead. He knelt long beside the lifeless body, clasping the stiffening hand. The realization of his bereavement brought upon his tender heart a crushing weight of grief that he had never known, and that only time could lighten.

With choking voice Si asked two or three of his comrades to assist him in lifting Shorty's body out of the ditch. They bore it to a grassy spot, under a spreading tree, which Si chose for his companion's resting-place.

"He's mine," said Si, "'n' I'll bury him!"

Procuring a shovel he dug a grave. An unspeakable sadness filled his heart as, with the help of another, he gently wrapped the body in a blanket, and they lowered it into the ground.

"HE WAS MY PARD."

"I wish ther' was some preacher here," he said, "to say sich a prayer 's Shorty desarves. 'Tain't a Christian way to kiver him up 'thout nothin' bein' said!"

Si hesitated a moment, and then knelt beside the open grave and reverently repeated the Lord's prayer.

"That's the best I kin do," he said. "My pard wa'n't a saint, 'cordin' as folks jedges 'em, but I hope God 'll take him up to heaven. If ther' don't no wuss people 'n' him git thar it 'll be a good 'nuff place fer me!"

Then Si softly covered from sight the body of his comrade. He rudely carved with his knife a piece of board and placed it at the head. It bore the inscription:

SHORTY

Co Q 200th Ind.

HE WAS MY PARD.

CHAPTER XLVII.

THE END COMES AT LAST, AND SI PUTS OFF THE ARMY BLUE.

THERE was no more fighting for the 200th Indiana. The rebel army whose guns it had so often faced was routed and scattered as no other army had been during the war. As an aggressive force it had almost passed out of existence. Its torn and battered fragments were gathered and transported to a distant field of operations, but they took small part in the closing events of the mighty struggle.

For some months the 200th was engaged in lazily guarding the railroads against imaginary foes, moving about from place to place, seemingly with no other purpose than to promote digestion.

Si grieved long and sorely over the death of Shorty. The sorrow of a bereaved husband or wife was never more sincere and poignant than that of Corporal Klegg for his heroic and helpful pard. He did not realize until he was gone how much he had leaned upon Shorty, and how he had been strengthened and comforted, through trial and suffering, by the companionship. For a time he was inconsolable, but the passing weeks and months gently assuaged the bitterness of his affliction. There were few of his comrades who had not also been called to mourn the death of those near and dear, and he knew it was the part of a good soldier to bear with resignation the manifold trials that fell to his lot. Gradually his wonted cheerfulness returned, but faithfulness to the memory of Shorty would not permit him to seek another "pard." It seemed to him sacrilege—as when Hymen clasps new ties over a freshly made grave. The daily round of duty in camp and the changing scenes of the march diverted his mind from his bereavement, but he never sat down to his coffee and crackers, or rolled himself in his blanket at night, without a lonely feeling that clouded his heart with sadness.

One evening the members of the little band that remained of the 200th Indiana were gathered around the blazing camp-fires. Dry cedar rails were plenty and there was no restraint upon their use. The fangs of the orders against foraging had long since been drawn, and those once sonorous proclamations lay idle and meaningless in the order-books of the generals.

Cedar rails were the soldier's favorite fuel, particularly when the weather was cool and a quick, warm fire was wanted. Nothing else responded to the match so promptly and furiously, with a roaring blaze that speedily tempered the chilliest air, and diffused comfort and cheer throughout the camp. The only fault of the cedar fire was the constant cracking and snapping, almost as loud as a volley of pistol shots, that scattered the glowing coals over a range of many feet. Millions of holes were burned in clothing, blankets and tents during the war by the sparks and blazing fragments that shot from heaps of cedar rails. But this annoying characteristic was freely forgiven; and when going into bivouac on a cold or stormy night, the soldiers pitched their yells in a higher key if they found that the adjacent fences were of cedar.

On the evening in question the men piled high the crackling fires and circled around them in fine spirits. They had potatoes and chickens galore, for that section of country had not been overrun and devastated by the hostile armies, and many of the boys had recently received from the North a fresh supply of "fac-simile money." This was simply counterfeit Confederate currency. Perhaps it could scarcely be called "counterfeit," in the sense in which the word is usually applied to spurious money, for it was intrinsically worth as much—a cent a pound for old paper —as was the so-called money of the alleged Southern Confederacy. The "fac-simile" bills, in denominations of from five to five hundred dollars, were printed in prodigious quantities by enterprising men in the North, and sold at the rate of about twenty-five cents for a thousand "dollars." It was a fair imitation of the cheap and poorly engraved stuff that was issued by the government at Richmond. Bushels and bushels of the counterfeit bills were sent down to the army and found a ready market among the soldiers, few of whom were disturbed in their seared and leathery consciences. If they argued the question at all, they had no difficulty in making themselves believe that it was as valuable as the genuine Confederate "money."

It was largely used to lubricate the wheels of trade with ignorant whites and negroes, for chickens, milk, vegetables and other "truck." A soldier with his pockets stuffed with "fac-simile" was a millionaire, and cared nothing for expense, squandering his pelf with the greatest prodigality. He would freely give twenty dollars for a canteen of milk, or a hundred for a fowl; while the guileless people who received such enormous prices were deluded with the belief that they were accumulating wealth at a bewildering rate, and would soon become bloated aristocrats.

No doubt, judged from a high moral plane, this practice could not have been commended, but the need of chickens was urgent, and the boys thought they could "buy" them with less friction than to steal them. If there was a hitch in trade because a citizen objected to taking "fac-simi-*lee*," as he called it, another soldier was promptly at hand with a supply of what he said was genuine Confederate money, and this was likely to be satisfactory, as only an expert could detect the difference. Frequently actual

Confederate currency was captured in considerable quantities and was diffused among the troops. This and the "fac-simile" were largely used in the game of poker. Fabulous sums were staked with a recklessness that recalls ante-bellum days on the Mississippi.

Seated around the snapping fires, the men of the 200th Indiana abandoned themselves to jest and laugh and song. They told stories and recounted many an incident, gay or sad, of their life in the tented field. They exhausted the

AROUND THE CAMP-FIRE.

repertoire of army songs. It may well be imagined that they sang "with the spirit and with the understanding also," such selections as "Just Before the Battle, Mother," "Tramp, Tramp, Tramp, the Boys are Marching," "When this Cruel War is Over," "Kingdom Coming," "Wake, Nicodemus," "Battle Cry of Freedom," and a score of others.

Then came those rollicking songs which were indigenous to the army. They were, in spots, glaringly defective in sense, rhyme and meter, but they were familiar to every soldier, from Virginia to Texas. "Dixie" was parodied, beginning in this way:

> I wish I was in de land ob cotton,
> Cinnamon seeds and sandy bottom,
> Look away, look away, look away to Dixie land.

An epitome of the four years of war was given in the following verses—varying somewhat in different parts of the army—which went galloping to the tune "When Johnny Comes Marching Home." The terse statements of fact contained in this song cannot be questioned, however much the reader may dissent from the convivial sentiments in the closing lines of each verse:

> In eighteen hundred and sixty-one,
> Free-ball! Free-ball!
> In eighteen hundred and sixty-one,
> Free-ball! Free-ball!
> In eighteen hundred and sixty-one,
> The war had then but just begun;
> And we'll all drink stone blind,
> Johnny, fill up the bowl!

> In eighteen hundred and sixty-two,
> Free-ball! Free-ball!
> In eighteen hundred and sixty-two,
> Free-ball! Free-ball!
> In eighteen hundred and sixty-two,
> They first began to put us through,
> And we'll all drink stone blind,
> Johnny, fill up the bowl!

> In eighteen hundred and sixty-three,
> Free-ball! Free-ball!
> In eighteen hundred and sixty-three,
> Free-ball! Free-ball!
> In eighteen hundred and sixty-three,
> Abe Lincoln set the niggers free;
> And we'll all drink stone blind,
> Johnny, fill up the bowl!

> In eighteen hundred and sixty-four,
> Free-ball! Free-ball!
> In eighteen hundred and sixty-four,
> Free-ball! Free-ball!

In eighteen hundred and sixty-four
We all went in for three years more;
And we'll all drink stone blind,
   Johnny, fill up the bowl!

There was another, decidedly bacchanalian in its character, but which was not as bad as it seems—that is to
say, it was often sung with great apparent relish by whole
companies when in a condition of most praiseworthy
sobriety, and by many who never—in or out of the army,
on "Saturday night" or at any other time—for a moment
thought of enforcing the "right" so vehemently declared
in the opening lines. The first part was sung to the appropriate tune "We Won't go Home till Morning," switching off to "America" at "So say we all of us:"

And every Saturday night, sir,
We think we have a right, sir,
To get most gloriously tight, sir,
   To drive dull care away!
   To drive dull care away,
   To drive dull care away,
It's a way that we have in the army,
It's a way that we have in the army,
It's a way that we have in the army,
   To drive dull care away!
     So say we all of us,
     So say we all of us,
      So say we all.
     So say we all of us,
     So say we all of us,
     So say we all of us,
      So say we all.

To the cursory reader there may seem to be an unnecessary amount of repetition in this, but the words were so
easily remembered that all could sing it after once hearing
it; and besides the iteration gave an emphasis to the
propositions that at once silenced all cavil. By the time
the soldiers got through singing it, "all of us" were fully
agreed.

It was late when the last song that anybody could think

of had been sung. The tension of strict discipline was somewhat relaxed, and more latitude was permitted than when in a campaign against the enemy. At length, when the oft-replenished fires had burned to embers, the men knocked the ashes from their pipes, crept into their "pup" tents and lay down.

An hour passed, and all save the guards were in deep sleep. Suddenly the sharp rattle of the long roll was heard, mingled with the blast of bugles, as one after another took up the alarm. And *such* a long roll it was! The drummers pounded as if for their lives, and the buglers blew their most piercing notes.

The startled soldiers came tumbling out of their tents, dragging their muskets after them and buckling on their accouterments as they ran. In half a minute the companies were formed and were hurrying at a double-quick out to the color-line. It was a moonless night, and the darkness of the oak wood 'was but feebly dispelled by the flickering light of the smoldering fires. Everybody wondered what was the matter. It had been supposed that there was no armed force of the enemy within a hundred miles, but the only thought suggested by the wild alarm was that an attack was imminent. Every ear was strained to catch the sound of shots on the picket-line, but nothing was heard save the turmoil of the assembling troops, and the hoarse voices of the officers as they gave the necessary commands. It was a moment of anxious suspense.

An orderly from brigade headquarters dashed up and handed a message to the colonel of the 200th Indiana, who read it by the dim light of a fagot. Leaping high in the air he gave a yell that an Apache chief might strive in vain to rival. The men thought he had gone crazy. When he came down he discharged another yell, and then handing the paper to the wondering adjutant told him to read it to the regiment. The adjutant glanced at it and yelled a duet with the colonel. Then he read an official copy of a telegram from the secretary of war, announcing

THE SURRENDER OF LEE'S ARMY.

If the inmates of a score of lunatic asylums had been suddenly turned loose in those Tennessee woods the scene could not have been more ragingly tempestuous than that which followed the reading of this dispatch. Officers and men danced and hugged one another and shouted and yelled, rending the air with every kind of sound within the compass of human voices well practiced in the making of noises. These men had done a good deal of yelling before, but never anything that could be compared to this hideous din.

When the noise had partially subsided, from sheer exhaustion of the vocal forces, the soldiers began to cast about for other means to continue the racket. It mattered little what it was—the more discordant the better—only so that it helped to swell the unearthly chorus. They tramped about beating furiously with sticks and stones all the camp-kettles and tin pans and cans that the camp afforded. All the brass bands in the division were playing but nobody could distinguish a tune. On all sides were heard the shriek of fifes and rattle of drums, and the buglers almost blew their heads off in their efforts to contribute to the prodigious uproar. One regiment after another began to fire muskets. The men took the cartridges from their boxes, poured in the powder, rammed down the paper for wadding and blazed away. The balls they threw upon the ground; there was no further use for them. The artillery opened, and battery after battery sent forth its thunders to echo among the mountains. The fires, heaped with wood, blazed high and the forest was aglow.

Men did everything imaginable that was grotesque and ridiculous. They climbed trees and yelled from the branches; they made heroic speeches from logs and stumps;

they turned their garments inside out; they rode one another on poles—and all the time yelling like maniacs.

Then there came an order from the general commanding
for the issue of a double ration of "commissary" to all the
soldiers. Many excellent people would no doubt say that
this was a highly reprehensible thing for the general to do.
Probably it was, and the men ought to have poured it
upon the ground instead of down their throats--but they
didn't. This was before the days of the temperance crusade,
and the provocation was extraordinary. If there ever
was, since the world was created, a valid excuse for a temporary lapse from sobriety, that occasion furnished it.
Years of toiling and suffering such as others know not;
of weary marches and lonely vigils, in summer's heat and
winter's storm; of facing the cruel missiles of war, amidst
scenes of death and human anguish; years that had
thinned regiments of a thousand men down to a hundred
—all were past, the end had come, and before the eyes of
those scarred and war-worn veterans were blessed pictures
of peace and home. It is not possible for mortal man, except he was one of them, to understand and appreciate the
thoughts that filled their hearts. Is it any wonder that
they indulged in these wild and extravagant demonstrations of joy? Above personal feeling were the consciousness of victory at last, after all the blood and wretchedness, and the patriotic rejoicing over a nation saved by
their valor and sacrifices. Let him who would cast a stone
at those who behaved so boisterously that night, be sure
that *he* would not have made a fool of himself for the
time being, had he been there.

At the brigade headquarters a horse-bucket full of egg-
nog was made, and the general and his staff indulged in
copious libations. After several "rounds" they sallied
forth, took possession of the instruments of the band, and
formed for a parade through the camp. The general
headed the procession with the bass drum, which he

pounded so furiously that he broke in the heads. The staff officers blew ear-splitting blasts upon the horns they carried. As they marched around, regimental and company officers and hundreds of soldiers fell in behind, until the column of howling lunatics was a quarter of a mile long. All night the "jamboree" was continued, and the morning sun looked upon hundreds still engaged in "celebrating," with unflagging zeal.*

The next day came the baleful tidings that President Lincoln had been assassinated. The revulsion of feeling cannot be described. Thousands of strong men, whose eyes had long been unused to tears, wept like children when the news, which they at first refused to believe, was fully

LEADING THE JAMBOREE.

confirmed, and they knew that "Father Abraham," whose name had been a thousand times upon their lips, in song and story, had been stricken down by the hand of a murderer.

---

* The foregoing is a feeble description of a scene in the camp of the Fourth Corps, in which the writer participated to the utmost of his lung power, on that memorable night in April, 1865. There are yet many living who will testify to the fact that the picture here drawn falls far short of the reality.

A few weeks later the remnant of the 200th Indiana was ordered to be discharged. At the capital of the state the survivors were paid and mustered out of the service. The tattered and faded flags of the regiment were deposited in the State House, and the men who had so grandly followed them were feasted and honored by a grateful people.

Few of the discharged veterans went home with their "soldier clothes" on. Nearly all bought complete outfits of citizen's garb, discarding the blue garments that they had so long and honorably worn, but which they hoped never to put on again.

Si Klegg was not yet of age. His tanned face bore abundant testimony to his long exposure to the elements, but when he was shorn and shaven, and arrayed in a new suit of clothes with all the trimmings, he was as fine-appearing a fellow as one could wish to see. A great happiness

AFTER A VISIT TO THE TAILOR.

filled his breast when those of the little squad that remained of Company Q left for home. The parting was not without sadness, for few ties on earth are as strong as those that bind the hearts of men who so long marched and fought and suffered together. But he was going home, conscious that he had acted well his part, and had done what one man could to bring the final victory. Si Klegg was but an atom of the mighty army; but it was the united efforts and sacrifices of a million such as he that overthrew the rebellion and saved the nation from dismemberment.

The "Company Q boys" received an overpowering welcome at home. The people of the village and from the adjacent country turned out *en masse* to greet them as they alighted from the train. Farmer Klegg and his wife and Maria, proud and eager, were there; and joyful tears flowed unchecked as they twined their arms around son and brother and pressed him to their beating hearts. Annabel was there, with moist eyes and a flush upon her soft cheek. Si had grown brave now, and as soon as the family embrace relaxed he advanced and put his arms around her as unflinchingly as if she had been a rebel battery.

Tumultuous cheers rent the air, the band played and banners waved in honor of the soldiers returned from the war. A sumptuous dinner was served to them in the town-hall, and the village orators exhausted their eloquence in giving them welcome and glorifying their deeds of valor. By the time the speakers got through, the veterans were pretty well convinced that if it had not been for Company Q the war would have been a failure—on the Union side.

Then the boys were taken in charge by their respective friends. In anticipation of Si's return, his mother and sister had for days done little except cook, and he found himself in a land flowing with milk and honey.

That night Si had the "best bed" in the house. As he threw himself upon it he sank down in a sea of feathers that almost covered him. Of course he could not sleep in such a bed, and in the morning, when his mother went to call him to breakfast, she was amazed to find him lying on the floor.

"Tell ye what 'tis, mother," he said, "I didn't like ter go back on yer nice bed, but 'twa'n't no use. I swum 'round 'n them feathers purty much all night, but I couldn't git ter sleep t'll I bunked down on the floor. That's a leetle more like the beds I slep' on 'n the army. I b'lieve t'night I'll rig up a pup-tent, put down some rails ter lie on, 'n' take my old U. S. blanket 'n' crawl in. Then ef you 'n' father 'n' Marier 'll jest git a gun apiece 'n' keep shootin' purty cluss to me all night, I kin git a good squar' sleep."

CHAPTER XLVIII.

Si Finds it Much Easier to Get Married than to Get a Pension.

IT is scarcely necessary to say that Si Klegg and Annabel were soon "mustered in." They fell early victims to the malignant connubial epidemic that devastated the ranks of the soldiers and sweethearts for two or three years immediately following the war. The parents of both thought they were "ower young to marry yet," but their feeble opposition on this score quickly melted away before the fierce heat of affection's fires in those young hearts. So parental objections were waived and there was a wedding.

Most of the young soldiers began, as soon as they were discharged, to think about getting married. They had fairly earned the right to enjoy the pleasures of wedded life, under their own vines and fig trees. They seemed to have little difficulty in finding "pards," and everywhere was heard a joyous chorus of marriage-bells.

During his last year or two in the army Si had had few dealings with the sutler, and had strictly kept his promise to Shorty not to play "chuck-a-luck," so that with his vet-eran and local bounties he managed to save a few hundred dollars. This sum, comfortably augmented by marriage portions, enabled him to buy a small farm, on which he and Annabel entered upon a quiet and uneventful life.

Si was more fortunate in this respect than thousands of his fellow-soldiers who—even though not impaired in health or disabled by wounds—found themselves thrown upon their own resources, at a great disadvantage as compared with those who had remained at home. They had given years to the service of their country, just at the age when they would otherwise have been fitting themselves by education and business training to fight their way in the scramble for position and wealth; and now their previous plans were deranged or wholly broken up.

Promotion was much more rapid in civil life, after the war, than in the army. People soon began to call Si "Captain," then "Major," and in a year or two he was addressed as "Colonel." This galloping advancement in rank was very general, until there seemed to be no privates or corporals left. A stranger would have supposed that the enlisted men were all killed in the war, or that the army was made up in accordance with the suggestion of the late "Artemus Ward," who, in 1861, proposed to organize a company composed entirely of brigadier-generals.

For a time after laying off his uniform Si Klegg had the feeling common to the disbanded volunteers—the very sight of blue clothes was hateful to him. He was thoroughly disgusted with "soldiering" and tired of the war; he never wanted to hear of it again. But as the years passed on memory recalled with constantly increasing vividness the scenes of the past, and awakened in his heart a yearning to once more grasp the hands and look into the faces of his old comrades—those who marched by his side, and with whom he touched elbows as the 200th Indiana faced the battle storm. A few of his fellow-soldiers of Company Q had remained in the neighborhood, but nearly all the members of the regiment were scattered to the four winds.

Si was rejoiced one day when he saw a call for a reunion of the survivors of the 200th. His work was pressing, but he told his wife that the farm would have to run itself for two or three days; he was going to that reunion if they had to live on hardtack and—bacon all winter. He told Annabel that she and the children must go, too—for by this time there was a thriving crop of infantry that gave promise of being ready for the next war.

So they all went to the reunion. The veterans

THE NEW CROP OF INFANTRY.

came from far and near, responding to the summons as promptly as they did so many times when drum and bugle called them to duty. Tears moistened their eyes as they met again and clasped one another in their sturdy arms.

The veterans sang the old war songs and fought their battles over around the camp-fire, and their wives and children en-joyed it almost as much as they did. Some of those who never smelt powder or heard a bullet whistle told the biggest stories — just as they have been doing at every gathering of soldiers since the war. Strident orators, whose courage never rose to the point of enlistment, at all—of that class aptly described as "invincible in peace, invisible in war"—talked long and vehemently, trying to instruct the old-soldiers in lessons of patriotism and valor. The "boys"—for so they still called one another—had such a good time, that with a tremendous and unanimous "aye" they voted to hold a reunion every year. These meetings bound together even more closely than before the hearts of the comrades.

The war had not long been over until the politicians, irrespective of party, began to bait their hooks to "catch the soldier vote." Eminent patriots, who, yielding to the importunities of their fellow-citizens, had consented to become candidates for office, often called around to see "Colonel" Klegg and secure, if possible, his ballot and his influence in their behalf. They talked grandly of their love and admiration for the brave defenders of the flag, and made picturesque promises what they would do for those who so faithfully served their country. These promises were usually forgotten as soon as the polls closed on election day; nor were they recalled by these men with defective memories until another political campaign made it necessary to scratch around again for votes. Si felt a laudable interest in the welfare of his country, and like a good citizen he marched in torchlight processions and yelled himself hoarse at mass-meetings and barbecues. He swung his hat and shouted when the election returns showed majorities for his side; and when the other fellows came out ahead he mourned because the country was "going to the dogs," and he had fought and bled in vain. But the ship of state kept on her course just the same, and he found it really made little difference which political party was at the helm.

Not one in ten thousand of the two and a half million men, who so promptly responded to their country's call in the day of her calamity, paused to inquire whether he would be pensioned in case he should be disabled by wounds or disease. When Si Klegg signed the roll of Company Q he did not even know what a pension was.

He knew only that the government needed his services, and he offered them freely, without a thought of the future.

Si came out of the war in good condition, so far as surface indications went. His physical vigor was seemingly unimpaired, and his friends said his army life had "made a man of him." His wound had not disabled him, although it continued to give him trouble at times. As long as he was able to make his way in the world he refused to entertain the idea of being a pensioner.

But as the years went by he began to grow prematurely old—as did nineteen out of every twenty men who endured so much. Every now and then Congress passed some new pension bill, and each enactment was closely followed by a bombardment of circulars from three or four dozen attorneys, in all parts of the country, assuring Si that he was entitled to its benefits, and offering to undertake his case for a consideration. At length he began to think about it in a serious way. He heard a good deal about the overflowing vaults of the United States treasury. The government seemed to have more money than it knew what to do with, and Si felt that he had borne an humble part in bringing the country into such a condition of boundless prosperity. But for the sufferings and sacrifices of such as he the Nation—with a big N—would have long since ceased to exist, and in its stead would have been several little nations, unworthy of capital letters. Why should not the government, rich and prosperous and powerful, secure him and Annabel and the little Kleggs against want, if so be that early decrepitude should result from his years of service in the army?

When Si heard some people grumble because such large amounts were paid each year for pensions, and heard them denounce the soldiers as "coffee coolers," "beggars" and "dead beats," it only awakened in him a feeling of pity for their ignorance and narrow-mindedness. He heard such expressions from none except persons who stayed at home during the war, some of whom grew rich out of army contracts.

For a time Si Klegg prospered, but at length reverses came. One year a drouth burned up his grain, the next floods drowned it, and the next it was devoured by flies, grasshoppers, locusts and chinch-bugs. Little by little his health gave way. The seeds of disease that were insidiously sown during those months and years of exposure to the elements, sprang up and brought forth a crop of ills that in course of time almost unfitted him for manual labor. He began to find it necessary to wear patched clothes. His wife was obliged to "make over" her dresses. The children began to get "out" at the elbows and knees and toes, and when the circus made its periodical visit they had to stay at home, provided they could not crawl under the canvas.

Then Si said: "I believe I'm as much entitled to a pension as anybody else, and I'll see see if I can make Uncle Sam think so." He did not then know how dull of comprehension "Uncle Sam" is, sometimes.

So one day he drove to a neighboring town to see a pension agent, who had sent him half a bushel of circulars during the previous ten years. From the perusal of these he had come to believe that all he had to do in order to get a pension was to ask for it.

"Let's see," said the agent, briskly, "what kind of a case we can make out for you. Been wounded?"

Si bared his arm and showed him an ugly scar.

"Mule kick?" asked the agent.

"No, sir!" replied Si, with some asperity. "Piece o' shell, the day the 200th Injianny went up the ridge."

"That's good—twenty dollars a month for that. Got any 'rumaticks,' from lying around on the ground?"

"Plenty of 'em."

"Good again; they're worth ten dollars a month more."

By the time they got through with the list of his ail-ments Si began to think he would be a millionaire in a few years.

The agent said he was very busy that day but he would give him a blank application to fill out which he promised to forward directly to Washington.

When Si got home he thought he would go over and talk with one of his neighbors—a veteran comrade who had succeeded in getting his claim through the government "circumlocution office," and was drawing a pension. Si thought his friend's counsel and assistance, based upon his own experience, might be of service in preparing the papers.

Together they filled out the application. Si hunted up a magistrate, made oath to it in due form and mailed it to the attorney. Then, in the course of a couple of weeks he began to look for his pension. He thought that a week ought to be abundant time to decide a case so clear as his, and two or three days each way were a liberal allowance for the mails to do their part of the work.

But day after day passed and Si heard nothing from Washington. At the end of a month he began to grow fidgety over it, and called again upon his neighbor to ask him what could cause such long delay. The latter, re-membering his own tribulations, laughed to himself, but was loth to cast a shadow over Si's life by telling him that he would be fortunate if he got his claim through in three or four years.

"Better go and see your agent," he said, "mebbe he needs to be stirred up with a sharp stick."

So Si took another "day off" and drove over to call upon his attorney. To his dismay he found that his application was lying in a pigeon-hole, not having been sent to Wash-ington yet. The agent said he had forgotten it, in the multiplicity of his business cares. Si gave him "a piece of his mind"—the whole of it, in fact—and the agent prom-ised to lose no time in rushing it along.

Then Si went home and waited again. As the weeks passed he wrote several times to his attorney asking about it but without eliciting any reply. At length he determined to "blow him up," and wrote that he believed he would take the case out of his hands and try some other agent. Then the agent wrote, telling him with some warmth that he need not expect to crowd matters; the officials at Washington were very leisurely in their ways, and it would probably take him as long to *get* his pension as it did to *earn* it.

This was discouraging to Si. It seemed to him as though the government cared nothing for him, after it no longer needed his services. But there seemed to be no other way, and he settled himself down for a long job of waiting.

Six months later, when he had almost forgotten that he had ever applied for a pension, the post-master handed him a big letter which he saw at a glance was from his attorney. His heart gave a great bound, for he was sure that at last his pension had come, and he had no doubt it was a liberal one. With a smile upon his face he tore open the envelope and found—a lot of blanks, with a demand from the Pension Office for his "hospital record."

That evening he went over to see his neighbor about it.

"Haven't you got a good hospital record?" the latter inquired, after Si had shown him the papers.

"That's what I hain't got, pard," replied Si. "I never was in the hospital only jest that night arter the fight. I reck'n the docters had all they could 'tend to 'thout spendin' no time keepin' records. The gin'ral sent me a furlough the next day and I came home for a spell. All the rest o' the time I was carryin' a musket 'long 'th the rijiment."

"That's bad," said his comrade, "but I had the same sort of trouble, myself. The people at Washington take lots of stock in a good hospital record. It helps mightily in getting a pension. A month in a hospital, even if you wa'n't very sick, counts more 'n three years of trampin' an' fightin', at the front. If I ever go into another war I'm going to stub my toe or something, if I can't get hurt any other way, just to get back to the hospital long enough to make a 'record.' Of course we didn't know anything about these things then, but I'll be sharp enough for 'em next time."

All that Si could do was to write a statement that he had no hospital record, and setting forth the reasons why such was the fact. It took six months more for the Pension Bureau to digest this, and then Si got another letter. This time he did not allow his emotions to get the advantage of him. He opened it with a vague hope that it had brought him what he wanted, but really finding what he expected—more blanks, and a requisition for further information. He must get the certificate of the surgeons who dressed his wound, and who treated him at various times for the diseases which resulted in his disability.

"I don't know what I'm goin' to do," he said to his neighbor, whom he regarded as his sheet-anchor for advice and assistance. "I never did take much medicine in the army, only jest once 'n a while when me and Shorty wanted to play off from fatigue duty. The doctor that dressed my wound, he moved away, to Patagonia or somewhere, a good many years ago, and I don't know anything about where he is."

"You ought to have made him sit right down an' write out an affidavit an' swar to it that night, as soon as he got your wound tied up," replied his friend, with a laugh. "I've got a boy growin' up, an' if he ever has to go to war I'll put a big flea in his ear."

"I guess that would have been a good thing," said Si, "but the fact is I had my head purty full of somethin' else that night, an' I didn't think of it. But that would 've been a nice place for a doctor to be makin' out papers, wouldn't it—he a-sawin' an' cuttin' legs and arms and the ground covered with men groanin' and dyin' all around

him? It'd be a fine thing for him to let 'em die and go
to makin' out affidavits!"

Acting upon his friend's suggestion Si went again to see
his agent, who told him the surgeon's testimony would be
valuable, and he had better try and find where he was.

During the next few months Si found plenty of amuse-
ment for his leisure time in writing to every old member
of the 200th Indiana he could hear of, in the hope of getting some trace of the lost doctor, squandering an acre of
his wheat in stationery and postage-stamps, but without
success. He informed his agent, who after a while communicated the fact to the Commissioner of Pensions.

It took the usual time to unwind the red-tape and untie
the knots, and then another lot of blanks was sent to Si,
with instructions to get the affidavits of his company
officers, or of some of his comrades who personally knew
all the circumstances.

Again Si called upon his friend. "I don't see," he said,
"why them fellers can't b'lieve what I've told 'em. I don't
think anybody 't knows Si Klegg 'd have any idee he'd lie
'bout such a thing and sw'ar to it besides."

"Fact is," replied his neighbor, "they think every soldier
tells the biggest kind of whoppers, an' every man's affidavit has to be propped up by a lot more or they won't go a
cent on it. You've got to prove that you ain't lyin'.
It's tough, but you'll find it's true. 'Tain't no use to kick
agin the United States Government."

"But I'm afeard I can't get 'em. One of our officers was
killed in that fight when I was wounded, and the other
that was there has died sence the war. The pension folks
can't get any testimony out o' *them* unless they're fust-
class mejums. I reck'n sperits ain't no good at Washington—leastwise not that kind. All the boys is scattered
'from Dan to Beersheba.'"

"I reckon you'd better try an' hunt some of 'em up, if
you can't get at any of the officers. It takes two or three

of them that was only soldiers to count as much as one officer in giving testimony. I don't believe the boys used to lie in the army any worse than the officers did, but the government seems to think the officers has all got converted since the war."

Then Si buckled down again to the work of writing letters. Many weeks elapsed before he succeeded, but he at length found himself in the possession of an array of affidavits from his old comrades that he was sure ought to satisfy even so insatiable and exacting a person as his Uncle Sam. When he mailed these to his attorney he believed they would settle the matter in short order These affidavits covered his wound and also fully set forth the hardship and exposure he had endured, which he considered ample to account for the diseased condition of his physical system.

With a placid confidence Si patiently awaited the effect of this broadside. By the time another section of his hair had turned gray he heard again from Washington. The envelope did not contain a pension certificate, but a call for more affidavits—of all the doctors who had treated him since his discharge from the army, setting forth his present condition, and why he had permitted his health to fail. He must present a schedule setting forth in detail all the different kinds of medicine he had taken and the quantity of each, and what for; with exemplified copies—to be filed as "exhibits"—of all the prescriptions he had had filled at drug-stores since the war, these to be accompanied by the photographs, autographs and certificates of the clerks who filled them, with affidavits proving their good character for veracity, and whether they were married or single, and if so, why; also the affidavits of credible persons who actually saw Josiah Klegg take, drink, swallow, gulp, ingurgitate and absorb, all and singular, the doses of such medicine aforesaid alleged to have been by him so taken, drank, swallowed, gulped, ingurgitated and absorbed; also he was required to state, to a certainty, the name of the individual who struck the late lamented "Billy Patterson."

Si had already laid in a considerable stock of experience with official circumlocution, so that all this did not surprise him much. He had ceased to wonder at anything. He did all he could to comply with the requirements, sent on the affidavits—and waited.

Months rolled away, and then still another voracious demand. Solomon wrote in Proverbs: "There are three things that are never satisfied, yea, four things say not, It is enough." If he had written a few years after the American civil war he would have mentioned five things instead of four which "are never satisfied," and "say not, It is enough." The fifth would have been the United States Pension Bureau.

This time it was a call for proof of "prior soundness." Si could not quite comprehend what that meant, and he went over and asked his neighbor.

"Why, that means," said the latter, in reply to Si's question, "that you've got to prove that you were sound and able-bodied when you entered the service."

"Of course I was—sound as a dollar. It'd be jest wastin' time to go to provin' that. I never heerd of so much nonsense in all my born days. 'Pears like they think at Washington that all a man wants is to git his pension in time to pay his funeral expenses!"

"I agree with ye, comrade, but all the same you have to do it. The government takes it for granted that every soldier was a weak, puny, sickly thing when he enlisted, and would have petered out if he hadn't gone to the war."

"The 'listin' officer had a doctor there and he examined me from head to foot and said I was in fust-class order."

"Oh, *he* didn't know nothing about it, of course; and you was so fierce for going to help save the country that you probably lied about it—anyhow they think you did, and you've got to prove that you didn't. You'll have to go back and show that your grandfathers and great-grandfathers died of old age. Then it will be necessary for you to prove that you would not have been taken sick, or bit by a rattle-snake or struck by lightning if you had stayed at home during the war. You see you might have been killed at home, and if so, going to war saved your life and you ought to be very thankful for it. The government supposes it did you a great favor by giving you the opportunity and the privilege of enlisting, and unless you can prove that it didn't there won't be much of a show for you!"

Si had no difficulty in establishing his "prior soundness." The pension authorities could not think of anything else, reasonable or unreasonable, that could be asked for, so they devoted a few months to sending "special" agents into the neighborhood, to work "on the sly," and find out Si's reputation and his physical condition, that the Bureau might reach a conclusion as to whether he and his witnesses had told the truth or not.

At last, five years after he had filed his application, he got word one day from his agent that his pension had been granted. A day or two later he received a letter bearing the trade-mark of the Commissioner of Pensions. Hastening home he gathered about him his expectant family, broke the seal, and drew out the document that was to raise them to a condition of opulence. He began at the top and read down till he came to the important point. Then they learned that the name of Josiah Klegg, late of Company Q, 200th Indiana Veteran Volunteer Infantry, had been placed on the pension roll at the rate of one dollar and seventy-three and three-quarters cents per month!

Si looked at his wife and she looked at him, and the children looked at one another. He read it again. He wondered if the clerk who filled it out had not made a mistake and left out the word "hundred" after "one." Then he did some heavy thinking.

"If they'd only put on that other quarter of a cent," he said at length, when he had sufficiently recovered from his amazement so that he could speak, "I wouldn't ha' keered. Looks as though Uncle Sam was about as poor as I am, don't it, wife? Let's see"—and Si figured it out—"that 'll be about twenty dollars a year. If I should live a thousand years that 'd be twenty thousand dollars! I wish I could live that long, jest to spite the government. I b'lieve I'll jest send this pension back an' tell 'em I don't want it; and I'll tell 'em that if Uncle Sam 's so hard up he'd better pass 'round the hat an' we'll all chip in to help him out!"

Si fully made up his mind to decline the pitiful allowance, and went to see his agent to get his assistance in writing a letter that would raise blisters on every department of the government he had fought and bled for. The agent told him he had better hang on to it. True it was not much, and it would take a year's allowance to pay the attorney's fee, but after a while he might get an increase; or, better yet, perhaps a bill could be got through Congress that would do him justice.

After thinking it over Si concluded to reconsider his decision. He was favorably impressed with the proposition to try Congress. The Member from that district had often told him—in election campaigns—that he would do anything for him that lay in his power. Si had an exalted idea of the Member's influence in the halls of national legislation, and he would see him at once.

There was to be another election that fall and the Member was again a candidate. He told Si it was a shame that so worthy a soldier as he should be granted such a beggarly pittance, and he would introduce a bill the first day of the next session. So Si "took off his coat," as the politicians say, and labored unceasingly to secure the Member's re-election. The result was in accordance with his wishes, and he threw his hat in the air when the count of the votes showed a majority for the Moses who was to lead him out of the wilderness.

Soon after the opening of the ensuing session of Congress Si received a copy of that thrilling periodical, the *Congressional Record*. A marked paragraph caught his eye, and with a palpitating heart he read that a bill had been introduced "To increase the pension of Josiah Klegg, Company Q, 200th Indiana." This brought happiness to Si's heart. With a sublime faith in the Member's magic power, he had no doubt that the bill would pass in two or three weeks, the vaults of the United States Treasury would be opened, and he would be invited to help himself.

But months passed and he heard no more of his bill. He ventured to write to the Congressman about it, and the latter said in reply that he was devoting all his energies to the herculean task of pushing that bill through—in fact he was not doing anything else, giving to it his entire time and attention. The truth is that probably he had not thought of the bill since he introduced it.

Si believed what the Member told him. He did not know that every year thousands of such bills were thrown into the hopper of the congressional mill, to cancel campaign obligations, and that not one in twenty of them ever got beyond the capacious pigeon-holes of the committee-rooms.

For five or six years Si watched that bill. When the next election came around the Member called upon Si and pointed with pride to the fact that he had introduced the bill; if he was elected again he would certainly get it through—and Si "took off his coat" again and yelled for him at the mass-meetings.

During this Congress, having re-introduced the bill, the Member shoved it along another peg by getting a favorable report from the committee. Si felt greatly encouraged at this, but his hopes fell again when Congress expired and the bill died with it. The work all had to be done over again.

Once more Si helped to swell the Member's majority and then the latter determined to see what he could do. By adroit management he contrived to advance the bill rapidly and at length got it before the House. He made a speech on it, which was "the greatest effort of his life," recounting with fervid eloquence the gallant exploits of Corporal Si Klegg, and denouncing the parsimony of the government toward him. The appeal was irresistible, and the bill passed by an overwhelming majority. The Member sent a telegram that filled with joy the hearts of the Klegg family.

Feeling that the success of the bill would be a feather in his own cap, and a shining example that would greatly help him in the next election, the Member spared no effort to steer it through the Senate. Securing the interest of the senators from that state, they took hold of the matter and in due time it passed that body. Another telegram went singing over the wires, conveying to Si the glad tidings.

A few days later there was another dispatch, which read: "The President has vetoed your bill," and there was woe again. Si received by mail a copy of the message which set forth in elaborate phrase the reasons why executive approval had been withheld. The principal one was that no evidence had been adduced to show that Josiah Klegg did not receive contributory injuries at the hands of the defeated nine, while acting as umpire of a base-ball game.

"LIGHTS OUT!"

APPENDIX.

THIS volume has far outgrown the original purpose of the author. He found the subject so fruitful that he became panic-stricken as the pages multiplied, and "threw overboard" much that he intended should have a place. Hundreds of pages could have been added without exhausting the theme, however much so ponderous a volume might have exhausted the patience of the reader. Notwithstanding his dismay at the size of the book, the writer ventures to add a few pages which will assist young readers and others, who were not soldiers, to understand the organization of the army and some features of the service which did not enter into the experience of Corporal Klegg and Shorty. The "veteran" may "skip" this if he chooses, but he will no doubt find something to interest him in the corps badges and bugle calls, which are given hereafter.

Since the war there have been many and radical changes in the arms, equipments, tactics and regulations of the United States army. Whatever this book contains applies to the army as it was during the war. The volunteers stood on the same military footing as the soldiers of the regular army. Their treatment and service were in all respects the same, and there was no difference in their courage or fighting abilities. They marched and fought side by side, in honorable rivalry.

Theoretically there was the same happy state of equality so far as the regular and volunteer officers were concerned; practically there was usually more or less friction between the two classes. That this should have been so is hardly a cause for wonder. Nothing else can be expected until the millennial dawn, when "The wolf also shall dwell with the lamb, and the leopard shall lie down with the kid; and the calf and the young lion and the fatling together; and a little child shall lead them." Then there will be no need for either "West Pointers" or volunteers. It is not strange that a regular officer—who if not "to the manner born" was at least bred to it by years of military study and practice—thought he knew more about war than one who left the plow, the anvil or the counting-room to buckle on the sword; and that he chafed and grew restive under the authority of a volunteer who outranked him. The regulars did not comprise more than a fortieth part of the army, though the proportion of officers was somewhat greater.

The unit in the composition of the army was the company organization.

A full infantry company contained, in round numbers, one hundred men. It had three commissioned officers—captain, first lieutenant and second lieutenant; and thirteen non-commissioned officers—first or orderly sergeant, four duty sergeants and eight corporals.

An infantry regiment was composed of ten companies, designated by letters from A to K inclusive. The letter J was omitted, on account of the confusion that would arise from the similarity in writing, of I and J. There were a few regiments with but eight companies each, and a few with twelve, but very nearly all were organized as above. The field officers were colonel, lieutenant-colonel and major, having rank in the order given. The regimental staff officers were a surgeon, with the rank of major; two assistant surgeons and a chaplain, ranking as captains; adjutant and quartermaster, with the rank of first lieutenant. There was a non-commissioned-staff, consisting of sergeant-major, quartermaster-sergeant, commissary-sergeant, hospital steward and principal musician. A regiment when full to the maximum had thirty-nine commissioned officers, and one thousand—more or less—non-commissioned officers and privates. In official returns all except the commissioned officers were "lumped" as "enlisted men."

A regiment of cavalry usually contained twelve companies, L and M being used in addition to the letters designating the companies of an infantry regiment. The general organization was similar to the infantry, except that the cavalry regiment was divided into three battalions with one major for each. The care of horses also required saddlers, shoers, etc.

A regiment of artillery consisted of twelve companies or batteries. Each battery, usually, had six guns, was complete in itself, and in almost all cases served independently. No regiment of light or field artillery, for obvious reasons, served as such, in the same compact sense as a regiment of cavalry or infantry. The batteries which composed it were widely scattered—often in different departments, hundreds of miles apart. Scarcely half of the field artillery had a regimental organization at all. There were some two hundred and thirty "independent" batteries, so called, organized in different states and duly numbered, as 6th Ohio or 10th New York Battery.

Each of these three branches or "arms" of the military service had its distinguishing color—blue for infantry, yellow for cavalry and red for artillery. The body of the uniform worn by all was blue—the trousers light and the blouse dark. The distinctive colors appeared in the corded seams, the trimming of the jackets largely worn by the soldiers of the cavalry and artillery, the field of the officers' shoulder-straps, and the chevrons of the non-commissioned officers. Artillerymen usually wore upon the front of their caps or hats a brass device representing two cannons crossed, and the cavalrymen wore crossed sabers. When a man was properly dressed it was easy to tell at a glance to which arm of the service he belonged.

Five-sixths of the fighting was done by the infantry soldiers. This was not because they fought any better, but because there were six times as many of them as of the cavalry and artillery combined. The cavalry was largely employed in scouting, picketing, "raiding" and other important service requiring celerity of movement; the great battles were fought chiefly by the heavy masses of infantry. It took two years to learn how to use cavalry to the best advantage, and to get a body of good riders, inured to the exposure and hardship incident to their peculiar service.

During the early part of the war the men who marched with burdened backs looked with envious eyes upon the cavalrymen, booted and spurred, as they galloped gayly about, with clanking sabers. The "walk soldiers"—or "dough-boys," as the cavalrymen called them—thought that those who rode horses had a "soft thing." "Who ever saw a dead cavalryman?" was their favorite conundrum—and everybody gave it up. But there came a day when this question was no longer asked—when the "yellow jackets" were often seen in the forefront of battle, and the bodies of the slain and the wounded thickly covered the ground. After the cavalry had become thoroughly seasoned, had learned the art of fighting on horseback, and was organized into a distinct aggressive force, it became a most important factor in the struggle. The history of the world records no more brilliant achievements in war than those of the Union cavalry under the leadership of Sheridan, Custer, Wilson, Kilpatrick, Buford, Stoneman, Grierson, the Greggs, Averell, Pleasonton, Hatch, Torbert and many others. No less can be said of the dashing southern horsemen, led by such men as Stuart, John Morgan, Wheeler, Forrest, Fitzhugh Lee and Hampton.

During the last year of the war cavalrymen did much hard, solid fighting on foot, as infantry, and against infantry. Moving in large bodies they were enabled to cover long distances with a speed impossible to infantry, and strike the enemy at a desired point. Every fourth man, at a distance in the rear, held the horses of three comrades who went dismounted into the fight. Sometimes the horse-holders had more than they could well manage, when the enemy tossed a few shells among the animals, occasionally stampeding them in the most effectual manner. In 1863 and 1864, particularly in the western army, a considerable number of infantry regiments were supplied with horses and served as mounted infantry. These were chiefly armed with the Spencer repeating rifle, and did most excellent service. Well drilled in the tactics of infantry, and usually fighting as such, their swift movements made them exceedingly troublesome to the enemy. Wilder's famous brigade of mounted infantry, which served so conspicuously in the Department of the Cumberland, may be cited as an illustration of this style of marching and fighting.

The fact is that until a man "got used to it," riding a horse was about as hard as marching and carrying a knapsack of reasonable size. On reaching camp at night the infantryman had nothing to do but to look after his own comfort, while the cavalryman had his horse to feed, water and groom. He was required to take good care of his horse, and to make this his first business. The supplying of his own wants was a secondary consideration. On the whole it may fairly be doubted whether the cavalryman had any appreciable advantage over him who trudged along on foot, save in the matter of foraging. He scoured the country and had the first pick of the chickens and pigs and the fruit of orchard and field, and he did not leave anything for his more slowly traveling comrade if he could help it. In this sphere of activity the average cavalryman was "a terror."

The minds of the infantrymen were further poisoned by the belief that the artillerymen had altogether too easy a time of it when on the march. It was conceded that an equitable share of the fighting fell to the latter, and that they did it well. But it was exasperating to the weary plodder, with smarting feet and aching bones, to see the artillerymen strolling along with nothing to carry but their haversacks and canteens, their knapsacks and blankets being piled upon the caissons and "limbers." This drove the iron into the infantryman's soul. Each piece of artillery, and each caisson, battery-wagon, etc., was drawn by four or six horses, with numerous drivers, one of whom rode the "nigh" animal of each pair. If a gunner or "powder-monkey" tired of walking he would exchange for an hour with one of the drivers, the latter being glad of a chance to stretch his legs. These things had a disquieting effect upon the temper of the foot soldier, and caused him to bewail, in sheolic language, the cruel fate that led him to enlist in the infantry instead of the artillery.

Batteries going into position under fire were often seriously embarrassed by the killing and wounding of horses. Artillerymen were provided with knives, with which they slashed the harness and cut loose from a dead or disabled animal, and the remaining horses dashed on with the gun. Sometimes when going at a mad gallop, a killed or wounded horse was dragged along the ground a great distance. Occasionally a battery in action lost so many of its horses that in case of retreat or change of position the guns had to be hauled by the men, details from the infantry perhaps assisting in the work. For this purpose long ropes were provided, and in this way many guns were saved from capture.

Late in the war several regiments of "heavy artillery" were recruited. The name was attractive, particularly when coupled with the expectation that the duty would be confined to manning the heavy guns in the forts. This pleasing fiction quickly filled to overflowing the ranks of these regiments. Some of them took the field with as high as eighteen hundred men each. But instead of sitting down behind the big guns these regiments were armed with muskets as infantry and ordered to "go in." They did so, suffering tremendous losses in the battles around Richmond.

Each infantry regiment habitually carried two silk flags, which, together, constituted a "stand" of colors. One was the regulation "stars and stripes" and the other, sometimes called the "banner," was often a state flag, bearing appropriate devices, presented by friends of the regiment. The colors were the rallying point of a regiment. If it lost its colors it was liable to become a disorganized mass. The appearance of a long line advancing with waving flags illustrated in the clearest manner the force and beauty of the words (Song of Solomon vi: 10) "terrible as an army with banners." It was esteemed a high honor to carry the colors, and the color-bearers were men—usually sergeants—of tried courage. Each regiment had a color-guard of six or eight corporals, detailed from different companies, who marched with the colors, and whose specific duty it was to defend them in battle. It was a post of danger, as the enemy's hottest fire was often directed at the colors, and at close quarters extraordinary efforts were made to capture them, as trophies of valor. It was not uncommon in a battle for several successive color-bearers to be shot down, and sometimes not a man of the color-guard escaped the deadly missiles. Others, to take their places, were never wanting, and the instant a flag went down the staff was seized by other ready hands, and the ensign was kept waving amidst the smoke and din of conflict.

As we have seen in the experience of the 200th Indiana, full regiments on taking the field were rapidly decimated by the ravages of disease and bullets. Scarcely more than half of the men enlisted proved to be physically able to "stand the service," and battles fast thinned the ranks. New organizations were constantly going to the front, but a "veteran" regiment having three hundred men was a large one. Some regiments were fortunate in occupying the less exposed positions in battle, while others, which had the "hot" places, were not infrequently, for the time, almost annihilated. There were repeated instances in which but one or two officers and a proportionate number of men of an entire regiment escaped unhurt. In some cases regiments became so reduced that they could not maintain their organizations, and were consolidated into "battalions," with others which had similarly suffered. It was always a heavy cross for its members when "the good of the service" made consolidation necessary, and a regiment or brigade or division lost the individuality under which it had made name and fame.

Some regiments received from time to time large accessions of recruits, by which they were kept well filled. Here and there one bore upon its rolls from first to last, the names of two thousand or twenty-five hundred men. Many high in authority strenuously advocated the policy of using the new levies of troops to fill up the old, depleted regiments, instead of organizing them separately. Wisely or otherwise the latter plan was generally adopted, and many of the veteran regiments continued but mere skeletons. It was urged, with much good reason, that raw men would sooner learn the thousand-and-one things that they must learn, if in direct association with those who had mastered "soldiering;" and that they would more readily acquire confidence and steadiness under fire when touching elbows with the tried veterans of many fields. The principal difficulty lay in the fact that those who spent time and money in recruiting expected commissions as officers.

Many regiments adopted—or were so christened by others—grotesque or suggestive names by which they were universally known through the armies in which they served, being scarcely mentioned, except officially, by their numerical designations. As examples may be mentioned the Pennsylvania "Bucktails," the "Orange Blossoms"—a regiment chiefly raised in Orange county, New York—and a Wisconsin regiment known as the "Wildcats." The 50th Illinois got the name of the "Blind Half Hundred," which it retained to the end. The 8th Wisconsin carried the eagle "Old Abe"—well known to every soldier of the Army of the Cumberland—through the war, and was always called the "Eagle Regiment." Some regiments took upon themselves such blood-curdling names as "Tigers," "Avengers," etc., suggestive of peculiarly sanguinary habits. Many soldiers to this day speak with evident satisfaction of their regiments as, for example, the "Bloody" 99th Rhode Island.

Of course officers received more pay than enlisted men. The difference was, however, more apparent than real, as an officer was required to pay out of his wages, all his personal expenses—clothing, food, etc.,—rarely less than $40 to $50 a month. The enlisted man was paid from $13 to $25 per month and "found"—that is, he received in addition his clothing and rations. The government kindly loaned the officer a tent to sleep in, but if it was lost or destroyed, and he failed to satisfactorily account for it, he had to pay for it. Company or "line" officers received from $100 to $120 per month, the pay increasing rapidly with the higher grades.

Rank was denoted by shoulder-staps as follows: second lieutenant, plain strap with clear field; first lieutenant, one bar in each end of the strap; captain, two bars; major, gilt leaf; lieutenant-colonel, silver leaf; colonel, spread eagle in center; brigadier-general, one star; major-general, two stars; lieutenant-general, three stars; general, four stars. The rank of "general" cannot be acquired by regular promotion. It can only be created by special act of Congress. U.S. Grant and William T. Sherman are the only persons who have ever held that rank in the United States Army. An act was passed authorizing the appointment of George Washington to that grade, but he was not appointed. Only Washington, Grant, Sherman and Sheridan have held the rank of lieutenant-general; Winfield Scott was a lieutenant-general by brevet.

A brigade contained three or more regiments, there being no fixed number. Early in the war, when regiments were large, rarely more than four were placed in one brigade. In 1864 many brigades contained from six to ten regiments each—and these brigades were not more than half as strong, numerically, as those which at the outset had but four. As a general thing three brigades made a division and three divisions a corps. The corps operating in a department constituted an "army"—as Army of the Potomac, Cumberland, or Tennessee. The corps were distinguished by badges. The colors, red, white and blue, indicated the divisions—first, second and third, respectively—as, a red trefoil or clover-leaf, First Division, Second Corps; white triangle, Second Division, Fourth Corps; blue star, Third Division, Twentieth Corps. A badge was worn by every soldier and also marked the wagons, tents, etc., of each corps.

No badge was ever adopted for the Thirteenth Corps. Neither

FIRST.   SECOND.   THIRD.

FOURTH.   FIFTH.   SIXTH.

SEVENTH.   EIGHTH.   NINTH.

TENTH.   ELEVENTH.   TWELFTH.

FOURTEENTH.   FIFTEENTH.   SIXTEENTH

SEVENTEENTH.   EIGHTEENTH.   NINETEENTH.

TWENTIETH.   TWENTY-SECOND.   TWENTY-THIRD.

TWENTY-FOURTH. TWENTY-FIFTH.   POTOMAC CAV.

WILSON'S CAV.   **ENGINEERS.**   **SIGNAL CORPS.**

was there a badge for the Twenty-first, as that corps was discontinued in October, 1863, when it was consolidated with the old Twentieth Corps. The corps so formed became the Fourth, and thus continued till the close of the war. Up to that time corps badges had not been generally adopted in the western army. Soon after this the Eleventh and Twelfth Corps—which had been sent from the Army of the Potomac to reinforce the Army of the Cumberland at Chattanooga—were consolidated and became the new Twentieth Corps, which took as its badge the five-pointed star of the Twelfth.

One of the inexplicable things about a battle was the small proportion of casualties, even in the bloodiest engagements, to the amount of ammunition expended. To illustrate: In a battle with, say, fifty thousand men on each side, lasting two days, each soldier would fire, on an average, one hundred cartridges. If one bullet out of one hundred struck a man, none in either army would escape being hit. At Chickamauga the killed and wounded were about thirty per cent., so that the ratio of men struck to rounds fired—saying nothing of the artillery—was less than one to three hundred. One who goes through a long, hard battle is amazed to find himself alive. He wonders—and well he may—that any can escape.

Some of the more familiar bugle calls have been heretofore given. The following will touch responsive chords in the ear and memory of every soldier:

The Reveille.

The General.

The Assembly.

To the Color.

Dinner Call.

Church Call.

Officers' Call.

Retreat.

Tattoo.

The following are some of the more familiar cavalry calls:

The General.

Boots and Saddles.

To Horse.

The Assembly.

To Arms.

To the Standard.

Stable Call.

Sick Call.

Fatigue Call.

A few general facts relative to the war, condensed into the briefest possible space, will be of interest. The various calls for troops made by the
President of the United States were as follows:

April 15, 1861, three months	75,000
May 3, 1861, three years	500,000
July 2, 1862, three years	300,000
Aug. 4, 1862, nine months	300,000
Oct. 17, 1863, three years	300,000
Feb. 1, 1864, three years	200,000
March 14, 1864, three years	200,000
July 18, 1864, three years	500,000
Dec. 19, 1864, three years	300,000
Total	2,675,000

In addition to the above, militia to the number of about 150,000 were
called out for short periods, to meet critical emergencies.

The following shows the total number of men furnished for the Union
army, in all branches of the service, by each state and territory:

Alabama	2,576	Nebraska Ter	3,157
Arkansas	8,289	New Hampshire	34,629
California	15,725	New Jersey	81,010
Colorado Ter	4,903	New York	467,047
Connecticut	57,379	New Mexico Ter	6,561
Delaware	13,670	Nevada	1,080
Dakota Ter	306	North Carolina	3,156
Florida	1,290	Ohio	319,659
Illinois	259,147	Oregon	1,810
Indiana	197,167	Pennsylvania	366,107
Iowa	76,309	Rhode Island	23,699
Indian Nation	3,530	Tennessee	31,092
Kansas	20,151	Texas	1,965
Kentucky	79,025	Vermont	35,262
Louisiana	5,224	Washington Ter	964
Maine	72,114	West Virginia	32,068
Maryland	50,316	Wisconsin	96,424
Massachusetts	152,048	District of Columbia	16,872
Michigan	89,372	Colored troops	93,442
Minnesota	25,052		
Mississippi	545	Total	2,859,132
Missouri	109,111		

Included in the above are 86,724 who paid their commutation after
having been drafted.

There were organized from the volunteer forces, at various times, 258
regiments and 170 independent companies of cavalry, 57 regiments and
232 separate batteries of artillery, and 1,666 regiments and 306 independent companies of infantry—equivalent to a total of 2,047 regiments.

In addition there were 30 regiments, of all arms, in the regular army, which numbered, first to last, 67,000 men.

The following is a very nearly correct statement of the loss of life:

Killed in battle	61,362
Died of wounds	32,081
Died of disease	186,216
Died in captivity	35,000
Various causes	2,146
Total	316,805

The number of Union soldiers wounded in action was 280,040, and 184,791 were captured. Typhoid and other fevers swept away 43,715; diarrhea in its various forms, 44,558; lung diseases, 26,468; small-pox, 7,058; measles, 5,177.

The total number of interments in the various national cemeteries is 318,870. This includes a considerable number of civilians, Confederates, and the dead of other wars. The following are the most populous of these cities of the dead:

Arlington, Va.	16,264	Beaufort, S. C.	9,241
Nashville, Tenn.	16,526	Richmond, Va.	6,542
Vicksburg, Miss.	16,600	Poplar Grove, Va.	6,199
Fredericksburg, Va.	15,257	Stone River, Tenn.	6,145
Memphis, Tenn.	13,977	Corinth, Miss.	5,716
Andersonville, Ga.	13,714	City Point, Va.	5,152
Salisbury, N. C.	12,126	Hampton, Va.	5,424
Chattanooga, Tenn.	12,962	Little Rock, Ark.	5,602
Chalmette, La.	12,511	Mound City, Ill.	5,226
Jefferson Barracks, Mo.	11,490	Gettysburg, Pa.	3,575
Marietta, Ga.	10,151	Winchester, Va.	4,459

Blood was shed in 2,261 battles and skirmishes. In 149 of these the loss in each, on the Union side, exceeded 500.